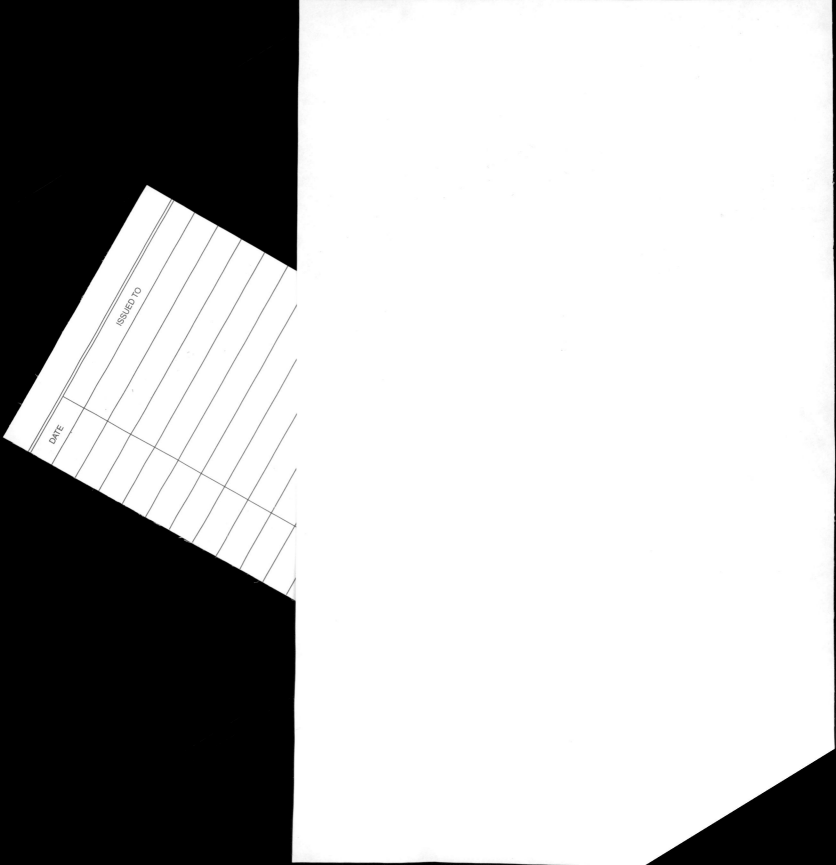

DATE

ISSUED TO

By Wonders and By War

A Novel
by
Carol Williams

May 29, 1780
His jaw hardened.
His foot grew heavy on the ground.
Mine! he thought fiercely. . . .
My life belongs to this ground!

- Joggi Lienhardt, A Carolina Partisan

Chicago
Swiss American Historical Society
1999

BY WONDERS AND BY WAR

Cover illustration and map by Betsy Thorne

Library of Congress Number: 99-70614

International Standard Book Number: 1-883294-83-5

Printed 1999 by
Masthof Press
220 Mill Road, Morgantown, PA 19543-9701
for the Swiss-American Historical Society

To Leo Schelbert

Thy dead shall live, their bodies shall rise.
O dwellers in the dust, awake and sing for joy!
For thy dew is a dew of light,
and on the land of the shades thou wilt let it fall.
- Isaiah 26:19

THE FAMILIES IN THIS BOOK

The Lienhardts

Johannes Lienhardt, born 1734 in Wildhaus, in the Toggenburg, Switzerland; emigrated to South Carolina 1756, settled on Savana Hunt Creek near the Congaree River; married *Magdalena Frillig* 1758.

Magdalena (Madle) born 1737 in Zurich, Switzerland; emigrated from Amsterdam in 1757; m. *Johannes* in Charlestown, South Carolina.

Their children: *Jacob (Joggi) Lienhardt*, born late 1758
                Heinrich (Heiri) Lienhardt, born 1760
                Barbara (Babeli) Lienhardt, born 1762;
                    married Conrad Meyer 1778
                Catharina (Cathri) Lienhardt, born 1765
                Johannes (Hans) Lienhardt, born early in 1767
                Andreas Lienhardt, born 1770
                George (Georgi) Lienhardt, born 1772
                Anna (Anneli) Lienhardt, born 1775

The Näffels

Rudolff (Rudi) Näffels, born 1740 in Wildhaus, Switzerland; emigrated to South Carolina in 1744; orphaned in 1745, only survivor of family; married *Margaret Allen* in 1769; eventually settled on Indian Creek near the Enoree River.

Margaret, born 1748 in the Shenandoah Valley of Virginia; family moved to South Carolina in 1756.

Their children: *James Fraser (Jemmy) Näffels*, born 1772
                Katherine (Katy) Näffels, born 1776

The Rieders

Elsbeth Rieder, born 1717 in the Rheinthal, married *Hermann Rieder* in 1735; emigrated to South Carolina in 1737; settled near the Congarees (Granby); widowed in 1751.

Hans Jacob Rieder, son of *Hermann* and *Elsbeth*, born 1738; married *Maria Beckman* in 1756.

Maria Beckman, born 1737 at the Congarees.

Their children: *Narcissa (Nissi) Rieder*, born 1758
               Wilhelm (Willi) Rieder, born 1760
               An older son and a daughter were born in 1756 and 1757.
               Other children were born after 1760.

Simmi is the son of *Hans Jacob* and *Calli*, a slave.

SOUTH CAROLINA

1780-1781

1

"And here we see her!" Hans sang out just loud enough for Cathri to hear him across the field.

The cart coming out of the woods was unmistakable. Elsbeth Rieder was the only woman in the Congarees who used such a conveyance. It was hard to imagine her square wide figure on horseback, and, of course, walking was not to be considered by a person of her consequence.

"And here we see her," Cathri giggled, glancing ahead to see if their father had heard them.

If he had, he ignored them. Cathri thought her father might regard Elsbeth's visits much as they did.

Hans and Cathri were hot, dusty, and scratched from the wheat bundles they were binding. Their father, Johannes Lienhardt, and their older brother, Heiri, moved tirelessly beyond them with swinging reaphooks. Cathri and Hans moved, sighing and suffering, Hans as slowly as he dared. The day had long lost its freshness.

The afternoon sky was cloudless, this May of 1780 like the May of any other year, only more so. The warm air was filled with the cackling, crowing, clucking, and cheeping of tame fowls, the high indefatigable wing-beatings of wild ones, the humming, buzzing, fluttering, and darting of lesser wings. The ground and the air were alive with the reach of root, bole, and leaf.

Their wheat crop was a good one. This six-acre field would yield seventy-five bushels. Their father was a good farmer. He knew how to nurture land, even the thin-soiled sandy ground which made up part of his acreage. He knew how to pen cattle for their dung and move crops from field to field to let the land rest sometimes. He worked hard and made his children do the same—even his daughter of late, although their mother did not approve of that. Perhaps her disapproval arose from the difference in their origins; she was a merchant's daughter, but he was a peasant's son.

Cathri did not really mind the outdoor work itself, only its grueling pace, its overmastering dailiness. She liked light and air better than the confined darkness of indoor tasks. She would have been surprised to know that in this trait she was very like her mother, for Cathri found it harder to please her mother than her father. From her mother usually came a correction or minor criticism, or if not that, cool-eyed appraisal. Cathri had not the small swift hands of her mother. But it did not take too much skill to use a hoe or a rake, to pull up weeds or to drop seeds. Once her father had said, "You'll make me a farmer yet, girl." The glow on his face warmed her too.

Hans did mind the work. He worked only because he had to. "I don't see why we can't have slaves to help us," he said for the fourteenth time. "Papa could if he would."

"He thinks it's wrong to own other people and you know it."

"But that's what they're brought here for! And if they're going to be here, they may as well help us as somebody else! And besides, we'd be better to 'em than some people are. Than plenty of people are!"

Cathri did not answer. You could never get anywhere arguing with Hansli—or Hans, as they called him now. Of course, Papa was right. . . . Yet some people, and people she'd been taught to respect, did have slaves. And it was surely tempting to think how good it would be not to have to work so hard all day and every day. . . . But wouldn't it be strange to have people in their house and fields who weren't in their family? How would they treat them? She always felt uncomfortable around the black people at the Rieders'. Slaves. Wrong. You knew it was wrong when you looked at a little child and knew he didn't really belong to his mother and father. But why did so many— *Stop thinking about it. We don't have any and we won't.*

"Wonder what she brought?" Cathri asked, returning to Elsbeth. "Come on, guess. What do you think she brought?"

"I'd say a jar of goose grease."

"I think she brought us a nice bottle of turnip juice wine."

Hans' mirth shot up in a cackle. "How about pigknuckle preserves?"

"Or rutabaga pie."

They were laughing out of control. "Collard cakes?"

"Ah, we're being mean, Hans. Frau Elsbeth's good. It's just—it's just—"

"That she's so continual."

Hans had the exact word, and Cathri was so tickled she lost her breath. They worked awhile in silence except for snickering.

"'And here we see him at last!'" Cathri exploded again, her voice breaking high, with Frau Elsbeth's inevitable greeting, especially of the young.

"'The first time I ever saw *her*—'"

"'The first time I ever saw *him*, he was squalling his head off and red as a beet and he puked all over my good bombazine—'" Cathri moved out of Hans' reach as he came at her with his sheaf.

She stopped suddenly. "Hans, is that Mama?"

"Jo-han-nes!" came the faint cry.

Everyone in the field stood still. The call came again. Their father hallooed in response.

"You chaps keep on what you're doing now," he called to them as he started toward the house.

Heiri stood still a long time, made as if to follow his father, stopped again.

Heiri was nineteen, Cathri fifteen, and Hans thirteen. Their oldest brother, Jacob, called "Jakie," which they pronounced "Yockie" and wrote "Joggi," was twenty-one. Once a Ranger attached to the regular army, he was now part of the so-called "country militia" which had been called down to help the Continental Army shut up in Charlestown. However, an older sister was married to a Loyalist in the British Army outside the city. Charlestown had been under siege since the twenty-ninth of March. Now people were saying it might have to surrender.

Heiri still stood there. Cathri watched him take off his hat and wipe his face. He was a husky boy with thick, light brown hair and fair skin burned ruddy brown. He had a snub nose and light blue eyes with a perennial fleck of laughter in them, which gave his face a look of pleasantry always seeming on the verge of mirth.

But for the last few months the look had been only a seeming. Heiri had few funny sayings now. He did a man's work, rivalling his father in endurance and night-time weariness.

Once Cathri had heard her father assailing Heiri beyond the barn. "What is it you want? Go join him if that's what you want! Go do your part in trampling and plundering other men's fields! Is that what you want to do?"

Heiri only bent his head and moved away.

Cathri hurt for her brother. She understood her father. Surely it was better to raise crops and make things grow, even if soldiers did come and want cows and hogs and horses and half your grain crop. And at least a little of what they took might go to feed Joggi. But if Joggi could go off to fight, why not Heiri? She knew why. Because somebody needed to stay and help Papa.

Now Cathri saw Heiri going slowly toward the house.

"I wonder what she did come for," said Hans. "You think maybe she brought news?"

"Get busy, Hans. Don't make Papa have to scold us."

"I bet it's bad news."

Cathri started to say, "Along with the collard cakes," but the jokes no longer seemed funny.

Madle Lienhardt listened with controlled face as she spooned cool clabber into a cup for her visitor. Elsbeth was in full spate. Her feelings had been dammed up for over an hour as the cart joggled through the sandbeds. There was no use to talk to Primus, her attendant, because he was almost deaf—or pretended to be, she said—possibly from having to listen to his mistress for forty years. Nor could she talk to her son, Hans Jacob.

"Madle, he walks away from me! He walks out of the room when I try to bring it home to him. 'Willi's gone!' I tell him. 'He's lost, your own son!' And Maria's as bad, shuts herself away from us every chance she gets. 'What do you think?' I ask, 'What will happen?' but no comfort do I get from him, from her, from anyone! And they're gone, Madle, oh, I know it! Gone forever, our fair boys, never to be seen again! Tumbled into some pesthold, dragged off to some ship to be sunk to the bottom of the sea or to rot in some godless place like the ones at Savannah, hanged or killed already for all we know, and here we are left to mourn and grieve, and what do they care for mothers and grandmothers, that do such wickedness?"

"Frau Elsbeth, we don't know these things!" Madle set down the cup and looked out the little window with an ashen face. She had already called Johannes.

"I tell you it's over! That no-account Heinrich Heller that slunk back here with his tail between his legs, he says it's as good as over! He says the guns stopped already once twelve hours while they dillied and they dallied, they said this, they said that, and then had no more sense than to start it up all over again and the whole town tied up tighter than a horse-break. And how they thought to defy a King's army God alone knows."

They did defy it with success, thought Madle dully, *four years ago, some would say defied it twice and thought they could do it again*. But she might have said, "I too had your misgivings." She picked up the cup, sprinkled sugar in it, sprinkled too much.

"Oh, I said," cried Elsbeth, "God be my witness, five years ago I said it would come to this, when those slick-tongued, call-themselves-gentlemen, oh so polite, oh so fine, came mincing up here to stir up our men and bait up our boys. 'Liberty!' I said, 'I've got liberty.' I told every-one then, 'I've got a good big house, better than any I would ever have had in the old country, the plenty that goes with it that the good God gives me to enjoy, all I want in this life, I've got all the liberty I want now, what do I want with more? I've got all I can see to now with lazy young-ones and Hans Jacob and Maria to worry me to my grave! Oh, Parliament and King George! What have I got to do with Parliament? And King George, he's across the water, which I know I'll never cross again, let King George alone! We live here in peace! Don't be stirring up and brewing up mischief for us here too! Keep it in that godless city down there!' But no, such bilious fools can't rest till they've got everybody else stirred up in their own stink!"

Madle put down the cup and spoon by Elsbeth with a small clatter.

"Aye-God, fine liberty they've got now," groaned Elsbeth. "And fine liberty for our poor striplings!" She half-lifted the cup, set it down again. "Aye-God, they couldn't see it was only their own liberty those high and mighty ones wanted, to loll back in their great mansions and lord it over the rest of us who work hard and live honest lives and want nothing more than to live out in peace the years God gives us. So learned, so high! And look down on us poor Dutch-speaking folk till they come up here to toll off our men! And never a penny for a church or anything else for the taxes we pay year in, year out, but what we provide from our own pockets. Though what Pastor Theus means when he takes their side I'll never know. And now he sees what they've come to he'll sing another tune."

Madle said, "Frau Elsbeth, boys like Joggi and Willi—if they have been spared and if the city does surrender—then it may be they'll be sent home. The King's army, they're not savages." Yet came the unbidden thought: Four years ago they were willing to send savages upon us.

Elsbeth sucked a little clabber from her spoon. She was sixty-three years old, and although she had lost her last tooth, her skin was still smooth across her wide, flat cheekbones.

"What? Has Charlestown surrendered?" Johannes stood dark against the light in the doorway.

"Oh Johannes!" Elsbeth rose in a commotion of thick skirts and grasped Johannes' extended hand. "What will happen now, what will they do to us? Will they come here? Oh, our poor boys—though you're lucky, you've got one on their side with Conrad Meyer for a son-in-law. I always said the Meyers know which way to jump, it took a smart girl to catch him—"

Why, thought Madle angrily, *must she always come out with such things?*

Johannes interrupted Elsbeth, "What have you heard, Frau Elsbeth? Who was the messenger?"

She groped for her chair. "Oh, it was that flap-eared Heinrich Heller, trust him to get his own skin out in time, he left in the night five days ago, he said, no six—or seven now it may be—said he came through swamps and branches because the King's men are thicker than yellow jackets all over the roads and every bridge for miles around—"

"When did he get here?"

"Yesterday, or no, day before yesterday morning it was, he stopped at Chesnut's store or whoever it now belongs to, Ulrich Keller said, said Charlestown's locked up tight, thousands on thousands of King's ships and King's men raining shells on the city day and night, he said, digging their way in and tunnelling up through ditches to get close enough to shoot down every man, woman, and child in the city, said they'd be in the streets in two days if not before. Johannes, what will happen?"

Madle sat down. Her face was turned away from them. Johannes moved toward her.

After a silence, he sighed, "Well, if they use the sense God gave them—Charlestown, I mean—surely they've laid down their guns. Madle," he stood behind her, his hand on her shoulder, "remember, it's not Indians they surrender to."

She glanced up quickly. "I said as much. Surely they're not without mercy. They're Europeans too."

"It may even be," he said slowly, "that our son will be paroled. In Georgia, I hear, most have been paroled and well-treated."

"Paroled?" asked Elsbeth. "What's 'paroled'?"

"It means they're free to go home if they give up their weapons and promise they won't fight again."

"Fight again! I'll say Willi Rieder won't fight again! Not if once I get that boy under my hand!"

Another time Madle would have smiled. She knew that Joggi would never again be under her hand if he ever had been, nor was it likely that Willi would be under his grandmother's either.

Johannes said, "And even if they're kept as prisoners, it may be only for a short time—if peace does come. I pray God it will now."

But the hope in his voice sounded weak. Could peace come so quickly after five years of war? Though much of the fighting had been distant, yet with troops camping at the Congarees and at Sandy Run, and with the marching and countermarching up and down the roads, it had been disturbing enough to break up their own family. Although many families seemed unaffected now, in the early days a scattering of young men had been induced to join the Whig side, and more men had yielded supplies to it at one time or another. Still some families continued strongly, if not so openly, loyal to the British government.

"Peace?" Elsbeth was curiously silent a moment. "Yes, but what about all the grain and cattle we've lost, who'll pay for that? Hundreds and hundreds of pounds worth Hans Jacob supplied and not one penny has he ever got for it—and what good will his notes be now? When I think of the horses, the barrels of beef, the barrels of flour—"

Johannes too thought of the little sheaf of paper notes in his trunk.

"—and two bolts of new cloth Dorcas and Dinah worked six months from dawn to dark on the loom at, not to mention ten sacks of dried beans I didn't want to let go, but Hans Jacob said, 'You'll get money for everything, you'll be paid!'"

Madle rose abruptly and threw down the cloth in her hand. "How can you speak of such things, Frau Elsbeth? My son is worth more to me than all the horses and grain in this country!"

Elsbeth stared at her as did Johannes, for never had Madle flared up at the older woman like that. Others might laugh behind her back, but Madle never. She said there was a side to Elsbeth that others didn't see.

The old face darkened. She bent her head, sniffed a little, and primped her mouth shut.

Heiri came into the room. "What is it, Mama? What's happened? Is it about Joggi?"

"I want no more talk. We know nothing yet. We'll not speak of what might have happened till it does. Twenty-three years in this country, I've learned one thing if nothing else. The evil that may come is bad enough, but you cannot fear till it comes. Heiri, tell Andreas and Georgi in the garden to bring me water and tell Anneli to come inside."

Johannes said shortly, "It's likely Charlestown's fallen to the King. We know nothing more."

Heiri stood a moment, looking from one to the other of them. The color was gone beneath his brown skin. He turned and went out.

Johannes too stood irresolutely. "We thank you, Frau Elsbeth, for bringing us news. We'll hope for the best." Then he was gone.

Madle sat down opposite Elsbeth, sat unspeaking.

The older woman sighed. "I know it's true, Madle. I know the children are more than all the goods saved or lost. My mouth goes on, but you know it's the young ones I think of most. Your own dear child, the first time I ever saw him—"

But some frail antenna stopped her, and they sat awhile longer in silence.

2

In the evening five-year-old Anneli, a sweet-faced slender child with brown braids, stood at her father's elbow and asked the blessing. Andreas and Georgi peeped sideways, trying to make each other giggle. Cathri with bowed head felt guilty. On the sidetable sat a large jar of strawberry preserves from Frau Elsbeth.

The five children and Heiri sat three to a side on benches, their parents in armchairs at the ends of the table. Johannes had made the walnut table ten years ago. At one time he'd wondered if he'd made it too short, but since the two older ones had left, and with the loss of little ones over the years—to croup, to summer fever, and the last two stillborn—he knew that from now on there'd be plenty of room to keep boys' elbows from jabbing one another.

The ten- and eight-year-olds were shock-headed boys in homespun shirts and wide-legged breeches. Andreas was darker than Georgi, already slimming up. Georgi would be stocky like Johannes and Heiri.

With the blessing over, their mother's gaze quelled the boys—that and their greedy enjoyment of thick potato soup and crusty bread, their anticipation of strawberry preserves.

Heiri ate without appetite. He glanced occasionally at his mother. Her admonition, "Sit up straight. Don't hunch," dinned into him down the years, sometimes made him poke the younger boys in the back to save her the trouble, but tonight he did not notice their manners.

His mother was forty-three years old. Her dark hair had white wings at her temples. Grief and care lines ran together around her eyes and at her mouth, but unlike most women of her time and place, she had not doubled her girth or even much increased it in twenty years. Her cheeks and mouth were not yet sunken, although the flesh was stretched thin across her fine bones. A few people marveled at her persistent appearance of elegance. Her husband, too, marveled when he really looked at her, but for him her beauty was less in her face or figure than in her mind and spirit. For Heiri it was in her voice, a musing tone, a love-note remembered for many days, and in her hands, the quick light stroke across his cheek or shoulders—not the stinging slap of childhood discipline.

Her daughters were least aware of her physical beauty, but they were very much aware of her cleanliness, her capability, and above all her durability, crossed by her fierce, obsessive care when they were sick or troubled. For Hans, Andreas, and Georgi, her beauty had mostly to do with clean shirts and clean beds, with fresh bread and tarts, and with the flowing lines of her dress as she sat her horse on a Sunday. For Andreas years later, its memory would be in a patch of bird's-foot violets in the sunshine or the fragrance of a little bouquet brought into the house.

Even tonight a few stems of sweet-shrub in a cup blended their crushed allspice aroma with the other smells of the room.

"Will you finish the wheat tomorrow?"

Johannes didn't look at his binders, but Cathri flushed because she knew they could have done more if they'd tried.

"I'd like Cathri to help me tomorrow," said Madle.

Johannes was slow to answer.

"Couldn't Hans and Heiri finish the wheat?" she persisted.

"If it's fair. And if I can have Andreas. Grass is taking the corn-field." He was silent awhile. "You too, Rabbit. It's time you started using that little hoe of yours in the cornfield along with your brother."

Georgi's face brightened because anything Andreas did he wanted to show he could do it better.

Madle's eyes darkened. Too much to do. Too many acres for two men and a half-grown boy. She would not include a half-grown girl. Madle had not favored Johannes' acquisition of his last tract.

"With five sons, Madle, we'll need more land. Six hundred acres is still a small holding in this country."

Four sons, she'd corrected him silently. *I doubt you'll ever see Joggi work this land again.* For even at Hansli's age Joggi had been restless. At sixteen he'd gone to his cousin Rudi up the country for a while, and at seventeen he'd jumped at the chance to join the frontier forces against the British-incited Cherokees. Johannes still blamed Rudi for luring him away. Madle did not. She knew her son. And the second one too. Under her nose morning and evening, yet in some ways as removed as Joggi was. She too could have cried, "Well, go if that's what you want!" But the truth was, she knew he did not want to.

Hans startled them by pushing back his half-empty bowl. "What will happen to Joggi now?"

The spoons stopped chinking. Cathri felt sick-weak, was furious with Hans.

"Papa, what will happen?" Hans asked again.

Johannes' face expressed nothing. "If God wills, he'll come home safe." He resumed eating. "Heiri, I'll expect you to take charge of these fellows in the morning. Get them out early."

No one said any more. They understood by Johannes' words that he'd go tomorrow to Congarees, or Granby as people called it now, to learn what he could.

To keep from worrying his mother Heiri ate strawberry preserves and butter with the rest of them and gave Hans a look when he said he didn't want any. As his father rose, Heiri did too. Though he usually went to bed soon after supper, tonight he said, "I'll check the barn. I thought I saw the door open."

Johannes grunted and sat down by the fire as Heiri went outside.

Heiri breathed the night scents of new leaves and small bloom, of water and tangled vines from the creek below the house, of animals and the trampled barnyard. It was black dark, for the waning moon had not yet risen, but Heiri needed no light to try latches. When he returned to the house, Beno, their young watchdog, was waiting in the dooryard.

Heiri came in through the back gate but walked around the house. He stood awhile at the front gate, then opened it, snapped his fingers for Beno, and began walking down the lane that led east to the High Road.

His feet knew the sandy ruts as well as did Beno's feet pounding ahead of him. He smelled the ordered rows of young corn to his right, the heavy-limbed orchard to his left.

He was not a rambler like Joggi. The smell of wild woods was not an intoxication to him. Yet tonight he felt an almost unbearable urge to plunge into the river woods beyond the High Road, to call his brother. Soundlessly he did call, *Oh Joggi!*

He passed through the strip of woods that grew between their house and the ancient Indian path that was now the great road, then walked again between fields. A shift of air brought the scent of pine needles down from the ridge, but he stopped a hundred yards west of the road.

No, I will not leave with only a written line. If or when I go, I'll tell them so. She can cry then, and he can have the satisfaction of railing me out to my face. She will cry less for me than she did for Joggi, and Papa will be angrier.

And the others? Heiri saw their smooth cheeks, the glint of their eyes, the mischief in their curling mouths, and he smelled the scents of yeast bread, spices, woodsmoke, and candlegrease. He balled his fists as he used to do when he was trying not to cry. *Why here? me? now?*

He did not share his father's hope of peace. Somehow he knew there was a hard way yet to go. He might have escaped or ignored like everyone else the militia drafts, but another call he could not escape.

Yet he kept that perennial doubt: Can I do it?

His father had gone out to fight just after Heiri was born, but he never talked about it.

The soil beneath Heiri's feet was black with a thin overlay of sand. He knew the feel of it cut by his plow blade and his hoe; he could always smell its sweetness as he scored it deep. A blade must cut into the earth for seeds and fruit. It was in the Bible, approved of God. A blade in the flesh? To cut a man's flesh? Well, that was in the Bible too, or at least swords were. Generation after generation had done it, had had to. Couldn't he? The drill at the muster ground was one thing. To end someone else's life was another.

I don't know, and I don't want to know. But I'll have to go and find out. And if I can't kill like a man, maybe I can die like one. But I don't want to do that either.

He whistled to Beno, ranging out by the road. As Heiri waited for the dog, the smells of young corn, potato vines, and the rampant tender grass were poignantly sweet about him.

They groaned on their knees in the dark, Johannes aloud with words he found hard to say in the light. "God, spare our firstborn, oh God, spare our boy! Oh Father, Thou knowest! Oh, let us see again his face!" Over and over Johannes groaned his prayer and Madle whispered it.

Finally their agony eased and their words stilled. Johannes put his arm about Madle and helped her up, and they lay down in the pine-posted bed where their children had been conceived and born.

All except Joggi. Joggi had been conceived in the time of his mother's grief for her dead lover and his father's pain for the girl who had married him because she knew nowhere else to turn. Conceived maybe on their sad journey up from Charlestown or perhaps in the hut where the Rieders had given them shelter.

Joggi, both like and unlike the others. Always wanting to go out from the rest of them. *But I moved out,* Johannes reminded himself many an anxious night. *I moved down valleys and rivers, across other lands, moved over an ocean, and so did she. What wonder the boy's like he is?*

But in the daytime, when Johannes looked at the swell of his grain-fields, the rich wall of trees that bordered his creek, he yearned, *Why can't he love it as I do? Surely it's what the good God intended for us—not slaughter and burnings, smoke and rage. Why?*

He knew why. *It was* for *them, because I loved them! For* them *I aimed a musket and steeped my soul in that stench. But how can the boy plead such a cause?*

Johannes always left the argument there. *I don't know. My son is not me.*

Neither of them was asleep when the dog began barking. At the first eruption Johannes was out of the room. Madle heard him drag up a chair to get down the musket, heard him lift the bar and scrape open the door, heard him shout to the dog, then the continued excitement at the gate till gradually it faded.

She rose swiftly. On the porch the night breeze shivered about her. The moonlight was so faint she could see nothing. Then she became aware of movement beyond the gate where Beno whined.

She hurried down the steps. "Johannes!" she called low. Her hand on the gate, she heard him say something. She called, "Johannes?"

"It's Joggi."

She opened the gate and ran, her feet tender to the sand.

Down the lane, two bodies huddled in an irregular shape, one above the other. "Help me, Madle."

She knelt in the sand, embracing, feeling, moaning. She ran her hands over his head, his tangled hair, unshaven face; she felt his shoulder bones and backbone. "He's starved. He's skin and bone," she mourned.

His words came faint but pleased. "You saved me something to eat, didn't you, Mama?"

As one, Madle and Johannes put their arms around the huddled form and lifted him and, gently propelling, felt his feet stumble along between them. Tears gushed down their cheeks.

At the gate Johannes said, "Back, Beno." The young dog did not know Joggi, but his tail whipped from side to side. As Johannes reached to push open the gate, the body between them sagged. "Ohh," Madle wailed softly.

A shape loomed in front of them. Heiri said, "Let me, Mama." He took her place and he and Johannes lifted Joggi up the steps. "I can get him in, Papa, if you'll open the door."

"In this room or in the bed?" asked Johannes.

"Let's cradle him before the fire," said Madle. She had felt the shuddering in his body.

Heiri lifted his brother and brought him in. Johannes was already stirring coals, laying kindling, and crashing wood into the chimney. Madle brought a pillow and quilt she'd dragged off the bed, and they eased Joggi into an armchair.

He opened his eyes. "I knew I'd get here." He still had that pleased note in his voice.

Light flared. Madle in the shadows was pouring milk and tearing off bread.

In the brightening room they knelt and hovered and saw a narrow, sallow face with sunken eyes and a half-healed cut down his forehead and aslant his left cheek. Joggi turned his head several times from side to side. "Lay out all day yesterday in the cane this side of Sandy Run." He was smiling. "But I got here."

Heiri and Johannes stood back as Madle brought the bowl. "Can you eat, child? Can you hold the bowl?"

He leaned his head on the pillow, looking up at her. "Try me." Yet he did not raise his hands.

After a moment his mother lifted the bowl and he opened his mouth. "Not too much," she murmured. "Now take a little bread." His mother fed him.

"Wait now. Not too much at one time. And broth would be better. Heiri, put a cup of water in the soup pot. Get warm water from the kettle. Johannes, if you'll get down that hunk of beef, Heiri can chip some off."

They saw a little brightness in the sunken eyes. The shaggy head turned, looked into shadows where firelight gleamed on cupboards and crocks, a great book, a few pieces of delftware. "I never thought—it would look so good."

Johannes laid his hand on the ragged shoulder, felt the knobs of bones. He stooped and curved his arm lightly around his son's shoulders. "Welcome home, Joggi. Praise God and welcome home."

3

His family had learned not to ask Joggi where he'd been and what he'd been doing. They waited till he told them, and if he didn't, they kept on wondering. Even his father had finally learned that.

That he'd been in the woods and swamps for many days was apparent. How he'd gotten the wounds on his face and on his leg he did not say, nor did he say how he'd gotten out of Charlestown. Had he been sent out? Or had he sneaked out? The last thought turned Johannes' face grave.

Too much like Rudi, Madle's cousin, who, even though married and supposed to be settled, Johannes feared was still too much of a backwoods adventurer.

Joggi slept and ate and slept again. He moved out of his parents' bedroom into the loftroom, where Madle took food to him at midday and examined and poulticed again the angry wound above his knee, a long, deep cut close to the bone. She fed him beef broth and later as much custard and chicken stew as she could get down him. He was no longer feverish, only weak and lightheaded. She forbore to wash him.

The loft was partitioned into two rooms, one for the boys, the other for the girls. Originally there had been no window at all, only spaces between the logs under the eaves for ventilation. Later Johannes had cut a window in the girls' room and had paneled it to keep out winter drafts, but the boys' unpaneled room still had only the upper part of the chimney for warmth and the spaces under the eaves for light.

In the late afternoon, sunshine slanted between the great high beams. Joggi saw Heiri sitting on a trundle bed with a streak of sunlight across his face. The smoothness of his brother's cheeks seemed remarkable to Joggi.

Heiri said, "It's me."

Joggi closed his eyes awhile, opened them to look at his brother again. Heiri didn't say anything, just sat there, a pleasant lump. Joggi imagined that if he said, "What do you want?" Heiri would say, "Nothing."

Joggi's eyelids fluttered down. No need now to force them open, to raise himself ever so slowly, wary of the broken stick or the crunch of leaves, to grit his teeth, to listen and will to move on.

Heiri said, "Are you all right, Joggi?"

Joggi thought about it. "Yes," he answered.

The sound of a girl's voice calling fowls rose from below. Joggi heard the bawling of cows in the far woods and suddenly longed to hear the dingle of cowbells.

The ropes creaked on the trundle. Heiri said, "I've got to go now."

Joggi opened his eyes. He smiled and lifted his hand. Heiri saw the curve of his brother's lips in the half light. Joggi saw sunlight bar the wide back as it disappeared down the steep stairway in a tumbling run.

He watched a dirt dauber crawl in and out between the logs. He fell asleep and a five-year-old Heiri was stumbling after him in the woods, half-crying, half-laughing, "I found you, Joggi!"

The sunlight was gone. Spaces between the logs merged into their darkness. He heard the sounds of his family coming in below, noisy, then subdued. He wondered if he was able to get up and go down the stairs, thought about it awhile and decided that whether he could or not, he wouldn't.

His mother came with light and food. Later he heard his brothers getting into the other beds, and the air seemed close with so many people breathing it. He felt the familiar pall of the old unbearable suffocation. Strange he never felt it in a tent or a hut. He imagined himself lying on a rock ledge on a hillside. Gradually spring airs drifted across his face, across the house smells, the smells of his brothers. In their blending he slept.

In one way Joggi had not changed, for in little more than a week, thin as he was, he began to regain vitality.

When he came downstairs, life surged around him. Georgi and Andreas shouted and wrestled in the yard. Hans groaned and clowned about all the work he had to do, much as his oldest brother had once done, though Joggi didn't remember taking nearly so many liberties as Hans did. Heiri and Johannes almost exploded with vigor as they tossed the last wheat sheaves into the wagon. Cathri soared up steps and sang in the fowlyard, in the garden, at the spring. Madle opened doors and windows, put out bedding to sun, baked and polished, and brought in a spray of red trumpet honeysuckle. Small Anna was a joyous sprite before and behind Joggi as he walked about the place he hadn't seen in almost two years.

Only Barbara was missing, Barbara grave-eyed and competent like her mother.

After their midday dinner, everyone sat on the porch for an hour, females busy with handwork, older males lounging, but the two youngest pressed into shelling English peas. Johannes had learned early that an after-dinner rest hour was needed to survive the climate of this country.

The sky was a fierce blue through the oak leaves. Beyond the sounds of amiable family bickering and the "pot-rack" of guineas in the orchard, Joggi heard the shrieks of a mockingbird diving at something.

Dark-eyed and hollow-jawed, he stared into the implacable blue and wished more than anything else that he could see it again as beneficence, or if not that, simply as home-sky. He wished he could be Andreas or Georgi.

Words moved within him, but already a stirring on the porch was ending the hour, and with the rising of a light breeze in the oak branches he stilled his words.

In the shadows of the big room that night he did not still them. "I'll tell you how it was. I feel obliged to tell you."

As Johannes looked at the thin, bearded young man, he was appalled at the strangeness and contradictions of his feelings—longing, envy, anguish. It was as if in his son he saw every man he'd ever vied with, marched with, and struggled alongside of . . . or maybe even been rebuffed or scorned by. Son? He shook his head slightly to clear it.

"This is what finally happened. . . . After we lost the battle . . . there were two more with me in the Santee Swamp, and then we met up with three others and we joined together to do what we could. We had muskets, or I had my rifle, and at first we had two horses. Later we got more. It was near a creek, I never learned the name of it. . . . We hid and saw fifty horsemen, and we knew they were the enemy. So we left our horses and followed them and lay close to their camp till night. Then we decided it was too few of us to try anything, so we started to crawl off. But in the dark somebody stumbled over a half-rotten log pen, and it fell in and made such a clatter they heard us and came after us, but we got away.

"Next day we decided to ride back the same way. We hoped if we could meet up with others of ours, maybe we could do something. And sure enough we happened on four more. That made us seven, so we hid by the road and toward evening we saw the same troops, though now they were many more, and we saw the sallow-faced officer that led them." Joggi's jaw muscles hardened. "I'd seen him before. At Monck's Corner when they came on us, dumb as we were to get caught so, I saw him across the fire. His troops stick men like hogs."

"How did you get to Monck's Corner?" Johannes couldn't help asking.

"I was with some riflemen attached to cavalry, Washington's cavalry. We were under General Huger."

"Washington?"

"Colonel William Washington. He's cousin to the great general."

"But—" Johannes didn't finish, somehow couldn't ask, "How or under what circumstances did you leave Charlestown?"

Joggi guessed his father's question. What if he said, "I just left"? Because that was what he'd almost done. Why should he stay in that trap if he could get out? He'd find better ground to fight on than in that cattlepen.

His father would not understand. *"When you start something, Joggi, stay with it to the end." That's what I intended to do, Papa, only it appeared to me the end down there was not a good end. I thought there'd be a better one somewhere else.*

But as it turned out, he'd left under orders, for his militia company had been sent out as support for the cavalry that was trying to keep the outside communication route open, and unlike many others, he'd been glad to go.

Johannes changed his question, "When was that? When you fought at Monck's Corner."

"It was the second week in April. . . . They charged us at daybreak when we slept inside a church, hewed us and slashed us, and drove us across a bridge. Those of us that got away, we scattered in the swamp. . . . It was a bad time after that. So many men in the woods, it scares away game, and if you do see something, you're afraid to shoot when you don't know who'll hear you, especially if you're anywhere near a road or a settled place. But after four days a woman and two slaves hunting cattle, they came up, they were French poeple, and they took care of me. I stayed with them a week, and two others on our side, they hid them too. It was after that, after we left the French people, that we joined up together the way I told you.

"Anyway, we all had horses by then, I still had my rifle, and we followed the horsemen till dark. Only this time we stayed farther back but close enough to mark where they stopped and see where they posted pickets. Finally after the moon set, it was about two hours before daylight, we sneaked up almost to the edge of their camp, and we set up a holler and did some shooting. We hit a few and drove off some horses, and I doubt very many of 'em went back to sleep that night."

"Did you all get away?" asked Heiri.

"All but one." Joggi shook his head. His eyelids hooded his eyes. "Then we made a bad mistake. We stayed together. Two days later we paid for it. We shouldn't have stayed together, because he sent men to track us."

"Who sent men?"

Joggi cursed. His words were as alien in the room as a wild beast looking through the doorway would have been. "Banastre Tarleton, 'Benny' Tarleton, they call him, the officer that leads them. One of our boys had heard about him from the North."

"Is he English?"

"He is, but not the men he leads. They're Tories. I won't say 'Americans,' though they were born here same as we were. But they have good trackers, I will say."

American, Johannes said silently. *Our son is American, Madle. But you see there are still Americans who take the other side.*

"But they didn't get you," said Johannes.

"Oh no. After I'd tumbled off my horse, I rolled into a slough of water and they overrode me, and by the time they came back I'd crawled up under a big bunch of roots the high water had washed loose. They never found me." He'd heard them beating about for a long time. "But I lost my horse and my gun."

"When was that, Joggi?"

"Two weeks ago maybe. Or ten or twelve days. I don't know, I lost track of time."

There was a long silence.

Johannes gazed at his son. *So starved and wounded with everything lost, you came home. At least you came home.* "Where did you get your hurts?"

"This?" touching his knee. "It was that last time. A greencoat's saber."

"And your face?" asked his mother.

Joggi looked puzzled. "I don't know. I must have run into something one time or another. In the woods maybe. I've been lucky though. I've never caught a bullet. Not even at Savannah. At Savannah men on both sides of me got cut to pieces."

His hearers were suddenly stilled.

"Grapeshot smashed all around me at Savannah. But none hit me." His voice still held a note of wonder.

And how could you stay in the middle of it? Hans wondered but dared not ask.

Joggi was leaning forward now with his elbows on his knees, his hands clasped loosely between them. His tale was over. His listeners thought about it, what they could understand of it.

Joggi sat up. He looked around at them. "Mama, Papa, all of you, I'll have to go again."

"No!" Johannes said loudly. He stood up. "You must stay home! Besides, if Charlestown's surrendered—"

"Oh, we're not beat yet! There's more than one of us that left and didn't surrender as I've no doubt *they've* surrendered by now."

Madle did not move. "But you'll stay till your leg's healed."

Johannes paced to the fireplace, stood a moment, went to the door as if he would go out, turned around. "Joggi, you've fought your share, more than your share. Two years or the biggest part of it you've been under arms. You fought in Georgia and you've fought in the low country. And now it's *over!"*

"Papa, it's not over! If they've won down there, don't think they won't come up here too! And if they move up here—it's not over, it's just started!"

King's troops in the Congarees. Twenty years ago they'd been a welcome sight. *How glad we were,* Johannes remembered, *to see Montgomery's Highlanders stepping along in the May sunshine and Grant's a year later. . . . But four years ago it was not those high-styled redcoats that gave us protection. It was men in huntingshirts like Rudi and boys like this one of mine. It was men in red coats that put the devil in those poor benighted Cherokees.*

Johannes said heavily, "We'll just have to wait and see, Joggi." He sighed, "Wait and see."

Joggi did not answer. Everyone in the room felt how long and heavy that "wait" was.

Madle said, "And while we're waiting, maybe we can all find an hour or two for living the way God meant us to without strife? At least in our own home without strife?" Her blue eyes were shadowed. Her mouth curved half-smiling with a slight tremor at one corner. It was the unexpected tremor that moved them all.

Johannes came back into the room and did something he seldom did. He bent over his son, put his arm around his shoulders and embraced him hard. He said, "Well, I'll tell you one thing, fellow, you'd better get some meat on those bones before you think about going anywhere."

Firelight flared as a piece of oakwood burned in two and flames licked up each side.

Georgi slid off his bench. "Joggi, we got something to show you tomorrow, just Andreas and me."

Joggi looked up slowly. The dark and sunken look had left his eyes. His mouth curved upward. "I bet I know what it is."

"Bet you don't."

"In a nest maybe or out of it?"

The little boy looked astonished.

Cathri said, "Nissi Rieder asked about you, Joggi, the last time I saw her. She asked if we'd heard anything from you. She said they hadn't heard from Willi since February."

Joggi said, "What's today? Friday? Do you still go to divine service? How's Pastor Theus these days?"

And so, thought Cathri with a lift of spirit, perhaps day after tomorrow they'd all go up the Big Road together to St. John's, be almost a whole family again. And perhaps—perhaps they might even see Barbara! Though it was probably too much to hope for.

4

On the last Sabbath in May, the gathering for divine service was sparse. When word of Charlestown's final surrender reached the Congarees, a number of the St. John's Reformed congregation decided it would no longer be prudent to sit under a minister of Whig persuasion. Oddly, however, a few Tory families did appear for the first time in many months.

The Reverend Christian Theus, born sixty-three years ago under the slopes of the Calenda, had labored for over forty years beside wider, slower streams that the young Rhine at Domat Ems and in even wilder places than the valleys of the Grisons. He had trudged and ridden through swamps and across pine ridges and up and down sandy paths to preach to, console, cajole, and remonstrate with his flock. He had baptized, married, and buried them. He had struggled to implant in their children the rudiments of religion and of a common education. In a few he had tried to implant the desire for advanced learning. Until his escape at fourteen, young Jacob Lienhardt had been force-fed a fair amount of Latin because he'd had the brains for it. But most such young Jacobs as Theus encountered were far too heedless for the pastor to have had much success as an inspirer of learning.

That Pastor Theus was a learned man most of his parishioners knew but did not appreciate. Perhaps it was because he entered so fully into common life. He walked more often than he rode. He never refused a cup of cold clabber. He was as interested in the production of good beef and good flour as anyone else was, and he enjoyed the wild fruits of the land— blackberries and rosy little plums in summer, persimmons in the fall.

But as an advocate of radical politics—and that contrary to the views of many of his flock—this elderly, orthodox Swiss-born clergyman shocked them.

Some people thought he'd gotten his Whig notions from his lowcountry connections, for three of his nephews were commissioned officers in South Carolina regiments. Also his sons in the lower parts of Georgia were said to be Whigs, and one had been serving with the rebels.

Centuries ago, Protestant Theuses had fled west from Salzburg to a valley of the Grisons or Grey Leagues, and in those same valleys contentious common people had struggled alongside of and against various gentry for some autonomy in their own lives. How much of that mindset had a fifteen-year-old boy absorbed before he went away to school in Zurich?

But in 1730, when his parents emigrated, they left not so much for freedom, at least not religious freedom, as for better chances for their sons. Their oldest, Jeremiah, did indeed prosper as an artist, a painter of the well-to-do in Charlestown. Their third son, Simeon, became a vintner and left substantial property at Monck's Corner. And the second one, Christian, became a country parson—perhaps not the distinguished man of God his parents had envisioned when they named him. Or was he? He knew the meaning of his name, given and surname.

His parents and brothers were dead now, and his older children lived elsewhere, though he still had four daughters and two young sons at home. He had few expectations to live up to. His wife had long ago accepted his imperfections. As for his flock—contentious, divided, and wayward as they were—he knew the impossibility of pleasing all of them. Not that he had ever conceived it his duty to please them. But how *had* he come by his views?

In 1775 he had made a clear if ineloquent statement of them. Also he had supplied provisions to rebel troops. However, he did not preach his politics from the pulpit as some Presbyterian ministers did—though he no longer prayed for King George's health. He said what he thought only in ordinary conversation. Some people thought he was naive; many thought he was foolhardy. Only a few admitted he was brave.

He did not look like a brave man. He was short and would have been rotund if his calling had allowed him to be less active. The hair he had left was salt and pepper gray, and his plain face was reddish brown. Occasionally one saw a glint of shrewdness in his dark eyes, and sometimes, when he was not looking harassed, one might see a kindly flicker there.

Young Jacob Lienhardt—Joggi—had seen it a time or two. Today, at the bidding words, when his pastor's eyes lighted on him, Joggi was astonished at their gladness. But when Theus sat down, his expression was impassive, and once more Joggi had the feeling that Herr Pastor knew or guessed everything he'd been up to.

No, not everything.

Out the open windows, beyond the cleared space of the graveyard and the pastor's fields, he saw the wall of mighty trees that descended the river bluff.

No, Herr Pastor could not know the feelings that took you when you caught your enemy's blade and grappled with him and felt your blade in his guts. The young man Jacob shut his mind, or tried to, against what he'd known over the last four years. . . . The surprised look of the first man he'd ever killed. The unshaven fuzz on the cheek of a Tory—fourteen or fifteen?—when he'd turned over the body to strip it of clothes and weapons. A woman and her children shivering while his side burned their house. The mindless look of a girl-child the other side had raped. . . . Oh, he was rich in such memories—beggar lice, cockleburs, sandspurs that clung or stuck into him worse than the residue of actual battle.

Sometimes when he eyed a wild creature before he pulled the trigger, he groped with the question: *Can even this be blameless? How did I get to be part of this darkness?* The menace of the dark men in the woods he'd gone to warn the others about when he was nine years old.

Now he could see only dimly the words on the old illuminated panel at the front of the church. They no longer gleamed, were barely visible. "Let him that is athirst come."

Thirst? I doubt that any here know what thirst is.

Everything was smaller. The people were fewer and shabbier than he remembered, the old seemed older, the young younger, yet all were depressingly the same. There were the Rieders, most of them. Except Willi. Joggi tried to shut another door. "Willi, you sure you don't want to come?" Willi was not sure, but still he wouldn't come.

Herr Rieder was now only an ordinary-sized man, the lines under his eyes more raddled than ever, the eyes that sometimes looked at you tiredly, sometimes looked past you. Joggi dreaded having to speak to Willi's father. His mother—perhaps she wouldn't speak at all. Nothing ever seemed to matter much either to her or about her.

He was aware of the slender form beyond her. Narcissa, or Nissi as they called her. He couldn't see her face, for she wore a deep bonnet. He supposed she was not yet married. He wondered at it because she'd always been so pretty, but he was mildly glad. She was his own age. Willi was a year younger.

They had an older brother and sister, married and gone, and younger ones, whom their grandmother was keeping in order in a front pew. They had also a mulatto brother. If he was here, he'd be sitting with the other slaves at the back. Was he the only dark-skinned Rieder? Probably not, Joggi realized now, as he remembered the people on Hans Jacob's place, not all of whom were African-black.

His thought shifted to his own father down the row, the round head set absolutely square on his shoulders. His eyes never looked away. Joggi reached toward that presence, and as his awareness of his father deepened, the tangled leaf-green curtain, deceptively shadowed, became smooth-hewn paneled walls with solid doors and bars, a place to rest in as he'd rested on the bearskin rug before the hearth years and years ago. He tried to rest there now.

Outside, after the service, Theus had done no more than clasp his hand firmly and say, "I thank God to see you, Jacob," when Elsbeth was upon him, and Theus moved away.

"And here he is! Here we see him!" Elsbeth was speechless a moment. "Oh Joggi, Joggi!" Her face was working. "So you're back!" Her mouth moved soundlessly as she gathered words, phrases, surmises.

"And now you see, now you know for yourself what this wise old head saw five years ago! Now you've gotten a bait of it, haven't you, of all such prancing and ramping about as you young ones have been up to! Well, I'm glad you're at last home, Joggi, for your dear mother's sake, but now you know what it's brought us to, and you know what it's like to bring us to yet, aye-God, and our Pastor too," raising her voice, "and his family and the rest of us who won't forsake him! 'Not go to divine service?' I said, 'I'll not hear of it, let our Pastor be ever so rebellious! I'll go there as long as my old legs hold me up. It's God's house!' I told them. 'Let others do as they please!'" She looked beyond Joggi. "And there's your sister, I see. Oh, she and that set walk high on the road today, no doubt! Well, if the King's soldiers come here, they can take me to jail along with Hans Jacob and our Pastor, guiltless though I am, and all the rest of you. 'And let it comfort you,' I told him, 'to know what you've brought on your wife and your children and your old mother at last!'" Her darting look jabbed Joggi. "Where's Willi?"

"He stayed in Charlestown, Frau Elsbeth." Joggi hesitated. "His duty kept him there."

"Duty? And what was your duty? What was your duty there that—"

Joggi interrupted firmly, "My duty was to leave, Frau Elsbeth." He smiled.

She hushed. That smile. Fifteen, twenty, twenty-one years fell away. The chuckle started in her eyes, twitched her lips. "You scapegrace! You good-for-nothing rapscallion! You always were the nimblest little rascal I ever knew!" She stopped and eyed him again, her smile twitching in and out of her sunken lips. "The first time I ever saw you, there you were trying to pull out of your dear mother's arms, trying to get to old Elsbeth, not that it was me you wanted to get to either, just wanted to pull off and be somewhere else! Let me hug you! You're not too big for me to hug yet! Or take a switch to either! Take a switch to you and Willi both is what I'll do if I ever get him back here!"

Her square old frame did not feel in the least fragile to Joggi.

He shook the cold hand of Hans Jacob Rieder and bowed to Maria, Willi's mother. It was a smooth bow which somehow, sometime he had learned effortlessly. He turned to Nissi and saw a stranger's face inside the deep bonnet, a middle-aged woman's face. And he remembered sickeningly what he'd heard a year ago about some of the Rieders being down with smallpox. Some Germans had brought it up from Georgia.

But Joggi did not look away from Nissi. He recognized her in the eyes. A derelict houseplace where someone still made fire and tried to live.

Her look also met his directly. He was not sure what it said but at that moment it impaled him.

He did not bow to her. Instead he turned to her father. "May I have the honor of waiting on your daughter this afternoon, Herr Rieder?" He glanced at her again. Her pitted face had reddened. He added, "If she's willing to spend a while talking over old times."

Joggi had only a little more education than most of the backcountry Swiss of his day. Yet from his mother he had learned correct speech, and he had a knack for good manners that his merchant grandfather Frillig, whom he had never known, would have approved of.

Hans Jacob let his surprise show, though in a moment he cleared his throat and said heartily, "Why, come ahead, Joggi, come ahead! Nissi'll be glad, we'll all be glad to see you!" He winked, "Johannes, they think we're old, they think we've forgotten, but we remember how it is, eh?"

Joggi sensed Nissi's cringing at her father's words as she moved away. He felt the same.

Hans Jacob turned to Johannes, lowered his voice. "What do you think, what will all this news mean? I tell you, it looks serious!"

Joggi walked across the churchyard toward his sister Barbara, and again he was startled.

She was standing with an older woman who wore a dark mantua of watered silk although the day was warm. Barbara too wore silk, but he did not observe her clothes, rather the fact that she was well along in pregnancy. She was eighteen and had been two years married, but even though he'd seen her once since her marriage, in his mind she was still a fifteen-year-old girl.

Their eyes met. Hers were the same deep blue as their mother's. They showed surprise and gladness; yet he saw hesitation, even a reserved dignity in her manner.

They said each other's name, clasped hands, then embraced clumsily.

The older woman said, "Well, I'm glad to see you, Jacob, though I didn't expect to see you yet so soon."

"*Grüss Gott*, Frau Meyer."

"And how was it in Charlestown when you left?"

Joggi's face clouded. "Raining, as well as I remember."

She looked puzzled, then laughed. "I've no doubt the sun's shining there today. At least for some. Well, if you had sense enough to know finally you chose wrong, I'm glad you left. We're certainly willing to let bygones be bygones. And I hope when others arrive here soon, they'll be as generous."

"If you mean the redcoated kind, Frau Meyer, I know little about their generosity. I haven't experienced it. But," he smiled, "I'm not yet convinced I chose the wrong side. And that wasn't why I left."

"Then let me give you some advice." Her voice was tight and high. She had not been talking about the British arriving but about ungenerous homecoming Whigs. "You'd better not tarry too long hereabouts. There'll be changes. That some will welcome and some will not."

"Thank you, Frau Meyer, for your advice." He bowed. "Barbara, have you heard from Conrad lately? I hope he's well."

Barbara's downcast face was pale. "Yes, we heard last week. He's well."

They stood awhile awkwardly until Frau Meyer moved away. Barbara lifted her gaze. "Oh Joggi, I wish . . ." She did not continue. "But," she lowered her voice, "you won't change, will you?"

Little Barbara. Babeli. Annoying little sister because she never turned away from the truth, always knew it and told it. Seeing her now, he realized how much like Mama she looked. "When have you been home?" he asked gruffly. "They didn't tell me anything about you."

"It's been a long time. At first it was the distance. Frau Meyer doesn't like the ferry." The Meyers lived east of the river. "Now I don't ride much."

"How did you come today?"

Barbara said they were staying with the Gallmans, a long-settled Loyalist family who lived a few miles up the river. "You should know that it's risky for people like us to live without men to protect us, Joggi. There's hard feeling against us here."

"Here?" He was unbelieving.

"Yes, here. Though more over there." She gestured across the river, nodded toward her mother-in-law. "She's been cursed and spat at."

He looked away, his face sober. "Do you come often to divine service?"

She shook her head. "It's the first time in months."

"Why today?"

"To see the looks on some faces," she answered low, "and because she feels safer now."

He responded quickly, "But you're not afraid."

She was silent. "I'm not afraid for myself." Again she was silent, then said swiftly, "Oh Joggi, why is it all so—why do we have to be on—sides? I'm not against anyone!"

He did not answer at once. At last he asked vehemently, "Babeli, why did you marry him?"

Her wondering eyes were the intense blue of sky. "You don't know?" Her expression changed and she looked away. "I hope you will one day, Joggi." Her voice deepened, was someone else's. "Oh God, I hope you can!"

As he looked at her uncomprehendingly, he saw her expression change again as she saw someone beyond him. It was her mother.

Hesitantly at first, then swiftly, Madle and her daughter came together. Joggi looked at Johannes behind them, and his father's face was streaked with such joy and pain as he had never happened to see there before.

5

That afternoon Joggi rode into the wide, trampled yard of the Rieders' two-storied house. The house was set a hundred and fifty yards back from the High Road and had been built by Hans Jacob's father, the immigrant planter, miller, tanner, and Indian trader, who had laid the foundations for his family's prosperity. The Rieders had far more land and possessions than the Lienhardts did; yet there had developed between the two families an enduring relationship, which resulted from more than their Swiss origins and a remote tie of kinship. Perhaps it had begun when Johannes worked for Hans Jacob his first two years in the country. The bond was strange because Johannes was different from Hans Jacob in many ways.

Joggi did not see Herr Rieder among the men lounging on the veranda as he rode up. He lifted his hat and bowed slightly, but, barely slacking his pace, he rode around the house to the broad-porched ell, where the women sometimes sat in the afternoon and where children often played.

Yes, there, unbelievably alone, sat Nissi Rieder.

Joggi hitched Roker, his father's horse, to a post and mounted the steps.

Nissi rose to receive him. In green-figured muslin with a silken light-green overskirt, her body still carried the ways of beauty, but unlike other women her age, she wore her hair loose about her ravaged face. Again it was her eyes that held him. The fine arch of her brows was not gone. She had hazel eyes.

She saw a slim man of below average height, his beard trimmed and brushed, his black hair curling neatly at his temples, his face beatified by the red-ridged scars on his forehead and cheek. Although his clothes were obviously not his own, their very looseness gave him an air of— difference. Nissi caught her breath at the violence of the movement beneath her breastbone. His hand was hard and warm.

He saw that her hand was as young and shapely as it had ever been. He raised his eyes again to her face. "Nissi." The corners of his mouth curled upward.

Hers trembled a little. She looked away, then back at him. She too began a smile.

Relief washed through him. Nissi Rieder. He saw Willi in her smile, and somehow that brought Heiri and the rest of them here.

"Sit down, Joggi. I'm glad you came." But her voice was no girl-voice. Her skirts settled gracefully about her knees as she sat down.

He looked about him. The same big old chairs with cowhide bottoms. The old fig tree that was the only green thing in the yard and the same size it had always been.

"Do young ones still climb in the fig tree?"

"Sometimes."

"When Frau Elsbeth's napping?"

A black girl came out with a salver and offered Joggi a glass of wine and some little cakes.

The wine was home vintage. With the port of Charlestown closed, he wondered if Herr Rieder was still able to enjoy his afternoon rum punch. He remembered the time he and Willi had sneaked too much of it. Herr Rieder had seemed to laugh it off but Herr Lienhardt hadn't. Joggi never forgot the price he'd paid. "It wasn't what you drank, but the way you drank!" thundered Johannes. "When you're old enough to drink openly with self-control, I'll have no word to say to you."

Later Joggi wondered if even his father drank always with self-control. Most men he knew did not. Just let them get into the enemy's stores. Occasionally he wondered at his own sometime indifference that let him leave it alone. He didn't think his father's words or punishment had anything to do with it.

After a while Nissi asked low, "Why didn't Willi come with you? Nothing's happened to him, has it?"

"No, he's all right—or he was the middle of April. I hope he's still all right."

"I thought you were both in the same company."

"We were."

She was silent. Joggi was suddenly tired of having to justify his presence. It had been a mistake to come here, even to come home. If he could have survived, if he could just have made it up the country—

"I was ordered out. He wasn't." But that wasn't the whole truth either. Nissi's silence asked for truth. "No, we were given a choice. He didn't want to go. I did."

"Was it taking a risk to go?"

"Not as much as staying there, I thought. At least that was how I saw it. There was risk fifteen or twenty miles away."

She didn't ask what the risk was. He set down his glass on the little table in front of them.

She said, "You don't care what people think about you, do you?"

He glanced at her quickly and saw again a faint smile. He relaxed a little. "Not most people." His gaze moved across her scarred and pitted face. "I hope you don't think less of me—because I'm here and not down there."

"No, of course, I don't. Being a prisoner would be hard. For you."

He kept looking at her but decided she was not mocking him. He looked away. "You can't always help what happens to you. Sometimes there's no way to help it."

She did not answer, and he wondered if she thought he'd been talking about her. After a while she said, "But it doesn't make sense to get killed either if you can help it. You'd rather be killed than be a prisoner?"

"You don't know you'll be killed. And you've got a chance to win something."

"What?"

"A chance one day to win a victory."

"To kill somebody else?"

"It's better than to be killed."

There was no shade in the yard except beneath the fig tree. The sun beat hot on the steps and on the wide boards at the end of the porch. The line between sun and shade was hard, definite.

She shook her head. "I don't understand it. I'm glad you're here. I'm glad you didn't stay in Charlestown and I wish Willi'd come with you. But I don't know why you were there to start with." Her voice gained force. "'The rights of my country,' I heard Willi say one time. Joggi, nobody's come here to take anything from us that I know of. My father, my family, they live here the way they always have. What is it that's worth—killing people and risking being killed for? Is it something completely outside my life?" She paused, said low, "Joggi, I understand about death coming when you can't help it, as you said." *And,* she thought, *I understand about wishing it had taken you after it's gone.* "But I don't understand about—going out to kill or be killed. Is it because I'm not a man?"

Joggi leaned back, stretched, didn't answer. His mind felt brittle and old.

How do other people get to be "the enemy"? she was asking. How could you be so against other men you were willing to suffer and die to destroy them? He looked into the sun-dazzled whiteness of sky. If you thought along those lines too long, you'd either go home or head for the far back-country.

. . . Ah, the far back-country. That was where you got your answer. There, too, men killed without thought. The back-country held freedom. And it held danger because it held men. No matter how far back you went, there was always danger. No freedom without it. . . . Freedom and danger, why were they so entwined? And what about loyalty? But loyalty to whom?

As always when he let his mind so drift, Rudi Näffels' words came to him. "Joggi, there's a time to put down your musket. I'm saying there'll be a time you'll have to not shoot. There's a time to remember the good that's been done for you and to you. In fact, most of the time, I hope you come to see, it's better not to shoot. . . . But there's a time you have to. You ask your Papa about it and he'll tell you."

Rudi said, "I went with Pickens because I can't see letting us all get scalped and burned. Look, I know a Cherokee. I know and respect more than a few of 'em. But they've got some ways I want no part of and you don't either, and a government that would bribe and use Indians against helpless people, not against armies, I tell you, not against armed men, that government I don't respect. I'll fight that government." Self-mockery twisted his smile. His voice rose. "And what right does a government across the ocean and thousands of miles from here, what right's it got to try to regulate my life? 'Regulate!'" He spat. "I got a bellyful of that a few years ago, I can tell you! I want no part of being 'regulated!'"

But it was a present irony that most of the South Carolina Regulator leaders from the sixties had taken the Whig side just as Rudi had. Oh, a few were Loyalists, like Moses Kirkland and the Cunninghams. And who wanted to fight on the side of Kirkland?

Too many did. Joggi thought of his brother-in-law. But he'd never liked the Meyers. . . . Well, he didn't much like Herr Rieder either. But his son Willi—well, Willi was his friend.

It was a snagged web, a many-sided, wormy web bunched in the crotch of a tree. What made a man your friend or your foe? It was hard to decipher the faces in the trees. How was the friend's face different from the hated enemy's?

Too many stories of troops who'd shot up their own side by mistake.

He shook his head, sighed inaudibly, and glanced at Nissi, but he couldn't see her face, for the curtain of her hair had fallen forward. She was looking at her lap. "Nissi, remember how we used to play 'Hide and Go Seek'?"

"Yes," she answered distantly.

"Remember the time I climbed on top of the scuppernong arbor and lay up there where it was so thick you couldn't see me from beneath? I lay looking down through the leaves and I could see different ones of you when you came in. Sometimes you'd look up but you never could see me, it must have been the way the light was.

"I remember Willi looked up one time and I almost moved. Then he went and stood at the edge of the arbor awhile. I wanted to come down. . . . But then I didn't either. It was like Willi was—I don't know. . . . Finally all of you gave up and called me but I wouldn't come, and after a while you stopped playing. When I finally climbed down and came around the house, you were all so mad at me you wouldn't play anymore."

They looked at each other, probing for the same meaning, but they did not find it.

"You didn't come when we gave up," she said.

"No. . . . Somehow I couldn't. You were on the other side."

And we didn't play together again for several months, they remembered.

Nissi looked at his brown hand clasping his knee. She remembered its grip. Once they'd been playing some game and he was It. She'd hidden but he'd found her, and when she dashed out, he'd caught her wrist so hard she'd grown angry and cried. He turned her loose quick, and he and Willi taunted her, "Crybaby!" How strange to yearn for that grip.

"Joggi, where was it you'd go when you wouldn't let Willi or Heiri go with you?"

Her dark hair still clouded her face, her face blurred. She was no longer a silken, petted girl, Hans Jacob Rieder's daughter. Nissi? That was still her name. And her hazel eyes were still clear, though questioning. Where did you go? she'd asked.

I'll say words but they'll hide me like the scuppernong leaves. . . . He thought now that he wanted to be seen. Perhaps this Nissi would come up and lie beside him. He wanted her to come up.

He leaned back in the old porch chair. Hot sunshine baked the board steps and baked the fields and pastures almost as far as his eyes could see. . . . Where there's running water and filtered sunlight on the sandy bottom and minnows dart. "Oh, places up the creek I used to go, I guess you mean. A long way off from any sound about the place—the axe sound and—others. I'd go where I couldn't hear anything but wild things. Free things."

She turned toward him, pushed back her hair in a gesture that was infinitely moving because it so gracefully revealed her poor face. "You wanted to be free of us all, didn't you?"

"Nissi, I wanted to be in those places where things have their own life, where there was so much to see that I didn't know about. I can't tell you how I felt—myself—not like in the field or at home, anywhere else around other people."

"Do you still feel like that?"

"No." He met her look. "Not anymore. That's all gone." He didn't say, "As your girl-beauty has gone," but the words said themselves.

Yet his hand moved the distance between them. Hers cupped to meet it. They sat awhile so. She moved her other hand to cover his, and now he felt as if two wings enfolded his hand.

She felt its life. *If a strong brown bird were caught so*, she thought, *if it would let me hold it, this is how it would feel.*

Slowly with a smoothing movement she withdrew her hands. Never, never must she hold him too long. She smiled at him.

Old woman? No! he cried. His smile flashed too.

After a while she said, "Freedom. Is that what you think the war is about?"

He shook his head. "At least, not my freedom. . . . I don't know." He stood up. "It's what you do. You get into it and you have to do it."

"You wish you weren't into it?"

"No, I don't mean that either." He spoke with sudden force. "I believe it's our country, and they have no right to try to hold us down. And I don't mean to give up either. I'm not the only one. We'll go somewhere else. We'll fight in North Carolina or Virginia. Nissi, I believe in our side! I do! Only—" He stood at the porch rail, saw the far line of trees—long, neat, and even. "It costs so much," he said low. "I'm not talking about death and starving. I mean," he turned to her, "I just wish it wasn't our own kind of people we fight."

She rose and took a step toward him, put a hand on his arm. "I wish Willi had come with you," she murmured. "Not so he'd be here safe, but to be with you. I wish he were here to go with you."

As he gazed at her, he saw that whatever came, her eyes would always cancel the outrage of her disfigurement. Their looks meshed.

He said eagerly, "Nissi, if we could be children again, we'd go up to one of those places on Savana Hunt I was telling you about. Listen, I'll take you one day, I will! We'll go there, hear?" His voice caught light, a spring wind.

"Yes, Joggi, we will go there." Her voice was as warm as the afternoon humming of bees.

He had never kissed a woman in this way—the tentative, tender preface, the ultimate seal.

"Nissi Rieder, don't you forget me," he said at last, only because words seemed needed to mark the moment.

"Joggi Lienhardt, don't you forget me," she said because she wanted him to hear her words and to heed them.

After she had watched him mount his horse and leave, she said aloud to God, to the world, "Today it's the seventh day of May in the year of 1780! I'm alive, God! Do You hear me? I'm alive!"

Elsbeth, who had not overheard their conversation but had been peeping out the window at their leavetaking, kept saying over and over, "Well, bless God! Bless God!" She would have broken into laughter if she could have seen her granddaughter's eyes.

When Joggi rode around the house, he saw that the front veranda was empty, for the men stood at the fence along the road. They were looking toward the south.

He drew rein. "What is it?"

Several glanced at him but did not answer. Their looks seemed uneasy.

"Why's everybody out here? Who's coming?" he asked.

An old man sniffed, frowned, and spat. "Nobody yet. But they will be soon."

Joggi sat on Roker, gazing down the road. He knew who they meant. King's troops.

One man held up his hand. "Listen! Do I hear something?"

At first there did seem to be a drifting murmur of voices, a distant drumming. They strained to listen. The sun-baked air was still. No, not yet.

But Joggi in his imagination did hear the far-off sound of drumming, drifting and receding. This side of Tom's Creek. Past Herr Theus's, past the church. Now it came more strongly, the definite ta-ta-tum, ta-ta-tum, ta-ta-tum-tum. Moving up the High Road, moving up toward the Congarees, swiftly, louder, to Granby to reclaim their old provincial mid-station.

Suddenly, Joggi dismounted and drew back in unreasoning panic at being weaponless.

In his ears the drumbeat was loud, smart, quick with its perfect control of feet moving and arms swinging. The sounds that had first seemed to float in the sunshine were solid and hard. The moving parts would be solid and hard. The shrill of a fife cut the air.

He must not stay here longer. He must not see the impassive faces sweating, the red shoulders swinging in tireless strength. Let the men by the fence wait for them. He'd leave tomorrow.

He'd not go home by the road as he came but back through the woods, cross the creeks at shallows. He must say his goodbyes tonight. *I must move fast,* he decided.

No, wait. He would make one more joyous space around the tender thought: *I'll circle far enough back to find the place where I'll take her one day.*

6

The brothers walked away from the house in the dusk. They moved toward the branch where the air was sweet with bay bloom and running water, went by the wagon road their father had made to his fields beyond the creek. They stopped on the bridge. Even and well-lodged, the beams were as firmly fixed as they had been ten years ago. In the dusk Joggi could see the bushes still kept cut at the corners of the bridge. It would still be easy for boys to get down the bank and play in the sunlit shallows when they had time for play or when they stole it.

Tonight the water was lightless. The night would be moonless. He wished he were already on his way, had not let himself be persuaded to wait until morning.

The house was too bright. There were too many faces turned toward him. Restless, he had said, "I'll step outside a few minutes."

Heiri had said, "I'll go with you."

They stood on the bridge above the rushing waters of Savana Hunt Creek, its myriad plashings intensified into a rich, muted roar. Shrillings came out of the grass. Something plopped into the water.

Heiri said, "Where will you go?"

The silence between them lengthened. Joggi said, "It's better I don't say. So if somebody asks, you won't know."

Does he think I'd tell anybody? Heiri pondered. *And who'd want to know besides us?*

An owl whooshed down across the bridge but the frantic shrilling of its prey could scarcely be distinguished among the other sounds.

Joggi said, "You can guess. There's not much choice."

"I'd like to go with you."

Could Heiri be serious? Yes. Joggi could not see his brother's face but he imagined its earnest look. "You'd better stay here. Papa depends on you."

"I don't know about that."

Such a tone from Heiri? Joggi felt mingled incredulity and exasperation. He tried to think how it would have been to stay here these last two years, hoeing, plowing, milking, woodcutting. Well, Heiri had chosen it. Or at least he'd not chosen to leave.

"Sometimes it's hard to be nothing but a pair of hands," said Heiri.

"What are you talking about? You know you're more than that."

They were looking west where it was still light above the trees. To Joggi the shape of his brother's head seemed large, yet very young.

"You think you're the only one ever wanted to get away?" Heiri asked.

"Well, why didn't you?"

"I'm not brave. I'm a coward, maybe."

"Heiri, shut up such talk."

Heiri thought, *You don't want to have to think about it, do you? It's easier not to think about a brother and how he feels.*

"Heiri, you think I left here because I was brave? Brave's got nothing to do with it! It's what you *want* to do, that's why you go! You go ahead and *do* it!"

"Joggi, it's always been easier for you. To move out. Maybe because you're the oldest."

"Easy? It wasn't always easy. Easy's got nothing to do with it either."

"But hard has."

Joggi did not answer.

Heiri wished he'd ask, Why is it hard? Then he might be able to answer, Because of love. But they'd never say that word.

"I ask myself," said Heiri, "why I'm here when you and Willi are off fighting. I'm on the same side you are."

Joggi did not ask again the obvious question. Unspoken also was an invitation. Heiri waited for it.

At last he said, "Can I go with you in the morning?"

"No!" The harshness of his answer hurt Joggi's throat.

Heiri jerked his head around, but his brother was moving away, moving back the way they had come.

Heiri sounded almost, but not quite, as if he were laughing when he called, "You never did want me tagging along after you, did you?"

"No, I didn't! I don't now! You'd start crying and I'd be responsible for you!" Joggi's words burst forth of themselves.

Heiri made a funny sound in his throat.

Joggi stopped still. "What I'm telling you is," he spoke with angry emphasis, "you do what you've got to do because *you've* got to do it, not

because of somebody else! It's because *you* want to go, not because of me
or Willi or anybody else!"

Slowly Heiri began walking toward his brother's back, though he
wanted to go the other way, move across the bridge to the fields beyond.

"Joggi, you don't know anything," Heiri said low. "You don't know
anything about living with people or what it's like to—to—"

"And you don't know what it's like to be all by yourself! Because
that's where you end up—by yourself."

"Why, I thought men fought together. And helped one another out."

"Yes, they do, we do. But there's a time— You listen to me, Heiri."
Joggi turned and they stopped and faced each other six feet apart. Joggi's
anger had dissipated, even his shame for the way he had spoken. Now he
said clearly and distinctly as when he had used to give his catechism
answers, word-perfect, "There's an hour or maybe it's a second, when it's
you by yourself, and that's what matters more than anything else. No
matter what anybody else does or doesn't do, it's what *you* do that
matters. That's why I'm telling you, if you go, you must go on your own."
After a moment, he continued, "*When* you go, Heiri. You'll go." And
Joggi thought that these words were the nearest to a gift he could give his
brother.

They moved away from the creekside and followed the road through
the cornfields back toward the house.

After a while Heiri said, "When I go to muster drill, we follow
orders. We don't do anything on our own. It must be I *am* ignorant. I thought
a lot of it was doing what you're told to do."

"It is. But whose orders you think I'm following now? See, that's
what I'm talking about. If—*when* you go, you won't be following somebody lockstep. And it takes what's making you go now to make you follow
somebody else's orders later on. Heiri, that's what so many don't know. Its
why so many break and run."

The brothers walked side by side, each breathing different mes-
sages in the air.

Joggi said, "I think sometimes about Papa, when he came to this
country. He didn't follow anybody's orders."

"He came with a friend, though. I've heard him tell of a friend."

"But that wasn't why he came. He didn't come as a tag-along."

Heiri accepted the word. No, their father was not a tag-along.

As they moved up the slope, the angles of the barns loomed black
against the sky.

"All right, I'll tell you then," said Heiri. His voice sounded husky, almost as if he'd been crying. "I've waited so long, I'm half ashamed—"

"Ashamed! Now? Why, now's the time they'll be quitting in droves! And you've waited and got to be such an old man! Old-man Heiri! You must be all of nineteen years old!"

"But besides I don't know where to go! I don't know who to join up with. That's why I hoped—"

Joggi cut in, "Heiri, I'll tell you one word. Rudi."

"Cousin Rudi?"

"He'll know. And you know where he lives too."

Heiri sighed, "I think I do. And maybe I can just manage to get up there. By myself." And in these last words Joggi heard at least one note of his brother's old comic self-deprecation.

"You will." Deliberately injecting a superior older-brother note into his voice, Joggi said, "I told you you will."

As they opened the dooryard gate, the dog bounded toward them, fawning and cavorting. Joggi bent to take his cool muzzle in his hands, to feel his skull and scratch behind his ears.

Heiri went ahead, paused, said over his shoulder, "Mama'll be wondering what's happened to us."

"Tell her I'll be in directly."

Heiri still stood on the steps.

"Tell her I want this fellow to know me when I come home again."

Heiri opened the back door, and although light and voices pushed out, Joggi walked around the house. He stood at the front gate and looked down the lane toward the High Road. He wondered if he'd ever come home that way again.

He wouldn't leave by it. In the morning he'd move northwest through the woods on whatever horse Papa gave him. He'd move parallel to the south bank of Saluda, try to cross at Island Ford, depending on who guarded it now, if anybody—no, maybe he'd better cross earlier at Kennerly's Ferry if he could, that might be safer—and make his way toward the Enoree. Heiri with him? He couldn't imagine Heiri with him, didn't even want to try.

He turned his back to the gate and looked west.

The stars were out, brilliant in the black sky. In the morning when he left, the thinnest sickle moon would be behind him. It would follow him over his shoulder.

He remembered the first time he'd ever seen that crescent moon emblem. It had been on his father's cap when his father had enlisted to go against the Cherokees. He remembered the first time he'd seen it on a battle flag too, the surge of identification he'd felt. That old blue flag would be furled by now. Also the one with the stars and thirteen stripes.

He knew boys from Georgia. And from North Carolina and Virginia and from Maryland and Delaware too, and no doubt he'd know others farther north in time to come. They really weren't very different as far as where they came from was concerned; they just differed from man to man the way he and Willi differed. Oh, they said things a little differently sometimes, used expressions that often seemed comical to one another, and they spoke of other rivers and settlements. Yet he'd known a Virginian from Fincastle who was not even Dutch that he'd felt closer to than to a blood brother.

You couldn't separate the people in this land by where they came from. And you couldn't separate its parts either. It varied marvelously, but mountains were brothers and swamps were sisters. Creeks in Georgia had the ways of creeks in South Carolina though the lay of the land might change a creek at its different levels.

Yet even so, after you'd recognized all kinship, you came to know there was a stamp on you of where you came from that was as much you as your hair and hide. He'd felt it the first time they'd recrossed the Savannah River, and always he felt it the closer he came to the Congaree. He had no words for what it meant to see again Savana Hunt.

Men talked of lands to the west. Rudi talked of pulling up and going there one day. *Maybe I will too*, Joggi thought. *I sure want to take a look over there if I live long enough.* Now he thought somberly, *maybe I'll be forced to go. Not allowed to come back here.*

His jaw hardened. His foot grew heavy on the ground. *Mine!* he thought fiercely, *whether I stay here or not. My life belongs to this ground!*

He stood inside the dooryard fence, leaned against its gate and drank in the shapes of yard tree, roof angles, the scent of smoke and sweet corn and faintly of earth-trampled dung. The great brilliant stars hung high.

He drew a deep intake of breath; his chest grew large. He felt a thing growing inside him that belonged not only to the ground but also to the air above it, a force welling up that belonged to this depthless air, whether night-black or cloudless blue, that overarched trees and water and all wild places. And roads and homely barns. His body grew powerful with the force of it.

"Do you still feel like that?" Nissi had asked, and he'd said, "No."

He hardly ever said *God*. His upbringing had been too religious for easy prayer or blasphemy, and even now he did not say the word. But he recognized in the vastness of its power, recognized in rapture, a thing inside him from beyond himself that he'd been given.

7

Two weeks later the marchers Joggi had not stayed to watch would move into and beyond the Congarees. These troops, which included American Volunteers and Loyalist militia, would be part of the force that would fan out over all of South Carolina to garrison such places as Georgetown, Beaufort, Cheraw, Camden, Rocky Mount, and Ninety Six and to make other strongholds at ferries, fords, and crossroads. Three companies of Royal Fusiliers would be left at the Congarees to encamp for a while around the old Kershaw-Chesnut Store, that now belonged to Wade Hampton.

Sir Henry Clinton reported the capture of 6000 to 7000 prisoners in Charlestown. In his count he included Continentals, seamen, militia, and all other adult free males in the city. The regular troops commanded by General Lincoln, who, according to an English journalist, "limp'd out at the Head of the most ragged Rabble I ever beheld," were sent first to barracks, then on board ships. The town's inhabitants were paroled to their homes as were the lowly militiamen, "Poor creatures," who were allowed to "creep out of their holes" and "to go Home and plough the Ground," which was said to be the only place they were useful.

Parole was offered all rebels in the country who would lay down their arms. In return they would receive British protection. Most Whigs felt obliged to accept these terms. They had fought and lost. After the fall of their capital, many patriot leaders outside the city, such as Andrew Williamson, Andrew Pickens, Isaac Hayne, and LeRoy Hammond, felt obliged to surrender with the understanding that they, like the humble, would be allowed to stay home and attend to the "ploughing." Since there was no longer a unified army in South Carolina, for them the war was over.

Numbers of people who had never actively supported the rebellion but who had been pressured into giving it lip service were glad now to make their loyalty to the old order known. Everyone was expected to take the oath of allegiance to the King if he desired British protection.

Johannes attended to his plowing and had not yet made up his mind to take the oath. Did he need British protection? From whom? Indians? Rogues? Or from the British themselves?

Heiri still attended to his plowing.

A week after Joggi left and a week before the troops arrived, Willi Rieder, a paroled prisoner of war, came home. He was not as ragged as Joggi had been or as starved, but with his flesh honed down to the bone he had the appearance of someone from elsewhere, a man from northward or perhaps an itinerant missionary. For the first time Elsbeth thought she saw in him the favor of his grandfather Hermann, and, wonderful to relate, not once did she reprimand him or tell him what to do.

Cathri Lienhardt could not get Willi Rieder out of her head. She saw him at divine service with his grandmother and she thought he was beautiful.

Only a handful of worshippers were there, and the few who came looked uneasy. They wondered if another Sabbath might find their pastor without a congregation. They never considered that it might find the congregation without a pastor.

Johannes had pondered a long time before coming. Madle had decided him. "We serve God, not earthly lords. It's the Sabbath day."

The worshippers sat stubbornly scattered in their regular pews, and the house seemed lighter than usual. Was it the uncrowdedness? The windows were open to the June morning. But as the service began, the empty spaces seemed to fill with an air as richly palpable as the sunshine outdoors, and the scattered worshippers seemed not so far apart after all.

They sang Luther's *"Ein' Feste Burg,"* "A Mighty Fortress." It was strange that with so few to sing, the hymn sounded out with such power.

Theus took his text from the Ninety-First Psalm: "He that dwelleth in the secret place of the Most High shall abide under the shadow of the Almighty. I will say of the Lord, He is my refuge and my fortress, my God; in Him will I trust."

Herr Pastor's face was as round as ever, his stature neither added to nor diminished. His voice was unemotional, slightly pedantic, sometimes a trifle unsure in its delivery. His sermon was not extemporaneous; it never was. He did not believe God was honored by the spur-of-the-moment mouthings of such ordinary servants as he. The sermon must be wrought in the study with much prayer. But today his words got out of the study. It was as if he were standing before each family's hearthstone. He made no specific allusion to their temporal situation, but he spoke entirely of the sovereign power of God.

Later when they sang the old hymn of praise, "*Man lobt dich in der Stille, du hocherhabner Zions-Gott,*" they felt borne up by notes beyond their singing. Within the age-darkened walls and the scents of summer, they moved into a greater simplicity that was at once a part of where they were and yet beyond it. They felt enfolded and at the same time free. Some of them would go glad in that great simplicity all day.

Elsbeth never cried in church like some, but today after service she took the pastor's hand and said, "God keep you, Christian." Elsbeth and Herr Pastor were the same age and had known each other for forty years, but this was the first time she had ever addressed him by his given name.

Everyone lingered near the door. The Lienhardts, except for Heiri, stood in quiet order for the greeting of their few friends and neighbors.

Madle clasped Willi's hand and smiled through a prism of tears.

Willi asked, "Where's Heiri?"

Johannes answered, "He wrenched his back yesterday. It seemed best he stay home and rest it."

"Tell him I hope I see him soon."

"Come down and see us, Willi. Come down any time," Johannes said.

Cathri gazed after him as he left with his grandmother. Had he looked at her? Had his look included her too? But he was twenty years old. How could she expect him to notice her?

She thought he was the most handsome, the most heart-moving, the most wonderful male person she had ever seen in her life, so fine-featured, so upright, so—noble! And his grave hazel eyes—so dark and deep and fine—she thought that if he really looked at her, she would faint even though she had never fainted in her life.

Willi Rieder. Could he really be this person? That undersized, persnickety, stand-offish boy that neither she nor Hans had liked very much? No, that was not this Willi.

She was wearing her rose-figured bodice and skirt that had been made up for her new at Easter. She loved wearing it because its dainty pattern became a part of her cheeks, her hair, her motion, made her dainty too. Had he glanced at her? And could he see she was no longer a child even though she was five years younger than he was?

Willi Rieder. She let his name slide in and out of her mind as they started home. She imagined him riding among them. There ahead were Papa and Georgi on Roker, Mama and Anneli on Mama's mare, and Hans and Andreas in front on the two young workhorses. She herself rode the little sorrel . . . and Willi rode with them.

She was glad she'd forgotten the old foot-mantle she was supposed to wear to protect her skirts. "It's so hot, Mama!" She wondered if he'd noticed how she rode out of the churchyard no longer doubled up behind someone else like a child. She kept behind the others on her little horse.

They forded Tom's Creek near the footbridge.

Suppose he *would* come after them; suppose he *had* decided to ride home with them to see Heiri. No, how could he do that when he'd left in the cart with his grandmother? But say he'd left his horse nearby. A black horse, like the one Herr Rieder rode, a tall, powerful horse. Any minute now he'd be coming up abreast of her. He'd see how well she sat her sorrel, see her in dainty rose and green, and he'd spur up and really look at her. He'd say . . . . Behind her she heard the wet black legs of his big horse splash powerfully through the churned-up stream. Soon he'd come up. He would look across at her, not smiling . . . those deep-seeing, serious eyes . . . just move nearer, look across at her, and say . . . "Catherine?"

"What's the matter, Cathri?" her father called back, turning, drawing rein.

"Nothing, Papa."

"You'd better come along then."

She glanced behind her. The trees that lined the creek hid the road beyond it. This side the creek, the road was lengthening. Empty.

The road was empty. Not there to see her in rose and tiny green leaves. She rode alone. She would be like the Key Maiden of Tegerfelden, who wandered by the little river, Surb, forever.

Willi, I love you! I love you, Willi Rieder! Do you hear me?

The trees along Tom's Creek heard her, and the white road.

The Key Maiden died of love, but I won't die! cried Cathri.

Her hilarious brothers rode ahead hallooing. Papa and Mama jogged in front of her with Georgi and Anneli clinging to them. They were going home to dinner and the long afternoon.

Empty. But no! The woods and fields stretched full around her, full of him and how she felt, different from any way she'd ever felt in her whole life! She felt so alive that the very sunshine and sky and leaves were full of it all! How could anyone ever die of love? *Willi*—so wonderful a name she couldn't get enough of saying it!

No, he was not here, but he was somewhere, would come sometime, maybe even tomorrow. Oh, everywhere on this road and over and above it, the sunshine itself was full of his name and of their being alive!

8

"Cathri, can't you do anything I tell you?" Her face tightset, Madle swung the pot out and took the lid off the reeking mess of turnips and greens. "How could you sit there and let the whole pot burn up?"

Her eyes already filling, Cathri moved out of her mother's way. With a thousand summer scents drifting through the back door where she'd sat churning, she hadn't smelled anything else. With her imagination drifting, she'd forgotten what seemed to be her primary function on earth.

"How much water did you put in?" her mother demanded.

"You said not to put too much."

"How much?"

"A cupful like you said."

"I said a cup and a half and I said to keep checking."

"Mama, I thought you said—"

"Cathri, you don't listen! You don't pay attention! You don't pay attention to a word I say!"

In one swift movement her mother turned the pot upside down and dumped its contents into the slop bucket. "And what will your Papa and the rest of them have for dinner now?" She splashed a gourdful of water into the pot. "Don't just stand there, hand me a basket!"

"Oh, I'll hurry and pull more, Mama. Don't you want me to—"

"No, I don't." Her mother was already putting on her bonnet. "You get that pot scrubbed out. I want two cups of boiling water in a clean pot when I come back, the same pot, mind you, and scrub it clean, and two slices of bacon. But no salt. I'll salt it myself."

"Do you want me to finish the butter?" Cathri knew it was a foolish question as soon as she asked it.

"Yes, please, Cathri." Madle regarded her daughter's tear-flushed face, tightened her mouth, and went out.

Cathri put her head on the table and sobbed. So unjust! "She *did* say a cupful, she did! Just a little over a cupful and not too much!" *And to watch it. How could I know it would boil so fast? Hasn't she ever forgotten anything in her whole life? Hasn't she ever done anything wrong?*

There was no end to Cathri's sins anymore. Too much salt in the hominy this morning. Did she salt it twice? The bowl broken last night. "It slipped! It just slipped out of my hands!" A jug of honey left uncovered that ants had gotten into. And worst of all, the slit she'd cut in Georgi's new shirt she'd been sewing. But she hadn't meant to! "Mama, I didn't know it was folded like that!"

"Because you don't keep your mind on what you're doing!"

No, she didn't. How could you think only of turnips and greasy bowls and jug stoppers all day long? Wasn't she ever supposed to think of anything but cookpots and the endless seams of cloth to be sewed with stitches never quite tiny and cramped enough to please anyone? Wasn't she supposed to have *some* freedom, at least in her mind? Nobody to talk to, nobody to see. More people might be coming and going on the High Road than ever before, but *she* never saw anyone with their house blinded by trees and her parents forbidding them to go anywhere near the road. And no sister, no friend to talk to, nobody. Who could talk to a child like Anneli? And Barbara might as well live across the ocean.

Lately she'd been missing her older sister more than ever, especially after seeing her that time at worship. Now Cathri thought of Barbara every day. Thought of her waiting for the birth of her child, thought of how it might be with her, how mysterious it was, wondered. Wondered what it must be like to have a husband—to marry and sleep in the bed with a man, a boy . . . . Her mother had talked to her about it once, mostly warning, but what she'd said seemed so unbelievable and unclear that Cathri hadn't wanted to think of it anymore. Yet the thoughts would come back. And now remembering Willi's eyes—hadn't he looked at her? How had his eyes pierced down into her heart if he hadn't?

The mystery that anyone *masculine* could be so wonderful. How could a *man* come to possess your heart and your thoughts and everything about you?

She grew still, rested her forehead on the smooth board.

If she could only see him again. It seemed like a month since that Sunday, though it was just ten days ago. Last Sabbath they had not gone to divine worship after all. Papa said it would be better to have a quiet Sabbath at home. Her heart had sunk in such desolation that she'd turned away to keep them from seeing her face.

"Why are you crying?" Anneli would demand.

Cathri had so looked forward, she'd been counting the days, how could she bear another desolate day, another empty week?

Her tears welled up again. She began to cry hard, cried till her throat ached and her eyes burned. At last she grew still and then began to feel ashamed. How hideous she must look, hot and red-faced, with a stuffed-up nose and swollen eyes. What would they say when they came in? Mama would think it was because of the scolding. Well, it was. Still she felt horribly ashamed. She saw herself as a clumsy girl in a short brown-checked skirt and a dampish brown bodice handed down from her mother because her own clothes kept getting too small. She felt as drab as old Frau Kesler. She reached for the loathsome pot, a scrub rag, and a spoon to scrape with. The black scrapings caked under her fingernails, ground into her fingertips as she scraped, scrubbed, and rinsed.

She heard Beno barking outside but wouldn't go out to look. Whoever it was, she couldn't bear for anybody to see her the way she looked now. It was probably someone for Papa, some old man. One of the children would run to call him. Or Mama would hear and come. She wiped her face again, and reached up to loosen her hair.

She hated braids. Why couldn't she wear her hair loose sometimes the way Nissi did? Nissi's curled so pretty, and hers tried to curl too.

"You can't work with all that hair tumbling down your shoulders, Cathri. Besides it looks so hot on your neck, get it up off your neck and your shoulders. It makes you look like a slattern."

Well, Barbara didn't look like a slattern when her hair was loose. She looked beautiful.

Barbara. Oh, if only—

Cathri hurried to measure water into the pot and swing it over the fireplace—but forgot to stir up the coals and replenish the fire—and moved quickly, softly toward the front door, keeping well to the side of it so she could peer out unseen.

Georgi and Anneli were already at the gate, swinging it open. Cathri felt all the blood drain away from her heart; her whole body grew weak and warm.

Him! He was getting off his horse. The children stood by the open gate. He was coming in! Oh no!

She slipped into her parents' room to the side of the big room and moved to the looking glass by the open window. She saw the same freckle-bridged nose, the swollen eyes and flushed face, saw the faded old bunchy bodice that made her look big as a house. She pushed it down farther inside her skirt, tried to make her waist look smoother. She tied the pot-smudged apron tighter, then untied it and flung it on the floor as she heard voices on the porch.

"Come in, Willi. Or it may be cooler out here. Georgi, bring out two chairs."

Her mother's voice carried well, but she couldn't hear what he said.

"Oh, you must know you're always welcome. And you'll have dinner with us? How is Frau Elsbeth? And your mother?"

His voice had a murmurous quality, more refined than their own brisk tones. The Rieders didn't speak like the Lienhardts; at least, his mother and Nissi didn't. *His* mother didn't spend all her time instructing and correcting children the way hers did.

She heard Heiri's name mentioned, also her father's.

"Cathri!" her mother called. From inside the doorway she called again, "Cathri!"

Cathri moved to the open window, sat on the sill, swung her legs over it and slipped to the ground.

Inside, Madle surveyed the empty room. There was tepid water in a pot over the fireplace, and the fire was almost out. In the churn by the back door, puffy specks of half-churned butter floated in buttermilk. Mid-morning, company, and no dinner yet.

Madle closed her eyes in disbelief. What in this world had gotten into that child?

Johannes, Heiri, Hans, and Andreas were hoeing out grass and hilling up corn. Their crop was excellent, the weather was fine, and they were making such progress they would finish the field by mid-afternoon. Everyone was working steadily with no talking. The only speaker was a bob-white at the edge of the woods.

They heard the barking at the house. Hans and Andreas looked up hopefully and slackened their pace. Johannes too paused, then bent again to his work.

"Must be somebody," Hans remarked.

No one answered and Hans went back to work. In a few minutes they heard Georgi's high-pitched "Papa! Oh Papa!"

Johannes straightened and watched the sturdy little figure come pounding down the row. "Who is it?"

"It's Willi! Willi Rieder!" Georgi skidded to a stop, panting. "He wants to see Heiri, Papa! And you too, Papa, if you can come!"

Johannes drew a long breath. To see Heiri. Just to see Heiri. Come in the middle of a morning to interrupt a man's work and break up a whole day. Why couldn't he have waited till dinnertime, or, better still, late afternoon? These Rieders, these people that didn't work themselves, how would they like it if somebody came and stopped all work in their fields in the middle of the morning? Not one bit. He knew how Hans Jacob drove his people. But that young Willi likely didn't know what work was all about.

"Go on, Heiri. You'll have to go. But he could have picked a better time." Johannes resumed hoeing.

"What about you?"

Johannes didn't look up.

"He asked for you too," said Heiri. "It may be news."

Slowly Johannes straightened his back. He sighed and planted his hoe in the ground. He looked at Andreas and Hans. No use to go off and leave them here; he knew them too well. "All right. You've both done good work this morning. You can knock off till dinnertime, but this afternoon we've got to get back out here and finish this field no matter how long it takes. Everybody hear me?"

"Yes sir!" They dropped their hoes. "Can we come too?"

"No. You find something else to do. Go cool off if you want to."

Each boy packed the blade of his hoe with earth to make its handle stand up and mark the place he'd stopped, then headed for the creek.

As he walked home, Johannes observed the strong stalks, the gray earth soft and grass-free around the plants they'd worked. Ah, it was a beautiful field. Never did it fail him, this satisfaction, this almost exultation. How do men live who can't work the ground? he wondered. Do they ever know what they miss? It's part of what we're made for. But some don't know it. Sometimes he felt a wondering pity for such men. Other times he felt chosen.

Heiri was walking ahead. He too sensed the life of earth around him, but he also felt the beginning of something tumultuous inside him as well as in the pulsing air.

Willi saw the strain in Frau Lienhardt's face. He was half-sorry he'd come. He wondered now what he'd thought to find here. Joggi wasn't here. What was Joggi's home supposed to give him that his own didn't?

Well, it used to give him—something.

He'd always liked Joggi's mother. Her vitality moved out to her fingertips, but it didn't agitate everyone around her. She neither nagged nor did she oppress others with her silences. As a child he'd always begged to go home with Joggi, and once there, he never wanted to leave. In this house there were no rending tides to surge in and drown a child. Here everyone was who he was from the inside out. You knew who everyone was.

As for Joggi's father, the one word Willi thought of for him was *steadfast*, and although Herr Lienhardt hadn't been overly tolerant of youthful vagaries, a degree of understanding was there. When he thought of Herr Lienhardt, Willi thought of one of those big rocks that cropped up near springs and creeks in the sandhills. He used to think Herr Lienhardt was like that because of where he came from, the old country his grandmother talked about. As a boy he'd wished he could have known his own grandfather who came from there too. But now he was not so sure. Now he thought the country had little to do with what a man was. It was the choices you made. That he'd already made.

How he wished he'd taken Joggi's way of getting out of Charlestown. If he had, his present might not be so difficult. . . . Yet if he had, he might not even have a present. If Joggi had barely made it home alive. . . .

Sitting across from Frau Lienhardt, Willi feared to mention her son's name. He glanced at her small sinewy hands, so different from his mother's plump soft ones. Why did he always think of this woman as a lady? She did tasks that only black women did in his home. Yet the way she said, "Willi, you give us great pleasure in coming," spoke of high gentility.

"Are there more people at the Congarees these days, Willi, or do there just seem to be more passing? We don't always hear them, it depends on the way the wind's blowing, but it does seem there's more coming and going on the road lately."

"Yes," said Willi, "and too much for some of us."

"When they hear the music and drums, the children are wild to go and watch, but we don't allow them to. I suppose you see and hear everything."

"Sometimes I wish we didn't. I wish our place was miles away."

Madle saw the young man's hands tighten on his crossed knees. After a while she said quietly, "Joggi said it would not soon be over."

The name spoken brought again the low voice pleading, "Come on, Willi!" and he saw the intense face shadowed in the lee of the wall that windy April day.

Madle rose. "I hear Johannes and Heiri now. If you'll excuse me, I'll go inside."

Willi rose too. "Frau Lienhardt, I don't know where Joggi is, but wherever it is, I'm going too. If I can. It's either that or—"

The desperation in his voice stopped her.

"—or join those against him."

Heiri and Johannes washed their faces and hands by the back door. As they came through the house they heard voices, and at the front door they found Madle and Willi facing each other.

Willi looked pale and distraught. He turned quickly, "Herr Lienhardt, I'm sorry I've come in on you like this. I'm sorry I've interrupted you."

Johannes put out his hand. "Welcome, Willi." The young man's looks and apology had already done their work.

"I wanted to see all of you again," Willi said low. "I keep remembering how it used to be, how I used to come down here and spend the night with Joggi—and Heiri."

Johannes' face spread in a smile. He put his other hand on Willi's shoulder, grasped it briefly. "I think we'd all like a taste of those old days again. Sit down, Willi. I'm glad you came." And he realized he meant it. What was a cornfield compared to a boy's need? "How's it been with you? Not easy to get back into our kind of life, is it?"

Willi shook his head. He glanced at the father and son, didn't know how to start. Johannes took the other chair and Heiri eased down on the porch with his back against a post.

"You've been gone—how long?" asked Johannes.

"Not as long as Joggi. I went the autumn of '78."

"And you were under—who? Not Colonel Thomson."

"No. I was under Colonel Robert Goodwyn."

"Oh yes. Colonel Thomson used to head up all our militia in these parts. I know he leads Regulars now. Or did."

Willi was silent.

"Then was General Richardson your commander?" asked Johannes.

"Most of the time. At Purrysburg and Charlestown he was. At Stono it was Williamson." Another silence fell. "But Colonel Thomson was at Purrysburg and Stono when we were."

"Not in Charlestown?"

"No. The Rangers were outside."

Johannes sighed inwardly. He had let it all become distant and blurred, his son an indistinct figure in some place he'd never seen and tried not to imagine. In the early days with Joggi in the upcountry, Johannes had suffered much. Later he deliberately put away his own images of the low country.

"Ah, you've seen all that country, Willi, more of it that I ever did. I've never even seen the Savannah River."

"You wouldn't want to now—or the country alongside it. Not the way it is now."

Johannes did not ask what he meant. Again the silence grew.

"I thought you and Joggi were together." Johannes decided to worry the subject further. "And I know he served under Thomson."

"We weren't together till Charlestown. It wasn't till after Savannah that his time with the Rangers was out and he joined our company." *And never belonged there,* Willi thought.

Another silence stretched long.

"Well, you've both followed good men. Richardson and Thomson are great men. They've served this province long and well."

State, not *province*, Willi wanted to correct Herr Lienhardt. "You know them?"

"Oh, I've seen both many a time. We marched under Richardson in '61. Colonel Richardson he was then. And Major Thompson, he was part of it too, with his Rangers."

"Where was that?" The Indian War it must have been. The middle-aged man across from him suddenly looked different. Willi's father had never marched anywhere that he knew of, except at muster drill when he was obliged to.

"Into the mountains. About the time you were born, Willi. And another time," Johannes added quickly before Willi could speak, "Colonel Thomson and Colonel Richardson, these gentlemen and one other, they put their own bodies between two bands of men about to battle. I know you've heard of that. At Bush River in '69?"

Willi shook his head.

You young ones, Johannes thought, what you don't know. "You see, I was on one of the sides getting ready to fight."

Heiri remembered about his father's taking part in the banding up of men to control outlawry—they'd called themselves the Regulators—but he'd been only seven or eight at the time, and he'd forgotten if he ever knew that part of it. He glanced at his father. So hard to think of him anywhere else but here.

"Those men prevented much bloodshed that day. Saved all of us from what we'd have been sorry for later. I have great respect for those men. I hope you young ones understand that. Why it grieves me they've lost."

The older man's shoulders were clad in a homespun smock that hung unbelted for coolness. No more unmilitary or unadventurous a figure could be imagined. *Yet,* Heiri thought, *he's marched with great men, and in spite of what he says, he's seen cities, mountains, and oceans I'll never see. My own father.*

"I'm not against a man going to fight, Willi. I know there are times he feels he must. But I know what it costs him. Heiri, I know what it would cost you."

Heiri met his father's look. He had to look away.

He heard Willi's quick intake of breath. "Did you know, Herr Lienhardt, that the order's come now, that we've all got to serve with the English or be their enemies?"

"What?" The other two spoke together.

"It's posted. Posted at Granby. Return to your alliegance, they say, and serve us or be considered King's enemies."

In the silence they heard Madle's voice at the back of the house expostulating with someone.

"Who do they mean?" asked Heiri.

"First of all, they mean me, the ones of us they paroled."

"You mean," asked Heiri, "they say you must fight for *them?*"

Willi's mouth was a bitter line. "We have till the twentieth of this month to 'resume the character of British subjects,' it says, and 'take an active part in forwarding military operations.'"

"But I thought when you were paroled—" began Heiri.

"After the twentieth of June all paroles are null and void."

Johannes digested the words. "It's not right. Not right to force that service on those who've laid down arms. I can see them maybe asking for volunteers, but to compel service when you've surrendered—no, it's not right."

"So that means," said Heiri, "you now have to—"

"Enroll to fight against our own side."

"What about those who never took arms?" Johannes asked.

"They mean everybody. All single men to serve six months here and in North Carolina. Or Georgia. Fathers of families to serve here as needed. Everybody in the militia has to be ready to serve."

According to provincial and state law, all able-bodied men from sixteen to sixty except slaves and the clergy had always been subject to militia duty, but under state government the service might as well have been considered voluntary. However, the recent sounds of fife and drum along the High Road told a new order.

"What it means is," Heiri said, "you've got to fight on one side or the other."

"What it means is being drafted to serve in Tory regiments," said Willi.

"No," said Johannes.

"Oh yes, sir. They've put out handbills everywhere. Go to Granby and read one."

No one spoke. Beyond the paling Johannes saw his ranks of breast-high corn waving in the morning breeze, on the left side of the lane his dark-fruited peachtrees.

"What does your Papa say about it?" he asked.

"He thinks it won't hit him. He thinks his beef and corn will buy him off. And me too, he says. Maybe it will."

Both Lienhardts were surprised, Johannes troubled, by Willi's cynical tone.

"He ought to have seen some of the country plundered and burned that I've seen," said Willi.

"But that could be all the more reason to seek protection," Johannes said quietly. "They do offer protection, I understand."

"Yes. And they offered parole to us militiamen too. In fact, they insisted on it. Our general wanted us to be considered just citizens, but they wouldn't hear to it; we had to be paroled prisoners of war. Now you see how they keep their word."

"I wonder how many men are still in arms against them," said Johannes. "Does anybody know?"

"To my knowledge there's been no sure news from the North. But I don't think they've had time yet to take over North Carolina. Or Virginia. Or any other state either. That's why Clinton went north. He left another lord in charge down here."

"No," said Johannes slowly, "they've not yet won it all. That's why they're so hot after us here."

Again they fell silent. How many this side of the North Carolina line still carried arms? Where was that lean, dark-faced spirit who'd left here three and a half weeks ago? How many were there like him and where were they?

Johannes stood up. "Willi, I'll leave you two for a while. Stay on and talk with Heiri. But don't go before dinner. You must stay and take dinner with us."

Johannes was unaware of boiling pots and sputtering griddles as he walked through the house, barely aware of the small braided head of Anneli as she sat on the back steps stemming strawberries or of the head of flowing tresses of his older daughter, who was bringing water from the spring. He had to get outside the house to consider these tidings against the spread of fields and sky.

Heiri said, "Well, I'll have to go, Willi. Soon as I can tell Papa and Mama, break it to them after dinner I think, I'll have to get ready and go."

With the large fair head turned away from him, Willi saw only the curve of a sunburned cheek. All at once he felt a vast easing. "When?"

"Early in the morning."

"Then I'll go with you. Is that all right?"

Heiri smiled before he chuckled. "You know it's all right. Tomorrow morning? You think that'll be time enough?"

"Good. We'll meet—where?"

They considered. No public place and not at Willi's house by any means.

"How about our old millpond, Heiri? Where the tailrace goes in the creek. We can cut back through the woods from there. I'm not sure we ought to go on any public road."

They talked about horses. Heiri thought he'd be given one, though he wasn't sure which one or how suitable. Willi said perhaps in that case he ought to bring two. They argued a little but finally settled it that each would bring the best he could.

"Have you ever been north of the Saluda, Willi?"

"No, I haven't."

Suddenly Heiri's eyes were alight with laughter. "Well, I haven't either, but we'll find our way. Don't you worry about that."

Why did food always taste so much better here? Usually Willi couldn't abide turnip greens, but here they were as tender and succulent as the youngest greens he could imagine with just enough flavor for taste. And these crisp light potato cakes, he was ashamed to take another.

Willi glanced around the table, especially at the woman at the end. One woman to prepare for all these? The girls helped, he supposed. Cathri was half-grown already. He couldn't remember the little one's name. In fact, he'd forgotten the boys' names except for Hans. He'd also forgotten that people could look so healthy. But who wouldn't with food like this? The children's enjoyment of dinner and their pleasure in having company was the dominant mood. Heiri said little. He seemed absorbed only in his dinner.

I wonder if he's thought what kind of dinner he'll have from now on. Though he'll probably come well supplied in the morning, better than I will. Willi had not yet decided when, what, or if he would tell his family.

All doors and windows were open to the scents and sounds of outdoors—flower fragrance, a rose in bloom by the fence, a privileged hen's clucking in the dooryard and a new brood's cheeping. Willi had been saturated in home smells and sounds these last weeks. And the softness of a featherbed, the long mornings of uninterrupted sleep, the clean clothes brought into his room by dark hands.

He'd never dreamed his mother would be so glad to see him. Or his father.

There was a stir at the table as Cathri and her mother brought bowls of strawberries and clotted cream, but just as Cathri set a bowl in front of him, the bowl tipped sideways and her hand slipped. Juice and cream splashed out, and a couple of berries jumped onto the table.

"Oh!" she gasped. He tried to help her pick up the berries, but as their hands touched, she jerked hers away, and juice and berries flew against his shirt.

"Oh, I'm so sorry!" she whispered, drawing back.

"It's nothing, don't mind." Glancing up, he saw the girl's face was scarlet.

She held a pink-stained apron clutched against her breast and kept whispering, "Oh, I'm *so* sorry! *so* sorry!"

Her mother came with a cloth. "Well, Cathri!"

Willi said quickly, "I moved my elbow, Frau Lienhardt, it got in her way. It was my fault."

"Oh, but your shirt." Madle retrieved the berries and blotted up the juice on the table. "If you'll take it off after dinner, we'll rinse out the stain before it sets."

He turned on the bench smiling. "Then I'll have to rinse out Cathri's apron." The girl had moved away, her pink cheeks shining wet.

He looked at her. More like her father than her mother. Just a soft, open-faced child's look. Like Heiri's, the look Heiri used to have sometimes when he didn't understand or was distressed about something. Poor girl, distressed about her mother's scolding?

When they were all seated again, he tried to smile at her but she never looked up.

Cathri's heart was melted, was flowing out into the sunshine and sky. He had tried to take all the blame. She was lapped and bathed in that sweetness like the fresh pink strawberries and cream. But now she almost wished him gone and wished herself away, for she could not bear to look at him again—his face, his goodness—so she could remember the feel of his hand and his soft cream-colored shirt and the spreading strawberry stain. With her head bowed, the fall of her hair on one side hid her face.

Heiri and Hans stopped eating and gazed at their sister. If Heiri had been alone with her, he would have given her a quick hug and called her "Doodlebug." He wondered, *When will I see her again? Or see all of them?*

Madle did not look at her daughter. She was overwhelmed by a rush of such tenderness as she had not had for Cathri in many a day. *Oh, my poor darling!*

Johannes gazed out the door, already sensing the empty spaces without his son.

9

Dark and green, it flowed between richly overhanging trees. The afternoon sun shone on the scow fastened to the opposite bank, on the ferryman's house and barn above it, on the cleared grassy slopes beyond. Heiri and Willi led their horses in the shade at the edge of the wide trampled way descending to the river. The sun was hot and they were drenched with sweat.

"Wait," Willi said.

"What is it?"

"We can't cross here."

Heiri stared at the sunlit water. The scow was only a stone's throw away. He saw horses but no one outside the house. *Why can't we? Won't they pole over to us if we call?*

He had never crossed a river in his life, but he had watched travelers and wagons being ferried across the Congaree at Friday's. He was relieved that this river was not nearly as wide as the Congaree, for he was worried about Roker. Sometimes they'd put horses on the raft, but more often they'd swim them alongside it. Would he be able to hold Roker fast or would the horse take such fright he'd drag him into the water, and one or both would be swept downstream? They said the Saluda had dangerous rapids. To Heiri it looked smooth enough here, though he saw that the current was swift. This river was different, unexpected, like a suddenly seen woods animal.

Willi was drawing back beneath the trees.

"What's wrong, Willi?"

"See all those horses?"

Three were tethered near the building and six or more stood in the barnlot. "What about 'em?" Their number did give him pause.

"Do they look like ours?"

Heiri squinted against the light. Yes, there was something different about those big gleaming nags.

Willi said, "They look to me like troopers' horses. And there are too many there."

Heiri and Willi stood straining their eyes and ears. The trees and grass were motionless, the air still. The green waters were so inviting. *I wouldn't mind swimming it myself,* thought Heiri. In the trampled clearing a few yellow jackets worked low to the ground.

A faint drift of voices came from inside the house, then it grew louder, and a man appeared in the doorway. In the shadow of the porch roof, another man, unseen till now, sat up on a bench he had been stretched out on. Both men walked to the edge of the porch and looked across the river. The military dress of the first man was unmistakable.

"Move back," whispered Willi.

They backed their horses beneath the great oaks and sweetgums into the understory of box elder, viburnum, and greenbrier. When they judged themselves hidden, they stopped a moment to listen, then turned their horses and made their way up the slope through the woods. Heiri, who had followed Willi down, now went ahead of him. Without thought he angled westward from the way they had descended.

He had joined Willi an hour after daybreak, and the two had ridden by circuitous paths along ridges and branches, skirting fields and avoiding roads, until a few hours ago, when they had come out on the old Charlestown-Ninety Six road, the same one they called the High Road that ran west of the Congaree. Afraid they might miss the turn-off to Kennerly's Ferry, they had ridden boldly along the road, noting signs of heavy passing. Willi had not said how ominous those signs looked.

"We're such fools, Heiri. Or I am. I should have known."

"Known what?"

"They'll have men at all the crossings now. They left out from the Congarees day before yesterday. They left at midnight and I knew it. When they came through here, they made sure to leave the ferry guarded, and you can bet all others are too. We're just three or four days too late, that's all."

Why didn't you tell me? Heiri wanted to ask. *Did you think if I'd known, I wouldn't come?* For a moment his face reddened. *I know I'm ignorant, but I'm not that much of a coward.*

"Who marched out, Willi?"

"Three battalions of King's troops and a bunch of militia. Four or five hundred men. Couldn't you see back there where they passed?"

"Where are they headed?"

"Ninety Six, it's said."

"But that's not where we're going."

"No, and that's why I thought—but I didn't think. Or I didn't think enough. Because it sure looks like they're going our way. Or some of 'em have. They crossed the river down there."

"I thought Ninety Six was this side Saluda. You think they all crossed over?"

"I don't know whether they all did," Willi sighed, "but I know a dragoon when I see one. They could be strung out on both sides."

The two fell silent. Had the men on the porch seen them? They'd been looking straight across the river. Would they think it worthwhile to ferry across just to catch two suspicious-looking travelers? Willi doubted it but he wasn't sure. No one was likely to trail them through these woods, he thought, but the troopers could gallop up the wide path and maybe cut them off when they emerged on the main road. Willi knew that only King's friends, or those who claimed to be, now crossed the Congaree at Granby.

Heiri and Willi led their horses through a pathless way. Heiri carried a musket, Willi a rifle. Heiri had never shot anything other than hawks. He'd never even killed a deer. He'd fired at one a time or two and missed.

"How could you miss?" his father had expostulated, laughing. "Anybody that can shoot a hawk!"

He just wasn't a hunter, Heiri said.

Now they labored through tangled glades and up steep ascents. The air was close and humid beneath the canopy of riverine trees.

"So we're following the King's army," said Heiri. "So if we catch 'em, they'll think we've come up to join 'em." He meant it for a joke but Willi didn't laugh.

"We should have left five days ago. Or at least four. If I'd just come on down there and we'd started then—"

Five days ago I was digging potatoes, grubbing for those big fine potatoes, Heiri thought. He remembered how cool and damp the earth was although the sun was hot on his back.

"Let's rest a bit," he said. "And I'm thirsty. I wouldn't doubt if these animals don't need a rest too."

They had stopped for only a brief nooning. Their eagerness had kept them going for almost nine hours, and it would take its toll on their beasts if they weren't careful. Heiri had been deeply affected when his father offered him Roker. His first impulse was to say, "No, I can't take him, Papa," but something in Johannes' look stopped him.

Now they found an open place and tethered the horses loosely to let them browse on the long grass.

The young men sat without talking. Finally, Willi took a rolled-up bundle from his saddlebag and lay back with it under his head and put his hat over his eyes. Heiri sat leaning against a tulip poplar, his eyes wide open. This was already foreign country to him—the narrow greenish river, the increased steepness and the richness of these slopes. He took some of the earth between his fingers, dark red clay. They rested an hour.

"Willi."

Willi stirred.

"You awake?"

Willi sat up.

"Think we better be moving?" asked Heiri.

Willi rose and stood motionless as Heiri got up more slowly.

Willi said, "Is it any use?"

"What?"

"Is it any use to go on?"

Heiri gazed at him.

Willi went to his horse. "If we can't get across the river—this way we're headed straight for Ninety Six and that army waiting for us. Or if not them, a gang of Tories."

"You think the whole river'll be guarded? Every last ford and ferry?"

"How many places to cross are there? That we know of."

"Papa said there's another one at Saluda Old Town. And beyond that the Island Ford."

"And that one's as sure to be guarded as Friday's. It's the main crossing at Ninety Six. You see, there are just not that many places to cross. That we know about."

"We might find another one."

Willi was silent.

"Well then, we'll just have to go around Ninety Six the same way we went around Granby, and we'll cross the river above it. *Sneak* around it, Willi. I think I might be able to sneak—with you along to help me."

Willi was still funbling in his saddlebag.

"You really want to go back?" Heiri asked slowly.

Willi turned. Two looks were quarreling on his face. A wry grin won. "No. Let's go on."

An hour later, only some four miles from the river but considerably farther upstream, they came out on the old main road in the westering sun. Widened and sunken by decades of feet and wheels, nevertheless the road showed no marks of recent trampling.

They stood in the slanting sunlight. "I don't believe any army's come along here," said Heiri. "Not lately."

"No," Willi said after a moment. "They all crossed at Kennerly's. They're using the road along the north bank. When they get to Island Ford they'll cross back."

"Why would they go that way?"

"Better road maybe. Or better plunder. I've heard it's thick settled over there. More provisions to take and steal. Or maybe they've got more friends over there and hope to gain more, I don't know."

"Then why can't we use this road? If they're all across the river. At least we can go a little faster on a road. And not get so bunged up."

Heiri had scratches on his neck from a hanging tangle of catbriers as well as earlier scrapes and tears from low limbs and thickets. He removed something crawling at the edge of his hair. A tick.

They scanned the earth for fresh hoofprints.

"All right, let's chance it," Willi said briskly. "Let's go."

The ground was mostly level now between woods and fields. The land was higher, the road more nearly straight except where it wound down across the creek bottoms. They passed two houseplaces set back from the road. They heard the lowing of cows. Heiri looked across the green corn to a far dark tree and a rooftop. They did not see anyone, but they smelled smoke. The air lightened, freshened. The evening was calm with bird sounds in the woods. It was strange, Heiri thought, that now he liked it better when trees hung over their way. Because he felt more sheltered?

"Wonder how far we've come?" he asked.

"Hard to say, we've come so roundabout. Twenty-five miles maybe. Or you've come more like thirty."

"How far would they go, Willi, in one day? As far as we've gone?"

"No, they'd stop sooner. They've got more to carry and more to do."

"They wouldn't keep on till dark?"

"Not unless they were trying to catch somebody."

"How many miles usually?"

"Twelve. Fourteen. Sixteen. Depends."

Heiri meditated. *If we've come twice as far as they go in a day— then they may not be so far ahead of us.* "Wonder where they are now?"

Having no idea, Willi didn't answer. He pictured the encampment spread out in a field or pasture, their officers in somebody's house. They'd have sent light troops ahead to scout the way and there'd be coming and going, dispatches sent back the way they'd come. There'd be tents, fires, men getting their supper, men at ease, the camp guards stationed beyond the fires. Men organized and the wild of uncertainty shut out. He longed to be by such a fire, though not one of those. To be with his own kind, his place achieved and his duty allotted to him.

"What I'm thinking," said Heiri, "if we push on tomorrow and the day after, keep to this road and keep pushing on, if they're not in too big a hurry, we might pass 'em. Get up there before they do and get across ahead of 'em. You think there's a chance of that?"

"They'd send ahead. They've already sent men on, you can be sure of it."

"But if the main part of their army hasn't got there yet, the river might not be so close guarded as we think."

"We can hope so. But I hear this country's thick with Tories."

"Not everybody's a Tory. We might find somebody that would know a good safe ford. And tell us."

"Maybe. Trouble is, you can't tell one from the other by his looks. A Whig from a Tory, I mean.

"That's true." *But aren't there people like Papa, people of good will who'd help anybody?* he mused. *Would Papa help a King's man, give him direction about roads and such?* he wondered. Either way, it bothered him.

"Tomorrow's Sunday," he said softly after a while. "Would they march on Sunday?"

"Oh yes, they'll march any day. We do too. But then," Willi added, "you'll take another day for rest now and again. And sometimes you'll lie up a week or more, sometimes a whole week waiting for somebody or something."

To idle a whole week. Heiri had never done such a thing in his life. *What kind of soldier will I make?* he wondered.

Maybe I'd do better to just keep going. On till I come to the mountains Papa told of. Find me a valley to scratch out a field and hide in till all's over. If I had me some tools and seed I'd be tempted—though it would be lonesome. If I didn't have Willi I might be tempted. He glanced at Willi's lean serious face. *It's why I'm glad I'm with him. It'll take Willi to keep me going. And maybe me to keep him going too. I think Joggi is wrong.*

Shortly after sundown they camped above a creek that had been meandering near the road for several miles. Heiri was too tired to fall asleep at once, but he would not allow himself to think of home. Instead he imagined the valley he might find, imagined it until it merged into the way he'd already come.

In the morning Heiri was sore in unaccustomed places, Willi only slightly less so, and it was hard to move on.

"Roker, I'll tell you what, old boy," groaned Heiri, "if we could swap legs, I'd be willing for you to ride me."

They led the horses awhile to work the stiffness out of their own bodies. The country continued rolling, richly wooded, interspersed with fields and pastures. They met a man and some children in a wagon. They drew aside to let the wagon pass and spoke a greeting, but the man did not respond. The children looked back with scared faces.

"We must use English now," said Willi, for without thinking they had spoken German.

"Then you'll have to do the talking."

The sun beat down hotter than the day before. They welcomed long woodland stretches. At noon they shared more of their homecooked food, Heiri his sweet potato pie and Willi his peach tarts, and they rested longer than they had the day before.

But by mid-afternoon heavy clouds were darkening the west and soon thunder was rumbling across a lowering sky. Then lightning began to crack close, and when the sky split, they dismounted to stand under some dogwood trees at the heads of their shivering beasts, but the torrent beat the leaf canopy into their faces. It was a long, hard pour. After it moved east, their clothes were washed clean of sweat but were trashy with broken leaves and twigs.

The road was slick mud. In some places water ran in rivulets; in other places it stood ankle-deep. When they came to a creek, they found the road so flooded on both sides they could hardly tell where the channel was.

They eyed it uncertainly. Heiri rode in first, and though the flow was swift and the descent uncertain, Roker kept his footing and brought his master up safe on the other side. He was a wise, brave horse, Heiri thought affectionately. Roker was thick and square-made, a dark bay with white hind feet.

Willi's young chestnut was less fortunate. Just as he came to the step-off, an uprooted bush borne down the stream dashed against him, and suddenly horse and rider were down, thrashing and kicking in the creek waters. Mercifully Willi got clear but was tumbled over before he managed to stand up in the breast-high waters.

"Help me, Heiri! Get hold of Shine!"

Heiri, already on the ground, shouted, "Catch hold of that branch, Willi! I'll get Shine out!"

He kept his footing in the current and managed to reach the horse's head and catch the bridle reins. Tugging firmly, he got the horse to his feet and struggled him up out of the water, while Willi pulled himself up the bank downstream, using some bad language. When they had felt the limbs of the trembling animal and afterward walked him, they thought he seemed all right. Willi, however, had wrenched his right knee getting clear of Shine. He felt his knee and grimaced as he took off his sopping clothes to wring them out and clenched his teeth as put them on again and mounted his horse. As they rode on, his knee began to swell.

The road continued hazardous for miles. Once they heard distant gunfire. They stopped, listened, wondered. Did it come from across the river? Neither spoke.

Their progress was slow because of rocks and mud. Sometimes Heiri dismounted to lead his horse, but for Willi walking was painful now. He rode silent and somber.

Heiri looked at him worriedly. Finally he asked. "Think we better find a place to stop?"

"If you want to."

Heiri looked at Willi uncertainly. Yes, he decided.

The sky was clear and sunlight shone horizontally on grass and leaves. The high ground to their left had little or no undergrowth under the big trees but plenty of grass. Moreover, they could tell they were approaching a bottom. Heiri did not relish the prospect of another creek.

When Willi dismounted, he could hardly stand. His knee was so swollen he could hardly get his breeches leg up to examine it.

"What you need is to wrap it up tight," Heiri said. "Put cold rags on it and then wrap it up tight."

"Cold rags from where? And wrap it up with what?"

Heiri considered. They could cut up a shirt, he had an extra one, but he didn't want to. Or a strip of blanket? Too hot. He thought of the two long linen strips intended for bullet patches. Why not? The cloth could wrap Willi's leg now and be used for patches later. Besides, he carried a musket and only a rifle required the greased cloth patch which you could use for a musket ball if you needed it but not if you had paper cartridges. His father had given him the cartridge box full.

When Heiri brought out the cloth, Willi protested, but Heiri said, "It'll still be good when you're through with it. Besides you're sure to need yours for your rifle, and I've already got paper cartridges."

"I should have brought a musket too," Willi brooded. "What did Joggi take?"

"He took a rifle. It was his old one. That's one reason I brought the cloth, in case he needs it when we find him. So I'll go fill up my kettle."

The branch below was high but did not look formidable. Heiri watered the horses and found a sizable stand of maiden cane for them. He filled his and Willi's canteens and the little kettle his mother had made him bring.

"How'll you cook without a kettle?" she'd demanded.

"Mama, I'm not going to cook!"

His father laughed. "Take it. You'll be glad of it!" Yes, he was glad.

Heiri brought up cold water several times for Willi to wring out his compress in, and afterward they bound up the knee as tight as they could. Willi said it felt better.

With the woods so wet they decided against making fire. They were glad of the bread and boiled potatoes they still had. They shared some of Heiri's dried apples, and they both had dried beef strips to chew on, but each could have eaten twice as much as he had.

As they lay down in their damp clothes, Heiri thought they really should have tried to make a fire. The night sounds grew louder around them and he thought of wild beasts. Wolves were said to abound in the upcountry and panthers. Was this upcountry yet?

He was about to say, "Willi, I think we'd better make a fire," when completely unbidden there sounded in his mind the words, *When thou liest down thou shalt not be afraid.*

Where did the words come from? He saw a round, gray-stubbled face and heard a pastoral voice. He remembered that today was Sunday.

He said in the dark, "I wonder if they had service this morning at St. John's?"

After a while Willi's voice came as if from a far place. "I don't know. I wonder too."

"Wonder what'll happen to Pastor Theus now?"

It was a hard question. "You think he'll take the oath?" Heiri asked.

"He's not done it so far," said Willi.

But could he continue to hold service under the very noses of the British if he didn't? And if he didn't swear loyalty, who'd come to service? Still . . .

"I don't think he will," said Heiri.

"No, Herr Pastor wouldn't go against his belief for all the King's army. And to think," Heiri heard a faint chuckle from Willi, his first in two days, "to think how many times he beat us for flouting authority. You too, Heiri."

"I didn't flout authority. I followed you and Joggi."

They talked of their tricks and ruses and of the times the old man had outfoxed them.

"I hope he's kept safe," said Heiri.

"I do too."

Heiri thought, *I'm glad I had him for a teacher. I'm glad my parents saw to it I had him for a teacher.* He sensed that he'd gotten more to keep him going than the food he'd brought from home. He forgot about wild beasts as he dropped into sleep.

10

In the morning they were itching all over from redbugs, the barely visible mites that burrowed into the skin. They were less disturbed by their tormenting whelps, however, than by the condition of Willi's leg. It was ominously puffed and discolored. Willi could hardly bear his weight on it.

Heiri finally found a sapling from which he made a rough crutch. He was glad for the hatchet Papa had told him to take.

"What if it was your left one, Willi? How would you ever mount your horse?"

"I'm wondering how I'll do it anyhow. You'll have to help me."

Heiri got a fire going and they had boiled corn-mush and bacon broiled on a stick. Willi did not eat much.

He gasped as Heiri helped him get his leg over the back of Shine.

"At least the horses had a good bait," said Heiri. "You ought to have seen that rich cane."

The sun was already over the treetops as they rode out.

Where is that army? Heiri wondered. *Starting so late, can we get ahead of them if we've even caught up with them yet? We didn't come as far yesterday as we meant to. But say they'd go fourteen miles a day. If they've been on the march four days, that's fifty-six miles. Say we've come forty-five from the Congarees . . . or maybe not so far. . . . No, we've not come even with them yet. We'd have to go twenty-five today or better, and we're starting late. . . . Well, all we can do is push on and hope.*

It was going to be another broiler. Willi's face grew flushed and his eyelids drooped. Heiri did not like his looks at all. After a while he stopped trying to talk to him. *But it's just a sprain, no broken bones,* Heiri told himself; *we both felt it.* If it had been broken, he couldn't have stood on it yesterday. Just keep off it and it'll get better in a few days.

"Willi, does it pain you when you ride?"

The answer was slow to come. "It hurts some."

Heiri tried to think what his mother would have done. She had all kinds of remedies for pain and inflammation, but the best was her cool, strong hands. And her sure, quiet voice. "Drink this now, drink all of it." Bitter tea. Willow bark.

Next time they crossed a branch, would Willi mind if he chipped some willow bark? If they had a covered vessel to put it in, it could steep in water as they rode. Why, his canteen, of course; he'd put it in his own canteen.

When the woods gave way to cleared land, he thought about turning off on a field road and asking for information. They caught sight of people in a distant field. A woman might help them, Heiri thought. He worried that Willi had caught some other ill from lying in the wet.

"Did you see those people over there?"

Willi glanced aside but did not answer.

"Wonder how far we are from Saluda Old Town?"

Again no reply.

The next stream was more than a creek; it was a small river, the Little Saluda. Here there was a narrow bridge of sorts but it sagged partly under water. Heiri eyed it doubtfully.

He dismounted and began taking off his shoes and stockings. "I'll walk it first."

As he sloshed through the water, he judged that the bridge would bear them. No planks were missing. Even so, he thought it would be better to lead the horses over it. Then he thought, *But Willi can't hobble across it. Still I'd be scared for him to risk it on horseback; it's deeper than that creek was. . . . But why can't I ride him over on my back? He's lighter than I am.*

As Heiri came back across, he called, "I'll lead Roker over and then I'll lead Shine. Is that all right with you?"

Willi was staring at the dark stream.

"And I've been thinking—what if Shine was to stumble or make some misstep? Why don't you slip off and let me be the horse this time?" Willi frowned and Heiri said quickly, "I know it's hard to get off and on, but if you could slide off easy on my back, I know I could bear you up, and it might be better than to take another risk."

"No, I can't do that. You just lead your horse across and we'll follow."

There was a short silence. "I don't know how much weight this bridge will bear. Maybe you'd better wait till I get Roker across." Heiri paused. "Then I'll come back and lead Shine, be at his head to steady him if anything—"

"I think I can steady my own horse."

Heiri's face flamed. He led Roker onto the planks. As he glanced down, the water flowing over his feet gave him an illusion of swaying. He had a momentary feeling of unsteadiness.

When he came up on the other bank, he turned and saw Willi leaning over his horse's neck.

It's his pride, Heiri said to himself. *And he feels so bad. I'll just have to stand here and pray he makes it.*

And the horse and rider did. Heiri smiled widely as Shine's fetlocks came up out of the water. Willi's face had lightened.

"I'm glad that's past," Heiri said.

He was relieved when Willi answered, "Me too," and added, "We've got to start learning how to swim these creeks and rivers."

"I don't know that Roker's ever swum a river in his life. You think he would—with me by him?"

"Sure he would. I know Shine would, wouldn't you, boy?"

As they rode on, Heiri thought, *I forgot to look for willow bark, but maybe getting over by himself was better for him than willow bark.*

Signs of habitation were becoming more frequent. They passed fenced rolling fields of corn, old fields now turned into pasture, and forests where cattle browsed among the great trunks. The oaks and hickories looked immense to Heiri. His eyes took in every detail of the growth and the lay of the land.

Twice they met single riders. This time they only touched their hats. The riders rode armed.

They came to a crossroads. It was clearly a main-travelled road to the river and would surely lead to a ford or ferry. Should they risk it? But they decided that even if they did succeed in crossing the river here, they might be too near the British to go safely on.

"Maybe by late afternoon—or sometime tomorrow—"

They had no idea how far they had come.

An hour later when Heiri was beginning to look for a resting place, two horsemen came thudding up behind them. "Hold up!" they cried.

Heiri and Willi turned.

The men looked fairly ordinary. One was somewhat undersized. The other had a bushy brown beard. They wore dark-dyed homespun and carried rifles. "Where you come from? Where you headed?" demanded the bushy beard.

Willi said in English, "We come from the Congarees. Near Granby."

"King's friends be you?"

"Who wants to know?"

The men exchanged glances. "You going to Ninety Six?"

"We head that way."

Heiri noted that the two had moved apart so as partly to flank them.

"And what might your business there be?"

Willi said angrily, "Why must we tell our business to strangers? Are you King's men that you have authority to stop us on the road?"

"Where's the King's army?" asked the smaller one.

"Why must we tell you? Who are you?"

"Look here, do you know Neely Carghill?"

"Not to look at, no," answered Willi. "We've heard of him."

Heiri never had.

"What do you hear?"

"I hear he's loyal."

In the silence Heiri meditated speech.

"We heard the King's army was coming this way. Do you know aught of 'em?" asked Bushy Beard again.

Heiri spoke. "They went over Saluda at Kennerly's Ferry." He gestured widely. "The King's army is over there." Heiri's German accent was much thicker than Willi's.

"Dutch be you? Come now, what's your business?"

Heiri disregarded Willi's restless movement, would not look at him. "We go to find my brother."

"Where is he?"

Willi broke in. "You know where Jacob Meyer lives?"

The smaller man motioned with his hand. The two drew back and spoke low. Heiri heard "Dutch" and "no harm to 'em." Heiri and Willi were beginning to turn also when the strangers confronted them again. "Tell us your names."

"If you tell yours," answered Willi.

They exchanged names. The strangers were Gill Stewart and Ephraim Giles.

"One thing you might like to know," said the bearded man, "I hear Ninety Six jail's full of rogues and rebels."

"Then why aren't you there?" demanded Willi.

For a moment it looked as if the man would charge them. He whooped and laughed. "Eph, I do believe this little Dutchman's got more to him than we thought. Reckon we'd best let him go? Or teach him his manners?"

Heiri had paled but he edged his horse forward. *I'll grab the big one—though I fear Willi's in no condition for this.* But Willi's hand had already crept to the knife at his belt.

Both movements were noted. The smaller man said low, "Best let 'em go their way, Gill. It may be we'll meet again."

While Heiri and Willi sat motionless, their challengers wheeled and spurred back the way they had come. The travelers watched them out of sight.

Neither spoke for a while as they rode on. Finally Heiri asked, "You think they were Tories?"

Willi shrugged. "Who knows? But I think if there'd been three of 'em, we'd have soon found out."

Later when they had hidden themselves from the road, they rested and ate the bacon and stiff corn mush they had saved from breakfast. Heiri asked, "Who is Neely Carghill?"

"I don't know. I just guessed."

"Who is Jacob Meyer?"

Willi grinned. "Nobody. A good German name." He turned to look at Heiri. "Would you have told them where Joggi is?"

"How could I when I don't know? If you mean would I have told him we're trying to join up with Whigs, I'm not a complete fool, Willi. But we have to have some reason for being on the road. May as well tell what truth we can."

Willi did not answer.

Heiri wanted to say, "And no use trying to make people mad either," but he didn't, for it might make Willi mad, and the last thing they needed was to quarrel.

He almost said, "How's your leg," but forbore. Instead he said, "Well, I doubt they know anymore about us than we know about them. That may be good. I hope so."

But was it good? What if they were Whigs and could have helped us? Whigs weren't famous for their gentleness anymore than Tories were.

Would he have taken the chance of trusting them if it hadn't been for Willi?

As they splashed through another tree-smothered creek, they glimpsed the roof and wheel of a gristmill downstream. Later they passed a cabin with a broken roof and, farther on, the briar-covered chimney of one long destroyed, but soon in the distance they saw a wide substantial house with numerous outbuildings. Now the country, which had been high and open, began to descend. The trees hung closer, heavier; and they knew they were nearing the river. As they crested the next rise, they saw before them a crossroads and, about four hundred yards below it to the right, the river. They knew where they were.

Saluda Old Town had been the chief settlement of the Saluda Indians before they removed to the North a half century earlier. Perhaps one of them returning might have found still some traces of their old fields and orchards, the weirs in the river which had once been theirs. After the Indians left, the site became a habitation of white hunters and adventurers until Ninety Six grew into the chief trading center of the region. Because the lands around Saluda Old Town were rich and already partly cleared, migrating Virginians in the 60's and 70's were not slow to claim them. Now the angle between the Saluda and the Little Saluda was filled with their small plantations. Still, a tavern house, the ferryman's house, and a couple of other old houses marked the ancient site, and it retained its Indian name. It was also a terminal on the road north from Orangeburg to the country across the river.

Heiri and Willi slowed their pace. To stop or go on? A big house fronted the road ahead and they saw outside it a number of men and horses. There'd be no sneaking around this place. The land was open on all sides.

"You think we ought to stop and ask about crossing here?"

"I don't know." Willi looked away, his mouth twisted in its peculiar way. "Yes. I don't know."

Heiri reined in. "Willi," he said low, "if it looks dangerous or not right, we can just ride on by."

"That's so."

The crossroads lay in a depression between two rises. The house by the road was high and double-roomed with an ell in back and a wide porch in front like most houses in the region. As they rode toward it, Heiri did not feel afraid but simply expectant.

More men came out of the house. Heiri glanced at Willi. His face was gray. Now Heiri saw most of the men had guns. It was then that his own legs began to feel mushy.

Suddenly he whispered, "Let me talk, and you talk German, Willi. No English."

The eight men outside the house stared silently as the two approached.

Heiri touched his hat, drew rein, and said in his heavily accented English, "My friend, his leg is hurt."

"What's your business on this road?"

"My friend. In the water his horse is fallen. See?" Heiri pointed to the swollen knee.

Willi sat slumped and his face was indeed haggard.

"Tell us your names and business."

"Heinrich Lienhardt. Wilhelm Rieder." He waited a moment. "We seek Jacob Meyer."

"There's nobody by any such name in these parts."

Someone standing behind the others murmured, "Maybe up past Big Creek? I heard there was Dutch come in there last winter."

"Who is this Jacob Meyer?" The speaker was a youngish heavyset man who wore steel-buckled shoes and a white linen shirt.

"My uncle. We go to—work for him." Heiri tried to look earnest and hopeful but feared he looked guilty because of the lies he was telling.

"Are ye Whig or Tory?"

"Swiss. We're Switzers."

"Ahh!" One spat. "Blockheads."

"Come now, be ye for King or Congress?"

"For my friend!" cried Heiri in distress. "Help for his leg!"

"Then get him down and we'll look at it. And see what else you might have about you."

As Heiri made a hesitant movement, Willi hissed, "*Nein!*" and clapped spurs to his horse. Without thought Heiri did the same and they were halfway up the slope ahead before they heard the shouting behind them. They pressed their horses, and as they reached the crest, they looked back to see men mounting to come after them, others emerging from the house.

"There!" cried Willi, pointing to a growth of trees below to the right, for all the land to the left was open.

They galloped downhill across a hemp field. Glancing back, they saw that the men had not yet topped the rise. Roker stumbled in the soft earth, but Heiri pulled him up. Now Willi was under the trees. Just as Heiri plunged into a sheltering thicket, he looked back and saw riders topping the rise. Not waiting to see what they did, he too pushed among the willows and alders.

They can't help knowing which way we've come, thought Heiri, *but if they didn't sight us, they'll have to look for our tracks.*

"Make for the river!" Willi called low.

Branches whipped their faces and scraped their sides. The horses heaved and their riders whispered encouragement, knowing the poor beasts had been tired and thirsty when they'd stopped. Ahead they saw sunlight parting the leaves. The river? It was a creek. Heiri did not know whether to be disappointed or glad.

"Let's listen a minute," Willi whispered.

At first they could hear only a high twittering in the treetops. Then they heard a far away scattering of voices in the woods to the west. As they listened, the voices receded. They stood very still but could detect no movement in the woods.

At last Willi whispered, "If we go down this creek, it'll take us to the river."

"But it looks like it runs back the way we've come."

It did. The creek running east paralleled the road. Then Heiri remembered noticing at the crossroads how the river curved north, and they concluded that the creek's mouth must be very near the settlement. Still if the men were out searching to the west, the mouth of the creek might be the safest place to be. Well, it depended on who'd stayed home and how long and how thoroughly the men searched.

Are we sure they're Tories? They must be. Whigs wouldn't now be so bold as to challenge unoffending travelers, but Tories could be under orders to stop every one.

"Willi, we could move back that way," Heiri gestured east down the creek, "and maybe hide till all's quiet. It might be the safest place to be."

Willi sat biting his lips.

Heiri waited, finally countered his own suggestion. "But if there's no good hiding place—two horses and all—and, too, I think we have now a chance to get ahead of the troops, but if we delay too long—"

They could catch no sound of any alien movement in the woods. The horses swished their tails against the tormenting flies. A woodpecker resumed his hammering. Dragonflies darted above the creekside.

Heiri saw a sandbar downstream. "One thing, it looks like an easy crossing here."

Willi sighed. "Then let's at least cross the creek. And hold north and try to get to the river."

It was a bold, clear-flowing stream, and after watering the horses, they angled across it without mishap. They slipped between the trunks of willow and river birch, under the white limbs of a giant sycamore, past great sweetgums and tulip poplars furred with poison ivy. In places the ground was boggy with standing pools. Heiri went ahead on foot to scan the way. When they stopped to listen, they heard only the faint rushing of the creek behind them until it too faded. Surely the river would be ahead? How far north would it loop?

At last they saw light and sky through the branches. On they hurried and this time they emerged to view a wide canebrake.

"But look, Willi, here's a path!"

Sure enough a beaten path led west along the edge of the canebrake, bare red earth marked by cowdroppings. Without much hesitation they turned along it.

The sun beat in their faces and sweat trickled into their eyes and down their necks. To the right the cane was head high. They came to another path that branched off through the cane itself.

"You want to try it?"

"May as well." Any path to the right should bring them nearer the river.

Now the cane was above Heiri's head, taller than Willi's on horseback, a wall on both sides of them. However, as they plunged on, the path divided and after a hundred yards divided again, each path becoming narrower. At each fork they tried to bear north or northwest but the path kept turning.

Finally Heiri said, "I don't know, Willi. You think this path goes anywhere?"

"A path has to go somewhere."

"It looks like just cowpaths to me."

"You want to go back?"

"Let's go a little farther and see."

But a little farther they came to what was plainly a couching place for animals with no path out but the one coming in.

Going out was not as easy as coming in. They continually looked at the sun for direction as they tried to return to the main path, but their trail seemed always to be veering east. After a while they knew they were in an entirely different part of the canebrake.

Heiri was about to speak when Willi whispered, "Hush!"

It was jingling of horsegear and was coming nearer. They dared not move but stood still amid a swarm of tiny insects and prayed their horses would make no sound. The cavalcade passed fairly close and as it passed, Heiri and Willi distinguished low words.

"They've either slipped past us or they're hid somewhere we can't find 'em."

"What about—"

Heiri and Willi couldn't hear the rest of the question or its answer.

"Well, we've combed these woods to a fare-ye-well," someone said louder, "and I know they couldn't ha' got beyond the first branch."

"Probably hiding somewhere along the riverbank."

"If they are, Billy and Jim'll find 'em."

"Might be across it by now."

Another voice rose. "Well, I seriously doubt they're worth the trouble we've already been to, and it's my judgment it's too hot and the game's too trifling to keep on." Heiri recognized the voice of their inquisitor at the crossroads. "Though I didn't like how they broke and run. Let too many like that slip through and we'll have more trouble again than we can handle."

"Not many's slipped through though."

Heiri and Willi stayed still for a long time. Both were thinking, *If we'd kept on that path, we'd have run straight into them.* Heiri rested his head against Roker's sweaty neck.

When the woods had been quiet a good half hour and felt safe, Heiri whispered, "At least, we know now which way the path is."

As they emerged from the cane, they saw the roofs of the settlement across a field. There was no question now as to their direction. Heiri mounted and they rode away as fast as they dared.

11

With the canebrake to their right, they were relieved to find themselves once more on their original path. They did not ask what they hoped to find at the end of it. They knew only that a path went somewhere, as Willi said, and they were still moving up the country and the river was somewhere to the right.

The canebrake ended and trees closed in overhead. Now the path descended past granite outcroppings. "Look!" they cried together.

Through maple and river birch they saw below them the fathomless black-green river. The path did not descend to it, however, but continued along the bank some ten feet above.

"Willi, we're bound to come to a way down somewhere, or this path wouldn't be here!"

As they rode scanning what they could see of the bank below, they spied a little tongue of land pushing into the water.

"Here!" cried Heiri. "Look here!"

Between two boulders a broad gullied way sloped off the path, turned and disappeared. It was clearly a place for dismounting.

"I'll jump off first and see how it goes," said Heiri.

Willi watched Heiri's shaggy head out of sight.

The throbbing pain in his leg felt somehow remote, as did the ringing in his head and his heavy heartbeat. The will to go on, to evade enemies, to hold to his purpose of arriving at some place beyond this river now dominated him. Get over the river. West, north. Find those who would let him be who he was, no question of who he was, his duty clear. Though before that happened, night would come and he must get off this horse, a necessity he both dreaded and longed for. Getting off would mean he must get back on. Yet Heiri would make him do it. And when he'd done it, he'd have to go on.

Heiri called up the bank, "We'll have a time getting the horses down but—" He broke off. "Here's a boat!"

"Is it?" Willi's voice rose.

"Though how we'll manage the horses—"

"How about oars?"

"I don't see any."

"Look about you! Look in the bushes! Or look near a trunk!"

"You're right! Here's one!"

"You think I can get down there?"

"Yes, but wait and let's think a bit. There are things we need to consider."

Willi peered at the opposite shore. Could they find a path through those trees? They'd need a sloping bottom and a sloping bank. It all looked steep from here. You couldn't get a horse out of deep water up a vertical bank. What was the use of a boat if they couldn't get the horses across? He couldn't go without a horse. Willi clenched his teeth. Shine stamped. Both horses switched their tails constantly against the yellow flies.

Heiri appeared, managing to look both cheerful and serious at the same time. "It's a way down there and there's a good boat but—"

A deep voice sounded behind them. "Don't take that boat."

They were too startled to speak. A large black man stood in the path. "That be my master's boat. You can't take it."

Willi said, "We must cross the river!"

"You can't take Master's boat." The man moved a few steps obliquely to be nearer the boulders and gulley. Much bigger than either of them, he wore gray ragged trousers and a colorless shirt.

"Who is your master?"

"Master Charley Carson. He need his boat."

"Where is he?"

The man nodded toward the river. "Over yonder. When he come back, he need it."

"Does he live back there?" Willi pointed toward Saluda Old Town. The man nodded.

Charley. Not Jim or Billy. "When will he be back?"

"He be back when *they* gone."

"They? Who?"

"Men want to kill him. Say they take him to Ninety Six jail. Might hang him too."

The black man regarded them without change of expression.

Willi said, "Two men along the riverbank, Billy and Jim, have you seen them?"

"Yes. They back down yonder." Heiri and Willi paled, as they remembered how they'd shouted up and down the bank. "They be gone now," said the man.

Willi spoke low, urgently. "They hunt for us and the men on horses hunt for us too."

"Why they don't find you back yonder?"

"We went in the canebrake. When they passed us, they couldn't see us."

The man's face changed. He threw back his head and laughed, his laughter a kind of high and low humming. He smiled widely, the notes of his laughing ranging the scale. "Hid in that canebrake! Hi, hid in the cane! Didn't go in there, did they?"

"No. At least, not where we were."

"Oh no, not there! Not today!" He was still laughing.

"Why won't they?"

"Last man go in, he not come out. And one before him neither."

They stood mystified, but the man merely kept laughing. Willi began, "Can't you—" when the man said, "You want to cross over yonder?"

"We must."

"You go to Chappell Ferry. Go on up to Chappell Ferry, Mistress Chappell, she get you 'cross the river. Good people up there."

"How far? How do we go?"

"Four, five mile. I tell you how to go."

"We can't cross here?"

He shook his head. "Too hard here."

"But the boat—"

"You drown your horses, sir. Master don't swim his horse here."

Then it must be too steep. "Tell us the way then."

It took a while to tell. They must keep to this path a mile or more, then skirt a wide bottom and find a certain oak tree, cut through woods, always moving toward the sun and veering away from the river to avoid the swamp where the river made another loop north, skirt more fields and avoid a plantation house—"They keep to the'self"—and at last strike the road to the ferry.

Willi's face clouded. "Can't you come with us?"

The man shook his head. "I keep care of Mistress. Master tell me, 'John, you stay and guard Mistress. And the little chaps.'" "Gyard," John pronounced it.

But couldn't he go part way? To the oak tree?

No, *they* would find out; then who would guard his mistress?

Willi offered money, but John said, "I be gone too long and they know something. They watch our house. Time I get back now they ask where I was."

Again they felt the creep of unease. It must have showed on their faces for John picked up a string of bream from the bushes and held it high. "Been fishing."

Heiri urged low, "Willi, we'll find it. We've come so far I know we'll find it. We better move on while the sun's still up there." He said to John, "Thank you. You helped us much. We thank you. Wait."

He bent to get a small purse from his saddlebag, and as he drew it out, Willi did the same. Each gave the man a shilling, but Heiri did not throw his; he gave it into the man's hand. He wanted to shake the hand in farewell, yet did not do it. He felt a half-familiar overlay of shame as they turned away. He looked back and saw John still in the path. Heiri raised his hand. Slowly the slave raised his.

It was almost dark when they emerged on the ferry road. At least they hoped it was the ferry road. Their horses were stumbling and neither Heiri nor Willi had spoken for a long time.

Now the land was descending, and they thought they could tell by the trees below where the channel ran. To the left of the road, almost hidden by a rise of ground, they saw a housetop, and without a word, Heiri turned toward it and Willi followed. The house in its fenced yard was high with double rooms below and above and chimneys at each end.

Heiri hailed as they approached; Willi echoed weakly. Dogs barked and a woman appeared on the porch, then a boy and a girl.

Willi pointed and said huskily, "Is that Chappell's Ferry?"

The woman came down the steps.

"You—you are Mistress Chappell?"

"No, Chappells live the other side." The woman stopped, her arms folded.

"We want to cross the river. Mistress Carson's servant, John, said people here would help us."

"Not this late. Daylight's the time to cross."

"In the morning early? We must cross soon." They strained their eyes toward the river.

The dogs barked but kept back. The woman moved to the fence. She was about his mother's age, Heiri thought. The planes of her face were shadowed. "Why are you in haste?"

There was a moment's silence till Heiri said, "We go to find my brother. He fights for America. We go to fight too."

"Light down. Andy! Come help these boys with their horses!" She opened the gate.

With no hesitation Heiri dismounted, but when Willi slipped from his horse, he would have fallen if Heiri had not been there. "My friend, his leg is hurt."

"Nancy! Come help Andy!"

The woman was as tall as Heiri, and as she moved to help support Willi, the strength in her shoulder moved into Heiri. A boy and a girl took the horses' reins.

"How did he get his hurt?" the woman asked low.

"The water was high and his horse fell. He hurt his leg in the stream."

"Are you Germans?"

"We're German-Swiss. From the Congarees."

She steered Willi toward the steps, where the three struggled up and at last stood beneath the porch roof.

"I thank you for your help." Heiri's voice trembled. "For my friend I thank you."

Hearthlight and candlelight opened the house to them.

Their supper was stewed corn, new potatoes, and boiled fowl. Three children younger than the boy and girl crowded the board comfortably. Heiri looked about him in the shadowed room, at the different kind of chimney stones, the placement of the window, the chairs and shelves and tables, the one fine piece of furniture against the inner wall— some kind of press, it must be—and the writing desk near the window. He recognized it for a desk because Herr Pastor had one too. He saw a big spinning wheel; his mother had only the little flax wheel. It was different from home. Yet not different either because it had fire and food and sheltering beams.

The woman was Mary Culbreth. After she examined Willi's leg, she said it would surely mend if he could keep off it for a spell. She bound a mullein poultice on it and gave him a bitter drink she said would lessen the pain and swelling—willow bark tea. Heiri smiled all over his face.

"You've a touch of fever, but that's like to ha' come from lying out in the wet and other ills."

The travelers told of their three days' journey as best they could. Heiri spoke more than usual in his limited English.

"And you mean to tell us you came through all that nest of Tories clear up from Little Saludy?"

Stewarts and Thompsons and Turners down there, she said, were well known-known Tories. And Willi had guessed right; Neely Carghill was one of their leaders, though she had never heard of Ephraim Giles. Aye, Saluda Old Town was infested with Tories too. Charles Carson had barely escaped from his home as had the Towles near here, and Mrs. Chappell's own husband and their two sons. They'd all gone to join whatever resisters they could find in the upper country.

Did they know aught of the British army? she asked.

Willi told what he knew.

Andy and the girl, Nancy, listened with grave faces. The boy looked to be about fourteen, the girl several years older. Heiri's glance kept straying to her. Her skin was fair and fresh, sprinkled with freckles; her eyes were green in the candlelight; and her hair was curly with gold glints. She looked different from any girl he'd ever seen. When their glances met, Heiri dropped his gaze.

"Well, you did right well to come so far," said Mrs. Culbreth. "It was either good chance or the Lord's guidance one. I'm thankful you found us." She rose and lifted down a great book from a shelf. "Now if you'll join us, we'll have a Psalm and prayer before retiring."

The language of the Psalms was familiar enough to Heiri in German that he understood some of the English. "'Yea, in the shadow of thy wings will I make my refuge till these calamities be overpast.'"

A deep hard knot loosened—homesickness, fear, he did not know what else.

He looked about him at the mother and the still, young faces. He remembered other faces he'd seen today—those of the armed riders, the bushy-bearded man, the well-dressed arrogant questioner at Saluda Old Town, the ones that had thronged about their horses. And John.

When they knelt—only Willi kept his seat—Heiri could not follow the prayer so well, nor did he bow his head but he looked up open-eyed at the smoke-dark beams. *God above, do You truly see us? Did You lead us into that cane and hide us? How did we come here? Did You lead us to John? Do You know us here tonight?*

Do You know me, Heiri?

The house was as solid as his father's house. The voice of its mother beat through its air, beyond its walls.

Suddenly, he bowed his head, bowed his shoulders and squeezed his eyes shut.

Heiri was offered a bed upstairs, but he said he'd stay down here with Willi.

"We'll set the dogs to watch at front and back," Mrs. Culbreth said, "but from what you tell us, I doubt there'll be disturbance. Now if you were well-known in these parts, it would be another matter."

The girl with her cloud of glinting hair brought them bedding, and as Heiri went to take the unwieldy bundle, he smiled at her. She did not smile back, but her eyes had gold-green lights.

"Thank you," said Heiri, "thank you!" He wished he knew more to say.

Their weariness was so great that their limbs melted into the floor as soon as they lay down, and they lay as if glued to it until Andy shook them awake just before day.

The fire was ablaze and the mother and daughter, seen against it, stirred pots and clinked lids. Heiri smelled bacon sizzling.

He clambered to his feet and stretched the sleep from his body. Willi groaned.

"Help that one up, Andy. Help him outside."

"Water?" Heiri cupped his hands and made motions of throwing water on his face. "Outside?"

"Aye, you want to wash. Andy, take 'em to the spring. Nancy, fetch a towel and scrub-rags."

Outside, the sky was beginning to pale.

Willi asked for the crutch Heiri had made him and said he could manage by himself, that his leg didn't hurt as much as it had last night and now he was up, he felt better all over.

Heiri felt an upsurge of spirit. "Willi, I'm sure glad!"

Long wet grass bowed over the path and brushed their feet and ankles. Below the spring ran a little rivulet they could barely see in the half-light. They took off their clothes and stood in the stream and scooped up water in gourd dippers from a bucket. They gasped and expostulated as the cold water doused their heads and arms and shoulders. Andy, who was helping Willi, suddenly tipped a dipperful of water down Heiri's back. Heiri bellowed, laughing, and Andy flung another at him. Heiri backed away; Andy followed, his face devilish. Heiri backed into the bushes, grinning, but Andy flung another dipperful at his chest. Suddenly, Heiri lunged forward, caught the boy around his waist, twisted and turned him headdown and dragged him scuffling to the bucket where he poured several gourdsful over the red head.

"Andy Culbreth, you better stop that foolery! Mother says make haste to breakfast!" The severe young voice castigated them all.

Abashed, Heiri turned Andy loose, who, with a grin and a parting splat of scooped-up water and sand from the stream, leaped up the path.

Willi had already decorously withdrawn into the bushes to dry and dress himself, and Heiri found himself momentarily alone in the little stream in the growing light. With his muddy feet, dripping body, and touseled hair, he felt much as he had when his mother had separated him and Joggi in their roughhousing years ago. But the green eyes didn't look at him.

Grabbing his breeches, Heiri too dashed behind a bush and began trying to drag them on over his wet self. Lacking a towel, he peered over the bush. The girl was still dipping her pails in the spring, though in a rather leisurely manner. Heiri wanted to come out and hunt his shirt but couldn't because of his half-dressed state. And he'd have liked to offer to carry her pails.

At last she left and he found his shirt on the ground where it had been stepped on. He remembered the towel, found it on a bush, and tried to dry his thick hair and smooth and comb it with his fingers, but long before he finished, Willi had gone. Halfway to the house he remembered the scrub-rag he had not used and went back to hunt for it but never found it. He felt about six years old.

By the time they had fed and watered the horses it was clear daylight. Andy was sent to call Mrs. Chappell, who plied the ferry herself.

Now the travelers stood outside the gate with their horses saddled. The children and Andy waited restlessly to go down and see them off. Nancy was not present.

Mary Culbreth, who had supplied them with potatoes and fresh cornbread, addressed Willi. "Mind you drink that tea I give you ere you lie down tonight. And keep that knee bound tight the way I showed you. Don't be putting weight on it for at least three more days." She turned to Heiri. "Young man, I ha' no doubt you've come so far you'll find your way safe above Saludy. Mistress Chappell can likely tell you more of roads and paths than I can. But you ask the good Lord to guide you as you go, and I ha' no doubt He will."

Heiri looked earnestly at her strong-boned face as he held out his hand. Her grip was as strong as her face. "I thank you. I thank you in God's name." He wished he knew more words. He said, "I have your goodness here," and put his hand on his breast.

Willi said, "We will not forget your kindness."

They began their procession to the river, the children running ahead, Andy leading Shine, Willi hobbling after him, and Heiri leading Roker. Heiri glanced back once to see Mary Culbreth still standing by the gate. But no Nancy.

Heiri's face was a study.

Twenty minutes ago he had just saddled Roker and was tightening the girths when a skirted figure appeared suddenly at Roker's head. The light was clear now. He observed her with astonishment, saw again the amber flecks in her green eyes. He saw how her hair curled behind her ears and at her temples. She was almost as tall as he was. She moved closer.

"Harry?"

He nodded.

"Leenart? Lennart?"

He nodded again.

"Harry Leenart? Harry Lennart?"

He shrugged, smiling, bemused.

She looked at him a moment longer, then abruptly hooked her right arm around his neck and kissed him. Heiri, dumbfounded at first, came to life and put both arms around her.

Simultaneously they drew apart. Nancy gazed a moment longer.

Heiri looked for the devilish expression he had seen on Andy's face, but it was not precisely that look he saw though the light danced in her eyes.

"Come again when ye can, Harry Leenart or Lennart." And she was gone.

Roker had not understood the additional grooming he'd received after he was already saddled.

Now as they descended the grassy slope, they saw a great white roll of fog ahead of them. Only when they reached the water's edge could they see the broad boat moored to the bank and in it a cloaked woman. She watched them come. The boat was flat with square bow and stern and was attached by pulleys to a cable stretched from shore to shore, but it was not nearly so large as Herr Friday's on the Congaree.

"How much to cross?" asked Willi.

"Two shillings each. An extra shilling if you wished to transport your beast."

Heiri counted out three shillings, Willi two, Heiri half ashamed of not trusting Roker to the water. *But he's too good a horse to take risks with,* Heiri justified himself. *Besides he's Papa's and he's never swum a river before, and I won't put him through it.*

The woman took their money without speech. She was older than Mrs. Culbreth, perhaps as old as Willi's grandmother, but tall and stalwart.

Shine was unsaddled again and Willi's belongings removed. Standing close to Roker's head, Heiri watched everything. When the boat finally moved, Willi sat in the stern and drew Shine's bridle reins close. Now the young chestnut was moving into the stream and soon only his head was visible above water. His heart pounding, Heiri said low, "See, Roker! Now you may have to do that another time." So intent was he on the horses that when he looked back, Andy and the children were only shapes in the mist. He waved but could barely discern their answering signs.

Now Mrs. Chappell was walking the length of the boat, wielding a long pole; yet the boat itself seemed stationary; it was the rope that seemed to move. The creaking of the cables and pulleys, the light plash of water against the boat's low side, and the soft thrashing of Shine's body were curiously intimate sounds, closed in by the fog. Now the horse's neck rose, now his shoulders, and the trunk of a great tree loomed.

The woman was making the boat fast, and Heiri moved to help Willi get up and saddle his horse. And now easily, immediately they found themselves where for three days they had strained their wills and wits to be.

Both looked back across the river but could see only the roll of fog. Ahead of them the land rose again in grassy slopes.

"Have you heard where the King's army might be?" Willi asked Mrs. Chappell.

She looked at them sharply from under her heavy brows. She had not questioned Andy Culbreth about her passengers.

"We must keep out of their way. Can you tell us how to go?"

Her face relaxed. "Well now, I'll do my best."

The British had not yet passed, she said. How far away they were she did not know. A mile up the ferry road they'd come to a fork and if they bore left, in about three more miles they'd cross the Ninety Six Road. That was the place to be wary, for that was the road the British would likely come. After crossing the road they must proceed northwest for two or three miles, then strike a well-marked path that would take them northeast across Little River, Bush River, the Enoree, and the Tyger—on up to the Pacolet and northern waters of the Broad, which was where most men were heading. "I hear it's a right smart of 'em gathered up there."

"Does the path go near Indian Creek?" asked Heiri.

"Aye, it'll take ye across the head of Indian Creek."

No, she'd heard no news of any fighting up there yet. Only of the butchering of Americans by that fiend Tarleton three weeks ago east of the Waxhaws. Hadn't they heard? American soldiers caught unawares and having to surrender, but that bloody butcher just hacked them to pieces, no mercy on weaponless men, just slaughtered them all. So much for British "clemency." She reckoned that would show many a one the nature of their "clemency."

Today was June the twentieth, Willi reflected, the last day to enroll as a British subject. He wondered what his father had done.

Heiri stood with downcast eyes. For the first time since he had come out, he thought of going back. Suddenly all the longing he might have felt every hour of the last three days—for mother, father, home, brothers, sisters, for the dog and the paths and the sandy rows—it swelled his heart almost to breaking. Will I ever cross this river again? The question loomed before him like the dark post with its cable disappearing into the fog. He wrenched his mind away from it.

They were again on horseback. When they had ridden up the long slope, they looked back once to see that the mist was rising. Now they could see the entire surface of the water, the narrow dark green river and the cable across it. But everything else on the southern shore was obscure.

12

A man and his child were riding along a path above Indian Creek. Although he was only forty, the man's black hair was already grizzled. He was smooth-shaven, but lines were cut deep about his mouth and eyes. His eyes were dark. Their look was intensely personal, the look of a man who saw one truly, and the expression about his mouth, so bitterly lined, was curiously sweet.

The man was Rudi Näffels, Madle Lienhardt's cousin. The child was his only son, James Allen, or Jemmy as they called him, almost eight. At home was a four-year-old sister, who they now dared hope would live. Other brothers and sisters had not.

"See that rock, Jemmy? Tell me what you notice about it?"

"A bird sat on it?"

"What kind of bird?"

"A joree."

"How you know?"

"It's a place he'd like. . . . See where he hopped?"

Why not? Rudi chuckled. The two got off the horse and examined the signs. They concluded that a snake had probably sunned there that morning, a raccoon had been digging about the rock, and something else too, probably a fox. They found a piece of eggshell. Jemmy knew it was a bluebird's. "Did the fox leave it?" he asked.

"Not this one. The bird dropped it. They carry off the shells after their young ones hatch out."

"Why, Daddy?"

"I don't know. Maybe to hide what just happened."

"From a fox?"

"Maybe. Or from a snake or some other bird. It may be there's something inside the shell the other creatures smell. They have powers we don't have."

Rudi rose stiffly from where they were squatting. He was of middle height with wide, heavy shoulders. He glanced at the light on the ridge across the creek. "We better go on. Your Mammy's going to whip you and me both if we don't get on home."

The boy acknowledged the necessity, his mother's temper being no minor consideration. Besides they had had no dinner.

They had ridden out that morning with a bag of meal and a half bushel of potatoes for an old woman in need. Her husband dead and her sons away, Martha Laird had recently been plundered of almost everything she had.

She had accepted Rudi's offering speechlessly, her face working with words she could not say.

"It's from Jane McGrew," Rudi said, speaking of his wife's Granny, who was twelve years dead.

Martha turned away, her face crumpling.

"How's Margaret?" she asked later.

He hesitated. "She's better."

Martha pursed her lips. "Well, you can thank the Almighty he's spared you this one. And I've told you afore he's somehow got the look of his great-granny about him, though how or in what feature I cannot say. You can pray he'll live as enduring as she did."

"I do." To Rudi it was one of the unexpected graces of life that so much of what was thought to be lost forever returned in a child. He saw it daily. He liked to think also that there might now and then be a look in his children of his own lost parents and brothers and sisters, whom he barely remembered, even of his grandmother perhaps, the memory of whom he kept as a far brightness.

"Though as for that slip at home, she's her mother all over again and more. Aye, she'll lead you the pretty dance one day." The old woman eyed him sternly. "You're too fond, Rudi Näffels. I tell you now, you're too fond."

Rudi laughed and changed the subject. "Have you heard any news, Mistress Laird?"

"News!" Her face turned grim. "What news would you have when the whole country's jangling with broils and brangles?" Two of those who had taken her stock and provisions were sons of old neighbors, members of their own meetinghouse. "Well, Mary Fraser was here yesterday, but she's heard ne'er a word from Aleck. Though I daresay she'll hear when he's shot dead or hanged."

"And James Fraser?" James was Mary Fraser's brother-in-law.

"They presume he's still at the North."

Rudi's face too was grave.

"Aye, he's gone like the rest of 'em," Martha sighed. "Though never a one to bide hereabouts, I must say. Yet who'd ha' thought he'd make such a fighter?"

"He's a good man."

"So some ha' judged. Though for my part I'll take one less bookish."

As he left, Martha gave Rudi a packet of herbs. "They missed my store of physic, too trifling, no doubt, for King's service. Tell Margaret if she'll take an infusion of this the last thing at night, it may help her condition."

Rudi thanked her. He noted the bare shelves, the few vessels on her hearth. "Are you sure you'll not come home with us? Margaret would like much to see you." He added, "You'd do her good," thinking it might lure her away.

"And leave my house to more robbery? Though it's little they'd get now. Like enough next time they'd burn it down for spite if it was left here empty. No, you can tell Margaret I still ha' left the few old cuddies that were too quick for the clumsy villains, and they've took to laying again. And I ha' yet the little garden truck that was not stripped off. What with such providence and the remembrance of Christian neighbors," her somber face cracked in a smile, "I'll make out."

She would, Rudi thought. *Such women could endure as much rigor as any man. Maybe more. Even so,* he thought, *it was wrong of those Laird boys to rouse so much ill will, no matter how strong their convictions, and leave their mother to bear the consequences.*

Now it was an hour later and Rudi was suddenly conscience-stricken as he and Jemmy mounted the horse a second time. "Pick up your feet, Frisker!" They had been gone far too long.

Today was one of Margaret's dragging-out and scouring-up days, when she worked as if driven. "I can't abide to live in dirt! I'll not sit back and fall into slack and shiftless ways!" It was little sitting back she ever did, thought Rudi, but did not say so. Moreover, what did she mean by dirt? Fire and earth were what they lived by. Smoke, soot, and ashes were to him a fact of life.

"Ah, Margaret, I lived houseless too long," he would say.

"And no doubt would do it again if you could," was her retort.

He usually laughed as he made his escape. That was partly what he had done this morning, though both of them agreed on taking assistance to Mistress Laird.

"Mind you get back afore noon," she'd admonished as they left. "Famish yourself if you will, but not the young one."

For once he was angered and looking her straight in the eye, he said, "I'll come back when I'm ready. And Jemmy's no nursling." He rode off before the light of battle had a chance to flare.

But now he felt only repentance. God knew he'd suffered in the loss of their children, but what was his suffering compared to hers? They had lost their firstborn to the strangling disease when it was over a year old and later three others to the mysterious summer fevers, the smallest one last summer. And then, there were her miscarriages, the last one in March. Childbearing was always very hard for her. "You're someways not built for it," Martha told her, adding obscurely, "It may be you're too strong."

And yet how enduring. Straight, strong, true. Tart and tangy sometimes with that unexpected sweetness like the best russet apples that made the best pies. He wouldn't have her any other way, he told himself as he had many other times, then grinned. *Now tell the truth. Wouldn't you? Maybe once a month? On scrub days?*

Well, consider what she had to put up with. Him.

Go on home now. Meet it like a man. She's had far too much to grieve her without your riling her. Make haste now.

But as they rode on, Jemmy chattering about one thing and another, he suddenly drew rein and whispered, "Hush!" and stilled the horse. He had heard a thrashing noise in the willows down the other side of the creek.

He sat motionless. Now it was horses splashing. Soon they'd be on this path. He listened to hear which way they'd turn. He discerned low voices. German words?—*diese Weg?*

As soon as he perceived that the riders were turning toward them, he whispered, "Hold tight, Jemmy," and spurred up the slope. Although there was little cover, for the trees were widely spaced, the riders might miss him if they were intent on their way, and even if they didn't, the intervening distance being what it was, they might not meddle with him. *Most men,* he thought, *were not so hardened as to offer harm to a child. Though I shouldn't have brought him. Fool!* he raged, *not to have thought of something like this!*

Better to stop still; motion would draw attention. Through the low hanging limbs of a hickory he watched the path.

It was two men, not overlarge, one rather scrawny, the other quite young, a look about him of—whom?

Rudi's eyes narrowed. That boy had a familiar look. Wonderfully familiar. Suddenly he bellowed, "Heiri Lienhardt! Heiri! Where you going?"

The fresh face turned, flushed rose-red. It was scratched on cheek and chin, darkly grazed beneath one eye, and already a little hollow-jawed, yet nothing could diminish that look of intense and hopeful joy.

"Rudi!" Heiri said softly, then shouted, "Cousin Rudi!" spoke again softly, "Now God be thanked!" yelled in jubilation, "Rudi! Oh, Rudi Näffels!"

The sallow-faced boy lost his dogged, fixed look. "You sure, Heiri? You sure?"

"Of course, I'm sure, dumbhead!" Never would Heiri have called Willi that in other circumstances. "It's our cousin! You know him!"

Rudi was down the slope. He and Heiri embraced and pounded backs. They were much the same size although Heiri was fair. Rudi lifted his son off the horse, and as Heiri embraced the child, he knew a quickening in his arms, for he thought of his own little brother.

Willi still sat his horse but he stretched out his hand.

"Willi Rieder," said Heiri. "You remember Willi, don't you? Joggi's friend? And mine. You remember him, don't you, Rudi?"

Yes, Rudi remembered the quiet boy, remembered the not so quiet father, remembered more than he cared to. But he'd never forget the one outstanding service the man had done him years ago. Twenty years ago through sheer overbearing bluster, Hans Jacob Rieder had forced Rudi's release from a seeming legal entanglement with the unscrupulous old man down Orangeburg way who had victimized him as a child.

Rudi searched Willi Rieder's face. As the young man's gaze met his, Rudi saw something that he knew intimately, that softened him immensely. "I'm glad to see you," he said in German. "Welcome in God's name."

Color suffused Willi's face. "I don't know anybody I'd rather see now—" he almost said "Herr Näffels," "—Rudi." He felt wondrously lightened.

Rudi asked where they'd come from.

From Chappell's Ferry, they said, coming for two and a half days, though it was only thirty-five miles away. After the first few hours above the river they'd dared not trust themselves to marked paths and until today had traveled only early in the morning and at dusk. The country was alive with armed bands, especially back toward Ninety Six. Even this morning they'd almost run headlong into a large troop that must have been coming from some battle, for some of the men wore bloody bandages and a few looked seriously hurt.

"Where was it?"

It was hard to say because they themselves had gotten so entangled in creeks and branches they didn't know how far back it was. The men were heading southwest. "We judged they were Tories," said Willi.

"Why?"

"Because of their number and direction. You know Ninety Six is in their hands now. But one thing, wherever they came from, they didn't look like they'd gotten the best of it."

"And they sure were in a hurry to get somewhere else," said Heiri.

Rudi was silent a moment. "And where are you going?"

"To find you."

"Then you were going the wrong way."

"Were we? Then how in the world did we find you?" asked Heiri grinning.

"Fool's luck," Rudi grinned back. "Though that's not what your Papa would say."

They were quiet a moment, Rudi hearing as he'd hear all his life certain earnest, halting words: "Haven't you ever felt, looking back, there was someone with you or behind you? Turning you a certain way, you not knowing it then, but looking back . . . ."

"Rudi, we're trying to find Joggi. You know where he went?"

"Joggi? No, I don't, Heiri."Rudi looked surprised.

"What? Didn't he tell you?"

"I haven't seem Joggi."

"Haven't seen him!"

"No time lately I haven't. I've wondered about him. Many a time I've wondered."

Heiri felt a sinking heaviness descend. "But he said—or I thought he said—he as much as told me—" No, Joggi had said, "Go to Rudi," not "I'm going there." "But I thought sure he'd come by here!"

Rudi had not seen Joggi since this spring a year ago when he'd been with the Rangers. "But don't let it worry you he didn't come here. Like as not he fell in with others and went directly on." He felt Heiri's distress and tried to speak easily, convincingly. "That's what happened.

Some have gone from here too this last month and they're sure to be in bands now."

"Gone where, Rudi?"

He studied the two intent faces before him. He said slowly, "On the upper Catawba, some say." His voice became heavier. "In places near the Pacolet. But mostly I think above the North Carolina line." His voice quickened. "But tell me now, how is it down your way? How is your Papa? What does he think about—all these turns?"

"He's well. And he thinks like most people, I suppose," said Heiri. "He wants peace."

Rudi looked away. What had Johannes ever wanted but peace? Rudi felt a sudden longing almost like homesickness. He understood Johannes better now. How he wished he lived closer to him so they could sit down and talk together sometimes.

"But there can't be any peace if they try to force us into their army," said Willi.

"Who?"

"Why, the British."

"They can't do that," Rudi said quickly. "And I don't believe they'll try."

Heiri did not speak but his lips moved.

Willi laughed. "Oh, won't they?"

Silence fell. Finally Heiri asked in a low voice, shocking himself with his boldness. "Which side are you on, Rudi?"

Rudi's face darkened and he looked older. He put his hand on Jemmy's shoulder. "His side. And my wife and daughter's."

Heiri said, "But Willi and I, we don't have wives and children. And we're not willing to fight against our brother and our friends."

"What if your brother was on the other side?"

"He couldn't be," said Heiri. He never thought of Willi's older brother, George, nor of Conrad Meyer.

"There's many a good man hereabouts that's loyal, Heiri. Or that's not willing to rebel. A few I've respected all my life. Sometimes I tend that way myself." Rudi's mouth twisted in his old crooked smile. "Especially when I hear about some who've joined the Whigs."

"Rudi, I thought you—"

"Oh, I stood with 'em four years ago. And may again. But now, like your Papa, Heiri, I'd rather have peace." His voice, which had sunk low, rose. "And I'll not leave my family alone."

Jemmy was looking curiously from one face to the other. He did not understand German for they spoke only English at home, but he sensed the seriousness of their talk and felt oppressed by it. He kept looking at the young man who'd hugged him. Only his parents ever hugged him so close. He felt this big boy must belong to him in some way. In the ensuing silence he pulled Heiri's sleeve. "I bet I can throw you down!"

"What?" Heiri looked at the brimful-of-challenge, upturned face. It had a thin little nose over which the freckled skin seemed almost transparent. The lips curved sweetly.

"Bet I can wrassle you down!" Jemmy grabbed Heiri's arm and clamped himself about one of his legs, almost unbalancing him.

Not quite understanding Jemmy's words but understanding his action, Heiri quickly bent over in such a way as to loose the little boy's hold, then scooped him up and held him at arm's length with his feet dangling above the ground. "Who can throw who down?" he cried.

"I'll get you back!" Jemmy squirmed in glee.

"Oh? How you get me?" Heiri gave him a sudden twist and toss and Jemmy was over his shoulder. "Hm? How?"

The boy gasped joyously, "When I get home and get me some dinner!"

Heiri flipped Jemmy over to land on his feet in front of him, stooped and held the wriggling body before him. Their looks met in delight. "Want your dinner, eh? So do I."

"Then come on home and we'll get it!" exclaimed Rudi.

Heiri blushed and stood up. "Oh, I didn't mean—"

"Of course, you'll come home with us." Rudi spoke English now. "Though it may be nearer supper than dinner. It's three miles on." And he couldn't help wondering what they'd find when they got there.

"We could eat now," said Heiri. "We have food for all. Though," he added grinning, "maybe not so good."

"No, save it and come home with us. Eh, Jemmy?"

"Yes, come on." The boy was already at Frisker's stirrup. "Heiri?" He hesitated. "Willi?"

It was the child's saying his name that made the difference for Willi. Why must he always feel like an outsider, he asked himself. He remembered the day, less than a week ago, when other children had welcomed him. He remembered the open doors, the bent heads, the potato cakes and strawberries and cream. But it was not the food that drew his longing backward. It was the young, unmarked faces. He remembered the innocence of brown hands fumbling to right a bowl and her whispered "I'm so sorry!"

Today as they rode through the summer woods, it was childish hands clutching a pink-stained apron that he thought of rather than her mother's wise charm. He glanced at his own brown hand on the bridle rein. In the mishap of that day they'd brushed it. And something else had brushed him, not of the girl herself but of some strange grace that always drew him back there. . . . What? A man and woman and children? Would he always be the outsider?

Rudi thought, *It just can't be helped. The boy's my own kin and few I have of such.* She'd liked Joggi well enough; he hoped she'd like this one too. And she was always avid for news. Margaret was ardent in her politics, far more so than he was.

Rudi was not in the habit of praying about daily vicissitudes, but he did prayerfully hope she'd finished the scouring and was done with her scouring mood.

13

"Stay out, Katy!" Although she had built a great fire in the fire-place to help dry the floor, it was still wet in the corners and under the table. "Don't you come tracking in here yet!" Her voice was sharp.

Katy stood looking through the back doorway. The cool damp floor would feel good to her feet, but her Mammy's hand would not feel good on her bottom. "I'm hungry!" she called.

There was a clatter and clang. Then came a different voice with an underlying rounded note like a soft hand on her cheek. "Well, you sit down on the steps now like a pretty girl and I'll come bring you your dinner. We'll both eat out there today."

Eat outside! Just her and Mammy! To sit side by side on the steps, just the two of them, was better than honeycakes! Her Mammy's voice, though severe just now, her all-knowing gaze had yet for Katy the aura of High Presence that overarched all her days. Daddy was the one who picked her up, but Mammy was the one who bent over from above. Ground and sky.

"Katy, did you put water in the hens' troughs?"

"Yes, ma'am."

"Well, take your little broom and brush off the steps again. I'll be out directly." Katy's ear caught again the rounded note that was rich enough to permeate all outdoors.

To the sounds of thudding and thumping inside, the scraping of chairs and table legs, Katy took her broom to sweep and sing, mostly to sing. Her singing was high and very melodious, but she made up the words and tune.

Inside, Margaret glanced at the moving sun on the floor by the window. Long past noon and the floor not dried and the other room yet to do, the front porch too, and she'd thought to have it all done by noon. When they got back. But them not yet back.

Oh, and Jemmy starved to death! She had given Katy a piece of bread and butter earlier but what would Jemmy have got? She straightened, put her hand to her back. Maybe Martha would give him something. But what would she have to offer? A woman robbed, a lone woman robbed of her very foodstuff and household goods by a gang of villainous, lowdown—"King's loyal subjects," they called themselves! Hell's subjects was who they were! Anybody that would— A door of the old cupboard flew open as she dragged it into place. She slammed it shut with such force that she jammed it. Oh Lord ha' mercy, now it would take *him* to get it open again. Open it he would without e'er a reproachful word, but she'd have to ask him, and after the way he'd left this morning she'd rather be hanged, drawn, and quartered than to ask him to do anything.

Again she glanced at the sunlight. No use to wait. No use even to expect him. Doubtless he'd stay out till dusky dark this time. And the child brought in fagged out and starved nigh to death.

She surveyed the drying floor, hard-scrubbed with lye soap. It felt clean whether you could tell it or not. She thought it was getting lighter from its many scrubbings, and she wished her mother could see it—"We will not live in dirt!"—could see how she tried. Again she straightened and pressed her hand to her back. And heard another old voice, curling, half-laughing, Granny's. "Meggie, are ye trying to run him off for good?"

. . . Be fair. He usually found somewhat for the two of them to eat. He knew how to roast a squirrel and broil fish as well as she did, and to catch them. No wonder the boy was wild to go anywhere anytime with his Daddy. As he should be. Yes, as the boy should be.

And what about her own self? Margaret gazed about her. To spend every livelong day enslaved in walls and chimney stones, to crocks and bins and sacks and to pots and bowls and pails— She swung the kettle out from the fire, the heat burning her face, drying her sweat. Then smash 'em all and do without! she rounded back on herself. What if the bins were empty like Martha Laird's? And what if you lived on a dirt floor? Many a one does, with a flimsy, leaking roof and a stick chimney, no window, and only the one room for everything from birthing to dying. How can you be so thankless?

She moved to the open doorway, stood there, listened to Katy crooning on the bottom step. She gazed into the summer air, over the heads of the creekside trees, at the line of ridge beyond the shimmering light. She grew very still. Suddenly, she was released into it, freed by the line of trees against the sky.

Oh, after dinner I'll take Katy and we'll stroll up the creek. She thought of a hillside where a blackberry thicket overgrew the edge of an old field. We'll put on shoes and old clothes and go up there. Leave food in the pots, shut the door and forget the other room. And nobody would object to a blackberry pie.

She went in to dish up their stew, hers on a plate and Katy's in a bowl, with a noggin of milk for both of them and cold cornbread.

How good it felt finally to sit down, to give ease to the pull in her back and legs, and just to be outside. A mild breeze cooled her neck and upper arms. She and Katy sat side by side and enjoyed their silence, for both were very hungry, though from time to time they had to scat away the cats.

"Mammy, can I drop the chickies my crumbs?"

"If you're finished."

Children liked doing a familiar thing in a different way, she reflected. Like that winter during the blizzard when they'd brought their bedding into the big room and kept fire going all night. They'd slept before the fire, all five of them, the children curled up like squirrels in a nest between their parents' bodies arched about them. She remembered not the cold but the warmth. . . . The light breathing of the children, her own drifting in and out of sleep. . . . The shape of his wide shoulders against the chimney glow. The crash of a log, the play of light on walls and rafters. The cats were warm mounds against their feet. . . . Waking up warm, though snow and ice encased all outdoors.

The weather moderated later in the day, but the children wanted to sleep before the fire again, Andy begging, "Sleep all here, Daddy!" She had said firmly, "No," but could have cried for it.

. . . Shut that door. No more.

How many times those words had slammed doors.

She sat on the top step and Katy below her fed crumbs to a brood of baby chicks. Katy's skin was pale at the nape of her neck where her hair divided and fell forward. No more a baby's neck.

Never more a baby in her arms? Again doors gaped. She saw the half-closed press, infant linen folded. . . . Just about now or a week from now you'd be coming down. In the sweat and agony, the deep delving, the endless struggle to labor past death, how narrow the way, strait and narrow . . . and few there be . . . an eternity in one small form.

Many a time she'd held the little body on her knees, scanned its face, looked into its eyes; looked for her mother, grandmother, her distant father. Or Rudi and his unknown father. For the man it would be if spared, for her own grandchild, and one down the years she'd never see. Little one, who are you? Given when? That August day in the woods? That cool misty evening? Oh God, came when?

And gone. He was none of us. Was of himself. Here for a season and God took him. She had to believe that, did believe it, but no more understood it than she understood killing cold or a burned-down house. But she knew the reality of what had endured in her long-lived Granny and in her deep-eyed husband, in . . . was it the arch of that branch of the tree?

"Katy, make haste and we'll go blackberry picking this afternoon. Would you like to go?"

Katy squealed and danced up one step, down two, took a whirl in the yard, then frisked up the steps again.

"Wait— No, I reckon it's dry now. We can wash our dishes. Then we'll put on our shoes and go."

The cats went with them. The old gray tabby followed and her white and silver-gray offspring dashed ahead to ambush his mother. Margaret held her child's hand firmly. "Now wait, Katy, you'll have to walk with me."

This path was too overgrown, not used enough anymore. They kept the horses close these days, for her husband was not a one for unnecessary risks. Nor did he like her to leave the house very far. Yet she'd always felt safe in these woods. Never had she or hers been threatened by outsiders here. It was at a houseplace where you were most apt to be menaced, she thought. It was at home her brother had been shot down by outlaw thieves twelve years ago. Though no doubt if you spent all your time in the wild, you'd find danger there too. Her thought moved again to her husband and Jemmy.

Their land was well chosen for these times, she thought. It was surrounded by ridges and away from any main path. Her father had chosen well. Perhaps that was why Rudi was willing to remain here, though sometimes, she knew, it went against his pride to owe their home to her people, whom he'd never known. That was when she exerted herself to raise another pride in him. "And would you leave a place you ha' put so much of yourself into? You know it was naught but old fields and eat-out pasture before you came. And now with your orchards and the increase of stock and the newground you ha' taken in, why would you up and want to leave all you've done? Not to mention the girl's room and the front porch. You think I take no pride in what you've done?"

For in spite of his pleasure in woods-roving he was essentially a home-loving man and an industrious one. Though they'd never be rich. There was not enough good land here and he had no desire to amass more, for it would call for more labor and he'd said long ago he wanted no part of slave-owning. She didn't care about that. Only sometimes the very enclosedness of their life oppressed her.

They went to meeting occasionally, but he was not a great one for Sabbath-keeping. Oh, he'd go for the looks of it, but his religion was more in his ways than his tongue. He'd lived too long away from other people. And nothing would ever make him wholly one with Frasers and Lairds and Logans. Though they'd come to know his worth.

Better than anyone else she knew his worth.

Then how in the name of God can you live so contentious with him? she cried to herself. But who else that she'd ever known could be so downright exasperating, so infuriating?

His worse trait was making excuses for people. He would always see both sides of a fracas, and he always seemed to want to *understand* the other side, although if she'd shifted to that side, doubtless he'd have taken up for the one she'd left. But how could you ever engage to struggle for anything or against anything if you thought the other side might be half-way right? And he ought to know far better than she that there *were* enemies to overcome. The Bible said that. The Bible, all through it, spoke of the wicked. Those that murdered her brother, those that came down to scalp and burn, the ones that despoiled Martha Laird, who were they? The Bible might say, "Love your enemies," but it did not say you had to let them take over the land. Did it?

Well, she often sighed, *be glad he's stayed here with you. Would you want to be left like Martha or like Mary Fraser and with two young children to watch over besides? But,* she gritted her teeth, *just let e'er a one come trampling my yard, I'll meet him with a rifle barrel and I'll dare 'em to dark my door!*

He would no longer discuss it with her. It was as if those happenings were unrelated to them. . . . And yet he'd fought before she knew him. For years he'd ridden with Rangers, went twice as a young man into Cherokee country and fought in pitched battles on the Little Tennessee, when most of the rest of them, her family included, were huddled in forts. In the winter of '75 and the summer of '76, no one could say he'd shirked his part then. And she'd known how to endure his absence, too, for her pride in him. *You see now what he is!* cried her pride to all her neighbors and kin.

He was forty years old. Maybe it was his age. Maybe war was only for the young.

But I'm not old yet! We're not old! I'll not be an old woman yet, I'll not live one foot in the grave! And this thing that's making now, I want part in it! It's not lost yet, I don't care what they say, it'll come!

Margaret was thirty-two. She was the same height as her husband, lithe and lean, her dark hair today bound up under her cap, though sometimes she let it hang free as her child's did.

The hill was hummocky with clumps of coarse grass, and here and there grew sassafras bushes and young pines. "Watch out now, Katy! Watch where you step! Keep close to me or you'll get caught in briars."

Birds scattered from the thickets. The berries were huge, juicy, shiny-black. The sprays arched to the ground. *I should have brought another basket,* she thought. *We'll fill these in no time.*

The cats disappeared. *Oh, I wish I'd brought another basket.* Hers and Katy's little one were soon filled.

If he came home before they got back, would he guess where they'd gone? She hadn't latched the door so he ought to know she'd be back directly. *Well, no use to worry about it,* she told herself.

"We'll sit down and rest a bit before we start back, Katy. Take off your bonnet and let's cool off."

They sat in the thin shade of a pine sapling.

"Mammy, let's sing."

"What you want to sing?"

They sang "Frog Went A-Courting," all verses; "The Fox and His Wife," all verses; "I Had a Little Sheep and I Had a Little Lamb," twice over. Now Katy's head was in her mother's lap and her eyelids were drooping. Margaret stroked the hair off her damp cheeks.

This child with ne'er a granny like I had, no sister either, only me to guide her in woman's ways. What will her way be? . . . Oh God, spare her, spare this one to me and the son I have left!

Margaret's fingers threaded the tangled strands. Although her back was only slightly supported by the slender pine, she realized its pain was eased and all her limbs had loosed themselves. Her breathing was almost as deep and slow as the child's.

As she sat there, she began to feel the ground, began to feel it wide and deep, feel it alive. She wanted to lie down like Katy and press herself into it. *I don't come out enough anymore. Oh, I'd go easier if I'd come out more like this.*

So much given. All her days she'd had trees and sky.

She remembered the wideness of a Virginia valley from long ago, but Pennsylvania was before her time. Too much of contention there, they'd said, and people jogging one another for room. The Ireland her Granny remembered to her death had been a place of stone bridges and stone barns, and other folks' houses you could see from your window. Towns and stony places with never a blade of grass.

Margaret thought, *I'm glad I have not to contend with such. Here's where I'd rather be.*

How came I here? What ways and thoughts I had no part of before my time? Margaret knew the world was great beyond her knowledge. She knew of seas, cities, and kings; of kingdoms and cities gone and of the one to come; of France, Babylon, and the New Jerusalem. Of Philadelphia and Charlestown. Long Canes and Ninety Six and the Waxhaws. Duncan Creek and this place that was eighteen miles from the mouth of the Enoree River. This place on the hillside, where the sun streaked young grass and whitened sassafras and a brown and orange butterfly drifted. *But how came I here?*

Katy, where will your feet take you? Oh God, give her all I've had and more. More of the light than I've had and more of ease. And good ground for her feet and to get the fruit of. She looked at Katy's stubby little feet that were so hard to push into her shoes when she bunched up her toes. Margaret covered one foot with her hand and gazed beyond it, saw her own. The wonder of a foot, how it reached and balanced; all the ways it could take you. . . .

She gazed at the butterfly's flutter and drift, gazed at movement on the ground between the hummocks of sedge grass, at a patterned muscular tube. She sat still and watched the flow of it, its diamonds gray and yellow-edged on black, the narrowing row of buttons at the end. She sat very still.

She'd brought no weapon. No stick near to hand. No rock either.

She sat immobile, her breathing still slow and deep as she watched it loop and flow on its way. Then she saw the flattened gray-white shape six feet behind it, infinitesimal movements inching it forward. It was only then that she grew breathless, cold. The young cat's haunches shivered.

Margaret sprang up, grabbed up Katy, Katy too startled to cry. Again Margaret looked about for a rock or a stick. She stooped and drew off her shoe and hurled it in front of the cat. Instantly the snake coiled; the cat sprang back, crouched again; the dread whirring began and the cat's tail lashed from side to side.

No stick, nothing. Katy was whimpering now, but Margaret pushed her back and took off her other shoe, advanced and flung it low, underhand, between the cat and the snake, hissed, "Scat! Scat away!"

This time the cat sprang down the slope as the rattler arced its length and struck where the cat had been, coiled, and rattled again.

"Scat away! Scat out of here!" Margaret picked up the baskets. "Hold onto my skirt, Katy. Hold fast. Come now." She changed her mind and picked up the child. "You carry this one.

As Margaret stumbled down the slope, snagging her ankles on briars, the high, light rattling ceased, then began again. She glanced back but did not see the young cat at all. Instead, she saw the old tabby crouched below her on the path, slitted pupils intent in wide green eyes.

The weight of Katy and both baskets and her haste had Margaret gasping for breath. As she set the child down, she saw a rock the size of a fist. "Stay here, Katy, on the path, you hear me now? Don't you dare to move from here!" She hunted for another rock, found one.

Margaret stood a moment, a rock in each hand, then moved carefully, diagonally up the hill.

The rattling had stopped and there was no sight of the young cat, but she saw a shoe ahead of her. She moved slowly, her right arm drawn back. She saw the other shoe.

She looked all around in the hot sunlight but saw only grass and earth. Then, just as she stooped to pick up her shoe, she saw the looped and circled form some ten feet up the hill. Even as she flung the rock with all her strength, the light whirring began. She hurled the second rock, backed off and saw she'd hit its head. For a moment she watched it writhe and turn before hurrying back toward the creek for more rocks.

She stoned the snake until it was motionless, quite dead. Finally she put on her shoes. She'd like to have its rattles but she had nothing to cut them off with.

She glanced down the hill at Katy, small and pale in the shadows. Katy had not moved from where she had been told to stay.

No, I can't drag that thing home now. Besides I have the baskets to carry. Rudi'll have to come and get the rattles. The rocks will mark the place.

Not till Margaret reached her, did Katy begin to cry. Margaret picked her up, hugged her fervently and pressed her cheek. "It's all right now. There's nothing to hurt us. That wicked old thing's dead!"

Katy's voice was high, crooning, almost like her singing. "I feared, Mammy, I feared!"

"Oh no, my baby, there's naught now to fear! We'll go home and make us a blackberry pie. Are you ready to go?"

As they went along the creek, Margaret carried Katy part of the way. The woods seemed very still.

Many a chicken snake she'd killed and once a copperhead but never a rattler. She wished fiercely for Rudi to be home now. *Rudi, I killed me a rattlesnake!*

14

The horses and the berry-pickers were approaching the house from opposite directions. Margaret had a second of paralyzing fear before she recognized the foremost rider as Rudi. But who were the others, she wondered. And how much stew was there? But she could thicken and add to it; potatoes and carrots and onions cooked up fast.

Rudi saw her with the berry basket, a good sign, as she hurried by the garden paling. "Brought us some company!" he called.

As soon as she heard his voice, she knew his repentance and apprehension. *Pshaw, man, I don't care who you've brought.*

Whoever they were, their beasts were spent, poor creatures, and she knew they'd been in the woods a long time, not so much from their unkempt appearance, though their clothes seemed stout and respectable enough, but from a certain empty-eyed, hungry-faced look she'd always noticed on anyone who'd been long in the wild.

Jemmy was already racing toward her. "It's Heiri and Willi, Mammy! They're kin to us! Did you know they're kin to us?"

They were young and stocky, no more than Rudi's height. The one with the averted face was tending to his horse's gear as the other one came toward her. He had light eyes, a familiar cast to his face that she could not quite place.

Rudi said, "It's Heiri Lienhardt, Margaret, Joggi's brother, Johannes Lienhardt's son. And Willi Rieder, his friend from the Congarees."

The boy bent awkwardly in a kind of bow.

"Mammy, they've come to take dinner with us! We brought 'em home! We—"

She caught Jemmy's shoulder, pulled him around against her. "Jemmy, boys shouldn't talk so much. You let your Daddy tell it."

Rudi said, "We came up on 'em down the creek. Or they came up on us. Anyhow we met and here we are." He paused. "They're looking for Whigs." He added, watching her face, "To join up with."

"Then I hope you can find some," she answered tartly. "They're scarce hereabouts." But when she smiled, it transformed her face. "We're proud to have you. We're proud to welcome you here. And this is our Katy-love."

Katy slipped from behind her mother and ran to clasp her father's legs. "Daddy, I feared that snake! I feared that snake!"

"Tell Daddy what Mammy did to it," said Margaret.

Rudi picked up Katy and she tightened her arms around his neck. Such a light little body; he wished it were more solid.

Margaret said, "If you care to go up the creek when you find the time, that old field with all the blackberries in it, about twenty yards above the path, you'll find its carcass. I marked it with rocks. You can bring me its rattles. I counted ten." She turned to mount the steps. "You can give our company ease on the front porch while I set out dinner. Jemmy, you come with me." Her shoes made a dignified clack on the boards. She was glad she had them on.

Jemmy was torn between hunger and a desire to go with the men, but hunger won.

Once they began eating, no one talked. Margaret ladled out boiled meat and vegetables over and over again. On the third serving Willi tried to murmur refusal, but it was so half-hearted she ignored it. Heiri made no apologies for his appetite, nor did Rudi or Jemmy. Afterward, when they had been regaled with peach brandy, a great drowsiness descended upon the adult males. Margaret regarded them impatiently and knew she'd get nothing out of them now.

The young men rose and tried to thank her, but Heiri was thick-tongued and could not find his words. Willi spoke for both. "Frau— Mistress Näffels, we thank you deeply."

"I hope you'll bide the night here," she said. "You're welcome both to bide as long as you will."

Heiri found his words. "We thank you. We must go on."

"You'd do well to rest your horses," said Rudi. "They need good baiting and rest. And other care. They look to be good mounts, but if you don't watch out, you'll end up afoot."

Heiri and Willi glanced at each other, startled. "We always found good grass," protested Heiri. "Or cane. Or almost always."

"They're ill-loaded for riding, especially the chestnut. I"ll help you re-load. And other attention too they need."

The boys looked shamefaced.

"Tell you what you do. You fellows stretch out somewhere. It's too hot upstairs now, but, Meg, can we let 'em have a couple of pallets out front? You two take rest and I'll see to your beasts."

Their protests were overborne, and soon they found themselves prone on the front porch. Few domestic sounds reached them there. Drowsily Heiri wondered what had happened to the children. So quiet. Not even the sound of a fowl. The breeze that fanned him bore the scent of corn blades.

When he awoke after a hard sleep, it was late afternoon. Everything looked different, softer, fresher. The cedars, the rise of the field, the near high treeline gave it an upland look, less spacious than he was accustomed to, yet appealing.

Going to fight. I didn't know it would take so long and be so lonely. Over and over, places to stop off at and women and young ones to say goodbye to.

Willi's sleep had been heavy too. He lay with his eyes closed. His head hurt and also his leg.

Will we ever get there? he wondered. Where was *there?* Nearer than it was and yet farther back. He felt contemptuous eyes waiting for him to fail. He was trying to hide the way his knee still bothered him. He felt mortified about Shine and half-angry with Heiri, for he'd left much of Shine's care to him. But what did Heiri know about hard travel, a farmer's son who'd never been more than fifteen miles from home? Willi tried to imagine Heiri as a soldier and couldn't. Oh, if only they could meet up with others on the same quest they were, as Joggi must have, a troop of men who'd know where to go.

As Joggi must have. Where was he now? What if he hadn't met up with anyone? What if they never did find him? Cross another river, two or three and never find him.

Rudi lounged awhile beside them on the front steps, and Margaret sat just outside the door.

Finally she interrupted their talk of weather and animals seen along the way. "Have you heard aught from the North?"

"No," said Willi, "not down our way. Have you?"

He turned courteously toward her, but Rudi answered. "Nothing certain. Though some say Congress has give up on South Carolina and Georgia. Say they'll let the British have us in payment for their own freedom."

"I don't credit that at all!" Margaret said angrily. "It's all one country! Virginny and Pennsylvany, they would not go back on their kin!"

"Kin?" Rudi questioned.

"I have kin in both places. And I've heard tell of Dutch there too. Surely you've heard of the great Dutch settlements in Pennsylvany."

In the silence that followed she was sorry for her words. It was like she was throwing up ignorance and rootlessness to him. With no decent upbringing and all manner of mistreatment, how much could he know of race and kin?

Heiri said, "My brother says many in South Carolina will not give up. He says it's still beginning."

"And yet when men like Andrew Williamson and Andrew Pickens," said Rudi slowly, "when they've laid down arms and pledged their word to peace—I just don't know."

"Did you hear of the British colonel," asked Willi, "who murdered men in the Waxhaws, men that had already surrendered?"

"I heard something but didn't half credit it. Because of the fellow that was telling it. What did you hear?"

They told what they'd heard of Tarleton's massacre of Buford's troops in late May. "Joggi says he sticks men like you stick pigs," said Heiri.

"Aye, it's sword fighting. I hate a sword or a bayonet bad as a scalping knife," Rudi said.

Words leaped from Willi's lips before he could stop them. "It's hard to stand, them coming at you with blades! I'll take a bullet any day before that!" His voice trembled.

Heiri was dumb. Some of Willi's dread moved into him.

Suddenly Margaret felt out of place. Old rebukes, old rebuffs echoed. "Don't be meddling in men's business!" "I told you afore, it's unbecoming for a female to speak so bold in front of men."

She rose and went indoors. *I'd best look at the pie. And see what the children are up to, they're too quiet.*

But if I were a man, I'd learn not to fear it! I'd harden myself! I'd have to!

After she left, Rudi said, "I been studying the best way for you to go. I know there's a gathering up beyond the Tyger about six miles this side the Pacolet. It's near a place called Cedar Springs. That's the nearest encampment of Whigs I know of, and I think it's the place you should make for."

"How far?" asked Willi and Heiri together.

"Two days will get you there. Or will if you don't lie out too long. And meet no trouble."

"Are there marked paths?"

"I'll see you across Enoree and Tyger. I don't guarantee the easiest paths, but when you get across Tyger, you'll find more Whigs than in most places, and you can no doubt get good direction."

"You mean you'll go with us, Rudi? You'll go along?" Pleasure and excitement reddened Heiri's face.

"I said I'd see you across Tyger," Rudi said sternly. "That's two days I give you. I won't undertake to be gone from here more than two days."

To Heiri the gap of age between them seemed suddenly more than twenty years, but it brought a wave of strange emotion to him. *Oh, I wish—that I could wake up in some loft-room smelling dried apples and herbs. Or walk a tract of land on some creek. Ride over to see Rudi once in a while and the little boy. But I wouldn't be gone overnight either if I could help it.* In his mind he looked toward a fireplace and saw a girl's back. A reddish nimbus of hair. But he saw only her back.

"You think Joggi might be there?" Willi was asking. "You think he might have joined up with them?"

"It's possible, but I think it more like he fell in with some going up the old road west of the Broad. He must have crossed Broad River somewhere and headed for Catawba, maybe toward Charlotte. I hear it's a big camp up there too. That's where most would go from down your way." *If they go,* he thought of adding but did not. Rudi knew the Swiss and Germans of the Congarees right well.

Willi and Heiri too wondered who would go. They themselves had left so suddenly, they'd all lived so close-mouthed those last weeks that they'd known little of the thoughts and doings of neighbors. *We may be the only ones,* thought Heiri. *Just us two coming up among all these English and Irish, how will they receive us? Will they even want us?*

"Rudi, you think we ought not try for that place too, the place you say our people would go?"

"It's two or three times as far from here, Heiri. I couldn't undertake to guide you so far. And the sooner you can meet with friends the better."

Friends. Some of Heiri's bleakness left him.

"Have many gone from here?" asked Willi.

"Some have gone."

They waited for more words.

"Have many taken the oath?" It was hard to ask Rudi that question.

"I don't know. I judge a good many have."

Neither Willi nor Heiri was brave enough to ask Rudi if he had. Perhaps they would have been glad to know he had not yet sworn allegiance, although he was considering the necessity.

At last Rudi broke the silence. "We'll leave at daylight. But you come out with me now, both of you, and I'll show you how to load a horse. Heiri, I thought you knew better how to pack a horse." He would have addressed even harder words to Willi if he had known him better.

In the deep-drenched dawn, Margaret watched the riders leave with her husband in the lead, watched as they mounted the rise beyond the shaggy cedars. They would cut across ridges until they came to the Enoree and cross it at Musgrove's Mill if the ford was unguarded. She knew that few others than Rudi could lead them such a quick, sure way, and she gladly consented to his doing it.

The boys did not look back again. *Why was that one boy's face so familiar,* she asked herself. She saw again his smiling upcast look in the firelight as she'd pressed more food on him this morning, his drowsy look giving way to laughter, a certain—merriment at the impossibility of his declining another helping.

Was he like Jemmy? No, Jemmy's face was thinner, more like hers. And not like Rudi's either; his had an altogether different cast. No, it was a look of. . . . But it was not the features, nor a shape of nose or jaw or mouth. Something in the eyes. Who?

Maybe not anyone she knew now. Maybe someone from long ago, someone from childhood.

Pennington's Fort maybe in 1761, when they'd been penned up for months because of the redskins, Granny helping to hold them together, quieting the children. Granny's face, so wise and innocent. Yes. . . . No, some boy's face there. Some half-grown boy who'd come and gone with the men. Come and gone, never seen again. Some boy there, it must have been.

Margaret's face grew long. She watched until the three shapes merged into the woods. The house was terribly lonely even with the sleeping children in it. She felt terribly bereft.

15

The big pool fed by three springs was shaded by a giant cedar tree; hence its name, Cedar Springs. On a slope above it, Colonel John Thomas, Jr., son of Colonel John Thomas, Sr., who was in Ninety Six Jail, commanded some sixty Whigs from the region around upper Fairforest Creek. They were the bravest and most obdurate from what was left of the old Spartan Regiment. Many belonged to the Fairforest Presbyterian meeting-house, of whom it was said that there was not a Tory among them.

Fifteen miles away, on the south fork of the Tyger, equal numbers were as stubborn in their loyalty to the old government. A difference between the two sides now was that the Loyalists no longer had to lie hidden in swamps and hollow trees. The Liberty Men must now be the outliers. However, the camp at Cedar Springs was no secret, and it was large enough to afford some security to its liberty-loving neighborhood.

Here, there were daily comings and goings of scouts and foraging parties, of relatives bringing food and news. Every few days a newcomer would join it. Occasionally someone would leave for one reason or another, not to return. All who walked or rode in to volunteer service were welcomed, since most of them were already known to the men there. However, the arrival of two young Dutchmen from over ninety miles away was unusual. A couple of the men knew or knew of the Dutchman on Indian Creek, and one vouched for his good name. But Näffels himself had not brought the two into camp; they had traveled the last miles alone.

Their story, though difficult to follow, was listened to intently. The distance they had come and Willi's service in the low country, where Thomas and several of his officers had also served, were certainly in their favor, but ultimately it was their earnest manner that gained their acceptance.

"I will not fight against friends."

"I seek my brother. He fights for America."

But the men at Cedar Springs had never heard of "Yocky Linnert."

As Willi had foreseen, soldiering came hard to Heiri. Because of earlier militia drill Heiri knew the rudiments of military usage and he knew how to handle a gun. But handling it lethally was another matter. Sometimes his responses were a trifle slow. He would look thoughtfully at the officer a second too long. Also language was a barrier, not so much Heiri's lack of understanding as his lack of words. His red-faced silence began to provoke impatience. Eventually the others assumed him to be stupid, more ignorant than he was, and therefore he began to feel that way. Although he was quite strong and in some ways dexterous, besides being very willing to please others, he had not the knack of blending anonymously into a group. Willi tended to be embarrassed by him.

Several of the fifteen- and sixteen-year-olds began to play jokes on him—sly, unfriendly jokes. Heiri was well acquainted with good-natured pranks, but these were different, and Heiri knew it. He tried to smile when they stole his little kettle, stuffed it with rags, decorated it with squirrel tails, and pranced around camp wearing it for a helmet. But when he caught one of them putting a rough twig under Roker's saddle, he exploded into the forbidden language he'd infrequently heard from his father and came near to knocking the boy down. The boy did not need a translator.

Heiri took good care of Roker, the best he knew how, sometimes sorry he'd brought him so far from home. Once in shame, he leaned against Roker's side and wept. The horse raised his head, switched his tail a time or two, and stood perfectly still. Later Roker got into the habit of nuzzling Heiri's neck. He had never done that before. Perhaps he only wanted more grain.

Roker's backbone was sharper now. With so many horses in one area, forage was scarce even in the height of summer. Moreover, rations for the men were by no means plentiful, although friendly neighbors brought what they could. Hunting skills were greatly prized, but small game was scarce, large game non-existent, and shot not to be wasted. In the camp Heiri came to be valued chiefly as a hewer of wood and a drawer of water.

Word of enemy movement seeped in from time to time. The troops Heiri and Willi had seen hurrying toward Ninety Six on June 22 were Loyalists defeated in a premature uprising at Ramsour's Mill in North Carolina. However, most of the Loyalists Heiri and Willi had been dodging the last few days of their journey were from a regiment that the haughty Colonel Alexander Innes had just furloughed. In contrast to Innes, Colonel Patrick Ferguson from his base at Ninety Six was busy enlisting with energy and charm every man he could win to the King's service.

Lord Cornwallis had ordered the confiscation of rebels' property but had forbidden cruelty to their families. Yet eastward between the Broad and the Catawba, an obnoxious Philadelphian, Captain Christian Huck, not only destroyed Billy Hill's ironworks, but his Loyalist dragoons pillaged and burned houses, terrorizing women and children. They not only turned out a Presbyterian minister's family on a Sabbath morning and plundered and burned their house, but a few miles away they murdered a pious young man who sat reading his Bible. Meetinghouses were highly suspect as centers of rebellion.

The embodiment of rebels on the upper Catawba River was growing. By invitation it moved downriver to King Hagler's Branch in the Catawba Nation, where two hundred Catawbas joined it. The elected leader of all these men was Thomas Sumter, a former Virginian, a well-to-do planter from the Santee near Nelson's Ferry. Sumter had been sitting out the war for the last year and a half but the fall of Charlestown had impelled him to action.

Seventy miles west of the Catawba, Heiri ate his cornbread supper with the others. They had had a few potatoes three days ago but no meat for a week. In fact, they had had meat only twice since Heiri had been in camp. Once a man brought in a comb of honey in his hat, but Heiri did not taste any. He tried not to think of green peas and dumplings, fresh eggs, fruit tarts, milk, and butter. This bread was no more than water and meal and salt baked in an iron spider and rough at that. He chewed slowly to make it last longer.

"What did you grind up in this meal, Eli? Cobs and all?"

"Cobs help fill up your gut too, Joe."

"Fill is one thing. Rupture is another."

Their camp was just inside the woods which edged their drilling ground. The men sat back from the fires in the cooling dusk. It had been a long hot day, the twelfth of July. No one had come or gone but the scouts, who had not gone far. There was nothing to report. No one would have the energy to do anything in this heat.

"Dutch, you going to drink that spring dry?"

"Sure it's just spring water you got there?" Someone reached for Heiri's canteen, which Heiri had laid down beside him. The boy sniffed it and sputtered and coughed. "Whooee, boys! It's been something more'n water in here! No wonder he fell over that rock this afternoon. Take a whiff!"

They passed Heiri's canteen from one to the other, each sniffing it, some falling back in mock breathlessness, others merely smiling. "Must ha' been powerful brew." "Dutch, you got to lay off that stuff!" "Dutch, I'm astonished!"

Heiri grinned speechlessly.

As he often did, he imagined Joggi among these fellows. Would they devil Joggi the way they did him? He doubted it. Sometimes Heiri thought of leaving in the night and trying to go to that eastward place where Rudi said Joggi might be. But then he thought how it would look. Also he knew he might well be taken by the other side and either jailed or forced into their service. Or worse. Yet often he wished he had tried to persuade Rudi to guide them northeast instead of northwest. . . . Somewhere up Broad River, the northern arm of the Congaree. Was the country over there like this or more like his own? Yet what if he and Willi had braved it all and not found Joggi there either? Sometimes he felt feverish to move. This dawdling and idling about in one place staled the ground.

Heiri was not the only one getting restless.

"I'd sure like to hear more about that meetinghouse skirmish."

"What? Where?" Voices quickened.

"Ten or twelve mile below Fishdam Ford. Other side Broad River."

"Oh, that one." They lay back. Old news.

No one knew anything more, just that some McClures and their neighbors had attacked and beaten off a band of Tories at a meetinghouse several weeks ago, Mobley's Meetinghouse.

"I just hope 'twas true."

After a long silence, someone said, "I sure wouldn't ha' minded being there to help."

Another sighed. "When you reckon we'll ever?"

"Ever what?"

"Be anywhere to help."

Finally someone else said, "I reckon we're helping now."

"How?"

"You heard of any robberies or murders hereabouts lately?"

Their officers sat at a distance. Colonel Thomas was conversing with a brother-in-law, Captain Joseph McJunkin. The fires were dying, their rose becoming ash. Beyond the firelight, tree trunks were black, their shadows lost in the almost dark. The clearing in front was vague, formless with suggestions of shapes floating as if risen from the ground.

A man cleared his throat, said loudly, "Never fear, boys, your day'll come. Mayhap sooner than you think."

Older gruffer voices, "Aye, they'll come." "And more than one or two."

Into the stillness that had fallen over the entire camp came the pounding of hoofbeats. Before the men had all sat up and before anyone could get to his feet, into their midst burst the commotion of a heaving horse and a small figure rearing back to rein him in.

The colonel sprang up. Even in the dusk he knew her.

"You'll have to help me down, Johnny." Her voice was hoarse and weak. "I ha' been coming all day."

Others ran to help her. The woman was less than middle height, a sparc and compact figure. She stumbled as she touched the ground. Her dark hair straggled about her face and her hand trembled as she pushed it back. "I'll trouble you for something for my throat if you please. I'm parched wi' thirst."

"Mother, I made sure you was at Ninety Six!"

"So I was last night." She pulled away from her son's support and turned so that her back was against a tree trunk and she could face him and the others beyond.

All stood gaping. Thomas found his voice. "What? You came all that way today?"

"Aye. I crossed Island Ford afore sunup. And after I have a few swallows to clear my gullet, I'll tell you why."

As she drank from her cup twice full, whispers, murmurs ran through the dark. "Come all that way today?" "All that way in one day?" "Clear from Ninety Six! It's near sixty mile!" "Mistress Old Colonel Thomas!" "It's Mistress Jane Thomas!"

Her son and the officers, two of whom were her sons-in-law, hovered around her. Her voice rose. "No. It's my judgment to speak in the hearing of all."

They made some low response.

"You think I rode so far and half killed poor Jack to waste time feeding? I come to warn you and I thank my God He's brought me here in time! Now you listen and make what preparation you will!" Her voice was now as sharp and clean as a gutting knife.

All stood as still as trees.

She had ridden to Ninety Six to see her husband and to take him what comforts she could. "I had gone to rest. A woman had consented to give me shelter for a trinket I'd brought, and as I lay in the chamber above—it was last night I lay there—I heard two women speak. As clear as you hear me now I heard them." Her voice sank a little. "One said, 'On tomorrow night,' and I heard it plain as you hear me now, 'on tomorrow night the Loyalists intend to surprise the Rebels at Cedar Springs!'"

A chunk of wood crumbled and flared. She repeated, "'Tomorrow night the Loyalists intend to surprise the Rebels at Cedar Springs.'"

Her voice brought other voices across the miles, loud, at their core a voice of authority. They heard themselves spoken of with cold intention in a house many miles away.

"So I determined to let you know."

Determined. It penetrated Heiri's brain. All that way in one day. That little woman. About the size of his own mother.

"Surprise?" McJunkin gave a shout of laughter. "Hi, Mistress Jane, to be sure, you've took care of the surprise part of it!"

Thomas turned one way, then another, a brightness on his face not from the firelight. His lips, which had been tightly folded, now loosed in a broad smile. His officers gathered close and spoke low. Everyone watched in the brightening light.

The orders came, not over loud. "Build up the fires, big lasting fires. Plenty of oak and hickory. We want light." And pack gear and prepare arms. Speedily.

Immobile figures loosed, bent, strode. There was little speech.

The horses? No, leave the horses where they were. The men would merely move a short way up the slope to wait.

No one noticed when Mrs. Thomas left. Later those who knew her said she'd gone home. By herself.

They scattered behind their camp and watched it in the dark. The fires blazed and burned down, and men crept forward to replenish them. An owl called from elsewhere. Crickets and jarflies sounded far away.

Heiri held his gun loosely. He thought that what he felt was not fear, only a trembling, curious anticipation, an eagerness for what would happen, something like what he had felt that morning when they crossed the river in the fog. He thought once or twice of the horses secured behind them. He thought of the troop riding toward them, an armed knee-to-knee progression of men whose heads were covered with darkness, but he turned his mind away from them. He concentrated instead on the rose and yellow light where he and the others had rested hours ago, it seemed. That light was now the focus of all progression, beckoning and terrible.

Heiri was barely aware of the man to his left, a fellow named Jem Boyd, until Jem whispered, "You there, Dutch?" Heiri's whisper leaped out, "I'm here."

The man to his right moved a few times but never spoke.

The moon had not yet risen. The sky was heavy with stars. The clearing beyond the campfires stretched wide and dark. Who knew what swirled there? The cricket shrilling was scattered and sparse. As a few breaths of air stirred the leaves, Heiri felt the cool on his neck, felt his shoulders loosen . . . felt his thought narrow, felt it float above his neck and shoulders. . . . He jerked his head upright, shook it. He must concentrate—

It was the wind. No, a stir around him—hissing, whispering, "Listen!" He shook his head again.

More sudden than the coming of the woman on the horse was the eruption of movement around him, the slide and click of readying arms, and there before him in the light were dozens of men milling about on foot and two or three on horseback turning and reining. Heiri half-rose, crouched. Down among the campfires he heard exclamations, a broken-off command. He saw light on a drawn sword, a horse's curving side, saw scarcely a turning this way and that when shots flashed all around him. Heiri gaped as the men on horseback wheeled in several directions at once. One jerked spasmodically and slipped to the ground. The dark was thick with yelling, thick with smoke. Something thumped hard on a tree nearby. The figures in the light were turning in a welter of confusion.

Scarcely knowing how, Heiri raised his musket in trembling hands and shot. Then astonishingly his hands began the motions of reloading.

Boyd was cursing and yelling, "Good boy, Dutch! I believe you got one!" Heiri heard no sound from his empty-feeling right.

Guns blazed out of the woods again, and now there was forward movement all around him. He heard no clear orders but felt himself one of a wide shallow vat of objects, nuts or something, shaken and thrown forward.

"This way!" They ran at angles toward the the edge of the woods on both sides of the camp, avoiding the light, and fired at what they could see in the open as a scattering of shots replied. Now they saw dimly in the starlight figures running toward their horses, and the mass of those already mounted turning, already beyond the spring, and spurring down the shallow draw. After a few minutes there was no one in range to shoot at.

Heiri ran out into the open with the others. Across the slope and down the valley came the sound of horses running, and they could see the strung out mass of their enemies in full retreat.

"A hundred! More than a hundred!"

"Two hundred! More like two hundred!"

"Say a hundred and fifty! At least a hundred and fifty!"

As the men in the clearing hushed to catch all sounds, they heard nearer sounds, low and heavy from the ground. They saw shapes that had not been there before, the bulk of a dead horse, and they heard another one thrashing and struggling near the camp. Among the campfires they found more tumbled shapes.

"Dutch, I'd swear it was you got that'n!" whispered Jem Boyd, then louder to the others, "It was Dutch got him! I heard and saw it!"

But I shot only twice! Heiri wanted to say; surely it was not my shot!

They counted four enemy dead and five wounded. Of their own, only two were hurt.

An hour later came the order to break camp. The wounded would be taken with them.

Heiri was one of the diggers of the pit at daybreak. It was hard digging and the pit was not deep. A boy who had once tormented Heiri threw down his spade, white-faced, and ran off.

Heiri helped to lift the bodies and lay them down, bodies which had now been stripped of most of their clothes. The naked limbs were hard to manage in the grainy light. Their faces were like dead animal faces, he thought. Heiri wished desperately for some human-made pall to cover and restore them to human likeness. But only earth, clotted with roots and stones, covered them.

Women came just as the men were ready to leave. They brought fresh-baked cornbread and a basket of peaches, not enough fruit to go around, but the men cut and shared it so that each got a piece. They were relieved that the women took away the wounded of both sides. Before they went, one woman cut cedar boughs and weighted them down with rocks over the grave.

Thomas's men rode northeast along a hill road, and at the beginning of their march they talked a great deal.

"Reckon they'll tell everybody how they surprised us?"

"Come a long way, didn't they, to surprise us like that."

"And them outnumbering us three to one."

"Tell you though, it were a mercy it weren't daylight."

"Well, they picked the time."

"Aye, they picked it."

As the morning wore on, conversation slowed. They reviewed their relative positions in the woods.

"I made sure 'twas you on my right beside me. I'd recognize that old 'b'lam' of yours anywhere."

Heiri wondered about the man on his right. Who was he? Where had he gone?

Finally talk ceased. The last exchange was, "That Mistress Thomas now, she's a wonder."

"More than a wonder. God's angel, I'd say."

Three miles to the north they descended to a rocky bottom and crossed a creek, and in mid-morning they forded the Pacolet River. Roker held up his head and went as steady as a veteran, Heiri thought. Roker. Was it still Roker, Papa's horse? No, he could not believe that. They had come out into a country of great rocks and deep ravines, and Heiri thought that he, like Roker, would soon be someone else.

Willi rode near Heiri. He said little other than what the needs of the march required. Yet he stayed by Heiri all morning and when they stopped in the early afternoon in a thickly wooded cove, he ate his bread alongside Heiri and stretched out near him to sleep.

16

Goosedown feathers floated lazily about the yard. If they had split the feather ticks inside the house as they had the straw ticks, most of the feathers might have been saved, but the invaders had preferred to empty the bolsters and featherbeds outside, where the feathers would fly out of their way. Now four men were busy inside cramming the empty bolsters and feather ticks with what they wanted. Six other men had taken the big straw ticks to the barn to fill with ears of corn.

Madle and the girls huddled outside the yard paling, shivering in the August heat. The dog had been stilled with two bayonet thrusts.

"Where's your husband?" the soldier demanded again, coming nearer, yet seeming never to look at her.

She could only stare at him, her arms fastening Anneli and Cathri to her sides like a vise.

At the barn men were hitching her riding mare and the old horse, Spark, to the wagon.

It was a still morning. Surely the sergeant's shouts and the sounds of squawking fowls must have carried across the creek to where Johannes and the boys were working. *God!* Madle kept crying out. *Father!*

The privates too, not British like the sergeant, avoided looking at her now that she had obeyed their orders. With shock she recognized one of them as a Remster, another as Jacob Volck.

Anneli hid her face against her mother's side. Madle felt the waves of trembling that continually racked the child's body. Cathri stood watching the little windows on each side of the chimney. She heard the clatter and scrape of vessels inside the house. She kept thinking she would wake up.

They brought out the flour barrel and the meal barrel, both nearly full; and boxes, jars, and kegs of sugar, salt, saltmeat; sacks and sacks of potatoes and of dried fruits; crocks of butter and lard; and at last even the kraut barrel. The men in the cornhouse and at the barn wrestled barrels of oats, wheat, and newly shelled corn into the other wagon they had brought

with them, and the great ticks full of ears still in the husk. Two men were
using corn to toll and catch the fowls, mostly hens and geese.

Now they brought out the last of the house plunder. Madle would
not look at the stuffed knobby sacks and the baskets, but Cathri looked.
She could tell the shapes of candlesticks, plates, jugs, and jars, knew them
to be leaving their house, drawn out of its life perhaps forever. She saw a
bright spill of blue silk, her mother's treasured lutestring silk though not
worn in many a year, and knew that under it were yards and yards of lace
made long ago by small skilled hands in another country.

A man brought out two guns, Johannes' rifle and his old musket.
The man laid the rifle aside with the other goods but swung the musket
against the doorpost to smash its stock.

Two soldiers brought the Lienhardts' wagon to the back dooryard
gate to be loaded with household goods. After they loaded it, the sergeant
shouted and six men swung off down the field road beyond the barn while
three remained lounging at ease by the two loaded wagons. The fowls that
lay with legs tied together panted and flapped their wings in the dust.
Another man stood in the yard with the sergeant.

The sweating sergeant was square-faced and burned brown, not
much older than Madle's oldest son. The man with him looked middle-
aged—stringy, dark-haired, and gap-toothed. He kept stealing glances at
Madle. He said something low to the sergeant, turned suddenly and
assaulted her with his shout. "Where's your man?" He moved toward her.
"I say, where's your man? Hans Linnert! And Jacob and Henry! Where's
Jacob? Where's Henry?"

Madle's mouth quivered. She gazed wide-eyed into the threatening face, as her hold on the girls tightened.

The man came to the side fence, stood in the open gate. "Look
here, Sis." He bent and touched Anneli's chin. "Let's turn up your pretty
face now and tell us where your Dad is."

The girls felt their mother's body harden and seem to grow beyond its frame. "Keep your hands from my child." Her words were low,
but something in their cold clear English articulation stayed the man.

He straightened and laughed. "Oh, we know about Jacob, and we
know about Henry too, it may be something you don't know." He grinned.
"But we'll see to 'em, mistress, I make no doubt—if we've not already
done so."

A cow bawled in the woods. The men exchanged pleased looks,
and the gap-toothed man returned to the sergeant. Both men moved from

the yard to join those at the wagons and look down the field road. Presently out of the trees five milch cows along with three heifers and two yearlings appeared, driven by the soldiers. The gap-toothed man shouted, "Ha-ha! Good boys!"

Although she had not heard Johannes, Madle knew him as soon as she felt his touch. She closed her eyes and let her head fall against his shoulder. She drew a shuddering breath and whispered, "The boys?"

"In the woods."

"Be careful, Johannes. Oh please, for all our sakes."

"I will."

Cathri felt her mother's hold on her loosen as if some of its strength had gone.

Her father left them and went along the side fence toward the men beyond the wagons. They had not seen him come up for they were watching the approaching cattle.

"By what right do you take my goods and stock?"

Five heads jerked around.

"By what right—"

The sergeant stood rigid as he took the paper from his waistcoat pocket and rattled off what he had read earlier to Madle, orders for the confiscation from all rebels of such goods as were deemed necessary for the use of his Majesty's troops.

"Rebel? I've never shouldered arms against this government. How do you call me rebel?"

"Are you Joe-Hans Linnert?"

"I am."

The man held out the paper for Johannes to see. "Well, here's your name. Can you read?"

Three columns of names were written below the order. Johannes stepped closer, saw mostly unfamiliar names, a half dozen struck through. He made out "Christian Theus" in the English script and two other Theuses—why, they don't even live here!—found at last his own with two other Lienhardts listed below it. For a moment he was puzzled. *I thought I was the only Lienhardt in this country.* Then he realized they were his sons' names.

"But—I live in peace here!" He stepped back. "We fear God and harm no one! I have not raised arms against King George!"

"Your name's here!" snapped the sergeant. "Joe-Hans Linnert."

Johannes' fists were white-knuckled. Slowly he turned and surveyed the loaded wagons, but before he could take it all in, he heard shouting and a great commotion beyond the barn. The yearlings had broken loose and were now kicking up their heels across the field while the heifers and several cows threatened to swing out after them.

The sergeant cursed and shouted, and the three standing by the wagons ran to help their comrades. The sergeant watched a minute, spoke to the gap-toothed man, who turned with his gun in the crook of his arm to face Johannes. Now the sergeant too hurried toward the men and cattle.

A high-piled wagon hid most of this action from Madle and the girls. Cathri moved away from her mother, the better to see what was happening.

Madle had turned her back. She gazed eastward over the trees into the light beyond the river. Sometimes she could see in the high-piled clouds the peaks of Churfirsten. Sometimes she was able to think herself back into that mystic *Felsloch* on Wildhuser Schafberg, the cleft in the rock where one was always sheltered. Anneli still leaned against her, and Madle gathered her child more closely, willing for her too the rock's guard. But suddenly she turned to call sharply, "Cathri!"

The answer did not come at once and when it did, it was, "I'm here, Mama," somewhere beyond the back fence.

"Cathri, come here! Come here at once!"

A low-growing bushy fig tree at the fence corner hid the girl, but as her mother called again, Cathri appeared. "I'm coming, Mama." She moved slowly around the corner and along the side fence. "I just wanted to—"

"How could you frighten me so? Stay by me! How dare you to leave me, Cathri! Don't you dare to leave my side again!"

Cathri heard her mother's scolding as from a distance, an incomprehensibly normal sound like the calling of partridges at the edge of a field.

"How can you be so thoughtless? To add to our distress—"

Johannes watched the men running about in the field. Ten men to handle ten cows. The yearlings and a heifer got clean away. In different circumstances he would have laughed. Finally, however, the men achieved a semblance of control and drove the little herd up past the barn.

Again the sergeant and the gap-toothed man, who had never ceased to hold his gun on Johannes, exchanged low words. Now the latter came toward Johannes and jerked his head toward Madle and the girls. "Get back." He gestured toward the yard.

"What?"

"Get back in there, all of you. 'Less an you want to go with us. We're already half a mind to take you."

"Please come, Johannes," Madle called low.

With his wife's face hidden on his shoulder and Anneli's against her mother's side, Johannes watched the overloaded wagons move, and Cathri watched with him.

Pulling was hard work for the old horse and the mare, ill-matched as they were and not used to such heavy work. The lines bit deep into Johannes' face as the soldiers beat the horses on. Spark wouldn't last long. Finally the sergeant told the men to pull some of the bags and kegs off the wagon and shoulder them themselves, and after that, the procession moved slowly by the house and on beyond the front fence.

"Wait!" Johannes shouted suddenly. He broke away from his family. "Who is your captain? Tell me your captain!"

The lean-faced man wheeled and leveled his gun. "You stay where you be or you'll get something to stop you, I promise!"

Johannes stopped. He stood outside the fence and watched the wagons and his cows disappear beyond the screening woods in the east. He turned only at the sounds behind him.

Anneli had sunk to the ground sobbing, her head buried in her lap, and Cathri huddled crying with her apron over her head. The body of their dog was between them, his blood still bright on the thick rough fur of his throat.

Johannes went to them, stooped to touch Cathri's shoulder. "Go to the bridge and call the boys, Cathri." He picked up Anneli and held her against his shoulder, and unbelievably, even as the child's body clung to him, he felt the knots of shock and rage loosen a little. He looked for Madle.

She stood on the porch with her hand on the back of a chair, gazing at it.

Here's this chair, she thought. *They did not take this chair. I'll sit down. I must sit down now.*

It felt strange to give her body to ease at this hour of the morning, but it made the demand. She watched Johannes mount the steps with Anneli in his arms, thought how gray and strained he looked. He stood hesitantly by the doorway looking at her.

"Don't go inside yet, Johannes," she said faintly. "Let's sit here and rest awhile. Sit down awhile and rest."

Something in her voice compelled him. She did not hold out her arms for Anneli, but simply sat with her hands in her lap as if she were a woman of great leisure. He eased himself onto the bench against the housewall. The child had stopped her hard crying, but a convulsive shudder went through her every now and then. Johannes felt his body treasuring the feel of his child against him.

Madle sat gazing at the orchard. The silence about them held only emptiness.

"There are still some yellow apples on that tree," she observed at last.

"What's in the garden?" It was strange to hear his own voice ask so ordinary a question.

"I'm not sure. I can't think. The late butterbeans? Or maybe a few peas not shattered out."

"How about the late peas?"

She shook her head. "They have not come on."

"Melons?" he asked after a minute or so.

"I don't know. I did not see." She thought he was asking if the men had taken them.

They heard Cathri's calling, high and faint. Johannes listened intently but did not hear her again. Madle watched two tiger-striped butterflies flit over the sand.

"Remember," she asked after a while, "you remember the first meal we ever ate here?"

He tried to think. "Was it supper? Or dinner? Seems to me I remember Frau Elsbeth giving us our dinner to bring with us."

"No, our first meal was before that. When you brought me here that Sunday. To show me the house. The first time I saw Rudi."

"Oh yes! Before we got the roof on. I remember. You were— Yes, I remember."

"Do you remember what we ate?"

Yes, now he remembered. One of the best days of his life.

"We had roasted ears of corn," she said. "And wild grapes. Rudi had gathered them. And a watermelon. You'd put it in the spring to cool."

"We had cornmeal cakes. You made cornmeal cakes, I remember. I had salt and meal in my saddlebags."

Their silence said, No cornmeal now. And probably no salt either. But we'd still have the grapes.

"About this time of year too," he said. "The second Sunday in August. We moved here in October."

"In Wine-Month." She still used the old names for seasons. "It was the first time I'd ever seen our house. I remember how high it looked. And so clean."

Anneli sat up. She loved to hear them talk of the olden days.

"I remember how blue the sky was, looking up through the roof beams. Almost as blue as home." Madle's voice was light, murmurous.

"The sky?" asked Anneli. "You could see the sky? Inside the house?"

"Oh yes. The roof was not yet on. This porch was not here either. And no steps. Your Papa had to help me up into the doorway."

"And our rooms upstairs, were there steps up there?"

"Oh no, there were no rooms there either. Just the one big space below and it not yet divided, but it had a fine floor. And the outer walls were finished and the ceiling beams and rafters. And the chimney. But no windows yet. The light came all from the sky." Madle's voice was as light and soft as the August breezes that afternoon.

"But you couldn't live in it then."

"No. But it was already our house."

"And Papa built it all?"

"Yes, your Papa built it."

"Well, I had some help—"

Anneli leaned back on her father's shoulder, Johannes against the wall. The square-planed logs were as hard against his back and as solid as the day he and Rudi had heaved them into place. He took a deep breath and to the child it felt as if his body had grown wider and deeper.

He looked across the fields in front of them. Acres and acres now, stumps long gone. . . . But gone too was most of this year's harvest. In a few hours.

Well, God be thanked for that field across the creek. And the work-horses over there. And the brush cattle still scattered in the woods. The one old milker they'd missed. The heifer and yearlings that had got away. And maybe a couple of geese. Thank God they'd not gone after the hogs.

Madle sighed at last, said in a deeper tone, "We're still here, Johannes. You and all of us."

"If I'd only—"

"No, don't think such things now. Rest and be thankful." Her deeper voice belonged to now. "Rest here a little longer and be thankful to God."

But just then other sounds assailed them. The boys had come and had found the dog.

Johannes stood up. "Stay with Mama, Anneli. Rest a little longer, Madle. Now wait for me, hear, and we'll go together inside." Command and entreaty were mingled in his voice.

Madle looked up as she held out her arms to the child. The look between them held many looks—always and ever the look between a blue-eyed child and an earnest boy, the ghost of a look between a grief-stricken woman and a pain-ridden man, and a thousand composite clear-eyed looks between a husband and wife who knew each other better than they knew themselves, yet remained forever aware of something separate—this look encompassed them all. I'll try to, said her look. Maybe.

Johannes went to the boys. "Find a shovel if you can, Hans. If not, we'll hunt for something else. We'll have to find something."

Strangely none of the farm tools had been taken. Johannes buried the dog swiftly behind the barn where the ground was soft.

Georgi could not stop crying. At last Johannes spoke sternly. "Hush that bawling, Georgi, and come with me. When we can find something to put it in, I want you and Anneli to come back here and gather up every grain of anything you see and every ear of corn." Trails and little heaps of spilled grain ran inside and outside the cornhouse, some was left in the corners of the bins, and a few stray unshucked ears had been dropped at the barn.

"Andreas, go back across the creek and break seven green ears for dinner, no more, and make sure each one's filled out full but not hard. If it's starting to yellow, leave it. And, Hans, you go and hunt for old Bett. She must be farther up the creek. When you find her, try to find some way to secure her down there till evening. I've got to go back to your mother."

As he hurried to the house, food for the seven of them was foremost in Johannes' mind, though Madle was at the back of it. Pray God there'd be something left in the house to eat. Surely they wouldn't have taken everything.

But they had. Madle stood looking at the tumbled chairs and benches, the open cupboards and empty shelves, the great bare spaces along the walls. Even the cooking vessels were gone, only one pot left broken on the hearth, its contents dumped into the ashes, a meat and vegetable stew that had been simmering for dinner. A few festoons of red pepper hung on the walls, some bundles of herbs. A couple of crushed baskets, a torn sack, and a few rags littered the floor. Johannes picked up a basket and tried to straighten it.

"Anneli, take off your apron and put it inside this basket. For a lining. Like this. Now you go with Georgi and help him do what I told him. Remember, Georgi, every grain you see. And try not to get dirt in with it."

In the other room, mattress straw was scattered everywhere. Their chests were emptied of all but a few old books and a couple of worn out garments.

The treasures of the house had been few: six silver spoons, a very old silver tankard, two Chinese porcelain plates, some pieces of good Dutch ware—all brought across the water a generation ago—and a few precious trinkets belonging to Madle and the girls. They were gone now. Gone too was cloth of every description—their winter bedding laid up in rosemary and lavender, their good clothing worn only on the Sabbath, the boys' linen. . . . Oh, what could his Majesty's troops want with a small girl's lace-trimmed apron?

In the loft-rooms Madle looked dumbly at the looted chests, straw-littered floor, the stark bedframes and ropes. Must we sleep like beggars in the straw? Or on the bare floor? She looked in vain for the sacks of dried fruit hanging under the rafters.

As she groped her way down the narrow steps, she felt again an unusual weakness in every limb. Johannes had gone down before her and set chairs and benches to rights, closed chest lids, shut cupboard doors, and had now gone outside, saying something about water. She sank onto a bench by the table, wanted to put her head down on it. She looked at the darkened hearth.

Dinner. They must have something for dinner. What? She did not know. She must go to the garden and see what was there. If anything. And what to cook it in? . . . She could not think. . . . She must get up and clean up the mess on the hearth, see if there was some way to use the pot. . . . Water. But the pail was gone. The one outside? Did they still have a way to carry water? . . . No cups. They would have to lap like dogs. Or drink from their hands. Like Gideon's men in the Bible. The Midianites, the Midianites had come upon them.

Cathri, oh dear Father, where was Cathri, Madle asked in despair. She had not seen Cathri since. . . . Some errand it must be or some work outside that Johannes had set her to do. *But I need her here! Why have they all left me? Oh Father, I cannot—I have not now the strength. Georgi and Anneli . . . or Andreas . . . or Hans . . . .*

She heard something bumping up the back steps. She looked around and saw Cathri's back. Cathri was struggling with something she was dragging up the steps.

Madle turned wearily on the bench. "Child, what in this world—"

Red-faced and perspiring, Cathri was hoisting some kind of bundle over the doorsill.

Madle stood up. "Cathri, whatever have you—"

Cathri panted, "I got it off the wagon, Mama. When they weren't looking. There's another one under the fig tree. And I pulled off a sack of dried beans, and there's a pile of potatoes I managed to get out and throw under the bush."

"What! When? Oh Cathri!"

"Before you called me, Mama, when they all were running around after the cows and nobody was at the wagon."

"Child!" Madle looked at the bundle on the floor, for a moment speechless. "Does your Papa know? Has he seen this?"

"No."

"Go call him! No! Wait, let's look and see what's here!"

The long stout bolster tick was packed with pewter and earthenware and eating utensils inside the big kettle, along with various cooking utensils, another pot, and the large skillet. There was even a big pewter candlestick.

"The other sack has some clothes in it. Your blue lutestring, Mama. It was that made me do it. I couldn't bear them to take your blue lutestring."

Madle began to cry. She sat down on the bench and put her head on the table, but as she did so, she reached to draw Cathri down beside her. The child had never felt so warm and strong, yet as pliant as a little one. Madle raised her head and sobbed against her daughter's cheek and stroked her rough untidy hair.

"Please, Mama, don't cry, please!" Cathri sobbed.

"I have to. Let me. Oh, let me." After a while she began saying, "Oh, my brave child! Dear strong brave child!"

When the crying was over, they sat still awhile. Cathri felt a rare and serene pleasure such as she had never experienced in her life. As for Madle, she felt merely emptied of despair, with a clean, wide space for strength to flow into again.

She rose, still holding her daughter by the hand and went to the door. "Johannes! Johannes! Children! All of you! Come here and see what your sister has done!"

As they stood together on the step, Cathri's face was a study. Trying not to smile widely, trying not to cry again, she looked mostly gruff.

Again Madle drew her daughter to her, this time very gently, and kissed her brow. There was a world of words that would not be said. Yet somehow they were known. Known too, though dimly, was the fact that something between them was forever changed.

17

Dinner was late but they had it. There was no meat or bread and no salt for the fresh boiled peas and corn on the cob. Still, when they bowed their heads for grace, Johannes' thanks were not rote though the blessing he asked held a note of urgency. But at least they'd have milk from old Bett and some grain to boil out of the husks for supper and breakfast. The potatoes and dried beans they would save as long as they could.

In the afternoon, Cathri and the two youngest children went to pick gooseberries and grapes, Hans and Andreas to hunt cattle. Johannes stayed with Madle and together they heaped the scattered straw into pallets as best they could. They would have liked to burn it, for it was not in the best condition. They had intended to restuff the mattresses next wheat harvest.

They kept missing things—the clock, the looking glass, Johannes' razors—but they found the big Bible with the children's baptismal certificates on the floor in a corner, and some wooden bowls and even a gourd dipper.

Cathri's second bundle contained no other garments than the blue dress and one other of Madle's, but under them were the yards of uncut cloth Madle always kept on hand, along with their best tablecloth, and also her entire store of lace. She unwound a few inches from a spool, marvelling that of all their treasures this should have been saved, with its memory of other rooms and light.

"It may be we can sell some of it," she said huskily.

They discussed the possibility of the soldiers' return. But considering all they'd carried away, would they even miss what Cathri had removed? And if they did, would they come back for a parcel of pots and tableware?

"For the lace and cloth they might."

"You'd think they'd be ashamed to."

"We must hide it till we can think what to do with it."

They marveled again at their daughter's strength in lifting down the heavy bundles—it was the outdoor work made her strong, Johannes thought—and at her courage and above all her prudence. "And when I think, Johannes, how I've scolded her time without number for thoughtlessness and all her little mishaps—" Madle's voice broke.

"Madle, it was the good God guided her. No, don't blame yourself. It's hard for us," his voice too was husky, "to realize who and what they are. . . . It may be we try to keep them children too long."

When they had put in order what they had, Madle looked about at the house's emptiness and thought again of the days when it had been new. She'd been waiting for Joggi's birth. No, it was not like that time, could never be like that again. Then every bareness was waiting to be filled; every new vessel was a promise. No scars then, nothing broken. Or stolen.

Yet for all her shock of violation and loss, she kept having a sense of a kind of simplicity having come upon them. With only a bowl and a fork or spoon apiece, there was not much to wash up after dinner. And no baking or churning this afternoon or any time soon. She couldn't sew, at least not now, and she had nothing to spin. Her only care must be for what was still growing in the ground and the few dumb creatures that might be scattered.

After dinner Johannes said, "Come with me across the creek." He thought it might be good for her to leave the house. "At least we've got that field over there." And no enemy's feet had trampled that ground.

The absence of fowl life about the house was loud, but as they shut the back gate, they heard the distant pot-rack of a guinea and it heartened them.

"We have the sweet potato patch too. Had you thought of that?" he asked.

Oh, God be thanked for the lateness of sweet potatoes!

As they walked toward the creek, it came to Madle that their lives were too rigidly divided into separate spheres. How long since they'd walked together like this? Johannes, unlike most of his neighbors who did not own slaves, had never expected his wife to work in the field, for he had always set her a little above himself, not because she was a rich man's daughter but because of a certain quality in her which, as Willi Rieder perceived, bespoke gentility—though there was nothing genteel in her dawn to dark toil about the house. She accepted the bounds of her role, yet never quite realized why it seemed sometimes so enclosed. She thought of it as homesickness she'd never be well of.

But now as they crossed the creek and she smelled the fragrance of great white flowers growing above the bank, she became aware of a luxury of space and leisure about her. She loved the bird's-foot violets and woods iris the children brought her in spring, the red trumpet honeysuckle that had come of itself to the fencepost in their dooryard, but here were rich rooms of August scent and bloom no more than four hundred yards from her door that she rarely visited.

But the bees did. She observed them in the flowers, winging heavy-legged away in the warm air, and she had a sense of a world still unviolated and free. "Look at the bees working. Our honey's gone but not the bees."

Johannes thought, *Yes, the bees still work. They get robbed, but it doesn't stop them. It won't stop us. We're like the bees.*

Are we? Insect life, is that what we are? He thought of the hundreds and thousands of hours of toil in the garments and barrels and casks that had been taken off; the countless movements and manipulations of fingers, arms, backs, legs; his wife's and children's as well as his own.

Worker bees, is that what we are to them? Brute animals like cattle? Is that why they left us the tools? His mouth hardened. *God help me, how can I go there tomorrow and bow and beg before them?* He clenched his teeth. *I'll bow for Madle's sake and our children's, but, oh God, let me not have to beg!*

The big field across the creek was some of his best land and bore a good crop of late corn. *If they left me my hoes and plows,* he thought, *they left also my axe, and I'll build a new barn they'll never find. Oh, we'll work, we'll have to, harder than ever, but not, pray God, for them.* He thought of all he must contrive.

They appraised their small cottonfield differently from the way they would have yesterday. Now when the bolls fluffed out, they couldn't take the lint to hired spinners and weavers, but must use it as batting for quilts between themselves and the straw, between themselves and the winter cold. Thank God, Madle thought, for the two bolster ticks she could split and use to overspread the straw along with the heaviest new cloth, though she feared it would spoil the cloth for other use. Perhaps someone would trade them ticking for lace or for the tablecloth. Frau Elsbeth . . . For the hundredth time Madle wondered about the Rieders.

Johannes picked up a hemp sack one of the boys had left carelessly in the field. Madle's gaze fastened on it.

"Johannes! Where did you keep your sacks, the extra ones?"

"Well . . . now I think of it, I keep 'em rolled up and stuck up on those boards under the barn eaves. Why? What are you thinking?"

"We could spread them over the straw. If they're still there."

"They may be. They're not in sight and I doubt anybody'd think of looking up there for anything."

"How many were there?"

"I don't know. Six or eight maybe. With this one." He glanced at the sandy rainbeaten sack in his hand. "But I never thought I'd see the day my family would sleep on hemp sacks," he said heavily.

"If we could only get clean straw," said Madle. The condition of the old straw had not mattered so much with the layers of bedding on top of it. "I wonder about broomsedge straw, that loose part we comb out."

"There's a big patch up the other side of the orchard," he said doubtfully.

"Then as soon as the children get back, we'll go and get some, all of us, let's try it. Each one bring back his own bed."

"Or we could make our beds up there." Johannes could not keep bitterness from his voice. "It would be safer." No dog now to give alarm. Not even the old musket. "I don't know, Madle. I just don't know." Suddenly, he felt weighed down by despair.

She glanced at him quickly. "We'll make out." She spoke urgently. "Come now, you know we will." She rarely made affectionate gestures toward him, but now she reached for his arm and drew it about her waist. "I've always been safe with you," she said low. "You know that."

As they looked at each other, though neither smiled, the look between them was better than a smile.

"That's a good idea of yours about the sacks," he said. "You know the old saying . . ." But he was unable to continue with the trite old adage.

"Go ahead and say it."

"Well, 'Two heads are better than one—'" He waited for her to finish.

"'—even if one is a sheep's head.'"

And with that worn-out bit of banter a small homely brightness, like the stone jugs and the delft pitcher that were probably gone forever, came back to them.

The feel of their pallets that night would take getting used to. Nevertheless, the younger children went quickly to sleep, for they were exhausted and not just from work, but it was harder for Cathri and Hans.

Hans' anger was a deep-running fever that evening prayer and Bible reading could not touch. Until today he had never quite accepted Joggi's conviction as to who their enemies were, but he did now. He knew them now for his own. It was *his* clothes they'd stolen, *his* bed, the rifle Papa had promised *him* when they traded grain and stock this fall, *his* mother they'd robbed, the fruit of *his*, Hans', labor they'd taken off. Oh, if he were only a year older, if he were bigger for his age, if only he had a gun! For if Cathri, a girl, could dare what she did, surely he could find some way to get back at those overbearing villainous—he couldn't think of a strong enough word—scum of the earth! If he had his own horse or a gun— But now not even Papa had a gun.

He was half-angry with his father for making him stay in the woods, because if he'd been at the house, he could have helped Cathri and they'd have saved much more. He might have slipped the rifle out too. He was both admiring and envious of his sister, but he wished he could show what *he* could do. *If it keeps on, if this war keeps on, I'll get into it and I'll show 'em!*

He turned this way and that. To have broomstraw pricking your neck and to sleep on sacks like—like slaves. *Trying to make slaves of us! They won't make one of me! Some day—I'll show 'em! I'll show 'em!*

Cathri lay awake because there was so much to think about, there were so many feelings moving her in so many ways, not only the remnants of shock and fear but also surgings of love and amazement at love so strong it hurt. There was also this new protectiveness she felt for her little sister and even for her brothers.

In the woods this afternoon she and Georgi and Anneli had talked much more than they usually did—about the bounty of the vines and bushes, about the good things Mama would make from what they were gathering, about what they could do to help, such as hunting for guinea nests, maybe even salvaging some of the feathers, how they would think of things to do without being asked.

They did not talk of the events of the morning, however, nor about Beno. But when they came upon a wary-eyed heifer browsing at the edge of a clearing, Cathri called, "Good for you, Brini! Oh, you knew how to show those rascals your heels! They couldn't catch you, could they?"

Anneli gave a high excited peal of laughter as Georgi cried, "And they couldn't catch you either, Cathri!"

"They didn't even see her!" Anneli crowed.

Tonight Anneli lay very close to Cathri and although it was warm, Cathri did not push her away. When the child jerked and cried out in her sleep, Cathri held her even closer, though she whispered with some asperity, "Now hush, Anneli! There's nothing to be scared of."

But it was the thought of her mother that moved Cathri most. For the first time ever her mother seemed more like—not just Mama, but Mother. She was filled with the consciousness that she was a beloved daughter, as if only yesterday her mother had given her birth. She was conscious as never before of bonds that did not chafe but blessed her. She kept smiling and at the same time wanting to cry.

She remembered with surprise as well as satisfaction the goods and food she had saved for her family. She wished she could have gotten more but knew it would have been too risky. She thought briefly of her rose-sprigged dress but strangely not with grief. Her grief was more for her parents, her family's lost heirlooms.

She barely remembered to think of Willi. Tonight he was only a name after Heiri and Joggi, who were living their lives in far away places she could not imagine. "God bless Heiri and Joggi," she ended her prayers as she always did. "And Willi. And keep them safe." But her deepest yearning was for the ones underneath this roof. *Mama. And Papa, oh, God bless Papa! And Anneli. Georgi and Andreas and Hans.*

Yet always under her care and yearning were words which kept buoying her up, "My brave strong child!"

18

Johannes could not remember when he had last walked to the Congarees. Even today he might have ridden a workhorse, but he was afraid to risk it. His feet beat the sand in a dogged tread on the road that today was inexorable.

It was still early light when he passed Theiler's empty fields and pastures a mile above his own place. He considered turning off but saw no chimney smoke. He had not seen Theiler since mid-July, when their conversation had been guarded and evasive. They had shared no thoughts, only words about sickness, weather, and grain yields. Neither had inquired about the other's sons. At the Buser place Johannes saw housesmoke but no other sign of life there either. Buser's son had been in the same regiment as Joggi. Where was he now? Johannes had thought earlier of stopping at Buser's, but now he found himself going on by.

He wondered how many from hereabouts were newly enrolled in the King's militia. *Who am I to condemn them? Maybe they felt they had no choice. Maybe they didn't have,* he reflected.

Sunrise found him three miles up the road, and there he began to scent charred timbers. He hurried, straining his eyes, and soon, even from the High Road, he could see the shriveled sides of the great hackberry trees. He turned off and only too soon saw naked chimneys.

He thought that a black fireplace three feet above the ground was the bleakest sight in the world.

It had been a house as unpretentious as Christian Theus himself, its square logs overlaid with unpainted clapboards, yet important enough for distances to be reckoned to and from it. Built some thirty-two years ago, it had been a low house with two broad original rooms and others added as the family grew, with wide porches front and back, a kitchen detached to guard against fire, and a schoolroom also detached.

Johannes stared. The magnitude of the destruction astounded him. Fences were broken down, gardens trampled, grape arbors and orchards shriveled by the fierceness of the barns' and stables' and other outbuildings' burning. Seasoned pine made that kind of heat. No life remained.

When? Within the last few days, for the ashes were fresh. He wondered that he had caught no whiff of it. It must have been the way the wind lay. Or had it happened at night? No, the destruction was too thorough. It had been deliberate, nothing missed.

Mother, daughter, boys, Theus himself, where were they? Johannes felt his skin crawl. What had happened to Herr Pastor?

He looked toward a farther grove of trees, the ones around the church. The sky was empty above the trees. He began to run, heavy-footed, but even before he stumbled into the churchyard, he knew what he would see.

The shock of it was greater than that of the dwelling, for he had seen burned houses before. New waves of loss overwhelmed him, and he could only stare, all private loss sunk.

He whispered expostulations, clenched his eyes shut, yet had to open them to the hollow air. Only a week ago rough-hewn vertical boards had sheathed the homely structure with its narrow, pointed windows and square wooden tower capped by a little wooden pyramid that proclaimed to all the country what it was: housing for a well-joined pulpit, a little organ that somehow still did its work, and a fine old illuminated panel that said, *"Let him that is athirst come."*

And housing for how many comers, some dead before his time and others later . . . His boyhood friend whose bones were in the ground over there . . . And himself with his sad little bride and later the happier pair they'd become. Their firstborn son and every other liveborn child of their bodies thereafter. Housing for a thousand hours of comfort and prodding, of mind-wandering and endurance. And sometimes of piercing and healing.

He stared into the empty air. He could not fathom it. Mindless. Blasphemous.

Yet even in his tumult of feeling, old memories surfaced, blade-sharp, that had lain in his bones a long time—of swinging an axe against orchard trees and the doorposts and light framing timbers of Cherokee houses, of hacking and smashing the posts of their councilhouses, places of ceremony and gathering too; the multiple burnings. But he'd never tried to justify that destruction! He'd never even pleaded the necessity of his part in it! He'd asked God's forgiveness and received it. Understood too the cost, he thought. . . . But were there other costs? Retribution still to come?

But this was Your *house, God! It was* Your *word we heard and said and sang here! . . . But how much did we hallow it? When did I last come here to hallow His sabbath and His name?*

Sparse, hard tears wet Johannes' face as he turned away. *A damned coward's all I've been! Skulking down there, hoping to be overlooked while others paid the price, young ones like—* But he could not follow that path. *. . . And not just young ones either and not just high, ambitious leaders, but one of* us, *a man in some ways as ordinary as—my old coat, though he does have learning. An old gray-haired man.* He thought of prison ships and tales of jail conditions. What was *his* crime? Furnished a little beef to the Continentals a few years ago. Well, who didn't? Who could help it?

. . . No, his crime was in his speech. He had the courage to speak his beliefs. Well? Is a man who's worked to help make a country, is he to have no say in how it's run? For this to burn him out and make his wife and children homeless? And to destroy a house of worship?

He remembered the last time he'd seen Theus stand in his pulpit, wondered if this last Sabbath he had stood there alone and if he had known it would be his last. Johannes saw the pulpit and the great old Bible lapped in flames. He thought of going back to look for some trace of the metal-work of its cover, but automatically his feet had already turned him up the road although a deeper dread now clouded his purpose.

The road was so churned up by wheels and horses' feet that the shallow bed of Tom's Creek was more like a slough than a streambed. The footbridge was gone, and he followed a path upstream and found a narrower crossing.

As he angled back toward the road, he saw a band of troopers trotting down the road, their big mounts and plumed helmets making them look twice as tall as they were. His first impulse was to stay in the field where he was till they'd passed, but his second overrode it. As he came up on the road, the troopers were still several hundred yards away coming toward him. Since they were not using the entire width of the road, so wide-trampled was it now, he saw he'd have plenty of room to walk along the side. Nevertheless, as they came on, they widened their formation and all at once spurred their horses. Immediately he found himself scrambling across a ditch. They did not even glance at him as they passed.

His face was brick red. He stumbled along the ditchside in the field and felt himself trembling. He was conscious again as yesterday of a thing inside him that was hardening, larger now.

The bridge across Congaree Creek had been widened and strengthened. The waters flowed darkly as if from the depths of the land. As in no other place, there was something here that made all tenure on the land seem ephemeral. Whose land? Mine? Or these people's? Or an older, darker people? Or darker ones to come?

Away in the distance, high among its fields and orchards, rose the Gallman house. It had been a shelter for the whole community during the Cherokee uprising of 1760, but now he felt debarred from going there.

Oh, not all Gallmans were Loyalists, for it was a large family, scattered and divided as so many old families were, and he knew that a couple of them, mostly younger ones, had served in the State militia before the fall of Charlestown. Might still be doing so for all he knew. But Heinrich, who was Johannes' age and now owned this property, was outspoken in his allegiance to the King. And only a few months ago that house had sheltered Johannes' daughter.

Johannes longed to turn in and inquire if they had heard from Barbara or knew anything about her. He had not seen her since that Sunday in May. He and Madle had been hesitant to go to her at the Gallmans' but had expected to see or hear from her soon. When after two weeks no word came, he sent Hans to make inquiry. They told Hans that Barbara and her mother-in-law had gone back across the river. And there'd been no word since. Oh God, surely, surely she wouldn't turn—

Oh, why couldn't he go there? It was his own daughter he craved news of, his own first grandchild! Besides, if he must make some sort of peace or accommodation, what better place to start? Once he'd ridden daily in old Captain Gallman's militia patrol, and later during the Regulator troubles, they'd all stood together like the good neighbors they were. Neighbors we've been more than twenty years, good neighbors they were to all of us, father and son, why can't I go there now?

He plodded on. He couldn't go now because he hadn't gone six months ago. Or two months ago to see Barbara. Or last week. Because he'd be too much like a bug exposed by an overturned log, crawling about to find another one.

He wondered if they knew of the burning of St. John's. But how could they not know and how could they countenance such deeds? Why, old Captain Gallman helped build that house and their children were baptized in it same as mine were! The Heiri Gallman I know would never approve such a thing. Yet how can he side with those that do?

Johannes trudged on past harvested grainfields and close-cropped pastures. This was some of the best land in the province, deep brown soil that had made its owners rich—Gallmans, Fridays, Rieders. . . .

He thought of Hans Jacob. What's he done? What accommodation has he made? No doubt about it, he's made one. Johannes tried to imagine Hans Jacob going through what he himself had yesterday. And Frau Elsbeth, what would she have done? Lord God—he almost smiled—it would have given her a stroke. He must stop by the Rieders' place on his way home.

A thought flashed into his mind. *Then why not go there first?* Hans Jacob was sure to know the official he should see and would advise him what to expect. Moreover he might have news from other parts. And surely he'd know what was happening hereabouts and could tell him about the Theuses. Johannes thought, *The more I know the more it may help me when when I come to deal with all that—puffed-up mightiness.* At once the idea compelled him. He would talk to Hans Jacob first.

And why him? he wondered suddenly, and not Theiler or Buser?

Because, Johannes thought slowly, *he's been torn more ways than one. I can talk to him because—in some ways he's not only somebody I've known for twenty-four years but also—almost like kin. Or all the kin I'll ever have in this country.*

Hans Jacob? He shook his head, yet knew his way clear for the moment and had a sense of reprieve.

Chimney smoke drifted above the kitchen house. If he had been on horseback, he would have ridden to the back, but being afoot, he would go to the front door.

The yard was littered with twigs, and field grass was encroaching at the edges. He noticed old horsedroppings in the sand, weeds growing near the front steps. Was Frau Elsbeth ill? It was she who regularly harried the young ones to hoe, rake, and sweep the yards clean.

The two front doors that usually stood open in summer were shut. The glass-paned windows were also down, though their shutters were open.

He felt a growing unease as he went up on the long porch. It still had benches against the wall but no chairs. And no dog barked.

He called out first, then knocked. He called again, "Hans Jacob Rieder! Is anybody home? Herr Rieder!"

In the quiet he heard scampering feet, also yapping from far inside the house, then saw a face at the window. A moment later Nissi Rieder opened the door.

At the sight of her he felt his usual mixture of grief and guilt. *Thus but for the mercy of God might be one of mine, and who are we to be so spared?*

He never looked long at Hans Jacob's daughter for fear he might seem to stare and perhaps offend her. Yet today for some reason he gazed at her searchingly and thought he saw an eager light in her eyes as she curtsied slightly to his bow and greeting, and his ragged old embarrassment dropped off. He found himself speaking as easily as to one of his own children. "Nissi, I've come to see your Papa."

"He's in the field." She stepped back. "Come in, Herr Lienhardt. I'll go and get him."

He wanted to say, "Why, child, I knew every field on this place before you were born. I'll find him myself," but she asked quickly, "Have you walked? Then you'll be pleased to rest." She gestured toward a chair. "Please, sir, sit down. I'm sorry we have no—" she hesitated, "proper refreshment."

At that moment he heard a succession of what sounded like groanings and callings from the room to the left, Frau Elsbeth's bedroom chamber.

"Please excuse me." Nissi opened the bedroom door and shut it quickly behind her.

Johannes heard a volume of strange, indistinguishable talk and withdrew to the center of the room that had once been part of a great long one but was now partitioned into a reception hall and a dining parlor.

"I will, I will," Nissi said low as she came out the door.

Johannes went quickly toward her. "Frau Elsbeth, is she sick?"

"She's better now."

He stood silent. He was overcome with dismay, remembering his earlier thought of Elsbeth.

"Ten days ago she was struck. We thought she'd never speak again, but little by little her speech returns and she's begun to move her limbs now too."

"It was apoplexy? She was struck by apoplexy?"

"Yes, it must have been that."

Johannes wanted to ask how it happened, but he did not know how and he wished for Madle.

"She knew your voice. She hears and understands everything, and she reminded me," Nissi smiled slightly, "that you might enjoy a cup of clabber. I hadn't thought of it but she said you'd enjoy it."

Johannes felt his eyes fill and his throat thicken. Enduring Elsbeth. Who loved his wife and who loved Joggi. And that enduring tongue not yet stilled, thank God, not yet! But who'd have thought he'd be so glad? "Can I see her?" He must press her hand and say some encouragement.

"Later, Herr Lienhardt, it may be—though she's hard to understand now and it may be— We'll see. But if you'll please to sit down, I'll bring you something and then I'll go for Papa."

His body was grateful for the armchair. He looked about him. New furniture had been brought up from Charlestown some years ago when the room was divided, and the scarred old pine tables and benches and the old rush-bottomed chairs were removed. Yes, the good furniture was still here— the matched walnut tables and armchairs and candlestands, and he could see through the doorway into the other room the mahogany dining table with its side tables and set of chairs against the wall. But he saw no porcelain or plate, no candlesticks or adornments of any kind. He thought, *No wonder Elsbeth's in bed.*

Nissi brought him an earthen cup of clabber with a spoon in it and a big slice or cornbread in a napkin. He eyed it with sudden relish. He had eaten no bread in twenty-four hours, and he felt a rush of gratitude to Elsbeth. She knows what I need. She's the same stock I am. "Thank you, Nissi, it will taste so good."

He noticed now the girl's dress, the apron with its torn pocket, and realized he had never seen her so dressed. She must have seen his wonder, for she glanced at her clothes as if surprised herself. He wanted to say something to bring back her eager look, but he could only gaze down at the bread and the cup. "This to me is better than wine." He looked up. "You haven't heard from Willi, have you?"

"No, Herr Lienhardt."

He sighed. "Well, no more have we from Heiri. But it's not to be wondered at." He glanced at the cup and the bread. He couldn't sit and eat while she stood there. "And not from Joggi either. Though we don't worry about him as much as Heiri. Joggi's more used to fending for himself."

Her face changed slightly. "Yes, so he is."

"And then Heiri has Willi. I tell myself he has Willi to help him. I'm glad he has Willi."

"Yes, they have each other."

"And Joggi has his wits. He's always been at home in the woods and the wild. You know, it was a wonder how he got home to us in May. But when he sets his mind to a thing, he does it."

Her smile was sudden, her eyes lustrous. "I'll go get Papa, Herr Lienhardt," and she was gone out the door that led to the long porch beside the ell rooms.

Johannes smiled a little too and mused, wondering.

The clabber and cornbread were soul-satisfyingly good. At least there was no lack here of what it took to make good bread. He folded the crumbless napkin.

The house was very quiet. From time to time he heard steps above him and occasionally sounds from Elsbeth's room. Once he was tempted to go to her door but thought better of it.

After a while he heard noise down the road. He went to the window. Some dozen horsemen, like the troop that had run him off the road, came jingling by, the light glinting on their saber hilts, on the curved steelwork.

And how would you like to live where you had to see them every day? Yes, I'd keep my doors shut too. No wonder the chairs were gone from the porch.

Some thirty minutes passed. He grew troubled. *Maybe I shouldn't have come here, or at least not this time of day. He won't like my coming in the middle of the morning; I wouldn't like it. But then I've never known Hans Jacob to work alongside his people.* A new thought struck him. *Could the slaves have been taken off?* He tried to think how many Rieder children were at home. Only two or three old enough to work, not counting Nissi. Not much help for a place this size, especially if not brought up to work. He thought of Maria. He'd not even inquired after her, he realized with compunction. So often one forgot her. But it was little help she'd be in such straits.

. . . Oh Madle, and you there waiting for me! His impatience surged. *Why haven't I gone ahead to do what I have to instead of straggling off here?* Again he went to the window to gaze up the road toward Granby. *How long will it take me there?* Twenty-four-year-old memories of day after day waiting at European officialdom's pleasure recurred to him. He sighed and sat down. *Oh, God help me; God help us all.*

At last he heard voices at the back of the house, mostly women's, but among them was Hans Jacob's. He heard steps hurrying down the porch.

19

The man who entered the room looked both younger and older than the Hans Jacob Johannes knew, younger in body because he had lost flesh but older in the face because it was darker, sunburned like his own. It had a harder look, not the empty joviality it usually wore, at least to company. However, Johannes saw a light of greeting in his eyes, though Hans Jacob did no more than grasp Johannes' hand and say his name.

Johannes began to apologize. "I know I shouldn't have come to interrupt you this time of day but—"

"Don't regard that. What's the matter?"

"Everything. Though no more than's the matter with anybody else." Johannes tried to take a deep breath. The room seemed stifling. "Hans Jacob, I'm in a box. I know what I've got to do, but I've come to you, I suppose, to tell me how to do it. So maybe it won't hurt so much."

Hans Jacob stood looking at him. Never before had Johannes Lienhardt asked his help or advice. Both had been offered occasionally, but never had Johannes done other than evade the offer in a more or less friendly way.

"Let's go in the other room."

In the dining parlor Hans Jacob shut the door behind them— Johannes had forgotten that where they were poor Elsbeth might have overheard every word—but opened a front door and raised windows. "I can't stand keeping this place so shut up. Today's going to be hot as the devil." He pulled two chairs up to a window where they might catch a current of air. "Sorry I've got nothing to offer you, but I expect you know that story."

"Oh yes, don't mind that. Besides, your daughter gave me a feast of cold clabber and good bread better than anything in the world you could offer me. First bread I've tasted since yesterday morning. Not that I'm starved," he hurried to say, "but it's just that all our flour and meal got hauled off yesterday and all other food in the house. Though," he hurried on, "we've still got food in the field and some cows they didn't find and other things, so that's not why I've come, Hans Jacob, don't think that.

It's just that—I wanted to talk to you." Johannes' voice slowed. "Or to somebody that might know more than I do." Johannes leaned forward with his hands clasped between his knees, his eyes intent on the other man's face.

Hans Jacob eyed Johannes a moment, then shifted to look out the window. His body assumed its old lounging posture although he had no glass in his hand and he was bare-legged and wore no waistcoat. He said, "I've thought about you. I've wondered how you were making out." He gazed down the road that stretched long through August-ravaged fields. "You haven't gone yet and made your peace with—our masters?"

"Not yet," said Johannes heavily. "And now I've got no choice. Have I?"

There was a space of silence. "No. Unless you have some place to send your family."

"For what purpose?"

"There are bands up the country not lying down. A man could go and join one. If the other way stuck too hard in his craw." Hans Jacob turned back to Johannes. They looked at each other.

"How's it been with you?" Johannes asked at last. When there was no immediate reply, he asked, "Were you cleaned out too?"

"Oh, we struck a kind of bargain." Hans Jacob's voice was dry. "I let 'em have most of what they wanted, I say 'let,' you know what that means, in exchange for promise of payment which I may or may not ever see. No, they didn't leave me in starvation. Though if all my blacks were here, we'd be."

"They take 'em all?"

"The men and boys, they did. And the women that wanted to go with 'em. Poor fools thought it meant freedom."

Now Johannes looked away. Though they never discussed it, the other man knew how he felt about slave-keeping. That strange anomaly of these times struck him anew. Men talked so much of liberty, yet still kept slaves. The lines deepened about his mouth. "How about your stock?"

"Oh, same as with you, they couldn't round up everything. And their visits here—they were not unexpected."

"I wonder how I could have been so dumb!"

"You had no dealings with them till yesterday?"

"Man, it was not dealing! It was robbery! They took everything, took my children's clothes, broke or stole the poor couple of weapons I had left, stripped the house of everything except a few sticks of furniture, and destroyed much of what they didn't take! And my children slept last night on hemp sacks!" Johannes stopped for breath. The veins in his temples were throbbing. "Though I suppose I should thank them for not burning down my house. Like they did our pastor's. And our meetinghouse." Hans Jacob's face too had darkened. "When did that happen?"

"Three days ago."

"Where's Herr Pastor? What's happened to him and his family?"

"They left. They got word ahead of time and left."

"Then they're all safe?"

"As safe as Adam Summer can keep them. Though that's not to be spread about, Johannes, where they are."

"Adam Summer?"

"Has a mill up Broad River above Crim Creek. He's staunch for liberty and always has been."

"I've heard the name." Johannes leaned back. He said more quietly. "Well, thank God our pastor's safe."

As Hans Jacob gazed out the window, Johannes saw that the main difference in his face was in the tautness of skin about his mouth. You could see the line of his jaw. Not drinking, he thought. Nowhere to get it.

"Nissi said you've had no word from Willi."

"No."

"You think he may be at such a place as Adam Summer's?"

"More like to be with a man named Thomas Sumter. He's leader to most up there. Farther up the Broad than Summer's. Over toward Catawba."

"Then Heiri may be there too. And Joggi, I hope. At least if they're banded with others, there's a chance. . . ." Of what? Johannes leaned back, stared unseeing at a closed door. Footsteps pattered above. "Are your children well, the young ones?"

Hans Jacob laughed shortly. "They wouldn't say so. I tell 'em it's good the blacks are gone. One thing I'll say about my parents, both of 'em, they expected us to work, blacks or no blacks."

Well, I never knew that, Johannes thought. "I'm sorry about your mother's sickness, Hans Jacob."

Hans Jacob made a grunting kind of acknowledgement.

"Nissi said it was ten days ago."

"It was."

Johannes looked about him, persisted. "All this, losing your household goods here, would go hard with her. Though it goes hard with all of us."

One corner of Hans Jacob's mouth turned up, the other down. "She didn't lose overmuch. Most things were got out of sight six weeks ago. Though God knows now whether she'll ever be able to tell us where they're all hid."

Johannes thought it through, felt a moment's internal mirth. At last he contrived to say earnestly, "I pray God she'll recover." He remembered to ask, "How's Maria?"

Hans Jacob's face lightened with what looked like pure cheerfulness. He turned in his chair. "Johannes, I tell you she's better than she's been in years. She feels better, looks better, I can't believe how she's taken hold these last weeks. Johannes, don't ever think—" but he broke off. "Maria's fine."

Johannes said heartily, "I'm glad to hear it."

"How's Madle?"

"Well, it's been hard." Johannes' expression sobered. "The shock and other things. She's suffered in many ways these last years, I know that. She's always seemed strong and yet—I'm worried, Hans Jacob." And with those words his deepest, most troubled feelings rose. He leaned forward, gazed at the floor without sight, his arms resting on his knees. "Hans Jacob, I don't know that I could ever leave her again." He looked up. "Twenty years ago, even ten, then a man could go off and leave his family if he had to, more or less confident they'd not be molested while he was gone. We all stood by one another then and we could trust one another." He shook his head. "It's not like that now."

"No." Again Hans Jacob looked away. "And not just your family. Your house and land too. You know what would happen, don't you?"

"Same as Herr Pastor's?"

"Your whole plantation, you'd lose it all. Talk about twenty years ago, look how much more now you have to lose."

Johannes rubbed his hands down his face. "Aye-God, and I was twenty years younger too."

"How old are you?"

"I'm forty-six."

"I'm forty-two."

Johannes had thought Hans Jacob was older.

With his hands clasped behind his head, Hans Jacob again stared out the window. A procession of wagons and cattle appeared down the road. "You may not know that some men as old as we are—or almost as old—and richer too—they've left everything. Men across the river, they've done it."

"Who?"

"Thomas Taylor, for one. He's almost as old as I am."

"But he was already a big officer. And English. I'm no soldier, Hans Jacob. I never wanted to be one. If I'd wanted that, I could have stayed across the water."

"You're more one than I am. I'm sure as hell not."

"Hans Jacob, the thing I keep asking is, What's it for? We've already struggled and fought here. Yes, a time or two I went out with others to try and make it safer for my family, but when does it end? What more do we want than just—to live in peace and enjoy the good God sends us? We had that, didn't we, five or six years ago?"

Hans Jacob did not answer at once. "Some did maybe."

"Didn't you?"

A brooding look overcast the other man's face. He said gloomily, "You've struggled more than I have."

The train of wagons and cattle came closer, its noise invading the room. Hans Jacob rose and slammed the front door shut.

"I don't know, Johannes, either, except that one thing has started to come home to me. Now you know me—"

Hans Jacob faced inward to the room, and as he did so, its emptiness shifted with absences that became presences, its air alive because its very bareness made room for past presences—upcountry traders and packhorsemen who had eaten and drunk here; Catawba and Cherokee bands on their way to and from Charlestown; self-important officials; newly-come Swiss and Germans; hard-working, heavy-shouldered neighbors; and at the edges of the room a few silent, locked-in Africans—these shades all seemed to gather about them in the gray light.

". . . you know what I am and what I'm not, Johannes, but I tell you something that's come to me. You'll say it's been slow, but—what are we here for? Is it just to get goods and to keep our hides?" He looked at the dusty mahogany. The old pine furniture had never needed dusting, only scouring. "I think about my father. He got the goods all right, but I think he got other things too—though he died at thirty-nine. He died younger and his life was harder. But is mine better?"

The noise of wagons, chains, horses, and cattle could not be shut out. The two men did not speak until it had passed.

Johannes said, "It's not *my* land and *my* hide so much as . . . Ah, it's hard, hard; every way you look at it, it's hard."

"Damned hard. Sometimes I wonder if my people might not have had more sense to stay where they were."

"No, you can't think that. I can't. I was born there and I'll miss it till the day I die but—well, I was not free there. I had no choice but to serve others because of my lack. My father died in debt, he was a good man, but he was too good in some ways, and there was not enough left for my brother and me both when he died. I may have told you this long ago, did I?"

"No, you never told me."

"Well, it's why I left. I didn't choose to live bound under others. I came to where I'd be my own man, have my own land, take orders from no one—" He laughed but there was not much humor in it.

The noise up the road grew fainter. Johannes clapped his hands on his knees and stood up. "Tell me who I need to see in Granby. Tell me his name and where to ask for him."

"All right." Hans Jacob rose too. "If you want me to, I'll write a few words for you. I don't promise it'll help but it might. You can say you've come with this letter."

They stood by the dusty table.

"If I were you, Johannes, I'd play dumb."

"That's no problem. No problem at all."

Johannes did not see Elsbeth. Nissi, who appeared when Hans Jacob went for his writing materials, said another day might be better. Johannes wondered whose feelings were being spared and knew his were, for he was conscious of relief. "Tell her how much I enjoyed the refreshment. Tell her I pray God we'll have the pleasure of speaking together sometime soon." As he spoke, he felt like a coward if not a hypocrite.

Nor did he see Maria. They invited him to stay to dinner but he declined, for he thought the food would choke him when he remembered Madle and the children.

While waiting, he heard a skitter of footsteps on the stairs, and through the door which Hans Jacob had left open, he glimpsed a black woman and some small children—two black, one mulatto, and two white—and scampering among them a little brown and white fice dog. The children were running and the woman was scolding and herding them to the back of the house.

As Hans Jacob gave him the folded paper, Johannes saw a man he had always known, yet another man too, and beneath that one, another, a face beneath the blur of other faces. He thought, *No, man, I don't know you. God does, but I don't.*

20

Johannes had not been to Granby in three months. He was prepared for differences, but from a distance he did not notice any. He could still see down the long road almost to the other end of the village with its great shade trees overarching the trampled sand. To the left he saw the chimneytops of the Chesnut-Kershaw store, where the British headquarters were. The store had changed hands last winter when an enterprising young merchant named Wade Hampton bought it. This Hampton had also bought up corn for the Whig armies, but whether they'd ever gotten any God alone knew. According to Hans Jacob, Hampton was still at Granby. He must have made his accommodation too, thought Johannes.

As Johannes trudged on, he saw a number of shedlike structures newly thrown up. He noted also the disappearance of several orchards and gardens and the removal of fences along the widened road that had meant the disappearance of people's dooryards. A glimpse of the river showed him that the wharf had been extended and many vessels were moored there. Across the river the ferry was nearing the opposite shore. It was loaded with wagons and barrels. On this side the river men were rolling hogsheads onto boats. He heard cattle bawling from a distant enclosure and somewhere the beating of drums and shouts of command. Far more than yesterday's experiences, these sights and sounds—the trampled earth, the sweat-drenched black bodies wrestling with barrels, the continuous bawling of cattle, and above all the drumbeat—these brought back a time and place and with it a visceral wrenching.

Almost twenty years ago. Ten months of it. Then he had believed it was his duty. Perhaps it had been. *But I won't do it again! I can't do it!*

A breeze off the river had dried his sweat, but the air was still sweltering. He had walked seven miles this morning but now he felt more than physical fatigue. *I could hoe or plow all day and not feel so beat out as I do now,* he thought.

He tried to phrase what he'd say. "I come to swear . . . allegiance. To the King." *And become an enemy to my sons. And to my Pastor. . . . No! You can't think of it like that!*

Yesterday he'd intended to protest the taking of his household goods, but now he thought it would be useless. All he could hope for would be that his name be crossed off one list and added to another. And what would result from that? He shut his eyes and groaned. *God, help me! Oh God, help me be the man I've got to be!*

When the sentinel stepped out from the lee of the fence, Johannes told his name, residence, and destination and was allowed to pass.

Now, inside the village, the road that earlier was choked with dust seemed almost empty, at least of ordinary people. The civilians he saw were strangers. He noticed a few servants busy behind taverns and houses and several soldiers going in and out of a residence and he heard the usual clangor from the blacksmith shops.

He had to stop for a gang of slaves rolling hogsheads down a broad way to the river landing. Among them he recognized the mulatto Simmi Rieder and two other Rieder slaves. He nodded. Looks of recognition passed but no other sign, no words or smiles.

As his leaden legs took him on, he felt as if he went in a dream to a familiar-unfamiliar place. These wide old steps he had gone up a hundred times—yet never till this day. His head had a buzzing in it.

The ordeal was both worse and easier than he had feared.

Hans Jacob had told him that the official in charge was a Loyalist, Charles Stedman, commissary to the British army, whose main responsibility was procuring and dispatching supplies. Today, however, Stedman was absent, for he'd gone to Camden. Hans Jacob said his secretary would be in charge.

A deep porch stretched across the length of the two-storied Hampton store, that was built along the same plan as the Rieder house, only larger. As Johannes came up, he saw the blinds to the public room were closed, but one of the doors stood open.

Inside the great room and out of the hot sunlight, Johannes was struck first by its clutter and disorder, but as his eyes adjusted to the gloom, he saw it was almost empty of trade goods. A number of kegs and barrels stood about, unopened except for two or three with nothing in them. On the shelves he saw stacks of wooden boxes that looked to be still nailed shut, but of the store's regular stock—iron and tin vessels; boxes of needles, buttons, knives, and nails; assortments of shoes, hats and hosiery; displays of mirrors, combs, and scissors—of these goods the shelves were bare. Only a confusion of large farming implements was heaped in a corner. If he had come here to trade or buy, Johannes thought, he would have come in vain.

He saw no one in attendance, although he heard a sound of knocking from behind the house and voices in the room to the left. Since its door stood open, he went to the doorway.

Inside, the windows were open and he saw a large table littered with papers and writing materials. Beyond it stood a smaller table crowded with bottles, glasses, coins, and playing cards, around which sat three men. Two were in military dress, or rather undress, for they had discarded their waistcoats and neckcloths as well as coats and boots. The civilian was a tall young man with a high-bridged nose and slim hands. He wore an open-throated frilled shirt and light-colored trousers.

Johannes stood in the doorway until one of them noticed him. Though all three men looked up, no one spoke.

Without thinking, Johannes blurted out in German, "I have a letter for the Herr Commissary."

One soldier laughed, the other played a card, and the young man merely gazed at him from heavy-lidded eyes.

In his confusion Johannes could not think of the right English words. At last he said thickly, "The oath, I come to swear the oath." He felt as if his mouth were full of charcoal. "I have this." He held out Hans Jacob's note.

The young man regarded Johannes languidly as he clumped across the room and laid the paper in a bare spot on the large table.

The man flicked a glance at the paper. "Wait outside," he said and turned his attention to the cards.

Johannes still stood there until the man glanced up again and frowningly nodded dismissal.

For a while Johannes stood hat in hand just outside the inner room. In a few moments he heard the men laughing and their voices resumed. Presently the air exploded with oaths, laughter and the sound of a chair knocked over. One of the soldiers came to the door stretching. He saw Johannes.

"Damn you!" he shouted, "you're to wait outside!" and he gestured toward the porch.

The porch had a bench at its far end but the bench was in the sun. For some thirty minutes Johannes stood leaning against the housewall. At last when the bench was in partial shade he sat down. The sounds from the inner room were vague and distant.

No one came or went. The emptiness of the porch, the roads, all seemed exceedingly strange to him. He could not remember ever coming here to sell or trade and seeing never a soul to exchange a word of greeting with. Perhaps it was the time of year, he reflected. Or perhaps the time of day, the heat of the day. But again he had the sensation of being in a familiar-unfamiliar dreamplace.

When the sun was directly overhead, talk erupted in the outer room, and one of the soldiers and the tall, high-nosed young man came out on the porch. Johannes half-rose, but before he could speak—if indeed he could have gathered his words—the two men clattered down the steps, crossed the road and disappeared down a cross street toward the river. To a tavern, Johannes thought, for their dinner. Ten minutes later another soldier arrived, and the one within came out to follow the others. For a while Johannes puzzled over their rank, for their insignia was unknown to him.

Now everything was still. There was no sound within or without, no breath of air. A great tree which once had shaded the house was gone, and sun baked the brown earth and the raw stump. Although the air was like an oven, Johannes no longer sweated. He rose and walked to the other end of the porch. He felt lightheaded. He thought of going inside to ask where he could get water, but when he ventured to glance through the doorway of the inner room, he saw no one, only the littered tables. He returned to the porch, sat down and leaned his head against a post and shut his eyes. His body slumped. It craved to stretch out on the bench. He kept slumping and straightening until the sound of two men talking on the steps caused him to jerk upright. One of the soldiers left; the other went inside.

Presently the young civilian returned alone. He did not glance at Johannes, who watched him mount the steps but did not try to rise. From low on his bench Johannes observed the flare of the young man's nostrils and the curl of his mouth.

Again all was still. Now that he was wide awake, Johannes realized his head was throbbing. After a while he heard someone moving barrels in the store room. He went to the door and stepped inside. The soldiers were reaching into a cask, but when they saw Johannes, one of them straightened up and motioned him out with an angry jerk of his head, but Johannes continued to stand inside the doorway.

"Outside!" the man said vehemently in a low voice.

"I wish to see the secretary."

"Nobody can see him now! He told you to wait, didn't he? Now get out!"

"I have waited already long. When will he see me?"

"He'll see you at his pleasure! Now you clear out!" The soldier's voice was low, but both men moved toward Johannes.

He still stood a moment looking at them before stepping back.

On the porch he gazed at the far, dark hanging trees beyond the road and the houses. He saw upper-story windows, chimneys, the flat sky. He lowered his gaze to the house walls, the drawn blinds, the trampled earth below, and finally to the old porch steps near his feet. He thought, *I'll just leave. The simplest, easiest thing in the world will be to walk down these steps and go home, on down the road to our woods and creek and fields where everything will be real again.*

The porch and the two top steps were in shade.

All right, he thought, *I'll wait till shade darks the bottom step. That's three more. Then I'll leave.*

The line of shade had just touched the last step when someone inside bawled his name. As he stood up, he felt staggery. Inside the building, he was almost blind from staring at the hardness between sun and shade so long.

The tall young man sat at the table, leaning his head on his hands, his frills and his eyelids drooping. He was leafing through papers. Hans Jacob's note was beside them.

Johannes stood there until at last the secretary stretched a long, slender hand toward a sheet of paper at the end of the table and told Johannes to sign his name, or, if he could not write, to make his mark and he himself would write it in.

Johannes bent over the sheet and tried to read the words at the top of it, but although the light was good enough, he had difficulty with the English script. The pen was bad and his hand trembled. He wondered if they could even read what he scratched. He had always taken pride in his neat hand.

As he stood up, he looked again at the young man, the flushed face with pillow marks still on it. No older than Joggi, he thought. The same slim hands but whiter.

One hand tossed a folded square of paper across the table. "Your protection. Keep it on your person."

Johannes' hands were wide and big-knuckled with dark, protruding veins. Slowly, even with difficulty, as if his hand were too big and clumsy, he picked up the paper.

No questions, no explanations, no insults. It was as easily done as that. Perhaps it was Hans Jacob's note that had done the work for him.

Normally Johannes would have bowed in farewell, but now he simply turned and clumped out of the room, out of the building, down the steps, out of the dooryard and down the road through the burning sand. He understood now about shaking the dust of a place off your feet. Oh, if he could only do it!

21

They had started an hour before sundown, two hundred of them, riding southwest from McDowell's camp at Smith's Ford. For the first few hours they rode straight through the woods. They must slip by Ferguson's camp of Loyal American Volunteers in the night. It would lie only a few miles to their left on Fairforest Creek. With guides who knew the country, they crossed Gilkey's Creek in the woods, but as they neared Thickety about dark, they took to the road and set their horses to a gallop. They hoped to reach the Enoree by daybreak.

Joggi's mount was a strong young sorrel, foaled in the low country and taken from the British by Sumter at Hanging Rock. Joggi himself had not been with Sumter. He was part of a Georgia company that had joined Colonel Charles McDowell in North Carolina. The horse had come to him by way of Sumter's former commissary, James Williams, who along with the officers Brandon, McJunkin, and Steen and a few of their followers had separated themselves from Sumter—as well as some horses and supplies—and joined McDowell two days ago—to Sumter's great indignation. But Joggi was grateful to his captain and to Colonel Williams for the fine sorrel. His previous mount had been a hard-mouthed farmhorse, though when he'd first met up with the Georgians in early July, he'd been riding an old breakdown he'd found in the woods. Three days before that he'd been afoot.

His imprisonment in Ninety Six Jail had been the worst ordeal in his life so far. The caged shame of it and the loathsome disorder, even more than the stark privation that verged on suffering, had eaten into him. Also he was lacerated with self-disgust for letting it happen.

The last week of May had found him many miles up the country, already north of the Tyger, for he had decided to give Rudi the go-by. He was dead asleep in a Whig house when it was surrounded, and his hosts being notorious Rebels, he must share their fate. After eight days in private confinement, they were taken to Ninety Six, which had just been surrendered to Loyalists.

Joggi might have been there yet, might have died there if a woman who sometimes brought the water had not taken a liking to him. Perhaps it was because he was a little younger than most of the other prisoners, or perhaps because he seemed somewhat apart from them, though it was hard to be apart in such jam-packed conditions. At least he kept out of the continuous fights. Joggi rarely spoke to anyone, but a couple of times he smiled at the woman, and his look affected her strangely. When he sickened with fever, she used her influence with a certain sergeant, and means were found to get this particular prisoner paroled. Also the British commander was under orders to use discretion and humanity in pacifying the country. Well-known Rebel leaders were one thing, obscure German youths another. This fellow would probably die, but if he didn't, let him go home and be grateful and learn better sense.

In a shed behind the woman's hut, Joggi recovered, but he soon felt as much a prisoner there as he had in jail. On a moonless night he slipped away without weapons or food.

This time he knew not to head north. Instead he went toward the Savannah River, toward land recently ceded by the Cherokees. Traveling mostly at night, he ate wild fruits and ears of corn he stole from fields. The third morning, as he neared the Savannah, he met up with the Georgians, many of whom were former Carolinians or Virginians. When they'd learned earlier that Tories controlled the district before them, their main body under Elijah Clark had turned back, but a smaller troop under James Jones had decided to press on. Jones' men, like Joggi, planned to skirt the Ninety Six district and hug the Blue Ridge foothills. When Joggi joined them, however, he had a hard time keeping up on his poor old horse.

At last they turned east. They crossed the Keowee, the Saluda, the headwaters of the Enoree and the Tyger, and found themselves again among Tories. Pretending to be Loyalist militia, they learned of a Loyalist camp and had themselves led to it. On the night of July 13, the Georgians surrounded and attacked the camp, killed one man, wounded three, and took twenty-two prisoners, whom they paroled. Some of these parolees were the same Loyalists who had fled Cedar Springs the night before. Now Joggi acquired a good rifle and a better horse. The next day his company reached the North Pacolet just above the North Carolina line and they joined the North Carolina colonel, McDowell, who would later move down to Cherokee Ford on Broad River and then to Smith's Ford. The Georgians knew Joggi as Jake Lennard.

Tonight the trees hung heavy-limbed above them, clouding out the August sky, for in places the road was no wider than a path. Yet the cool night air was pleasant and they cantered much of the time. They rode without talking. When they crossed the Pacolet, only light splashes and the creak of their gear told their crossing. Joggi's sorrel picked his way surefootedly down the bank.

It was high, rolling country, the slopes broad and well-wooded. The clearings, though infrequent, were wide, for the country had been some twenty years settled. Every so often dogs in the distance would set up a barking, and sometimes the bulk of a house loomed near the road. Inside the house, its occupants would lie tense till the sounds of the riders merged into silence. A boy might get up to peer through a look-hole. A woman would start up suddenly and reach to the cradle close by. A man would pad barefoot back to bed, thankful the dark stream of riders was swift and at night. The people in the houses would lie awake a long time, never quite sure the sounds were gone, listening till the roosters crowed.

Some of the riders knew who lived in these houses, knew every landmark. They knew when they passed the burned-out meetinghouse, for it had been their own. But to the Georgians and to the overmountain men this was only country that they or their kin might have left five or ten years ago. Nonetheless, they felt a claim to it.

To Joggi the country was an endless flow of riding, fighting, sleeping—always on the ground with his gun as near as his arm—of leaping to the alarm; of mounting, dismounting, nearing, distancing. It was better when you were nearing. It was what you lived for, the chance to dash at the enemy, by cunning to be where he didn't expect you, to mark him down before he marked you—and to vanish to where he couldn't follow or find you. It was more than ever like watching from the top of the scuppernong arbor—only now with the sure purpose of descending to strike down the one who stood at the edge looking out.

Sometimes he thought of Willi with a tinge of bitterness, wondered if he'd ever see Willi Rieder staring at him from the other side. The British were said to have enrolled five thousand militiamen in South Carolina.

Of Heiri, Joggi rarely thought, for he did not want to think of him, but if the image came unbidden, it was usually of Heiri sitting on the trundlebed with a slash of sunlight on his face. Occasionally in a drowsing moment he was pierced by a curious longing to hear his brother's deep, even breathing. He never thought of Heiri being on the other side.

. . . Earle's Ford; Fort Prince; Fort Thicketty, or Fort Anderson to the British; Thomson's Plantation, that would later be called Second Cedar Springs or, by others, the Old Iron Works—the skirmishes, surprises, routs, and retreats had been continual since mid-July, although Jake Lennard had not been in all of them. The last one was on August 8, ten days ago, a running fight which started near the Cedar Springs and ended on a hill north of the Pacolet, from which, retreating, they'd taunted Ferguson's men on the other bank. Though hacked by the broadswords of Loyalist dragoons, they had brought down a number of mounted riflemen and had taken fifty prisoners. No one of the actions was a large success, yet all together they were a challenge if not a threat to the conquerors.

But now from the east they'd heard stirring news. An army of Continentals, a whole army, was marching down from Virginia, commanded by no less a general than Horatio Gates, the great victor of Saratoga! No, Congress had *not* abandoned South Carolina and Georgia! That was only another British lie.

Elijah Clark had led them to Sumter, for Clark had not stayed long in Georgia. The risks and hardships there were as bad as anywhere else. With an increased force Clark arrived at McDowell's camp not long after Jones did, and all the Georgians were reunited. However, for some reason Clark took a dislike to McDowell's ways and pressed on east to join Sumter. But their stay on the Catawba was brief. Almost immediately Sumter sent Clark west again. Gates was nearing the South Carolina line, and someone had to watch Ferguson's Volunteers and keep them distracted. Some of Clark's followers were disappointed to have to retrace their way, for the name of Sumter had acquired great drawing power.

Joggi had mixed feelings about the man who had stayed completely out of the war since the autumn of '78. But what had their other leaders brought them to? Loss of Savannah and of Charlestown. Be fair. And the day Charlestown surrendered, Sumter left home to fight. At least he hadn't let himself be caught or forced to take parole like Moultrie or Williamson or Pickens. Maybe the smart ones were those who stayed out. Or got out.

Yes, it was smart but was it right?

Well, you *lost no opportunity to leave,* he told himself. . . . *But when I left, I went with a troop. To fight. And to get beat. And then to get caught and have to take parole anyhow. . . . Well, so I broke parole, but if I'm willing to risk it, whose business is it but my own?*

Who am I to judge him? He's rallied almost a thousand men. They fought all day at Rocky Mount and if they'd had big guns, they'd have taken it. And they sure took plenty of spoil at Hanging Rock—including this horse I ride. . . . But why couldn't they have taken the post too? Instead of going crazy when they got into plunder and riding away rolling drunk.

Joggi wished he'd gotten a look at this leader, the man who promised his followers no pay but the spoils of winning. Too, he was curious about Sumter's followers. Were any from the Congarees? Clark's stay near the camp had been too short to find out.

Ah, what did it matter? What did any of it matter, leader or comrade either, except for the chance to fight. He liked this captain as well as any he'd ever served under, this Shadrack Inman, as smart and brave as they came. Besides, it ground his gizzard, as Rudi would say, to think of that rooster Ferguson strutting and enlisting Tory traitors—and maybe some that weren't really Tories. Was Rudi old enough to escape their hellish draft? Surely he wouldn't allow himself to be compelled as others were. But it was said Ferguson had a gift for drawing men.

Yet we have such leaders too, Joggi thought. Clark and Jones. And Isaac Shelby and John Sevier—though Sevier wasn't with them tonight but his brother was—leaders whom the overmountain men from Watauga and Holston would follow at a word, as fierce a breed as they came. *I'm glad they're on my side,* he thought. *But they're Georgians and North Carolinians. Where are ours? Where's Pickens? And old "Danger" Thomson we looked to for so long? Sitting home paroled. Well, at least, we have Sumter and the ones with him.* Maybe *it's a time for new names. . . . And what does it matter where you're from? We've all got the same fire, no matter where we come from.*

. . . Then why did he sometimes feel he never quite belonged to any of them? Because he wasn't Irish or English?

Sometimes he remembered the long imprisoned days in old Herr Pastor's schoolroom when he'd been as much a part of a closeknit band as he'd ever been in his life. And yet even then, in the deft execution of some devilment, in their shared glee, he'd have a sudden sense of not being one of them.

"'Hath God created thee naturally so wicked and perverse?'"

He could hear the very tones of old Herr Pastor's voice and his own parroted answer: "'By no means: but he created me good and after his own image, in the knowledge of God. . . .'"

Ah God, who—what am I now?

I'm one of these. And they're the ones I go with because I have to go with somebody now or die.

As for the boys in the old schoolhouse, he'd have no more hesitation in shooting one down than he would any other Tory if he saw him on the other side. The men before and behind him were all the friends he had.

He almost never thought of Nissi Rieder. The life she was in had nothing to do with where he was now. She was where there was no enemy, a far away place that was no longer real.

They reached Fairforest Creek around two o'clock in the morning. Their crossing was as noiseless as they could make it. Ferguson's old camp, where several companies remained, was only three miles down the creek from the shoals.

As the stream of riders flowed up and down the banks, some of them thought of their homes and families a few miles away. Major Joseph McJunkin thought anxiously of his father and sister. Colonel Thomas Brandon thought with suppressed fury of his house and lands.

They crossed their last steep-banked river, the Tyger. They had not stopped all night and their horses were very tired. The sky was beginning to lighten. A ridge line sharpened on the sky.

In the gray light they came out into an old Indian field overgrown with sumac and pine seedlings, for the land had not been burned off since the last withdrawal of the Cherokees and the disruptions of war. Here the leaders called a halt. They were one mile north of a rocky ford on the Enoree River where two hundred Loyalist militia were reported to be encamped around old Edward Musgrove's mill. Shelby, Clark, Williams, and their officers conferred and decided to send out scouts.

As the five men disappeared down the track, the main body also advanced toward the river. They stopped one half mile from the ford and bivouacked east of a south-running creek called Cedar Shoal.

The two hundred men were a lean-faced unsmiling lot, wearing nondescript backcountry clothes stained with dirt and sweat. Their faces were darkened by the smoke of a hundred campfires. After watering the horses, they let as many as could, get forage in the cane near the creek. Some of the men munched on dry corn they had crammed in their pockets before leaving Smith's Ford, but if the growing light suggested a better breakfast, they put the thought aside. Their craving was for a different kind of filling. They readied their guns and drew out knives for a last whetting.

Words were low and few. Mostly they listened. Bird sounds too were few. A loud-mouthed jay warned smaller birds away, the squirrels had moved on, and the men heard only a distant high hammering in a dead pine up the creek. The woods were so quiet they could hear the rush of water between the rocks. They leaned against trunks of trees or lay flat on the ground. It was now broad daylight.

Sudden gunfire crackled to the southwest. They counted the exchanges, tried to count shots.

"Eleven? Twelve?"

The men stood up. "I made out fourteen." They stood straining eyes and ears until they caught the sounds of plunging horsemen. Their scouts burst into sight. One had a grazed forearm and another was bleeding at his shoulder.

"A mounted patrol this side the ford! They come up after we did!"

"We killed one and knocked off two, but the other two got away!"

The encampment at the mill, asked Clark, had they gotten close enough to observe it?

Oh yes. They'd crossed upriver at Head's Ford and crept down close enough for good observation. But it was a right smart of 'em there, more'n any two hundred, more like four or five hundred.

"Are you certain?"

"Yes sir."

Although a low wooded ridge lay between them and the river, the two hundred partisans seemed already to hear the sounds of bugle and drum. Faces darkened. Four or five hundred were more than they'd bargained for. And the advantage of surprise was gone.

In the middle of their consternation a man on foot came hurrying toward them through the woods. He shouted, "Be ye friends to liberty?"

"Aye, man! Come forward!"

The newcomer was about forty-five years old and wore the briar-snagged clothes of an outlier but a still handsome wide-brimmed hat. Surveying the assembly, he picked out Shelby, came up to him, and gave his name. "I'm right glad to see ye. I'm a friend to liberty myself, though few there be here now, at least not so's to find 'em. I come over to relate our news."

He said that two hundred Loyalist regulars under Colonel Alexander Innes, as well as a hundred militiamen, had arrived last night from Ninety Six to join those under Major Fraser, raising their number to over five hundred. Daniel Clary from Ninety Six commanded the militia, and David

Fanning from North Carolina rode with them, both well-known Loyalist leaders. "We spied 'em the other side the river when they crossed Duncan's Creek. We made good count."

The commanders exchanged a few words. No use to think of running; their horses were too tired. But foolishness now to attack.

Their grim followers stood silent. They could hear drumbeats clearly across the river. No. They could hardly get away even if they wanted to. Besides, Ferguson's men were to their rear.

It was decided they would range themselves along a ridge and across the road to the ford. Let the enemy come up to them. "Drag up branches, dead wood and old logs! Hack off brushwood! Use anything you can find to make a breastwork!" They would deploy along the ridge about three hundred yards, curving their line at the ends. They'd have the cover of the trees, and their enemies would be attacking uphill.

"They don't know our numbers! We'll surprise 'em yet!"

They built their barrier breast-high in a semicircle across the road. Although the woods were fairly open, low bushes and the lay of the land would hide their preparation till the enemy was almost upon them. Shelby took the right, Williams the center across the road, and Clark the left, the entire force in one line with twenty horsemen on each wing and a reserve of forty men behind Clark.

"Oh, I itch to see them skunks come a-frolicing up here."

"Old Sweet-tooth is a-craving to bite one."

But how to draw them on, to draw the fight to their own ground? "We could wait here half the day."

"No, we must not give them time to counsel or plan."

"Then toll 'em up here right now. Send some of us to toll 'em up here."

The young officer with that suggestion was Shadrack Inman, and he volunteered to do the tolling. While their comrades watched, Inman and his twenty-five horsemen set off down the road.

Some ten minutes they rode between dew-drenched leaves toward the loudening beat of drums and the blare of bugles. Then they saw the river. The water was light-colored above the rocks but black-dark under overhanging trees. They scanned the opposite bank, a wide meadowlike slope with its patterned array of troops, a few companies still moving into formation.

Inman raised his sword, his followers spurred to a gallop, and the thudding hoofs help muffle the drumbeats. At the water's edge they reined briefly, then splashed in.

"Oh, you Wingfoot," whispered Joggi to his mount, "oh, you're fine!" His deepset eyes burned after his leader.

They pulled to a scrambling halt near trees on the farther bank and hitched their horses to low boughs, then scattered thirty yards up the slope and fired. The range was too great for effective shooting, but immediately the enemy commanders shouted and wheeled their mounts, and their foremost infantry began the advance.

Inman's small band retreated and sent out two more ragged volleys, then ran for their horses and dashed through the ford. On the north bank they deployed again and watched the enemy wade into the water. They waited, fired, and retreated, closing their formation, as the massed troops came on to a quickening beat.

Joggi looked back, saw them coming thick-ranked out of the water, moving at a jog-trot up the slope with gleaming bayonets. He felt the old thrill of fear, yet checked his horse and looked entreatingly at his captain. Let's give it to 'em full-face, Captain! his look implored. Perhaps Inman saw it, perhaps not, but he curved to the right and circled back. His men dismounted and fired again, then fled as if in panic, bending over their horses' necks. Joggi thought he might have hit one this time but did not look back.

Hoarse shouting rose behind them. "Look at the scurvy ragtag run!" "Huzza for King George!" came the roar. "Huzza for King George!"

The roar assailed the slopes, rolled in great waves back across the river to cheer the spectators crowding the windows and rooftop of the Musgrove house. "Rebel scum! Look at 'em run!"

Beneath the leafy branches up the long rise, grips tightened and sweat poured.

"Remember to hold it, boys. Remember, not till you see the buttons on their coats."

Now Inman's boys were in sight, wheeling and skirmishing up the slope.

Down the ridge the cheering quieted as report of the barrier ahead must have reached Innes, for the oncoming troops spread along the slope in a three-columned line.

Above them, Shadrack Inman yelled, "One last time, boys!" He turned his horse and rode straight toward the center of the advancing line, his men beside and behind him, the light blazing in their smoke-darkened faces. They fired their last shots, then scattered in different directions up the ridge. As the roar deepened below them, Joggi felt in his flesh the bladed drive.

At the barrier Inman's men were greeted with curses of endearment, for they'd done the trick they'd been sent for. They slipped through the line to secure their horses, then came running back. Joggi found his place behind a rail fence near the road, nearer to the center than to the Georgians.

He heard the excited voice of old Williams. "Keep steady, boys Each one find his mark," and repeating the wellworn maxim, "but wait till you can see the whites of their eyes!"

A musket volley crashed up the slope from a hundred and fifty yards away. Bullets bit the trunks and branches above them, and leaves and twigs fell on their heads.

"Reckon it's squirrels up there making a nest?"

"If 'tis, I think it's somebody shooting at 'em."

A hundred yards, another volley, again high. As the smoke swirled toward them, the mountain men squinted along their rifle barrels. Shelby's shot would be their signal. The breasts of the advancing enemy were covered with strong new linen and canvas, light-colored for summer, and their hands gripped good brown regulation muskets. Their officers rode confidently. Eighty yards, seventy.

One shot, Shelby's, and two hundred more blazed out of the logs and brush.

A terrible yelling arose in front and behind. Some of the Loyalists dropped, but their comrades kept on coming, blades glinting. The defenders shot again and again, but Innes' regulars on the right did not pause, and there seemed no end to their coming. Now they were at the barricade, a hundred blades charging, and the mountain men gave way, dashing for cover behind trees.

Far to the left where the Georgians were fending off Loyalist militiamen, Clark saw how Shelby's wing was outnumbered, saw how the right was being bent back across the ridge like a forearm out of joint. He shouted, and the forty reserves behind him ran low the length of the ridge.

But the center was holding. The fence kept up a steady fire, though the smoke was so thick, nothing could be seen beyond a hundred yards. Joggi was conscious of himself only as fingers to pour the powder, hands to ram in the charge, arms to lift, swing, and balance the stock, eyes to probe and sight the mark, the whole coordinated movement one note of a chord sounded again and again. He marked a man on horseback, shot, and the figure tumbled, yet others kept coming low-crouched out of the smoke.

Down the ridge on the right, wild shouts rose among the mountain men and a resurgence of movement.

"Innes is killed!" "Innes is shot!" passed from one to another along the ridge.

No, he was not killed, but they saw the Loyalist colonel taken up and borne away.

Reinforced by Clark's men, Shelby's surged back to the barrier. With Indian whoops the mountain men swung hatchets and rifle butts, slashed and stabbed with their knives. For a while they fought hand to hand among the logs and brush, then began to leap across the shambles and bear down on their enemies with terrible yells. Still, all along the line the struggle hung balanced, for the Loyalist recruits were not giving ground. Ferguson's training held. But another of their officers fell and another. Their Major Fraser was carried off.

"Forward!" yelled Brandon. "They're going to turn!"

"Roll into 'em, boys! Roll 'em down!" roared Williams.

The Loyalist attack was stalled, already turned on the right. Now everywhere the partisans clambered over logs and limbs with whoops and yells, and though the Loyalists had not yet turned their backs, they had to give way. Too many of them had fallen and not enough of their enemies. Too few voices were left to enspirit them. What they faced was too fierce.

The Loyalists gave ground slowly at first, then more rapidly, then in full retreat. Halfway down the slope the retreat became a rout.

Their yelling foes pursued them to the ford. They shot them as they splashed among the rocks, shot one across the river as he derisively turned up his backside, shot another one out of a tree. The windows of the Musgrove house gaped empty; the roof was vacant. The spectators had already grabbed their knapsacks and cleared the premises and were now on their way to Ninety Six. Some had recently been prisoners of the Whigs and had broken parole. At the ford the victors kept up their fire till they saw no more targets.

Up the ridge under a great Spanish oak, several men stooped above a body. They peered into its blackened face under blood-matted hair and recognized Shadrack Inman. They found seven bullet holes in him.

"Oh Lord, I made out how he galloped ahead of us all! Wouldn't wait for no one!"

"He rode to his doom. He rode straight in amongst 'em."

The sun rose over the trees. The August sun beat down on their husks of rage, unsparing. Jake Lennard—Joggi—as he looked at his dead captain, felt his insides wrenched and something inside him spill out he'd forgotten he had. He did not vomit or even weep, yet whatever it was that broke kept seeping out.

The Loyalists had lost sixty-three dead, ninety wounded, and seventy captured, a good half of the number engaged. A party patrolling downriver hurried back when they heard the firing but arrived too late to help. Part of the Loyalist force now withdrew a mile and a quarter from the river to bivouack for the rest of the day and to return to Ninety Six that night. They would march the first miles in close order with bayonets leveled for defense in flank and rear. The remaining Loyalists kept to the mill.

At Cedar Shoal Creek the partisans consulted. They had lost four killed and nine wounded.

"On to Ninety Six!" the men called. It was only twenty-five miles away. They could get there by dark. With so many troops out it was bound to be weak.

Were the horses up to it? Well, they'd had almost four hours' rest. Yes, now was their chance to take back Ninety Six! They exulted at the thought of it. Williams especially urged it, for his family and plantation were eight miles above Ninety Six on Little River.

They were already mounted when a rider and a spent horse came beating down through the woods behind them. At once they recognized something unwelcome in his look. The messenger said he came from McDowell, and he handed Shelby a packet. "Colonel Caswell's letter, sir."

The men watched Shelby read. Shelby handed the paper to Clark, who read it and handed it to Williams. They exchanged a few words. They scrutinized the messenger.

"It's Caswell's letter," said Shelby. "I know his hand."

The men saw it in their leaders' faces: some terrible loss.

It was worse than they guessed. The entire Continental army under Gates had been defeated by Cornwallis above Camden, virtually destroyed, and by a smaller army at that. Hundreds were killed, captured, or wounded; those who escaped were scattered, and Gates himself was in flight to Hillsboro, North Carolina. Among those lost was the brave General Baron De Kalb, who had refused to retreat and died after the battle of eleven sword, bayonet, and bullet wounds.

McDowell advised they retreat at once or they would be cut off. Ferguson was nearing them in strong force, and other British troops would fan out in pursuit of all resistance. McDowell was already on his way to Gilbert Town forty miles above the state line. They must move speedily if they hoped to join him.

The three leaders did not dismount for further talk. There was no need. All Loyalists would be immensely strengthened by Cornwallis' victory, even the ones just defeated. "We must leave the wounded," they decided, "but take the prisoners with us."

Somberly they mounted the prisoners, one behind every third man. The August sun shone hot on all indiscriminately as they hurried away.

Now other figures moved across the battlefield, smaller ones, stooping, turning over bodies, examining faces, a few reaching among clothes and into pockets. Sometimes wild sobbing broke out to mingle with the moans and calls of those still alive. Eventually men from the mill came to bear away the living, the several Rebels included, and to bury the dead. Shadrack Inman was buried by the Spanish oak tree where he had fallen.

The victors rode northwest, crossed the forks of the Tyger, and, certain already of Ferguson's pursuit, they stopped only briefly to feed and rest the horses. They drank from the rocky fords they crossed and, as they rode, ate green corn and peaches they snatched along the way. They rode all day and all night. The morning of August 19 found them sixty miles from the Enoree and across the North Carolina line, but their faces were so bloated and their eyes so swollen they could hardly see. Only after they crossed the North Pacolet, did they dare to stop. Yesterday Ferguson had been only a half hour behind them, though at nightfall— they did not know it then—he had given them up.

They decided that Williams would take the prisoners to Hillsboro and report their small victory to whatever Patriot authority was there. The others would join McDowell beyond Gilbert Town or, like Shelby, go home to recruit more men.

Jake Lennard received permission to join the South Carolinians and go with Williams.

22

Heiri wrung out the sweat-soaked breeches he had been swishing through the water and draped them over a bush by the creek. They were new canvas, but the sun was so hot they'd dry in no time. His wet shirt he'd dry on his body, for he could not like going about stark naked. Though he had a new shirt in his saddlebag, he preferred the old one. Its rips and holes made it comfortably airish. Also the small neat stitches that still held spoke of small neat hands.

Most of the men were asleep under wagons or other shade up the ridge where they were bivouacked. Exhaustion and heat had sapped every nerve and muscle of power to move.

Three days ago at Fort Carey down the Wateree, Sumter's militia and the regulars sent earlier by Gates had taken fifty British supply wagons and two hundred prisoners, but news of the Camden disaster next day forced them to retreat back up the Catawba. They moved mostly at night, cumbered with wagons, cattle, and prisoners. Some eight hundred and fifty of them, including the regulars, had halted this morning west of the Catawba on a ridge between Fishing Creek and the river. It was the same position they had taken after Rocky Mount in expectation of the attack that never came because of the swollen creek. It was a good site for defense, well protected by draws and deep ravines on all sides.

Now arms were stacked and horses unsaddled. Some of the men were cooking, some eating, a few still slaughtering beeves. Others were cooling themselves in the river, or a few, like Heiri, in the creek, but most of them, including the General, were sound asleep. A few sentinels stood guard downstream at the creek crossing.

Heiri still had trouble sleeping in broad daylight. For too many years the cry, "Up, boys! Sun's rising!" had routed him out, and although he could be as sleepy-headed as anyone, he could never quite still the echoes of that cry.

Heiri's cheekbones were high ridges with wide hollows beneath them, his face darkened by more than the sun. The full, pleasant curve of his lips, if it was still there, was hidden under the ragged beginnings of a beard. Anyone talking with him who had known him before might wonder if it was still Heiri.

Heiri seldom saw Willi, never sought him out. Willi was more apt to seek out Heiri, though not often. Willi had found old acquaintances among the followers of Major Thomas Taylor from east of Friday's Ferry on the Congaree.

Sometimes, however, Heiri would find Jem Boyd near him, and the two would assume companionship. Jem had stopped calling Heiri "Dutch," called him "Harry."

Jem couldn't sleep either. He was sitting up the bank, turning something over in his hands. "Hey, Harry! Look what I found me!"

Heiri glanced up. "Anything for the belly?"

"Not now. Might ha' held some such once." Jem was looking at a pottery bowl with an inverted rim. "Indian ware, I don't doubt. It was up yonder other side that rock."

An empty bowl. That was apt. "What you think was once in it?"

"Maybe a mess of corn meal?"

Wheat flour, Heiri thought, *would be better.*

"Couldn't ha' held much though," said Jem. "More like, say, some hickor' nut kernels. Indians set great store by nuts."

"Five or six eggs," said Heiri. "That's what I set store by."

"Well, we'll all get baited up today for certain."

"Oh yes." But there was such a thing as too much fresh beef in a shrunken stomach Heiri had learned. Especially in the heat.

The rifles of men felling cattle still cracked occasionally. They heard shots now down the creek. Heiri thought, *Strange place though to be shooting them.*

Jem thought so too. "How'd the beeves get down that way?" The shots sounded near the crossing, which was hidden by a bend in the creek.

"Maybe some broke loose."

Jem stood up to listen, heard no more. "I'm going on back," he called.

Heiri regarded his breeches on the bush, then took them and wrung them out as hard as he could and began to drag them on, aggravated with himself for feeling ill at ease without them. Who was to see him? Who was to care? He remembered a red-haired girl in the gray mist, her face now austere, now alive with—what? He knew if he curled up in some hollow and lost himself in the half-remembered, half-imagined look and feel of her she would become real. . . . But not now. Tonight maybe as they moved, to keep himself awake. He'd remember every detail of the night they'd come to Chappell's Ferry, build up slowly to the dawn's revelation . . . and stay there. But now he'd better go look for Roker.

Heiri could not believe he still had Roker. Shine was long since become rotting flesh and hide, put out of his misery after Hanging Rock. Although the militia did not fight on horseback, the chances of ambush, pursuit, and dangerous fords took their toll on their horses. Now Roker, like Heiri, was rawboned. Whenever Heiri tended him, he would try to see his father's legs clamping those brown sides, but it was becoming harder. He could not believe little Georgi had ever grasped that mane.

Heiri followed Jem up the ravine, the wet canvas chafing his legs.

The camp was spread out where the ridgetop widened on each side of the road traversing its length. Baggage wagons were drawn up to the rear and the horses browsed beyond them. Some hundred or so prisoners were confined to the rear also and had flung themselves on the ground to take what ease they could.

All was tranquil. Though most of the camp were asleep or in the river, knots of men lounged here and there—some playing cards, a couple of them betting on a louse race, one cutting up strips of leather for some purpose of his own, others ravening around a steaming pot or, somewhat apart, joyously passing a bottle. A refugee woman sat on a log near the road feeding her two children.

Heiri looked for Jem but did not see him. For some reason he thought of Willi. Likely asleep.

He was just about to cross the road when the place in front of him exploded with the crash and plunge of dragoons bearing down on them.

Men started up. No guns were to hand. Heiri ran, but everywhere hooves pounded and blades flashed. One slashed at him, caught his shoulder. Heiri threw up his arm to shield his head and stumbled. A horse reared and came down over him. He tried to roll out from under its feet, but a hoof struck the side of his head. He felt a bright black shock of pain.

Someone kicked and turned him partly over, left him lying twisted on his side. He felt the sun beating on his back. In the hot haze he was aware of man-shapes, giant pillars moving above and beyond him. Harsh staccato shouts sounded far away. Crying behind him rose and fell in rhythmic pulsation, then gradually ceased.

Heiri moved his head and pain and consciousness drained out of him and soaked into the ground, yet not quite all of it. He lay still a long time, his consciousness contracted small. Finally he moved his right arm; the other was pinned beneath him. His right eye was blind. His throat was afire.

He could not remember why or how he came to be here. Some battle—somewhere. He did know he was lying like the others he had viewed during the last two months in the jumble of ridges, ravines, and logs, where his bullets bit into trees and rocks and flesh. And now he too lay there. On his way to death. What he'd come out for. . . . But so soon. If only he could have found. . . . His thought ebbed.

Presently something lighted on his face. He opened the eye that was not sealed shut. Whatever it was flitted off, and his clouded vision focused on a nearby weedstalk with flannel-like, elongated leaves. Many white insects worked up and down its stem. Up and down the stem. Where are they going? What are they after? Up and down, hurrying, scurrying, for no reason he could tell. Sometimes one went out on a leaf by itself, but mainly they kept on the stem in a continuous coming and going.

A shadow covered him. He moved slightly. Hands grasped him, caught him under the armpits. "This one's shamming it! Get up, Rebel! On your feet! Stand up!"

He felt as if his arm were being torn off as he was pulled to his knees, and a great stone crashed in his head. Yet amazingly, dragged upright, he stood there weaving.

"One of you villains, come look to this one! Keep him up!"

A muddle of shapes about him, someone supporting him. "Hold on to me, Heiri. Heiri?"

He gasped. Someone drew Heiri's uninjured arm across his own shoulder. His left arm hung bleeding afresh.

Willi's voice. "Hold him up for me."

They tore up Heiri's shirt and bound it around the arm and shoulder. Heiri's lips drew back in a grimace meant for mirth at its being Willi.

"Take heart," someone else said. "You're up on your own two feet, and you still got your arm."

"Water!" Heiri croaked.

He was being propelled across the field. Willi muttered, "We got to march now."

Heiri sensed the shuffling of other bodies around him, heard cries of command to front and rear. He smelled something afire. His vision cleared; he saw flecks of floating ash. He clutched at Willi and mouthed the word again, his throat a cracked gulley.

"When we get to the creek, Heiri. Pray God, we go soon. They're burning what they can't take."

Heiri stood shivering in the heat, gazing dimly from one eye at hundreds of men like himself being marshalled into ranks. We're prisoners. He thought he saw Jem Boyd, then realized it was another man. He wondered—Roker, where's poor old Roker? As they left, Heiri saw many bodies still on the ground.

If the creek hadn't been fairly near, Heiri thought he never could have made it. Even there he could not drink as much as he craved, for their captors hurried them on. Men who had hats tried to carry away water in them. One let Heiri drink more from his. None of them got their bait of beef that day.

Through the rest of the afternoon they shambled along, over three hundred prisoners, on through the twilight and into the night, guarded by Banastre Tarleton's dragoons, a troop of light infantry, and the former British prisoners, who were jubilant at the reversal of role. They marched down the west side of the Catawba, that farther south would become the Wateree River. They climbed and descended long steep hills, passed the Great Falls, passed Rocky Mount, crossed Fishing Creek, Rocky Creek, and Crooked Creek. The next one would be the Big Wateree. They were on the road to Camden.

During the first hour the prisoners spoke little. Most were trying to understand what had happened, how it had happened. Eventually low sporadic questions and comments found voice.

There had been some resistance, some exchange of gunfire among the wagons, but the momentum of the attackers and their unpreparedness had been too great. The General? No, he wasn't among the prisoners, and he hadn't been seen among the dead either. He must have gotten away. Others too must have escaped. But many, many had been left on the ground.

Those in the river? "If they got away, I make certain they'd need fig leaves."

A man began to curse the leaders for their misjudgment and stupidity, but others shut him up, for their officers marched among them.

The realization of what awaited a number of them at Camden was swift for some, slow for others. To Willi it came slow. At first he was simply glad to be alive and unhurt. His main concern was to get through whatever discomfort lay ahead. He'd gotten through it at Charlestown; he could do it again.

And he'd see Heiri Lienhardt through it too. He could never quite rid himself of that—tie or whatever it was with Heiri, like a family connection you were half ashamed of, yet couldn't disown. Why he should feel ashamed, Willi never understood. It had nothing to do with social or military status. No, it was just that Heiri was still—Heiri. There was still too much of—Willi didn't know the word. Something he really didn't like to think about. He knew Heiri was unhappy, but it was something else. A kind of unbearable something. Unbearable for Willi.

However, now that Heiri was physically hurt, Willi felt distress for him, especially about his head wound. There was some bared bone, a great deal of swelling and clotted blood, but it hurt too much for anyone to probe. He hoped Heiri wouldn't lose his eye. The cut in his upper arm, though deep, was only in the flesh. It was to be hoped he wouldn't take fever. Still, Heiri was staggering along without help. Lienhardts were tough, Willi thought, and strong. Stronger than he himself was, Willi knew.

The glum men shuffling along talked low.

"You got nothing to fear. Or no more'n common. Me, I took protection. Fool that I was."

"And me, I must go and get myself paroled."

"Surely they won't—"

"What makes you think they won't? Him?" Though the elegant greenclad form was too far ahead to be seen, no one doubted which British officer was meant.

"It won't be up to him."

"No matter who it's up to, not a one of 'em but would hang a man that's broke parole."

"They give us no choice."

"Oh yes they did." The voice was heavy with sarcasm. "Said, 'You'll fight for us or against us.'"

Willi felt his scalp tingle.

As dusk thickened, the woods moved in on the road and the way narrowed. Horsemen no longer rode alongside the prisoners but drove them from the rear. The column seemed less compact.

Heiri stumbled blindly, his shoulder throbbing, his head a block of pain, yet some strength in his legs and his lungs kept pushing him on. It was like a will other than his own. Willi marched silently beside him; Willi's friend who'd helped him was far ahead.

For Willi the realization of what awaited him sank in. Oh, it might be days or even weeks before British officialdom found his name on their lists, but he didn't doubt they'd find it. He thought of giving a false name. But no, too many other Carolinians were in the King's service for him to get away with it, and the discovery of deception would make his doom only more certain.

But surely they won't doom me! Can this be happening to me? Surely God wouldn't— A vision of himself learning his catechism at school. Even old Herr Pastor had liked him. *Bind me and hang me? Surely there must be—Camden's not so far from Congarees. If I could just get word to—*

Others walked in grimmer certainty.

In the dusk Willi saw a man ahead of him stumble and fall, but when they came to where he'd fallen, the man wasn't there.

"Move up," someone muttered. The man abreast of Willi moved ahead and another from behind took his place. Some five minutes later Willi was again aware of men moving up on the outside of the column. They marched five abreast now, though some ten feet ahead he saw only four.

He whispered to the outside man who had just come up, "What's happening?"

The man said low, "If it's the gallows ahead of you, Major Taylor says work on up to the middle of the line and when it's a chance to drop off in the dark, you do it."

"Now?"

The man had already moved on.

The dusk was thicker and shapes were dimly visible. Willi felt a throb of fear and excitement. Why not? Couldn't he? Well, why not?

Where'd be the best place? The bottom of a hill where the bushes were close to the road. . . . But what if he were caught? Could he disappear quickly enough? It was too dark now to tell much about the lay of the land . . . . And how could he know what he'd drop off into? . . . But it was a chance! Do it! he urged himself.

And what about Heiri?

He glanced at the shape lunging along beside him. Willi bit his lip. *He's never been paroled like me. He'll just be kept in some jail or stockade and maybe even sent home. Besides, if I'm hanged, he'll have to go on without me.*

Someone else moved up in the dusk, moved past him. Willi kept his place.

What if he dies on the march? No one at home would ever know where or how he died.

He whispered, "Heiri, you see what they're doing up ahead?"

The answer came slow. "What?"

"Heiri, they're dropping off in the dark to get away."

Heiri did not answer.

"See, our guards are far enough back and so far ahead they can't tell what's happening. Heiri—" Willi plodded awhile in silence. "Heiri, they'll hang me at Camden."

"What? Surely not!"

"Yes, they will. I broke parole. I was paroled at Charlestown. They'll hang me, all of us that broke parole." He could not control the tremor in his voice.

"Then you better drop off too."

"Yes, I'll have to try." They were descending another long hill. Again the trees loomed high and close to the road.

"Heiri, I don't like to—leave you. Hurt and all."

"It's all right, Willi. I must not be too bad hurt. To keep going."

"You're walking stronger. Talking stronger."

Heiri made no answer. The force that propelled his legs through the murk and thickness, where did it come from?

"Wonder if they mean to march us all night?" Willi whispered. "Surely they'll make camp soon." He tried to think. *Where will the guard be less alert? When they're tired and sleepy too, wouldn't that be a better time? In camp, wouldn't it? . . . Of course not. Then we'll be guarded on all sides.*

. . . No, here where the woods are thick and dark, in a deep bottom like this one, I could drop off right here and roll into the dark, roll into . . . what? Fall in some gulley? Sprain or break a limb. Or make so much

noise I'd get caught. Or else be by myself, disabled, and everybody gone.
In the woods by myself, unable to go.

He tramped on. The ground rose. The moon appeared. It was in its
second quarter. As they climbed the long slope, the trees were more widely
spaced and the undergrowth thinned. At the top of the hill Willi could just
see the shape of the toiling column ahead. He could not see the prisoners
behind him or the train of wagons and horsemen following, but he felt the
oppression of tall strong men with pistols and blades.

How many more of these valleys? Even *they* must be bone-tired
now. One part of him dreaded to hear the command to halt, but another
part longed for it. *Tomorrow in daylight, when I can see and think better. . . .*
No, there'd be no chance in daylight.

"Heiri."

"What?"

"This may be the time. Down there if the woods get thick again.
What do you think?"

"I think so."

"Will you—" Willi broke off, for he did not know what he meant
to say.

At last Heiri said slowly, "You want me to try it too? Try it with you?"

"You think you could?"

"I—yes. Right now I could fall out as easy as keep going."

"Here, man, hold up, hold on to me!" Their pace had quickened
with the downhill march.

Heiri accepted the support, but after a while he said, "It'll have to
be one at a time, won't it?"

"I—yes, I think so."

"I'll go first."

"You want to?" Willi asked quickly.

"Yes. That way if they catch me, you'll hear 'em and know it."

"What if they catch me? How would you know?"

"They won't catch you."

The boughs above hung heavier. The understory was dense with
increased ground moisture and they smelled the sweetness of night-damped
leaves.

"I wonder it it's a creek down there," Heiri muttered.

Willi said, "When—when you drop out, don't go too far off the
road, Heiri. Lie there till the line's past and then I'll crawl back to you.
Get under the bushes but just lie still."

"All right."

"I'll be back," Willi whispered. "Never fear, Heiri, you just wait for me."

They tramped on. Already they were leveling off in the valley. Through the sounds of scuffling feet they heard running water.

"We'd better change places," Willi whispered. He broke his stride to let Heiri slip in front of him. A man behind them cursed. Willi said, "Push up, Heiri, and over when you can," but wondered, *Can he do it without me?*

Now Willi could just see Heiri's bare shoulders, one of them bound in that rag of a shirt, crowded among the taller men ahead. Suddenly the shoulders weren't there. Willi strained his eyes, craned his neck. He knew an instant's panic. Where was he? What happened? Willi tried to scan the verge of the road, looked over his shoulder but saw nothing.

The column moved on. Now he heard clearly the rush of water. He was trembling all over. *Before we cross that branch*, he told himself, *I've got to!* but his feet kept going on. Soon they'd be across the branch; the ground would rise and the trees thin.

"Let me by!" he hissed suddenly to the outside man abreast of him. "They'll hang me at Camden!"

Abruptly the man reached out to swing Willi in front of him with mighty strength.

Willi gasped, "Thanks!" then not trying to move up in the column, he crouched and scuttled off into the bushes, flattening himself, crawling, scrambling, scraping his flesh and tearing his clothes, until he judged himself some five or more yards from the road, where he collapsed and lay motionless, hearing only the pounding of his heart.

Gradually other sounds became audible—the tramping of feet, the scrape on earth and stone, pieces of conversation.

"Give me good dry cornshucks anytime. Sweetest bed in the world."

"Or pineneedles. Clean pineneedles. I favor the smell of pineneedles."

The horsemen were trampling the edge of the road, the very bushes, he thought. Anytime, one of those big hooves would come down on him. He smelled the steam of fresh horse manure. At last came the rattle of captured artillery carriages and the creak and jingle of wagons, which went on forever. More infantry. More horses.

Then abruptly the sounds were past. A long time Willi lay listening to the diminishing scuffle, thud, grind, creak and jingle, heard it recede up the long rise, finally become silence over the hill.

Now he heard the rush of water and a light breeze rustling the leaves. On the ground it was very still. For a long time he lay there motionless, and after a while there came to him a new sense of who he was. Wilhelm Rieder.

He did not dare take the center of the road but edged along in the shadows. After a while he called low, "Heiri." He had no idea how far back Heiri had dropped out. "Heiri!" he called louder, repeated the call.

He began to hurry. Would the fool have crawled off in the woods? "Heiri!" he kept calling and stopping to listen. Fear coursed through him. He'd soon be back to the place he'd dropped out.

Suddenly, at his very feet a voice croaked, "Willi?" and there was Heiri stretched out by the road.

"Man, why didn't you answer me? Didn't you hear me? I've been calling fifteen minutes or more! I came right by you!"

"I must have been asleep, Willi. I thought I heard you but then. . . ." Heiri's voice trailed off.

"Asleep! With them going right by you? You could have been stepped on!"

"I fell asleep. Soon as I lay down." Heiri's voice came slow and lazy. "I heard you, Willi. But it was like . . . in a dream."

"Well, we've got to move on! They'll be back patrolling this road at first light, maybe sooner, soon as they start missing men."

"Willi—you go on. I want to lie here. Awhile longer."

"Heiri, don't be a fool! Get up, man! You got to go!"

"Willi, I just don't . . . feel like it." Under other circumstances Willi would have judged from the slurred lazy voice that Heiri was drunk.

Impatient, exhorting and tugging at him, Willi got Heiri on his feet. "After we get over that hill, we'll go in the woods. Then we'll find a place to sleep. Right now we'll stay on the road. Let's get up where the bushes aren't so thick and we can tell better which way to go. Come on now, Heiri. You've come so far, surely you can go a little farther!"

To Willi their going was agonizingly slow. They shambled and lurched back up the slope that now seemed steeper and longer than any they had yet climbed. Willi kept talking, going over the details of their escape, saying what he had heard and done.

Heiri made little response. Finally he asked, "How far you think we are?"

"How far? From what? How far from what, Heiri?"

"The Congarees."

"Why—I don't know."

"Which way is it?"

"Congarees?" Willi's tone was sharp, but he did not answer for a while. "Oh, southwest. I'd say southwest."

"Which way we going?"

"North."

"How many miles would it be? To the Congaree River."

"I don't know, Heiri. I just don't know."

"A hundred miles? Two hundred?"

"You know better than that. More like—fifty or sixty maybe." Willi was silent, then said tiredly, "You want to go home?"

Heiri did not answer at once. A breeze sprang up. They felt it on their foreheads, and Heiri felt it cooling his arms and shoulders. When he finally spoke, his voice sounded suddenly awake. "Of course, I do. But I can't. We can't either of us, can we?"

Willi allowed himself a sigh. "No, we've been through too much."

"Which way we go then? The way we came?"

"We'll try to. But we have to get off this road. We can't go by this road."

At last Willi said, "I believe I see a clear way through here. Maybe down the other side this ridge we can find us a place to rest. Let's strike off here."

There was more moonlight here than in the valley. Up and over the ridge, between the great tree trunks they stumbled and dragged themselves along. Both of them had been without food since early moorning. Finally they found a small, clear glade in the shadow of a great rock outcrop. They thought they heard the trickle of water somewhere, but now they had no will to go and find it. "In the morning," said Willi.

Heiri lay motionless. Willi thought he was asleep till Heiri said, "Wonder where Joggi is now?"

"No telling."

Both could hear the far small trickle of water.

Heiri spoke once more. "Well, we did it, didn't we, Willi? We got away. . . . You got us away."

Yes, Willi reflected, *I did, and who'd have thought it?*

23

With Rudi breathing at last deep long breaths beside her, Margaret drifted into a light doze to the pre-dawn chittering of young birds.

"This will have to do us a long time," he'd said.

"Oh, we'll make sure it does."

She lay melted and serene, yet even so, she kept on the floor of her mind the need to wake him before sunrise.

They knew how to love. She knew how to love in deed, but he knew how to love in word too. In the dark he could say words she had never thought to hear in her days. "You are like the white flower that hides itself. But not hid to me." "Like a spray of fern. Curved like a spray of fern."

In the daytime she sometimes wondered when he thought of such sayings and if he saved them up. Once in a tiff she'd asked him, and he came as near to blushing as she'd ever seen him. Then she felt as if she had walked on something rare. Was there ever another like him?

Whispering, "Like the inside of a shell, white pearl shining," and she would walk light and young for days.

As for her, she could not say her love in words, only in her look and touch and the way she gave, gave wholly and often with ardor that was like the gift of summer rain.

"Margaret, you're the one woman in all this world would be so enduring strong." Over the years he had absorbed her patterns of English speech.

Will I be strong? she wondered.

"I'm a blessed man. Truly. You'll know—" He had paused a long time. "You'll know how to do."

"I'll try," she murmured. "But you make sure you come back. Hear me? You come back, Rudi Näffels."

"God knows I'll try. But there'll be plenty out to see I don't."

"I know," she whispered. "But you remember Jem and Katy."

"Oh, I will Every day I live. . . . But you first."

The dull of daylight filtered through the room. She opened her eyes. It was unmistakable day. That day had become this day.

She rested her hand lightly on his chest, whispered, "Rudi," said it again low. He stirred. "God knows I hate to wake you, Rudi."

Open-eyed, he looked at her. He thought now she was like a still pool behind a splashing fall. *I'll love you*, he thought, *to my days' end, be it now or later*. Margaret. Someone had told him once her name meant "pearl."

The Bible spoke of a pearl of great price that a man gave all he had for. He knew it didn't mean a woman, yet the gift of this woman was one of the reasons he knew there had to be God. This woman and their children. *How can God not be, with so much given to such as me?* he asked.

Her touch lingered. Yet even as they lay face to face, the day's need took possession. Simultaneously, quickly they arose and dressed.

They spoke low so as not to wake the children. Breakfast was a coarse, scant affair. "Here, you take the rest of it, else I'll be seeing you faint and famished all day." She bore down his protest, spooning her hominy into his bowl. "I can get dinner! Where'll you be getting any dinner? Out of trees?"

"Maybe. But don't worry," he added, "I won't waste powder."

It was late summer when they'd learned they did not live as secluded as they'd thought. Twice they were plundered by Tory troops. Or they called themselves troops, she said. "More like blackguard thieves!" The first time she and Rudi were caught unawares. After that, they'd hid what was left and the little yet to be gathered.

But it was not the loss of goods or even the insults of riffraff that at last roused Rudi, nor was it Margaret's smouldering. It was finally the matter-of-fact way they had ordered him into their ranks.

"I'll not be any man's slave, no bondslave to King of Britain or anybody else! You hear me, Margaret? It's not by your will or Congress's or anybody else's I go. It's because I'll not be slave to a pack of men! I'll support a good man. I'll not obey an unjust one."

She did not answer him a word although it was hard to keep words back and her triumphant looks. But she could not wholly suppress her fierce joy, for it sprang out of the tendrils of her hair and showed in the set of her back. Thereafter she made sure the children spent every hour they could with him.

He had almost finished his breakfast. She rose to throw another stick of wood to the back of the chimney. It was a dampish morning, mid-September, the cool of fall already in the air.

He said, "Make sure you don't delay leaving. I'd feel better to have seen you and the young ones to Frasers' myself."

"We'll go. Soon as Mary brings her wagon. Though it's little but us to go in it."

"Well, I'm glad we moved all else yesterday." He glanced about the dusky room. She would have to go. Only a few utensils and foodstuffs were left. Outside, only his horse remained. Hers and their one cow and the hogs and all the fowls they could catch were gone. The outbuildings were stripped clean. The house would be empty except for shelves, bedsteads, loom, and a few old sticks of furniture. Who knew whether either of them would ever see it again?

"Mind, you promised me not to be trying to come back here."

She sighed. "Aye, I promised. But I presume," she inquired dryly, "you'll not object to my sending young Aleck over here next week to collect a few more apples?"

"No. But don't you come back. I don't want to have to think about it."

"Like as not it'll soon be nothing to come back to."

"You can spare yourself the sight."

"I've seen burnt-out houseplaces afore. You forget I was born in the Valley of Virginny? And the day I first laid eyes on you, where had I been but to my brother's burnt-down house, remember that? And a God's mercy it was for you I went." She spoke of the time she'd found him hurt in the woods. "Oh," she said sternly, "I've seen many a houseplace burnt to the ground."

"But not this one," he said softly. He rose and went to her. "Spare yourself that grief, Margaret. And don't spend yourself so in anger. That's my part."

She drew back and looked at him, her hands on his shoulders, and shook her head. "Oh no, Rudi, you don't go to spend anger. I know you better than that. That's not why you go."

"No? Then why you think I go?"

Her expression lightened. "Well, one thing, you'll be out of earshot of my tongue, out of the reach of my clacking tongue."

"Margaret, Margaret." It was a half-laugh, half-groan.

Her face against his shoulder, she said, "It's because you're the man you are and ever have been. Well I know that. But not now because you're angry."

His look was somber. He dropped his arms from about her and went to the doorway, stood a moment looking out, went on the porch. "Margaret," he called, "will you come out here a minute?"

They stood on the high back porch and gazed across descending fields and the creek bottom, across the ridgeline of trees beyond. He reached to draw her arm through his, and she knew great gladness.

"Margaret, so much I don't know. So much I don't understand." He spoke heavily. "That our life should have so much hurt and wrong. Yet goodness too." He turned his head to look at her. He never spoke of the old years, of deprivals, misfortunes, misjudgments, perhaps seldom thought of them.

"Margaret, ever since I was old enough to take on man's ways, I found it hard always to know and to do the right. I'm slow to see it. Now you, you fly straight to your mark. But I look too much about me and see more paths than one."

Yes, you see more, she thought. *And maybe it's because you've had to.*

"But one thing I want to tell you. Now I don't remember where I came from. I know I had once a country and kin like everybody else but they were taken from me before I knew them. All I had left was—" he gestured outward, "—many paths. It was not then fifty acres to hoe and plow. It was much more. You understand? Twenty years ago, how it was then? It was much more."

As they gazed at each other, thoughts, impulses, joys timeless rose up in her. *Maybe why I was drawn to him,* she thought. *Yes, he's always had more than this little place on Indian Creek.*

"But now I see all of it," he said, "Not just mine, not yours and mine and Jem's and Katy's, but I see it belongs to more than us."

"'The earth is the Lord's and the fullness thereof,'" she said low. "I mind how Granny used to say that."

"Yes, I know now He put us on it to live upright before Him. Or try to." Again he was silent awhile.

"Margaret, you know I'm not a pious man, but I do know there's no way you can live on this earth," his voice gained force, "without pain or at least the risk of it. I learned that a long time ago. A good man tried hard to teach me. You know him." She nodded. It was James Fraser he meant. He said, "It's a price we pay, all of us, one time or other. Time and again it comes due to pay. Most times we got no choice, but sometimes . . ." He sighed. "Time and again it'll come, the easy path and the rough one. Or maybe both look rough, but one's a little easier and when I've tried it, it's come to be hardest. It's apt to go down and get you in a thicket, and if you don't watch out, you almost can't get free. I've done it more than once. You know that."

"Ah!" she said fiercely, "you always found the way, the right one! It's just that you don't dash in and maybe do all manner of harm the way I do and then regret it!"

"Meggie, Meggie," he laughed softly. "Now you know better than that."

He stroked her rough hair, thought, *How could you have lived without her? . . . Even though a time or two you've knocked your head to think how you could go on with her*. He moved back to see her face, wanting to remember this look now above all her looks.

"Well," he resumed, "what I want you to understand—and see the little chaps understand it too as need comes—I do not go because they take our corn and cattle. Either side would do that. I do not go because of what I believe about the King or Parliament—or Congress either for that matter. The less I have to do with any of 'em the better. What it's finally come down to is, I've always walked free in this country or tried to, and I must do my part so we can keep on doing it. I'm sorry I've been slow to see it."

She did not answer a word but put both arms around him and held him as hard as she could.

"Ah, Meggie, you'll be squeezing the life out of me."

"Pshaw! Quit talking like an Irishman!"

"Who's made me one?"

After a while she murmured, "Now ha' you really walked so free as all that? These last few years, I mean?"

"As free as I wished to."

Jemmy had asked his father where the war was that he was going to.

"Other side of Enoree and Tyger, Son, and maybe up beyond Pacolet too, northward. Maybe in North Carolina by now."

They'd got beat awhile back, his father said, and he had to go help out.

"Will it be the ones that came and took our corn and everything?"

"Maybe. Maybe some of 'em. But it's men from across the water mainly. They're the ones in behind it all."

"Then they're the wicked villains!"

"They do what others tell 'em to, Jemmy. Maybe they wouldn't be so wicked if left to themselves."

"You have to go stop the ones that tell the others what to do."

"We have to try. I'll do my best."

"They won't tell me what to do! If they come here again and tell me, I won't do it!"

"You'll mind your Mammy and do what she says."

Jemmy knew his father had gone off to fight before, but he barely remembered it. His mother said he'd fought the redskins. Now it was Britishers and the scurvy Tories. And that strutting coxcomb, Patrick Ferguson, she said.

Jemmy accepted his father's leaving as he'd accepted his absences for hunting and trading; yet he knew this absence was different, for they too were leaving home. He looked forward to being with young Aleck and William and Sarah and the rest of them. He looked forward to being with so many children. If only his father's absence weren't part of it. He'd seen his mother once with a staring look on her face as she stood in the yard. He came up to her, wondering why she stood so still and what she was staring at. He said something but she didn't seem to hear or even see him. At last she answered sternly, "What, Jemmy?"

This time he knew his father was going into danger, knew that they all went into danger and change. He was not afraid of the danger, but he dreaded such looks as he'd seen on his mother's face that day.

Katy did not know what their leaving meant. She held up her arms to her Daddy, smiling a little, for she almost always woke happily, felt herself picked up and carried outside, still in her nightgown. Her Daddy's horse stood saddled and tethered to the post by the steps.

Katy felt his wordless, convulsive hug and kiss before being handed to her mother.

"Jemmy, take good care of Katy. And mind your Mammy and Mistress Mary."

Mammy set her on the ground but held on to her hand. Daddy got on his horse and rode off. Katy watched his back above the horse's moving haunches.

Mammy still stood there holding her hand so tight Katy began to pull on it. "Mammy, I'm hungry," she murmured, but Mammy didn't answer. Finally with the silence and hurt to her hand and the damp and gray and no breakfast yet, Katy's mouth primped and her eyes filled. Jemmy turned and went stamping up the steps, but Mammy stood still there till Katy began to whimper.

Rudi did not look back. As long as they could see him, he rode his accustomed way, but once he was in the woods, he turned off the creek road and struck up the ridge on a path of his own. Because he was traveling by day, he would not risk going by roads and beaten paths, although it really did not much matter. Like a gray fox he would know how to pass unseen.

The acorn crop was already falling. Nut-fall would start soon, and it looked to be a heavy one, he thought. The big green hickory balls weighed down the lower branches so as almost to brush his hat.

Hunting season would soon be here. The fall hunt. His mouth thinned into a bitter line, a look no one had seen on his face for a long time.

24

It was not named for one of the Georges but for a man named King, who lived at the foot of it, King's Mountain, a long narrow monadnock extending southeast across the North and South Carolina line. Patrick Ferguson, camped on the southern end, thought his site so well taken that he said even God Almighty could not dislodge him. Strange blindness of Ferguson.

Well, the Reverend Samuel Doak, who had prayed over the "mongrels" and "backwater men" gathered at Sycamore Shoals on the Watauga twelve days earlier, had told them to take as their battle cry "The Sword of the Lord and of Gideon!" This they did and also the same wild Cherokee scream the Tories had heard at Musgrove's Mill so that a Tory captain remarked as the battle began, "These things are ominous. These are the damned yelling boys!"

Ferguson never fought more bravely than on the mountaintop. He was cut down by six or eight bullets as he attempted a last desperate charge through the tightening ring of Virginians, Carolinians, and overmountain men. The "mongrels" had retreated down the mountain from his bayonet charges once, twice, three times, yet never very far and always, when the charge receded, to dodge from tree to rock uphill again and to make sure their enemies who reached the top were fewer than those who had descended. Within this narrowing encirclement the Scotsman met his doom.

So did some two hundred and forty of the nine hundred loyal Americans who followed him, either killed or wounded, almost a hundred shot after they surrendered. The Whig password that day was "Buford" in memory of "Tarleton's quarter" at the Waxhaws. Ferguson's body was divested of valuables and wrapped in a raw beef's hide to be buried down the slope, his grave eventually marked by a rock cairn. Other bodies were buried in shallow pits which wolves later dug up.

The partisans, with a red-headed commander-in-chief named Campbell, paid a lesser price. Of their nine hundred and forty, twenty-eight were killed and sixty-two wounded. Among the dead was that devious Presbyterian elder, James Williams, who had schemed in vain to lure these Whig forces to his own Ninety Six neighborhood. By his death he erased perhaps some of the anger and disgust he had aroused among other South Carolina officers. At the end he fought for the mountaintop as bravely as anyone else, and his mortal wounding was mourned by many if not all. So was the death of young Major William Chronicle, who fought under the old German, Colonel Frederick Hambright, with the North Carolina Lincoln and Gilbert Town men. These were the volunteers from just over the line that Rudi Näffels had joined.

On the day after the battle, the evening of October 8, Rudi and Joggi Lienhardt sat side by side devouring beef and sweet potatoes, the first food they had tasted in two days. Both were red-eyed from lack of sleep and still grime-faced. Although they had lain down a few hours the night before, the continuous cries of wounded and dying men had haunted even the sleep of exhaustion. Nor would the raging in Joggi's blood be stilled. Today the deeps of his eyes still smouldered. He ate ravenously, barely tasting what went into his mouth.

Rudi ate more slowly. He almost said, "Mind how you gorge yourself," but caught himself in time.

"You plan to keep on with these North Carolina boys?" Rudi asked.

"I don't know. How about you?"

"I don't know yet either."

"Brandon's South Carolina. So's Hammond. But with old Williams gone, I don't know what they'll do." Williams had died of wounds that afternoon.

Joggi had already told Rudi how he'd followed the South Carolinians to Hillsboro, North Carolina, Williams having been commissioned to report the Musgrove Mill victory to Governor Rutledge in exile. Joggi and a few others had remained with Williams, Brandon, and Hammond as they beat about the country recruiting in North Carolina, also in their altercations with Sumter's officers. More than once Joggi almost left them. "I'd just about decided to try to join under Sumter, but when I heard how they'd got whipped and scattered in the Waxhaws, I decided I'd stay with the ones I knew. I'm glad now I did. Though I've sometimes thought I'd have done better to keep with the Georgians."

"Not if you'd been with those at Augusta you wouldn't have," said Rudi. Whig prisoners at Augusta had been turned over to the Cherokees.

"I wouldn't have been caught."

Rudi glanced at the thin face. "Better mind such talk as that."

Joggi did not answer but he reiterated to himself, I wouldn't have been caught again. It was as if by his own determination he knew himself under a fixed decree.

"So you're now a sergeant. Sergeant Lienhardt."

"If I were English or Irish I'd be now a captain. Or at least a lieutenant. Not that I care for such."

"Old Colonel Hambright, he's German."

"I'm Swiss," said Joggi, "not German."

Rudi shot him a glance of amusement. "I thought you were American."

For a moment the charm of an old Joggi smile lifted the corners of his mouth; then his face settled again into its somber cast. "What's 'American'?" The other day it had been white paper in their hats as opposed to pine tufts.

"Them." Rudi gestured toward the overmountain men who lay reclining around fence-rail fires, "and them," gesturing toward those from the Waxhaws, the North Carolina foothills, and the valleys of Virginia. "I'd say they're American."

"How about you?"

Rudi did not answer at once. "Yes, I'm American. Though maybe not like some."

"The tree bark was scaled off pretty clean all around where I first saw you. You were on that mountaintop quick as anybody."

"Yes, and I stopped shooting quicker too."

Joggi looked away.

Rudi said no more. He had not joined those who kept on killing men after the show of white flags. He thought Joggi might have been.

"Aye-God," Rudi said heavily, "I don't relish this work anymore."

After a while Joggi asked distantly, "Why did you come?"

Rudi thought the question not worth answering. He groaned, "I never thought I'd find the ground so cold and hard."

"When's your guard duty?"

"Not till morning, thank God."

"Well, mine comes before that." Joggi rose in one upward flowing movement.

"Joggi," said Rudi, "here's a thought for you. When all this is over, get you a good wife. That's sound advice from an old American."

"So you *are* one of the blue hen's chickens."

"No, just an old knocker that's maybe known it rougher at times than you have."

Joggi hesitated as if he wanted to say something, then merged into the shadows and was indistinguishable from the ragged figures around him.

That supper was the last they would have for some time. The country through which they were passing was thinly settled, and the armies of both sides had recently marched and countermarched through it. They sent out foragers to take from Whig and Tory alike, but barns and cornpatches were few and far between, often already stripped, and most of the remaining cattle were well hidden. About all to be had now was pumpkins.

They moved northeast toward Gilbert Town, marched into the dusk to put as much ground between themselves and pursuit as possible. Every so often the name of Tarleton would be rumored through the camp. Wounded companions, borne carefully away on horse litters through country too rough for wagons, must now be left with whatever friends they could find along the way. Soon it grew apparent that some of the unwounded were departing also. Colonel Campbell issued stern orders to counteract straggling and desertion.

The prisoners were made to carry two guns with flints removed, but their number too, imperceptibly, gradually diminished. Backcountry Loyalists were as well able to contrive escape as Rebels were. Five brothers who took turns carrying a sixth because he was ill, managed to lag far enough behind in the dark so as to disappear in the waters of a stream they were fording. Another prisoner was not so lucky. Darting into a hollow sycamore tree by the wayside, he was seen by Colonel Thomas Brandon, who dragged him out and hacked him to death with his sword. At Gilbert Town the prisoners were confined in the same pen Ferguson had used for Whigs. Raw pumpkins and unshucked corn ears were thrown to them as if to hogs.

Beyond Gilbert Town the ridges stretched long above wooded valleys. Rain succeeded frost and October leaves hung sodden or were ground underfoot.

Rudi knew this country well. He had hunted it many a fall and spring in years gone by. Sometimes he rode beside Joggi, for the men were not strictly marshaled in their companies. He remembered the first time he'd seen the dark-haired little scrap on his mother's breast in a large, peace-filled room. Then he would think of his own son, his own babies and would try to hold them close-cradled in his thought.

The cousins found frequent opportunities for talk. They spoke of Heiri and Willi.

"Young John Thomas went over to Sumter right after that first skirmish at the Cedar Springs in July," said Rudi. "I don't doubt they stayed with him.

Heiri and Willi in those summer woods? It was a revelation. And to think when he'd been at the Catawba with Clarke's Georgians, he might have been near them! Joggi was gripped by excitement, though at the same time by a sense of loss. "If I'd just known, if I'd just tried— How'd they look, Rudi, when you saw them? Were they in health?"

"Willi was getting over a bad sprain. Got thrown in a freshet. Other than that, considering they'd been a week in the woods, they looked all right. Maybe not quite so heavy as when they started out."

"What were they riding? What did they carry?"

Rudi told him.

"And they got through all that country with nobody laying a hand on 'em?"

"Oh, I think a time or two somebody tried, but they got away."

Did better than I did, thought Joggi. *They got joined to a troop while I was still in jail.*

If I'd just known when I was in the Waxhaws, he thought feverishly. *Known what? What would you have said or done? Congratulated them for being braver than you thought they were?* Joggi felt a strange stirring in him. *Willi that I've known all my life and Heiri, my own brother!* Something opened in Joggi, a hunger he had never experienced—to be with own kind and ride beside them to whatever would come. Better even than being with Rudi, he thought, though Rudi's companionship had brought an astonishing release of words.

He glanced at the older man. Grizzled and heavy; deep-lined face. Rudi must be close to forty, almost as old as Papa.

Mama and Papa. They were far and small, infinitely removed. . . . But Heiri and Willi, they'd be grimed and shelterless like he was. *If I could just get to them*—the thought struggled—*maybe I'd get—get back to—*.

But it was almost four months since Rudi had seen Heiri and Willi. So much had happened since then, so many mischances, that terrible beating above Camden. One or both could be penned up now in some stockade, sick or hurt. Or worse. Best not think of it. Yet from then on Joggi's thought sometimes drifted southeast.

Another time he wondered aloud, "Reckon old Cornwallis is still in Charlotte?"

"If he is and if he's got word what we did, I doubt he's sitting there so easy as he was."

"Wonder who he's sent out after us."

Rudi shook his head.

"That damned Benny Tarleton, I'll be bound," said Joggi morosely.

"Well, maybe one day we'll catch him too."

"I don't know as I want to. Too much like getting hold of the devil himself."

"What? I didn't think you'd mind that."

"If you'd ever had his damned greencoats come slamming down on you, you'd mind it. Don't tell me you never been scared, Rudi."

"Oh no, not me," Rudi grinned.

Every evening they talked. Joggi still had much to tell. Although they spoke German at first, almost without thought they slipped into English, for it had become their daily speech; indeed, it had been so for Rudi since his marriage.

"I hear Hammond may soon turn back with Lacey's men," said Joggi. "If they do, I'm going with them."

"They tell me Daniel Morgan's come down to Hillsboro. Now there's a man I'd follow anywhere."

"Have you ever seen him?"

"I think I did. He's from way back, even before my time. But he got his learning same place I did."

"Where's that?"

"In the back parts of this country. Though not to compare myself with him."

"Wasn't he at Saratoga? Like Gates?"

"He's no Gates. He's one of us."

"But he's regular army. You'd have to enlist to serve under him."

"Yes, and if I can get to where he is, I may do it."

Joggi was surprised. He had not realized Rudi's commitment was so strong. He thought of enlisting again himself. . . . But no, this way was best. This way you had better chances and more freedom to choose your way. If he'd been with the Regulars, he'd have missed King's Mountain. This way you could fade and strike again, even if you got beat, and everything not be all over and done with the way it had been at Charlestown and Camden. This way it went on and on.

Nevertheless, he sighed. "Rudi, you said one time, 'when it's all over.' Sometimes I can't think of it ever being over."

"Oh yes, Joggi, it'll be over. For all of us. One way or another."

The phrase echoed in Joggi's mind. *Oh yes, one way or another.*

The next night it was over for nine Tories. One after another they were swung off the limbs of a great oak tree in the glare of pineknot torches. The tenth man escaped when his young brother, under cover of an emotional leave-taking, managed to cut the cords on the condemned man's wrists and the two got away in the night.

Some thirty or more prisoners had been tried and sentenced to hang that day as thieves, housebreakers, and murderers, although if asked to consider carefully, most men, certainly his former neighbors, would have found it difficult to adjudge Colonel Ambrose Mills guilty of any crime other than being a Loyalist officer. But then what had been the crimes of the Whigs hanged at Camden? Or at Ninety Six a few days ago? Or the ones tortured and massacred at Augusta?

Yet that display of violent brotherly grief and the swift quickwitted rescue among the nine bodies hanging motionless in the lurid air, in some way it moved many men to say, "It's enough." Shelby intervened, "It's enough." The other officers concurred, and the rest of the condemned were pardoned.

In the middle of the night Joggi stole off alone and threw himself on the damp ground.

He tried to efface the picture of men standing firm on the earth, straight and soldierly, breathing, noosed and tied; then jerked up from the ground, suddenly every last kick and quiver stilled, their shapes hanging long and dark, neither of earth or sky.

Who were they? Where were they? How could men so full of thought and feeling suddenly not be? Many and many a time he'd seen men die, and some he'd put on the ground himself, but seldom had he let himself ask, much less try to answer such questions. He's gone to heaven. He's with a merciful God. Or, he's on his way to hell, God damn his soul.

Sometimes at night Joggi thought of crawling off into some hidden place like the woods-room he'd found as a boy in the Congaree Swamp, a room completely walled in and roofed by smilax and dogwood leaves. There he would lie until he became part of earth itself, earth's creatures passing over and through him. There with the smell of earth, all human scent gone and only rocks and the dripping trees and rain, his bones bared.

He wished to hell somebody would cut down the bodies and bury them or at least let them fall to the ground. But he knew they would not. They'd ride off tomorrow and leave the nine long shapes suspended between earth and sky.

It poured rain again next day as they hurried toward the upper Catawba, which they forded breast deep. They had only corn ears to eat, sometimes roasted, more often not. At Quaker Meadows, the home of General Joseph McDowell, they were better provisioned and invited to make free of his fence rails for firewood, but it was slow work to make even such seasoned wood burn in the damp and wet.

At last with rivers in full spate below them, they began to feel safe. Now by common consent Sevier and his men, also Shelby's, took their leave for the journey home through the mountains. Lacey's men also returned to South Carolina to try to unite with Sumter and those who had gathered again to him. Joggi Lienhardt went with them.

Rudi kept on with the Virginians. Others from the various commands who hoped to serve under Morgan did too. There were now only a few more troops than prisoners, even though many prisoners had escaped along the way, a hundred during one wet evening's march alone. Any man caught was killed immediately. Nevertheless, quite a few prisoners were paroled, and many enlisted then or later to serve with the Whigs.

The last week of October, Campbell, Cleveland, and Shelby, who had not gone home with his men, arrived at the Moravian settlements beyond the Yadkin and camped first near Salem, then near Bethabara. The Moravians were neutral. Also not having yet been visited by the military, they were well provisioned. Here the troops settled down with their prisoners.

Once Rudi had been to Salem and had never forgotten it. Never before or since had he heard such a power of music. He remembered also the ordered harmonies of the life there. At that time he had almost, just almost, decided to become part of it. And if he had, what would he have become, he wondered. A different man. Without Margaret.

. . . No, he and Margaret were meant for a different music. Who he was and who Margaret was, drawn together, made a harmony of their own. In spite of their sometimes seeming dissonance, they'd made a oneness. Their music was meant to be. At least he'd become enough of a Presbyterian now, he thought, to recognize that whatever was meant to be would be, and would be best. And whether he ever saw Margaret again or not, it was ultimately not in his hands but would ultimately be good, though maybe bitter indeed before that.

Nevertheless, the music he heard one Sabbath at Salem stirred him again as deeply as before, took him for a time into a world where he either woke or dreamed, he did not know which, into a different mode of being, and became a different man. This music affected him far more deeply than the sermon he listened to a week later on an open hilltop, even though that discourse was full of strong theology and good Republican principles.

Yet he recognized that right theology was more apt to serve him now than was music. "The sword of the Lord and of Gideon!" Was it truly the sword of the Lord? Well, it had certainly brought down some Midianites. On the whole he thought it probably was. The Lord would not allow arrogance to go unpunished. *Or cruelty either,* he thought tiredly.

25

In spite of two major victories in South Carolina—Charlestown and Camden—the British kept losing men. In the last six months of 1780, they lost almost twenty-five hundred killed, wounded, or captured in smaller battles and skirmishes, while the American partisans lost only about eight hundred. The British held towns and forts, but they could not control the countryside. In the low country a dark little Huguenot named Francis Marion was so wily in his raids and evasions that even Tarleton finally gave up chasing him, saying the devil himself couldn't catch the damned old fox.

Cornwallis, who had marched to Charlotte in anticipation of his North Carolina invasion, was obliged to return to South Carolina. In late October he moved sixty-five miles south to the village of Winnsborough, where he camped at Mount Zion Academy. Meanwhile, Sumter, the Game-cock, kept flying back at his antagonists.

Again men rallied to Thomas Sumter. With the news of King's Mountain, their number multiplied. Again, however, Sumter let himself be attacked resting in camp, but this time the outposts were vigilant, and the attackers bungled. Sumter, who was caught in his tent, fought off his assailants and ducked under a tent flap to spend the rest of the night shivering under a riverbank. In a chill predawn hour he caught a stray horse and clung to its warm neck and sides, thus saving his life, he said. Even his own men did not realize until daybreak that they had driven off the enemy with little loss to themselves and more to their opponents, for in the confused dark some of the partisans scattered as usual. This skirmish occurred November 9, east of Broad River at Fishdam Ford.

The next day Sumter crossed the river and moved southwest toward the Enoree. He continued to be joined by volunteers, including a troop of Georgians, until his force again numbered about a thousand men. As soon as Cornwallis heard about Fishdam Ford, he sent Tarleton in haste across the Broad River.

The men who had been at King's Mountain had come into Sumter's camp while it was still east of the Broad. At first Sergeant Lennard could find no one who remembered the particular Harry and Willie he kept asking about, much less knew what happened to them. Some rosters of former commands were incomplete or unavailable at this time and place, nor were there official lists of casualties and prisoners from all the battles and skirmishes. At length Joggi found a man in Captain William Goodwyn's company who said, yes, he remembered Willie Rieder, though he was in another company, and he thought their officers had been killed or captured. Willie was a quiet little Dutchman, but he hadn't been seen since Fishing Creek. Could ha' been caught or killed there. So many were.

How about another Dutch boy with him? "My brother."

"Ne'er other one with Willie that I recollect. There was two, three other Dutch boys in our company Willie had acquaintance with." The man gazed intently at his questioner, whose eyes looked out from blackened hollows, his mouth bracketed with deep-cut lines. "But I don't recollect one of your favor."

"He wouldn't look like me. He'd be sandy-haired. Heavier than me."

The man shook his head.

"He wouldn't speak much English. Came in with them under Colonel John Thomas," urged Joggi.

The man answered gloomily that too many boys had come and gone. Who could know where they'd all be now? Or where they lay.

Sumter was west of the Broad moving toward the Enoree when Sergeant Lennard's patrol met up with another small party riding south from the Tyger. Challenged, the group said they were Liberty Men from the upper Fairforest region who were on their way to Sumter. They were a man in his forties, two men in their twenties, and a boy of sixteen. One of them had already served under Sumter, but the older man was spokesman. When they'd heard what happened to old Ferguson, he said, they'd determined to come out again. "Jem here, he said he'd undertake to bring us down, so we come on."

The four accompanied the patrol back to camp, positioned in the center and kept in view. It was a pretended Whig who had led the way into Sumter's tent that night at Fishdam Ford. In camp, however, the newcomers were vouched for by Major McJunkin.

That afternoon Sergeant Lennard spoke with one of them as he tended his horse. "Your mount looks like he's seen considerable service."

"Aye, that he has, poor old bonebag."

"You tend him good."

"Best I can."

Joggi rested his hand lightly on the horse's rough brown shoulder, reached and drew his hand lightly down the neck, felt it shiver. The horse had no blaze marks. Every rib showed. Yet there was something about the shape of the head and the way he lifted his white-stockinged hind feet that caught Joggi's attention. "Had him long?"

"About six weeks."

Joggi stood silent.

The man was examining the hoofs for stones or anything else lodged in them. He said, "Come across him loose in the woods."

"So you took him up. I've done that."

"I needed him. I might ha' found a more handsome brute, but I knew this one's master and I knew he was a good horse."

Joggi felt his skin tighten. He asked low, "Who was his master? What happened to him?"

The man straightened up and glanced at the lean unsmiling face.

"The one that had him, can you tell me his name?" The question came harsh and impatient.

"What for, Sergeant? Excuse me asking."

"I'm trying to get word of—my brother. This horse—he looks like one my father once had."

"How did he name him?"

"We called him 'Roker.' We're Swiss," Joggi said as if explaining the name, although it did not, for one of the little girls—Babeli, he thought—had fastened the name on the bay colt out of her head.

The man's startled look changed to a wide grin, but it vanished quickly as he turned away. He caught the bridle reins up close and said, "Old Roker! Hear that? Beats all I ever heard! Roker! Damnedest name for a horse I ever heard. Well, Sergeant," he said over his shoulder, "I guess he's yours."

"No, but you tell me about the man that had him!"

"This was Harry's horse, Harry Lennard's."

"Was?"

"No, I shouldn't ha' put it that way. Harry got caught and marched off with two-three hundred others that day Benny-Bedamned surprised us all between the river and Fishing Creek."

"You saw him a prisoner—Heiri Lienhardt?"

The man nodded. "I saw him. And a God's mercy it was I wa'n't with 'em. I would ha' been too if I hadn't ha' tripped and fell down a gulley. How I was missed in all that beating over the ground I'll never know. But you can believe how low I lay."

"How come you to know what happened to my brother?"

"Because when I could tell by sounds they were leaving, I crept up and spied what they'd done. Though at the time I wished I hadn't."

"You saw Heiri Lienhardt amongst 'em?"

"I saw him. Saw him stagger off bloody-headed and all, poor devil. And sorry I am to have to tell you."

"Was he bad hurt?"

The man drew a deep sigh. "I'd say so. Looked like he'd been trompled and slashed both. You know how they deal, sons of hell that—" He began to curse, but when he saw how gray-faced the other man was, he let his words die, and their violence dissipated across the back of the old bay horse snatching at a few tough blades of grass.

He said, "Look here, I'm Jem Boyd. I'd like you to know I thought a lot of Harry. A more generous-hearted, obliging boy I never saw and one that would do his part in any scrape or skirmish. If you're his brother, Sergeant, I'm proud to know you." Jem held out his hand.

Joggi took it and said his own name.

Jem was sallow and lean-faced like Joggi, not over tall. He too had dark, deep-set eyes, but they were quieter than Joggi's.

The two talked on. Jem led the horse into some dry cane by a little branch. Joggi asked more questions. Jem told what he remembered of Heiri from the time he first knew him at Cedar Springs.

"The other boys deviled him some at first, but when it come to a brush, I took note he'd be at your side. I never once knew him to run save as we all had need to."

Joggi felt a hard swelling in his throat. He asked about Willi Rieder.

Jem remembered less of Willi. "But come to think of it now, it was him helping poor Harry away that day. Yes, I recollect, it was him that was marching alongside your brother and helping him on."

So Willi too was a prisoner. Joggi took a little comfort in that knowledge for Heiri's sake.

Suddenly he was conscious of pride. Never in his life had he felt such a sense of brotherly pride, yet at the same time a hollow fear.

Perhaps Jem saw it. "Now you sure you don't want to take old Roker? Him being your Daddy's horse and all? I don't doubt but I'll make out to find one somewhere else."

"No, you keep him now. Maybe later on— I'm obliged to you more than I can say."

"Well now, you must cheer up, Sergeant! Look at it this way. It was one chance in a thousand you'd come across his horse like this—the one horse in a thousand—or no, say one in ten thousand, and the man riding him be one could tell you news of your brother. Now that's a wonder I'd say. It's a thing to tell!"

Strange indeed. Joggi felt something loosen and his spirit lighten a little as he looked into the earnest face of Jem Boyd.

He went up to Roker, took the bridle reins and lifted the horse's head to the level of his own, tried to look into the big eyes, but the horse thrust his head against Joggi's shoulder. "Roker boy. Oh Roker boy, you remember me?" Joggi spoke softly in German.

Roker stood very still. He made no other response as Joggie kept on talking to him in German, but he did not toss his head or try to pull away either.

"He knows you!" said Jem. "Be sure he knows you!"

They crossed the Enoree, crossed Indian Creek, set their faces toward Ninety Six and the late James Williams' plantation, which was reported to be a weak British outpost.

On the way Sergeant Lennard led his patrol along a certain path he knew above Indian Creek. They passed several farmsteads, where the fields were ragged and brown, the old cornstalks stripped and knocked over every which way. They saw few signs of life about the houseplaces. One had only bare burnt chimneys left.

On up the creek the path narrowed, overgrown with bushes, but when they emerged into a clearing which was part of what some still called the old Allen place, it was evident that others had used the path recently. The blackened shade trees in the distance told why. Even the outbuildings were gone. Yet down a derelict field in front of where the house once stood, a double row of cedars still marched strong and green.

The soldiers scarcely paused. They followed the path on up the creek, past an old blackberry field and into deeper woods where at last the path merged with a wider one.

At this time the men did not know, Sumter did not know, that Tarleton was coming up fast behind them. Two days later, November 20, they did.

It was already too late that afternoon for Mrs. Blackstock to rush out and say she would allow no fighting on her premises, even if she did have a patriot husband serving with other troops up the country. The riflemen were already deploying behind the stout rail fence along the lane, and Hampton's sharpshooters were moving into the strong log outbuildings about her house. Twigg's Georgians were marching down the pasture to wait this side the branch, and the rest of the troops—Lacey's, Hill's, McCall's, Bratton's, Taylor's, and Winn's—were being drawn up along the wooded hillside that flanked the lane. The partisans occupied a high place backed up against the Tyger River. They were brought to bay before they could cross it and melt away; yet even so, the place was one of Sumter's choosing.

Once Sumter had learned of the pursuit and reversed his course, Tarleton with all his infantry and artillery had not been able to catch the Gamecock. Only cavalry could do that. Therefore Tarleton decided to forge ahead with only his Legion cavalry and the pick of his infantry mounted, the Sixty-Third Regiment. He would crash down upon the ragtag as he had so often before. What if they were a thousand to his two hundred and seventy? Such rabble had never been known to stand to a cavalry or bayonet charge. Oh, he'd hold the creatures pinned till the rest of his force came up; then he'd destroy them. Only now it looked as if the Gamecock would flash his spurs at once. Good enough. Let him.

What was it determined a man's allegiance or disaffection? Both sides had deserters. The night before, one of the Sixty-Third Regiment had slipped away and warned Sumter of Tarleton's approach; thus Sumter's rapid retreat. That afternoon a woman who had watched the dragoons gallop by cut through the woods to bring the news that Tarleton had left his artillery and the main body of his troops and was coming up fast with only two hundred and seventy men.

In the cloudy late afternoon, the two hundred and seventy green coats and red coats were bright in the dun November woods. They pressed close on Sumter's rear guard, on Thomas Taylor's wagons that were hurrying up with captured foodstuffs from down in the German settlements.

Now the green and red halted by the creek that edged Blackstock's pasture. The infantry was ordered to dismount, the dragoons to stand. They saw the Georgians waiting, and as they gazed, they saw some four hundred more militia come hurrying down the pasture.

Major Money raised his sword. The red-coated Regulars charged at a brisk trot across the branch and up the hill with bayonets leveled. The militia fired, but their fire was too soon and ineffective. Before the militia could finish reloading, they seemed to feel bayonets almost at their rib cages. They whirled and ran. It was the old story.

The shouting British charged up the pasture, chasing them. But they charged too far. They chased too close to the buildings.

Rifles thrust between the logs took aim. Sharp eyes searched for epaulets. Major Money fell and two lieutenants, and many a bright coat crumpled, some on the other side of the house still chasing militiamen. The fire from between the logs was effective.

Down the slope at the foot of the lane the Legion watched. Above them to their left, dun-colored men eased down through the ragged trees, moved down upon the flanks of green jackets, sabers, and chargers. Joggi Lienhardt brushed and ducked under bare-leafed vines, their grapes all gone to possums and foxes now, their frail leaves crumbled by frosts and pounding rains. His eyes were intent on the bright fruit below.

Fifty yards. The vintage of cracking rifles was twenty dragoons brought down.

Tarleton shouted and flashed his sword, and his Legion charged uphill, up the lane where other dun coats waited, positioned front and side.

But this time the rabble were hard to get at behind strong fence rails, bushes, and tree trunks. It was risky business for dragoons. From above them the bullets whistled. Above them eyes burned and blood sang to see the bright forms topple and the horses stumble, the dismounted struggle back down the lane, now clogged with their dead companions and screaming, thrashing horses.

Load and shoot, load and shoot. Joggi Lienhardt slid out from cover, his eyes afire to burn into the struggling mass and discern the man who had once tried to ride him down, the one who had trampled Heiri.

Banastre Tarleton called retreat.

But he had his own loyalty, for he dismounted in a rain of fire to pick up the dying Major Money.

Toward the close of the battle Thomas Sumter, as careless of his own safety as Tarleton had been, was shot in the shoulder. Later Tarleton would write to Cornwallis that Sumter was said to be dead, and Tarleton and Cornwallis would rejoice to be rid of, they said, one of the greatest plagues in the country.

Tarleton reported a victory because next morning he was able to move up and occupy the ground at Blackstock's. The rebels had slipped across the river in the night, leaving their campfires burning as a ruse. The British troops had lost ninety-two killed and a hundred wounded. The cowardly rebel militia lost three killed and four wounded.

Across the Tyger the various commands under Sumter dispersed for the time being. They lacked the ammunition or the artillery for another engagement. Tarleton pursued them to the Pacolet River, then turned back.

26

On Savana Hunt they heard little of the war after the news of the American defeat at Camden. Their days were spent in hard labor, struggling for food and warmth: for Johannes and the boys digging, hewing, dragging, and hauling; for Madle and the girls the unending toil of gathering and preserving food and sewing quilts and clothes. Johannes built a new smokehouse far up the creek and a rough little barn for the remains of his crop. The younger children scoured the woods for every kind of fruit and nut—for gooseberries, elderberries, muscadines, haws, crabapples, and persimmons; for walnuts and hickory nuts to grind and use for pudding. Madle, Cathri, and Anneli spent every spare daylight hour huddled over sewing on the porch until cold weather drove them indoors. Then they would sit by an open window until raw air chilled them to the bone.

Madle tried to use prudently the lace that had been saved. She humbled herself and went to see old Frau Gallman, but she would not accept as a gift the needles, scissors, and thread Frau Gallman offered her, would take them only in exchange for lace. The older woman exclaimed, "Ah, it's Appenzell! It's been years since I've seen Appenzell lace."

"Not Appenzell," Madle said proudly. "St. Gallen."

She debated between selling her tablecloth or cutting it up for garments. In the end she traded it for a bolt of quilting cloth. She thanked God every day for the new cloth Cathri had saved.

Johannes would not risk taking their scant store of corn to the mill; they ground it daily in a homemade mortar. One morning in September he found a large sack of cornmeal hanging on the front gatepost. Two weeks later Anneli spied a keg of wheat flour just inside the gate. They never knew who had brought either gift. Hans Jacob said he knew nothing about it when Johannes questioned him. They went to bed early—hard work made them sleep sound and they had no dog to give alarm. Madle thought the gifts came from Frau Gallman.

In mid-September Hans Jacob came to tell them he'd been to Camden but could learn nothing of Willi or Heiri. He'd spent two days inquiring not only of officials but of everyone else who came and went, especially of the women who were allowed to speak with the men in the stockade. He said he'd inquired for both Lienhardt boys. "So maybe they got back safe to North Carolina."

"If they were even in that battle. We don't even know they were in it."

"Aagh! If I'd just known whose company they were in!"

Johannes let his mind range blindly over ridges to the northwest.

"They ought to have sent us word!" Hans Jacob said angrily. "Willi can write! What does he think I sent him to school for? Surely he could find some way to send word!"

"Has anybody come from up that way?"

"Not that I know of." Hans Jacob's mouth hardened. "But I got another word last week. My oldest boy's turned Tory."

"What, George?"

"Yes, George." Married five years ago, George Rieder owned large acreage beyond the forks of Broad and Saluda. "I named him right, didn't I?"

"What's that got to do with it?" Johannes said sharply. "I've got a George of my own."

"You can be glad he's under age. . . . No, I'm talking like a fool. And," Hans Jacob said heavily, "he may be the wiser of my sons."

Johannes did not speak his thought—pray God they never meet at opposite ends of a gun barrel. At least I'm spared that fear. So far. He thought of Conrad Meyer.

"How's your mother?"

Elsbeth was stronger but had not perfectly recovered speech. Maria was in health; so were the others. "Though they work hard enough, poor souls, these days."

"You do too, don't you?" Johannes ventured a half-smile.

Hans Jacob's mouth relaxed as he glanced down at himself. "You think it's good enough for me, don't you?"

"Maybe. The work itself won't hurt us. At least not you and me." Johannes hesitated. "How's Nissi?"

"Well enough. She'd have come with me, but Maria said she couldn't be spared."

Johannes thought of his last conversation with the girl, her look when he'd mentioned Joggi. Joggi had gone to see her in May, he remembered.

His compassion groped toward her. Cruel for her. He'd known that ache himself. Hard on the young, harder on them than us in many ways, he thought.

At that moment the men heard an eruption of shouts from the back of the house where the boys were cutting wood. Georgi came tearing around the corner laughing, pursued by Andreas. When he saw his father, he skidded to a stop and dodged back the way he had come.

Johannes raised his voice. "All right, you boys! You remember what I said!" But he chuckled low to Hans Jacob, "Well, at least mine still sometimes kick up their heels, for which I thank God though I can't let 'em know it."

"Reminds me I'd better get back and see what mine are up to."

The men stood at the front gate. When Hans Jacob had arrived, he had brought a bag of salt, and Madle and Johannes were distressed to have nothing to offer in return. But now Johannes thought of something. He said, "We haven't got a thing to put it in, but if you'll tell Maria to send some kind of jug or jar, we've got honeycomb to spare. If she'll send Nissi and someone with her, we have more than enough to spare. You tell her. Tell her to send Nissi."

"I will." Hans Jacob unlooped his horse's reins from the fence post. It would be a dire day when he walked instead of rode.

"We must let 'em be young while they can," said Johannes. "Or try to."

Hans Jacob seemed to understand him. "Aye-God, it's never easy. For them or us."

Johannes thought, *He's a father like me. Strange, I've known him for twenty years, and never saw him as that kind of father.* But Johannes thought of Simmi and his look grew sober.

Beneath the bright red dogwood berries in October, leaves turned rose between the veins. Wild cherry was salmon pink, but star-shaped sweetgum leaves still floated green. The turkey oak merely rusted.

All day a mockingbird sang from the ridgepole of the house or of the empty barn. Towhees, thrashers, and cardinals foraged in the weeds at the edge of the yard; and flocks of robins passed across wasted fields for a harvest of their own. Madle and the girls sat on the porch sewing until swifts and martins cut the evening air in wheeling flights.

They named their favorite birds.

"Which is yours, Mama?"

"Oh, I'll say the wren."

"Tell why."

"Oh—I like the way she builds her nest so close to us. She knows we won't harm her. Or 'they,' I should say. They both build it." In June, wrens had built in a gourd dipper hanging over the rain barrel, and Madle would allow no one to disturb them. "Then too they work so hard. And they're brave. So tiny and so brave. Now what's yours, Anneli?"

"Let Cathri say hers next."

"Well—" Cathri rested her work in her lap. "The redbird. I'll say the redbird."

"Why?" asked Anneli.

"He's bright. And the way he chirps and hops. And he's easy to see."

"Tell more," said Anneli.

"Well, he's red. I like him because he's red."

"The mama's not."

"Yes, but the mamas and papas are supposed to be different. Now you tell yours."

The little girl twisted her hands. Jays, no, and not mockingbirds. Sometimes they'd swoop down and peck you. She did not know the names of many birds. She thought of bluebirds that sometimes flashed in the orchard. Then she caught her breath at the thought of a bird she'd seen only once. "Oh, mine is yellow with black wings! Bright, bright yellow with black wings! I saw him once on a fencepost!"

"A goldfinch?" asked her mother. "It must have been a goldfinch."

"Tell why you like it," said Cathri.

"Because—because it was so yellow and—it was there just a minute, just a tiny, tiny minute, and I saw him!"

With a soft laugh Madle reached to hug the child to her. Small-boned and fragile as a bird herself, Madle thought with a pang of fear. Could she get this child through the winter? Her cheeks were too pale. Madle knew the little girl spent far too much time hunched over sewing; yet Anneli could push a needle in and out in a fairly straight line even if she wasn't quite six years old.

But we must have quilts for winter! Madle's fingers moved faster, then paused. "Anneli, I thought I heard a hen cackling. Go look for the egg. And while you're at it, walk outside the garden fence and see if you can find that guinea nest. Take your time now. Cathri and I, we'll work and not talk for a while."

Daylight hours were lessening. With wooden shutters pulled in and no candles, their only indoor light was from the fireplace. They had talked for years of glazing the windows, but Madle had never pushed the matter and now she blamed herself. She had not foreseen the day when they'd have no candles. Their beeswax was too precious for working candles, and they had other needs for tallow. The fireplace gave light for rough work only, like grinding corn or cracking and picking out nuts or getting the seeds out of cotton lint. The last task was Georgi's and he hated it. Andreas helped him in the evening, but Madle had not the heart to drive Hans to it.

She grieved for Hans. When Johannes spoke to him sharply, Hans never answered a word. Indeed, he said little to anyone. He was doing a man's work and sat bowed over the table at night as if too tired to eat. She never told him now to sit up straight. She grieved for the thinness in his shoulders. And in Andreas too. They were growing up too thin, not getting enough eggs and milk and butter. . . . But God be thanked for what they did have, she told herself. And Georgi and Cathri seemed sturdy enough, though Cathri too was slimmer. Once Madle noticed her smoothing her waist. Well, near sixteen was time for a slender waist. And other things.

Madle yearned toward her daughter. Cathri worked and thought ahead almost like a grown person. *Where now is my dreamy child?* Madle mourned.

It had begun to come to her that she seldom talked to her daughters in a leisured way. One daughter already gone and what had she ever gotten from her mother but lessons? What do they know of Madle Frillig? When I'm gone, what will they remember of me but how to make butter and roll out dough, or how to make shirts and petticoats?

As they sat sewing in hot September, in cooler October, little by little she spoke of the past as she had rarely done before. Oh, she'd told them stories and sung songs when they were little, but she'd left all talk of the old country to Johannes. Why? she asked herself. Because she feared the cost of bringing out memories?

On a fall afternoon she spoke of snow. "In midday it lights a whole room. It's a different kind of light, I wish I could describe it to you. It's not like ordinary daylight but it's like—a clearness that comes inside the house, even with the cold—all have glass windows there—and it makes the work seem light and easy in your hands. . . ."

"And if you go outside in the afternoon—it gets dark very early there—you look up the meadow and it's so smooth even to the woods . . .

the shadows are violet, then blue close up to the woods, and it makes—
a clearness in the world. Everything distant seems very near, every far
off rock so distinct and clear. . . . Though you mustn't stay out long. And
you're always glad to come inside."

"I bet it's freezng cold," Cathri said. "You'd have to wear plenty
of clothes."

"I remember when I was little it snowed," said Anneli.

"Last winter? Why, that was only a skim! The snow at Wildhaus
would be as thick and heavy as fifteen quilts and you'd never see the ground
from St. Martin's Day to Easter! Why, even in summer the tops of the
mountains were white, or at least the highest were. There'd always be
snow on the peaks." She saw the wash of white on juts of rock, immortal
shapes. "Now I'll tell you the names of some of them. . . ." And she named
the row of teeth to the south they called the Churfursten. She spoke of
Wildhuser Schafberg to the north. She had climbed its lower slopes, she
told them.

"You, Mama?"

"Oh yes." And over behind it, she said, was great Säntis, the highest in all that country. "It's really in Appenzell, Appenzell joins onto
Toggenburg, but Säntis belongs to Toggenburg too because everywhere
you go you see it. More than anything else it would always tell me I was
coming home to Wildhaus."

"Where would you come from, Mama?"

"Well, when I was little I lived also in Zurich." She paused. How
to explain that divided childhood? "Now Zurich is a city, a great city."

"Oh, tell about Zurich!" said Cathri.

"But first tell more about Wildhaus," said Anneli.

Madle fell silent. How to describe the green sweet reaches of
meadow and the distant music of bells, the rough snowmelt of Thur and
the dark spruce forest she'd sometimes feared?

"Wildhaus is a village, nothing like what we have here."

"Not like Granby?"

"Not in the least like Granby. The houses are not lined up like
boxes as they are in towns. Though Granby's not a town either, though it
likes to call itself one; that is, it's not like Charlestown."

"Oh Mama, you've been there too, haven't you?" Cathri's voice
rose in excitement. "And Papa's been to Charlestown!" And Joggi and
Willi, she remembered. "Oh Mama, do tell about when you were in
Charlestown!"

Tell of that February spring? Those crisp cruel days? Her face grew still. They glanced up at her.

"I'll tell you about another city, a city I lived in when I was a girl, though older than you are, Cathri. I'll tell you about Amsterdam."

And another day I'll try to tell again of Wildhaus, she thought. *Perhaps of the day I climbed to the summer pastures where Johannes and Matthys were. Who was Matthys?* they'd ask. *A boy with the loudest whistle of anyone I knew. And I loved him with all my heart and soul. Till this country devoured him.* . . . No, she would never tell them that.

"Now Holland is a country at the edge of the sea—"

"Oh, tell about the sea!"

"And do tell about the ship and being on it and coming to Charlestown!"

"One thing at a time, girls. I will now tell about Amsterdam."

Her talk moved in a clear, instructive way along the canals and streets and shops of a city. She named some of them, described how they were built, what goods were sold there—though she never spoke of her merchant father's house with its mahogany and Chinese porcelains. Her words were as orderly and precise as when she explained how a seam must curve to fit a shoulder. Yet at the edges or underneath her description, there sometimes sounded a different note as when she spoke of windmill sails or the masts of shipping or the great old church towers. Her daughters glanced up, searching her face. And it seemed that always at the edges of their mother's talk there was light and sky, always at the edges of it something she could not quite describe. Finally it came to Cathri that it had to do with light. Something moving in the light that enriched it beyond the light.

". . . and there were always birds in the trees along the canals singing." ". . . and on windy days you'd see gulls and other birds of the sea."

And Cathri heard beneath her mother's voice another's. Whose? Oh, incomprehensible!

The house shadow reached almost to the fence. Beyond it lay gray and tangled fields, flattened by frost, and beyond them low drab oak woods with leathery leaves. But here and there rose high green plumes of longleaf pine that years ago her father had spared from his building. They spoke to Cathri, they had always spoken to her, she thought, of what was beyond her sight. Lonely and far away.

Oh ever again? Ever? High rich air, rose-sprigged with beauty . . .

"In the springtime storks would come to nest in the chimneys, great white long-legged birds from far-off places. . . ."

Beyond the pines. . . . Far off and gone. Oh, ever, ever?

In November there were days of wind and rain, then cold. When it cleared, Hans Jacob Rieder brought another bag of salt and also news of the astonishing defeat of a thousand Loyalists and that British officer Ferguson up near the North Carolina line. "What I heard and, mind you, it was only third- or fourth-hand, was Ferguson's dead and every man of his force was killed or captured. Over a thousand killed or captured on top of that mountain!"

"On top a mountain!"

"Yes, one called King's Mountain—but it sounds like no king's mountain to me!"

They call them mountains here, Johannes thought, *but they're not like those I'll never see again.* Yet he felt a lift of spirit, and he tried to squeeze every drop of news he could from Hans Jacob. Who'd been in the battle? Where had they gone afterward?

Hans Jacob thought it was mostly Virginians. "But some of ours too, I believe. I told you it was third- or fourth-hand. But one thing I do believe and I tell you now: they're not lying down, our boys aren't. They're still in arms, hundreds of 'em."

"In this province?"

"Say 'State,' Johannes, say 'State!'" Hans Jacob spoke with energy. "In the State of South Carolina! Men from Georgia and North Carolina are banded with 'em, men from all parts!"

"Where?"

"Up the country and down the country. In the swamps and mountains both—or foothills, I should say—banded up everywhere. Except," he added sardonically, "right here."

"You know what, Hans Jacob?" Johannes' voice rose. "I wish I was twenty years younger!"

Hans Jacob darted him a quick look and beat his hat softly against his thigh. "Tell you something. Some folks I know better be careful before they discredit a Toggenburger."

"How about a Rheinthaler?"

"Now that's another story."

"Come on, wouldn't you? If chance offered? Say it came this way?"

Hans Jacob looked narrowly along the fence and past the leafless orchard. A smile crept about his mouth. He looked like his mother in one of her candid moments. "Give Willi the shock of his life. Not to mention George."

But as both men thought of their sons and their unknown whereabouts, their excitement dwindled.

"There's talk of building a fort at Granby," Hans Jacob said after a while.

"What for?"

Hans Jacob shrugged.

Johannes observed, "Well, maybe that says something too. If they've won the war, why now build a fort here?"

Hans Jacob shrugged again.

"It must be they expect something," said Johannes.

"Not from here, you can be sure. Still—" Hans Jacob gazed toward the empty woods; the lurking smile returned. "You could be right. It could be a whole new army making up, up there."

Along with the news and salt Hans Jacob also brought Nissi. She had wanted one of the children to accompany them, but her father said he would not go riding about the country with a parcel of whining young ones.

"Just Uli, Papa. He'll be no trouble."

Her father was adamant.

Well, perhaps Uli would whine but he was not a "parcel."

Why did she want him? he asked her.

She could not say. Maybe it was because she'd whipped him yesterday for almost no reason. But she thought it might be that she wanted him as a social diversion—or to distract her from her own intensity.

Why do I want so desperately to go to the Lienhardts'? she asked herself. Little of Joggi could she expect to find there; he'd been gone too long. But perhaps there'd be something he'd handled that would bring him before her. It was years and years since that day he had told her not to forget him.

As she had also commanded him. Now she knew her command had been vain, for she found herself forgetting him hours at a time, even an entire day. As when a day turned drearily sick and her arms ached with strain and her face settled into sullen anger. As when she carried out Elsbeth's slop pail or bent over a washtub and felt only the poison of her own resentment. Yet even worse was her sudden fear of never seeing him again.

Desperately she would try to rally her thought and senses. *As long as he breathes the air. . . . As long as I do not know he no longer breathes the air. . . .*

Sometimes she would go into the scuppernong arbor and look up through the mesh of leafless tendrils and vine at the empty sky. As she swept out the sodden leaves that had floated gold to the ground, she tried to see some expression of his face.

At Savana Hunt she made conversation with his mother. There was, as she'd expected, considerable distance between them. Frau Lienhardt did not look old or sound old, but she seemed to Nissi far removed in time. Like the strange little wooden angel her grandmother had brought from the old country—and who knew where it was now?

"No," Nissi answered the inquiries, "she tries very hard but she still has this constriction in her throat so she can't form her words very well. We understand some things but others we can't."

Cathri and Anneli sat silent, their eyes bent straining on their work in the dim chill room. Frau Lienhardt's look was grave.

Nissi spoke of her mother. They talked of Pastor Theus. He was well and all his family, the last they'd heard, up at Herr Adam Summer's.

As Nissi rose to go, Frau Lienhardt said, "Nissi, please give your dear grandmother my love. Tell her especially that Madle Lienhardt sends love. And Joggi too. Tell her these words for Joggi."

Nissi felt a breathless wheeling inside. She exclaimed, "Oh, have you heard from him? You know where he is? He's here?"

Madle stood quiet a moment. "No, I have not heard. But I know he loves your grandmother and she loves him."

Madle read the girl's face. Dispassionately her thought moved toward her. *So it has been given you too—that terrible gift. God help you.*

Nissi perceived no aura of kindliness in the small erect figure. She sensed none of the personal warmth she had felt in his father. As the blue eyes regarded her, Nissi thought, *How like, yet unlike they are to Joggi's eyes.* They were clear and deep with something unassailable. What knowledge, what place? Oh where, what is it? The place Joggi said he'd one day take her?

As she turned away, her glance took in the poor bare room. Starved and robbed. *Well, so am I.*

Will beauty ever return? Not to me, ever.

Why had he said, "Don't forget"?

His mother was saying, "Cathri, carry the honey jug and let your Papa fix it to the saddle or however it's to be carried. Wait a moment, Nissi. I have something for you." She hurried from the room.

Nissi waited in surprise. Frau Lienhardt returned with a small folded packet of cloth. "It's only enough for a handkerchief. Or perhaps one day the throat of a gown."

Nissi unfolded the cloth. She drew in her breath.

"My daughter, Cathri, saved it when all else was taken. It's only a small piece. I'd like you to have it."

"Frau Lienhardt, it's so beautiful!" Nissi gazed at the fragile fabric, richly worked.

"I myself made it when I was about your age, I suppose. When I was alone."

"Oh, would you teach me how to make lace like this?"

"I have never made lace in this country. There's been no time or need here, and I think I may have forgotten how." Then Madle said softly, "You must learn to make your own beauty."

Nissi did not know what to say, but Madle saw now that the girl's eyes had great power of speech. She held out her hand.

Nissi took the small sinewy work-hardened hand.

"You make your own beauty, Nissi. Learn to make it."

Again the two women looked at each other. Nissi's face lengthened, drawn and haggard. *How? When all I have is ugly, inside and out?*

"Don't forget now. Give your grandmother our love, Joggi's too. Don't forget."

As she rode home behind her father, Nissi kept thinking, *Give her Joggi's love. What an unexpected gift. A gift? To whom?*

Well, I'll do it. And she wondered if perhaps the very saying of his name to her grandmother might charm him again to her.

27

For the old woman—at sixty-three she both looked and felt old—misery came and went with the changes of weather. The cold got into her bones, heavy damp cold, and she would sit huddled before the hearth, rising only to stir the stew which the Dutch boys provided, for one of them could snare rabbits. They had stacked enough wood in the dogtrot so she could keep good fires now when rain hissed down the chimney. The boys were handy about the place, she must admit. They'd even rigged up shelter for her one old horse, for the barns and stables had been burned last summer. She herself had put out the fire at the house.

It was fury at not catching Edward at home that made the blackguards try to burn her out. And her own tongue. "Oh, you ha' murdered Michael and Andrew, to be sure, but I'm thinking you'll not be catching Edward yet awhile! Or not till he's paid you back, him and his friends, for your thieving and murders!"

Tom McNulty had knocked her down.

"Is it for the time I fed you, Tom? At my own table? Alongside my own boys?" She struggled to get up.

"It's for your foul rebel tongue, you damned old snaggletooth! And be glad it's not a bullet! Now where's Edward?"

She held herself up, panting. "If I knew, you think I'd tell such scum as you?"

For a moment she thought she'd said her last say. Another man cocked his pistol, "We're King's men, loyal and true!" but Tom, glowering, told him not to waste the bullet. Nor could they waste more time. When they dragged her out of the house to fire it, she found herself strengthless.

She still could not remember, did not understand how she'd managed to put out the fire. Beat it out with an old wet sack, she thought, as they rode off. She remembered crawling over the old step. Afterward she wondered if they'd really meant to burn it as they had the outbuildings.

But with most of her cattle slaughtered and provender stolen, it didn't matter much about barns and such. Her children were gone—daughters married and moved from the country, two of her sons in their graves; and in spite of her defiant words she was not sure Edward still lived. Until a day later when he came calling in the dark of night, naked as the day he was born, telling how he'd evaded Butcher Tarleton's dragoons at Fishing Creek. He'd been in the river and that was how he'd got away.

All next day Edward lay sweating behind an old chest pushed against the eaves in the loftroom while she broke God's Sabbath to sew him up a pair of breeches and a shirt from two of her petticoats. When he left that night, he took her last hidden firearm, though he had neither powder nor lead for it.

"It was Tom McNulty knocked your mammy down, you remember that! From the same pack that killed Michael and Andrew!" Those were her parting words. She said nothing of her fear of the months ahead, of the giddy spells she'd been having. She knew she no longer had strength to cut wood and haul it in, and how she could catch and butcher the couple of hogs left, much less the yearling, she did not know.

But the day after Edward left, the starving Dutch boys crawled up out of the pasture, one of them just about dead. She had to be convinced they were Whigs. She judged them not much in the way of soldiers, or at least not the one that did the talking, to go by his looks and his size, but she finally decided they were honest and she struck a bargain with them.

"I'll see what I can do. I'll tend him best I can, though I can't undertake to promise he'll live. But I'll do for you, if you'll stay and do for me. At least till after cold sets in. Or till my son comes back."

She fed them from her hidden store of salt pork and meal and poulticed the hurt one's wounds, first with warm wet ashes, then with slippery elm bark. As for his head wound, "A broke head heals best with little meddling. It'll have to heal of itself."

And it did. Though the sight in the boy's right eye was damaged and the side of his face would be permanently dented.

It had taken her a while to know what to make of the two. They could tell her no more of what happened at Fishing Creek than Edward had except for the account of their capture and escape. Well, their escape showed they did have some wits, even if they had let themselves get caught.

She thought the one called Harry was simple. He would try to smile at her every time she came near him and he always said "Thank you" with his thick tongue for whatever she did. He never jerked or yelled at her ministrations. She thought he must be like an animal, not feeling the pain—until one time she saw his expression when he didn't know she was by. Her words were never more than "Drink this," "Sit up," "Turn this way," "You can come eat now." The other one had to help him.

As for him, a womanish kind of boy, she thought. Too many fearful looks for her liking. However, one fact made her stop short of contempt. He was undoubtedly a far piece from home. How had he come to be in the Waxhaws? And to be sure, he'd got himself away from the British and his friend too. From down on the Congaree River he said they were. She'd heard the Dutch settlements were thick down there. But it was another race, another kind.

Yet one trait he had in common with every male she'd ever known. He was blind when it came to seeing what had to be done about a place to keep body and soul together—water to tote, wood to gather, fences mended if vermin weren't to eat up every blessed thing you raised.

"I'm too old to wait on grown men without help! I'll try to wait on him as long as he can't do for himself, but I have to have help!"

Thereafter, he'd stepped more lively, but he was so awkward at some tasks—woodchopping, for instance, that she wondered what kind of sorry people he came from.

For the first several weeks he kept away from the house in the daytime. He wanted to know how far it was from the public road and other settlements. It was on the edge of Catawba land, she told him, leased from the Catawbas. The Indians had recently left, having sent their women and children to Virginia, for their warriors fought with Sumter. She did not mention McNulty and his gang. Happily they did not return. They must have thought they'd finished their work, she decided.

As October drew on and the hurt one mended, both Dutch boys began to move about more freely. Now, but only to herself, she called them by name. That Harry, once he recovered strength, she could see he knew more how to do, both inside and outside than Willy. He had a great deal of strength and suppleness though for a while he was more or less one-armed.

Late one afternoon when he happened to come in with an armful of wood—Willy did most of the cutting and Harry the toting—she let her knife slip as she sliced salt pork, and gashed her hand. She cried out involuntarily and he hurried to her. He helped her stanch the flow of blood and bound up her hand almost as neatly as she she could have done it herself. Then as she sat in a trembling faintness, for she'd bled like a hog, he went ahead with supper for her, frying out the meat and mixing up meal and water for the johnnycake, but when she started to give directions he became confused. She rose impatiently to take charge so that he drew back. Still he didn't leave but continued to hover behind her, and she snapped, "Get out of the way." But it was awkward trying to move the heavy iron spider almost one-handed to stir the coals, and she dropped the tongs. As she stooped, she grew dizzy and staggered and might have pitched forward if his hands had not caught and raised her. "You come away." Gently a strong arm helped her to her chair. She sat there with her lips trembling, her eyes half-closed against the blurred shape moving between her and the fire.

. . . The strangest feeling she'd known for many a year. Cared for. Her burden wholly lifted. The vast freedom of it. She felt no compulsion to do anything.

After a while she went into the other room and lay upon her bed, continuing in that strange feeling. And yet it was so natural it fitted her like a fine, well-made garment. When if ever had anyone helped her like that? Never her husband or her children unless they were asked and that was seldom. She was the burden bearer. Yet something in her bones responded so naturally to that lifting that it pleasured her whole being. Perhaps beyond memory some one else had helped her once like that.

Supper was good. She knew the boy observed her to see what she thought of it. Perversely she would not eat much. To herself she pretended to find fault with the meat. Too crisp. Fried out too much.

It was not until several weeks later that she called him by name, at last called both of them by name.

Years of heavy rain had sunk and begun to rot the poplar log that served for a step at the back door so that now it lay sloped into the earth and was too far below the doorsill for her to step down on it. The boys jumped it, but she used the front porch although it meant extra steps for her.

One afternoon she heard a thumping outside. She opened the back door a crack and saw Harry rolling and tumbling a big hunk of log toward the house.

"Lord, that's too thick for the chimney," she muttered. "What's he thinking about?"

He left it at the woodpile and went back down the hill. A short time later both boys appeared, lugging as many rocks as they could carry, which they dumped near the back door.

Through a partly opened shutter she watched as they dug and prized out the old half-rotten log, then proceeded to lay the rocks in the hollow it left to make a kind of trough. Lord, they were going to lay that log there in place of her old step! How could she use a step like that? It would throw her down. She was past the age of balancing on a footlog.

She was about to remonstrate with them when the sound of her pot boiling over called her, and before she could return to the window, she heard the axe. When she looked out again, she saw they had split off two sides of the log to square it and were working on the third side. She watched them. Harry was doing the splitting she noted with approval. They were leaving the fourth side round and were chip-chipping with the axe on its widest side to smooth it. Now she understood. The round side would lie in the rock trough that would serve as a good foundation to secure it and keep it from rotting.

She was divided between curiosity and annoyance. Who were they to move her old step Jess had laid nigh thirty years ago? And to make so free with her trees! What kind of wood was it, oak? Well, if it was, it would not rot in her lifetime or the next generation's either. Jess had used an easier wood.

As she watched them take turns chip-chipping away with the axe, she thought of the adze, the plane, and the other tools she'd hidden under the floor of the room across the dogtrot, where she never let them go. But she made no move to fetch them.

They saw her watching. Harry grinned, and even Willy half-smiled. She turned away. Well, since they'd taken charge, let them do it to suit themselves. After a long time she heard a fumbling and thumping near the door, heard them talking low and knew they were putting the log in its trough. Still she would not look. At last all was still.

Some twenty minutes later she opened the back door. There below her was a broad step, somewhat rough, but perfectly level and seated securely in its rock foundation. Below it, for a lower step, was a smooth flat rock. The boys were out of sight.

She stood awhile looking at it, then returned to the hearth but left the door wide open. She heard no sound, did not know where they were or what they were doing.

Just before dusk she went to the door and called, "Harry! Oh Harry! I need a turn of wood!"

When he came laden up the back steps, she was waiting for him. The steps were easy, shallow, and wide. But it was not until he dumped his load that she remarked, "Looks like you're on the way to being a fair hand for a journeyman carpenter."

Later she called, "Harry! You Willy! Come on in to supper now!"

Willi moved in an unthinking routine, in some ways not unlike that of his old militia company, except that here his tasks were more menial and he had less restriction on his thought and time. True, he was restricted by his commitment to the old woman for Heiri's sake. Yet that commitment did not erase his unease.

For a time it was a blessed simplicity to spend his hours in domestic chores and eventually in trying to salvage the little that could be saved from the ruins of this farmstead. When Heiri grew well enough to join him outside, sometimes the work was even enjoyable. Still beneath Willi's acceptance of the day's pattern, questions stirred him. *Is this all I'm good for? Gathering acorns and building hogpens? What's to become of me or of him?*

But Willi sensed no unease in Heiri. Heiri had changed. He was no longer just a follower and companion. In some intangible way Heiri was his own man now as he had not been before. It was not in what he said or did but in something Willi sensed that he did not understand. The old mirthful simplicity had returned, but there was no longer anything clownish about it. Heiri seemed utterly serene.

Nor did Willi understand why Heiri always found more favor with some people than he himself did.

Well, Heiri was likable. Everybody always liked Heiri even if they did laugh at him. And Willi supposed it was natural for the old woman to feel closer to Heiri than to him because she'd brought him back to life, you might say, for he'd lain in a raging fever almost a week, and it had been a question one time whether he'd even live. And naturally Heiri felt gratitude and showed it. It was he who'd thought of replacing the old step. *Yet I helped plan and build it*, thought *Willi, and I was the one found that big flat rock.* Not that he was jealous. How could he be jealous of the regard of such a poor old creature as that? Still he puzzled over the difference between other people's response to him and to Heiri. Something about himself that was not as attractive. Some lack in him that made him seem insignificant . . . . That rich brown strength of Simmi. . . . No! Let thoughts like that be gone forever! Always he'd do his duty and try to do right. He always had, hadn't he—at least among men and boys? In the war—*but I came back. I was always there.*

If only he knew what was happening in the world! Where did they fight now? Where was John Thomas? Where was Sumter? Was he still alive?

He knew the old woman was violently partisan to the Whig cause; otherwise she would not have taken them in, but she knew no more of outer events than he did. She spoke of her son's return. "He'll bring us word. He'll know."

Day after day Willi cut and stacked up winter wood and later, along with Heiri, did his best to repair and replace the burnt, broken, and rotten amid the weed-grown fields and empty woods.

One morning before Heiri was able to be outside, he felt so cut off from the world he had actually struck out through the woods in hopes of the mere sight of another person. He followed a path until it joined a well-trodden way and finally emerged into a clearing with chimney smoke in the distance. Under cover of the woods he skirted the field till he could see the house. It was a poorish place but its buildings looked intact. He watched for a while, saw a girl go in and out, an older woman, some children. He considered going up to talk with them and began to plan what he'd say. But he thought of how ragged he looked. Would they be alarmed? Or hostile? Which side were they on? Their buildings still stood. How would he account for himself?

As he stood there, a man rode up. Willi watched the man dismount, then gloomily turned away. On the way back, he got lost, and the sun was setting when he reached his place of refuge. He must have walked ten miles, he thought. Although she raked him over because she'd had to fetch in the water and wood, the old woman asked no questions.

Sometimes Willi thought he would simply leave and let Heiri do as he wished. *It's not as if I haven't paid the debt, or at least my part of it. And if I stay much longer I'll find myself plodding behind that old horse. She's sure to have plow irons hidden somewhere.*

In early November Willi thought, *If I'm going, now's the time. Soon it'll be too cold to lie out without a blanket.*

But what about provisions? If he just knew how far he'd have to go . . . He wondered how much she'd give him if he asked, how much she had yet to give. . . . Maybe after they butchered. As soon as it turned cold enough, they'd butcher, first the hogs, then the yearling. After that, if the weather moderated as it usually did. . . . He was glad Heiri knew all about butchering.

In front of the evening fire in November, they cracked white oak acorns for boiling, then drying and grinding into meal. She talked disjointedly of lawsuits and killings. In North Carolina her husband, Jess, had killed a man in a land dispute. Here in the Waxhaws he'd aimed to settle away from the Augusta County Virginians who were filling up the country, and with the help of the Catawbas he succeeded. Having come out of the back parts of Pennsylvania, Jess hated a Shawnee almost as bad as the Catawbas did, and it was easy for him to fall into friendship with them here. He'd enjoyed the friendship of their beloved King Haigler until Haigler was slain by Shawnees in '63. In the spring of '64, Jess too was shot and scalped while hunting with Big Otter when a Shawnee revenge party came skulking southward and ambushed them at Little Sugaw Creek. The Catawbas in turn followed the Shawnees almost to the banks of the Ohio and brought back to her their scalps and Jess's gun.

"Catawbas are true. No matter what's said. A Catawba will stand by you to death. Oh, they ha' their own ways. Some folks will tell you, 'I hate a redskin like I hate a rattler, ne'er a one of 'em but's cruel and treacherous.' Well, I say the Catawba knows his enemies. And he knows a friend too and he'll stand by him till death. They ha' stood by me and mine."

Willi said, "They have fought with Sumter in all his battles." He paused, added, "I believe they were with us in Charlestown."

"Indeed, they were!" the old woman said sternly. "They went out long before the rest of 'em hereabouts did. And gave their life blood too!"

Willi was silenced. To him the Catawbas were strange fearful beings who fought alongside them but camped apart.

"Aye, Indians is Indians and you can't make whites out of 'em, but I say the Catawbas ha' got as much right to the good of this land as any Christian I know. . . . Drag that backlog up to the front, Harry, and throw on another one. I tell you now, if Big Otter was on the river this season, we'd never want for meat."

Willi felt abashed, for even if he'd had a gun, he knew he was not a good hunter and he supposed she knew it too. Still they'd managed to supply her with rabbits and she ought to appreciate that.

"No, I'll tell you what their downfall is," she resumed, "it's their love of spirits. Something in 'em, Jess used to say, a something that's different, and they can't hold out against it once it gets inside 'em. 'It's their ruination,' he'd say. . . . Though a fine one he was to talk."

She gazed into the fire, her gray hair straggling about her hooded eyes. She might have pointed to that scar on the chimney stone there, made by a blow of Jess's axe when she'd dodged it. She'd spent that night in the woods and much of the next day. There were other scars about the place from reelings and ragings, as well as stray bullet holes. But men had ever rotted grain for whiskey and few of them knew when to leave it alone. Though she thought maybe Edward did. At least it did not make him mean the way it had Jess and Michael.

Heiri, sitting on the floor astraddle of a vat of acorns to be crushed, considered her last words. Spirits only made him foolish and sleepy. Oh, he liked well enough the taste of wine and rum punch, but he'd been warned too often that it was a dangerous liking so that seldom, even when they captured large stores from the enemy, did he partake much of the spoils. "'Wine is a mocker. Strong drink is raging and whoever is deceived thereby is not wise.'" Old Parson Theus had done his best to embed those words in the minds if not in the flesh of his charges, though with limited success.

Heiri guessed that for Kate the fellowship and comforts of the meetinghouse had been sparse—"Oh pshaw, just say 'Kate!'" she'd snapped at him, impatient with his attempts to put "Mistress" in front of her name, "Mistress Kate Reid." He saw she kept the Sabbath more or less, but he never saw a Bible, though for all he knew she might have one in the other room. Now impulsively he asked where the nearest meetinghouse was.

Still remembering Jess, it took a while for her to understand Heiri's question. She said there was a meetinghouse ten miles below on Lower Fishing Creek that old Parson Richardson, the one that hanged himself, had preached at. "Too much religion can addle your brain I've always heard said. And I partly believe it. . . . Though some ha' maintained 'twas his wife did it." But another meetinghouse stood about the same distance to the southwest, she said. "And I'm bound to say it's been a good man there these fifteen years. One that's took up for his country. I heard he went with Sumter and got burned out like the rest of us. Simpson. Parson John Simpson."

"Simpson!" exclaimed Willi. "Oh, I've heard him preach! You have too, Heiri."

"Our pastor is also for liberty," said Heiri. "Our pastor at Saint Johanns on Congaree, Herr Christian Theus."

The old woman grunted.

Heiri said, "Men who know God's Word, they can see truth. Better than we can." The right and the wrong, he meant. Injustice that must be opposed even though it cost dearly.

"Now that's as may be, Harry. There's some as profess to know it I wouldn't give a groat for, for all their rant."

Heiri could not answer. He had not the words even if he'd had the answer clear in his mind. What he did have, still had, was the heavy conviction that lay like a log half-buried in earth: *I cannot let others wholly pay the price. Before God, I cannot let my brother alone pay the price. I must take my place beside him. But where?* he asked as he had so many times. *Oh Joggi, where?*

Sometimes he had sensed his brother with him at the creek's edge, in the summer leaves. But these days Joggi seemed farther away. Heiri did not think of him as often now.

He thought more often about this place and the people who had lived here. He wondered about sons and daughters who would go off and leave their mother alone. Sairy was somewhere in Georgy, she'd said, and Peg's man had gone over into the Holston country in North Caroliny. As for Annie, she'd just up and gone off with that Anson County man. "She might be dead now for aught I know." Kate spoke as of stock that had wandered off. Heiri was shocked until he noticed the twist to her mouth, the bleakness in her eyes. It was the same when he'd asked her about the two fresh mounds among the rock markers at the woods' edge. Her two sons killed last summer, she told him and then went into a tirade, much of which he couldn't understand.

Sometimes when he saw her sharp, protruding shoulder blades as she hitched her way down the steps, her big rough hand grasping the rail he'd put up, he wondered how it would be to bring forth so much life and see it leave you. He thought of his own mother but never considered her bereft, for she still had life, he thought, had it in herself. But poor old Kate?

Well, she'd given him back his own. She and Willi together. For he knew as clear as day that his life had been given him again. And by those two. And by the good God through them, he thought. Oh, he knew it.

It had come to him late in September when he'd awakened to sunlight slanting through the open door, such a clarity of knowledge as he'd never had. He felt himself newly born into a purpose as large as the fields and sky above him, yet as precise in its crafting as any leaf or wing. He'd felt its ascending power and a kind of release. After that his body mended more rapidly and he was soon well.

Now his mind was often exercised with the thought of some purpose for which he had been restored. Right now perhaps it was only to serve Kate. To pen her hogs for fattening, to rig up better stabling for her old horse, cut plenty of cane from the bottom and get him in condition for next season's work. He did not consider who might be doing the work.

". . . I might ha' gone to meeting sometimes if it hadn't ha' been for the way they shunned us when we first come here. It all went back to what happened in Anson County. But I couldn't help what he did! And the other man would ha' done the same to him if he could ha'! That Bill Dawes was a liar and a thief! And Jess was never one to be run over!" Her words ground out the old rut afresh. "Well, his brother—Joe Dawes, I mean—he'd already got to be a big man down here and he set 'em all against us when we come."

"Which side is he on?" asked Willi.

"Side?" It took her a moment to understand. "Oh Lord, child, Joe Dawes has been in the ground ten years or more. Of course, he left a big generation." She cleared her throat judiciously. "No, I'm bound to say the most of 'em's come out for the right. Or so Edward tells me. 'It's a queer turnout,' I said, 'you to be fighting alongside Dawes and against McNultys.'"

Catawbas, Dawes, and Reids. *Who are these people*, Heiri wondered. *And Lienhardts. Who is Heiri Lienhardt?*

A friend and brother. To Willi Rieder, to Joggi Lienhardt. A son to Johannes Lienhardt and—Mama. To Kate?

Last week he had built a coop and nests for her few half-wild fowls in hopes of encouraging them again to domesticity. Even though it was not their laying season, this morning he'd found an egg.

She looked at it in wonder, looked at him. "Now, Harry, I don't know what kind of spell you ha' worked on that old buff hen, but whate'er it is, you keep on a-working it, hear?"

November brought more rain. The boys' feet were almost on the ground. Soon as the beefhide cured, she told them, they could cobble up leather shoes. She helped them make coats from some old canvas she had, for both boys turned out to be fairly handy with a needle. They trapped several coons and she helped them make caps. She used some of the rabbit fur to make herself a warmer cap and mittens. Yet the misery in her body grew worse.

Torrents of rain continued into December. One morning she did not get up. At last Heiri called her, listening at her door, and she groaned in answer. He went inside and helped her up, wrapped her in a quilt, and brought her before the fire. After an hour or so she began to move about. It was the cold and damp in her bones, she said.

How to keep her warm at night. Heiri puzzled his brain. The big cluttered room where she slept had a fireplace she never used. He thought that if they kept fire there, it would get some of the damp out of the room. She said, No, the chimney was not safe. He said he'd examine the chimney, make it safe. She said, No! she was not going to risk the house burning down over her head!

Heiri made a ladder and climbed up on the roof to peer down the chimney, went into the room without her permission to peer up the chimney. He saw daylight between some of the rocks, knew how to mend the defect and did. At last, with her permission, he made fire in the room and thereafter kept it burning almost continuously.

"Well, you the ones got to get up the wood. If you want to do it."

She never said she slept better, but her morning groans were fewer.

They had stacked enough wood in the dogtrot and in the dooryard to last well into spring. She complained it was getting to be in the way. Willi answered it should be cut ahead so it could season. What Kate suspected was, the two were getting ready to leave.

She knew the signs. That Willy was restless, had been for a long time. She was surprised he had not gone off in the fall at the time most males took to the woods. Waiting for Harry she surmised, though Harry showed no sign yet of wanting to go. Still she did not take even Harry's presence for granted. She simply accepted it as she would have a prolonged spell of fine weather.

He was unlike any son or lover she had ever known. If she had ever had a servant, she thought, a good servant, he would have been like Harry. Yet he was more than a servant. She did not know how to categorize him.

His conversational abilities did not improve. But perhaps there was no need, for he seemed to understand most if not all of what she would have said to him.

She lent him scissors and a piece of looking glass to trim his hair and beard—so she could get a good look at his face, she told him. Sometimes when she said some scolding or snappish word to him, he would cock that good eye at her with a brightness in it enough for two eyes, and his lips would curve as pretty as a girl's. She would wonder, *Who is it, what is it come to me here at last?*

Dusk fell early now and the boys were still outside on a misty December evening when they heard hallooing in the woods to the front of the house. Willi heard it first. They listened a moment, then went inside.

"Somebody's calling," said Willi.

"What?"

"I hear somebody coming."

Kate went out the front door, Heiri and Willi behind her. They saw two riders drawing near, the sounds of their horses already loud, but their forms were indistinct in the half-dark. One of them hallooed again and shouted words.

Kate cried out and went hobbling down the steps as fast as she could. "Edward? Oh Edward! Is it you?"

A tall man dismounted. "Well, yes, here I am, Mother. Didn't you expect to see me?"

"Oh, I made sure you'd be back! Oh, I knew you'd come!"

They embraced quickly, hard. "This here is Ephraim Giles."

Now, the men were hitching their horses to the porch post. "We come by to see how you do. And we've not eat all day."

They were crowding into the house. The other man was not as tall as Edward, yet the two filled up the room. "I won't deny we're froze to the bone. And wet! Lord God, that last creek was ice." They crowded to the fireplace, where Kate was already clattering pots. "Been riding since before daybreak, nigh fifty miles we must ha' come, clear up from Little River over beyond Winnsborough."

Heiri and Willi, who had stepped backward, slipped out the back door and stood outside, hearing the rise and fall of voices, the man's, then Kate's. They withdrew farther from the house, not wanting to eavesdrop. "Should we see to their horses?" Heiri asked low. They were unsure. They stood awhile longer. "We better go back in," said Willi.

Edward Reid was hunched close to the fire. He looked up from under lowered brows. As they came in, Kate said, "Here they are."

Heiri and Willi said their names.

Heiri said, "Your mother, she saved my life. Your mother and my friend."

After a short silence, Edward said, "She tells me you got took at Fishing Creek."

"Yes."

Again there was silence. Willi began a halting account of how they had escaped and come to be here. When he finished, Edward merely nodded.

"I understand you were there too," said Willi.

Again Edward nodded.

"She needed us to help her," said Heiri. "We stayed to help her. But she helped us first."

"Edward, you wouldn't credit the wood these boys ha' chopped and toted! You can look out in the morning and see how it's piled up. And the butchering and other things. So many things." She paused, said low, "I don't know how I'd ha' made out without 'em."

"Aye, you told me." Edward straightened up. "I'm obliged to both of you." He stretched out his hand. "For seeing to things."

The smaller man, who was squatting and baking his back, rose also for the handshaking. He looked vaguely familiar and his name sounded familiar too, but there had been so many like him in the last six months, so many to come and go. . . . The man said, "Where you from?"

"Near the Congarees," said Willi. "He's from down on Savana Hunt Creek."

"Remember latter part of last June? On the road below Saluda Old Town?"

Light broke for Willi—the two men who'd challenged them! "You and another man. Stewart?"

"Aye. I knew I'd seen the two of you. This here little fellow, Ned, he like to ha' fought me, what with me being in company with that damned Gill Stewart. We might ha' had a right smart set-to if I hadn't ha' pulled old Gill back. Did you think I was a Tory?"

"We didn't know." Little fellow! Willi thought indignantly. How big did Ephraim Giles think he was? Yet in spite of himself he grinned. "Wasn't your friend one?"

"No friend of mine. Just happened up with him."

"We heard afterward he was Tory," Willi said.

"Well, Eph's as good a Whig scout as you'll find anywhere," said Edward. "Come on up to the fire, boys. We don't mean to crowd you out."

"Your horses?" Heiri asked. "Can we tend the horses?"

After a few minutes Heiri went outside again with Ephraim, and they cared for the tired beasts as best they could although there was no adequate stabling.

As Kate listened to their talk, she basked in the pleasure of four male voices in the room again, of getting supper for a crowd of men. She felt great relief at Edward's arrival and wellbeing, also satisfaction at his acceptance of the Dutch boys. But there was another circumstance, a vague probability she would not consider.

Edward had much to tell, most of it heartening. They heard of new battles: King's Mountain, Fishdam Ford, Blackstock's; names of new generals: Nathan'l Greene, Dan'l Morgan. General Sumter had been wounded at Blackstock's but was recovering. Francis Marion was giving 'em hell in the swamps. That damned Benny Tarleton, though, was still ranging free in spite of his comeuppance at Blackstock's.

They said Sumter lay no farther than fifteen miles up the river at John Price's rock house near Tuckaseegee Ford. Greene, the Continental commander, had moved into the Cheraws, but Morgan was still on the Pacolet. Old Cornwallis was lying low at Winnsborough. Edward and Ephraim had been sent from Sumter's headquarters to scout around it.

Willi's face was flushed with excitement. "I knew it! Heiri, I told you!"

Willi inquired of the whereabouts of other leaders such as Thomas Taylor and John Thomas. But when Kate put food in front of them, all talk stopped, and immediately after supper the travelers were ready for sleep.

"We got to be gone by sunup, Mammy."

She did not protest.

A curious silence ensued. Heiri and Willi looked at each other, and inexorably Heiri felt himself nod and Willi heard his own voice say, "We'll start out too when you do. If you tell us the way. Though we have no horses and no guns."

Ephraim and Edward exchanged glances and nodded also.

"Tell you what, boys, what if Eph rides on with one of you and I come after afoot with the other. Or other way around, however you will. You want to ride on, Eph, and take one with you?" The quality of the air was changed.

They agreed it was a good idea. Each pair would have a guide and a gun. Now the air was mellow with camaraderie.

Ephraim and Edward soon lay down before the fire and dropped off at once into hard, deep sleep, but neither Willi nor Heiri in the loftroom slept very much that night. Nor did Kate. She rose long before day to make their bread for the journey.

Heiri realized that even if they'd had more time to prepare for leaving, there was not much more they could have done. For the last time he and Willi brought in water in the predawn blackness and great turns of wood for both fireplaces from the high stacks outside. They had been preparing for departure a long time.

Eph and Willi left first, riding away in the drizzle.

"As I can," Edward told his mother, "I'll swing back by, now and again, to see how you do. And come April I'll be here to put seed in the ground."

They did not embrace this time. Edward lifted his hand and turned to go.

She stood on the porch with her hand gripping the bannister. An old black shawl was pulled around her shoulders. Her face was white.

Heiri, who had been standing apart from them, now came back and mounted the step. His shaggy head was on a level with hers. The wet had already damped his shoulders, and fine droplets clung to the hairs of his fur cap. The sunk-in place at his temple was dark in the faint light.

He had been going to hold out his hand but instead he felt his arms go around her and felt her quick convulsive holding of him. Then she let him go.

"I will never forget you," he said thickly, low.

She did not answer for she could not. More deeply than he, she would remember him till her last day.

28

"On this ground I will beat Benny Tarleton or I will lay my bones."

Maybe it was because Morgan knew he could not get away. The Broad was rising in front of him and the British were close behind. Or maybe it was because he was tired of falling back and wanted to fight. Or it might even have been that he was goaded by the measured words of Andrew Pickens, that taciturn honorbound Presbyterian elder, who at last had broken his parole and come out. Pickens said that whether or not Morgan decided to try to get his Continentals and Virginians across the Broad into North Carolina, he and the Carolina and Georgia militia would stay and make a stand.

Up from the Pacolet, across Thicketty they had retreated already. Men, wagons, and horses had toiled all day, January 16, and reached at nightfall an open rolling woodland known for decades as Hannah's Cowpens. That morning they had left their breakfasts half-eaten on Thicketty Creek with the sudden news that Benny was this side the Pacolet, only six miles away.

Daniel Morgan had been a hero at Quebec, a hero at Saratoga. He was a veteran Indian fighter. He called himself the Old Wagoner and his body was scarred by the flogging he'd received in Braddock's army in '55 when he'd knocked down the British subaltern who struck him. He was from Battletown, Virginia. He was also a professional soldier who knew that part of his duty was to preserve his little army.

In the weeks past, he had been harrassed by one trouble or disappointment after another. Davidson of North Carolina, whom he had counted on to muster at least six hundred militiamen, brought him only a hundred and twenty in late December. Pickens' arrival about the same time was heartening, but he too had gathered far fewer of his old command than he'd hoped for. It was the same with the Georgia leaders who had served under Elijah Clark, now wounded. To cap it all, Thomas Sumter absolutely refused to cooperate in furnishing provisions for the troops trying to subsist in the already scoured country. Sumter would not acknowledge Morgan's authority to supercede his own.

News of the enemy did not allay anxiety. The British had been reinforced in December by thirteen hundred and fifty fresh troops, now slogging up the country by way of Camden. Cornwallis had at last broken camp at Winnsborough and was moving his thirty-five hundred up east of the Broad to catch the remaining Rebels after Tarleton should have broken them. And on January 15 a report came in that Tarleton himself had not only his five hundred and fifty-man British Legion but a total of eleven or twelve hundred men that included infantry and artillery. Morgan, what he could count of them, thought he had less than a thousand.

January was cold and rainy. Morgan was in misery on horseback. His sciatica was killing him.

In camp, on the march, the militia kept straggling off, hunting forage. Professional soldiers cursed the southern habit of every man riding to war on his horse. Volunteer soldiers cursed these tactical retreats. They'd come out to fight, not to run away. Better to ha' stayed at home if they weren't a-going to make some kind of stand. A man couldn't help worrying about his wife and young ones huddled back there on Beaverdam Creek and him getting farther and farther away from them.

It was nearly as ragged an army as could have been assembled. True, John Eager Howard's Maryland and Delaware Continentals and William Washington's dragoons wore uniforms, but the six-month Virginia militiamen, former Continentals, wore only a semblance of buff and blue, some not even that. The rest wore whatever they had—nondescript wool coats and breeches, battered hats or caps of every description—and many were shoeless. But they were almost all veterans.

The Carolina and Georgia militia followed Joseph McDowell, Benjamin Roebuck, John Thomas, Jr., Thomas Brandon, Harry White, James Jackson, John Cunningham, James McCall. They followed Andrew Pickens. They were men who had fought at Musgrove's Mill, at King's Mountain, at Blackstock's. Some were men who had not had time to fight at Fishing Creek. But they were also men who had never yet learned to stand the bayonet charge. They had not the training or weapons for it.

That the rivers were brimful of water seemed no obstacle to Tarleton, who was doing what he liked best, hounding hot on the trace of his foe to overtake him unprepared and cut him to pieces. His orders would be "No quarter. Take no prisoners."

So on the evening of January 16, Morgan decided to make a stand. At the Cowpens. Regardless of the fact that it was Tarleton's kind of country, cavalry country. Maybe the pain in his body goaded him insensibly, maybe even the old ridges on his back. In himself he must always have wanted to fight. He was from Battletown, Virginia. And he knew a few things Benny might not know.

All night long the general loomed large among the campfires, all six feet two of him, as he went from group to group and explained to the men the plan he had worked out with the officers. He joked with the boys, helped the young dragoons to fix their sabers, told them all how their sweethearts would love them, their families would bless them for what they were going to do in the morning when the Old Wagoner cracked his whip over Benny. The men might lie down at last for a little sleep but Morgan would not.

Earlier Rudi Näffels had dozed off and on. The day had been grueling. But he kept dreaming of Katy as he often did, little Katy running up to him crying, "Daddy! Daddy!" holding up her arms. Margaret had left her to go and fight snakes. Jemmy? Where was Jemmy?

How could he stand it, if he was still here tomorrow this time, not to go and see about them?

Joggi Lienhardt had told him the house was burned down. Probably every Whig house on Indian Creek was gone by now. God only knew where Margaret and the rest of them were.

He knew she was valiant. Except in the matter of childbearing she was as strong and resourceful as any woman he had ever known. But Katy was so little and frail, his son yet so tender. His arms hungered for his children to hold and shield them as they hungered in a different way for Margaret.

As if ultimately he could shield any of them, he told himself bitterly. He had not been able to shield Andy.

But it was God who took Andy! they said. God's will be done; Andy was with God! It had cost him much to give up that child. Yet at the last he'd been able to. But to give up his children to hunger, to fear? And to abandon Margaret to the roughness and savagery that would destroy what he loved most in her?

He turned on the ground in great bitterness of spirit, rose and moved away from his comrades to pace back and forth, went farther away to be more alone.

In the past he had not been much of a praying man but now he was learning to be one. He had learned at last that when you emptied out your soul, turned it raw inside out, then a word would come, or a sense . . . yet not so much a feeling as knowledge . . . and a great calm of order and control came upon you.

That night finally in the hour before dawn, he lay down and rested deeply. Margaret and the children would be all right.

Joggi Lienhardt did not lie down but sat laughing and chaffing with the others as he cleaned his rifle, inspected every bullet and patch, checked every buckle and strap, and honed his knife. He would be in the advance party of riflemen who would skirmish ahead of the Georgia and Carolina militiamen and draw the British on.

How shrewd of Morgan, he thought, to put the militia in front of the others and direct them to fire only two or three shots when the enemy should come within fifty-yard range, then to retire and reform behind the Continentals and rejoin the battle on the flanks. That way there'd be no question of their having to stand that charge. Their only work would be to weaken it with good shooting, aim for the men with the stripes and epaulets. The enemy did not aim, just fired volleys, which might not do much harm from a distance, for they tended to shoot high—but, oh, the stab of those glinting blades coming at you with the drumbeat and the squealing fifes getting louder and louder and the big legs churning toward you in all the confidence of their wellfed beefy power. They never dodged behind trees. It was hard not to shoot too soon, and when you did wait, harder yet to stand and reload.

He had ventured to say as much to Heiri earlier, but Heiri only looked at him with his calm gaze that even the droop-lidded cast in his right eye could not change. "Don't worry, Joggi. I'll stand."

Heiri and Willi would be behind him in John Thomas' regiment, and Rudi farther back among the Virginians with whom he'd enlisted for six months. The Virginians would fight alongside Howard's Continentals.

Amazing they were all in this one place at last. Not about Rudi perhaps but about him and Willi and Heiri. The three of them together once more as they must have been a hundred times when they'd ranged the Congaree woods—him in front, Willi next, and Heiri last. Though this time not Heiri last. And, oh God, he was relieved about Willi. As to what he felt about Heiri, he had to cover it with silence. . . . Oh, it felt so good to be with his own again! He'd never dreamed it would feel so good. Tonight he felt he could drive back Benny all by himself.

After Sumter's wounding and immobilization at Blackstock's, his command had partially disintegrated. Some men had gone home. Others lay out in small hidden camps—"flying camps," they were called—waiting for some chance or change. Eventually some of these drifted back toward the Catawba, where Sumter, still convalescent, continued to maintain his network of scouts and foragers and to amass supplies. It came as a shock to some of his followers when word leaked out that Sumter would do nothing to help the little army on the Pacolet.

"I can't see the sense of us just sitting here. I say if somebody's going to make a push for you, then you go to help."

"Old Morgan, he's one more fighter's what I hear."

"But he's from northward. Like Gates."

That name gave them pause.

"Trouble is, them from northward, they don't know our country. Or us. How we do here."

"Morgan's not like Gates. My cousin says he's more like us. Says he got his learning same place he did."

"Where's that, Jake?"

"In the back parts of this country."

"Oh, I know he was in that old Indian war, but then so was Gates. And up there in New York, Saratoga, both of 'em was up there too."

"My cousin said Morgan's a man he'd follow anywhere. Last time I saw him he was going all the way up to Virginia, he said, to enlist under him."

"When was that?"

"King's Mountain. Or right after it."

The controversy ended. The word of a man at King's Mountain meant more than all the reputed glories of Saratoga.

When a messenger rode into their camp several days later to relay Morgan's call to all Carolina militia to turn out, Jake Lennard and some others made up their minds. Early next morning they left Crowder's Creek and headed west.

Eph Giles had hunted up Heiri as soon as he'd made his report to Sumter's headquarters. "Your brother leaves light tracks," he said, "but I believe I found him for you."

"What?" Heiri could hardly believe what he heard.

"Or rather I found out where he's been. You know that little branch on Crowder's Creek about five miles up from the iron works? He's been camped over there with some others. Till they left out four, five days ago, him and fourteen others, left out for the Pacolet."

"Joggi Lienhardt?" Heiri's voice broke with excitement. "My brother? Eph, you sure?"

"Well, they call him 'Jake,' that's short for 'Jacob' you told me his name was, Jake Lennard. It's 'Lennard,' same as yours. He's from down your way too; Dutch, they said, but you can't tell it."

"Oh, *danke, danke!*" Heiri gripped Eph's hand, then turned away, afraid Eph would see him cry. Eyes squeezed shut, he kept whispering, "*Oh Herr Gott, Herr Jesu, danke!*"

It was the first sure news he'd had of Joggi since last May on Savana Hunt.

Eph said it was chance that had given him the information. Talking with a man at Colonel Billy Hill's he'd learned of Captain John Moffatt's departure. When he'd asked who all had gone with him, the man tried to enumerate them. Most from hereabouts but a few from other parts. He'd mentioned a mettlesome Dutch boy from down on the Congaree.

"Willi!" shouted Heiri. "Oh Willi! Come here!"

After listening, Willi said, "You mean they went to join Morgan?"

"Wouldn't ha' gone for nothing else."

"Then we must go too!" exclaimed Heiri. He stopped short; his face sobered. "Eph, how can we go?"

Eph squatted by their scanty fire to warm his hands. He did not answer for a while. Willi waited tensely.

Eph stood up. "Well now, I tell you, boys. Me and some others, we don't favor this laggardly way here, and we aim to set out ourselves. If you boys are of like mind, why, we'll be glad to have you along. But we can't hang back. What I mean is, you'll need good horses."

And that was where the hitch came, for neither Willi nor Heiri had a horse. Both were assigned to duty with the supply wagons.

"If we ask—"

"Aagh, Heiri!" Willi said low. Why would Heiri be so simple? He asked Eph, "Have any of the other troops gone? Or any other officers?"

"I hear Colonel John Thomas has called out his. Whoever will. He's the one I'm a mind to join."

"Why, Willi, it's our old regiment! Colonel John Thomas! Willi, it's a sign!"

"Where is he now?" asked Willi.

"I have all ideas he's already on the Pacolet. He was headed toward his old home district last I heard."

The other two were silent.

"Well, if you boys can see your way clear to come, you can meet us at daybreak day after tomorrow morning. You know that big old rock on Tawny Branch? We'll meet there. But hear me now," Eph concluded sternly, "I'll trust you to keep all quiet."

Eph limped away. Lying out in the cold got into his joints and sometimes he felt like an old man.

"Willi, we must go!" exclaimed Heiri.

"How the devil can we, Heiri, without horses?"

"Maybe Colonel Thomas, maybe he'll give us horses."

"And him forty or fifty miles away? How you think we can get to him?"

"We can walk! We can follow a trail, can't we? Eph and them, they'll leave us a trail."

Willi did not deign to answer. You did not join a militia company without a horse, and Heiri knew it.

Yes, they were armed now and they knew the country fairly well. And many a man when he felt the call to more urgent duty elsewhere simply absconded, and depending on the circumstances, usually no one thought worse of him. But to take horses not theirs? Neither Heiri nor Willi felt up to that.

In the glum silence Heiri concluded their only choice was to ask for horses. That's what he'd do. But he wouldn't tell Willi.

When the sergeant scowled and sent him to the lieutenant, Heiri found that officer talking with the captain. Thus Heiri had to explain his motives and plight to both officers. The captain looked at him hard. The lieutenant was shaking his head slowly when the captain said low, "Let's send him to the General, Ben. Let him speak with the General."

The lieutenant lifted his eyebrows. Heiri stood astonished.

"Sir, General Sumter?" he ventured.

"Yes. Just tell him what you told us. Don't be afraid. Just tell him what you want to do. Grimsley!" the captain shouted. "Take this man to headquarters and see he gets speech with General Sumter." To the sergeant's startled look, he added, "You needn't wait for him." As the sergeant turned to slouch off, the captain said, "Grimsley. Lennard. Before you go, a word—" and was it a wink? "—don't tell him who sent you. Unless he should ask."

Fifteen minutes later Heiri stood in the entry hall of the rock house. He could see inside the room where a man at a table sat writing although his arm was in a sling. It was broad daylight outside, but the blinds were pulled shut because of the cold, and the only light was from candles and the hearth. Dazedly Heiri heard Grimsley's voice. ". . . Private Henry Lennard. . . ." His knees were mush.

Heiri saw the man lay down his pen, heard him say something. Grimsley beckoned Heiri into the room and, dismissed, took himself off.

"Well, what is it?" In the dim light Heiri could not see the impatience on the general's face but he heard it in his voice.

Many a time Heiri had seen this man in the open air, usually on horseback, and he had wanted to keep his distance. Yet always he had been impressed with the authority and power of the figure before him. Now the man looked taller than ever with firelight behind him and candlelight casting up shadows. The lines in the hollows of his cheek make his face look long and lofty, his firm chin and well-carved mouth expressive of power and command.

"What is it you want, Private?" the general repeated sharply.

"Sir, I wish a horse."

There was absolute silence. It came to Heiri that Sumter was about the age of his father. He tried to associate the man with his father but could not.

"Sir, I wish to go to my brother. He—" His voice gave out.

The general waited. Heiri thought again of his father, his father's giving him his own horse. Sparks flashed up the chimney and something caught fire with a flare of light. Sumter moved slightly and light fell on the moving of his shoulder as if to ease discomfort.

He got his arm hurt too. Like me. Heiri drew a deep audible breath. "Sir, I have not seen my brother in seven months. He went first to fight for liberty. I came later. I have now at last heard of him." He paused. "He went west to the Pacolet. I wish to join him."

Sumter continued silent.

Heiri thought of more to say. "I got took at Fishing Creek. My horse, my gun, all was lost." He paused again. "My friend helped me get away, we both got away, and when I was well of this—" he gestured toward his head and eye, "—and this—" he touched his shoulder, "—we came back." He stopped. The general seemed now on the verge of speaking. Heiri concluded. "I have now no horse. Of my own. I work now with cattle and wagons."

In the gloom Heiri could not see the change in Sumter's face, the relaxation of taut lines, even the hint of a smile. A militiaman who'd come and ask for a horse! Instead of just taking off with one.

"Well, Private—Henry, it may be we owe you a horse. What sort was it you lost?"

"Oh, a good, good horse, sir! My father's good riding horse! My father's own, a strong horse and wise!"

The general reached with his left hand for a scrap of paper and dipped his pen.

"And one also for my friend, Willi Rieder? My friend that helped me get away from the enemy?"

"Oh, two of you?" Heiri was about to explain how Willi was also a friend of his brother when the general asked, "How did you escape?"

"We fell down in the bushes and lay there. In the dark till they passed us by."

Sumter nodded—now Heiri saw his smile—folded the note and handed it to him. "Take this to your captain. You and William Rieder to be given a horse and a stand of arms apiece. And also—" Heiri did not hear the irony in the phrase, "—a month's leave."

As never before Heiri wished for the right words. All he could say was, "Sir, I will come back! If I live! If God wills!"

When the soldier had gone, the general mused awhile, his lips still curving in a half-smile. German. It all went to show how easy it was to misjudge a man of another sort or condition. He knew what it was to be misjudged. And misvalued.

Who'd sent that boy in here? He didn't want to know. *I'll give you work,* he thought fiercely, *all of you, one day soon!*

Sumter frowned, sighed, then had to laugh at himself for the contradiction in what he had done. Well, there went a horse and musket for what it was worth. Two horses, two muskets. They couldn't say he'd sent them nothing. His anger took hold again. Maybe one day they'd learn how to value such men and what they'd done to hold on to the country when there was no one else to do it.

Six of them met at the big granite rock on the thirteenth of January. In some ways the cold rain favored them, for few horsemen were abroad. In the afternoon they passed south of the long rough crown of King's Mountain. The next morning they came to the Cherokee Ford, found it unguarded, crossed, and took the south-leading road to Grindal Shoals on the Pacolet. They forded Gilkey Creek in a drizzle, then stopped well off the road for a long nooning, where they baked corncakes and tried to dry out, huddling as close to the fire as they could. Heiri felt the familiar aches and pains in his back and shoulder. Willi's knee was nagging him again. He had not ridden so hard in months. He thought of what he was approaching.

It seemed to Willi his whole life was to be only an endless ordeal of trying to get somewhere he wasn't. He never thought now of waking up to ease in a paneled room. Just to get where he was supposed to be, that was all life held. Where was it, that place or condition? Would he always be pushing for—pushing to *be* what he was not?

He thought now he would not ever be really a brave man. What he did was mostly because others pushed him, other people or some circumstance, and he never knew whether to be glad for it or not. And yet what was it that really made him move? It had to be something more than just submitting and taking the easy way out. The way he went now was not easy.

Well, he supposed he ought to be glad for poor old Heiri. Heiri was one of a kind. Willi admitted that too. *He's got more to him than I have. To have braved the general himself! Never in a thousand years would I have done that.* Though the way Heiri told it, he'd had no choice. *He's so dumb*, thought Willi. *And stubborn. And maybe that's what it takes. Too dumb to know what you can't do and too stubborn to stop doing it. No!* Willi contradicted himself fiercely, *do Heiri justice! He's not dumb! He's just—Heiri.*

Now wouldn't Joggi be surprised if they did find him. But like as not when they got there, wherever it was, Joggi would already have gone on somewhere else. In a way Willi did not much care. At least not the way Heiri did. Why should finding Joggi be so important?

. . . Oh, if I'd just gone out that time last spring in Charlestown, he agonized, and he heard again the low insistent voice, "Willi, come on!" *wouldn't everything be different now? Wouldn't I be different?* . . . *Yes, different all right. Dead in some swamp.* . . . So he'd refused to follow Joggi then, but he'd been trying to catch up with him ever since.

Why? Willi asked. *What does it matter where Joggi is?*

Because he went out free. He always has been free. He's always done what he wanted to do. He's independent of everyone. He went out free.

Well, I've come out too. . . . *But did I come out free?*

He thought of where he was going. This evening, tomorrow, whenever or wherever, it would be the furthest thing from freedom he could imagine—hemmed in right, left, in front, behind. Was that what he wanted? . . . *Well, no matter*, he sighed, *I'll do the best I can. And maybe when it's over, maybe some day at long last when it's over.* . . . His mind went blank. He could think of only one end and he must not dwell on it.

Heiri decided he would not even try to join Joggi's company when they got there. He would go with Eph to Colonel Thomas, let Eph do the talking and Colonel Thomas could put him where he would.

He wondered how many of his old companions he might find, especially the ones he'd first known at Cedar Springs. Some of those boys had fallen, he knew. With his own eyes he had seen two die. He thought of Jem Boyd. It could well be that Jem's long bones also lay gnawed and covered with leaves on the ridge above Fishing Creek. Yet somehow Heiri did not think so. Maybe tonight, he thought, he'd see Jem! And Billy. And Ike. Even Abe he'd caught that time playing a trick with Roker. . . . Now he was thinking of them all as friends. How had it come about?

He was startled to realize how many people he now thought of as friends. Ned Reid. And Eph Giles. His thought reached back. Rudi's Margaret and Jemmy and the little girl. Red-haired Andy Culbreth and his mother. And Nancy. Like as not she'd forgot him by now but never would he forget her, though her image came less frequently than it once had. . . . And Kate, dear old Kate! *Lord God, I owe her so much.* And Willi.

That a life like this could bring him so much friendship, he marveled, more than ever he'd known in all his years before. It made the other side, the hell side—not bearable but. . . . He would not think of the coming military action. He had learned it was better not to till it stared you in the face. Nor did he think much about Joggi, about what he would say to his brother or what his brother might say to him. He was afraid to.

They got soaked again crossing Thicketty Creek and twenty minutes later ran headlong into Morgan's army. Before they knew it they were surrounded by an advance party of horsemen, but with Eph along they had no trouble establishing their credentials. Absorbed into the retreat, they retraced the way they had come.

By late afternoon the entire body were making camp back on the other side of Thicketty. Howard's Continentals and Washington's dragoons, who rode in from Wofford's ironworks, where they had been having their horses shod, these units achieved an orderly encampment. Among the militiamen there was considerable coming and going as various ones scattered out to hunt for forage. By nightfall, however, most of the camp had acquired a semblance of order.

Eph, Heiri, Willi, and their companions were received by Colonel Thomas and the others in such a way as to put Heiri and Willi in a glow. Willi had almost a feeling of coming home. *Have I found it?* he wondered momentarily. *Is it only this good fellowship after all?*

As for Heiri, when Jem Boyd grabbed him exuberantly and told him about Roker, Heiri could hardly believe it. "After all this time? Jem, I—oh *mein Gott*, yes! it's him all right!" The two did not hesitate to swap horses. Now only one thing was lacking.

After supper Heiri asked Willi to go with him. He had found out where Moffatt's company was camped. Willi felt somewhat reluctant but he went with Heiri anyhow.

Most of the men around the campfires on the other side of the thicket seemed to have their backs turned to them—brown-shouldered backs with shaggy hair hanging loose over their shoulders or pulled back and tied with a thong. They looked like a thousand others that Willi and Heiri had been with in the last six months. The men paid no attention to the shapes coming out of the dark and hesitantly approaching their fire.

Heiri scrutinized each face he could see. One man noticed him and looked up curiously. Heiri, keeping in the background, began to circle the group to look at other faces. All were strangers. Men of the right size and color looked unfamiliar. His heart beat hard. He felt the beginning of a terrible emptiness.

By this time others had noticed the two figures.

"You call! You ask!" Heiri whispered, returning to where Willi stood in like perplexity.

"We're looking for Jake Lennard!" Willi called loudly.

Heiri mouthed silently with dry lips, "Joggi! Joggi Lienhardt!"

The men stared back at them. Blonde-streaked heads, black touseled heads, bushy brown beards, scraggly beards, scarred cheeks, one face remarkably smooth. A man slapped another on the back and that one got up and came toward them. Still Heiri did not recognize him.

"Joggi!" cried Willi, one low intense word uttered in such gladness as to be almost pain.

"Oh *Herr Gott*, Willi Rieder!" The two gripped hands, stood a moment looking at each other. Willi gestured toward Heiri.

Heiri stood dumb as a stone. So did Joggi. Each in the smoke-wreathed gloom looked for his brother.

Joggi was first to move, Heiri to speak. As they clasped each other, Heiri said, "Well, Joggi, I found you," and his brother heard again the old pleased note he'd heard a thousand times.

Joggi said nothing, but Heiri felt a grip in his brother's arms that he never had before.

Heiri woke early in the predawn hour of January 17, stiff and cold. He knew something of what the day would bring. Yet instead of getting up to stamp and shiver before the smouldering coals, he kept lying there. He thought of Savana Hunt, of how it felt to run almost in a tumble down the stairs from the loft-room. He thought of his mother as she moved before the fire, the sound of her voice; of Cathri and Georgi, the last ones up, slow-voiced and sleepy-eyed. He thought of taking down the milkpail and the cloth and of dipping warm water into the pail for washing the cow's udder. He felt his hand slap lightly the coarse-silk flank, "Saw, saw," felt the weight of the stool as he adjusted it, heard the sharp satisfying ping as the jet of milk hit the side of the pail. He moved with his father among the beasts, helped to bring in the pails, felt their heft, and helped his mother pour their warm and frothy contents into pans. His sense was not of taste but of sight and sound, what it felt like to do these things.

He lay in the dark seeing how the sun rose over the river swamp and the nearer oakwoods, rose clear above their wheatfield. He saw the spreading green of winter wheat, saw the brown of old cornfields. Thought of hitching up a plow to Early to take him across the creek, and felt the skip of the plow on the path, on the planks of the bridge, felt the easy plunge of its blade into the loam of the field. They'd begin plowing in February.

He did not think of these things with nostalgic yearning. They recurred to him as experiences. Somehow they were better than the fire. They made him whole.

When moments later the drum began to beat up the chill gray air and the shout rang out, "Up, boys! On your feet! Get ready! Benny's coming!" he sprang up not as someone torn from a dream, but rather as one who knew who he was, where he came from, and what he had before him.

In a different part of the camp Joggi too sprang up, with elation. Nearer at hand Willi moved with the old familiar churning in his stomach, of resolution and of dread.

Distant from all three, Rudi made his preparations the way a man does when he knows he has a thing before him that's got to be done.

29

The rain was gone. The sun had not yet risen but the day was dawning cold and clear. In the distance greencoated horsemen and redcoated footmen were easily visible to the riflemen scattered among the winter trees, Georgians to the left, Carolinians to the right. Most of the riflemen recognized the slim greencoated figure on horseback who coolly surveyed everything before him.

Tarleton was surprised that the Rebels were drawn up for battle. The sparsely wooded ground rose gently before him, dipped slightly and rose again to another crest beyond.

He had to move back as the advancing rifles began to crack. He signalled fifty dragoons to gallop out and drive the riflemen in. They had hardly reached full gallop when the Rebels' firing multiplied. Horses screamed, riders cried out and fifteen men, some of them officers, toppled from their saddles. The troop faltered and wheeled. The riflemen too fell back as ordered, reloading as they ran.

Jake Lennard, already smoke-black, did his work with dark-faced intensity. He knew how to reload running, when to turn, steady his long barrel against a tree to aim. He had not been chosen at random for this work. As he ran, his body was all one leap and motion, turn and twist of dexterity, every sense of his body coordinated as one. He was doing what one might have said he was born to do.

As the greencoated cavalry fell back, a rage of purpose took hold of their commander. Then let it begin!

Swiftly he deployed his troops, lined up his infantry—so swiftly, so eagerly that one battalion did not have all its officers in place when he ordered the advance. This battlefield was made for him—terrain, circumstances—everything perfectly suited to his ways! Then let it begin! And no quarter, no prisoners!

Except for a battalion of Royal Fusiliers, Tarleton had seasoned troops—regulars and loyalist British Legion—with two artillery pieces and ample cavalry support. The good red wool of their coats warmed the

air and the green livened it. The blue of the artillerymen's jackets made a
brave, bright assertion. Fifty fearsome Seventeenth dragoons trotted on
their flanks to hem in the Rebels when they broke and ran. The fieldguns,
called "grasshoppers," which divided the line into thirds, were ordered
not to waste their shot on the militia but to fire at the Continentals lined up
fifty yards behind them and at the cavalry on the farther rise. Behind their
own line, Scottish Highlanders and two hundred dragoons of the British
Legion waited in reserve. Drums beat, fifes shrilled, the grasshoppers
jumped on their carriages as they hurled their rounds. The red and green
came running under their famous colors with a lusty British shout and
bayonets leveled. So great was their din they might not have heard the
wild whoop up the field.

In front of them, Turkey Creek, Beaverdam, Little River, Tyger,
Crane Creek, Reedy Branch, Keg Creek, Brier, Long Cane, and Buffalo
waited. They'd faced it before; they'd felt it before, but they knew they
had to wait. Their muskets had an accurate range of only fifty yards.

Willi took deep ragged breaths, his throat knotted and mouth dry,
every pore of his body sweating, and he felt his head would explode. His
hands were big and wet. His musket weighed a hundred pounds.

Heiri glanced at him, saw just the bearded chin, for Willi's hat was
pulled low over his eyes.

Heiri felt only taut readiness. If he thought of the men coming at
him, he had to think of them as men with work to do like himself. His was
to keep them from doing it. He might not like it—he never liked felling a
steer—but at times you had to do it. Not that he thought of these men as
steers. They had chosen, he had told himself again and again, to risk their
lives as he had. All must take their chances.

He watched the advancing helmets, made out "G 16 R" in the growing light, saw shaven clamped jaws, gleaming buttons, polished straps,
musket and blade driving straight at him horizontal to the ground. He noted
a man to the fore, a big man with a sergeant's stripes, knew he was the
one.

Closer and closer the big legs pounded. Willi saw him too, aimed
the best he could. *Oh God!* Willi screamed inside, *How much longer!* The
seconds were interminable.

Quick and harsh came Pickens' shout, multiplied: "Fire!" "Fire!"
"Fire!"

A sheet of flame and smoke. The big sergeant pitched forward.

"Stand, boys! Stand and fire again!"

The line in front was checked momentarily, yet kept coming on. "Stand, boys! Stand! Give 'em one more!"

Heiri's mouth was drawn back in a hard grimace. Before him alien shoes scuffled, alien hands grabbed frantically at the winter grass that rose to meet them. Pain was all of it. No bullet or blade had touched Heiri's body. Yet he was all pain.

From a far distance, it seemed, came the order to turn as they had been told it would and to file around to the left and back. Mechanically, gratefully Heiri obeyed. The pace was quick. The militia hurried, closing ranks to fill the spaces of those who had not waited. Where was Willi? Ah, there ahead.

Down the field Tarleton watched with careless satisfaction. True to form the militia had broken. Now it was time to set the staghounds on them.

The redcoated Seventeenth dragoons wore brass-crested, high-plumed helmets emblazoned with the death's-head and under it the words, "Or Glory." They thundered out.

Willi heard the hoofbeats, looked back, saw the gleaming horses and sabers.

The militia scattered, ducked, and dodged behind trees. Blades swung. Gun barrels tried to parry them. The dragoons scattered also, the better to ride the ragtag down. One came straight at Willi.

Willi leaped to run for the cover of a scrubby tree, but as he did so, his knee gave way. He gathered himself half up and tried to scramble away as the rider rose in his stirrups to swing his blade. The horse checked and reared. Willi fell again and, looking up, saw Heiri above him, a great figure with his gunstock raised against the saber.

Willi rolled sideways and managed to get out of the way. Heiri did not.

Willi gained cover, looked back and saw Heiri down, saw the horseman lean low and saw the blade come down again and again.

As Willi stood holding himself up by the tree, a whirlwind of whitecoated cavalry, swept down the rise, William Washington's one hundred and twenty dragoons. Almost before they knew what was happening, the scattered British assailants—shocked and outnumbered—became the assailed. Those who could, fled. The sounds of hoofbeats and clanging blades moved down the field.

With great relief the militia now hurried through the trees to the rear. Mindlessly Willi limped after them, hardly conscious of the grind in his knee. Others kept running. Dimly he heard some officer haranguing them into order. "Form, men! Form!" The men nearest Willi obeyed and he did too. Now they were behind the Continental line where the battle was roaring, and their own officers were yelling and cajoling, getting them ready to rejoin on the right where their marksmanship was needed.

Most of the militia had escaped the cavalry charge unhurt. Young Lienhardt was an exception. He died exactly twenty years and three months from the October dawn when he had first seen light.

The regulars on both sides shot volleys and in the enveloping smoke most shot blindly. The British shot high.

But Rudi Näffels had brought down too much game in his time not to know how to make his bullets count, even in swirling mists. He'd had practice with blades also. Not that these men were game. They were enemies trying to take his country. Not that they were personal enemies; they were his country's.

He fought not out of loyalty to his comrades, although he now felt a certain amount of that, and not because of his admiration and approval of Daniel Morgan—he had a great deal of that—and not even, in one sense, to protect his family, for if that had been the case, he would have stayed at home. He fought for his country. Foreign-born as he was, he knew it was his country. He knew it deeply, intimately, the way a man knows his wife is his. It belonged to him and the likes of him, not to the men coming at him. Neighbors they might be, some of these in the green coats, but they were alien.

So Rudi let loose his old primal urges and fought with as much power and skill as ever he had as a young man and with more passion. He grappled as he would have with a savage trying to hurt Margaret. He killed as he would have a beast rushing at Katy or Jem. But when the savage or beast threw down his weapon, his face became human and Rudi's did too. Twenty years ago that might not have happened. Now he did not need Howard's shout to make him give quarter.

Tarleton had sent in the Highlanders and also cavalry to swing to the Rebels' right and attack their flank. John Eager Howard had seen the approaching danger. He ordered the Virginia militia on the right to turn and face the threat to their side, but they misunderstood his order as relayed and wheeled about-face and began marching to the rear. The Continentals saw them, saw their perfect order, and thought they themselves must have missed a command. They too wheeled and followed, and so did the other Virginians on the left. In an instant the entire line was retreating over the rise and up the one behind it.

The British saw victory and came on pell-mell.

Morgan, who had been with Pickens and the militia, was appalled. He thundered up to Howard. "Are you beaten?"

"Do men who march like these look beaten?"

But the British rushed headlong after them—light infantry, Fusiliers, the Legion—though many came leaderless.

Then—who would have believed it?—almost at the crest of the farther rise, those ragged blue backs turned and fired point blank and charged down the rise with bayonets.

The British reeled. The Rebels were on them like wolves. Shock and dismay became panic. At the same time Washington's dragoons swept around behind the British to block their retreat. Fusiliers threw down their arms and begged for quarter.

"Give 'em 'Tarleton's quarter!'" ran up and down the Continental line—it was Virginia Continentals whom Tarleton had massacred that day at the Waxhaws—but Howard cried, "No! Give them quarter! Good quarter!" Howard's command prevailed.

It was the beginning of the end. The Highlanders, deserted by the Legion cavalry, fought on valiantly against Pickens' militia, now blazing at them from the right. The artillerymen fought to the death but it was no use. For the British the battlefield was now chaos. In less than an hour after it had begun, it ended.

Banastre Tarleton escaped with the remnants of his Legion. Of his one thousand and fifty men, over seven hundred were killed, wounded, or captured. Morgan lost only a dozen or so killed and sixty wounded.

It was a remarkable victory. For the Old Wagoner, for Billy Washington's dragoons, for John Eager Howard's shabby Continentals and for the fierce Virginians. And for Andrew Pickens' grimy militia.

Joggi as usual was tuned to so high a pitch he could not wind down. Never had he been part of such a victory! It was greater than King's Mountain! They'd beaten regulars! And not just a skirmish either but a pitched battle! Oh, not like last year in the low country! Here they'd won! Oh, it was sweet and with surely no bad aftermath as at Musgrove's Mill with its news of Camden at the end, and at Blackstock's with Sumter taken off in a litter. Today surely there'd be nothing to spoil the taste, or very little, for their losses were so few. Except that Benny'd got away.

But they'd have to leave quickly. Make no doubt about it, the General said, Cornwallis would soon be on them. They must cross the Broad as soon as possible. Well, Joggi didn't mind that. This field was no place he wanted to linger.

But Heiri and Willi, where were they? He couldn't wait to see them!

The battlefield was a shambles. This was the part he hated most. He was not in general a shirker, but this part he was always tempted to try to get out of—the disposal of dead and wounded. If and when they could stay long enough to take care of it. To avoid it he would volunteer for any other service, no matter how hard or dangerous. He disliked even the routine duties of listing and guarding prisoners. It would be heavy work today. He thought enviously of the cavalry and mounted militia pursuing Benny.

He must find Heiri and Willi at once while all was still a joyous confusion, before the officers began detailing duties and he had to assume responsibility.

Now where were they? During the fighting he had not caught sight of either, but then he he'd not had his mind on either. Where'd they been? How did they feel now? A thought edged the back of his mind. A few militia had broken after the first fire. But not Heiri and not Willi! Oh no! and he was glad they'd got here in time, wouldn't have missed their being here for anything in the world!

Joggi ranged the sections of the field where the militia were clustered, a few already sprawled out resting. He made forays into various groups. Men relayed his question. Anybody here seen Willy Rieder? Harry Lennard?

"I saw Willy while ago." "He was just here." "Willy was over there."

Nobody said it: I've not seen Harry. Not since we first marched out. Nobody wanted to say it. Had Harry run?

Well, where was Willy? Maybe he'd gone to his horse, gone to get something from his saddlebag.

The horses were tethered behind the camp. Willi should not have gone there yet but he might have. A thought *would* obtrude. If Roker was still there—

Last night Heiri had told him about the horse. "Can you believe it, Joggi? After all this time! And I'll swear he was glad to see me!"

Now with growing worry Joggi thought, *I'll go look for Roker. At least that will tell me. . . .*

He had just passed the outskirts of the field when he saw Willi. Willi was sitting under an old cedar tree, still and alone. One twisted tree limb drooped low, partly hiding him; yet something caused Joggi to glance there.

"Willi?"

Willi turned his head and looked at Joggi. The expression of his face was set and strange. As he stared at Joggi, it changed.

Joggi stared back, called again sharply, "Willi!"

Slowly Wili got up, ducked under the limb and emerged into the light.

He looked at Joggi. Joggi saw now that his red-rimmed eyes were pain-dark. "Heiri's dead."

Joggi's mouth moved.

"Heiri's dead, Joggi. He got killed with a broadsword."

"No!" Joggi shouted. "How could he?"

"I'll show you. I've been dreading—"

"How could he? The damned clumsy—"

"Come with me."

"Wait! You tell me! Where? How?"

Willi stood silent. He looked away and began to tremble.

Joggi went up and grabbed his arm. Still Willi did not speak. Joggi wanted to hit him. He wanted to shake that look off his face. He gritted his teeth, said low, hard, "Willi Rieder, you tell me about my brother!"

Willi said, "Right after we marched off. I stood, Joggi. I swear to God I stood. I fired two times. When our orders came, I went with the rest—"

"Heiri?"

"Oh, Heiri never runs! Why I stood near him. Why I always stand near Heiri if I can. Joggi, your brother—" Willi's voice broke and he made a gasping sound. He sank to the ground and bowed his head over his knees and his shoulders began to heave.

After a few seconds Joggi sat down beside him. His mouth, heart, insides—all bone-dry—but he sat by Willi. It was not the first time he had sat by a sobbing man and wished he too could cry.

Willi told him how it happened, how his knee buckled under him and how he was caught. "Joggi, he saved my life! Heiri saved my life, Joggi!" Willi's voice crumpled and he started crying again.

Joggi stood up. "All right." He reached down and pulled Willi up roughly. "Now shut up, Willi! You show me where he is."

There were great wolfpits about the Cowpens, dug under trees and baited for the trapping of wolves. Bodies would be disposed of there, for there was no time to dig graves. They must cross the Broad before Cornwallis caught them.

"My brother's not going into any wolfpit!" He did not care whether he received permission or not, he'd dig with his bare hands if he had to.

He did not have to. Heiri had friends enough to help and to see that the mangled body was buried the best it could be under the circumstances. They even found a cloak to wrap it in, but it looked strangely small in the earth. Most people had always thought of Heiri as a big boy even if he wasn't tall. Well, Heiri's gone from it, thought Rudi Näffels. That's why it seems small.

They buried it not far from where Heiri fell, where surprisingly the digging was easy. Rudi found a rock to mark the place, wondered if any of them would ever come back there.

He stood by Joggi with suffering eyes. He had always remembered this younger boy as having a special gift for laughter and tears both. He thought of Madle, whom he loved, how she would bear it. Aye-God, she'll have to, he thought sadly. And Johannes.

Well, Johannes would take it as he'd taken other griefs, simply absorb it. Not that he wouldn't feel it. He'd feel it all right. It will become a part of him and stay with him to his grave. As with me. Rudi realized suddenly how he and Johannes were alike. Perhaps all men were. He wondered if Joggi knew that yet. You have to take it into yourself, boy, open up and take it in.

The gaunt boy's face was a mask. Not a boy, Rudi corrected himself. In years he was a man. Yet something in him stunted or arrested. Oh God, he's too young for all he's gone through. I must keep an eye on him. Rudi rested his hand lightly on Joggi's shoulder, but it was rigid as a post, not even a movement of recoil.

As for the Rieder boy. . . . Rudi sighed. If it had not been for him—
*Ah Lord God, who knows what devils torment him, aye, will go on
tormenting him? At least, he told us all that happened, was man enough
to tell his part in it. We owe him for that.*

Rudi sighed again. *I'll have to keep an eye on both of 'em.* He had
given up the idea of asking leave to go look for his family. He'd just have
to trust and hope. And certainly this victory would do much to assure their
safety.

"Joggi, thank God for how your brother died," he said low. "You
know how proud you can be of him, don't you?"

Joggi nodded slightly.

They left the Cowpens early that afternoon. In the evening Rudi
went looking for Joggi but did not find him. Willi said dully he had not
seen him since that morning. Inquiring of Captain Moffatt, Rudi learned
that Lennard never crossed the Broad. No one knew where he was.

Joggi had struck out through the woods. He was going home.

30

The armies were moving northwest, northeast. Joggi circled southwest, southeast. Not that he consciously planned a route. He went by instinct, keeping to wooded ridges, avoiding roads and fords where Tories might lurk. Even so, he passed the edge of many a ruined homestead and much desolation. He avoided the old battlegrounds at Cedar Springs, Blackstock's, Musgrove's Mill. They belonged to another time. The time that was now he did not understand. If he had thought once to lie down and be no more, that thought was gone. He felt a formless hunger, an inchoate urge. He must return to the place he had come from.

He brought Roker with him. He led the horse more often than he rode, for the way was rough. Winter forage was poor. The first night he found a little fodder by moonlight in a wasted cornfield. Getting the horse home had become an obsession with him. He barely thought of his family's reaction to his reappearance.

For himself he found some meal and dried meat in a saddlebag. A legacy from Heiri.

January nights continued cold and it began to rain again. People could not remember another fall and winter of so much rain. The second day found Joggi near Bush River. After nightfall he tried to sleep huddled under the branches of a thick red cedar but he was unable to stop shivering. At last he got up and staggered on, leading his worn horse, thinking perhaps he might find shelter in the half-burned ruins of some farmstead if he struck the road he knew to be near. Sure enough, in about an hour he saw a clearing and the shapes of buildings. He circled to approach them cautiously from the rear. No dog gave tongue. Either the place was deserted, or the rain and wind muffled other sounds. He found a door into an empty stable, where he rummaged about and found also some hay to bed down in. With himself and the horse under shelter he sank quickly into sleep, intending to be up and gone before day.

He woke to the sound of Roker's champing. It was full light and a tall, white-haired man stood looking down at him. Joggi sprang to his feet.

"Well, if thee's slept thy nap out, come on up to the house and we'll give thee breakfast."

Joggi stared in confusion as the old man pulled down more dried peavine for Roker, then realized he'd stumbled among Quakers.

When he emerged from the stable, he saw an orderly arrangement of outbuildings, poultry yard, garden plot, and orchards. The rain had stopped. Before him was a large, double-roomed log house.

Inside, two young women and several children drew back as the old man urged him up to the fire in a ten-foot-wide chimney, and in a kind of whirling daze Joggi crouched before it. Soon a mild-faced younger man appeared, a son or a son-in-law, Joggi did not catch which.

Breakfast was plentiful and hearty but he thought that his insides must have changed, for the civilized food—milk, bacon, and eggs—tasted strange. He felt as awkward and out of place as a woods creature sitting in a chair with tableware in front of him.

He told them who he was and where he was going although they did not question him. They seemed incurious as to any news he might have and he did not tell them any.

Once, as he looked across the table, he observed a child staring at him. The child was dresed in a homespun shirt and loose dark trousers much like what his own young brothers wore. The child's cheeks were rosy and round, unbelievably clean. Joggi stared back and felt as if he looked through an invisible shield.

He glanced at his own hands, grimy-gray, was conscious of his scarred, hairy cheeks and black, matted hair. A tear in his shirt was pinned with a locust thorn.

The child kept staring with his spoon halfway to his mouth.

The old man said "Jonathan, if thee's through with breakfast, thee can leave table."

Joggi felt as if he himself were somehow at fault and said, "Most like the boy's never seen such a fellow as me. It's six months since I've sat down under a roof."

The young man glanced at him with a momentary gleam of curiosity as the women with pleasant, rueful smiles passed him a dish of hominy and another of eggs.

The old man said, "Oh, there's been others like thee to pass this way. No doubt it's us seem strange to thee."

Joggi could not think of an answer.

After they finished breakfast, the old man asked if he'd stay for dinner but Joggi declined. The two men accompanied him to the stable and gave his horse corn. Roker, not finding his breakfast too civilized, ate ravenously. There were several stables attached to the barn but Joggi saw no signs of horses. Either they were hidden, if there were any, or they had been taken off by combatants.

As he prepared to leave, he said, "I thank you both—all." He felt there was more he wanted to say but he did not know what it was. He repeated, "I thank you for food and rest."

The old man had bright, dark eyes and now his look held Joggi's. "Young man, I find my heart moved toward thee." Joggi stood still. "It appears thee's got some trouble. More than common."

Joggi's deep-sunk eyes gazed back.

"Our heavenly Father lead thy way."

Joggi glanced down. Any words coming to his mind seemed either unmannerly or hypocritical. At last he said, "Sir, I thank you." He busied his hands with the horse's gear as he prepared to mount.

The old man caught a bridle rein. "Stay. This word comes for thee." He paused. Joggi waited, half annoyed, half wondering.

"Young friend, I feel much exercised to tell thee: Look to the rock!"

Joggi was startled. Again the bright dark eyes held him. "I do," he said low. For a moment his gaze was locked with the old man's. He nodded and tried to smile.

He swung up on his horse and looked down into the old face that had gladdened now and was soft with light though the day was overcast. Joggi caught up the reins and turned Roker.

The old Quaker cried after him, "Look to the rock, young friend! Look to the rock! Isaiah fifty-one!"

Joggi rode straight toward the woods, away from the road, and the Quaker fields were soon behind him.

Look to the rock. Herr Pastor had been a good teacher and Joggi a good scholar in spite of himself. He knew that Scripture. He even knew its context. "Look to Abraham thy father and to Sarah who bore thee." There were few rocks on Savana Hunt Creek, but, oh God, surely his father and mother were there!

It was almost dark when he forded Saluda some five miles below the mouth of Little Saluda. The water was swift and deep at the deserted shoals where the river widened, broken by islands, but Roker swam strongly. Afterward they came upon an abandoned, dirt-floored cabin where they sheltered for the night.

In the morning Joggi struck straight across the ridges, mile after mile of pine and blackjack oak, old ocean floor raised up, its dry white sand untouched by human habitation. The big brown oak leaves still hung tough and leathery, but here and there the green of long-leaf pine burst crisp in the dull air. He rode straight southeast. He would not pass through Granby.

Early in the afternoon he recognized shapes of land, and at midafternoon he reached the head of Savana Hunt Creek. He wondered if Roker knew where he was. The horse was plodding more wearily now and Joggi did not press him. For a while they went along the ridge some distance above the creek but presently they descended. There were still some five or six miles to go, and for hours their way had been withered and dry. Perhaps there'd be cane or a little grass by the creek, not yet winter-killed. At least they could drink.

They came upon a sheltered glade and he stood for a while watching the horse snatch at the green grass. He sat down and leaned against a big gum tree.

He had had nothing to eat since yesterday afternoon, when he had finished Heiri's beef and the Quaker bread; yet he did not feel hungry. Instead, he had begun to feel peculiarly clearheaded, although he was not really thinking about anything of significance. As he sat there, he grew conscious of the freshness of the air—a cool effluence of titi, bay, and smilax leaves and the running water—and he inhaled deeply.

The water trickled small over shallow shelves of sand. He thought back to times he had played and bathed in this creek. It was too shallow here to bathe. And too cold. He looked at his hands. It would take more than cold creek water to cleanse them. Still he thought of going on downstream to look for a deeper pool to wash in.

The chill inflow of air was an elixir. Something inside him caught a glint of light on a bead of dew. It glinted in and out. It sparkled again, caught. He did not move. That minute glint of freshness burst and renewed itself again and again. He sat a long time on the bank, must have sat there an hour when suddenly he realized he no longer saw or heard the horse.

He got up and listened but could not hear him anywhere.

He followed the tracks up the ridge. They went east, straight along the ridge above the creek. Roker knew where he was going. Joggi could only follow him.

The shadows were getting long but Johannes stayed where he was, driving down the saplings he had felled and trimmed yesterday to extend the enclosure for his cattle. The dank air muffled his axe blows. He was far enough up the creek that the sounds would not carry to the house.

They had been robbed again in late December although the military had gotten much less this time—a cow, a keg of flour, and a middling amount of corn from the old barn—but that was too much. Thank God, they had not found the new barn and smokehouse, where the rest of their food was. He and the boys were careful not to make paths there. Nor did the soldiers plunder them of household goods as before. Perhaps the officer in charge took pity on the woman of the house, who was ill. Either that or they scorned the poorness of what they saw.

He and Hans had been hauling up firewood on a drag. The soldiers had eyed Early speculatively, then turned away with a joke about the horse's age. Not old, Johannes knew, just overworked and underfed. His animals' condition grieved him almost as much as his family's.

All he knew to do he did. Work from dawn till dark. Hew, grub, contrive, and pray. He was almost prayed out.

He was glad for the work. It kept the dread at bay. Occasionally, as he made something new or better, the burden lifted, but after a day or two it descended as heavily as before. That was why he had come out this afternoon even though it was the Sabbath. It was hard to keep the Sabbath with no divine service to attend. He could not sit or lie abed all day, though his body might need the rest. He had come out this afternoon to look for a strayed steer and had ended up driving down the stakes even though each blow served only to tamp in his guilt and unease.

He had profound fear for Madle. Four weeks ago she'd had some kind of spell—a sudden seizure of trembling, dizziness, and nausea that left her white and exhausted. It was not apoplexy. It passed off fairly soon and did not affect her senses or the use of her limbs, but it left her weak and frightened. All of them were frightened. Although she rarely coddled herself, she'd kept to her bed for a week and even now avoided great exertion. Cathri and the children did much of the work about the house.

If he ever tried to think of life without Madle, his imagination failed. Twenty-three years this March, if they lived, they would have been married, and long before that she had been his light, his star. He could not honestly say that every day he had marveled and thanked God for her, but many a day he had, deeply. He could not contemplate losing her. Yet fear continued to dog the edges of his thought, along with that other anxiety that weighed on him more and more since winter had deepened. Weighed on her too, he thought, might have brought on the sickness.

If only this war. . . . Oh, let spring come! Let him once more begin to plant!

During the summer and autumn he'd managed fairly well not to brood too much over his sons, he thought. He told himself Joggi was as well able to take care himself as his father had been at that age. He's returned once; he'll return again. As for Heiri, he too was now a man. He had to be a man.

As Johannes worked, he tried to excise memories of Heiri as they'd shared tasks. He tried not think of Heiri except when he prayed at night. He had Hans. And Andreas and Georgi. . . . But they were not Heiri! And sometimes, especially as night drew on, there came down on him such fear as he could hardly endure, so that if he was alone, he had to stop work and fall down and cry out loud to God. He had done it this afternoon.

One after another he drove the big pointed stakes into the creekbed, trying to drive down his fear. Suddenly between his blows, his ears picked up other sounds. Somebody coming, coming quietly. And it wasn't one of the children for they would have called. Gripping his axe handle, he moved up the bank.

Joggi heard the thuds of the axe and knew almost certainly who was making them. Only two that he knew on Savana Hunt could heave an axe with such power and one would not do it again. Guided by the sounds, he descended.

The man who waited for him was grim-faced almost beyond recognition.

"Papa!"

The face did not change, or if it did, Joggi could not see it in the fading light.

"It's me, Papa! It's Joggi!"

Still gripping his axe, Johannes came forward, gray in the winter woods. He shook his head slightly as if perplexed and he might even have tried to smile but Joggi had stopped where he was.

"Joggi?" Johannes half-frowned, half-smiled. "What—where have you come from?"

"I came from back that way. I heard your axe and I knew it was you. Papa—" Joggi stepped forward, again stopped. Suddenly he could say no word. His silence became terrible.

Creekwater rushing over roots and sand prolonged the silence.

Johannes said heavily, "You've come to tell us something."

Joggi had not thought much of how he would tell it, had thought only that his father must know first. Let his father tell his mother and the others. But now he felt the unaccustomed thrust of owing them more than just to bring himself home. And what had he to bring them?

He reached out to close his hand around a small trunk, seeking the feel of it. He looked at his father and mouthed his brother's name. Then he dropped his eyes, no longer able to meet his father's look, and turned his head aside.

His father came up and grasped Joggi's shoulder. "Is your brother dead?" he asked harshly.

As Joggi looked up, the big hands gripped his shoulder so hard it hurt; then he felt himself flung away. His father turned and tramped off, his feet crashing through bushes and shrubs, till some dozen yards away he stumbled slightly, then lowered himself to the ground. There he sat with his back to his son and his head bowed over his knees. In the gray light Joggi watched that back, still and unmoving.

After a while he took a few steps forward and called low, "Can I tell you how it was?"

"I don't want to hear it now."

It grew darker. Johannes continued to sit bowed, unmoving. At last Joggi went nearer to him. "Papa?"

Johannes looked up. Even in the half-light Joggi could see how his face had changed. He had never seen that face before.

Johannes groaned and made a partial attempt to rise, then as if with great difficulty he heaved himself up. "Yes. She'll worry." He looked about him, saw the axe and went to pick it up. "I have to go." He shouldered the axe, then stopped and looked back at Joggi. "Where were you intending to go?"

A bleakness he had never known came over Joggi. "Here," he said faintly.

Johannes made no answer.

"I was coming to you. And to Mama."

Johannes turned and went tramping up through the woods. Joggi stayed where he was for a moment, then followed his father.

Johannes went on, never looking back, never saying a word.

At last Joggi called, "Papa!" There was no answer.

Joggi hurried, caught up, caught hold of his father's arm. "Papa, you—you—"

Johannes paused slightly, then jerked away and Joggi grew more afraid.

"Papa! Stop! Stop and talk to me!" He had begun to think. How would it affect his mother and the children if his father came in like this? "Wait. I know it's late, but you mustn't go home right now or else— Mama—"

"Ah yes, your mother. And do you care that much for her? Do you begin at last to care what your mother feels and suffers?"

Joggi recoiled as if struck; yet even as he recoiled, he recognized his father's anger as at least sane, but it broke something inside him. He cried out, "You wish I hadn't come? You'd rather we'd just disappeared and you wouldn't know anything about it? I thought you'd *want* to know how he died—how he was buried—" Hard tears hurt Joggi's throat. "I thought you'd want to know—and be proud—" He was crying as loud as a child. "I thought you'd want me to come! I too am your son!" In the darkening woods he stumbled and caught against a tree and cried as he never had before, never in the five years past. He was crying worse than Willi. He was on the ground.

And then he felt his father's arms about him.

"Oh my son, God forgive me! Oh my dear son!"

Joggi turned his head from side to side, burrowing it hard against his father's breast.

31

If Johannes ever thought to conceal anything from Madle, he found it difficult, and so tonight greatly as he feared to tell her, he knew he could not wait until morning. And, oh God, what of Joggi? The house, the neighborhood was not safe. Yet cold and starved as the boy was, what was he to do? Bring him home anyhow and take the chance.

Very little light shone between the cracks of the shutters. Only the smell of smoke told of warmth and light inside. It was deep dusk. The outside work was done, for the old cow was dry and the heifer would not find her calf until March. These were lean days.

Johannes stopped in the lee of the old barn. "Wait, Son, I must tell you something." They had been walking in silence. "Your mother's not well. I fear to tell her this news but I know I must. And it may be—it may be your coming will help her. But you must know—" he put his hand on Joggi's shoulder, no longer rigid, "your mother—she's had some kind of spell."

"What kind of spell? What happened?" Joggi asked sharply.

Johannes told him.

"You think I should wait to—"

"Oh no. I know now you must come in."

While they stood there, the door opened and Andreas and Georgi came out to get a backlog they must have forgotten. The two at the barn waited till the boys had gone inside, then walked up to the high little house that loomed so black against the sky.

The smells of sizzling bacon and of stewing apples met them. Cathri was tending to the supper, Anneli was picking out nut kernels, and Madle sat near the hearth with a piece of coarse cloth in her lap, stitching more by feel than by sight. Andreas was scratching letters on a smooth piece of wood for Georgi to copy. These days they did not keep the Sabbath rigorously.

At the scrape of the door opening everyone looked up. Anneli gave a little cry but Madle was first to move. Dropping her cloth on the floor, straight to Joggi she flew and clasped him, murmuring and crying.

Joggi held her close. He was so drained, yet so pliant and newly opened that he wept too but not as he had before. "Mama," he kept saying, "Oh Mama!"

"Come up to the fire. Let me see you."

He steered her to her chair and Anneli pushed up her own stool for him. Madle sat crooning and crying and stroking his matted hair, laughing softly and looking into the scarred face of her firstborn, and Joggi almost forgot why he had come home.

He knew in her what he had always known, that curious combination of care and knowledge that make up authority, that underlying mother's stratum of forbidding and forgiveness—something to jerk away from, something to rest in. He smiled his own upturned smile, like hers. He saw no signs of her illness.

"You came back."

"I had to."

Madle glanced up at Johannes, who stood near the door not moving. She looked back to Joggi. "Have you seen your brother?"

Joggi's face changed. His body seemed to weaken and harden at the same time. The great dread door swung open.

"Yes, Mama." He lunged. "We met at last four days ago—no, five. The night before the battle—" Joggi's voice sounded weak and high, unlike his own, "—he found me at last. For the last time he found me."

Everyone waited. Again Madle looked at Johannes.

In the long silence she began to understand, and the children did too as they saw it in the faces of their parents. Still they waited, making no move or sound.

At last Joggi's words came again, crushed soft and strained as though through a sieve. "My brother—Heiri—was brave and good. He died—saving another man. Be proud—all of you. Be proud of Heiri Lienhardt."

As Cathri burst out crying, Hans crashed his fist into a chimney stone. Madle half rose and stretched out her hand to Johannes. Joggi rose with her and the shock of her piteous gesture and blind face opened him up again; he would have helped her, but she turned to his father and Joggi gave way as his parents groped out of the room.

When the door to the other room was shut, whatever sounds might have come from behind it were covered by the sounds in this one—Cathri's gasps and sobs, Andreas' broken whimpers, and the younger ones' louder crying. Only Hans did not cry. He sat nursing his bloody knuckles, white-faced. Finally Cathri rose from her half-crouch and reached for the two younger ones to draw them into her arms. Andreas leaned against the wall with his face hidden.

Joggi gazed sightlessly at the fire until the smell of meat burning caused him to get up and pull the skillet off the coals. He glanced at the other pots, one of dark-flecked hominy grits and one of apples. He sat down again.

It was Andreas who spoke first. His throat was swollen against sound and tears kept rolling down his cheeks, but he said in a strangled voice, "Joggi, tell us more—about Heiri. You said—please tell us more."

Joggi looked at this dark-haired boy. He had been away so long he hardly knew Andreas. Yet Andreas was his brother. Like Heiri. He was Mama's and Papa's. Was Heiri's brother. Was his own. Andreas himself. He did not know this boy; yet he did because he was his own brother. Like Hans and Georgi. And Cathri was his own sister just as Barbara was. There came upon Joggi an awareness of the whole being of his family. And that was why he had come home.

Joggi looked into the shadows where Cathri sat huddled with the little ones. "I'll try to," he said low.

Andreas said beseechingly, "Cathri, let's try to listen," and Cathri murmured brokenly to quiet the children as she drew them forward to the fire. Hans said nothing, kept his eyes fixed elsewhere, but as Joggi spoke, his white face at last turned toward him.

Joggi told them all he knew, talking in the old family language, German, as he had not talked in years. He remembered everything Heiri had told him the night before the battle and he related all of it. He told them everywhere Heiri had been. He told of Heiri's service and of his wounding in late summer and of his recovery, and how he and Willi had at last made their way to the west. He told them everything Willi had said about Heiri's death—and what those who knew him had said. Long before he finished, the door to the other room opened and his parents were listening too.

Joggi told of the burial. "Rudi was there. And Willi Rieder. I said the words, all I remembered. Papa, Mama, I cannot say it meant to me what it should have, but I said the words. And another man, he said a Psalm. He said things about Heiri. . . . Heiri had good friends, Papa. . . . Rudi marked the place with a big stone. He fixed it in the ground so you could find it if you ever went there. I think you could find it years from now. If you ever went there."

His family sat quieter than they had been. For Joggi as for them, although his outpouring of words did not lessen their pain, yet it gave it shape and defined its limits. For Johannes the terrible fact was no longer a champing beast but a dark and human-faced companion.

He groaned heavily, "Aye-God! Aye-God!" and buried his face in his hands, but shortly afterward he looked up, straight at his oldest son. "But I thank my God you were there. We thank God for that, Joggi. And that you found your way home to tell us."

The words echoed in Madle's mind from some other time. That was what she had said to Johannes before this son was ever born, years ago when grief for another man was beginning to be assuaged by Johannes' faithfulness. But tonight, even before that memory came clear, something else came clear. She saw in this boy Johannes' son as she had never seen him before. Oh, he might not favor his father in looks—he greatly resembled her own father, a fact that had secretly pleased her—but tonight she realized that Joggi was indeed Johannes' son in the ways that mattered most. For that she too thanked God.

One of the children stirred. "Mama, are we going to eat anything?"

Johannes said quickly, "When did you last eat, Son? I doubt you've eaten all day."

At the same moment Madle and Cathri rose, nor did Madle sit down again until everyone was seated around the table.

As they were finishing the meal, Joggi thought of something else— that poor old horse. Somebody needed to go out and see if he'd turned up anywhere. When Joggi mentioned it to his father, Johannes was astonished as they all were, and he and the other boys lit lightwood torches and hurried outside.

In a few moments Georgi came bounding up the back steps and flung open the door. "We found Roker! He's out there! He pushed inside a stable! He pushed in all by himself!"

And so that night and thereafter tending Roker gave some of them a little comfort. But Johannes said the horse must not be kept near the house. They'd build him a stable by the new barn.

They needed any comfort they could get. The next morning Madle had another spell, this time a terrible griping in her chest as she sank white, trembling, and clutching at her breast, while Anneli and Georgi ran crying for their father.

Madle remembered everything she could of grace and light. It was not that she was unwilling to mourn for her son, but she knew that if she gave way to grief again, it would gripe and tear her to death. She prayed for a loosening of the clawed thing. For the sake of her family it must be prized out. She used the only lever she had.

She tried to remember dawns with rose-flushed skies and the light on Heiri's face when he laughed, remembered the sturdy feel of his warm little body when she held him, its child's perfection when she washed him, and the giggles of her oldest eight- and ten-year-olds as they played and teased each other. I have him yet. No one can take that from me. Her consolation was not so much in his present life—it was infinitely removed from her now—but in the eternally indestructible fact of him.

Some days, even as she struggled to blot out her fear for the others, she rested also in a consciousness of the wider, deeper life that comprehended them all, each one's givenness. She rested in the knowledge of their being together beneath this roof, even Heiri incomprehensibly having come home somehow, all here at last. Except one. When her thought touched Barbara, it brought no ease. Oh, my daughter! What have you undergone and your mother not there! But she must close her thought to that child now.

In the dark, chill room where she lay, she would try to rest, remembering light. The light would be of high places with summer sun on rocks and grass and valleys below. The sounds were of bells and the twittering of small birds.

Anneli knelt at the foot of the bed and tried to reach carefully, softly up under the covers near her mother's feet for the flat piece of soapstone wrapped in a rag, to exchange it for a warmer one. But all Madle's resting was fringed with domestic care.

"Tell Cathri not to forget to wash that old shirt of Georgi's today so we can use the good parts for patches to mend Joggi's. . . . Cathri, get Hans to help you pull together the beds upstairs. If you'll do that, they can spread both quilts wider and maybe they'll sleep warmer. . . . Make sure Georgi washes his feet tonight. Are you keeping the kettle full? . . . Don't let Anneli take off her cap. Where's your father? I have not heard him yet."

"He's working away from the house, Mama. He took his dinner with him."

"Where is he working?"

"I'm not sure."

No, Cathri was not sure. He had gone up the Road. And maybe it was not a lie to call it work, for he had gone heavily.

"Tell him to go ahead and bring down some of that beef for your dinner tomorrow, not to keep saving it. Bring down five thick slices, each as thick as your finger. A slice apiece for himself . . . and Joggi . . . and Hans ... and half a slice for the rest." Somebody would be left out, Cathri calculated quickly. "I'll have only the soup. The beans have soaked long enough, so you'd better get them on the fire." *I have them on already,* Cathri could have said but did not. "And let them cook slow. . . . Watch. Let Anneli watch. Don't let anything burn."

Cathri did these things routinely and if not as well as her mother, yet acceptably. What she did not do well, found most difficulty in doing at all, was in caring for her mother's personal needs. Her mother's modesty and reserve had always been such that to help her bathe and change her gown, to help her in even more intimate ways was a reversal of an entire life pattern that Cathri found almost unbearable.

If only some woman like old Frau Schombert, nurse and midwife who'd always come as needed. . . . But Frau Schombert had died three years ago. If only Frau Elsbeth. . . . But there was no one now, just the feeble and old or the burdened and young. And Mama herself had probably as much knowledge, at least of common ills, as anyone else. . . . If only Frau Theus—or Herr Pastor, who might have known of someone farther away. . . .

Papa had gone this morning for any kind of help that might be available. He would stop by his neighbors' who were still at home in the hope that someone might know of anyone with knowledge to treat such a case as Mama's. There was no physician at Granby that they knew of, or no one for people like them. Now Granby was a walled fort. No use to go there.

Sometimes Cathri tried to understand what had happened to them. Why had so much changed? . . . *War.* . . . *Why did it happen to us? We had nothing to do with it. Why should war happen to us? Oh, what is life that so much ruin can come down on you? Is it because you're bad and deserve it?*

She knew she had sinned many a time; been selfish, resentful, and lazy; been angry with her little sister or her brothers; and worst of all had had bad feelings against Mama. And how many days she'd forgotten God, forgotten to thank Him for Papa and Mama and for her brothers and sisters and for clothes and for food. *Is it because I wasn't thankful, because I sinned, because we all sinned? Is that why Heiri was killed?*

Sometimes despair said, Yes. Other times, most of the time, common sense told her, No. Heiri was killed because a British soldier sabered him, because Heiri was where the war was. . . . But he was good and he helped Willi! *Oh, why didn't God keep him safe? Papa and Mama prayed for him. I did too every night—or almost every night. And why did Mama get sick? . . . And why hasn't Barbara at least come back to see us? Does she hate us?*

Cathri could not understand what life was. She could not fit the beauty and promise with the squalor and pain. *I love my mother!* she cried. *I love Hans! And Andreas and Georgi and Anneli! I love Barbara! And God forgive me that I loved Heiri more than Joggi*, she wept. *Oh God forgive me that I'd rather it had been Joggi.*

Her mother's flesh was blue-veined and white like that of a fowl beneath its feathers. Cathri shrank from its nakedness, thought, *oh God, I don't want to care for her in these ways!* and hated herself for her feelings. *Oh Mama, dear Mama, don't die! Dear God, oh please God, let her get well again!*

32

At first it was hard for Joggi to know what to do with himself and hard for others to know what to do with him. He had not been part of their life for a long time and his mother's illness was now its center. Moreover, his presence was dangerous not only to himself but to them, should word get out.

Rest, good food, cleansing. Harder in January than in May, in the downright penury which he had never experienced in this house before. The fire still blazed and the housebeams stood, but he was shocked by the bareness and lack of common comforts—candles, good clothes, and warm beds, plenty of everything for everybody. And yet it was no different from what he had seen elsewhere, he told himself. Nor had it burned to ashes. Who are we to escape?

He thought of his words last May, "It's not over, Papa," and hated their truth. Would to God it had been over then.

He spoke very little of what he had known and done. A time or two Hans and later his father tried to question him about battles and rumors of battles, but Joggi's answers were brief and almost non-committal. October's exhilaration was crushed like last year's leaves. The sun that had glittered on January frost now lighted the gray interlacing of bare-boned trees against a flat sky—though the changeless green of pines still brushed the horizon.

Early in February the weather moderated. He helped his father put up a lean-to stable for Roker, and for the first time in years the two shared tasks. Joggi was humble in deferring to his father.

Alone, he brooded because there was so little he could do to help them. Except leave so there'd be one less mouth to feed. But where would he go?

Well, go anyhow, he told himself. But if he did go, he thought his life was done. . . . Then where was his life? He shook his head. He felt as if some nerve in him had been cut.

It had been second nature to replenish his shot and powder inmmediately after the last battle, and, of course, he still had his gun. Now one morning when he noticed deer tracks up the creek, he realized he did have one thing of advantage to his family. When he mentioned going hunting, Johannes approved, so long as he kept away from the river and the High Road. And other people's land.

"I hate to say it, but I'm afraid it wouldn't do for *anyone*," Johannes emphasized, "to know you're here. I don't mean I'd suspect a one of our neighbors of intending harm, but you never know who might drop a word, not meaning to, and with times the way they are—you never know what temptation can do."

They talked about families in the neighborhood, the whereabouts of the men. Some of the younger ones had been drafted into British service, even several who had served with the Americans. Because of this dividedness and because of the destruction of St. Johns, neighborly ties had weakened. Fear kept people separated.

Joggi asked about the Rieder's.

Johannes sighed. "I've been thinking about them, Joggi. What you told us. They need to know Willi's alive, at least the last we heard. I should have gone up there already to tell them. Hans Jacob Rieder, he'd have done as much for me, I know."

"You want me—"

"No!"

"I could go at night. I could circle back through the woods."

"No, Joggi, I'm the one. It's just—I'm afraid I won't do it right. And with your mother sick—and so much else on my mind...."

Johannes had obtained only commiseration from his neighbors when he'd gone to seek help. He'd found sickness and want in other households too and had been too disheartened to go farther than the nearest houses. He kept postponing the trip to Rieder's.

But Madle was slowly mending. By the second week of February she was sitting up most of the day, and now she urged Johannes to go to the Rieders. "Besides, I want news of Frau Elsbeth. Take her some of our honey and the walnut meats. Tell her I send my greetings and I long to see her." The next morning Johannes went.

The British had taken over Hampton's establishment at Granby with all its storage facilities and had built a stout stockade around it, complete with ramparts, bastions, ditch, and a necklace of outward pointing stakes. It was Fort Granby now, fully manned, and Johannes was not about to go up the Road or anywhere near that place. He went a longer way to the west, taking paths Heiri had followed last June when he had gone to meet Willi. It was a cold bright day and late in the morning, when he arrived at the Rieders' back door.

Maria, heavily shawled, came out on the windswept porch. Hans Jacob was not at home, she told him.

Johannes was taken aback and hardly knew what to say.

"I'm sorry. He's gone up the river," she was murmuring. "I don't know when—he said something about being delayed. . . ." Her voice trailed off.

Johannes stood silent. In the harsh sunlight he saw white strands in Maria's black hair, the network of lines about her mouth and eyes. She had always been a very handsome woman, and he had never noticed these agemarks before. But then he had never much noticed her face at all.

"Well . . . I'd like to speak with you, Frau Rieder, if I may."

She looked surprised but stepped back and opened the door.

The room that had once been their indoor kitchen was almost as bare as the Lienhardts', stripped of almost everything but people. A slave woman and a girl sat huddled near a glass-paned window sewing or mending something. At the back of the room children played jackrocks on the bare floor.

Johannes hesitated. "Please, I must speak with you alone," he said low.

Maria's face lengthened. She told the woman and girl to take the children to the kitchen house and help Rose. Her murmurous voice sharpened. "Mind, I'll be out soon myself."

Johannes took the shuck-bottomed chair she offered him before the fire, a poorish, sullen fire at the back of the chimney. Maria sat opposite him, still wrapped in her shawl. He thought, I must tell her at once.

"Frau Rieder, I came to bring news of Willi, good news. We have word of a big battle fought up the country, a victory at a place called the Cowpens. Have you heard?" She half nodded, kept her look intent on Johannes' face. "Willi was there, we have sure word. He was not hurt in any way." Johannes' flow of words waned. "Few of ours were lost."

Maria shut her eyes. Her face broke up. Tears came from under her tight-closed lids as she whispered her thanks over and over, *"O Herr liebster Jesu, O Herr Gott!*" over and over, and, "Oh Herr Lienhardt, Johannes, how I do thank you!"

He thought, *We live so separated. It's wrong we live so separated.*

She asked, "And—" then paused as if to change her question, "was there other news?"

He heard himself saying, "It took place on the seventeenth day of January. I'm sorry I didn't come sooner to tell you. Please forgive me. My wife's sickness—she has been so sick, though she's better now. But all I can tell you, all I know is, the Americans won a victory on the seventeenth day of January, and afterwards the armies were going into North Carolina. And when the battle was over—Willi Rieder was alive and well."

"Oh, how I thank you for bringing me word of him! The first in *so* many months!" She was looking directly at him, her gaze not lowered or distant, and for the first time he saw the swirl of feeling in her eyes. "Who brought the news?" she asked

It was the question he had not been able to determine how to answer. Now he found himself unable to lie, yet afraid to speak of Joggi. He shook his head. "I cannot say."

She scanned his face. Maria was not used to reading men's faces. She did not care to read them. Yet now she discerned something in this man's face she almost understood. But not quite.

She let it go. Like other men he wore a mask. Let him keep it. But one fact she had heard clearly. "You mentioned—" she resumed formality, "Frau Lienhardt has been ill? I'm so sorry to hear it. What was it? But you say she's now better?"

Briefly Johannes told her what he could of Madle, and Maria made concerned responses. He remembered to inquire about Elsbeth.

Amazingly Elsbeth had recovered most of her speech, Maria said, although not wholly the use of her body. "Nissi stays with her much of the time. She's with her now. Would you like to see her?"

Hurriedly Johannes declined. If Elsbeth could speak, she might ask questions, and he feared he might not be able to evade them as he had Maria's. Then too there was Nissi.

He pleaded the necessity of getting back to Madle, though he relayed her greeting. He had already set down their trifling gift. Now he took his leave. It had not occurred to him to ask Maria as he would have asked Hans Jacob, for news of the country.

She followed him out of doors. The sky was swept clean, a brilliant blue. "I wish you'd stay and take dinner with us. Hans Jacob will be so sorry.... Oh, how can I thank you, Johannes, for this good news!" Never had he seen her smile like this, and never until today had she addressed him by his Christian name. As he bowed in his old-country way, he tried to answer her smile.

She stayed on the porch to watch him leave. The wind blew up the fringes of her shawl, but her eyes were bright.

As he tramped through the woods warily—he would not risk a horse, least of all Roker—he hunched against the wind with his hat pulled low about his ears. He felt relieved and glad he had gone, yet was vaguely dissatisfied with himself.

Why hadn't he told her about Heiri? He didn't know. Not wanting to lessen her joy? Or not wanting to stir up his pain? Yet he felt somehow dishonest.

Also he knew he was wrong not to have seen Elsbeth. Old friend as she was, who had stood by Madle, cared for his children, surely to look in and at least speak to her was the least he could do.

But it would have meant more than just speaking. Most likely she'd have asked about his sons and he might have told her all. She didn't need that grief, he told himself. Nor did she need to be troubled by Madle's illness. No, it was better he hadn't gone. But Madle would be disappointed. He'd have to tell her the truth.

It was a long tramp across the sandy ridges, through pine glades and across the thick-fringed branches. Once he caught a glimpse of a soft brown form, a white scut, and he wondered if Joggi had had any luck. He wondered what Joggi did the days he too vanished, though they weren't many.

It broke Johannes' heart to see how the boy would come up to his mother, then move back, not knowing what to do. Cathri was now so efficient and every child so quick to anticipate their mother's wishes that there was little even Johannes could do for her.

As for his own work, he knew that what brought him satisfaction had once been only drudgery to Joggi. But Joggi was different now. It worried Johannes. He was not himself. In his very docility he was not himself. In a way Johannes understood it. He knew those raging fires, how they could leave you as sere as a blackened field. Or empty as a burned-out house. Yet a field would green again. But a house?

Johannes shook his head. *He's known far more of burning than I ever did. And younger too.*

As Johannes drew near his own woods, he heard the crack of a rifle, a distant crash, and for a moment he was startled until he realized what it must have been.

As he hurrried toward the sound, he heard other movement, then saw the back of his son kneeling by the brown shape on the ground.

"Joggi! You got one!"

Joggi turned his head, but his face showed no triumph. "I did. Though it could have been a cleaner shot." He wiped his bloody knife on the dead leaves and stood up. "Well, it's good you've come along. We can go ahead and dress it."

He'd said "we." And Johannes thought as they worked together and he talked of how Madle might enjoy the fresh venison that Joggi's face grew a little less bleak.

33

In South Carolina there are always certain days in February that say "spring." Maybe a whole week the word will be in the sky, the air, the slant of the sun's rays, the crumble and smell of earth, especially damp earth. It works up various urges, among which is the planting urge.

In 1781 as in other years this urge would be primary, for men knew that if they did not plant, their families would not eat. And it took a man's strength to break up the earth. In February it was hard to hold men in camps. In March it would be almost impossible. Wise leaders let their men go home. Others devised journeys and adventures. On February 16, Thomas Sumter left the Waxhaws with several hundred men for a quick foray into the lower country, a series of surprise attacks on British posts. The first would be on Fort Granby on the Congaree, where Sumter hoped to capture supplies.

But for men already at home there could be other calls. With under-the-earth stirrings and over-the-earth flights, a man might hear also a call from some place he had not yet gone or only dimly remembered. He might see something that looked like a path in heretofore trackless woods. He might remember waterways that wound among hills he'd never seen the other side of and folds of land against a far horizon. He might envision great broad roads and rivers. Or narrow beckoning ones. On Savana Hunt a young man heard names like Watauge, Tenase, Cuntucke. An older one suddenly remembered Strasbourg, the hills behind Basel, and the nightingale-rich woods above Mannheim.

Where? Where? Far.

Away up the creek Joggi helped his father clear newground, dragging the best timber to higher ground for later use. Johannes was determined to move some of his planting ground farther from the High Road and let parts of the old lie fallow if need be.

"Look at this good rich soil, you can see how black it is. Deep too. See how high the trees grow?"

They looked up the trunk of a soaring poplar, estimated the length of its fall.

"I'll deed you some of this tract when times are settled. If you want it. It goes a good half mile back in there."

"Who owns beyond it?"

"Unclaimed, far as I know. I'd hoped to get claim to some of it myself. Maybe we can when times change."

When times change. The only change Joggi hoped for now was that he might begin sleeping all night. And that his mother would get well.

Not far away was a gentle slope that he thought perhaps only he knew of, where a giant hickory and great oaks drooped their limbs almost to the ground, where there were coverts for every kind of wild creature. Many a time he had sat there motionless and watched them rustle among the grass and leaves—ground birds, squirrels, rabbits, mice. Or had climbed the hickory and felt himself free, no hoe or axe to claim him there. When he was a child.

He tried to remember if Heiri ever slipped away by himself. *Maybe he did and I didn't know it. But Heiri was different-natured from me. Yet he too played and swam in the creek. And he always wanted to ramble after me. But never to go as far as I did. Or stay away as long. He was always the one to say, "Let's go back." One time he cried to go back. . . . But in the end he went as far as I did. Farther. And stayed there.*

Oh, why did he insist on going? *Heiri, it was* not *I who led you, it couldn't have been!*

But engraved on Joggi's mind were Heiri's "Can't I go with you?" And that last night at the Cowpens: "Well, Joggi, I found you."

. . . Heiri, that war had nothing to do with following me! It was— the cause, the country, what we wouldn't give up to the enemy that wanted us body and soul! Freedom, Heiri!

Joggi heard again that suppressed voice by the bridge last spring, "Joggi, you don't know anything about living with people."

For the hundredth time he wondered if he would have gone to Willi's help as Heiri had. Probably he wouldn't even have seen Willi in trouble, for he would have been too intent on his own retreat or evasion. No, he was different from Heiri all right. His lip curled. He was a fighting man. Whereas Heiri was—just a man.

Oh God, what was it You put in him and left out of me?

His father was talking about a new house site. "Stop awhile and come up this way with me. I want to show you something I've been thinking about."

He followed his father.

"See what a prime site this would make for a house?"

As they surveyed the great old hickory and the oaks, Joggi felt only sadness at the distance between himself and the trees. Never again would he climb that tree.

His father said, "See those oaks? One of 'em would make a mighty fine shade tree. And if you put the house to the right over there, you might even leave the hickory. Cut off those bottom limbs though. You wouldn't want those limbs dragging the ground."

No, Joggi thought, *no limbs for children to climb.*

His father's hands and shoulders lookcd as broad and strong as ever. He saw them eternally hewing, lifting, and shaping. Suddenly he asked, "Did you always like to build and make things?"

Johannes looked at his son, then looked down and scraped a little trench in the ground with his old worn shoe. He examined the soil, smoothed it over. "Oh, I don't know. Well, yes. Maybe it was because I had to." Johannes raised his head, looked toward home. "Coming here as I did, if I was to make a life for myself, I had to learn how to do here and to make things. Yes, I enjoyed building." Because it was for you and for her, he wanted to say. For all of you. "It was what you had to do, especially those that came here new the way I did."

But few are doing it now, Joggi thought. The silence lengthened. He said, "But now it's different."

"Yes, the times are different." Johannes drew a sighing breath. "It was hard then in many ways, but I know this time's harder."

They stood in the pale sunlight looking at the crossed patterns of gnarled limbs and heavy boles, where light made white strips above or beside wider bands of shade.

"But, Joggi, I think as long as we're in this life, we'll have things to struggle with. Or against. Just when you think you'll have some ease or you'll soon have everything fixed the way you want it, why, then there'll come down on you some trouble, sometimes something worse than anything you ever thought of. To knock you down to where you almost can't get up."

Johannes was colored gray and brown like the hickory trunk, like the few dry oak leaves left hanging. "But you do get up, Joggi."

The young man's face was gray too but patternless as an overcast sky.

Johannes said, "Another thing too I tell you." He made a quick upward gesture. "He knows how we go. He does not forsake us."

Joggi cried out, "Then why did He let Heiri die?" He flung up his head. His eyes flashed fiery dark. "Why did He forsake Heiri? Why wasn't it me?"

Johannes' eyes and mouth took on the deepening look of suffering, but he kept his gaze steadfast on his son. "I don't know, Joggi. Maybe it was—appointed to Heiri. I don't know."

"And maybe," he said after a little while, "there's a good life for you yet to live. Here on this earth."

Joggi turned to go back the way they had come.

They cut and stripped the limbs off the downed trees to make huge brushpiles. Joggi had wiry endurance but not the lifting strength of his father. Yet together they accomplished a great deal. Sometimes the younger boys helped in the newground, but more often now Johannes put Hans in charge of the lighter work with Georgi and Andreas. Today the three were breaking up corn and cotton stalks in the fields across the creek to prepare for plowing. Everyone worked from dawn to dark and went to bed early. Even so, after supper the boys had an hour or more before Georgi was the first to collapse into sleep.

Joggi had been thinking about that hour. "Do you know there are chalkbeds a couple of miles over that way?"

Johannes looked puzzled.

"About two miles from here," Joggi said. "You can see seams of white chalk in the clay. It's in a red clay gully. If you could spare one or two of the boys one afternoon, or maybe on Sunday, we could go up there and bring some back. I'm thinking that old board they try to make their letters on has got so dark, chalk might mark it better than charcoal. Maybe easier to clean off too." He paused. "If Georgi went with me to get some, he might be more willing to use it."

"Why, yes," Johannes said slowly, "come to think of it, now I do remember that place. Not far I think from the path I took to Rieders. But I'd never have thought of that use for it."

"It would have to dry out and cure. And it may be too crumbly, I don't know."

Johannes was silent awhile. "No harm trying. Go ahead." He topped a trunk with vigor. "Tomorrow if it's fair. Take all three. God knows it's a hard enough life for 'em now."

The two worked on in silence. Joggi said, "That piece of board leaning by the wall in the old smokehouse, I was wondering what you use it for."

Johannes thought a few moments. "You want it for your scholars?"

"Scholars!" Joggi could not help smiling. "Georgi and Anneli?"

"Well," said Johannes, "if you give each one his own writing tablet, they might get to be scholars. Cricket may even get ahead of Georgi." The faces of both had relaxed into smiles.

Presently Johannes said again, "No harm trying." With one blow he severed a last limb. "I'll take my drawing knife and see if I can't smooth that board and polish it up a bit." After a few moments he said, "Some of these Lienhardt boys do have heads on their shoulders. Herr Pastor told me that a long time ago. I'm beginning to believe him."

Joggi said, "Andreas is your scholar." *But I'm afraid he'll never have the chances I had*, Joggi thought.

At first Joggi had thought it was a game the boys were playing at night with their crudely marked board; then he realized what Andreas was trying to do.

There had been no school for almost a year; in fact, Georgi had never attended school, and Andreas was trying to remedy the lack. But with only a coal from the fireplace and a piece of old board for a tablet that had gotten darker and dirtier with use, the business was crude and difficult, and Georgi was not inspired.

One night Joggi had said, "If you took some fresh chips and drew a letter on each one, that way you could move them around and make words. Teach him to read words."

Andreas and Georgi looked up. "You mean chips from the woodpile?"

"Mama and Cathri burn 'em all," said Georgi.

"I have to pick up chips every day," chirped Anneli.

"But I think Mama could spare you some," their mother said, "if you put them to good use." She sat with her family in the evening now although her hands were quiet in her lap. "That's a good idea, Joggi."

What kind of chips? they asked.

As smooth and strong as possible. Try to get all the same size. Or whittle them down.

"Oh, and Hans can draw the letters!" exclaimed Cathri. "Hans makes beautiful letters."

The young ones were shocked at her praise of Hans. Cathri herself was shocked. She had meant it for teasing but it came out truth. Hans was struck dumb. When he recovered, he said gruffly, "Ah, there's nothing to write with. You can't write with a smudgy old coal."

"You can write with a quill pen," said Madle. "If your wood's smooth enough." She glanced at Johannes. "It's been a long time since we've made ink here, but we still have plenty of soot and water—if we can think of something to mix it in. Though for a pen—"

"Oh, Hans can pluck one from the old gander!" said Cathri.

"Hah! And get goose-bit? Not me." Their couple of geese that had escaped the marauders were very ill-tempered.

Everyone laughed at Hans except Andreas, who said, "Oh Hans, you can get one! You're smart enough to think of a way!"

"Let Joggi do it."

"Oh no," said Joggi firmly.

The young ones would not leave Joggi and Hans alone. At last Joggi said, "Look for a crow feather. That's the best kind. Herr Pastor said so. Keep your eyes peeled for a big black crow feather."

Their enthusiasm fermented and bubbled. Georgi wanted to take a light and go outside right then to get chips. Anneli said, "Why can't I learn letters?"

Madle drew the little girl close to her as she so often did. "Would you like to begin?" She had taught the older girls to read and write but had not yet begun with this one, her baby.

"All right, we'll set up school," said Johannes. "Three nights a week. Joggi can be schoolmaster."

"Oh no," Joggi said laughing, dismayed. "Not me!" He thought, *What have I started?*

"Why not?" asked his mother with a touch of her old asperity. "And Hans and Cathri can be assistants."

Hans groaned and Cathri was alarmed. "No!" they cried like Joggi, but Georgi, Andreas, and Anneli were gleeful. "Yes!"

Joggi shook his head. He meant it. Or thought he did. He glanced at Hans and wondered if the gleam he saw in his eyes was eagerness.

The next day Joggi's mind went out of control. All day it was busy with word lists—geography, spelling—words for all of them, Hans included. It occurred to him that of all his brothers, he knew Hans least. It could even be that Hans knew more words than he himself did.

When he began reckoning up his own store, he was astonished to realize the size of it and all that he had to tell. He was more astonished to discover that he wanted to tell it. His mind formulated patterns and procedures. The lack of physical implements would be no deterrent.

Late in the day he said, "I've been thinking, Papa. Maybe I *can* help the boys more than I thought. What we talked about last night."

It took Johannes a minute to recover the subject. His face lighted. "Yes, I know you can." After a while he said, "We've still got the old Bible. And a few old books in my chest the soldiers despised."

Joggi had not thought of the Bible although it had been the staple of his own education. His mind had envisioned a freer world than the one between those boards.

Of course, the Bible contained quite a variety of printed matter, all kinds of words and doubtless many he'd forgotten. Some stories too that young ones liked. At least he had, some of them.

He heard again Herr Pastor's reading voice, dry and stiff. Moses, Samuel, Elijah. . . . So many were about old men, men born old, like Herr Pastor. . . . Really? How about David?

Joggi had always liked David best. Because David was never old. Even when he died "full of years" and a young girl had to sleep with him to keep him warm though he "knew her not," yet somehow David was always young—killing a lion, killing Goliath, evading his enemies. An outcast and a fugitive. Always struggling with somebody or something. Sinned a great sin, two sins. . . . But "a man after God's own heart." That didn't make sense. Joggi's thought took a long leap: strange that Christ should be called the Son of David. Because Christ struggled even harder than David?

. . . Oh, I can't get caught up in all that again. Let parsons tell all that. All I know is that words give shape and sometimes make things clear. And it may be that in trying to give words and letters to my brothers— Joggi did not include the little girl—*I can. . . .* His thoughts stopped. He did not know what he hoped for. Something about the untracked simplicity of Georgi's mind that beckoned him. He'd find a path. Or make one.

In bed a few nights later after a schoolmastering session, Joggi realized he had ceased to feel oppressed by the rooftop and the nearness of brotherly bodies. He had even consented to let Georgi instead of Andre as sleep next to him, and though he stayed awake long after the others, the closeness of the hard young body somehow made him feel that he belonged where he was. With Georgi's warm back wedged against him, he was fastened down securely to where he was, far less likely to turn and toss with the turning of trails, or to lie only half asleep with the rise and fall of hoofbeats beating in his head.

34

By the third week of February, Johannes had cleared five acres of ground a mile and a half up the creek. With Joggi's help the largest trees had been felled and the limbs and brush piled in a dense row around the border. Normally much would have been burned, but there could be no telltale burning this year. Next came the toil of chopping out roots. Stumps would be dug up later, though some not for years.

Their food was not plentiful; still Joggi was eating better than he had eaten on the march. His clothes were almost as ragged as they had been, but in deference to his mother he had trimmed his hair and beard and gotten rid of the smoke grime that seemed to have been ground into his skin. He seldom smiled, although he was not above a chaffing remark. He had been at home a month and not seen a soul outside his family. Until February 23, when Herr Rieder came calling.

Rieder came by the path Johannes had used several weeks earlier. Thus he found both Lienhardts at work in their clearing.

Joggi heard and saw him before Johannes did and almost failed to recognize him. They exchanged looks of astonishment. This boy was not the one Hans Jacob expected to see.

Johannes masked his unease as he went forward.

Hans Jacob spoke heartily in his old way. Tethering his horse, he said, "I'm sorry it's taken me so long to get down here. I've been trying to come every day since you came to tell us about Willi, but it's been just one thing and another every day, so I said this morning, 'I'm going down there today, come hell or high water, I'll go today.' Joggi, I'm glad to see you," shaking hands, "mighty glad." He paused. "Where's—how's Heiri?"

There was a brief silence. Johannes said, "Heiri's not with us, Hans Jacob. He was killed in that battle. It was Joggi came home to tell us."

Rieder's face changed. "Johannes! Oh man, I'm sorry!" He moved forward as if to grip Johannes' arm or shoulder, but something about the other man's look stopped him. He turned to Joggi, who was staring at the ground. "Oh, I am sorry! Why didn't you—" He faltered. "You didn't say anything, Johannes, when you came."

Johannes took a deep breath. "I wasn't up to it at the time. And, Hans Jacob," he spoke hurriedly, "you realize you're the only one besides us to know Joggi's here. You know how dangerous it could be if—if word got out. That's one reason I said nothing to Maria. About Heiri. I was afraid one thing might lead to another."

"Oh, I'll say no word! You can rest assured of that! Oh no, I'll not say a word!" He looked from one to the other, but their faces seemed to forbid more questions. He said heavily, "Well, that news you brought us, this knocks it to pieces—or takes from the satisfaction of it. If I'd known before—though what I could have done or said. . . . " He shook his head, his face now taut with the strain that made him appear so different from the old Hans Jacob.

"Will you come on up to the house?" Johannes asked.

"If it's all the same, I'll just talk here. I came to tell you—and I brought a thing or two, though I didn't know, I had no idea how it would be."

They stood silent a few moments. Johannes was about to speak when Hans Jacob said, "You've been busy here, I see. You've made a big clearing."

"Yes, and I couldn't have done it without this fellow."

"Looks like good ground. Will you put in a crop here this year?"

"I'll try."

"In hopes of keeping it?" Hans Jacob half smiled.

"In hopes right now of planting it. If my seed holds out."

"If you're short, I can let you have seed," Hans Jacob offered quickly.

Johannes was annoyed that he'd revealed his need.

Hans Jacob continued, "I can't begin to plant what I would ordinarily. With so few hands. We'll do well to get a third in the ground of what we usually do. Will you plant a full crop?"

"We'll try. We'll need it."

To Joggi it felt both familiar and strange. How many times as a child he'd stood listening, not listening, to such conversation? And even now what did he care about acreage and corn yields? He felt like a tired young hound between two old watchdogs. Yet he was trying, he told himself, trying as best he could to aid if not match his father's lift and heave, at least to be part of his world. Although Joggi's efforts were without deep desire, he kept feeling he had to complete something, the tasks he'd slighted or run away from, the tasks he'd left for Heiri. Many times the thought came that he was doing Heiri's work.

"Well, what's happening up the Road?" asked Johannes. "Anything new?"

"You haven't heard?"

"I don't hear anything, Hans Jacob. I don't go anywhere, talk to anybody. What's going on?"

"Well, I'll tell you. One reason I came this back way instead of down the Road." Hans Jacob shot a glance at Joggi. "You don't know about Thomas Sumter trying to take Granby?"

"What? No, I heard nothing. When? What happened?"

Joggi stood very still. "Trying," he'd said.

"Some couple hundred men with him, they came from up the country, came down through the Forks and down this side the river. Up through the woods back of Mathias' land."

"What? When?"

"Four days ago, early Monday morning. Must have been three hundred of 'em. They just appeared out of the woods and came right up to the fort, right up to the walls. They built a kind of log tower or turret and climbed up inside it so they could shoot down over the walls."

"Were they surprised?" Johannes felt a lift of excitement. "Those inside the fort?"

"Nah. We were but they weren't. Some weasel slipped in to give warning and they'd already sent to Camden for help. But I tell you, all day Monday and Tuesday those fellows sure kept 'em pent up inside, kept the whole fort surrounded all the way to the river, and I think they might have taken it if word hadn't come Wednesday morning about the troops on the way from Camden. So they had to leave in a hurry."

Joggi turned away, refusing the question that burned his tongue.

Johannes asked it. "Which way did they go?"

"Straight down the Road, down toward Sandy Run. Toward Amelia."

"What?"

"You didn't hear 'em pass?"

"I've been working back here every day and Joggi with me. The others must not have noticed. So much comes and goes, and I try to keep the young ones away from the Road."

"Well, I guarantee you they didn't tarry. The Rebels, I mean. Or Whigs, I should say. I've got in the habit of using *their* words."

Another time Joggi would have corrected, "Americans."

The three stood silent. Johannes looked about at his stumps and fresh cut limbs. "Well! Right here!"

It was almost a year since a Whig force had passed through the Congarees but it seemed longer. They tried to think what Sumter's descent into the lower country might mean. Johannes glanced at the expressionless face of his son, then at Hans Jacob. "What you think it means?"

Hans Jacob shook his head.

"Any news from anywhere else?"

"Nothing much beyond what you brought. Or what Joggi brought."

Joggi had walked away. He picked up an axe and grubbing fork and went to another part of the clearing. His walk was as loose and lithe as it had always been, yet his body seemed slighter. Both men gazed after him. Johannes' face lengthened. Hans Jacob's did too, for he had wanted to inquire further about Willi.

"Was Joggi hurt in that battle?" he asked low.

"Inside some way, Hans Jacob. A man can get hurt more ways than in his flesh."

"His brother's death?"

"Yes, that but—I don't know." Johannes shook his head. They looked at the distant figure bent tearing at the roots. It looked strangely like that of a thin, fragile old man. "I'm just glad he's here with us."

"Johannes, tell me about Heiri. If you feel like it."

"He was cut down by a trooper, that's all. They buried him on the field. Rudi Näffels was there. And your son, Willi. Only twelve were lost on our side, but Heiri was one of 'em." Abruptly Johannes changed his tone, changed the subject. "How's Maria? How's your mother?"

No, it was not just Heiri's death that was the matter with him, Joggi could have told them, though that had brought it on. It was as if there was now a stalemate inside him between the dark and the light. He had thought one time that rage had consumed all light and turned it into its own dark joy, but he had learned that that was not so, that evanescent light still lurked at the edges of what was no longer rage but was now a grayness, a nothing.

He had caught the first fresh glints when Rudi brought news of Heiri and Willi after King's Mountain, and he'd learned they were trying to find him. Later, Ephraim Giles' report about Heiri's capture along with the unbelievable recovery of Papa's horse had stabbed him with a strange deep mingling of pain and discovery. But it was not till Heiri and Willi arrived at the Cowpens that the light's power invaded him. In a way, it was old, familiar, even troublesome because of its demands and revelations. Yet it was also new and invigorating. A brotherly hand that was stronger than he'd ever realized reached to grasp his. He'd experienced it with joy, the sight of that familiar, dear—yes, now he admitted it—dear, battered face and all it brought with it. It was what he had been starving for for months, maybe years, and he had not known it. But when the face was obliterated, the hunger was not obliterated, nor strangely the light that hung about the edges of his despair, sometimes intensifying unbearably.

He asked himself again and again why, even if his old battle zeal was gone, even if he could no longer summon up partisan rage, why he could not now muster personal fury at those who had killed his brother. But he felt only vague detachment. When he thought of the war still going on somewhere, when he thought of his former companions, he felt no guilt that he was not with them, and he refused to think of himself as a deserter. He would have been glad to hear Sumter had taken the fort, but he knew he would not have lifted a finger to help him do it.

A few nights ago Joggi had dreamed he was hanged though not killed, hanged by men he knew, who paid no attention when he tried to tell them who he was. They rode off and left him hanging, rode off in the time between daylight and dark and left him suspended between earth and sky. He felt the pain of his body's weight and its elongation, felt the roughness of the rope beneath his chin, and he longed for oblivion, but he could not die, nor strain as he might, could his feet quite reach the ground.

When he woke up, it took him awhile to know where he was. He lay a long while in that awful twilight, terribly abandoned. Gradually, however, he got hold of the present, and as he did so, thankfulness pervaded every pore of his being. He felt the bedstead beneath him, the rough mattress on its hemp ropes, was aware of the roof and walls and floor of the house. He heard the light breathing of Hans and Andreas, the heavier breathing of Georgi, knew them by name, and he thanked God literally for where he was.

He was in this house where he'd first seen light. He was here where they knew him. His family called him by name. Old Pastor Theus had christened him Jacob. He was alive, who he was.

He did not soon go back to sleep. He did not want to but to bask in that rich reality, for as he lay there, he had the strangest sense of being cared for. It was almost as if the hanging and abandonment had been real, but now his life was saved. The care was all about him, incomparably rich.

The next morning he remembered everything, both the dream and the waking, and although his feelings faded, yet he kept the knowledge.

While Joggi was struggling with roots, Rieder said, "I'll tell you what would do her most good. Of course, you may not want him to. Or he may not."

"What's that?"

Hans Jacob nodded toward Joggi. "Send that boy of yours up to see her."

"Oh, I don't know about that, Hans Jacob." Johannes was slightly alarmed.

Although his mother's bodily health had improved, Hans Jacob said, she was sunk in gloomy lethargy from which she roused only to fly into fits of wild agitation or anger. "My poor Nissi, I don't know what'll ever become of her. She gets the brunt of it."

"Why's that?"

"She's the only one can stand it. And now the only one *she'll* have about her." In all the years Johannes had known the Rieders, he had never heard Hans Jacob call his mother by name. "But one thing she's had in her head lately and that's that boy of yours." He gestured toward Joggi. "She thinks something's happened to him, and when she gets a thing like that in her head, nothing can get it out."

"That's strange." Johannes wondered, but he sighed and repeated, "I just don't know, Hans Jacob. Situated as you are, I told you my fear. Then too I can't answer for him."

"Johannes, I'm not sure it would be that much danger. Right now. Oh yes, I came this back way, but with the big scare at Granby, I think some people may be lying low for a while."

"You have much company?"

"Not from *them*. They know they've got all they can get from me for the time being. As for others, people don't visit these days. Nobody at my house anybody wants to see." Hans Jacob sounded unexpectedly bitter.

"I was ashamed I didn't go in to speak to your mother."

"Well, it was hard enough anyhow. I see that now."

"Did you say anything to her about Willi?"

"Yes, and that's what got her stirred up about Joggi. She wanted to know why nothing was said about him or Heiri, but especially about Joggi. You know she's always been partial to him."

"Well, I may speak to him. But don't look for him. And don't say anything to her either. But—if you want to tell Maria about Heiri—it's all right. Just—I know you'll be careful."

Hans Jacob had brought a sack of wheat flour as well as his regular gift of salt. Johannes tried to thank him warmly, wished he could be more grateful. "Madle, all of us, we certainly thank you, Hans Jacob. I don't know what we'd do—well," he interrupted himself, "we'd do without."

As Hans Jacob was getting on his horse, Joggi came across the clearing to say goodbye.

"Did I tell you," asked Johannes, "this fellow brought back my old riding horse?"

"No! You don't mean he kept him all that time!"

"It was Roker, the one I gave Heiri. Yes, he got hold of him up there and brought him back. Get him to tell you about it sometime."

As Johannes picked up Rieder's gifts, the thought struck him: *But he doesn't know what he really owes me. Or my son. Shouldn't I tell him? Wouldn't I want to know?* But somehow it was knowledge Johannes wanted to hold on to.

Several days later after talking it over with Madle, Johannes told Joggi what Hans Jacob had asked. Joggi surprised his father by saying immediately, yes, he'd go.

35

He felt two ways about it: he wanted to and he didn't want to. He was startled to realize his eagerness to be going somewhere, anywhere, and as he left that circumscribed area of woods and field, he had a heady sense of being himself again. At the same time he confessed he had little zeal for visiting old Frau Elsbeth, merely a nagging sense of obligation, for he knew she'd always been fond of him. Ever since he could remember she'd been there—scolding, indulging, ranting, once or twice even shielding him from someone else's wrath. No, he could not pretend she didn't matter. The main reason for his reluctance, he realized, was Nissi Rieder.

His visit to her last May was now a very small cameo, still a troubling one because he knew he could not ignore it. He remembered how they'd promised not to forget each other. He had not forgotten her. But neither had he forgotten her father and mother or her grandmother or others he had grown up with. True, he had known her a little better than some. But what after all did he remember about her? It was he who had opened himself to her, not the other way around. Why? What had caused him to pour out his thoughts and feelings like that? Who was she more than any other girl? He could not remember.

He thought of Rudi's words. "After this is over, get you a good wife." A long time, he thought, before he'd be ready for a good wife. If ever. A good girl maybe, friendly like the one at Ninety Six. But a wife? He shook off the thought.

Yet in spite of a faint underlying dread, his spirits lightened as he went through the woods. Six weeks at home, the longest he'd stayed in any one place since—Ninety Six jail. But home wasn't jail, was it?

He noted the fern fronds uncurling, the cracks of green in hard buds. Two or three weeks and it'll be another season, he thought. How long can I stand it? March maybe, help Papa plow and plant, but April? May? Last April was two lifetimes away.

He went in daylight because of Elsbeth. Dusk or the end of the day would be a bad time for her, his mother said. But his father cautioned him to try to slip up to the house unseen if possible. His father was more concerned about risk than he was. "Papa, they can't make me serve. Nobody can compel me against my will." Or catch me either, he wanted to add. He had not told Johannes about his imprisonment and parole at Ninety Six.

"They can make you uncomfortable trying. And maybe the rest of us too. Have you thought of that?"

"All right, but I don't see how I can go in broad daylight and guarantee nobody'll see me."

"I'm not asking you to guarantee it. Just be as careful as you can."

Joggi felt a tinge of anger, wanted to say, "And how do you think I lived to get back here?" but he would not talk back to his father.

It was a clear day, still damp from recent rains and moderately warm. When he sighted the Rieder house from the edge of the woods, he scanned the fields around it. He saw someone working at a distance, but too far away for recognition, he thought. Even so, Joggi felt exposed as he hurried down a field road.

As he came through the orchard, two dark children emerged from the kitchen house with a large bucket. They had thin arms and legs and it took the strength of both children to carry the heavy pail back inside.

Joggi mounted the steps of the side porch. The leafless fig tree looked smaller than it had last May. The cowhide chairs were gone.

The woman who opened the door said the master was not at home but she would call the mistress. Waiting, he wondered if the woman knew him.

Like Johannes, Joggi was surprised by the change in Willi's mother. What had happened to that languid woman? She spoke to him warmly, welcomed him and drew him inside, looked at him directly, and Joggi was momentarily cheered. However, when she began almost immediately to question him about Willi, he had to force his words.

"He looked well. As well as you'd expect. He wrenched his knee last summer crossing a creek in a freshet and it sometimes still gives him trouble, but he was well." "Oh yes, he walks all right, but mostly he rides. Every one rides most of the time." "Sometimes beef, mostly corn, but he seemed hearty enough. The last time I saw him." Joggi looked away from Maria, for he was still seeing Willi under the cedar tree.

She must have sensed his distraction or distress, for she said hurriedly, "Oh, forgive me! I was so taken up about Willi—you know or maybe you don't know. . . . Oh, your dear mother—I was so sorry to learn about Heiri. Please tell your mother and father how grieved I am, we all are."

Joggi bowed slightly. "Thank you."

"And tell your father—"

But just then Nissi came in. He rose. Although she did not seem surprised to see him, her face had reddened, and she hardly looked at him as she spoke.

Unsmiling, he greeted her, but he did not advance to take her hand. Light through the glass windows was hard on her face. She was a haggard, pitiable girl.

Her mother said, "I was saying to Joggi how grieved we are. About Heiri."

Nissi said, "We are. Yes, we are." Her voice sounded faint and stifled.

Joggi grew more and more depressed. Their words meant nothing. As always, everything here was artificial, and he was part of it. He said abruptly, "Herr Rieder said—or he seemed to think—how's Frau Elsbeth?"

After a moment's silence Maria began to speak of her mother-in-law's condition.

"Do you think I might see her? Herr Rieder said she might like to see me."

The women exchanged glances. Maria said, "Yes, if she's awake, I'm sure your visit would be much appreciated. If she's awake."

He fastened on the word "awake," and hoped she would not be.

The girl left the room and Maria continued to make conversation, asking about his mother. Joggi asked if they'd heard anything of Herr Pastor.

Maria believed he was still at Herr Adam Summer's above the Forks. She spoke of the destruction of St. Johns. Although he knew of it, Joggi did not want to hear more.

The door opened. "My grandmother will be very pleased to see you, Joggi." Nissi's voice was sweet and high, quite different now. As he glanced at the shabby, sallow-faced girl, suddenly his heart was moved a little toward her because she could yet speak like that. Then he saw her as he had seen her last spring in the churchyard. Who she was. Still.

Neither spoke as he followed her through the cold, unused rooms until they reached the bedroom door off the front hall. "She's changed, you know. I hope you won't be too shocked."

The room was overly warm and smelled of sickness. It had the same high bedstead and two old chests he remembered, but only one chair and a plain pine table, and none of the sacred china and other fine clutter that had been such hazards to small boys.

The old woman sat by the fire swathed in a quilt, her head sunk between her shoulders, making her neck seem even shorter than it was. She peered up, straining to see him in the semi-dark, for the window curtains were drawn. When she recognized him, she began to cry.

He bent to take her hand, but as she clutched at him, he took both her hands in his own.

Her mouth worked soundlessly.

"Now, Frau Elsbeth, you'll make me think you're not glad to see me."

"Oh you—Joggi Lienhardt! Oh you—bad boy!" she exploded. She frowned and smiled in rapid succession, clutching and shaking her fists still enclosed in his. "First time—first time I ever saw you—"

"I was squalling and red as a beet." He let go her hands.

She laughed excitedly. "Nissi!" She beat her fist on the arm of her chair. "Move—oh, you know!"

Nissi brought up a stool. Elsbeth directed its exact placement alongside her own chair, and as Joggi sat down, her flabby lips moved in and out. At last the dam broke and her speech came flooding.

"Your dear mother, I have not seen her in—oh, they tell me she's sick like me—oh Joggi, what awful times, such cruel times to strike us down and leave us low, flat on my back I've been till just a week ago, or no, two weeks, when I first set foot on the floor. Oh, tell me how she is."

Joggi told Elsbeth about his mother but stressed her recovery. Elsbeth was turned and bent forward toward him, frowning, straining to hear and understand everything. He was relaying Madle's greeting when she interrupted him. "And what now are you doing? Why are you now at home?"

Her question was like an arrow between his shoulder blades. After a moment he said, "I'm helping Papa."

She sniffed. He saw her eyes were no longer clouded. "Where's Heiri? What's he doing?"

Inadvertently Joggi glanced up at Nissi, who shook her head slightly. Joggi said, "He's not here."

"I know that." She pursed her lips. Her face darkened. "I asked you where he is now."

He tried to think what to say. He resented having to lie but was about to say, "He's up the country," when Nissi said, "You know, Heiri went with Willi."

Elsbeth looked from one to the other: Joggi silent and Nissi with her serious, anxious look sitting on the edge of the bed for there was nowhere else in the room to sit.

"Oh, so you've told him what to say to me, have you?" Elsbeth's voice was harsh, sarcastic. "Told him what he could say and couldn't say. Oh, I know how you keep things from me! Don't deny it, all of you! They think I've lost my mind, Joggi. They think my brains are cracked!"

"Oh Grandmother, you know—"

"I know I'm not blind! I know I've still got some of my wits if not all, and I know how you try to keep things from me, and, yes, I know how you talk about me behind my back too, all of you, plot and plan against me, plot and plan! 'Take her to the madhouse! Shut her up!'" Elsbeth's eyes darted wildly. "Put me out of my own house, will you? My own house my own dear husband built, this very house with his own hands—"

"Oh Grandmother—"

"I'd like to see 'em try! A sin to heaven! Oh, I've told Hans Jacob, I've told him to tell her—not once in a week, not once in a month, two months has she ever come near me! 'Tell her,' I said, 'tell her I'm here yet!'"

"Grandmother!" Nissi bent over the old woman, put her arm loosely about her, and said low, caressingly, "You know, you know all that's not so!"

"Not so? Can you stand there—get back! Can you stand there and tell me Maria Rieder's not laughing and kicking up her heels to the skies because I'm—because I'm—" Elsbeth's voice broke and she began crying with loud, high sobs.

Nissi looked at Joggi with despairing eyes.

"Shall I go?" he asked low.

"I don't know." She shook her head. "Yes. Maybe."

In her agitation Elsbeth had pushed her cap askew and one of her plaits had loosened and looped across her forehead, giving her a sad ridiculous look. Joggi longed to be out of the room.

He half-rose, sat down again. He took her cold, knobby hand. "Now, Frau Elsbeth, I'd hoped— You want me to go? I came only to see you."

"So now you see me! You see what I am! Go and tell everyone, tell everybody what a crazy old woman I am!" She jerked her hand away, tried to rise but could not, and fell back sobbing, her head bowed and hunched between her shoulders.

Nissi leaned against the wall near the hearth with her eyes closed and tears running down her cheeks.

Again Joggi almost rose.

Elsbeth raised her head. "Go! Go! What are you waiting for?"

He said, "Frau Elsbeth, I walked a long way to see you. I walked six miles and I'm tired. You won't even let me sit here and rest?"

She peered sideways at him like a bedraggled old owl. Suddenly her face primped up like a child's. She bowed her head again and began to moan, "Oh Joggi, I've been so sick! Nobody knows! Night after night in this room, day after day in this one chair. Nobody comes, nobody cares. Who wants to come and see anybody that's old and sick like me?"

"Frau Elsbeth, I've come."

Nissi walked behind them toward the door and he heard it close. Elsbeth kept moaning and trying to catch her breath.

Presently Joggi said, "You remember that night Willi and I hid under your bed? How you found us and dragged us out?"

Elsbeth stilled momentarily, said in a different tone, "Yes, and I made you dance for it too, didn't I, both of you!" But she groaned again. "Aye-God, I remember. Much I remember, Joggi. People you never heard of. Places you never saw and never will. Oh God, have mercy."

She lifted her apron to dab at her eyes, then wiped her whole face and tried to push her hair up under her cap. He saw the sunken hollows in her wide flat cheekbones.

"Joggi, you don't know. What it's like," she whispered. "Yes, I remember. How it was, how everything used to be." Her voice, her eyes were sad now with an expression he'd never seen in them before. "Joggi, that's all I have left now. To remember."

He thought, *How strange is life. Heiri gone, and poor old Frau Elsbeth still here. Yet her life too gone in a different way. . . . Is it? Has it gone?*

Suddenly he wanted her to know about Heiri, for it was as if her knowing would bring her back and bring something of him back too.

He said, "Frau Elsbeth, I didn't tell you a while ago, but Heiri is dead. He was killed in that battle. I came home to tell Papa and Mama. That's why I came. Why I stayed."

She sat in silence, such a long still silence that he grew afraid until she began to clench and unclench her hands. "Oh, poor dear little Madle.

Oh, Johannes!" She closed her eyes, shook her head a time or two, but did not sob again, only moaned softly every once in a while, "Ohh!"

They sat without talking for some time. He saw that now she was staring at the fire. It had burned low and he was about to rise and put wood on it when Elsbeth spoke.

"Joggi, years ago—before you were even thought of—well, you were thought of but not yet born, not yet named—your mother would come to see me." She was not turned to face him but was looking at the coals. "Oh, I know she didn't want to, she had to come here for milk, but I'd call her in and talk to her or just talk *at* her, you know how I do. Johannes was building his house where you now live, but they were staying here in a rubbishy kind of place it was then, it was all we had to offer. Well, she had lost much and gained little, she was new in the country and such a frail kind of girl. She'd sit here. . . ." Elsbeth voice faded. She breathed a long sigh. "Yet so strong, Joggi, so strong! You see, you know what she became. So many of you, such fine children, and I wished so many times I could be like her."

Elsbeth fell silent again. Joggi simply sat and wondered.

"But what I'm trying to tell you, what I'm getting at if I can say it. . . . You're her child! You are! . . . Heiri was, I don't know how it is, but in some ways—Heiri, strong like your father, always a strong boy from the time he was born, stronger than you and a good boy and I loved Heiri but—" She looked at him questioningly as if he might tell her how to say it.

The silence between them deepened.

"He was good and brave, Frau Elsbeth. Better than I am. He died saving another man's life. And it's so hard—" his voice was husky, "—to lose him—when I know he was so much better."

Again neither spoke for a while.

"What's 'better'?" Her voice gained some of its old vigor. "No, he was not like you, he did not have in him that mischief, that daring, but do you think because he was good, do you think you are now bad?"

Joggi did not answer.

"Well!" She sniffed. "You're alive, aren't you? You can walk out of this room on your own two feet, is that wrong? You have yet the hope of life, the hope to marry a wife and, yes, if the good God spares you, blesses you as He's done so far, the hope of getting one like yourself one day—or no, please God, not like *you* to worry us all to our graves, but maybe, who knows, one like—" At last her voice crumpled. "Oh, little Heiri and my little Willi and all of you!" But again, after a moment, her tone resumed vehemence. "Get you a wife! Marry Nissi! Oh, what's a face when it's her heart and all the rest she'll bring you? The rest of her's not ruined, the best of all, and when she's had two or three babies and one a girl, then name her. . . ." She could not go on, but her fierce old eyes challenged him to utter a word of dissent.

Joggi sat shocked, hardly daring to answer. Suddenly, he smiled. "Little Elsbeth? Bettli?"

She gave a crow of laughter, nodded and whispered, "Bettli."

"Well, you'll have to give me time. A good bit of time."

"Psh! Do you know how old I was when I married my husband? Seventeen. And Herman only a year older." She leaned back and took a long breath. "Well, work it out for yourselves." She closed her eyes and said abruptly, "Call Nissi. I need to lie down."

In the hall the girl hurried toward him with strained and anxious looks. He tried to smile. "She's all right. I think she is. Or better than she was."

"Thank God," Nissi said faintly.

Joggi returned to wait at the door as Nissi helped her grandmother rise. When Elsbeth was standing, he went to tell her goodbye.

She gave him her hand. "Well, come again. Of all the rest of 'em you're the one that came. Others talk and send word but you came. Never tell me you're not a Christian boy, Joggi, now hear me?"

As he turned to leave, she was shuffling toward the bed with Nissi beside her, but halfway there she stopped and called, "Don't go till Nissi brings you something to eat or drink, something—though God alone knows, such slack, such sluggardly ways, what she'll find in this house to bring."

He stood in the hall doorway that led to the side porch. When the room door opened, he called to Nissi and then went onto the porch. She followed and they stood in the bright daylight.

"No, I don't want any refreshment," he said low, "but I did want to tell you, I hope I did no harm, I told her about Heiri."

She looked down, said gravely, "Well, time will tell."

"Nissi, I think I would have wronged her not to tell her."

She did not answer.

"Another thing I wish to say." He paused a long time and stared into the flat February sky. When he turned to her, he saw that her eyes were dark and burning.

"Nissi, I don't know how to say it. I have to speak the truth. To try to. Last May—when I was here and you let me talk so much about how I felt and thought—I remember how you answered, more than in words." He stared into her eyes, but for what, he did not know.

"Nissi, I'm not what I was then. I can't ever be again what I was then."

She shook her head slightly, her lips widened yet compressed in some emotion. Pain? Or was it pity?

"Because—when Heiri was killed—I don't know, but it was like— I was the one that killed him. Can you understand?"

All she could do was shake her head a little, not in denial but as if in pity. He thought, *What have I said? Is it simply that after all?*

Her brown plaid dress had discolored stains about the bottom of her skirt. As he looked at her, he thought of Elsbeth's words, of the living heart and flesh beneath the dress. "Nissi," he said, stopped. No other words came.

They looked at each other, open-eyed. They began to read. Grief, guilt, and loss. Each read the other's looks, exchanged.

And slowly, unaccountably, Joggi began to feel great release, then lightness, and something like smiling began inside him like the glint of light he'd seen at the creek the day he first came home. He kept looking at her—dumb, mysterious—with a life of her own hidden under the ugly winter of her dress and the mask of disease on her face. He put out his hand to touch hers lightly. "I remember you now," he said low. "I remember it all. Do you?" How was it? What had she given him?

"Oh yes. I remember."

Though she had no answering smile, he took her hands and held them loosely against his breast.

Although her body surged ever so slightly toward him, she kept her place, but her mouth trembled. "I love you, Joggi." Her voice was rough and low. "No matter how—anything—I love you."

In the depths of her eyes, he saw a force of being that was as real as his father's or his mother's. As real as his lost brother's. He too stood still. Now he shook his head gently though not in negation, said at last softly, "I thank you. God above, I thank you, Nissi Rieder."

He felt the light move into his head and into his eyes but when he spoke it was barely above a whisper. "I have to go. It's not enough time now." He dropped her hands. "But—is there any way. . . ." He left the question unfinished.

"I don't know." She looked about her as if to see who might be near or even at a distance.

Unaccountably he picked up a faint prickle of unease and said hurriedly, "Nissi, my father may be right. He thinks it unsafe for me to come out like this and maybe I ought not to come so openly again but—" as she looked away, he saw the droop of her mouth, thought of her leaning against the wall crying, "—but there's a place—if you could ever come, bring somebody with you if you wanted to, somebody you trust. Look, Nissi, do you know the way I came today? The path that goes behind your millpond, goes back of Haghabucher's swamp?"

"Yes, I know it." A slight breeze lifted a tendril of her hair curling at her temple.

"It's clear this time of year. There'll be logs across the creeks if you walked. Though it might be better to ride. Have you ever ridden that way?"

"Oh yes. Not lately but I remember it."

"Nissi, there's a place just as you come to our land, it's a chalkbed, a red clay bank with lumps of chalk sticking out of it. I took the children there once. I could go there again if you wanted to come." When she did not answer, he said, "Would you?"

"Yes. If I can."

"When?"

"I'm not sure, Joggi. I can't tell. You saw how it was today. It's hard to know how she'll be from one day to the next."

"Tell her," he urged. "Tell Frau Elsbeth you're going. I think she may want you to." He hesitated. "Shall I bring Cathri or somebody else along?"

She did not answer at once. "As you like."

"I'll come this Sunday afternoon and wait for you. And if you're not there I'll come the next. And the next."

For the first time she smiled. "Oh Joggi Lienhardt!" she whispered. Belief broke through and transformed her face. They stood leaning a little toward each other, neither quite daring to move.

Voices inside the house violated their stillness. Joggi said quickly, "I must go," and without another word he turned and ran down the steps. His movement was swift and vibrant across the yard, through the orchard, and across the field.

She did not stay to watch him disappear into the woods. She returned to her grandmother's room, but it was not the place it had been. It was a place where she saw him still.

36

The day his enlistment was up Rudi headed for Indian Creek. There'd be plenty of fighting yet, as much as anybody wanted, but right now he had to go home.

He believed they were going to win. Eventually. Anybody that could keep an army together the way Greene had, even after losing, well, he deserved to win—not that deserving had anything to do with it either.

Masterly the way that Rhode Island Quaker had led the enemy a chase through North Carolina in the cold and dark of January, February; up muddy roads and across flooding rivers—the upper Catawba, the Yadkin, the Deep, even to the south bank of the Haw across the Virginia line, where Cornwallis had given up at last and gone back down to Hillsboro. And then what did the chased do but come after his chaser and try to have it out with him at Guilford Courthouse in mid-March?

If only the North Carolina militia or those Maryland recruits. . . . But at that age I'd probably have run too, thought Rudi. *And Campbell's North Carolina riflemen fought like demons, same as they did at King's Mountain. But it was how the outnumbered enemy fought that beat us. No doubt about it, they were tough and brave. But they paid a bigger price than we did. No wonder Cornwallis went off to Wilmington to meet the ships. So what use to win your ground when you can't sit down on it? And we got away. If you've got a general that can save his army to fight again the way Greene did, why, you've got a prime general.*

But no general alive could force a militiaman back into immediate service when his time was out, not if he was haunted by the cries of his children and his wife's anxious face. Like many another, Rudi could stand it no longer.

He'd said as much to the friend he'd met up with after Guilford, an unlikely friend for him, Captain James Fraser of Lee's cavalry. Jamie was the last person he'd ever have expected to make a cavalryman, Rudi thought with amusement, remembering Jamie's struggles with the ill-conditioned nag he'd ridden up the country that time to find him.

At their first startled recognition, friendship had not broken through the formality of rank, but that night Jamie sought Rudi out and they sat by the fire apart from the other men.

The bond between them was deep; they had loved the same woman. Jamie of his own will had given up his chance with Margaret when he more or less haled Rudi back to her, Rudi being then in no state to present himself to any woman. If it hadn't been for James Fraser, he'd reflected many a time, he hated to think what he might have become.

So that March evening, both men could not help remembering another time when they had sat by a campfire.

"My son has your name—James Fraser. Did you know that?"

"Mary said you called him 'James.' I didn't know about the 'Fraser.'" Jamie shifted his big body. He was the same fine figure of a man he'd always been and looked unscathed. His boots shone in the firelight. Lee's men were well shod. "Who is he like?"

"I don't know. Sometimes I think I see the favor of Meg's Granny in him. Mostly he's like himself. Smart little beaver. . . . You have a son?" Rudi did not say "sir." The dimness of the fire made it easier for them to talk as equals.

"No, we have only the one little lass." Jamie was married to a Philadelphia girl. "We had a son in midsummer but lost him the second of September."

"You get to see him?"

"Yes. But I've not been home since."

Rudi's voice roughened. "We lost children too. It's a grief like no other." Both men were quiet awhile. Rudi said, "I've not seen mine since mid-September. I left Margaret with Mary."

"I'm glad of that." Mary was Jamie's sister-in-law.

"But it's come to my mind lately I might have done wrong. Though I don't know why. What's the last you heard from Indian Creek?"

"Nothing since October. When I got word about Aleck."

Rudi was relieved that Jamie already knew of his brother's death. He had feared he might have to tell him. "I'm sorry, Jamie, sorrier than you might believe. We'd got to be right good neighbors."

Jamie made acknowledgment. Aleck had been shot from ambush by a former neighbor when he'd stopped by home on the way to King's Mountain.

Rudi said, "I think sometimes about afterwards when all this is over. I wonder if we'll ever be able to settle down together the way we were before, those of us still here. With so much to forget. And to try to forgive."

Jamie shook his head. "No way we can do it in ourselves."

"God knows what I'll find when I get there," Rudi sighed. "I heard they burned our house." He had already told Jamie he was going home. "I don't say I won't come back," he had said, "but right now I got to see about them."

"You're lucky you have a chance to."

Now Rudi said, "I'll make sure your family gets word of you."

They talked about where they had been, the fighting. They talked late, found themselves talking without reserve as they had that time long ago.

"You've got to be a great man, Jamie. I'm proud to say I know you."

"Oh no, Rudi. But yes, I've learned a bit outside these back parts. Still I think sometimes I knew as much of worth that day we talked—where was it? Up the hill above some wild creek? Twenty Three Mile? Twenty Four?"

"It was Twenty Three Mile Creek. Twenty-three miles from old Fort Prince George."

As they sat in the chill dark, Jamie could see yet the great monarch butterflies flitting among the stalks of orange milkweed in the meadow clearing. He remembered his growing recognition of the rare seed buried in that blending of weakness, hurt, and compassion in this man he'd gone so far to find.

Rudi said, "You showed me something as important as anything I ever learned in my life."

Jamie did not answer.

"Showed me my power. Or the way to it. Helped me find my man's power."

"You already had it."

"You helped me to know it."

Jamie smiled in the flickering light.

Rudi asked. "Did you ever regret it? Seeing what it led to?"

"Oh yes. Indeed I did. Many a time."

"But not now." Rudi did not make it a question, but it was one.

Jamie took a while to answer. "No. Once you decide on a way, Rudi, if you know it's right, you can't dwell on any other. Cost what it may."

Both sat in deep remembrance. Finally Jamie said, "I finished payment some time ago."

"Your wife is named?"

"Anne."

Somehow Rudi knew to probe no farther. After a while he said, "Well, they tell me you're a grand fighter. But I will say I'd never ha' guessed you'd do it a-horseback. And you a parson."

"No, not yet. I had not yet got to my ordination when all this broke out."

"Why? I thought you had."

"I was ever slow to get to things." He glanced at Rudi with a half-smile. "You ought to know that."

"Will you get to it after this is over? If you're spared?"

"I don't know. I'm not sure I'll be fit for it. With the education I'm getting now."

"Well, Jamie, I can't think of a man I'd rather have preach to me than one who's had to go these ways we're going now. I'm thinking you'll know what to preach."

After another silence, Jamie asked, "How have you fared with all that parcel of Irish Presbyterians you live amongst?"

"Right well, all things considered. I'm not as 'speeritual' as some might wish, but they know me now and I know them. I know the good in 'em. You're a staunch people, you Allens, Lairds, and Frasers."

"I must say you don't seem slack yourself."

"It's because I'm Swiss," Rudi answered drily. "I know little about my people but from what I'm told, they're none to be ashamed of. At least in the old country."

"Man, they're some of the best soldiers in Europe. Always have been."

"Well, I hope I'm more than a fighter."

"You are."

When they parted, Jamie said, "Give Margaret—" he paused slightly, "my love."

"Aye, I will. And you take hers. And mine."

"I see she's got you talking like us."

"She has. And a right smart tongue she's still got to her too. Oh, she keeps me in the path. Will you come to see us one day?"

Jamie would not say yes. Too many chances between now and one day, he said. "Better not to promise."

Rudi plunged into speech. "I'll remember you to my last day, James Fraser. The best friend I ever had. Outside Johannes Lienhardt. And Meg's Granny."

Later, each thought that whether they saw each other again or not, it did not matter. That they had talked tonight was enough.

Naked chimney stones scarred by winter rains and a yard grown up in weeds were a sight too familiar to cause much surprise. Even so, Rudi felt as if he'd been kicked in the stomach when he reached Mary Fraser's place. He knew what to expect at his own house place, for Joggi Lienhardt had told him it was burned, but he'd thought surely, with Aleck dead, his widow would be left alone. Hellhounds! Anger and fear surged up in Rudi. He was trembling as he turned away. All gone—food and shelter, mothers and children. Where were they? Where had they gone?

He'd already passed the ruins of the Logan place. Was all Indian Creek burned out? His insides churned. The Laird place was next, but with those Laird boys the rampant Whigs they were, it was doubtful their house had been spared either. He rode on in dread and anxiety.

He continued to avoid roads and frequented paths, and he stopped often to look and listen, but the young leaves that gave some cover also obscured his view. The woods were noisy with April life that could mask other sounds. These parts were said to have become safer for Whigs after the Battle of the Cowpens but it didn't look like it here. Rudi knew he'd be shot in a second if he was seen by the wrong person.

The Laird place was two miles from the Frasers' home. From the edge of its clearing he saw an intact roof and he drew a deep sigh of relief. Even if they weren't here, surely Martha would know where they'd gone. But as he observed the house more closely, he saw its doors were closed, its windows shuttered. His relief slid back into despair. He saw a hen flapping her wings in the dust of the woodpile. Still, you never knew. Was Martha shut up inside? Or someone else? He moved down the edge of the woods for a better view.

He had left his horse farther back in the woods. He thought no one had observed his approach, but he could not be sure there was no one else at hand more cautious than he was. Many a man had been shot approaching a house, sometimes his own.

He continued to scan the premises. His keen sight showed him the churned up earth in front of the dooryard gate. No good sign. That path to the spring had been used recently.

He settled down to watch as the sun moved into mid-afternoon, but except for the hen sauntering about, he saw no signs of life. At last he concluded that Margaret and the children were not there, and as for anyone else, he'd have to take a chance and see.

With gun loaded and primed he stepped out from under the cover of trees and approached the side of the house where the only opening was a shuttered window. It remained shut. Looking across the dooryard paling from outside, he scanned the ground and saw tracks leading back and forth from the house to the front gate. Dismissing caution, he went around to the gate, saw many barefoot tracks, some of them children's. He hallooed, called loudly, "Anybody home?" called again, opened the gate.

The front door was unlatched. Inside, only shelves and bedsteads fastened to the walls remained. The house was empty of everything except a barrel turned on its side and a worn out broom. In the loft rooms he found only the trash of crumbled herbs and the scent of dried fruit.

Swiftly he descended to study the signs outdoors. Nine or ten people—children of different ages and several women. And a man, maybe two, or perhaps one a boy, the man wearing shoes. He was fairly sure it had rained here some three days ago. Judging from the superimposed chicken tracks, he thought the footprints were at least a day old, maybe two. One good sign: no hoofprints, no horses. But ten yards beyond the gate he saw the tracks of a cow and a calf merging with those of the people. Plunderers, raiders? Hardly, since some of those leaving were children. As he studied the tracks, he tried to suppress emotion at the sight of a small footprint.

He knew his work. He hurried into the house to look for any clue he might have missed, but except for a buckeye in a corner he found nothing. Jemmy carried a buckeye for good luck. But so might any other boy. Why would he discard it? Lost it maybe.

Outside, Rudi worked his way around the place. All the tracks led to the front gate and up the lane beyond it. From the deep impressions of toe and heel he could tell that those leaving had carried burdens. He saw that one child walked with a limp but the footprint looked larger than Jemmy's. He saw where sacks and kegs had been set down. These signs comforted him somewhat. Perhaps they'd carried provisions. He hurried toward his horse.

Back in the lane the ground was soft and sandy in places, but as it rose, it was more of eroded clay. He saw again the small footprint, knelt to look at it. "Now you don't know it's Katy's," he told himself, but just ahead he saw another, long and slender. "I know that's Margaret's!" he exclaimed. He could never mistake that foot. But she carried a heavy burden. He kept looking for Jemmy's tracks.

Where the lane came out on the road, the party had turned northeast. Now the tracks were overlaid with those of horsemen. The road rose, became increasingly rocky and eroded, and he had to work carefully, scanning the sides for signs in the bushes and for dislodged pebbles.

Where were they going? Why were they going? Safety? Food? Both, he concluded grimly. He tried to suppress his anger to keep his head clear. Was the man or men still with them? He was not sure. He saw clearly that one child, a boy, he thought, walked with a dragging gait. Fear increased the tumult of his feelings.

It was growing dark as he descended a long rise, but when he reached the soft ground at the bottom, he saw no sign of cow, calf, or barefoot people, only of horsemen. Dismayed, he realized they must have turned off the road somewhere on the ridge and he'd missed it in the long shadows. Well, no use to go back now. It was too dark.

He camped by a little branch, but sleep would not come.

Destitute! Oh, why hadn't he come on, a week, two weeks ago! He groaned and turned. After a while he got up to stamp his feet and walk, to stand and stare into the sky.

One thing, when he found her, she'd know who did it, and she'd not be slow to tell him.

Why had they burned the Fraser house and not the Lairds'? Because there was no longer a man to be faced for the burning of Mary's? Whereas Martha's sons were yet to be reckoned with. And not me? Well, that's a miscalculation I'll have to correct. And he'd thought he was coming home to plow and plant.

He lay down again but the night was too alive for sleep. He kept trying to think where they might be going. *God, tell me where they are!* he cried. . . . *Toward the river? Duncan's Creek?* Suddenly a memory surfaced: Gilchrist. Hadn't someone said one time that old John Gilchrist and his neighbors were repairing the ruined blockhouse by the river, the one used back in the Cherokee War? And wait a minute. John Gilchrist's wife, Sarah, was sister to Martha. But she'd died a few years ago. Still that would make John Gilchrist brother-in-law to Martha Laird. Miller Gilchrist, once a prominent man. But he'd had only daughters. Strong girls, said to be able to do the work of men.

Rudi watched the half-moon across the sky. He fell asleep but he did not know it, for he kept seeing Margaret's bent back, heard her calling him, "Rudi!"

The weather had turned fine. The sun shining through small tender leaves gave the air a softness and made it a perfect day for planting. Or for burning.

He found the place they'd stopped to rest or sleep. They hadn't made fire, but he saw where squirrels had garnered husks of half-chewed grain. He was thankful for the cow and calf that made the ridge trail easy to follow.

He kept thinking of Katy's little bare feet among these rocks and thorns. He decided the reason he could not be sure of Jemmy's was that several of the children were almost the same age and size. He tried to remember the ages of Mary's children.

The trail wound through a long valley, skirted a canebrake, later came in sight of a house with smoke drifting from its chimney. At the edge of the clearing, the signs were confusing, but it looked as if some of the party had gone down to that house.

Rudi rode a little way into the clearing and hallooed but no one appeared. He called again, rode boldly toward the house and shouted, "I come in peace! I look for my wife and children! I mean no harm!"

The door on the porch inched open and a face appeared in the crack, also the barrel of a gun.

"Can you tell me who passed by here yesterday or the day before? I seek my family!"

The door opened a little wider. A woman called, "Who are you? Who is it you want?"

"My name is Näffels and I look for Margaret Näffels and my two young children, a boy and a girl, along with some six or seven others! From Indian Creek. Have you spoke with any that passed?"

In the shadow of the porch he saw a youngish woman with long black hair dragged back from a pale face. She wore a single colorless garment.

"My wife and children that were burned out!" he repeated urgently. "Can you tell me anything? Anything! Where they were going—"

The woman came out on the porch still holding the gun. Behind her in the house there was a continuous noise like something snarling.

"I tracked 'em through the woods up there and it looked as if some might have branched off down here." Rudi advanced and was about to dismount.

The woman stepped back. "Then keep on tracking! We know naught of such vagabonds! Come inside that gate and you'll get a bullet in your guts!" She raised the gun.

Rudi's strength drained from him. The sound inside the house rose. He recognized it as a man cursing.

White-faced, he backed away. He was getting light-headed. For a split-second the woman had looked like Margaret.

Back in the woods he found the way his people had left. He was forced to conclude that whoever had gone to the house must have gotten the same kind of treatment he had.

37

As he moved into the afternoon, the trail grew easier to follow, for now Rudi saw more signs—the scuff marks of a stumble, a rag snared on a root sticking out of a bank. Farther on he found a big iron skillet and retrieved it for its owner. But it had been a long time since he had seen the little footprints. Perhaps someone was carrying her.

The roof of a gristmill rose among the trees by the creek that emptied into the river downstream. Approaching with his usual care, he stopped to scan the clearing. In the middle of it, some hundred and forty yards to the left of the mill, stood the miller's house, a large house with a full upper story. Smoke drifted from a chimney. Fields stretched on all sides, and down the field opposite to the mill he saw the old blockhouse with a new palisade fence around it.

He caught the sounds of voices, saw a large fenced garden back of the house where a number of people were working, saw in the field two plowing and two dropping seed. He spurred his horse and came out of the woods with his heart pounding. He shouted, hallooed. The faces in the garden turned toward him, almost all of them women. He dismounted and, leading his horse, hurried up, scanning every face, but recognized no one.

"I seek my wife! And my little son and daughter I left with Mary Fraser! Are they here? From Indian Creek?"

"And you be who?" called a stout woman with a hoe.

"Rudi Näfels! My wife, Margaret, and my children, Jem and Katy, that I left with Mary Fraser! I found the house burned down, but I tracked a parcel of folk from Lairds' on Indian Creek yesterday and today, and I hoped mine might be amongst 'em—"

While he was speaking, a tall, sunk-jawed woman, who had left the garden and was coming toward him, interrupted, "Why, Rudi Näffels, are you so addled you don't know me? Quit clacking and let me have a word!"

Martha Laird's bonnet almost hid her face. Rudi strode toward her. "Where's Margaret? Is she here? Is she all right?"

"She's where she needs to be, flat on her back, all she's been through of late. Now don't get in a stew," Martha said strongly. "She's well enough."

Rudi clasped both Martha's hands in his. "And Jem and Katy?"

"Katy's fine. And Jemmy'll do well enough, I think, now his Daddy's come. No, now what ails you?" For maybe the first time in her life Martha had her hands kissed. She frowned to keep from smiling.

"Where are they, please? Oh Mistress Martha, take me to them!"

"Now you hold on a bit! You'll have to wait. You can't go busting in like a heathen savage!" But as she looked at him, her voice softened. "Rudi, she's—well, in about two months and the Lord wills, and this time with me to have the tending of her it's like He may—two months and you'll be getting you another young one. Now you just look up. This time I believe she'll come through fine and the babe too."

Rudi's face wore a mixture of relief and dismay.

"She got overtired with all that dragging through the woods we had to do. And other things. Now remember, you ha' the two young ones you want to—"

"Why did you leave Indian Creek?"

"For one thing John Logan came and got us. And with all that happened and none but women and a couple of boys to look out for 'em, well, he persuaded us to come on here where we'd have better protection. All thought it was taking too much chance to stay there. I hated it, but—" she quirked her mouth downward and sighed, "so I came on too. With Margaret in the way she was. You say you went by my place yesterday? I reckon it's ashes by now."

"No, it wasn't yesterday."

Another woman came up. "I'm Annie Gilchrist." Her voice was hearty and authoritative. "Joe!" she shouted. "Bring us a noggin of ale! So you come up from Indian Creek. And where before that?"

Martha told Rudi to stay where he was till she returned. A boy took his horse and Rudi followed Annie Gilchrist to a bench under a great walnut tree.

A robust, fair-haired woman, Annie took off her bonnet and fanned, as she set to work questioning Rudi about where the soldiers were and had been; what they were doing, had done, were going to do. She kept him talking steadily although at times he hardly knew what he was saying.

. . . Over in the Waxhaws, he answered. Still a sizeable army under Greene. No, Daniel Morgan had resigned and gone home; his health was so bad he could no longer sit a horse. No, they weren't giving up. They had more help now. Cavalry from Virginia under a fine leader, Henry Lee, "Lighthorse Harry," they called him. Did she know that James Fraser, brother of Mary's Aleck, rode amongst 'em? Yes, Pickens was still in the field and would have a good-sized following once the men got back from planting. Just as he'd come home to do. But who was it had done all that devilry on Indian Creek and why had they been able to rampage so freely?

The woman's face reddened in anger. "Who was to stop 'em? Not that some wouldn't ha' tried if they'd had the bullets. But what could women do against men with guns? Pack of scavenging scum!"

Rudi, who had kept looking toward the house, saw Martha come out with one child holding her hand and another behind her.

Katy did not rush forward as her father did, but she turned loose of Martha's hand, and as he caught her up in his arms, she laughed a little whimpering laugh.

The feel of her. More of arms and legs and eyes than when he'd left and, oh, so light, but his Katy. He held her off to search her face, now rose-flushed, said her name again, closed his eyes and kissed her several times, then set her down to look for the other child.

Martha had drawn him forward. Jemmy looked up and almost smiled but not quite. "Daddy?"

Rudi knew it was Jemmy. His freckles were pale in the thin transparent skin across his nose. He too was taller, but the look in his eyes was unfamiliar. The boy dropped his gaze and did not move.

Rudi said no word, merely bent forward and opened his arms.

The child's body felt long and awkward. There was something almost resistant about it.

"Jemmy? You not too big for a hug, I hope." He moved the boy back to look at him, but although a smile trembled at Jemmy's lips, he did not quite meet his father's look.

Rudi straightened up. "Well, let's go see your Mammy. You've took good care of her, I know."

Jemmy turned his head and Rudi knew at once he'd said something wrong. "Son? I know you've done the best you could in every way." He reached to draw Jemmy to him again, and as he did so, the boy flinched and stumbled. "Why, what is it? You've not got hurt, have you? Here, what's happened to you? What happened to your leg?" He saw how one-sided Jemmy stood. Rudi glanced at Martha, who stood grim-faced, holding Katy's hand.

"Jemmy got his leg hurt, Daddy!" came the shrill little voice. "It was the bad man that hitted him and hitted him and threw him, threw him—" Katy's voice rose higher and higher.

Martha interrupted, "Hush, child, I'll tell it. Rudi, it would not become me as a Christian woman to say what I would about that pack of— vermin that burned Mary's house down and turned 'em out in the field. Your boy got thrown off that high back porch of Mary's and it's the Lord's mercy it didn't kill him. But I'll let Margaret tell you."

As Rudi looked at his son, he realized what had changed. It was the brightness of countenance gone, that clear and eager look to greet all comers and everything new. Rudi wanted to pick up his son and carry him away to himself.

"You tell me now," he said to Martha in a low hard voice. "Tell me straight. Come aside and tell me now."

Martha looked at him a long moment. "Sit there, Katy, on the bench, and, Jemmy, you sit there beside her and keep her, and then in a little you can take your Daddy inside to your Mammy." Martha moved stiffly across the yard and Rudi followed.

Her face was gaunt and scoured. "Well, it's not that much to tell. When they come to put 'em all out with naught but the clothes on their backs—well, your Jemmy had the misfortune to cross one."

"How did he cross him?"

"Oh, he said something or other, like children will, 'You better leave us alone,' or some such, you know how boys are with any spirit to 'em, but him no more than—how old? Eight, nine?"

"Going on nine." Rudi felt the beginning of that terrible emotion he had almost forgotten, that bitter compound of hate and rage that tore at your guts worse than any stab or blow. "Who was it?" he asked, almost strangled.

"I mislike to tell you."

"You may as well. She will if you don't."

Martha appraised his look. "Well, I reckon you've got a right to know. I'll tell you if you'll make me a promise."

"I make none."

"Hear me out. You must promise you'll not seek him out. If he comes to your hand, it's another matter. If the Lord gives him into your hand, I don't say you ought not to pay him back, but with things the way they are here, I mean with your wife, you ought not to go off after him. Oh, I know," she raised her voice, "it's not my place to tell a man what to do, but it's my judgment, Rudi Näffels, and I will say I've come to know you for a reasonable man—and a good one—and you'll not take it amiss when I counsel you so."

Her words hung weighty between them, countering for a moment his rage. When one of her kind began to talk, she did not lack force.

He looked toward the two sitting on the bench, the young sapling, the son of his own scarred body, who had been such a whole, unsullied child. Now broken and scarred too. Rudi's pain was more unbearable than any he'd ever felt for hurt of his own.

"Who was it?"

Martha continued to eye him sternly. "You'd not take off after the creature today, would you?"

"What?" he exclaimed impatiently. "No, nor tomorrow neither! I'm not a brute beast, Mistress Laird! But it would be better if I had not to discuss it with Margaret. Is it a man I know?"

Martha gave a long sigh. "Aye-me! Well, it was that Micajah Fonder. I don't know whe'r you know him or not."

"Who was he with? Does he follow another or does he lead his own band?"

"He goes with Bill Lee. I know you know him. But I wouldn't doubt they're rampaging well beyond Saludy now."

"When did it happen?"

"It was the second week of March. We'd just commenced to break up gardens when they come on us like locusts. We'd all known to hide our things, the little we had, and I make no doubt it was that, there being so little to plunder, that brought out their hellish spite."

"Margaret—she took no hurt?"

"Not in her body that I know of. But for the hurt to the boy, well, going through that was bound to take its toll." She groaned, "Oh, Lord ha' mercy! ... All right. She was coming out the door with Jemmy in front of her. The child broke from her and said something about like what I said, and the ugly brute savage grabbed hold of him and knocked him about and then when the child was trying to get away, he grabbed him again and threw him over the railing, just slammed him onto the ground. I didn't see it, but from what they said, you can thank God, Rudi Näffels, it didn't cost him his life. Thank God Almighty for no more than a broke leg. Well, it happened so fast, Mary said, almost before they knew it, before they could move, Margaret rushed down, children screaming and all, Margaret was to him at once, but she did not lose presence of mind. As soon as she knew what the hurt was, she ran for the axe and wrenched off the door to a fowlhouse and they eased him onto that and bore him out in the field. And after a while—" Martha paused. "Well, by that time the vermin were firing the house, and Mary's oldest boy, I mean the oldest at home, David, he came and got me." Again she paused. "We splinted the leg as best we could and bore him over to my place. With barns and everthing afire, I persuaded 'em all to come home with me." Martha shut her mouth, finished. Rudi wondered what she had not told but had no thought for it now.

"How's his leg? You think it's like to get better?"

Martha's face was tight. "Some better maybe. He won't use the stick anymore. But I don't doubt he'll be marked for life. You see, Rudi—" She shook her head slowly. "It was like more than his bones got broke. Oh, I don't mean in his mind or his head, but Jemmy's—he's not like other children. In some ways."

No. He'd had too much of the sweetness of life in him. And now it was drained out. Rudi looked away at the blue and the far, light grayish green of the woods.

Martha wished he would curse. Another man might have.

She followed him toward the children. He picked up Katy and held her against his shoulder, stroked her hair and kissed her cheeks. "You go with Mistress Laird now, Katy. I'll come on in a little with Jemmy. Tell Mammy I'm coming. Tell her I'll be there in just a little. With Jemmy." He said to Martha quietly, "I thank you for all you've done. My own kin—" his voice shook, "they could not ha' done more."

As Martha led Katy away, Rudi could not see the tears in her eyes. Rarely did Martha Laird cry.

Rudi eased himself down on the bench by his son and put his arm loosely about him. "She told me some of what happened, Jemmy, what caused you to get your leg broke. You want to tell me any more?"

Rudi felt the boy begin to tremble.

"If you tell me, it would help me to know how it was. I'm your father and I need to know."

Jemmy just sat hunched up and trembling under his father's arm. Finally Rudi reached and cupped the boy's chin, gently turned his face up. "Look at me, Jemmy. You got nothing to be afraid of. If you'd tell me, I think it might help you. It might not help your leg, but it'll help you."

Rudi saw speech quivering on the boy's lips, like water heaped at the rim of a cup. He waited.

"I was scared he'd come at Mammy! I ran at him because I knew she couldn't fight him and I feared what he'd do!"

"What? Why did you think he'd hurt her?"

"What he said! He was a damned villain! A hell-bound villain, that's what he was and they all are!"

To Rudi such language from Jemmy told him more than anything else could have. The lines around Rudi's mouth deepened. His face darkened. He did not speak for a while.

"Well, nobody hurt her, did they? You took her hurt for her. Had you thought of that?"

Rudi felt Jemmy grow still.

"Didn't anybody tell you that?"

The boy looked up, whispered, "No sir."

As Rudi gazed down, he tried to smile. "Even though the fellow *was* too big for you. You ran at somebody too big for you, didn't you? No wonder you got hurt. Still you did it for a good reason and you got nothing to be ashamed of. Hear me, Jemmy? You got nothing to be ashamed of. I'm proud of you." Holding his son's gaze, Rudi tried to will his own life and power into him.

Jemmy's face did change. Was it relief? The boy drew a long shuddering sigh and turned his face against his father's shoulder and began to cry. Rudi said nothing, just held him there and had the oddest sensation of peace. He gathered his son closer and Jemmy nuzzled against him as Katy might have done.

"Now," Rudi said as Jemmy sat up and began to sniff and to try to wipe his nose and eyes, "let me tell you something. Or let me ask you something. You ever get stung by a yellow jacket?"

Jemmy cleared his throat. "That time in the garden." His voice was frail and high. "That time we were digging out that old stump. And that time in the orchard. I thought it was bees but you said yellow jackets."

"Yes, you been stung at least twice that I remember, maybe more. It hurt a right smart, didn't it? But after a while it quit. Now was it your fault you got stung?"

Jemmy looked uncertain.

"No, it wasn't your fault. Anybody could've been stung. I could've. Now how about this. What about snake-bite. I know you never been snakebit, but say, what if you had? Say a copperhead or a rattler bit you, how'd that be—compared with a yellow jacket?"

"Bad. It might kill you unless—unless you could get the poison out."

"Yes, it would be a serious thing, all right. I got bit by a copperhead once. Come up on him by an old log, stepped right on him because I wasn't watching where I was going or thinking about him being there, and he struck me. Now I've told you, haven't I, what to do when you get bit by a copperhead or a rattler?"

"Yes sir. You got to lance it quick as you can and suck out the poison and spit it out. To keep it from spreading through you."

"That's right. Good. Now Indians, they'll use snakeroot or some other herb they claim'll do the job, but I wouldn't take that chance. Besides, when I got bit, there was none to hand, so I just lanced it and sucked out the poison the best I could. Though I reckon I didn't get it all because my whole leg swelled up big as a bolster, but I lived through it. And now you want to see the place?" Rudi took off his shoe and showed Jemmy the white marks inside his ankle. "I had to nearly 'bout turn myself inside out to get at it, but I managed. Now all I got is that scar." He looked hopefully at Jemmy. "You see what I'm saying?"

On the boy's face Rudi saw a shade of the old bright curious look.

"Jemmy, you got bit by something worse than a copperhead or even a rattler. A man can bite and put his poison in you too. He can do it different ways. Now a brute beast is mostly just trying to protect itself, but a man—well, his poison's of a different nature and it's harder to get rid of. Oh, a man can be better than a beast, but he can be worse too. I'm sorry you had to learn it so soon." Rudi's voice sank low and somber. "But most of us do in time. And what you got to do . . . is to get his poison out of you. And that's hard. I know."

How? the gaze asked.

"I wish I could tell you some easy way, Jemmy. I'd hoped you'd be spared such for a long time." Rudi looked away. *If only I'd been there!*

"Daddy, I tried not to be scared! I tried not to!"

"Jemmy, you listen to me. I think that's the poison he tried to put in you, making you be scared and ashamed you couldn't help yourself, but you got *nothing* to be ashamed of! Anybody would ha' been scared! Somebody three times bigger than you? You got no more to be ashamed of than if you'd got snake-bit! You were trying to be a man but you weren't of a size yet for a man's work. But that doesn't mean you weren't one. And even if you had been grown, you could still have got the worst of it. You know that, don't you?"

Jemmy's gaze was fastened to his father's.

"Oh yes," said Rudi. "You think I never got the worst of a fight, never got knocked down and kicked and beat? Oh, I have. But I don't like to think of it, much less talk about it. I put it out of my mind. Oh, it'll happen. There's too many mad dogs loose in this world for it not to happen to some of us, Jemmy. But the thing you got to hold on to is, you got no more to be ashamed of than if you'd come up on a rattler in the woods, same as most do in one manner or another. You were trying to stand up for your Mammy and that was right, though it's like you'll bear the hurt in your body for a long time. But just because it's in your body, it's not got to rule your mind. The men off at war, many a one of 'em has got hurts as bad as yours. Or worse. Only difference is they weren't bit by mad dogs. But I think, I hope, his poison'll soon get gone. Just knowing what it is may help. You think so?"

Jemmy's pale face was still turned up to his father's. He gave a sudden short nod.

"Well!" Rudi rose. "Come on, let's go see your Mammy!"

"Daddy, I can't run anymore or jump or anything."

"No. And maybe you won't ever be able to again." Rudi spoke quietly but sternly. "You did a man's work and it may be you got to pay a man's price. Face up to it. I know it's hard, but I know you got it in you to do so." He reached for Jemmy's hand. "I want to take a look at that leg this evening. Though it may not be anything I can do for it."

Rudi wanted to keep on holding Jemmy's hand, but as they walked on, he turned it loose.

Margaret lay in a shed-room at the back of the house, the shutter of one small window slightly ajar

Martha, who was sitting in a low hide-bottomed chair with Katy in her lap, rose as he entered. "Now she's not to get up! I don't doubt she'll want to, but you tell her she's to do as I say and not get up for no object or purpose. You young ones come on out with me. You too, Jemmy."

As Rudi's eyes adjusted to the half-dark, he saw her face as a paleness with her hair spread dark about it. She looked younger as she always did when she lay in repose. As Martha and the children went out, he opened the door wider for more light and he saw that her eyes were alive like running water under trees. So often she made him think of cascades.

He held her raised a little from her pillow, waiting for whatever she would say.

Her arms and hands were not without strength. Her fingers moved through his hair, at the nape of his neck, at his temples as they always did. Still she did not speak.

He tried to be gentle in his greeting. He lowered her back on the pillow. "Margaret?"

Her hands slid down his shoulders, his arms, reached again to move her fingers across his cheek, to catch in his rough beard.

"Now what have I done?" he exclaimed. "Clean forgot to cut off my whiskers! Come in such a hurry, I forgot all about trimming up my whiskers!"

Wind rippled the water, a breeze from outside. "And forgot to put on your linen shirt too and your sprigged waistcoat," she said huskily. "Come out of the woods in such a way as to shock all civilized beings. Well!" She was smiling. Their gladness took them full force.

After a while she said, "Well, Katy knew you, didn't she? What did they—how did the children do? Did Katy—come to you?"

"Oh yes."

"And Jemmy?"

Rudi knew her meaning. "It was hard for him. And me. No need to deny it. But he's still our Jemmy. And I'm proud of him. I told him so."

"Oh Rudi, I'm glad! He's been such a cast-down child and I've not been able to encourage him. . . . Did he talk to you?"

"He did. Martha gave me an account of what happened. Afterwards, we two—well, he talked a little. I told him he did a man's work and not to be ashamed howe'er it turned out. I think that might have helped a little. But what I didn't tell him—" bitterness thinned Rudi's voice, "—was the man he worked for—I'm the one ought to be ashamed, not him."

"Oh Rudi, no!"

"Oh yes. You think I don't know? Oh, I tell you, it half kills me to think if I'd just been there—"

"No, you were right to be gone! We couldn't ha' held up our heads if you hadn't been! It's just. . . . I know, I know, and that our own child should pay such a price. And, Rudi, I search my conscience too! It's on my conscience and I have to tell you. I know if I'd just held onto him and got him out of harm's way, that was my work. If I hadn't said—if I'd just gone meek and silent—oh, Rudi, he took the brunt for me! It was my fault!" She half-rose, propped on her elbow.

"No, Margaret!" Rudi's chair scraped the floor as he got up. He went and looked out the door, his back to her. "It was a felon misbegot son of hell that will groan the day I catch him! You hear me?" His fist pounded the doorpost. "He'll curse the day he e'er laid hand on my son! I've already took my oath to it."

His shape was heavy against the light. Margaret lay back, her face still.

Rudi tried to quiet the roiling inside him. "Well," he groaned at last, "I oughtn't to speak so before you. Not ruin our joy today." He turned and came back to her bedside and pulled up the chair he had flung back.

"Rudi, will you push that shutter back? This air's so thick-feeling."

He did so, staying at the window. "I told Mistress Laird I'll not seek him out—yet. Not today or anytime soon. But he'll come to my hand one way or another." Rudi's voice was honed and thin. "I know that, I know it as sure as I live." He came back and lowered himself into the chair. "But I'd have you put it away from you now. Same as I'll try to. For now."

"One thing you ought to know. It was Bill Lee kept him off us, kept him from doing worse harm."

"What do you mean, 'kept him off'?"

"What I said. Fonder might ha' done worse but Bill held him back. So when—if you ever come up with any of 'em—remember about Bill Lee."

Rudi gazed somberly at the rough wall above her head. "Right now I mislike to remember about any of 'em." But he did recollect that years ago before they were married, she'd told him Bill Lee had brought her game a time or two. Then why now burn down the house where she stayed? "Tell me this. Are they the ones burned our house?"

"God knows, Rudi. It could ha' been. But it might ha' been others. Other gangs have marauded there too."

He looked about him. She lay in a borrowed bed in some one else's shed-room. No doubt her very bedclothes were borrowed, perhaps even the frayed garment she wore. He had never been one to take much pride in house trappings and clothing, but now, he thought, his wife and children were no better than paupers.

"Was anything of ours saved?"

"A little. We had hid some tools and other oddments. But the clock, my wheel—and of course the loom at our house—"

They fell silent. Then from somewhere beyond the walls of this room they heard the fluting of children's voices. They recognized Katy's.

And could it be Jemmy's too? They listened. Jemmy's voice, light and clear?

"I'll get you another wheel!" he cried. "And I can build another loom!"

"But the house," her voice still mourned.

"I'll build you another, Margaret, higher, broader! I've got my back and my arms still. As for other goods—well, cloth rots anyhow and kettles rust out, but there's still good hard wood around us and we've got the ground—"

"Yes," she broke in. Her voice too caught light. "The seasons of the year and the fruit of the ground, they can't destroy that, can they? Though some would if they could."

"And, Margaret, it may all be over sooner than many think. I tell you, there's been a turn. You heard about what we did at the Cowpens? I wanted to come home then and tell you myself, but a man like Morgan, I couldn't leave such a general then. And now we have Greene." He told her about Guilford Courthouse and repeated with more spirit all he had told Annie Gilchrist. His voice grew strong and Margaret's eyes glowed.

"Ah Rudi, and to think you had a part in it!" She stretched out her hand, laid it in his. "And with you there, we did too." They sat looking at each other, almost wonderingly, and in the quiet, their fire faded to a soft glow.

"You know, I've thought much in the deep of night." Margaret's voice was low, even a little halting. "I've thought and I've tried to come at it better—why there should be so much hatred—and willful destruction in our time. And I cannot come at it any other way than—Granny used to say it, and I believe it's in the Bible—the way is always hard and the gate's narrow—to life. Some don't get through it. Some don't even try, don't choose it. But I wonder . . . are we heading into—life?"

Rudi was perplexed, even disturbed. He knew what the text was said to mean in its original saying. Years ago at St. John's on the Congaree he had heard it preached when he was young and impressionable. It meant life beyond this life, didn't it? But not that yet for Margaret! Oh, she was still young, still in her thirties. His face must have shown his dismay.

"Rudi, you mistake me. I mean—good's got enemies. Good costs. Like now. Bearing life is hard. You've been with me, and you know it same as I do. Now what if—we're all—you, all of us—are bringing into life—something we can't yet see?"

He continued to regard her soberly.

"Like—our country. A new and better country."

He shook his head, "I confess, Meg, sometimes I can't see how the new will be much better than the old. When I look at some of the ones still in it. They're the same ones."

"But if you can get free of *things* sometimes. Sometimes I get so tangled up and boggled down with work and house plunder and all that— if I can just get out and get free of it for a while, seems like I can take a better start again."

He realized that in all their married life Margaret had never talked to him quite like this.

"Coming up here from Mistress Martha's, it was a long hard wearying way for all of us, but they lightened me of everything but the one burden I carry now. And I don't know, Rudi, how it was, but somehow I began to feel so free. It was strange. Have you ever felt like that? Everything behind you and out of the way—and you're free?"

Margaret's face had a cast he had never seen there before; yet it was poignantly familiar. Who? Where?

A smile of great joy gathered inside him. Her look was the one that had been about him from birth perhaps, the look he had sensed about him in earliest childhood, brought to its fullness that time he played with his wooden toys on the box by the glass window. The look he felt about him that day he lay hurt almost to death in the house that was ashes now, when Meg's Granny sat beside him.

He had no words. All he could do was to bend down and kiss her hand and to sit there smiling at her.

Later he said, "We'll do. God knows how, but somehow we'll do, won't we?"

"Aye. We'll do."

38

By the second week of April dogwood bracts were shriveled and the trees were well leafed out. Pines had flowered in March, their pollen dusting new leaves, and their tiny dry cones still crunched underfoot on the sandy path. Nissi heard whoever it was coming before she saw him. She knew it was not Joggi because she would not have heard him until he stood beside her.

Johannes saw the leap of dread in her eyes and said quickly without greeting, "He left before sunup. He left safely."

Her whole being made a settling, subsiding motion. "Where did he go?"

"He did not say. He said it was better not to. Though I myself don't think it would make any difference now."

She looked away, shook her head slightly with a slight rueful smile.

"But he left in good spiritis," said Johannes. "He was not unwilling to go."

He observed Nissi's quietness with approval. Why she was right for Joggi, he did not know, only that she was right. He was glad Madle agreed. Her looks did not matter, Madle said. And who was to say, Johannes thought now, that she had not beauty enough in her steadfast gaze? "You've heard nothing else, I suppose?"

"No, Herr Lienhardt."

"Well. Tell your Papa I'll thank him much if he'll let me know of any happening."

At parting Johannes took her hand and bowed. "Take care of yourself, Nissi. For my son's sake as well as your own."

When Nissi smiled, Johannes knew she had enough of beauty for anyone she loved.

Nissi thought she would never again know another spring like this one, even if years and years with Joggi were given to her.

Usually when they had met, they had sat on an old wind-fallen log near the chalkbeds, but sometimes they had wandered to other places. Once he took her a long way up the creek to a hidden glade, where they watched dragonflies flit among the ferns, sat so still they saw a raccoon come to fish, a mouse scuttling among old leaves, a turtle clambering up the bank through tufts of new grass, a green lizard puffing out his rose throat. They saw a slithering snake which Joggi said wouldn't hurt anyone, but Nissi could not help moving closer to Joggi.

Usually she sensed a kind of austerity in him that made him avoid much physical contact with her. They hardly ever touched each other, but if they did, the merest brush of his arm she would feel in her flesh for hours. That afternoon by the creek, after a length of time, he stretched out on the ground—he'd been in the field since sunup he said, grubbing and hoeing in the newground—and almost without volition she moved to pillow his head in her lap. She wanted to caress it, to touch his face but she hardly dared to. He lay with half-closed eyes. A squirrel ran out the length of a sweetgum branch and measured the distance to a limb in a water oak, decided not to risk the leap and scampered back.

Joggi took a deep breath, turned slightly toward Nissi, raised his hand slowly, rounding it behind her head, and she bent to his embrace. Yet in a minute or so she felt him withdraw and she too disengaged herself gently. He sat up, then stood up and looked away. She stayed where she was, crying, *I don't care! I don't care!* not wanting to remember her mother's words, yet at the same time adoring him for his control.

They met twice a week: late Thursday afternoon and earlier on Sunday. She always left her horse a half mile from their meeting place. Each of them came alone—except for the time after the one by the creek. That time Joggi brought Andreas, who hung around ill at ease for a while before disappearing. Nissi knew what Joggi was saying.

In the beginning they talked much of the past, avoiding all but commonplace references to the present. One day Joggi spoke of far off places. "I want to see the other side of those mountains. They tell me those ranges go many a day's journey, and on the other side they say there's rich wild meadow different from anything we've got here. I'd surely like to see it."

"I've never even seen a mountain."

He looked at her quickly. "Would you want to?"

"Oh yes! Yes!" She felt a rush of spirit, a fresh gale. With you, her eyes said.

He kept searching her face and it seemed to her they exchanged promises.

She never mentioned the war or fighting, nor did he speak of it for several weeks. Then one day he asked if she'd heard anything about where the army was.

She was startled. "Which army?"

"Our army," he said in a short voice. "What they would call around here the Rebel army."

She shook her head. She never saw anyone except her family. Her father talked little to them of public affairs, or if he did to her mother, it was not in her hearing.

Joggi changed the subject abruptly. "Tell you one thing I've learned. I'm not cut out for a schoolmaster. At least not that age." Georgi's age he meant. He had told her about the children's night school. Andreas was the brightest, he said, though Hans too was smart. But the trouble with Georgi, he didn't care enough, didn't try. "I know now how old Herr Pastor used to feel." Georgi had already let Anneli get ahead of him. "I hate to admit it, but she's quicker than Georgi and Cathri put together."

"Why do you hate to admit it?"

"She's a girl."

"Indeed!" Nissi frowned till she noticed a curving at the corner of his mouth. She realized how rarely she'd heard him tease or joke. "Well, your mother is too. A girl."

"And so are you."

"Does that mean you don't want to admit I have intelligence?"

"Oh, no." His voice softened. "But you have more than intelligence."

"What?" she could not help asking.

"You have—Nissi, you have—" his voice changed, "—in some ways knowledge. Like me. You're like me." Now his look was dark and piercing. "You—" He fell silent. "I don't know any other way to say it than just—you've come to be your own self. And we know each other." He smiled. "That's it. We know each other. . . . Oh, I don't mean I know everything about you, how could I? or you me, but we don't hide from each other. Do we?"

She spoke slowly. "Not our real selves. But I don't tell you all I think. Or you either. Do you?"

He shook his head. "No. Not now. No use to."

She thought of the old saying, "Time will tell." Yes, it would. In time they'd say it all.

That night she remembered to ask her father about the Rebel army, telling him of Joggi's question.

Hans Jacob knew when and where his daughter met Joggi Lienhardt, for she had felt obliged to tell both parents. Her mother made the most objections. Her grandmother alternately condemned and approved, according to her moods, but her father consented to their meetings.

"What do you think she's got to hope for?" he demanded of Maria. "Who do you think will marry her? Who'll be left to marry her? You want her to be a slave the rest of her life? As for what I can give her, it may be I'll have nothing left to give, have you thought of that? And even if I do, you want a bought husband for her? Is that what you want?"

"But—" A few years ago Maria would have thought, might even have said, "What does it matter?" but nowadays she spoke differently with her husband in spite of their sometime disagreement.

Hans Jacob could be vehement when he chose. "Let the girl alone! They're upright people! I trust Johannes Lienhardt to see she's not wronged. I'd trust Johannes Lienhardt with everything I've got."

"But it's not the father, it's the son!"

"Makes no difference, I know *whose* son he is. I know the father and he's the one I depend on. Now you let the girl alone."

"But something could happen to that boy—"

"Maria, you let her alone. It's little enough she's got to hope for so let her have what she can when she can. You want her to slave for you all her life?"

Maria was both shocked and dismayed, but when Hans Jacob took the trouble, he could bear anyone down. Later, however, when she saw the change in her daughter, the softness, the almost beauty that now possessed her, she wondered, was even somewhat amazed at her husband's different perception of the matter. After a while Maria gave up worrying and began to hope for the best.

Nissi relayed her father's news to Joggi. Word had seeped in, her father had told her, of the capture of a British post down the country near Beaufort, also of a sharp defeat beyond Ninety Six of a hated Major Dunlap, who was captured and later killed.

"Who were the Americans?"

"He said some were Georgians under—was it Clark?"

Joggi nodded. "That's right. Clark's a Georgian. What about Sumter?"

The last word on Sumter was that he'd gone back up to the Waxhaws. What he'd accomplished on his foray down the country, other than to give the British and Loyalists a scare, was unknown. As to the main part of the troops, all her father knew was there'd been a big pitched battle up in North Carolina which the British had won, but afterward they'd gone off to the coast. And the American general—

"Who?"

She didn't think her father had called his name; it was the main one from the North.

Joggi said, "Greene."

Well, he still had his army and had sent word he was returning to South Carolina. Of course, the British were still at Granby. And at Camden. And Ninety Six and no doubt all the other forts. Even so, the partisan troups were said to be moving about the country, but of their specific actions Hans Jacob knew nothing reliable. They'd had no word from Willi.

Willi. That name silenced Joggi. For perhaps the first time he felt a stir of discomfort at the thought of someone else doing his fighting. Old comrades might seem remote but not Willi. Yet the truth was Joggi almost never thought of him now, except as someone from his and Nissi's childhood. But today the speaking of his name brought Willi, wherever he might now be, strongly to the forefront of Joggi's mind.

Willi had gone with Heiri. Saved his life that time they were captured, so Heiri'd said. Well, Heiri sure paid the debt. . . . *But if Willi hadn't stood by Heiri after Fishing Creek, would I ever have seen him again? Heiri wouldn't have made it to the Cowpens. . . .* Well?

Joggi's face grew long, his mouth twisted.

Nissi followed his expressions with vague understanding, but she knew she had no other words for him. She knew he had a farther way to go, a way hidden from her.

She gazed at the ground, the tiny wormlike cones from the pines and the gray-green tassels from the oak trees littering the sand, patternless debris from the ageless flowering of great trees. She raised her eyes to look at him, wished she had some word or touch but did not dare take even his hand.

The sun was low for he'd come late, and in a few minutes he said he must go. She moved away when he did but stopped after a few steps to turn and watch him disappear down the path with his long, loose stride, straight-backed but with one shoulder hitched a little stiff. She stood watching, not sure he'd really disappeared.

The following Sunday she'd come early, fervently hoping he'd be early too, but of course he was not. She walked back and forth twisting her hands, sometimes muttering, "God! God! Bring him soon!" She thought of going to meet him but was afraid she'd miss him on the way.

As soon as he saw her, he said, "Nissi, what's the matter?"

"Calli told me this morning they know about you at Granby."

"Calli?" His eyes flashed and his face changed with an expression she had not seen before. Fierce? Eager?

"Simmi's mother. Simmi's the head of a gang of slaves they took from us, and since they put him in charge, he gets away sometimes and comes to see Calli."

"Oh yes." Mulatto half-brother to Willi. And to Nissi as well. Unthinkable, but true.

"Calli came this morning before good daylight, didn't even knock though I was already awake, but I didn't know she was in the room till I saw her standing there. She said—" Nissi paused to catch her breath. "She said Maxwell, he's the fort commander, said Simmi said he let fall, or somebody did, they were going to make a raid either today or tomorrow, Simmi wasn't sure which, on all the Rebels hiding out around here."

"Who? What Rebels?"

"Two across the river and some others up near the Forks, and he said they knew of one down on Savana Hunt Creek. He said they knew of one down here. Oh Joggi, I've been so afraid they'd come before—"

He interrupted, smiling, "Nobody's been after me yet, Nissi, not today." They'd had a quiet Sabbath dinner. "How'd Simmi manage to get hold of this?"

"Oh, he's got ears, and he's not stupid. No more than we are."

And he's warned us, thought Joggi, whether he meant to or not. It had never entered Joggi's mind to acknowledge, much less to think about the relationship between Nissi and the mulatto slave. Her brother.

"Does he know about us? Us meeting?"

"He may. I'm sure Calli does. Though I never said a word to her. And I don't know how she knew because I've never mentioned your name to her, Joggi."

"She saw me when I came to the house that time."

"Yes, and now I've no doubt she knows when I come here too—and where I come. As I think about it, she's bound to know even though I try to slip away. Oh Joggi, they always know more about us than we know about them. How glad I am they do!"

But I wonder if that's how they found out about me at Granby, Joggi mused. For if Calli had eyes, so had others. He turned around, looked west toward the empty woods, southeast toward home. But not northeast toward Granby. *Well*, he thought, *this makes it easy. Quick, just the way I wanted it.*

. . . But he must not think of the farewells. His family around the fire in that ordered world of their own making. His mother, who seemed so small to him now, who had not yet gotten her full strength back from her winter illness. His father so much older in the face, yet stronger than ever in his body, or so it seemed to Joggi. The children, Georgi, who liked to follow him about. . . . And Nissi.

He never failed to be stirred by the indefinable grace with which she moved. And the depths in her eyes.

"Well, I'll have to go," he said.

"Now?"

"No, not this minute, oh no." He caught her hand and drew her to sit down beside him on the log, and they enfolded each other without thought or words.

And now as they clung together as they never had before, each felt every pulse of the other's body and began to move silently, urgently to the place of no withdrawal.

Suddenly Nissi whispered, "Joggi, we must part now."

"No!"

"Yes!" With trembling strength she pushed his arms away. "I say so. Not till you come back."

"What if I don't come back?"

"You will!"

He did not answer. She moved away, still feeling his hands and his body. She rose. She knew she must do it now.

"Joggi, I know how you'd feel later."

"You don't know!" he said angrily and stood up too.

"I do! I know you! You said so! And I'll not give myself here in the woods like a—" She could not say the word.

Bitterly he said it. "Whore. Is that what you think I'd call you?"

"No, but I know that I want you to come back here without guilt. Or any feeling that you have to. Just want to, Joggi! Come back because you want to!" She was crying, tears welling and streaming down her sallow cheeks. "It's our future!"

He stood silent. Unaccountably he thought of Heiri, and he wondered if Heiri had ever loved a girl. "What if there's not a future?"

"Then I'll live as I did before. Not forgetting."

He shook his head slowly as if already grieving.

She took one impulsive step toward him, stopped. "Oh dearest love, please, please come back!"

"I'll try to, Nissi." His voice was light and shallow. "Hmph." The little sound he made sounded almost humorous. "I expect you're right. Well. . . . " He looked down and picked up the battered old hat he sometimes wore and flapped it against his knee. "I'll have to go, better try to find Papa, and I'd better hurry." Already he sounded distant.

They looked at each other a moment longer till abruptly he turned away.

"I'll come here tomorrow," she cried after him. "Please send someone to tell me you've gone safely!"

"Oh, I will," he called back.

"Be careful!"

But he was moving so fast that his words floating over his shoulder were lost to her.

She turned too, unable to watch him disappear. A short way up the path she plunged aside into deeper woods, where sure of aloneness, she threw herself on the ground and sobbed great body-wrenching sobs until she was worn out. It was almost dark and spring peepers were shrilling in the new grass when she reached home.

39

By the end of April more news of the war was coming to Savana Hunt, for it was getting closer. Sumter was again moving down Broad River, headed for Granby, and sweeping the German settlements of grain, horses, and cattle that were not well hidden. About the same time Greene advanced toward Camden, but on April 25 at the pitched battle of Hobkirk's Hill he failed to defeat Lord Rawdon. Again, however, although Greene lost the battle to a small tough army, he saved his own. And he was cheered by news that two days earlier Francis Marion and Henry Lee had forced the surrender of Fort Watson on the Santee by building a wooden tower and shooting down into the stockade that occupied an old Indian mound. Three weeks later in May, Andrew Pickens and Elijah Clark would begin the siege of Augusta. Pickens, unlike Sumter, obeyed Greene's orders. As the British were put more and more on the defensive, Loyalists began to seek cover.

Soldiers from Granby had visited the Lienhardts the day after Joggi left. Madle and the girls were alone at the house so they sent Cathri to find her father, but she brought back only Hans and tried to explain in German that her father was not to be found. It was true Johannes had gone off to hunt a cow that had calved somewhere in the woods. Since the men could not understand Cathri, they questioned Hans, and when he too seemed obtuse, the sergeant lost his temper and struck Hans reeling. Tears sprang up in Hans' eyes. Only Cathri realized how furious he was.

At first their mother had wrung her hands and looked pleadingly at the intruders, but when they struck Hans, she rose swiftly from her chair and came flying toward them, crying in her clear, correct English, "Leave my child alone! You have killed already one of my sons! You have taken the food off their table, the clothes off their backs, what more do you want? Do you fight children? Do men like you fight children?"

Madle was a small woman but Madle in anger was not small. With blue eyes flashing she was like a swooping bird with beating wings and needle claws.

The men had seen there was nothing in the house worth taking so they went outside to ransack the barn and smokehouse, trample the garden, and catch a couple of hens. A smaller party made a brief foray among the trees by the creek but soon came back with nothing, for the stock was far up in the woods. After that, the soldiers left.

That night Madle insisted Johannes must keep away from the house early and late from now on.

"Madle, they'll not want me."

"They may! You said yourself they compel men into their ranks! For spite they'd compel you!"

"But I'd feel so cowardly! Look how they treated Hans. Who knows what they'd do here again?"

"That's why you must keep away! And what does it matter how you feel? You must keep away from them!"

It was true that some older men had already been drafted for daily labor at Granby, slave labor not being enough.

"If you should be taken, Johannes, how could we go on?"

How could they? Johannes looked at his sullen Hans, who seemed angry with everyone. Only fourteen, and where did he get his height? There must be something in this air. But he was still only a stripling, far too young for heavy responsibility. Johannes sighed and gave in to Madle.

But the British never returned. Perhaps other news of the Rebels was beginning to disquiet them. Also they knew their quarry at Savana Hunt had escaped, and Fort Granby was already crammed so full of spoils they began to think now more of keeping what they had than of adding to it.

On a cool misty evening, May 3, Hans Jacob Rieder rode up to the Lienhardts' house. After Joggi left, Hans Jacob and Johannes had fallen into the habit of going the back path every so often to meet and talk. They had talked two days ago in the newground where Johannes worked on set days, but this was not one of them and Hans Jacob came on to the house.

Though the light was fading, he could still see the good stand of corn, also the harvested wheatfield near the house. Johannes had told him he knew better than to store all their grain in the new barn in case the troops came searching and he'd left a portion in the old barn to allay suspicion, and, of course, all that had been taken. But they had been able to replant the garden, for they had saved seed against the possibility of a late cold snap.

This evening a hard shower had driven everyone home early from the fields, and Hans Jacob found Johannes and the three boys washing their feet on the back steps.

"So much to do in the fields," Johannes apologized, embarrassed to be found in such humble activity, "we go to bed with the chickens. The rain stopped us early tonight. Come in and take supper with us."

"I know how it is. We quit too and I came soon as I could get away. No, I won't break in on you, but there's something I want to tell you."

"Boys, go on in the house and tell your Mama I'll be in directly."

"No, let 'em stay, Johannes. No reason they shouldn't hear too. I came to tell you there's a big party of Americans camped around Granby."

"No!"

"Yes sir! Sumter's men have the place surrounded."

"Again?"

Hans Jacob nodded. "And this time they may take it. They're camped on both sides of the river. This time they've got the ferry, and nobody from Camden can get across the river without a good fight."

Johannes whistled softly. "Why, that's news worth having." He committed himself. "Good news."

"I'd say so." Hans Jacob grinned and rubbed his hands together. "Of course, Granby's not free yet. They've got those artillery guns in there."

"Don't the Americans have any?"

"No, they say not. Still it looks to me like there are a lot more of us outside than of them inside." *Us.* Hans Jacob committed himself too.

"Well, it takes more outside," said Johannes. "Inside a fort, a few can hold off many. How many you think they have inside?"

"A good three hundred or more. Say three hundred and fifty."

"And us?" It felt good to say *us.*

Hans Jacob shook his head. "Six hundred maybe. I've not heard the count but I've seen the camps and it's a bunch."

"What about Maxwell? Wonder what he'll do?"

Hans Jacob made a contemptuous sound. "In my opinion, nothing. There's nothing to him. He's nothing but a greedy dog. Others too say he won't stand 'em out. Not without help."

"Well!" Johannes took another whistling breath. "Come on in, Hans Jacob, and take supper with us," he urged. He wanted to keep talking about the news.

"No. No, I need to get on back. I just thought you'd want to know. Knew you'd want to. You're about the only one around here I can talk to and know you'll not blab everything I say to somebody else." He turned to go, hesitated. "I suppose you've not heard anything from Joggi yet. You think he could be with Sumter?"

Johannes did not answer at once. "No. Somehow I don't think so. . . . How about Willi? Have you heard from Willi?"

"We've heard nothing." Hans Jacob's voice changed. He shook his head and said heavily, "God knows whether we'll ever hear from him again."

Both men stood silent until Johannes said, "We just have to trust the Father, Hans Jacob. It's the only way I can go. Whether the boy is here or above."

"I know. . . . Well, I must go." Hans Jacob had lost all cheerfulness. Johannes had never heard him sound so bleak.

Madle and Cathri were standing in the doorway. Madle said, "Herr Rieder, I believe Willi will return. I cannot believe Heiri died for no reason."

"Yes. Well." Hans Jacob had already shaken hands with Johannes and was about to mount his horse when a possible turn of meaning in Madle's words caught him. He stood still a moment, again moved to leave, then glanced at the shapes grouped around the doorway with a dim light behind them. "What do you mean, Frau Lienhardt? About Heiri? Dying for no reason."

"He died helping Willi. Hasn't Johannes yet told you?"

"Helping Willi? No, he hasn't."

Johannes said, "Willi told Joggi his knee buckled under him, and Heiri came and took the blow meant for him so he got away."

There was silence.

"I didn't tell you, Hans Jacob, because—I don't know why I didn't tell you."

"You should have told me," Hans Jacob said roughly.

"Yes. But it was hard to talk about it then," Johannes said low. "If you'd ever lost a son, Hans Jacob—" he shouldn't say that; it was like an accusation, "—you'd know." Johannes' voice held a note of pleading.

Still Hans Jacob did not speak.

"It's makes no difference," said Johannes. "Nothing can bring him back."

"It makes much difference. To Maria and me both. How can I ever—pay you back?"

"Don't talk nonsense!" Johannes exploded. "Heiri and Willi were friends! Each helped the other! As for us—nobody owes anybody anything—but to help when we can." Johannes spoke angrily; he couldn't help it.

Madle broke in, "I'm thankful Willi was with him, Herr Rieder. Heiri did not die friendless as he might have. It eases our grief to know that. Now do come in and eat with us. There's plenty of what we have, such as it is, and we'd be happy if you'd come in. We have so few friends to sit at our table these days."

"Well—" Hans Jacob hesitated only a moment. "If one of the boys will see to Diamond here. He's stood so long he'd be glad of a drink."

Johannes said, "Give him some of that cane we cut yesterday, Hans. Now let's go in and eat." He tried to sound hearty.

Johannes walked barefoot like his boys, not thinking about it now as they went inside.

Hans Jacob never seemed quite himself during the meal. Since this was the first time he had eaten with them in several years, Madle wondered if he was shocked by their fare—noodle soup, bacon, and cornbread. Normally Johannes would have been either ashamed or offended that his guest did not eat more, but tonight he saw that the other man had much on his mind. They did not resume talk about Granby. Even the children seemed unusually subdued.

Once in the quiet Hans Jacob said, "Your son for mine." He shook his head. "If I could only somehow thank—"

Madle interrupted, "No! Be glad! It was how the Lord intended it. We know that."

When they said goodbye, Hans Jacob wrung Johannes' hand. "I'll never forget what you told me tonight, Johannes, never. Never forget it."

Johannes could not understand why Hans Jacob's feelings should be such a burden to him.

The next morning, however, he had a new burden, a much greater anxiety. Hans had slipped away before daylight. He had told only Cathri where he was going.

As soon as he could get away, Johannes went to the American camp at the Congarees to look for Hans, but when he finally found him, the boy had already been issued weapons. Hans flared, "Whether you think I'm a man or not, Papa, I'm going to be one! They can't treat me like scum and me sit back and take it!"

Tight mouth, burning eyes. *Soon I'll have no sons!* Johannes cried in despair.

"If you try to do anything to interfere—" tell the captain his age, Hans meant, "—I'll never forgive you, Papa."

Looking at the boy, Johannes knew he meant it. After a few more words, Johannes returned home alone.

Sumter could not take Fort Granby at present without big guns, so on May 6 he left men with Thomas Taylor to hold the blockade until he should return. Meanwhile, he and the rest of his troops would try for Fort Motte some thirty miles down the Congaree. On the way, however, he learned that Marion and Lee were already besieging Fort Motte, so he headed due south for Orangeburg on the Edisto.

There he was not disappointed. On May 11, the Loyalists at Orangeburg surrendered to Sumter. Also on May 12, Fort Motte fell to Marion and Lee. And on May 15, unknown to Sumter, Fort Granby surrendered to Henry Lee's Continentals, who had come in his absence with a six-pounder.

When Sumter arrived next day, he was dismayed at Lee's assumption of command, and his followers were furious as they watched Maxwell and his men leaving peacefully as prisoners bound for Charlestown with their horses, wagons loaded with plunder, and the slaves Sumter had promised them as payment for enlistment. Sumter tried to placate his men with some hundred and fifty slaves he took from a few rich Tories nearby, along with their cattle and sheep.

Among the slaves carried off by Maxwell was Simmi Rieder.

But during this time the whole country was distracted by even more amazing news than the fall of Granby. On May 10 Rawdon had evacuated Camden. Many Loyalists went with him, and the Americans moved in to destroy all British fortifications as other Americans were now leveling the earthworks at Granby.

Thereafter, the posts in and around Augusta on the Savannah would fall to Clark, Pickens, and Lee: Fort Galphin on May 21, Fort Grierson May 23; Fort Cornwallis June 5. None of these American victories were bloodless for either side—except for one on June 6 when the British abandoned Georgetown to Francis Marion without a fight.

Meanwhile, not quite a year after Charlestown had surrendered to the British and all South Carolina seemed lost, Greene with his army of almost a thousand Continentals arrived at the Congarees on the way to

Ninety Six. With the fall of Augusta, the Star Fort at Ninety Six was the last major British stronghold in the Georgia-Carolina backcountry. The siege of Ninety Six began on May 22.

But its commander, Colonel John Harris Cruger from New York, was of a different cut from Granby's Maxwell. Cruger and his Provincials and loyal militia, though greatly outnumbered by the besiegers, were determined to resist. They had a high sense of honor and were resolute and capable defenders. All were American except for one British lieutenant.

And farther down the country, the British presence was by no means minimal. Rawdon, who had fallen back toward Charlestown, was still formidable. His leaving Camden was not to be considered retreat but strategy that gave him more freedom to maneuver and fight. Even so, the country beyond was stirring with many emotions—an intensifying of fear and hatred or a surge of exaltation and relief.

40

For Madle the light about the house in May was always different from that of any other time of year. The sunshine, the white sand, thc humming of bees, and the singing of the hens compounded with a light that seemed to come from elsewhere, yet was homely and humble as a feather or a grain of sand. It came like grace in the vibrant air to form about that vertical invisible thread that was always present.

For some reason now she did not fear the thread—fire, massacre, marauding, sickness, and death—for its line was immersed in this air that was both fragile and enduring, that seemed to come from beyond the horizon's ridge of pines, yet was also very much of her own dooryard.

In May she thought often of her lost children, believed they were not ultimately lost to her. Little Verena they'd had for so short a time, had lost in winter's cold. The last little crumpled face, only two days old. Her May baby that had looked like Heiri. Heiri himself was more present than he'd ever been. But Joggi was not. Nor was Hans, who, like Joggi, had left her before he ever went away. Perhaps it was because they were living their lives intensely elsewhere, she thought. And Barbara, oh Barbara, was a very present yearning. *Oh, I must see her, I must see her soon. I'll go to her myself. Johannes has said we'll go.*

Late last fall Frau Gallman had told Madle that Barbara and Conrad's child had come safely into the world but whether it was a boy or a girl she could not say, if she'd ever heard. Madle tried not to show her exasperation with Frau Gallman, who was in her seventies and showing her age. Yes, Frau Gallman said, the Meyers were still at home, so far as she knew. Conrad had been there on leave. He was now Lieutenant Meyer. The King rewarded *his* friends.

Early in May Johannes vowed, "I'll go to her. Yes. Soon I'll go to her, Madle."

"And I'll go with you," she answered with strength.

He looked at her in tender surprise but did not contradict her.

The very next day, however, came news of the American blockade of Granby and the seizing of the ferry, and no trip could then be considered. Later when Granby passed into American hands, it was still very much a military center. Greene's army stopped there on the way to Ninety Six. Sumter remained in the neighborhood amassing stores, gathering intelligence, sending and receiving orders, so that, according to Hans Jacob, there was no end to the military comings and goings through the Congarees. Again Johannes said they'd better not try to cross the river now.

Was Madle even able to make the trip? Both wondered. Fifteen miles, thirty miles there and back. Afoot? Or should they risk their horses such as they were? If they did, could Madle make the trip on a plowhorse? How many years since she'd gone that far? *I will!* she vowed to herself; *farther than that I'll go!* remembering rivers, mountains, cities, islands. She could make the old journey as clear in her mind as yesterday if she wished. But she knew it was a century ago, not just twenty-four years.

Her life had made a turning. *Why, of course, I'm mortal,* she told herself. *Why should I act as if I'm not?* She had prayed for a full recovery of strength for the younger children's sake, but even as she prayed, the thought would come, *Who am I to be spared?* She was forty-four years old but she did not feel that old—except for breathlessness when she hurried or stooped or climbed the loft-room stairs. But she knew that many a woman younger than she was had been taken, her own mother at twenty-eight, and many and many a child left orphan younger than her own.

Thinking of how they would manage if she were not here, she sometimes speculated idly on the prospect of Johannes' remarrying. She could not imagine it. But she thought of times when something he'd done or said had caused her to ask, *Do I really know him? Would he remarry?* At once she cried out, *No!* to the very idea, as indignant as if some woman were going to oust her next week. At first Madle was startled by this self-revelation, then amused by it. *I'm a long, long way from being a good old soul yet,* she thought. *Surely the Lord won't want me in heaven yet.*

She refused to think more of such things. *I'll never remarry nor will he. I know it.* But there came to her another application of that thought. The thread moved, twisted, grew terribly distinct in the air, a smoke-blacked rope. *God, spare him to me!* she cried. *Oh please, God, don't take him from me!*

Mercifully, a young hen began to cackle, its notes sweetened and mellowed by distance and sunshine. The line faded—fears, jealousy, tomorrow. The motes of air clustered and sparkled as before. Be glad in today! So much given today! She called to Anneli, "Come, little sweeting, let's go look for eggs!"

All the way from the garden they heard Cathri's robust singing. Madle closed her eyes in joy and blessing, sorry that her words to Cathri still tended to have too much instruction, tinged too often with impatience.

Cathri was beginning to sense some movement, some sweeping song or tide that would flow from the north or from the river or up the Road, perhaps even out of the western woods, some change coming to envelop her. She could not give it a name. A person? A piercing glance? Or was the coming only in herself? Her body changing, shaping to different uses and roles. Sometimes she felt in herself a great beauty that had nothing to do with rose-sprigged dresses. Sometimes she felt a strength that could leap down steps and fly to rooftops.

She did her work with ease, a slapdash ease, her mother implied smiling, but Cathri did not mind, did not mind the work either. She began to take some pleasure in doing things thoroughly and right. She saw her hands as smooth and shapely, made to shape and smoothe, to order and clean, made to make, to caress.

Joggi and Nissi's meetings had haunted her days, filled her with longing and vicarious joy. Someone for me too? Ever? She could not remember well the way Willi looked, not even his face, except in a wooden, formal way. She tried to visualize other boys, but that was even less satisfying. She might as well be thinking of Hans or Georgi. Someone more like Heiri or Andreas inside, she dreamed, yet different too, someone to come. But who? Who'll come ever?

The men who had thought to catch Joggi broke cruelly into her dreams. One with a curving, ripening mouth stared at her, and one winked, the one with the long scarred cheek and discolored teeth. Their attention made her skin feel wet and bare. The troops last summer had not seemed to notice her at all, but as these last ones addressed her, she felt their regard to be personal, and she feared it, loathed it, loathed them, and most of all loathed the heat and flush that enveloped her body. However, when the man slapped Hans, her fear and shame turned to fury. If she'd had a gun, she thought she'd have tried to kill one. After that—almost—she could have cried, Let no one come, ever!

Yet several days later when she went to the spring in the evening, turned with her full bucket and saw the sky a brilliant crimson beyond the darkened trees and smelled the sweetness of leaves and grass around her, suddenly she felt invaded by freshness and light. She smelled the faint woodsmoke, heard the birds in the oak tree twittering and the faint far lowing of cows. She cried aloud in joy, "Ohh!" and inwardly, *Soon, soon! Oh, I know it! Surely, surely!*

That night in the loft-room no spring airs drifted between the close-set logs, and she tossed and turned, yearning. *Oh, ever?*

After Hans left, she had to help more in the fields, for a man and two young boys could not keep up with the rampant grass. Along with her father and brothers, she hoed out grass and mounded up earth around the young corn. As she worked in the big field, Cathri felt out in the world. They were working near the High Road, which stretched up the long rise to the north and down to the bridge across Savana Hunt Creek and over a shallow rise to the south. This morning the road was empty, its sand rough with the passing of many horses and wagons, for it had not rained in several days.

As they worked, strung out down the long rows—her father far ahead, Andreas and Georgi on a row together trying to keep up with him, and Cathri last of all—she glanced every now and then toward the road, wondering if they'd see anyone pass. It was the first time she had worked here in many months.

Two crows crossed the field cawing derisively, perhaps at the workers as well as at the two scarecrows the Lienhardts had had such a time rigging up. Scarecrow clothes were hard to find, being already on people's backs. They always put two scarecrows here, for the field was broad, the oldest on the place. Its soil was soft and loamy from years of cultivation. Now the rhythm of the hoe's chop carried them along in the fresh morning.

Suddenly, through the thud of the hoe and the tear of grass came the sounds of horsemen. As the workers stopped and straightened, they saw some thirty riders topping the rise and cantering down the High Road. They came swiftly but showed no gleam of scarlet or green and little of brass. Still, although their clothes were nondescript, their muskets looked bright and new and their horses were good ones.

Johannes turned around and called, "All right, you chaps, keep on with your work now," and bent to his own.

Cathri obeyed, chopped out a few more clumps of fibrous roots, then could not help straightening to look up again.

They were all ages, young men and boys mostly, though two looked as old as her father. How were they different from the ones who had come after Joggi? Except for their clothes they seemed no different. Yet she thought she could see in their faces an austere look that the others had lacked. Most of the riders gave only cursory glances toward the field.

Cathri stood still. She fixed her eyes on one young rider whose glance flicked over her. His face was brown and smooth. He looked as if he might have come out of his own father's house that very morning. Something in his face, a shadowy brightness like the dew of the grass blades close to the ground, spoke to her. His mouth was firm. He sat straight. Oh you! she cried. Is it you?

That night as she dropped off to sleep, she took that face with her. After a few days, however, it became formal and wooden too and she let it go.

May passed. The season grew dense with leaves and cries of birds and the farm animals. Sweat and heat thickened around everyone's body. Cathri's patched bodice grew so tight that it split again and could not be mended. Any garment of her mother's was now too small for her, but Madle took her only other petticoat and cut a bodice for Cathri out of it. A strong linen-cotton cloth, it had once been royal blue with red flecks. Now the blue was dull but the red was still bright. Cathri remembered it from the time she had been no higher than her mother's waist.

The cloth made a wide and ample garment across her own shoulders and across her breasts, and now she could stretch her arms with ease. She did not think of this bodice as something old made over; rather it was an expansion of a strong garment into new use. It was for her, and it was made new for her. The color or lack of it did not especially become her; nevertheless, the feel, the new fit and freedom of it delighted her, made her spirit soar so that when she worked alone, she would often sing at the top of her voice. Her family, hearing her, sometimes marveled at the soaring power of Cathri's voice.

41

He was with the men he knew. He would go with them until he or they were dead or until the fighting was over. He believed he would see it over. The enemy was still fierce and forted up in places, aggressive on roads and at river crossings, but Joggi had begun to think of the day they'd be gone and he'd turn his horse toward Savana Hunt for the last time. And to Nissi. To Nissi.

He would not again forget her. The deep place where she reached him was alive. It would stay alive with the memory of his home hearth but even stronger and more consciously part of him than the family bonds that made him who he was. Yet he realized the strength of those bonds as never before. That three months had made a difference.

And a difference in the fighting too. Oh, its essence hadn't changed but its outer ways had. They weren't doing so much running now. He was one of the combined force of Georgia and North and South Carolina militia who assaulted Fort Grierson among the woods and swamps outside Augusta in late May. He did his part when they closed in to kill or capture most of that garrison. Later he saw Colonel Grierson, a prisoner, shot to death by a Georgian.

Tales of cruelty by the Tory commanders at Augusta were rampant. Therefore, when Brown was at last forced to surrender Fort Cornwallis in early June, Pickens made sure that that most obdurate Tory was strongly guarded to keep him from being murdered as Grierson had been. Early in the war, Thomas Brown had been tarred and feathered, the soles of his feet held to the fire and burned. After that, Brown had fought as hard as he could and got what revenge he could. Some Rebels he had hanged immediately after capture; others he had given to the Cherokees for torture. In his last fight at Augusta he placed an older prisoner on the bastion the man's son was firing at. No wonder the Georgians hated him. No wonder Clark saw him as a personal enemy. But Pickens made sure Brown was got safely to Savannah.

One thing was better now, Joggi thought, and that was the man he fought under, Andrew Pickens. A year ago it would not have mattered, so long as the man was bold and skillful.

Joggi had always respected the leader of the Georgia partisans—Elijah Clark was one more fighter—and he was glad to be near the Georgians again. As for Henry Lee, who could help admiring the dash of the man and the gleam of success surrounding him? But Pickens, that close-mouthed, long-nosed meetinghouse elder? The general was not quite as old as his own father, Joggi thought, early forties maybe, but something about him reminded Joggi of his father.

From '75 till the fall of Charlestown, Pickens had led the backcountry Whigs. At the Ring Fight, when Pickens' twenty-five followers found themselves suddenly surrounded in a field of tall grass by eighty-five warriors, his victory over them so impressed the Cherokees that they named him "Skyagunsta," "Wizard Owl." But after the fall of Charlestown Pickens took parole and refused to break it until Tories began plundering and burning his property.

What Joggi liked mainly about Pickens was not just that he'd do what he could to help a dying enemy—see that a Tory's widow got back her husband's jewelry, for instance—but that he was not too proud or jealous to cooperate with other leaders. If anyone could give war a humane and intelligent face, Joggi thought, it was Andrew Pickens. Was it because of his religion? Maybe. And then there was his air of calm certainty. Was that what reminded Joggi of his own father? Well, they said Pickens was a good farmer too.

Could I ever be like that? He could not imagine it. He'd be twenty-three years old in December. If he lived.

Joggi knew Rudi liked Pickens. "He may be Irish Presbyterian, but he's no hypocrite. I can't say I'd ever feel comfortable to sit down with him by a campfire, Joggi, but I'd feel mighty comfortable to lie down later and know he was there. And another thing, he knows how to fight, but as soon as he's won he knows how to stop."

Yes, he'd done both at the Cowpens, where he'd commanded all the militia. Where the militia had not run. . . . Where Heiri was killed.

Joggi could think about Cowpens now. It no longer obscured other memories. Yes, he saw a number of things differently now.

They were on their way to Ninety Six, which Greene and the Continental army, over a thousand, had already surrounded. The enemy inside the fort were far fewer.

Finally Ninety Six. Could they really take it? Joggi thought of the place with a mixture of anticipation and loathing. In his mind it stood for degradation and humiliation and not just his own. He remembered the heat, the darkness, the closeness, and stench of it. For him it reeked of helplessness and despair beneath the weight of power and lies. Well, maybe now he'd have some part in tearing it down. Though something in him shrank from even coming near it.

He did not relish siege and assault. He did better when it was man to man in the woods or open field. In its own way the siege at Augusta had been as bad as the one at Savannah, though on a far smaller scale, but of course they'd won at Augusta. From what he'd heard, Ninety Six, the way it was fortified now, would be somewhere in between. The jail, the town, the old palisade fort and the big new one with its wedge-shaped bastions, all were surrounded by ditches, ramparts, and every other kind of ingenious defense. All the same he'd rather be on the outside and not like at Charlestown. Well, maybe Ninety Six would be opened to freedom too. Joggi thought briefly of the woman who'd helped him last summer, wondered if she was still there.

Thank God, Granby was free. He had been immensely cheered by that news and hoped it would make a difference to his family. And to Nissi. As always he thought of her apart.

How different it was, Rudi thought—though here in these woods much the same. The same campfire smoke; the rivulets of sweat and your hands slick with it; the redbug, mosquito, and tick bites that tormented you day and night; the smells of men, horses, cattle; the earth and trees. But now the woods were stripped of the vines, brush, and saplings that were needed for the stakes and wickerwork of fraises, gambions, fascines, and who knew what other French-named traps and contrivances that went with fortification and siege. Though what it amounted to was simply earth and wood as it always did. And iron and lead. And iron-willed flesh and bones. It took an iron will to keep a man digging in this heat, tunneling through hardpan clay. Rudi was no shirker, but his forty-year-old body was glad for a spell of picket duty after three days' digging.

Though Greene's headquarters and the main camp were a half mile north of the Star Fort, the whole area was ringed and guarded so that no one from the village or forts could get out and no messenger could get in.

In front of the besieging army stretched a baked waste of stumps and ruined fields. Their focus was the Star Fort, but they must also take the palisaded town, the fortified jail, and the smaller fort on the rise above Spring Branch, which was the defenders' only water supply. These four works lay along the lines of an open angle, stretching west and northeast, with the village at the junction of the lines and the Star Fort northeast of it. Adjoining the village to the west was the brick jail and beyond it the Spring Branch and across the branch the Palisade Fort. Each place was fortified separately and surrounded to a greater or less degree by walls, earthen ramparts, embedded collars of pointed stakes called fraises, by ditches, and by a second barbed necklace of felled trees, the abatis. All four were connected by a protected ditch called a covert way. Hard to get into those strongholds, Rudi knew, especially the Star Fort. No one had realized quite how hard it would be till they got there.

Only way was to starve 'em out, Rudi thought, but everyone knew they had supplies aplenty in there. And what no one did know yet was how near the British were on their way from Charlestown to relieve 'em. So the plan was to try to dig up close enough to the wall to storm it. On the advice of that Pole with the unpronounceable name, Greene decided they'd work their way forward like moles, zigging and zagging up to the ramparts of the main bastion, sap it, mine it, and storm it—the fort with its eight wedge-shaped points.

It was a different kind of fighting from what men like Rudi knew. When it came time for the actual assault, no doubt the Continentals would bear the burden of it. Rudi was not so foolish as to mind. Yet he wondered—and others did too—if they weren't biting off more than they could chew. That Tory, Cruger, was an intelligent man. And decent, you had to admit it. . . . Aye-God, if it were only a matter of all the wrong being on the other side. . . . Rudi cast the thought away as he had a hundred times before. *His* wrong, the wrong done *him* had come from that side over there.

Rudi's company was camped a half mile south of the village, not far from Ninety Six Creek, near the old graveyard and the ruins of an old meetinghouse. It was very near the spot where Robert Goudey's large establishment had once stood. But barns, store, the old palisade wall— all were burned or pulled down now. Goudey had died in '75, never saw Ninety Six a fortress again and pass from Whig hands to Tory to Whig to Tory again.

In his mind Rudi saw Goudey's big store of square-hewn logs where he'd often traded his skins; its open porch where many a time he'd shared a swig from a jug, shared talk in a wide afternoon. He remembered a particular friend, wondered whatever happened to him. The half-breed children that had played about the porch would be young men now. . . . Wagon after wagon had backed up to Goudey's barns and store. But all of it now was charred bits of wood and tumbles of brick and rock.

He remembered when its palisade walls were new and green, '60 and '61, the woods alive with men. Twenty years ago the middle of May, an army of 2800 men had camped here, and the summer before that, 1600. He'd been here both times. Both times British and Provincials had been on their way to Keowee, aided by Catawbas, Chickasaws, and even a few Mohawks, headed for the mountains to punish the Cherokees. Then the red coats and cheap osnaburg blue had camped together. Today only those drab-clothed Rangers would blend into this camp. And the black Pioneers, who then as now did much of the hewing and digging. Though today the blacks who'd toiled to make these ramparts strong were now inside them, but there were still a few who'd been gathered from roundabout to help the attackers in their own hewing and digging. Twenty years ago the slaves had come mostly from down the country.

Twenty years ago the site of today's village was woods and fields. Twenty years ago Ninety Six had been only a stopover. The army's destination then was two hundred miles from here; their end the destruction of Cherokee fields and villages because that was the only way to fight an enemy you couldn't come to grips with—starve him, burn him out, make him want peace.

And it had worked. *More or less it worked*, Rudi thought. *It gave Margaret and me the peace we dwelt in on Indian Creek those seven or eight years, once the outlaws were got rid of. And the British and Charlestown let us have a courthouse up here.*

But then Charlestown and the British had to keep quarreling. And the British stirred up the Cherokees; that was the worst thing they ever did. And then they too came here, thinking to do to us what we'd done to the Indians. Only we didn't skulk away.

Didn't we? Sure we did, just like the Cherokees. Bided our time till we could strike back. But if they'd had the sense to leave us alone we wouldn't have struck. And now there are more of us roused than there ever were of the poor damned Cherokees, and we, unlike those scattered tribes— we're strong enough to hound our enemies out. We'll see 'em gone. We'll see 'em pay for their burning, their starving and crippling our children, the ones that did it!

Rudi's mouth twisted derisively. *Ah, how different am I after all from Running Elk? He loved his son same as I love mine. But would Running Elk, no matter whose side he was on, would he have struck mine down if he knew he was mine? No, and I don't believe he'd have let it happen either. But Bill Lee did. And Micajah Fonder, scum that he is, that I shared a fire with many a time, and some inside that town or fort too. Well, let 'em know how it feels to get instead of give!*

Yet even as Rudi formed these thoughts there would surge behind or under them a sick revulsion, and sometimes it rose into a cry. *Oh God, can I never get out of it? Caught no matter how I turn!* He would hold still a moment, then grab his gun or knife or something else to clean, oil, polish, or hone. Once, he got leave to go and still-hunt for a few hours. He brought nothing back, for there was little or no game here, but he came back calmer. He brought Margaret with him. Margaret, pearl. Strange he should now get his calm from her. . . . And remembering Jamie Fraser.

Lee's Legion was here. They'd come up ahead of Pickens three days ago. Rudi wondered if Jamie was with them, wondered if he'd ever see him again. But he and Jamie had had their say together.

One interesting occurrence: He'd caught sight of young Willi Rieder the other day, seen him out cutting withes for the baskets they filled with earth to build up the height of the trenches. Rudi couldn't help a sardonic smile at the sight of the rich Congaree planter's son sweating and hacking brush with the rest of the backcountry ragtag. *Well, give him his due. He was as ragged as any of 'em now and no doubt had earned his place among 'em.* Rudi remembered the last time he'd spoken to him. By Heiri Lienhardt's grave.

He thought of those two in the woods a year ago, Heiri and Willi, the day he'd found them. Remembered his own boy, his laughing response to young Heiri. He clamped his jaw on the pain.

He traced the steps his duty demanded, stood still to hear the faintest sound of leaf, earth, or twig between the boomings of the cannon. He knew as well as the general the importance of detecting any approach to the fort.

. . . That Cruger was a smart man, they said, and a good one. There'd been no atrocities after he took command. He must have something to him, and him from New York State, to make the Loyalist militia stick to him like that, especially when he'd given 'em a chance to leave.

Well, let 'em stay, be starved out, and be damned to 'em! Or be blown out! The Americans had a good strong network of spies spread over a hundred and fifty miles south and east. They'll know if those high and mighty lords down in Charlestown try to send an army up here. An American spy can outwit a Britisher any day.

. . . "American." The word kept tripping him up. *Those people inside Ninety Six would claim they're just as American as we are, he thought. But they're not! "American" is free! "American" is not lording it over a man because of his coat or his lack of one, or the way he can or can't sign his name, or who his daddy was. "American" is*—he traced the thought into a harder place—*my son's right to defend his mammy. Or his sister. Or his son.*

. . . To make the one who hurt them pay.

Rudi's mouth stretched in a bitter-sad grimace. Not American. Just human. Man's work. Cherokee, Tory, Whig. Britisher, Irishman, Dutchman. New York, Georgia, Carolina, and over the mountains. And across the water. No, he couldn't claim that work for American any more than he could claim pulling a trigger for American. Aagh! the old sickness rose in his throat. He was back where he started from years and years ago, the day he'd come up behind old Bruger with a clout of wood, struck him down and left him for dead. Sixteen years old. Never repented it, its poison in him still. *Ah, Jemmy,* he cried, *you got your daddy's poison in you early. But not from me! Oh, pray God, Jemmy, not from me!*

42

Willi ran in a half-crouch, straightened, aimed, and shot at a figure scuttling along the shielded ditch up from Spring Branch toward the jail and village. He dropped behind the scant cover of a stump to load, ran forward again and tried to keep sight of Eph leading them. Were there fewer bullets whistling? It seemed so to Willi. Were the intervals between the firing from the jail longer? No sound at all came from the swivel guns in the Stockade Fort. He peered to his right through a rift in the smoke, saw Lee's white-shouldered Continentals scrambling between the gaps their axes had cut in the fraise, two men clambering above the stockade wall. Glory to God! They were taking it!

Eph glanced back grinning, lifted his left arm over his shoulder and jabbed toward the right. Into the ravine and up toward the jail, its V-shaped rampart and ditch. Beyond it the village with its revetted walls, loopholes, and manned blockhouses.

Willi made a sudden diagonal run down the hill toward the little branch Eph had already crossed—he'd learned better how to favor his knee so as not to stumble—and began his half-crouching run up the slope toward the jail.

In the distance on the other side of the village, he could hear between the boom of artillery the yells and shouts, the crackle of musket and rifle fire. The yelling came from inside the abatis they'd cut through, from the deep ditch north of the Star Fort, where bundles of sticks were being thrown down to give the Marylanders and Virginians higher footing, the ditch where they struggled with long forked poles to pull down sandbags from the parapet above their heads, where they themselves were being skewered by long spears from above, were being clawed by the crossfire from loopholes in the angled walls.

But Willi's work was not there. His militia company had been ordered to support Lee's assault on the Stockade Fort above Spring Branch. Their job was to scour and skirmish to its north toward the jail, be ready to trouble or drive back any sortie from the smaller fort or from the village.

The time was a half hour past noon, June 18. The sun was as merciless as the down stroke of a saber.

The attack had begun at noon. It had to be today. Lord Rawdon's army of over 2000 men were slogging up through the sandhills less than fifty miles away.

Although for Willi it was still a fiendish tangle to struggle through, like the great collars of sharp-branched trees around the ditches, yet he seemed to know how to thread through smoke and shot to the place where he must be—alongside his brothers. It was strange how that dread of fear was gone and with it much of the fear itself. He did not even think about being afraid anymore. Not that he wasn't afraid sometimes, but he knew how to take it like the pain that came and went in his knee.

Eph motioned them to the ground. A rifle ball splintered a stump; another kicked up the dirt in front of him. Now the V-shaped rampart this side the jail loomed over them and Willi could see the top of the brick jail above its rampart, square and red through the hazy sunshine, its upper story glaring through an iron-barred window from which rifle barrels stuck out like spikes.

More shot tore the ground; a clod of clay stung Willi's cheek. Joe Morris grabbed his side and bent double. Eph motioned them back to where the steepness of the ascent would give them cover. Someone shouldered up Joe from where he'd stumbled. They'd have to wait for further orders, wait for the Delaware men. They lay in the sun and watched for any vestige of a target above or outside the rampart, waited under the bristling eye of that jail. A couple of them had been in it.

. . . Joggi Lienhardt, where was he? Willi wondered. He must be in the woods where the main body of militia waited. *What a turnaround, me here and him back there*, Willi thought. Well, no doubt they'd all get their share of hell before long. Joe Morris wasn't making a sound.

In their own stillness, the yelling and clamor from the Star Fort sounded louder, the artillery more thunderous, drowning out sounds from the Stockade Fort behind them. It seemed to intensify. Lying still in the sun, few could help the shiver that worked its way up their spines. Willi stared ahead, knew that when Eph rose, he would too, that his legs would take him, with or without pain, straight or obliquely up the slope or however Eph beckoned.

They lay still about fifteen minutes. Then they began to turn their heads. Some looked backward, looked at one another. A few rose slightly to change position. The shouting from the Star Fort had reached a higher

pitch. Somebody was getting it bad. A rider came galloping, circling out
of range of the ramparts, making for Lee's command. Suddenly, Eph's
men realized they were hearing no guns, only the clamor of voices. What
was happening? Had Cruger surrendered already? It didn't sound like
surrender, they thought uneasily.

The hell Willi had expected was different from what he'd thought.
It was hearing in the dark, even at a distance, even out of earshot, the
groaning of men in the ditch all night, the ones not yet dead. It was knowing
that the broiling weeks of digging, tunneling, hewing, and heaving, the twenty-
six gut-straining days were wasted. Their hell was admitting defeat.

Shortly after one o'clock Greene had called off the assault. Too
many men were dying in the ditch. When Cruger sent out two flanking
companies, one on each side, to drive into the Continentals with bayonets,
the attack on the Star Fort turned suicidal. Their enemy was too determined, too well prepared, his defenses too strong.

True, Lee was in the Stockade Fort, which seemed actually to have
been vacated earlier, but his men were halted before they could attack the
jail, and all supporting militia were pulled back.

From the hour's fighting in the noonday sun, a hundred and thirty-
four Continentals lay dead or wounded. Militia losses were not reported.
Lee said later that the total American losses were a hundred and eighty-
five. The British reported only eighty-five casualties.

"British." "American." The attacking soldiers had been commanded
by Lieutenant Richard Campbell of Virginia. One of Cruger's flanking
parties was led by Captain Peter Campbell of New Jersey. Nathaniel Greene
of Rhode Island ordered the attack. Major Joseph Green of New York was
in charge of the fort's defenses. Here as in other battles, South Carolinians
of the same name had fought on each side.

All that night as they prepared to leave, Rudi had a sense of reprieve. He felt some disgust at the waste of their toil but no bitterness as
the darkness of anticipation slid out of him and left him curiously light for
a while. Probably Bill and Micajah weren't even in there, wouldn't have
had the guts to stay and last it out.

The Continentals and militia crossed the Saluda at Island Ford early on June 20 and marched toward Bush River. Rudi was moving toward home.

Home. They passed naked chimneys, weeds, and ashes. But some of the peachtrees had fruit on them. Next day they camped near the remains of old James Williams' plantation on Little River where the British had made a fort and later abandoned it—Pleasant Grove.

Now Pickens was ordered to stop and remain near Ninety Six as a screen for the wagons of the retreating army, while the Continentals moved toward Indian Creek. But Pickens' command was already disintegrating. Men whose families weren't trying to follow the army as refugees hurried home to see about them. After what had happened at Ninety Six, the Tories would take fresh heart.

Rudi stood it as long as he could. Finally he too rode off toward the Enoree, promising like the others to return in a few days. He did not allow himself to hope in any way about the child that should have been born by now. He fixed his thoughts on Margaret, Jem, and Katy.

Joggi kept his emotions battened down. Willi tried to. Both remained with Pickens. The Congarees was too far away for them to go home, and besides they did not have the weight of anxiety that men like Rudi had, although Willi was troubled by Joggi's report of the Rieders, especially about his grandmother. He'd hoped that after they took Ninety Six, since Granby was now free. . . . But with that big army of Rawdon's up here, the British might retake Granby.

Willi was still in Thomas' upcountry regiment, one of four summoned earlier to help Greene, although it had formerly been under Sumter. Would they join Sumter again? Sumter was—but who knew where Sumter was? Still dawdling somewhere on the Saluda? Gone careering off down the country again? Or over to the Waxhaws?

It was no secret that some men, and not just General Greene, were beginning to have hard feelings toward Thomas Sumter for not coming to help them or at least trying to delay Rawdon.

"Just like at Cowpens. He wouldn't come and he wouldn't help."

"Thinks he's got to be the whole show or he'll not fight."

They could not remember a time when Sumter had actually joined forces with the Continental Army. He seemed to think the militia's work was different from the Continentals'.

"But it's all one fight! It's the same fight!"

And what about the militia at Cowpens? "You think they could have won without us?" asked Willi.

Eph shook his head. "Not there at the last when we come in on the right. And not at the start either when we give it to 'em coming. No, old Morgan said he needed us. And he did." Eph leaned forward to punch the smoky little fire that helped keep off mosquitoes. "Oh, I've scouted for Tom Sumter and I don't deny he's a rare fighter. I was with him at Hanging Rock, and I heard how he fought at Blackstock's, where he got hurt. You were there, Jake; you know. We know he's a fighter." Joggi nodded. Eph paused, spat, finished dryly, "I was with him at Fishing Creek too, where he went to sleep and we all got caught."

After a while Willi said, "Maybe we ought not to talk so hard against him though. I tell you one thing Sumter did." A smile played at his lips; his eyes were bright. "He gave us horses and guns, Heiri and me. When Heiri went and asked him."

Eph burst into a big laugh. "Lord, I'd forgot all about that. To be sure, he did." He chuckled. "Lord God, if that wasn't the beatin'est I ever heard."

Joggi said, "What you talking about?"

"Why, Heiri never told you?"

Joggi shook his head. He did not say, *He never had time to tell me. So much else to talk about that last night.*

"You tell him, Willi." It had occurred to Eph that the telling might make hard listening for Harry's brother. He rose. "I got to see about something."

When Eph was gone, Joggi asked, half-smiling, "What was it Heiri did, Willi?"

"Oh, he just went to the big General himself and asked for a horse. Asked for two of 'em. Well, some officer told him to, but would you have done that? I sure as hell wouldn't. I wouldn't even have gone to the captain. But Heiri, him a private, he just went right on in to the General, went in and told how he needed a horse to go to the Pacolet. Told him he'd lost his papa's horse and he needed another one. *And* one for his friend. To go help General Morgan."

"No!" Joggi exclaimed. "Heiri did that?"

"He did," Willi laughed and Joggi broke out chuckling. "That's what he said he did and I never knew Heiri Lienhardt to lie. Came back with two pretty good horses too and two stands of arms. *And* leave to join Morgan."

Joggi swore softly, his eyes misty-bright. He shook his head.

Willi said, "He knew we had to have horses to go with Eph and them, and the only way to get 'em was to ask for 'em."

The air was mellow with remembrance and the laughter that covered their pain.

"He'd never have stole one," said Joggi.

"Not Heiri." *Nor would I*, Willi thought, but he knew his reason would have been fear of being caught.

"Wonder what the General thought?"

Willi shook his head.

"Probably never met up with anybody quite like Heiri," said Joggi. "Probably why he gave 'em to him."

"There wasn't ever anybody like him," said Willi, looking at the ground. "He's why I'm here now, you know that?" He looked up at Joggi. "Oh, I don't mean what he did for me at the Cowpens, God knows that was everything—but I mean—well, Heiri just wouldn't let you quit. He wouldn't."

Joggi did not speak for a long time. They sat remembering older days and wanted to reminisce more but not quite yet. Yet their laughter had been a refreshment. Where from?

"Willi, you need to go see your family soon as you can," Joggi said suddenly. "If it's only a day or so. They don't even know you're still alive."

"I've been thinking about that. If we ever swing down the country. But the way things have turned out up here. . . ." He groaned, "Oh, if we could just have taken Ninety Six."

Joggi's face grew somber. "Aye-God. Nobody knows that wasn't in that place how good it would have felt. I could have taken a sledge hammer and battered that jail down all by myself." His jaw tightened. "But no use to talk." His look, his voice hardened. "I tell you, Willi, Ninety Six *will* go down. It *will* fall. They can't stay shut up in forts forever. We can beat 'em in the open; we've done it before and we'll do it again. Oh, we've lost some big ones, I know that, but we've won some too, and add 'em all up together. . . . And even the ones we lost—now look at Camden."

"Thank God, I never had to."

"You look at what's happened there. The worst we ever got beat, outside of Charlestown, was last summer at Camden. Think about it. And even April, when Greene lost there again, though not as bad as the first time, but you know what happened two weeks later, don't you?"

"Rawdon pulled out."

"And every last house and hut of the place burned down and every wall pulled down. Think about it."

They shook their heads in wonder. "I hear the same thing was done at Granby," said Willi, "though not by them. I hear, after they left, we pulled it all down. Though we didn't burn people's houses."

"And at Ninety Six," said Joggi, "it's not like Greene let his whole army get smashed the way Gates did last summer. He's still got his army." Joggi gave Willi a sideways look. "And we're still here, Willi, you and me and some more of us."

"For all the good we do."

"We do. You think we haven't so far?"

"The way some tell it, not much. Some don't seem to think so."

"Ahh, one thing I can't stand is this damned bickering and jealousy, this damned spite talk between us and the Continentals. We've got our work and they've got theirs. Sure, we helped to win at Cowpens, but don't tell me we could have done it without the Maryland and Delaware men. *And* the Virginians. I saw 'em in action. They do what too many of us can't or won't do, Willi. I don't want to hear anybody say a word against those men that fought in the ditch the other day."

Willi didn't answer. He wanted to say, "Yes, Herr Lienhardt," but did not quite dare to.

It was a long speech for Joggi. He thought, *I'm starting to sound like Rudi. Pretty soon I'll be sounding like Papa.* He decided to finish it off. "Those walls *will* come down one day, Willi. They're bound to."

The walls came down on July 10 on orders from Lord Rawdon. The surrounding country was depleted of food and forage, and the garrison was too far from Charlestown to be maintained. So Cruger burned everything at Ninety Six that would burn—buildings, stockade walls, abatises, fraises—and buried in the red clay of the great ditches and trenches everything they did not want or could not take with them—spikes, nails, broken swords and muskets, their cannon. Ironically, Rawdon had sent Cruger orders in May to abandon this backcountry post, but the two sets of orders never got through the Rebel network of guards and spies.

On June 29, Rawdon had marched half his army from Ninety Six back to the Congarees, leaving the other half with Cruger. Later Rawdon decided to move on to Orangeburg. The new recruits from Ireland continued to die of the heat on the way down as they had coming up the country, when they'd still been in red wool coats.

Early on a July morning, with the flames of the little town searing the dawn air, Cruger too marched out of Ninety Six. For a long time smoke smudged the sky behind him. Their houses, church, courthouse afire, the people of the town went with Cruger, many who had taken refuge there, many from Loyalist families roundabout. They followed the army to Orangeburg, began the long trek that would end in Charlestown, where they would join refugees from Camden and other places in a miserable encampment outside the city, eventually to be known as Rawdontown.

But other Loyalists refused to leave their land. They had lived here a generation, had worked as hard as any Rebel to build their homes, harder they thought than most, and would not give them up. Women, children, boys, old men —they'd stay and tough it out the best they could, depend on their courage and the few men they had left to protect them. One of their leaders was an embittered young man named William Cunningham, whose crippled epilectic brother had been murdered by a Rebel.

In the next twelve months, from the Piedmont to the sandhills, Cunningham would rage. Many a pool of blood would soak into the floor of a house, into the red clay of a dooryard, the autumn leaves on a road, the white sand of a camping place in the woods. Bloody Bill and the men with him would do their work. Man's work.

43

On Savana Hunt moods alternated between hope, fear, and despair. British troops came again to Granby on July 2, and the next day the country was full of their move to Orangeburg. Retreat? Or reconquest? Orangeburg had been taken from the Loyalists in early summer; now it would return to them.

A few days later the Americans—or Rebels or Whigs, call them what you would—trampled the hot sand and thickened the air with dust. They were following the British to Orangeburg, where Greene hoped to challenge Rawdon to a fight while Cruger and the rest of the army were still at Ninety Six.

Johannes' and his children's work in the field by the High Road was wasted. He'd known he should not try to plant there again, but habit had been too strong. Milky ears were torn from the stalks, green blades were stripped for forage, and most of the interspersed peavine with pods just forming was trampled. Johannes thought dully, *Well, God alone knows how we could have tended it to harvest anyway. Cathri can't plow. Andreas is still too young. I can't work my children to death.*

The sweating, red-faced young British were not allowed by their officers to stray too far from the road nor did they show the malice and spite of last year's marauders. Greene's Continentals did not invade the orchards and garden either, but some of the militia did and the newly-raised State troops that came later. And after them came other straggling bands as ruthless as any plundering Tory ever was. Indeed, some were the same men, who had just changed sides.

By mid-July the Lienhardts were left with little to be taken. The orchards were stripped, the beehives spoiled, almost every tame fowl caught and spitted. The old barn was empty and the new one almost so, for in May Johannes' conscience had made him take part of his wheat crop to the Americans in Granby though all he'd come home with were the same old paper receipts.

Yes, they were destitute or almost so. The only difference between them and the wandering poor Johannes remembered from his native Toggenburg was that his family had a roof over their heads. And also a little sustenance from the fresh cows hidden up the creek and the promise of a scant crop of corn in the newground. How they'd survive on that promise he did not know. The fields across the creek had been discovered and pretty well ruined.

Twenty-five years of toil. Twenty-five years from that May morning when he'd turned his back on the Solothurn hills to set off down the Rhine. Twenty-five years of struggle, grief, and toil, and what had he now to show for it? His children thin-faced and big-eyed, Madle pale and more quiet every day. If the fever struck now, they'd all be gone.

Johannes went to Granby on foot. He went by the Road even though he knew the bridge across Congaree Creek was destroyed and he'd have to go upstream to ford it. In Granby, what was left of it, the wreckage of palisade walls and outbuildings, the scored uneven hills of earth, he saw fierce-eyed men on horseback and a few loiterers, but no women or children, and few people he recognized. None recognized him. He did not realize how much his own appearance had changed.

Even so, with the walls down, it was good to walk unchallenged till he came to the military headquarters, still in the Kershaw-Hampton store.

He did not have to wait as long on officialdom as he had last summer. It was the same kind of weather, heavy sultry heat, but the officer who saw him had not been napping and probably not gaming either.

Wordlessly Johannes put his receipts before him on the table, then called up his English as best he could, but it was his grim simplicity that spoke best for him.

"They take all bread from my children. They take all their hands can hold. My wife, she has now no strength to live. My four children, two are little, they live in fear. Once it was King's men, now Americans. Three sons I give you. Two, God knows, my oldest and the other not yet fifteen years, God knows will I see them again. My second-born I will not see again."

The officer behind the table had listened with bent head. Now he glanced up at Johannes. He asked a few questions.

With some difficulty Johannes told of Joggi's long service, more easily of Heiri's, briefly the little he knew of Hans'. "He joined in May. I did not wish it; he was too young. Still he went."

"We'll allow you some corn and whatever else can be spared." The man wrote an order and handed it to an aide. "There are many others in your plight as you may guess."

He questioned Johannes about the bands that plundered him.

As Johannes tried to describe them, the officer's face became grim. "It won't happen again."

The officer stood up. He was in his early thirties, his hair was already receding from his forehead, and his skin was weathered nut-brown. His mouth was stern, but as his eyes met Johannes', they were dark with— anger? or compassion? Then he offered Johannes a courtesy no English-speaking official had ever offered him. He extended his hand.

It took Johannes a moment to realize what was meant. He clasped a hand as hard as his own.

"Thank you, Mr. Lienhardt, for your sacrifices. Your country thanks you."

Johannes was too moved to answer but merely bowed.

He trudged down the road with two pecks of meal slung over his back and an order for the same amount to be gotten tomorrow. He wished he had risked riding so he could could have taken it all home today.

As he approached the Rieder place, he was struck by its desolate look. He had paid no attention when he passed earlier, for his thoughts were too heavy and urgent, but now seeing a door on the porch half open, he decided to stop. He had not seen Hans Jacob in at least two weeks.

At the top of the steps he paused to listen. They were probably at the back, he thought. He put down his sack, knocked, and called loudly but heard no answer.

He moved to the door, opened it wider. Everything was gone from the dusky reception hall—tables, armchairs, candlestands—all gone. He stepped inside. The door to the next room was open and it too was empty except for the long, scarred mahogany table. He saw broken windowpanes by the fireplace.

The door to Elsbeth's bedroom was closed, but he rapped on it lightly anyway although he sensed its emptiness. Everywhere he heard only echoes.

Standing on the porch again, he looked at the trashy, grass-grown yard, the great trees, the trampled road, and he had a strange sense of gray sheets of time dropped about him, sealing him from the past.

He picked up his sack and went around the house but saw and heard no sign of life there either. On the backporch he knocked and called, then looked about. A limb of the old fig tree was broken and its withered leaves hung gray.

Had they left the country? Hans Jacob, had something happened to him? Surely not!

Johannes walked quickly past the empty kitchen-house and toward the outbuildings. As he passed the well, he noticed sandy footprints and recent splashes on the wooden platform where someone had stood to draw water, but the earth was so soft and churned up he could not tell which way the tracks went. Across the field the slave cabins looked empty.

He decided to try a path through the peach orchard that led to a wagon road beyond because he remembered where it went. Years ago he had trudged it early and late. Now he remembered Hans Jacob talking some time ago about adding onto and improving the old two-roomed cabin where he and Madle had once stayed. He said he was getting it ready for the family of the white man he'd hired to run his tanyard and his grist mill. But the tanyard turned unprofitable and the man left.

I'll bet that's where they are, thought Johannes, *or somebody is. But can they all be living together in such a place? And why would they leave the big house?*

Well, if you lived right on the Road like that and had any other house, wouldn't you move too? Wouldn't you do it now, even the distance you are, if you had another shelter farther up the creek? . . . But to leave such a big, strong house built by your father. . . . Still what was a house compared to your family's safety?

Johannes had not been this way in almost twenty-three years, not since October of '58, when they'd moved to Savana Hunt. Before that, he'd made this trip twice a day for water, and Madle had come morning and evening for milk. He thought of her young and suffering, remembered his own misery in having no better place to take her. But the memory of those days had been almost swallowed up by the later ones: the unbeliev- able joy that followed, her pleasure in the home he'd built for her, Joggi's birth, the birth of her love. Ah God, the sweetness of those days. And the miracles.

The crescent-shaped peachtree leaves hung heavy. The fruit was all gone, not even a stone of fallen fruit as normally there would have been. The cornfields beyond looked about like his own. Surely, surely . . . Johannes hurried on.

Yes, the low-roofed house had tenants. He saw open doors and windows, caught a whiff of smoke. He called from a distance, "Hans Jacob Rieder! Frau Rieder!"

It looked different from what he remembered. It had a bigger dooryard now with a fairly large shade tree and a porch. Two rooms had been added to the front and side, though the pitch of the roof was not changed. He remembered the stifling heat of that long ago summer.

The front door being open, he called again. No one appeared, but as he mounted the steps, he thought he heard a sound inside. He put down his sack and was about to knock when he heard a scuffling, a scrape and a groan, then a slow shuffling. He looked through the doorway and there was Elsbeth Rieder with a curve-handled stick over her arm, grasping the back of one chair and groping for another.

"Frau Elsbeth," Johannes called softly. "It's Johannes Lienhardt. I've come—I'm rejoiced to see you!"

With her hand shading her eyes, she peered against the light. "Johannes Lienhardt?" Her voice was slightly slurred.

He stood a moment gazing into the dimness, then went forward.

She turned loose the chair and tried to straighten herself as her stick clattered to the floor. "And here you see me, Johannes Lienhardt. Here you see me."

He was less shocked by her appearance than he might have been. His main emotion was shame for his avoidance of her. "Oh Frau Elsbeth," he murmured as he took her hand and bowed over it, "how glad I am—" He realized he was glad. "Please forgive me, Frau Elsbeth, that I've not come sooner."

"I forgive you. So here at last you are." She stood with a little smile and a brightness in her eyes. "And how is dear Madle? They tell me—oh, these awful time! Tell me she's not sick still, not sick like me! Oh, how is Madle?"

"She's—" he tried to lighten his voice, "she's well. She's up and about."

"Then she's not down, thank God. They told me she had some kind of spell, but I know she's too young still to be down like me. Though such grief—and you, Johannes. . . ." Elsbeth groped backward for her chair, staggered slightly, and as Johannes helped her to it, she murmured, "Such grief, Johannes. I know, I know."

He picked up her stick but she waved it away. "Drag that chair around so I can see you. I know you look for Hans Jacob, but spare me at least five minutes. Here you see me, Johannes. Here I sit alone."

"Where are the others?"

"They're out in some field, I didn't catch where he said, out there slaving. He's slaving, Maria's slaving, so's Nissi, all of them, young and old, black and white, though it's only two of 'em left, well, four if you count old Dorcas and that crippled boy, all of 'em out in this heat together. So would I be if my legs would hold me up to go, if my head wouldn't get in a whirl when I try to stand up. Yes, they work from dawn to dusk, Johannes, work their hands to the bone and what good will it do us when robbers and criminals—oh Lord have mercy!" Her voice broke. She dabbed at her eyes and sniffed back tears.

The low-ceilinged room was stifling in spite of the open windows, disorderly and crowded with furniture and boxes and trunks. These new rooms were no bigger than the old ones, he saw. The walls were of rough-planed pine, the floor too close to the ground. "How long have you been here, Frau Elsbeth, in this house?"

"Like a year it seems, at least two months—"

He thought it had not been a month, for he'd seen Hans Jacob two weeks ago.

"'Don't talk about it,' they tell me. 'Turn your mind to something else.'" She groaned, threw her head back and shook it frowning. "Well, I know I can't dwell on it or I'll have another spell, but when I look about me, Johannes, packed and crammed and jammed—'Why didn't you make it bigger?' I said. 'If you'd known that you yourself would one day live here,'—and so many people, and when I remember the peace I had, forty years, Johannes, forty years with my own bed and the peace of my own room and then to be rousted out, to be rooted up! But yet—" She sighed heavily. "Aye-God, I know I had to come down to it; I know it was for the best with vandals and intruders of every kind, every kind of lowdown no-good riffraff off the Road. . . . 'Well, it's a mercy,' I said, 'a mercy I have still body and soul together. When I think of all I've come through, all I've seen, it's not the first time I've been packed up.' Packed like fish in a barrel, Johannes. 'You don't know how it was, you have no notion,' I tell them. Two hundred souls of us packed up together, crammed chockablock full in that ship with all our goods and possessions, trying to keep what we had beside us and jerked this way and that—"

Johannes thought, *She has more memories than I have. And maybe more bad ones. My crossing was not like hers.*

"—nailed in the bottom of that ship, the 'hold' they called it, and it was a *hole* I can tell you, barred down and nailed inside it for two days and nights! With the waves above our heads and the storm throwing us this way and that like a handful of jackrocks, most of us with nothing to hold on to but one another, and we didn't know if we'd ever see the sky above and God's great sun again!"

He'd never thought of her having such memories. "How long were you at sea?"

"Oh, months and months, a year it seemed, but I can tell you this. We knelt down on the ground as soon as we had it under our feet again, knelt right there on that sand and thanked Almighty God for the ground beneath our feet. . . . But after that, oh so many died, so many poor souls." She shook her head slowly. "I can't tell you how it was." Her voice died away.

Presently she resumed, "But somehow I was strong. Somehow, some way I was strong and I didn't give way like some, I didn't give in to my feelings. 'You can cry and you can moan about home all you want to,' I said, 'but this now is my home. It's to be my home till the good God takes me to His.' . . . So we came here. We came here and he was a man that knew how to do things. Oh yes, he knew how to work and he knew how to use his head and we prospered. Oh, I don't say it wasn't hard, but we didn't let that stop us. 'Life's been too easy for you, Hans Jacob,' I tell him or I used to. 'Your father left you too much ease. If you had it more like your father—'"

Johannes shifted uncomfortably. Sickness had not changed her very much after all.

"—but then I know it's not easy for him now. 'Be glad you've got this place to come to,' I say. 'Don't be so proud you can't bend down a little. Packed up, yes, but at least we have a place to lay our heads without the fear of brigands and thieves coming in all hours of day and night.' Though I know they could find us here if they tried, but at least we're away from the sight of them and the hubbub up and down the road day and night, all times of day and night. But Hans Jacob *will* go back there to sleep and what sleep he gets I don't know. 'Well, do what you have to,' I tell him. 'It's your house now, not mine. You're a man. Do what you think you have to. It's not now my place—' but I tell you, Johannes," she lowered her voice and leaned toward him, "I'd not be surprised if he went one day to join Willi."

"Hans Jacob? You think so?"

"Yes, I do. 'Don't tell me about it,' I said. Though he hadn't said a word, I could see how his thoughts ran. 'Don't even tell me, I don't want to hear it. Your old mother, what does she matter, but your children—and your wife—' I'll do Maria justice, she's stood it better than I ever thought with nothing behind her but a life of ease, I'll do her justice at last. 'Maria,' I told her, 'you've stood it better than I ever thought you would.' So I told him, 'Well, make up your mind. It's not now my place to tell you what to do.'"

"What's got him thinking of joining Willi, Frau Elsbeth? Have you heard from Willi?"

"Why, bless God, Johannes, Willi came home! He came home! Though it was no more than a look-in-and-leave, but at least we got to see him, to know he's alive though black as a mulatto and starved half to death, I told him his legs look like a jaybird's. We tried to get him to stay, Maria begged him, we all begged him, but after no more than fifteen minutes, well, it may have been longer, nothing would do him but he was off again like a jughandle. But he whispered to me, and I told him, I said, 'Don't you say that, Willi Rieder, where your mother can hear you.' He told me," she leaned forward, whispering, "that he came home because Joggi Lienhardt told him I was sick."

"What? Joggi? Oh, he's seen Joggi?"

"Oh yes. Oh yes. Didn't you know that? Yes, they're together now as they should be in all their skirmishing about. 'Well,' I told him, 'I'm glad. Joggi was hurt when last I saw him, Willi, much hurt. Be a brother to him now. Not that you'll ever take the place of him that's gone, but still you be his brother.' I said, 'Encourage him. Try to uphold him. And, praise God, one day,' I told him," she paused and gave Johannes a sly, half-smiling look, "'you may be his brother in truth.'" She nodded several times. "In truth," smiling at Johannes, but he did not answer.

"'Oh yes,' I told him, 'the day will come, one day, when all this godless uproar, this wickedness,'" she raised a clenched fist and crashed it softly on the arm of her chair, "'oh yes, it will come to an end. You'll see.' I tell you too, Johannes, I may not live to see it but it will. I've lived long enough to know that. Such things do end."

And so have I, he thought, *so do I know it, and I ought to try better to hold on to it.* Again he remembered his unhappiness under this roof and the joy that had followed. Though never again would he know the like of *that* joy.

"So I told Hans Jacob if he wants to go, don't let his old mother hold him back."

"What's got him thinking of going?"

"It was the way they took off Calli."

"Who?"

"Simmi's mother, Calli. 'Don't worry,' I told him—"

"Who took her off?"

Elsbeth shook her head, squeezing her eyes shut, grimacing and frowning. "I don't know, Johannes, I can't tell one from the other. They're all villains and thieves as near as I can tell. 'King's men,' 'State's men,' I don't know, but I told Hans Jacob, I told Maria, 'Protection!' I said, 'what protection have you got now? What good's that precious King George's protection now? You'd be better off with another kind!' But at the same time, to encourage 'em all, I said, 'But I'll bet you pounds and pence she'll find a way to protect herself, even if you can't. Calli's smart! And she'll find some way to get herself back here too. Calli *belongs* here.' But it went deep, Johannes, deep. Calli is—not that there's been—oh, I'll speak plain though it's all in the past now, has been for years and years. Or do I need to tell you?"

"I know who Calli is," Johannes said shortly. Everyone knew that Simmi and two of Calli's other children were also Hans Jacob's.

Elsbeth was silent a moment. She puffed out a long sigh. "It's how this country is, Johannes, and it's how men are. You know it as well as I do. Oh, I don't mean *you*, but some men are, and when you've got men and women, black and white, all mixed up together, I tried to tell Maria long ago, but how can you change it? We know it's not right but how can you change it?"

The only way's not to let it get started, he would have liked to say and might have said if he'd been talking to anyone else. Years ago Hans Jacob had offered to sell him Calli and Simmi, practically give them to him. It had all been so repugnant, especially the idea of selling the child, that Johannes had given little thought to Hans Jacob's motive. Had it been to break the relationship? Probably.

"Well, I will say for Maria, her face was as long as his when they took Calli. In fact, I think she was as stirred up as he was. We all were."

"Hmp." His mild syllable expressed nothing like what he felt. Calli must have been supremely useful, he thought.

Again Elsbeth was silent. Then she burst forth, "I tell you, Johannes Lienhardt, she was one of us! not like the others! It was hard enough when they took off Simmi, but Simmi's a man, 'He'll take care of himself,' I told them. Johannes, you don't know how it is, but Calli was like us, she's one of us. And when they came and took her—King's men,

Congress, I care for neither, but when they took off Calli and like she was no more than cattle—'God's judgment on us!' I said, 'on you, Hans Jacob, and you too, Maria! God's judgment on us all!'" Elsbeth's voice broke and she began to cry. "Oh, when will we ever again get our homes and our people and our children back, get back the way we were? We'll never be again the way we were, never!"

Her gray face streaming, she was pitiable. He had to try to answer. "No," he said slowly, "it can never be as it was. But it *will* end. You said so yourself just a while ago. All bad does end sometime. And surely some good will follow. God's still in heaven."

"Then why doesn't He *do* something to stop this wickedness? I pray to Him day and night and why does He let it go on?"

"I don't know, Frau Elsbeth. One thing I try to remember. It's men that do the wickedness, not God."

She groaned and wiped her face on her apron. He began to think of leaving.

"How do you think it *will* end, Johannes?"

"I think," he said slowly, "the King will lose. You see now how many are changing sides. But it's not just that. When I think of my sons, how much they've given—I think—surely it can't be for nothing. And sometimes I think—" he heard himself saying words he had not meant to say, "it would end sooner if more of us did more to help it end."

"Just what I told him! Just what I told Hans Jacob! My very words!" She pounced. "Oh Johannes, I hope you'll go with him! Oh, how it would give me hope to know you went with him!"

Johannes was taken aback, did not know what to say.

"You've got your head on straight and always have had. Time and again I've said, 'You watch Johannes Lienhardt,' I said, 'he's one who'll know what to do. When the right time comes, he'll know it and you watch him. You'll find no slack and sluggardly ways in Johannes Lienhardt—"

Lord God, he thought, *let me get out of here*. "Frau Elsbeth, I must go now. I must get back to Madle, and I've got work waiting for me too. Tell Hans Jacob I came." He rose.

She looked up dismayed. "Why, you just came! You've stayed no more than—you just came!" She looked away and sighed, her face gloomy. "Well, I know how it is. I know how you all are."

"I'm sorry, Frau Elsbeth." He tried to speak warmly, gently. He remembered something he'd meant to ask. "I don't suppose Willi said anything about Hans, did he? My Hans?"

"Hans? Hans Lienhardt?" She stared. "Why should he?"

"Hans has left me. He went to join Sumter."

"Your Hans? Why he's no more than—eleven, twelve—how old is Hans?"

"He's fourteen years and six months old, but he's still too young. I opposed it but he was determined. He went without my leave and after they took him, I could do nothing."

She threw up her hands. "Oh Lord! oh God! Oh, the poor children, every child I ever held in these poor old arms, all gone, all slaughtered! Oh Lord, Lord, Lord!" She bent over her knees, her head on her hands, and burst into tears again.

Johannes put his hand on her shoulders, murmuring words, hovering over her until she flung up her head and cried, "Leave me! Go! Men are the ones to blame! Men who stay home safe and let these things happen and their children must pay!"

"Frau Elsbeth!"

She stirred impatiently under his hand. He removed it and stifled his words. He stood a moment longer, then said goodbye abruptly and left without waiting for an answer.

As he trudged home with his sack of meal, he tried not to feel angry. Her words were so unjust! But she was only a sick old woman, he told himself; her changing moods showed that. Of course, her words were unreasonable.

Yet they bit him all the way home.

44

Rawdon might be young—he was twenty-seven—but he had not obtained his command by being a hothead. With his troops outnumbered, he refused Greene's challenge to come out and fight in Orangeburg. He had a strong position in the village, and, as at Ninety Six, a two-story brick jail from which to rake his attackers. Moreover, Cruger and the rest of the army were on their way to Orangeburg, so it was wise to stay where he was and not fight.

Greene recognized Rawdon's good sense. Although for the first time Greene had the full support of the State militia—Sumter had joined him at last, also Marion—he saw the strength of Rawdon's position and he knew the condition of his own men. His Maryland and Delaware soldiers had been marching and fighting since January. Some were sick with malaria and almost all were spent to the bone, exhausted by the unaccustomed heat. Therefore, on the evening of July 13 Greene broke camp at Orangeburg and led his army back across the Congaree River and the next day over the Wateree to the High Hills of Santee. The High Hills were a twenty-five-mile-long range east of the Wateree which offered the nearest thing to mountain refreshment that central South Carolina had to offer. There Greene established a Camp of Repose. Marion and Sumter, however, along with Lee's Legion, moved south and east to harass the British any way they could. Pickens was sent to patrol the backcountry between Orangeburg and Ninety Six.

As Greene had foreseen, the British soon left Orangeburg and moved east to the lower Congaree near where it joined the Wateree to become the Santee. Rawdon was sick with malaria also. Surrendering his command to Lieutenant Colonel Alexander Stewart, he left for Charlestown, where he finished his five years' service in America by playing his part in an event which only further enraged Americans, the hanging of Colonel Isaac Hayne, an esteemed patriot. On August 21 Lord Rawdon left forever those marshy shores and sailed home.

The Dog Days lay like a thick lumpy blanket on the sandhills. The oaks and pines gave thin shade and the ground burned Cathri's bare feet as she hurried up the rise. She hoped no one would see her, hoped no one at the house would notice her absence. She carried cornbread from her own breakfast and a bowl of clabber covered with the milk-straining cloth which she hoped no one would miss from its peg on the wall.

Over the rise and out of earshot of the house she called softly, "Hans?" Hearing no answer, she called louder, "Hans!"

She had a sudden fear that the woods were empty. Why hadn't she pressed him to say exactly where he'd be? Their conversation last night had been so hurried. "Back up there in the woods, Cathri, just over the rise." Oh, if only she could have come earlier! But there'd been no chance till after breakfast.

It was so hot here. Maybe he'd hunted a place with more shade. "Hans, oh Hans!" she called softly.

The woods were mostly blackjack and turkey oaks with a few young pines, for her father had taken out the big pines for building. She noticed there were plenty of gooseberries. She'd snatch enough to fill the bowl on her way home. She wished she'd had the sense to bring a basket. A basket of gooseberries could be a reason for going into the woods.

"Hans, where are you?" she called. Oh, what if something had happened to him! He'd talked so weak and faint it broke her heart she'd had nothing last night to give him. She had gone outside to the closet just before bedtime—she was so glad she'd gone without Anneli—when she'd heard her whispered name.

"Oh Hans!" she called louder, almost crying. "Where are you?"

She caught his movement as he sat up under a low-limbed sparkleberry tree. She rushed toward him. "Hans, didn't you hear me? Why didn't you answer? I was so frightened!"

"The whole world heard you, Cathri. I told you—"

"Why didn't you tell me where you'd be?"

"I told you."

"But when you didn't answer, I thought— Here." She held out the bowl.

He turned it up and swallowed the clabber almost all in one draught.

"You'd better not eat so fast."

The bread was gone too.

Seen in daylight, he didn't look as bad as she'd feared. He had no wound that she could see. He'd already been thin as a rail. He wore the long-legged overalls and shirt he'd been issued as an enlistee, and the stout duck material seemed to have held up well. He was barefooted, of course, with no hat. No gun. But Hans had always been a neat-appearing boy, and now his hair straggled about his face. The fuzz on his cheeks was coarser than it had been.

"I'm sorry that's all I could bring you. If you'd just let me tell Mama and Papa—"

"No!" he interrupted vehemently.

"Hans, why not?"

"Because I said not to. Cathri, you better not tell them." He eyed her almost menacingly.

"But, Hans, what are you going to do? You can't go on staying in the woods."

"Where you think I've been since May?"

"But weren't you in camp?"

"We sure didn't camp in houses."

"But, Hans," she blurted, "food's so scarce now. There's just not enough—I mean for me to take it and nobody notice. Hans, we've been robbed again, worse than last summer, the worst of all. They took almost everything."

"From the new barn too?"

"Well, not *from* it, but they got what was there. Papa thought, we all thought, with the British gone from Granby and the Americans there, well, he let them have some wheat because, he said—and Mama told him to go ahead—he thought about you and Joggi. And too we needed so many things, but they didn't pay us, just slips of paper. But Papa went ahead and had the rest of the wheat ground too and brought it to the house—we didn't know how they'd be, some of them—and before we could turn around, they came and took it all."

"The British?"

Cathri shook her head. "No, they passed us by. And it wasn't even regular soldiers going to Orangeburg. It was just—bands of men." Her voice hardened. "Bands of men that call themselves Americans. They took food from the house and everything else they could put their hands on. From the garden, the cornfields, *and* the orchard. And trampled and tore up and ruined everything."

"Where'd you get that bread I just ate?"

"Papa went to Granby and they gave him a bushel of meal, somebody he talked to there. Oh, we've still got what little's in the newground, but you know how that bears, and a few sweet potatoes they missed. Yes, they even dug up our sweet potato patch. And tore up the beehives robbing them."

Hans' face was set hard. She didn't need to tell him how they did. He'd recently dug in somebody's sweet potato patch himself.

"I just wish," she said pleadingly, "if you'd just come on down to the house, Hans, come on home with me, we'll get food, we'll manage. We will."

"And have me too to feed? Don't worry, Cathri," his voice thinned, "you won't have to feed me."

"Hans!" She would have been angry if she had not been so distressed. "Think how Papa would feel and Mama too if they knew you were out here like this! Please let me tell them."

He ground out his words, "Cathri, I do not want Papa to know."

"Tell me why not!"

"Because—I just can't." He turned his face away, but she thought she heard his voice crumble. She saw his shoulders jerk.

"Where—where's the camp you were in?"

He turned to her. "You think if I knew I wouldn't try to get back there? That's what I hoped I'd find out. Though why I expected *you* to know anything—" He altered his tone to ask less roughly, "Have you heard of any troops about here lately?"

She shook her head. "Not since they all passed through here three— or, no, it's almost four weeks ago now, going to Orangeburg. But I guess you know they've left down there."

He did not answer. He had been at Orangeburg. Oh, he'd been many places, almost as many, he thought, as Joggi.

"I've heard it said," she spoke hesitantly, "that the fighting's mostly down the country now. We thought maybe—" Her voice trailed off. She did not want to say, "that that's where you'd be."

He seized her words for his anger. "You thought! You think! But you don't know! No, you don't know anything because you don't care enough to listen! People like you, what do you know or care? You just stay stuck back here in this one place and what do you know about men being shot to death and cut to pieces, every day men dying—" His voice broke on a falsetto note.

She stooped to pick up the bowl and laid the neatly folded straining cloth inside it. It was the absurd break in his voice that kept her from flaring back at him. Her eyes were downcast, her face flushed.

She wore no cap and Hans saw the nape of her neck bare where her braids parted. To him there was such humbleness in the way Cathri stooped that he compressed his mouth to keep it from quivering.

When she didn't say anything, he asked gruffly, "No sign of Joggi yet, I suppose?"

"No," she answered quickly, "but Papa told us when Willi Rieder was home, he said he'd seen Joggi. But Joggi must not have been with the ones coming through here or he'd have tried to stop by. At least, I think he would have." She added, "In a way I was glad not to see him. I'd have hated to think of him with men like that."

"Cathri, you don't—you just don't know how it is! You don't understand, you can't understand." Again he compressed his lips in a hard line.

"One thing I know." She straightened her back, put one hand on her hip, unconsciously taking a familiar combative stance before him. "When you fight, when you go to fight, I know you have to do things I couldn't do, I don't think I could do them—or maybe I could, I don't know—but I don't *believe* you have to be heartless and cruel to people that never harmed you—" "—to people's families," she was going to say.

He interrupted, "Why, what do you think it's all about, Cathri? That's how it is! You just don't know! You don't understand!"

She only looked at him. He was her nearest brother, always younger, always trying to catch up with the older ones, always trying to prove himself smarter or better at something than the older ones. Her look became a plea: Oh Hans, please come home!

As she gazed at his clamped mouth and his lead-colored eyes, suddenly she realized how much he wanted to come.

She looked about her and sighed, dropped to the ground. "We may as well sit down." She pulled her skimpy skirt over her legs as best she could, and after a moment he sat down too. His knees were drawn up high and bony in front of him with his arms clasped loosely about them.

Above, the small oval leaves of the sparkleberry tree were dull and leathery, but among the brown twigs there were still a few tiny white fragrances. Here and there in the white sand, young longleaf pines were a bright and feathery green.

Cathri said low, "If you'd tell me, Hans, I'd try to understand. Sometimes you've told me things before. That you didn't tell anyone else. You know I wouldn't say a word to a soul."

His face reminded her of a wizened stunted animal's. He looked even older than Joggi or Heiri, she thought, with a different oldness from Papa's.

Thoughts and feelings took shape within her, a voice coming, her own voice. "Hans, it must be so hard to go and live like that, have to do things and see things—you've never done or seen before."

He gazed at his feet. They were scratched and dirty but still shapely.

"Those men that came," she said, "all the different ones, really just boys some of them, the British and the Americans, but—I hated them all. When the last bunch came, and they were just as bad as the British, then afterwards I began to think about them and I thought—what made it so bad was they weren't like real people anymore. Just mean and greedy and—monstrous. It was like they—they didn't even see us, like—they were a different kind from us. But, Hans, you know they weren't—you know they weren't always like that, not all of them. They couldn't have been. Hans, what makes them get like that?"

For a while she thought he was not going to answer. He shook his head and looked away. At last he said, "Cathri, you think you've got the guts to do what you're supposed to do. You think you'll be strong and brave, but when it starts happening, when they start screaming—and half somebody's face is gone in a second and he's dead, he's dead like a cow or a hog, somebody that was talking to you a minute ago, you just can't control it. You can't control what you do. I ran like a deer. I ran. I turned coward."

His words hung gray beneath the leaves. She thought, *You're no more a coward than you've ever been, Hans. It's just that you never faced such things before.* She said, "When was this?"

"The first time it was a skirmish. We were camping on Saluda back in June. A whole regiment of ours—it wasn't the one I was in, but it was the one got caught at the Juniper Springs, almost the whole regiment, they were just . . . destroyed. It was awful. Everybody was talking about it. Well, right after it happened, we were on patrol, the ones I was with, and a band of Tories jumped us. And we scattered and I thought. . . . I didn't get back to camp till late that night because for a while I didn't even know where I was. It was like—I was out of my head. Though when I did get back, nobody said anything. Then I found out later the others had rallied and they drove the Tories off. They killed six, made 'em pay double for ours. But I still had all my powder. I didn't even fire a bullet."

In the long silence Cathri asked, "Where did you go after that?"

He sighed. There'd been another fight with those same Tories next day. Again his body had betrayed him, but no use to tell her about that. "Oh, we marched back and forth different places . . . when we finally broke camp, after everybody left Ninety Six. *We* never went there. Then some of the boys started leaving. Some were leaving all along."

"Leaving?"

"Quitting. Going home."

"Why didn't you?"

"Oh, I wanted to, don't think I didn't want to. But, no, I didn't leave." Again he was silent. "Finally they got more horses and we moved up the country. It was easier then to keep up, in some ways easier. But I found out, Cathri, I found out—it's not just riding along that makes you a soldier."

"How long did you stay? With them."

"Oh, I kept on till just a few days ago."

Cathri counted on her fingers. He'd been gone less than three months. Would that be long enough to make you a soldier?

He rested his head on his knees.

"Was there anybody else your age?"

He looked up. "Age has nothing to do with it, Cathri! I can shoot a gun! I'm a good shot! You know I've always been a better shot than Heiri. Oh, if I'd just—" He squeezed his eyes shut. "If I'd just had another chance, I think I would've. . . . Next time I'd have been more prepared. Instead, it was just—staying in camp or marching." He added low, "I was never sent on patrol again."

She was about to ask, "What did you do in camp?" when he continued, "Oh, I went to Orangeburg with everybody else but nothing happened there either."

"Did you come by here?"

"No, we crossed farther down the river. And after we left there, we went on down Santee, way down there, that country Joggi was in. Cathri, such swamps and woods you've never seen. Hot? Wet? You think you'll melt to your bones. And bit and stung by every bug you can think of. Listen, it's pleasant here, pleasant in our woods compared to down there. Down there . . . it was worst of all." His voice lost expression as he looked away. "They didn't even send me in. When they fought down there, I stayed with the horses."

In the long silence she did not dare speak.

"I was going to try so hard. I was so determined, I thought surely—this time I didn't even care if I did get killed." He shook his head slowly with his eyes closed.

"They'd already fought the night before. That morning too, at a bridge, I couldn't get its name, an English name, and that's another thing, Cathri." He turned to look at her. "I never thought how hard it would be, not knowing the English. Oh, I learned some, I picked some up right away, but just because you don't know a certain word, they think you're dumb! . . . Well, by the time we got there, us and General Sumter, the British had got inside a big brick house. Cathri, you've never seen such big fine houses as they build on the edge of those swamps. Fine rich houses with pleasure gardens and every kind of building for slaves to live and work in. Well, the British were behind those walls and shooting at us from every window. Some said we shouldn't have tried to go in there in the first place." He paused abruptly. "A lot of ours got killed. We fought hard—or *they* fought—but it was all to no good. Some blamed our general. Afterward there was a lot of blaming. I don't know."

Hans sighed. "Well, different ones left. General Francis Marion. Cathri—" his voice changed, for a moment was young and enthusiastic, "—I *saw* him! He's a dark little man and you'd never think, to look at him, he'd be so great, but, oh, I'd give anything to be under him! They say he *cares* about his men. . . . But he left. And that same night Colonel Lee left too with the Legion. Even some of ours. They say Colonel Taylor told General Sumter he'd never serve under him again."

Cathri did not understand much of what Hans was telling her, but one thought did occur to her: that if he had been allowed to fight down there, she might never have seen him again. Because he was not ready yet. Hans, you expect too much of yourself! she wanted to say.

"But you stayed on, didn't you?"

"Oh yes." Again he rested his forehead on his knees. "I was so far from home, I wouldn't have known how to get back here."

"How did you? Get here, I mean."

"Well," he raised his head, "we started back up this way. He sent us, the General. I heard *he* went off toward the Waxhaws. It was a long time getting out of the swamps but finally we took to the Road and I began to know where we were. Four nights ago, soon as I knew where we were, I left. I just up and left." Again Hans' voice gave way and he hid his face against his knees.

Cathri wanted intensely to move toward him. He was different from her but still the brother who was so close to her she did not realize till now how much she loved him. She said quietly, "If they were headed up this way—you said you wanted to get back with them, I don't see why you can't. If you'd only come on to the house, we could find out—"

"Cathri, I just told you! I left without leave! You think I can go home and tell Papa that? I ran away just like I told you before!" He squeezed his eyes shut. "All this time I've been gone I haven't done a thing but follow around and tend to other men's horses."

"Well, isn't that what somebody's got to do?"

"Aagh!" She'd never understand. To be the lowest of the low, to be cursed and even kicked. And worst of all to know that at the beginning if he'd just been brave and stayed to rally with the others, it might have been so different.

Cathri thought, *I must be careful what I say.* "Hans, maybe I *can* find out something for you." *Though I don't know how.* "What do you really want to do now?"

He gazed at her somberly. "I thought—I thought one time—maybe if I could join another company, I'd get another chance. Or if I could just talk to somebody . . . like Joggi. Oh, I know he's not here, still . . . maybe . . . I thought if I stayed near the Road. . . ."

"Yes. Maybe that would be the best." She did not really know, but it was something to say to him. "Hans, listen, I've got to go now." Quickly she rose. "Soon they're going to start wondering where I am and they'll ask me all kinds of questions, but listen. Don't you go anywhere yet, and tonight if you'll come to the old barn, I'll bring you something—" she hesitated a moment, "and I promise you, I promise, Hans, I'll do my best to find out something to help you." She tried to put encouragement in her voice. "But you've got to promise you'll come."

He gazed at her from under drooping lids. She held his gaze. At last he nodded.

Cathri was grown, he thought. As so often before, she'd already gone ahead of him. But she'd listened. And he'd never realized how much it always meant to tell her things. And for her not to despise him. A light breeze fanned his sweaty face.

"Hans, you know the corn's starting to fill out in the newground. And—" But he'd know how to be careful if he wanted to stay hid from Papa.

Again he nodded. He was glad she gave no more advice.

She looked at him long, still sitting on the ground. She struggled to keep back tears, seeing him with his straggling hair and his fuzzy chin resting on his knees. To leave him there.

But she had to. She did not even look back.

As she hurried away, her mind raced. *What am I going to do? I can't bring enough food without anyone knowing! How in the world can I find out anything without asking Papa? And how can I do it without making him suspicious? Oh Hans, if you weren't so—like you are! . . . And now I've been gone way too long and I know somebody's going to ask where I've been, and I just know Mama's already missed me, or if she hasn't, Anneli has, and she'll keep at me with questions till Mama hears her. Oh, my family! Why are they all so—like they are?*

She passed big clumps of purple-laden gooseberry bushes. As she topped the rise, Cathri clapped her hand to her forehead. The bowl and the cloth, she'd forgotten them! *Oh Father above, what must I do?* The bowl they could do without, but they had to have the cloth to strain the milk. Go back for it. She hesitated only a moment. She had to, no matter how late it made her.

The bowl and cloth were where she'd put them under the sparkleberry tree, but only smudges on the ground showed where Hans had been. She shook the ants off the cloth and brushed them out of the bowl. She ran almost all the way up the rise but before she reached its crest, she got such a stitch in her side she had to slow down. She stopped, panting.

Why should she run? She'd already been gone so long a few more minutes wouldn't matter. Either they'd missed her or they hadn't. And if they had, if Mama asked where she'd been—then she'd just tell her. It was as simple as that. She'd just tell Mama.

After all, he was Mama's child, and Mama had a right to know about him. Who did he think he was to treat his mother as if her feelings didn't matter? If Mama said one word to her, asked one question, she'd just tell her about Hans—well, not everything—and if Mama wanted to tell Papa, it was up to her.

And if Hans holds it against me, he'll just have to, I don't care. There's no sense in him lurking out in the woods like that, hungry and all by himself. Who knows what could happen to him?

He needed help and he was going to get it. She didn't care what he thought.

45

"He's so ashamed, Mama. You know how proud he is. I don't know how we'll ever get him here."

The lines in Madle's face deepened. Inwardly she was crying with happy relief but she was also fuming with exasperation. She'd have liked to take a switch to him. The hardest thing about being a mother was coping with boys trying to become men.

"He won't hear to Papa knowing. I don't know why he's so set against Papa knowing he's here."

Madle could have told Cathri. "If you start it, finish it." "Don't begin what you can't finish." "What you like has nothing to do with it, it's got to be done." Such maxims had been dinned into the boys' heads as soon as they could walk, and Johannes had done most of the dinning. It was part of the discipline of work. But had his father taught Hans enough of the discipline of courage?

Madle knew little about soldiering. It was what men did when they said public affairs had gotten to such a crisis that something must be done. It seemed always to have been so. But why the something absolutely had to involve killing or being killed she had never fully understood. Once long ago two Indians had invaded her house, frightening her almost senseless, but after she'd fed them, they went peacefully on their way. She had not liked their intrusion but she could not imagine trying to kill one of them. Of course, she'd had no child then.

Men said there were times you had to fight, times you had to take a stand or be run over. Yes, that was true. In a way. You could not let a child get away with willful mischief. Or wrongdoers like thieves and murderers. But were all those on the other side only wrongdoers? Certainly they could be cruel. But so could those from the side her sons were on. She knew it from recent experience, had guessed it all along.

She remembered from her long ago Atlantic voyage the startling beauty of a little French vessel dancing toward them just before its guns exploded, and afterward the likeness of a wounded French prisoner to someone she loved. She'd wondered then, What made him an enemy? . . . And now those French were their friends. Oh, this world!

. . . Well, Hans was on the way to being a man, trying to be one, and she understood something she would not have understood twenty years ago. It was that most men secretly did not like killing or the risk of being killed any more than women did. What they did like was being part of a large, controlling brotherhood, doing what women could not do. They liked being freed from the failures and frustrations of their own daily toil to venture out and subdue all things according to some larger plan or order that was greater than their own.

Madle thanked God for Johannes' care of her. She knew he had not only the physical but also the moral stamina to stand between her and danger no matter what it cost. And she had to admit he used good judgment. Most of the time. But she also knew there was still inside him, probably would always be, that something that was in Hans, had even been in Heiri, and more than in any of them in Joggi, whatever it was that made them leave home. And probably in Andreas and Georgi too one day. *If I'd been a man— But I'm not a man. I don't know.*

"Your father must talk to him," she told Cathri. "Only your father can help him."

"But how, Mama? How'll we ever get him here?"

"I'll speak with Hans myself. Tonight I'll go with you."

A heavy afternoon thunderstorm cooled things off, but Cathri and Madle agonized at the thought of Hans shelterless in the downpour. Feverishly Madle searched through a bundle of nearly worn-out garments she had hidden under the rafters, looking for something dry that Hans could put on. She measured more meal for bread than usual though she knew Johannes would notice and perhaps say something. Cathri stayed close by, helping her. They talked little but thought flowed between them.

Once Cathri said, "As much as anything, Mama, he needs to have his hair combed and tied."

Johannes was already asleep when Madle heard Cathri creep down the stairs. She waited some five minutes before sitting up and easing out of bed.

In the yard the dark was warm and humid. The moon had not yet risen and the shape of the barn was barely discernible. The crickets and treefrogs were so shrill she could hear nothing else as she groped her way around the barn. She strained to catch a voice. *Oh Father, what if he hasn't come!*

She was almost upon them when she heard Cathri.

"—soaked this afternoon!"

"It's not the first time."

"Did you find—did you find anything else to eat?" Cathri had already given him the bread.

Hans did not answer, thought angrily, *Stupid question. . . .* No, it wasn't, he knew that. It was just that he didn't want to tell her how he'd gorged on half-filled ears of corn, swallowing the kernels almost whole, and later baited himself on some ripe persimmons he'd found, but then either the corn or the persimmons hadn't agreed with him or with each other, and he'd cast up everything. Lying strengthless on the ground, his body had welcomed the rain. Afterwards, however, he started shivering in his wet clothes and couldn't stop. He lay there thinking how they'd feel if they came across his bones in the woods. He took a macabre pleasure in imagining it—until something in him said, *Shut up!* He pulled himself erect, stumbled down to the creek, and managed to kneel and bend over without falling in and scooped up water on his face. He put his feet in the water and sat there a long time, remembering. Heiri. Babeli. Little Andreas. . . .

Cathri was saying, "Hans, I didn't get to ask Papa anything, he's the one who'd know but—" She hesitated. "I did talk to Mama."

"What? Cathri! After I told you not to? Ohh. . . ." His voice wailed high.

It was interrupted by a deeper, softer voice. "Hans, how could she not talk to me?" A touch on his arm. It moved to his shoulder, claiming, embracing him.

"Mama!" He made one weak convulsive effort to pull back but failed against the softness and tug of her voice and hands.

Neither of them spoke. Madle cried a little as she stroked his head and cheeks. At last she said, "You must not blame your sister. I'd have found it hard to forgive her if she hadn't told me."

Cathri said gruffly, "Mama has a right to know about you, Hans. She has every right. And so has Papa."

"You didn't tell Papa!"

Madle tightened her hold, said swiftly, "No, no, Hans. Cathri told only me and only because I asked where she'd been. But, my dear son, please—you must stay with us. If only for a little while. Till you're strong again."

"Just till you're able to go again," Cathri said.

"And your father loves you, Hans. Please don't slight his love."

Love. A foreign word. He knew only scorn and contempt. He'd been battered by them and he couldn't take anymore. Was that why he couldn't face Papa?

"Your father will understand things, Hans. You left in such a hurry, it was such a surprise, so unexpected—"

"Papa never even thought about me!" Hans said wildly. "Nobody did! How I felt, what I thought! I was just somebody to stay and work while the others went and—" He broke off. And got killed? something mocked him.

His mother said quietly, "That's true. In a way. We were thinking only of how to get food and how to keep warm, just to live from week to week."

"But day in, day out just to grub with a hoe, day in day out—there ought to be more than just—slaving to eat and keep warm!"

"Yes, there ought to be. Sometimes there is."

"Oh Mama!"

Again she held him, stroking his greasy straggling hair. She whispered, "There will be more for you, little son, oh, I know there will be."

Her diminutive endearment undid him.

Cathri said, "Don't you think if we go on up to the house we can talk better? Mama, I know we left some of that stew broth in the pot. Hans, she cooked extra for you tonight. Though she didn't tell anybody."

"Hans, Papa probably won't even wake up he was so tired when he lay down so you don't have to see him tonight. You can wait till morning. If you'll stay."

Why should facing his father be so hard? Was his father his enemy? Why did he so want to run? It was not his body that wanted to run, but something else. Yet he knew his father was not a harsh or cruel man.

His mother's hand on his shoulder fell away.

He stood trying to firm his mouth. His stomach cramped; he shivered. There were some things you had to do. What you liked had nothing to do with it. He drew a long sigh. "All right."

Cathri's sigh was short. Thank the Lord he still had a little sense. For a while she thought it had all left him.

They started for the house, Hans and his mother in front, Cathri close behind so if he suddenly changed his mind, she could grab him.

What surprised Hans most was the wide gladness on his father's face. Johannes did not physically embrace him, at least not at first, but his smile did. It engulfed Hans like the broadness of those shoulders, warmed him as that big deep chest would have if he'd been held against it.

"Hans! My boy! I'm so glad—God knows I'm so glad, oh, God knows, Hans! Here, let's look at you. Oh my goodness, Mama, what more have we got to feed him?"

Johannes had come into the room quietly. He did not know what waked him. It was not a sound. Something else got him up, and he'd just stood there in the shadows until Hans finished his bread and bowl of broth. Tears still wet Johannes' cheeks as he surged into the firelight.

Hans turned on the bench, jerked involuntarily, clamped his elbows to his sides, but he met his father's look.

Johannes sat down by him and took Hans' right hand in both his, pumped it up and down. "Oh my boy, I'm so glad to see you, so glad!"

"I'm—I'm glad to see you, Papa." Warmth suffused Hans' face. A smile got hold of him. He *was* glad. Great God Almighty, he was glad!

"Here, let's make up the fire! I see you've already been feeding him but let's have more light. Cathri—"

"Shh," cautioned Madle. "You don't want to wake the children."

"No. No, that's right. Not tonight. I'm just—so glad,"

Perhaps it was Madle's silence or Cathri's that told Johannes not to ask questions. Or maybe Hans' look. He saw some kind of pleading in it. It was not the closed, sullen look that had exasperated Johannes all last winter and spring. Maybe now there would be something Hans would want to tell him. . . . Or maybe not. Anyway, not tonight. No matter, here was his son he'd feared he might never see again, come home!

"Well, let's put him to bed, Mama," he said more quietly. "That's what he needs now. How long's it been since you've lain under a roof, my boy? No, don't try to tell me, I can guess. But here's what we'll do, Mama: I'll go upstairs and get Georgi and bring him down to our bed. Chances are he won't even know he's been moved. Then, Cathri, you come up with Hans. No," he shook his head at Madle, "let Cathri do it."

"Be sure to straighten the bed, Cathri," said Madle. "You know what a tumble Georgi gets it in."

His mother brought him an old clean shirt with no sleeves. She helped him take off his damp filthy clothes, and as he felt the soft cloth on his body and the air on his naked legs, he began to feel like someone else, like Georgi, whose head lolled over his father's shoulder as Johannes came down the steps. He half expected his mother to get a basin of water and wash him. He knew he would not resist if she did. But she didn't.

Hans' legs were shaky as he mounted the stairs with Cathri behind him. Halfway up the stairs he looked back, looked back at his father, who'd come in from putting Georgi down, and stood with his mother at the foot of the steps. That unbelievable look on his father's face was like—fire— and milk, bread, honeycakes.

Too many feelings. He did not try to sort them out as he collapsed in the familiar, unfamiliar dark; onto the unfamiliar, oh most familiar bed. He did not even know whether he was glad to be in it or not. But he knew that something was. Something bigger than he was was glad.

Downstairs on the hearthbench, Johannes sat with his head in his hands. His lips were moving. Madle stood behind him, her hands on his shoulders. Finally he reached up and drew her down beside him. They sat there a long time whispering.

46

To think they all cared about him. The children—it was pitiful the way they gathered around him, his little sister even wanting to hold his hand. And Georgi laughing, Andreas smiling. He'd never imagined his own little brothers cared that much about him.

Nobody asked any questions. He thought Cathri or his mother must have told them not to. In a way it bothered him, but he was relieved not to have to talk. They had sweet milk and cornbread for breakfast. Later in the morning his mother boiled him an egg.

She sat near him while he ate, and as Hans really looked at her, he was shocked. She was so thin, her face so drawn. The wings of her hair at her temples were snow white. He'd never thought of her as old; she was just his mother. He tried to remember how old she was. Forty-something. Yes, that was old. Yet she still had that power of voice and touch. Squeezed in the middle as he was, he'd sometimes felt she didn't care as much for him as for the older and younger ones, but now he knew she loved him. And he knew he loved her. He had to be glad he'd come back if it made her glad. As to whether Cathri had done right to tell on him, that was another matter. He tightened his mouth.

Everybody else was out of the house this morning. Cathri and Anneli were gone to pick gooseberries and gather persimmons. The boys were checking their snares and traps. Last night's rabbit stew was partly the result of their skill. Hans did not know where his father was. He'd seen him for only a few minutes this morning, hearty and smiling.

Madle did not tell Hans that Johannes had gone to Granby to try to get more meal.

Though the day was already hot, at least it was clear. It was the blue sky as well as Hans' arrival that sent Johannes to Granby again. Whatever he obtained, hoped to obtain, he'd have to get it home dry. Also he had the feeling Hans didn't want him hovering about. Let his mother do the hovering.

As Johannes trudged along, damp sand kept getting inside his broken shoes and clogging them. He decided to take them off and carry them till he was nearer Granby. He carried also, wrapped in a mealsack, the large pewter candlestick they'd hidden last fall, the one Cathri had saved. With pewter so scarce, so much melted down for bullets, he hoped the candlestick would still be worth something, maybe to a tavernkeeper.

He had nothing else to trade. Except his labor. But even if anyone had anything to pay with, who needed labor this time of year? There seemed to be only one use for a man's body now, and Johannes was not even sure where that market was. From all he could hear, the armies were mostly resting in camps. It was too hot and there was too much sickness for anything else. And now this flooding.

At Tom's Creek the footlog was washed away and the water was almost up to his waist. Congaree Creek was worse. Lee's men had destroyed the bridge and cut down trees along the banks in July. He had to go far upstream to find a place he could wade. The swamps were drowned and green leaves trailed in the water. He saw a dead shoat entangled in some branches. Thank God he had no cattle near the river. His few were well up Savana Hunt.

Roker was recovering condition. Andreas and Georgi groomed him every day that Johannes could spare them from other work, and he allowed them to ride the horse occasionally. He'd have liked to ride him himself today, or even his workhorse Early, but he was still wary of the horse-hungry military, although it did seem as if the commander at Fort Granby had put an end to roving predators. God knows I wouldn't look so much like a beggar if I rode my horse, he thought.

It had occurred to Johannes that Roker was worth far more than a pewter candlestick. But if the military got him, they'd probably pay with no more than paper. And besides he couldn't think of selling Roker, not because the horse was his own but because of the ones he'd borne, where he'd been. No, things would have to be much worse for him to sell Roker.

As Johannes passed the Gallman place and thought again of Barbara, the old grief twisted his heart. Three weeks ago, tardily, he'd crossed the river, but when he reached the Meyer plantation, no one was there. The nearest neighbors he could find said they didn't know where the damned Tories had gone, maybe to Charlestown. The two-story clapboard house stood empty. But at least it stood. Unlike the Gallman house.

Johannes had not told his family that all that was left on the Gallman place were the great old chimneys. Twenty years ago its house fort had sheltered a whole community in the terrors of the Cherokee War. Now all was ashes and charred wood. Hans Jacob said old Frau Gallman and the rest of her Tory family, like their Whig pastor earlier, had taken refuge up the country among the Germans who tried to keep neutral and stick together. Several of the Gallmans now fought on the Patriot side, but so far as anyone knew, "young" Heiri, who was actually Johannes' age, was still loyal to the King.

For various reasons the Gallmans had always seemed to Johannes somewhat above him. Yet he never forgot that his own Heiri, though named for Johannes' brother, had had as godparents "old" Heinrich and his wife.

What would happen to their land if—or when—the British lost? For forty-five years Gallmans had tended this rich acreage, built it into a fine plantation. They had come from Canton Zurich in '36, some of them serving for their passage. He'd heard stories of how they, like other first-comers, had built huts, endured sickness and loss, but year by year learned to clear and work the woodland earth. At his death in '68, old Heiri, a young man when he came, left many acres, six slaves, a large house, and a long inventory of goods. From want to plenty, from plenty to want in forty-five years. How? Why? Hard work, favorable circumstances—and wrong choices.

The Bible spoke of building a house that would stand. *My house*, Johannes wondered, not meaning hewn logs, *will my house stand?* He still had Joggi, he hoped, and oh, thank God for Hans come home. Georgi and Andreas. Though he knew any of them could be taken at any time. But twenty-five, thirty years from now would there still be Lienhardts in the land? If the years ahead were like the first twenty-five. . . . *And yet I've had good years too, many of joy and satisfaction. Along with fear and struggle. And loss.*

God, bring us peace again! Oh God, bring peace! Oh, why is it—that want and suffering come when we've tried to live upright lives, wronged no man, tried to obey Your laws?

A cloud darkened the sun. He saw with dismay the bluish pile moving out of the west. He sighed. *What a fool I am. When I know it's rained every day for the last nine days. If I am fortunate enough to get meal, how will I keep it dry? Well, maybe I can get a keg. Or maybe the rain will hold off. Or maybe somehow I'll miss it. Please, God, don't let it rain on the meal if I get it! Help me, please, to find meal and not be caught in a downpour. If it be Your will,* he added dutifully.

The big Rieder house looked as desolate as ever. He decided to turn in to sit on the porch a few minutes and put on his shoes. As he stepped inside the dooryard, however, not noticing where he walked, he found himself hopping out of a patch of sandspurs he'd tramped down on. His feet were tough but the sandspurs were wicked. Standing now on one foot, now on the other, he pulled the stickers out, grinning, and cursing. He reminded himself of Georgi and Andreas. He sat on the steps rubbing his stabbed feet. Poor boys. Their feet were always on the ground. . . . Poor old Elsbeth. What would she say if she saw her dooryard like this?

Shod and on his way again, he glanced back once more at the broken windows by the lifeless north chimney. The trees were still, but clouds moved slowly across the hot, bright sky.

At Granby, however, he found more stir—riders coming and going, a wagon filled with barrels creaking up from the ferry, several men under a tree talking, and ahead of him two well-dressed women walking together along the sandy street, and finally, even more unusual, some small children playing in the lee of a house. He tried not to stare. It seemed strange to see normal people moving about.

But across a field came the sound of drums. He paused, veered off the road to stand in the shade and watch the company drilling. A hard-bitten lot, though some of them looked respectable. They were all ages, a few perhaps as old as he was. The sergeant's shouts were harsh and familiar. Oh yes, he remembered. Would his body, used now only to the axe and plow, still be able to march and move with alacrity? He liked to think so. The hot heavy air dulled the shouts and the drumbeat as he went on. He turned off toward the ferry where the taverns were.

An hour later with the old pewter candlestick still clutched under his arm, he thought, *I might as well throw it away. And throw away my shoes too.* He walked halting because a loosened sole was flapping. Well, when he got home, he'd cut a leather thong from somewhere or other and try to mend it. Mending old shoes was about all he could do. Never in his life had he felt like such a derelict.

He had visited the three ordinaries and none wanted his candlestick. He couldn't understand it. Only later did he reflect that these places, being necessary to the military of both sides, had not been plundered. The last keeper he applied to, a German who knew him, advised him to go to the commissary. He said meal was scarce everywhere, that the military controlled most of it, even his own supplies and unless— He broke off, scanning Johannes' appearance. "Go to Colonel Hampton, Johannes. It may be he'll give you bread."

Johannes' face was set in misery. I can't go there again. The memory of that officer, though he knew it wasn't Hampton, the one who'd treated him with such respect, the memory forbade it. He would not risk the coldness or annoyance or even denial he might meet if he went there begging again.

If I can't provide for my own, what kind of man am I? . . . But I could have if they'd left us alone. Or if I hadn't taken them wheat in May. So foolish. But I felt obliged, I can't let my boys pay all. So to go again now, hat in hand—with my candlestick and flapping shoes. . . . No. Nor did he feel this time the force of moral indignation as he had before. The officer's courtesy had robbed him of it.

I don't have to go. Yet. But, oh Hans, poor boy, so starved and gaunt. If only that corn in the newground was further along. . . . Still we're not quite destitute. Yet. Thank God for the couple of cows. And the yearling and the hogs. But it is a long time till frost. And how'll we ever manage the butchering without salt?

Do without. Like the Indians. They use only smoke. And why in August should I think *about butchering?* It was just—he wanted more bread for Hans. Johannes looked yearningly toward the big building he'd entered the last time he was here. And the time before that.

But a glance at the lowering sky turned him toward home. With his shoes in one hand and the old candlestick in the other—he didn't know where he'd left the sack—he trudged back down the Road.

Now he saw lightning and heard rumbles in the west. The wind rose. Ten minutes later the sky was roiling black, and wind was tearing at the branches of trees. He hurried almost at a trot. Just as he sighted the Rieder housetop, the first big drops hit, and by the time he reached the edge of the yard, lightning crackled all around, thunder roared and the deluge descended. Without more thought he rushed through the Rieders' gate, and forgetting sandspurs, bounded for the shelter of the porch. The blown rain sheets were so white he did not see the horses at the bannister rail or the men on the porch until he was almost at them, but the near crackling and almost simultaneous roar propelled him up the steps and under the roof.

Three men stood near the house wall. Johannes took off his sopping, battered hat and wiped his brow. He nodded. The men nodded back.

"Great God a'mighty, that was close!" said one in English.

"It hit something, that's sure."

The rain was a white curtain around the porch. The barrels at each end splashed and overflowed, and water began to pond up in the yard.

"Lord, when's it ever going to stop?"

Johannes stood at the north end of the porch, instinctively putting distance between himself and the men. Although they wore no uniforms, they were armed. All stood silent, hearing only the pounding, hiss, and splash of water. From time to time lightning split the air and thunder roared.

Better I got no meal, Johannes thought.

He became aware that one of the men had taken a few steps toward him and was saying something, but because of the downsplash off the eaves Johannes could not hear what he said. He moved from the edge of the porch.

"I said, 'Be you from hereabouts?'"

Johannes did not quite understand the question. "I come from the Congarees, from Granby. I go home."

The man nodded, kept looking at Johannes. "I knew a boy from hereabouts of the name of Harry Lennard. I wondered—I wondered if you might know aught of his people?"

"Harry Lennard?" Johannes repeated the English pronunciation. Its meaning penetrated.

"Harry Lennard," the man said, "a good Dutch boy. I knew him well but we had the misfortune to lose him awhile back. Up at the Cowpens."

Johannes could frame no word. His mouth working, he could only look at the man.

"You heard how we fought up there, didn't you? At the Cowpens, where we whipped old Benny Tarleton to a fare-ye-well? But that's where we lost Harry, I'm sorry to say."

Johannes said slowly, "Heiri Lienhardt was my son. I am Johannes Lienhardt. Yes, Heiri was my own son."

"Oh come now, you don't say so, come now! Listen, boys, hear that? Here's Harry's daddy! Matt, you remember Dutch Harry? The one got sabered at the Cowpens? Near about ruined the day for some of us, wonderful as it were. Well, sir!" The man extended his hand. "Be sure we thought a lot of your boy, sir, and I'm proud to know you."

A startled joy took Johannes. As always when he was deeply moved, tears filled his eyes. He grasped the man's hand. "Thank you, thank you," he said huskily.

"Aye, now I see the favor and I confess I wondered even afore I spoke. I'm Jem Boyd. Aye, I knew Harry almost from the time he first come amongst us."

"Harry was a mighty good boy," said Matt, extending his hand.

"I wasn't acquainted with him but if he was Jem's friend, he was mine too and I'm much obliged to his kin. I'm Billy McPheeters."

Tall, leanfaced, unsmiling, the men stood in a semi-circle around Johannes, but the light of their friendliness softened their faces.

Johannes said, "My first son, Jacob, he brought us news. He said Heinrich had friends, many friends. He said they stood by his grave."

"Aye, we stood there." Jem was silent a moment. "He was our friend and we sorrowed to lose him." Again all stood silent. "So I always said if ever I come this way, I'd do my best to find his people."

"You know my first son, Joggi?"

"'Yocky'? Oh yes, 'Jake' we call him. Yes, I made his acquaintance but a good deal later than I first knew Harry. Yes, I surmised he'd come here to tell you about Harry or I wouldn't ha' spoke so open."

"Jake Lennard? Oh yes, he's with us now," said Billy.

One of the old benches still stood against the wall, long enough for the four of them, so they sat down, arms on knees, leaning forward so they could see one another. Stirred with pride and this unexpected meeting, Johannes found himself talking unselfconsciously, even asking questions. They told him things about Heiri he didn't know, and it was as if more of his son were given him all over again. They spoke too of Joggi. McPheeters told him Jake was with troops who scouted around the north fork of the Edisto. He'd seen Jake a few days ago. He was well.

Johannes inquired about the positions of various troops. "What about Sumter's men? And General Greene's?"

The answers were less clear. "From what I hear the ones under Sumter are mostly furloughed. And Greene's, well, they're still in the High Hills." They themselves were on their way to Granby, they said, but did not say why.

The rain slackened and stopped almost as quickly as it had begun. Big drops were scattering from the trees when the men stood up and said they'd best move on. They were sorry they couldn't tarry longer.

Suddenly, even the sun was out and, moving from under the porch roof, they saw one another more clearly. Again they shook hands with

Johannes. Jem asked where he lived. "In case I might be able to swing back by here some day and call."

Johannes beamed as he tried to give clear directions in English—until he thought of something and his smile faded. "But we have not much now to offer friends except our roof and hearth. Our house still stands. You will be welcome to our house."

As the men mounted their horses, Johannes stood barefooted on the steps with the candlestick under his arm.

Jem Boyd regarded it curiously. "You said you come from Granby. Do they trade such goods there?" He nodded at the candlestick.

Johannes shook his head. "No. They trade nothing for this."

As Jem continued to look at him, Johannes felt compelled to explain further. "I took this to trade for meal but no one wanted it. But," he added strongly, "we will not starve. The good God always provides. We still have—" He broke off. Fear, unworthy fear. "We have enough for this day. And tomorrow. Only—when my son Hans came home last night, so starving, I wanted more for him."

As Johannes stood there—grizzled, ragged, stocky—a pewter candlestick of all things under his arm, to two of the men he had an unmistakable, an unforgettable look. Aye, he was Harry's daddy, all right. They raised their hands in farewell and turned to ride out of the yard.

Johannes called after them, "God go with you!" His thoughts were full of their gift as he trudged on home.

47

Mid-afternoon was clear when Jem, Billy, and Matt left Granby. Just below Congaree Creek where a trail diverged southwest toward the Edisto, Billy and Matt left the Road.

"We'll wait for you at the Big Cedar Pond. It's about six mile this side the North Fork. To your left if you strike the main path."

"I know the place. Give me one hour past sunup. If you don't see me by then, go on and I'll catch you. I'm right certain it's nothing but sandhills to the west of his place and fair going."

They transferred the rest of the load to Jem's horse. "You'll not have to bear it too far, young fellow," Jem said to his horse. The burden consisted of three fifty-pound sacks of meal—two of corn, one of barley—and a small bag of salt. With the load adjusted, the men raised hands in farewell. Jem continued down the road, leading his horse.

It certainly helped to know other men than just high-ranked officers, Jem thought. After Matt had delivered the letter to be forwarded to General Greene, and while they waited outside headquarters for Colonel Hampton's acknowledgement of receipt, the three looked about and asked a few questions. They learned the best channels of access to commissary stores for a hungry Patriot family. They'd already decided that a family that gave three sons deserved at least three sacks of meal, and they found someone who agreed.

Now as Jem strode along the road, he kept his eyes and ears open, for it was risky carrying a load this size alone. Several times, seeing or hearing riders in the distance, he withdrew into the woods. An hour before sundown he came to a certain turn-off in a field, and beyond the field he entered a screening band of woods. From its cover he sighted the Lienhardt house.

It gave him a queer feeling to know that here was Harry Lennard's birthplace. The tall little log house was like a thousand others in the country; yet somehow it looked different. He could not frame words for the difference. Weathered silver-gray, it said "home," and it belonged where it was. Although it was only some twenty-odd years old—he knew this from Harry—it had already taken root as if it would be forever a part of that creekside hill and the sky behind it. Jem knew that next year or even tomorrow might find here only earth and ashes. Yet strange, strange. It was already a place from the past, but it spoke to Jem also of years and years to come.

He wondered about Harry now. If—or since—there was a heaven— Jem more or less believed there was one, but he tried not to think much about it or of its alternative because he knew he was not fit for heaven, not now, though he thought Harry must have been—but if or since there was indeed a heaven, Jem wondered if it was very far from here.

Not that this place was more than earth and trees and log buildings. Still something about that sky to the west, the roll and lift of the land, the dark block of the house itself—he wondered. What had the man who built it, what had Harry's father built into it?

Jem called long as he emerged from the screening woods, and a child appeared, then a girl.

Harry's family was just that: his family, more of Harry. Jem was awed and grieved by the mother, the shadows in her face. He thought that the three youngest children somehow made up the essence of Harry, what Harry had once been. But the boy Hans was different, not like either of his two older brothers. Jem pitied him, yet felt he knew him though he didn't know why. As for the older girl, the curving of her cheek and mouth, the combinaion of modesty and directness in her look, these, he thought, made her resemble Harry more than any of the others did.

Most of Jem's talk was with her father. Johannes was overcome with emotion. His throat thickened. "God bless you, sir! God bless you and your friends! The Lord God, He sent you to us, I know!"

Madle took Jem's hand, looked up at him. "Thank you for this food, but more than that, I thank you for coming here. My husband has told me all your words—about our son. Both our sons. Tell your friends— I too thank them."

Jem tried to smile but he could not. They did not speak again of Heiri.

He let himself be persuaded to stay for supper. They assured him there would be plenty, especially with their provisions so abundantly replenished. Madle suggested the two men sit on the porch while supper was being prepared, but Johannes managed to whisper to her to send the boys running to the newground for fresh corn, also to the new barn for the rest of the sweet potatoes. They were thankful for another rabbit.

Jem was glad to rest. Johannes was less glad because of the milking, but tonight he knew he'd just have to trust it to Hans and Cathri.

"I'm sorry we have no drink to offer you."

"Don't let that trouble you. Cold spring water's good enough for me. It's what I'm used to."

"You will stay the night?"

"No, sir, I'm obliged to be on my way. Billy and Matt'll be expecting me." He hesitated. "We judged the three of us would be too many to come in on you."

"Oh no! All three, you all are welcome, all three." Though it would have been hard on Madle, Johannes reflected.

Last rays of sunlight yellowed the sand in long unshadowed strips and whitened the leaves of the oaks. A mockingbird performed vigorously in some treetop, and swifts wheeled high above the creekside field.

Peace, Jem thought. *That's what it is here. Just peace.*

Johannes asked, "What you think will come next? Where will the Americans go?"

Jem shook his head; he wasn't sure.

Quiet continued on the porch. They heard faintly the bawling of a cow. Johannes frowned slightly, aware that sound was carrying too far this way tonight.

Jem said, "Well, the British they're still down the Congaree just waiting and we're waiting. More or less. But it's my judgment in a few more weeks somebody'll move. Though I don't know where."

"You hear anything from the North?"

"They say old Cornwallis, he's still in Virginny. We hear there's a right smart fighting up in Virginny now."

Johannes glanced at the dark-eyed, lean young man. He was not much older than Joggi if any older; yet somehow he seemed so. Johannes asked Jem a question he'd never asked his own sons. "Why do you fight?"

Jem pulled in his lips, pursed them meditatively. "I've asked myself that. Many's the time I've asked it." He cleared his throat. "I think what it comes down to is—I think America ought to be free for the ones that live here."

Johannes thought of Heinrich Gallman, born in this country, lived here all his days. Why did he see it differently from young men like Jem? Alliegance. Gallman had a strong sense of alliegance to the old sovereign, maybe because he himself was older and had lived longer. *His* sovereign, he would say, *his* government. But what about Conrad Meyer, no older than Joggi? *Why do some feel loyalty more strongly than others? Why don't I? Because they have wealth and I don't? More of this world's goods to lose? But God knows I've lost. And may lose more.*

"Jem—" Johannes said "Yem," corrected himself, "Chem." "—Jem, you think we do right under God? I give my sons—or they give themselves if I will or not—and I think sometimes to give myself too. Then I ask, Why? A man can be so wrong, can go two ways, one so easy and so wrong, the other so hard—yet maybe still wrong." He paused. "I'm not now a young man. Fighting is more easy to the young. But I can still pick up a musket. If I have one," he smiled. "They broke my old one."

Jem appeared to muse awhile. "I say it's according to what a man feels in himself, the power of his own feelings. Now my daddy, he come out with us last fall when the crop was got in, and I'm proud to say he stood up strong when we fought at Blackstock's up on Enoree. But his leg got smashed there and after that, what with his laming and other hurts, his health begun to dwindle and he got disheartened. And now I misdoubt he's in the world. I've not got back to see."

Johannes was about to speak when Jem continued, "But he said last time I left, he said to me, 'Jem, it's as fair a land as you'll find, and you mark my words, it's meant for better things than these broils we see now. But, Jem,' he said and I did mark it, 'if it takes all this for us to be our own masters and better to come, then you do your part.' He said, 'You do your part.' And I conclude that's what I'm trying to do."

It was that simple, thought Johannes. Do your part. Or was it? "Are you a married man?"

Jem shook his head.

Johannes said painfully, "I'm sorry. About your father." He wanted to inquire about the rest of Jem's family, whether there was a mother or brothers and sisters, but he did not.

Because supper was late, the younger children were already drowsing when Jem prepared to leave, but Hans stood near to listen as Johannes and Jem talked of paths.

"Follow this creek to its head. Go west over the hills, come to the next creek branch and cross it and still go west. After that you hit your way."

"How many miles?"

"Nine, ten; two hours maybe. If you wait till moonrise it will go easy."

"I'd like to wait but I'd best start now. I promised Billy and Matt I'd try to catch 'em."

"Then I'll see you on your way till moonrise."

Hans broke in quickly, "I can show him, Papa. I can set him on his way."

"Hans, you ever go so far?" Johannes was surprised. "I think it's better for me, so dark now—"

Hans turned away so that Johannes could only imagine his expression.

Madle interrupted, speaking low in German, "Let Hans go, Johannes. You need rest. So far you've walked already today. Besides— let Hans go."

Johannes asked Hans, "You sure you been back there?"

"Yes, Papa," Hans said in a long-suffering voice.

Johannes regarded his son somberly. Finally he nodded.

Hans said eagerly, "I'll bring up your horse, Jem."

Johannes growled in an undertone to Madle, "Much better to wait till moonrise, it's too far in the dark." But afterward he sighed to himself, *Aye-God, he's gone farther than that, been longer in the dark than that.*

When they had gone, the thought occurred to Johannes, I should have told him to ride Roker. Yet obscurely he was glad he had not.

For a while they walked in silence, Hans ahead, Jem leading his horse. Jem followed more by sound than by sight, though occasionally he could discern the boy's light-colored back. At first the way was dense and winding and Jem was glad for a guide—they had tried not to make a regular path through here, Hans said—but after they passed the new field, the way was straighter and more open. They angled up a ridge, and the loud rush of creekwater on their left became a whisper. The woods on the ridge were thin with scrub oaks and scattered pines. They saw faint white patches of sand.

Jem called ahead, "You about ready to turn back? I think I can go on by myself from here."

Hans appeared not to hear him.

Gradually the light increased and in another fifteen minutes moonlight flooded the ridges.

Jem quickened his step to draw abreast of his guide. "Hans, I'll say goodbye to you here. I'm much obliged for you settting me on my way. I don't know how I'd ha' done without you back there, but it's time now I mount and go on."

Hans stopped. "I wish I could go with you," he said low. "I know I can't but I wish I could."

"Aye, I know. Well." Jem thought, the trouble was he did seem to know. He wished he didn't. "Maybe another time. Maybe you can."

The boy stepped backward but he still faced west. In the colorless light, Jem could see how angular and taut his face was. Jem had already put his foot in the stirrup to heave himself up, but he stepped back down and stood by the horse as if adjusting the saddle.

"Your daddy said you been serving down the country. You're a right young chap to ha' gone out already."

Hans made a self-deprecating sound. "I did little service. Mostly I—tended horses. Jem—" But he could not go on.

Jem knew he needed to be on his way, but he kept thinking, *It's Harry's brother.* "What is it you want to ask me?"

Hans took a long, ragged breath. "Did you ever run off? The first time? At first, did you ever get scared and just run?"

Jem laughed. "Lord God, how many times have I been scared? How many times have I run? Times you got to!" He chuckled again, then fell abruptly silent. His tone changed. "No, that's not what you're asking me, is it? I know what you're asking. Did I run in my first fight? No, I didn't, but I was—how old are you? Fifteen, sixteen? Now see here, I was twenty-one years old first time I ever heard bullets whistle and that made a difference. Listen, I've seen a good many join up about your age and nine out of ten ha' got to *learn* to stand. Now some do and some don't. Boys far older than you. But that's because they don't give themselves, or in some cases don't get the chance to learn."

Jem glanced about, thought of sitting down but decided not to. The boy needed to get on home or his people would be uneasy.

"Now I'll try to tell you what I think it is. Partly it's how you're natured—or for that matter how most of us are natured. Now here's a thing I know about that's somewhat like it. I was always mortally afeared of snakes, growing up, and anytime I'd see a rattler or a copperhead or anything even looked like one, why, I'd take to my heels afore I even thought about it, and I couldn't help it. Let me sight a snake and afore I knew it, my heels would be flying. It was in me and I couldn't help it. And I'm still natured that way, they fair make my skin crawl! Only difference now is, I *do* know that if one come up in my dooryard, why, I could kill it. I've done so. What I'm saying is, give yourself time. You might not ever stop being scared of something. But in due time, you'll learn to do what you got to do."

"You think so? Oh, I want to so much. . . ." Hans' voice trailed into longing.

"Tell you what. You build yourself up, get yourself stoutened up again, and a couple of months, say a month or so from now, maybe I can get back by here and it'll be so you can go along with me."

"Oh, will you, Jem? Oh, do come!" Then Hans caught his breath, said low, "But I must tell you—I left my company without leave."

"Was it the regulars?"

"Well—when I joined up, I 'listed with them under General Sumter. But I never got any pay. Except my clothes and gun."

"You still got your gun?"

Hans said even lower, "Another fellow took it. He—said he wanted it. He lost his."

Again Jem was silent, seeing it, understanding it. "How long did you serve?"

"Three months almost. I joined the fourth of May. I stayed till last week."

Jem meditated. "Now see here. I happen to know just about all them under Sumter ha' been furloughed, and why you weren't I don't know except you didn't wait to be."

Hans swallowed hard but could not answer.

"Now it's my judgment that it might not be thought, considering when you left, it being after that battle and not before it, it might not be thought too serious a matter. Now, mind, I'm not saying it was right. I do think it would ha' been better if you'd asked leave."

"Others went. Earlier. All along. They didn't ask."

"I know. But it's still no way to do." Jem hesitated. "Your brother would ha' wanted you to do it right. But hear me now," he hurried on, "you being where you were and the time and how it was, I don't see a reason in the world why you can't come back if you want to. But it's my judgment you should go with a different set."

"You think so? Oh, you really think so, Jem?"

"I do. Aye, I do. . . . You can handle a musket, can't you?"

"Of course, I can! And, Jem, I'll do whatever I have to, I'll mind the horses, I'll do anything if I can just join up again!"

It was as well Hans could not see Jem's expression. Poor boy, Jem thought, *what good is he apt to do in a place where it's hard enough for men. . . .* He thought of the boy's mother. "Now I'm bound to tell you," he said slowly, "there's another thing to consider. And that's the help you can be to your people. With two already gone—you think you might not do better to stay here awhile and help your family? Looks to me like your daddy—and your mammy too—could use your help."

Hans' whisper was vehement. "No, Jem! It's something I've got to—to overcome. I can't bear to be a coward!"

Jem was silent. "No," he answered finally, "that's hard to live with. Though some ha' learned to do that too. . . . All right, I promise you. Somebody, if not me, a friend of mine, we'll come by here. But one thing more. You tell your daddy about it ahead of time or we'll not take you. You hear that?"

Hans did not want to answer but Jem stood waiting. "All right," Hans said, "I'll tell him."

As Jem rode over the moon-bright ridge, he looked back once to see the boy still standing there, but his figure looked as unsubstantial as the hanging leaves.

48

Unlike Margaret, Martha Laird would not argue with him. With her mouth pinned shut she left the room. Rudi knew Margaret was still smouldering, but as she bent over the cradle to pick up the little bundle, the tightness about her mouth loosened, and Rudi, gazing, almost forgot the subject of their disagreement.

Johannes Allen Näffels was six weeks old. He'd probably call himself John one day, but he'd been christened Johannes after Rudi's own father. Until now Rudi had been afraid to name a child after anyone in his own family, for all had perished either at sea or within months of their arrival in South Carolina.

"But you didn't perish, Rudi. It's my judgment we should name him after your father." Margaret had waited for the naming until Rudi came in June, when the baby was two weeks old. At that time Rudi could hardly believe what he saw. After all she'd gone through, after all their loss, when they'd all but given up hope, what a blessed rebuke to them!

"As strong a babe as e'er you'll see!" cried Martha Laird. "Just look at him!" She pulled the clean rags away from the ruddy little legs. "Didn't I tell you, if you'd just do what I said—no, no!" she broke off. "God, forgive me, it's no work of mine. But ha' you e'er seen a more lusty young one?"

Rudi's face had not been used to such smiling lately. He felt himself swell twice as big as he was.

"Came through it fine," crowed Martha for the third time, "both of 'em, just the way I thought if she'd do as I bid. Though again I must say," she remembered piously, "it was the Almighty did it."

Well, He must have, thought Rudi. For who would have thought in the midst of such hardship and displacement she could bear such a hearty child? Yet he remembered that strange inner quiet she had shown him in April. She'd called it a sense of freedom. From anxiety? Or just from possessions? Whatever it was it had freed him too for the time being—

that and his knowledge of her and the children's safety. After the baby's birth she'd looked ten years younger, he thought.

But now four weeks later, she'd taken on all that burden again. It both grieved and exasperated him. Why she'd even consider going back to Indian Creek he could not understand. If only she could learn to take the day, this day, as it was given and not be forever agitated about something beyond it. "Can't you ever be satisfied?" he wanted to shout. But he must be very careful what he said. Too much was at stake.

Two days ago Martha had been assured that her house still stood, and both women wanted to return there. At first, all Rudi could do was splutter. The foolheadedness of it! Martha, however, refused to discuss it and went creaking out of the room. Then followed the period of silence. Margaret bent to attend to their son, and gradually both parents became wholly absorbed in the wonder of that small object.

"Ah, Meggie, I can't get over it," he repeated softly, "every time I look at him, what you did."

She deigned an upward glance, said ironically, "And all by myself."

He wanted to kneel beside her and hug them both but was afraid to just now. She was apt to be overly suspicious of what she called his cozening ways.

In their half-truce each sat basking in their son's satisfaction with his dinner. When at length he'd been eased of hunger, air, and other matters, he lay on Margaret's knees gazing sleepily at his parents, and Rudi leaned forward to touch him, utter a little nonsense, rouse a gurgle and a wet smile. Finally Margaret lifted the baby to cradle him close and sway him to sleep. All the while Rudi was good. He sat on the side of the bed in the crowded little room across from Margaret in the one low chair, and he did not say a word. At last she rose to put the baby in his box-cradle.

Rudi rose too. He went to the door to stand looking out. He waited while she moved about behind him and he wondered what she could find to do in such small space. He knew it was inconvenient here, probably downright uncomfortable at times, but where could she find comfort or convenience with safety now? He turned. She stood looking at him. He jerked his head, motioning her to come outside. After a moment she did.

He wanted so much to embrace her. She was more beautiful to him than any woman he'd ever known though it wasn't all in her looks but in what she was. Away from her he longed for her as he longed for the cool and shine of water on a sweltering day. He wanted to say that now. She saw it on his face and looked down.

"Meggie, you know you can't go back there."

"I do not see why not. An I have the strength to go."

"It's a risk we must not take."

"We?"

"We."

"Oh, you aim to stay here with us then?"

"You know I can't. Margaret, if aught happened to you or to one of ours and me not with you—" He swallowed hard. He did not know how to say it. *I'd go mad.* Jemmy's hurt had shown him that. "I could not bear it."

"And you think nothing can happen to us here," she said flatly.

"It's less apt to. You must see that."

For a while she did not answer. "Rudi, I tell you—it's no good place to be. Now."

"Why not? What's happened, what's changed? You didn't talk like this last time I was here?"

Again she was slow to answer. "I can't say anything's *happened.* But you can look around you and see—Rudi, too many people ha' come here."

"Yes, I do see it, I know it's more crowded, but—"

"No, you don't see. There's too much coming and going. It—makes me uneasy."

"But, Meg, that makes it safer! The more people here the safer it is! And with these stout walls, that strong old blockhouse you could all move into if need be—and that fence, those good heavy logs around it, oh, I've examined it, it's well set. There's not many places left like this one."

"Why not? I reckon you never heard of logs to burn? Of a log fort burnt down? All my life I've heard of it."

"Oh, military forts, but that's because—" Ninety Six, Granby, Camden— "they were destroyed by soldiers. There's no soldiers here."

"My brother was no soldier. His house, it had stout logs and it was no fort, no military fort, but it got burnt down. Men found reason to burn it and shoot him too."

"Margaret, that's it, it *was* a house and he was alone. Now it just stands to reason that two lone women in a house, they can't be as safe as twenty-five or thirty inside stockade walls."

She gazed toward the river. It was often pleasant here. It was high enough to catch a breeze when there was one. And sometimes she enjoyed talking with the other women. They stood in the narrow shade of the eaves.

"You showed good judgment to come here, Margaret," he urged warmly, "to bring Katy and Jemmy here. And now our little one."

"Aye, to come. But not to stay. I tell you, Rudi, too many people know about this place. It's the numbers I mislike."

He looked down the slope across the pasture, saw two horsemen riding away with sacks of meals. He heard loud talking around the corner in the well-yard.

"But with a gristmill, what can you expect? This time of year, anybody with anything to grind is bound to come."

It was true that twice as many people were here as there'd been two months ago. Some were already sleeping in the blockhouse, while others camped outside it. Also more men were on the premises. In a way that was good—men to help with heavy work and later to hunt. Could the men draw trouble? In spite of himself Rudi felt a prickle of unease. His face grew somber. But where could they all go? Too many houses and farms had been destroyed. There were too many Whig families with no shelter. The withdrawal of the armies had not meant the peace and security they'd hoped for. But that was all the more reason to stay here.

"Margaret—" He was frustrated; he didn't know what else to say. "The more people the better protection."

"I don't know about that."

He kept gazing at her. It was true most of the Tories still in the upcountry were said to be lying low. But who knew what the next few weeks would bring? There was bound to be major movement, some kind of action soon, maybe decisive. And if the two armies did engage . . . and if Greene should fail again . . . and if the British should be reinforced and come back up here . . . and even if they didn't, with any encouragement at all, the Tories, the ones still up here. . . . Rudi shook his head; he did not even want to think about it. Pickens' men could not patrol the entire backcountry. But how to impress that on her? He'd already told her as much as he knew or surmised about what would happen in the coming month. Yet now as always when they argued he could get nowhere.

"Margaret, I cannot stay. I'm persuaded you don't want me to. But I cannot leave you either unless—Margaret, I tell you, you must not leave this place! Hear me? You must not leave!" He paused, said low, "I forbid it."

Never had he said that word. He braced himself.

But when she turned and looked at him, her eyes were dark with something he did not understand. Unthinkingly, he reached to draw her to him, to press her cheek against his, and to stroke her rough dark hair. She did not resist but clung to him as she had last night.

"You said no one's said or done anything to harm or offend you," he murmured helplessly. "You told me that."

She drew a shuddering sigh. "Aye, I told you that, it's true. Squire Gilchrist and Mistress Anne, they're as good people as you're like to find, and many another here too."

"Well then, Margaret—" But he could not continue.

She released herself. "We'll do the best we can here, Rudi. You go on and don't be worrying about us. You go find Jemmy. I make no doubt he's out at the barn with the others. You'll want to be with him much as you can if you aim to leave in the morning."

Jemmy seemed gladder of his little brother than Katy was. That was natural, Rudi supposed, also natural that Jemmy should be a little less glad for his sister now that his mother asked him to give Katy more attention.

This morning some ten or twelve children were under a shed shelling corn, but as soon as Katy saw her father, she jumped up and came running to him, and in a moment Jemmy followed.

Maybe it was wishful thinking, but it appeared to Rudi that the boy's limp was less noticeable.

Katy flung herself against her father's legs with gleeful upturned face, and Rudi picked her up. "Let's go around the other side of the barn," he said. "I believe I saw a bench around there in the shade." He was pleased with the solid heft of Katy's body. One thing about being at the mill: they had good food.

Out of sight and almost out of sound of the others, his children pressed near him, one on each side. Katy had most to say. She told Rudi about her friend Hattie, about a big boy named Charles, who for some reason impressed her, and about a corn doll-baby Mistress Sally had made for her.

"And what about our little baby?" Rudi asked. "What you think of your little brother?"

Katy frowned. "Little Brother did bad. He did bad on me."

Rudi was startled, then laughed. He hugged her closer, said low, "And you never did bad when you were little?"

"No-o," she shook her head solemnly.

He drew back, cocked his eye, and saw a glint of mischief in hers, but she kept her mouth prim. Under her father's amused look, she squeezed her eyes shut, then opened them wide. "But I love Little Brother," she said virtuously.

Rudi laughed and hugged her again. He said low, "Let me tell you something. I got two boys. I got a big boy and a little boy." He paused for effect. "But you know what? I got me just one little girl." He bent low and whispered, "You're my only girl. And I love you."

"No-o, Daddy, you got two girls."

"Hmh?"

"Mammy's your other girl."

"Oh. Yes, well, Mammy's my big girl. But you're my little girl, and you're my only little girl. And let me tell you something else. You're my daughter." He reached his other arm around Jemmy. "I got two sons. Jemmy's my big son and now I have a little son." Rudi drew Katy off the bench and onto his lap. "But I got me just one daughter. You know that? Now who's my one daughter?"

"Me?" Her face was pink, her eyes bright. "I am!" she shouted. "I'm your one daughter!" She squeezed her eyes shut and butted her head against her father's chest, then slipped off his lap. "I'll go tell Hattie!" she cried, and not looking back, she skipped off onesidedly, for she had not yet learned to skip with both feet.

"Then go find Mistress Martha," he called, "and stay with her till I come get you."

He watched her, smiling, but with a twisting in his heart. One little girl. So short a time.

After a while he said, "Jemmy, you see now why you got to take up more time with Katy."

When Jemmy did not answer, Rudi said, "Jemmy, she's apt to feel displaced with your Mammy having so much more to do for your little brother." He paused. "I depend on you. To help her." He looked into Jemmy's face. "I depend on you to help all three, to be the man here while I'm gone. The way you have been."

Jemmy reddened, tried not to change his expression and made a gruff assenting noise.

Again Rudi felt the twist of pain. *He'll be grown up afore I know it.* After a few moments Rudi said, "Let me take a look at that leg again. I didn't have time last night to look at it the way I wanted to."

Jemmy stretched out his leg along the bench and Rudi felt it carefully from knee to ankle, then swung it down and gently worked it at the knee. "How's that feel? It still hurt?"

"Not much."

"How you mean 'not much'? Where?"

Jemmy touched the side of his knee. Rudi asked, "You wear that brace every night the way Mistress Martha tells you?"

"Most of the time." Jemmy evaded a direct look.

"You must do that, Jemmy," Rudi said sternly, "unless you want to go halt-foot the rest of your life. It's to keep you from twisting it when you turn sudden in your sleep and hurt it worse. You wouldn't want to have to start wearing it again all day, would you?" He softened his tone. "Though I know it's a bother to you. I wouldn't like to fool with it either," he smiled. "She says you still got some of that ointment I brought last time. Now you use it. You can rub it in yourself, you don't have to wait for your Mammy or Mistress Martha. It's a prime remedy for healing joints and I want you to use it."

Rudi had not told Margaret that the prescription came from a woman named Gray Cloud, but he thought Martha might have guessed, for she'd eyed it askance though she said they'd use it.

Rudi said, "I believe the bone's knit true. It's just that a joint takes longer to heal. But I'm satisfied it's mending and will mend *if* you do what I say."

Jemmy murmured some reply. Rudi had not meant to lecture, but it was just that a boy needed firmness. Margaret was strict in some ways, but with so much more to take up her time and in a place with other children and so many different influences, a boy could get out of hand. She had not given that as a reason for leaving, though he thought she might have. He was glad she hadn't.

"Jemmy, what's got your Mammy wanting to go back to Mistress Martha's house?"

Jemmy looked surprised. What was it flickered in his eyes? "I didn't know she wanted to."

"Oh, you didn't?" He was relieved it had gone no further than her own thoughts. And Martha's. *It must be Martha's idea*, he thought, *that stubborn, opinionated old*— He braked his anger. He owed Martha much, but he'd have to talk with her too. His face turned grim at the prospect until conscious of Jemmy's questioning gaze, he softened his look. "How about you? How you like it here?"

"Oh, I like it. Most of the time. I like being with the others. Most of 'em."

"It's a safe place for you, that's the main thing. It would be hard for me to go off and fear you weren't safe."

Jemmy was silent. Rudi slipped his arm around him again. He remembered the prattle and the open talk between them last summer. You couldn't keep it. Nothing good could you keep.

"Daddy, did you know Indians—will take a baby and bash its head in? Or any young one that can't keep up when they're taking you off? After they've killed your people."

Rudi was startled and angry. "What? What you talking about, Jemmy? Who's been telling you such?"

"Different ones. A man said—a man came here and said, he said the Cherokees are just waiting to come down on us like they used to."

"That's not so," Rudi countered swiftly. "You may not remember it, but we whipped 'em good back five or six years ago, whipped 'em good and proper, and you can be sure they remember it. Why, my general, the one I follow now, he was one of the main ones went up there. He led us back in their country, and we beat 'em in fair fight, I can tell you. And I'll tell you something else, Jemmy, they respected him for it. They even gave him an Indian name, they named him a name that means 'the Wizard Owl.' Now you think they're going to come back down on us when old Wizard Owl and others like him are out in arms?"

Jemmy fixed his gaze on his father.

"Don't you listen to such talk as that," Rudi said.

"But, Daddy—what makes Indians so mean?"

Rudi felt another stirring of frustration. He drew a long sigh. "Jemmy, listen to me." He waited a moment. "All men in war can be cruel. I said '*can* be.' Every color of man. War's cruel. That's why—I pray—and you pray too, that this one'll soon be over. That's why I leave you, you know that. To help get it over. Sometimes a man's got no choice, so it seems, but to do things he'd rather not do, and you're old enough to know that too."

Jemmy was looking at him earnestly.

So much I want to teach him, Rudi thought, *without him having to learn it hard the way I did*. But as Rudi held his look, Jemmy's fell away.

"But another thing I want you to remember, and I think I've talked with you along these lines afore—look at me now." Jemmy looked up and Rudi saw that his son's eyes no longer had that sweet clear look they once had had. His own face became somber, but he continued in a strong voice. "Indians have different ways from us. I've fought 'em and I've been friends with 'em for nigh on twenty years, some of 'em. But they love their young ones just like we do ours. And I've known a one or two, you've heard me call their names, that would stand by you as long and strong as e'er a white man would and maybe stronger. They got strong feelings. That can be good. And sometimes it's bad. But as far as all that about being took off by Indians, don't you even be thinking such things. You hear me? Don't you be thinking such a thing. I don't think of it, and you're my son, aren't you?"

"All right." Rudi felt a breath of relaxation under his arm.

"And I'll tell you another thing to remember too. Your daddy, he's got friends amongst 'em. Why, Running Elk, why, I wouldn't know where to look for a better friend. And you want to know my name? Anybody ask you, any Cherokee, you tell him Beaver Man's your daddy. Not many know that. But a Cherokee maybe would."

"But, Daddy, why—"

"I tell you what it was," Rudi interrupted. "It was Britishers got 'em all stirred up, and may be still trying to for all we know. I'll be honest, Jemmy. Some things I don't know. But one thing I do, and it's a fact—or was yesterday. The British are miles and miles from here now, away down the country from here, gone back down the country. And one day they'll be gone for good."

"But, Daddy," Jemmy moved under his father's arm, "what made the Britishers want to stir 'em up?"

"So they could win the war! Get 'em on their side! But we're not going to let 'em."

Rudi rose and pulled Jemmy up with him. Margaret was right. He did need as much time with Jemmy as he could get. He thought of staying a day longer, but he knew he shouldn't. "Come on, let's you and me go down to the river and follow that path back up in the woods. It's been too long since you and me been in the woods together. But first we'll want to go and tell your Mammy where we're going."

Five minutes later they were leaving the sun-baked pasture for the shade of box elder, sycamore, and river birch.

"Did I ever tell you about the time a big old sugarberry limb broke off and fell down on me? It was a high wind come up, and that big limb broke off, it was half dead but still heavy, and the wind come up so sudden and the limb fell down so hard it knocked me off my feet and pinned me where I lay so I couldn't get up, I could hardly move. Listen, Son, your Daddy wouldn't be here now if it hadn't been for Running Elk that day."

As they moved into deeper shade away from the sight of the house and the blockhouse, Margaret watched them disappear.

She thought, *I don't know how to tell him. I don't want to tell him. If I put it in words, he'll worry too much; he'll think it's something to do with my condition, and I won't have that.*

She had not even told Martha though she knew now that Martha sensed her unease. In the daylight it would often leave her mind completely, but toward night it would creep back, that awful dread, the terror that waked her in the dark, the sensation of being swaddled in vile-smelling blankets that she was struggling to get loose of, and when she did, it was too late, for already a ring of fire licked the top of the stockade wall, and the night was thick with the dark figures of enemies. She could see it through the open window of this room that was full of the foul smell, but only she was in it. Jemmy, Katy, and the baby were gone.

Nightmares, she told herself in the daytime, like the old ones long ago in the Valley of Virginia when she was little, so her mother said, and like the ones when she was thirteen years old during the Cherokee War. They'd started when the family came home from the fort on Indian Creek, where her mother died. At first her older sister had been soothing and sympathetic, but later she'd scolded Margaret and threatened to slap her if she kept on waking them up. After that Margaret begged to sleep with Granny. Eventually the nightmares ceased.

So they would again, Margaret told herself. They were simply old fears dredged up by the sight of that stockade wall. She tried to scold herself into sanity. *How can you be so weak-minded and so cowardly? You know it's naught but evil dreams as it was back then! Be ashamed of yourself, a grown woman to give in to a child's fear!*

But three nights ago she had waked up so terrified she gasped for breath, and not even the touch of her sleeping children could free her. "It's this place!" her panic cried. "Get away from it! Get away!"

She'd leaned against the wall shivering and sweating by the window, looking at the dark blur of the blockhouse roof against the sky. The night was ominously still. She stood there trembling against the rough wood as wave after wave of fear swept over her. At last she groped for the door and stepped outside. As she felt the cool stones and the wet grass under her feet, she began to hear the crickets and the frogs, and her trembling ceased. But she did not lie down again until just before day, and then she did not sleep.

In the morning she thought, *Maybe it is something about my condition.* She'd heard of women who lost their minds after childbirth, though she thought it usually happened immediately afterward. She debated telling Martha about it, but she feared to.

However, that very afternoon Martha had said, "Joe Phillips said he rode by my place yesterday."

"He did?"

"Aye, and he said the house is still there. I own I'm surprised to hear it."

"Well, I'm glad."

"If nobody's bothered it, it's a wonder."

"To be sure it is," Margaret agreed. "But maybe it's not meant to be bothered." She did not know why she added that; the words just came.

Martha's face was still. "Aye, it could be."

Both women were silent. They were sitting under a walnut tree, Martha darning clothes for women of the more active sort, for everyone shared work. Margaret was mending for her own children. The baby slept nearby in his box.

"Have you given e'er a thought to going back there anytime soon?" asked Margaret.

"I have."

Margaret said quickly, "Then I'd be pleased to go with you if you decide to."

She was conscious of Martha's searching look. "These are good people," Margaret said, "but I somehow have it in my mind to leave here."

Martha held up her big-eyed needle against the light to thread it with a strand of wool. "Well . . . it's mainly a matter of getting our foodstuffs and the cow back there with us. And our little bit of house plunder. I make no doubt John Gilchrist can help us if he's a mind to."

"They can surely use the room space here," said Margaret eagerly. "I make no doubt they'd be glad of that."

Again Martha did not answer for a while. She adjusted the garment in her lap. "You want to go," she stated.

"I do." Margaret put her work on the bench and said low, "Lately, I don't know why it is but—I fear to stay here."

"I know."

The two women exchanged looks.

"Well, I'll see what I can do," Martha said in her matter-of-fact voice. "I'll talk with John."

There was considerable grinding at the mill in spite of the condition of the country, and meal too for those able to pay. Martha had no money, but she did have a kind of promissory note from her brother-in-law that she had never called in. "Oh, I make sure he'll oppose it. It's how men are. But I ha' no doubt I can work him."

Three days later Margaret thought gloomily, Yes, it was how men were. But unlike Martha, she had been unable to work Rudi. She might have gone on arguing until she wore him down, she thought, but she was unwilling to. For this time her main reason was fear, and never before had she imposed that on him.

I'll just have to stand it the best I can, she thought despairingly. *Somehow. Let what'er will, come. Stand it if I can.*

If Rudi had seen her then, he would have thought she looked twenty years older.

49

Madle knew it was going to happen sometime fairly soon. She observed the misery in his face, his sudden anger at inert objects, his silences. She noticed his longer than usual absences from the house, the way he was building up the woodpile in the heat of August, and the way he started the boys on tasks that normally belonged to late September. He did things not really necessary yet, like cleaning out the spring and cutting summer growth back farther than usual from the nearer paths. She knew what he was doing.

She said no word. Sometimes, however, the two of them drew wordlessly close and held each other as they had twenty years ago.

Johannes was still not sure, but Madle was.

They harvested the corn and peas in the newground, carefully saving seed, and Johannes immediately began preparing the older fields for wheat. He kept Andreas by him, instructing the boy minutely in methods of sowing different kinds of grain.

Andreas, going on twelve, was not big enough to plow, but he could certainly use a hoe, and his mind was settled enough, Johannes thought, to hold on to what he learned. And maybe by next spring—how the boy was growing!—shooting up like Hans. All of them were growing, even on their less than plentiful diet, though more plentiful now than it had been. The rain with its lush growth had increased the cows' yield. Even Anneli was looking a little plumper with some color in her face. Now if they could only be spared the autumn sickness. . . .

He was always glad to see his sons gain height, but sometimes he was a little dismayed by it. "How did we manage to have such tall children, Madle? Is it this air, this country?"

Johannes was five feet seven inches tall, and Madle was not quite five two. The older children were an inch or so taller than their parents, but it looked as though Hans and Andreas would be considerably taller.

"I believe your mother was as tall as your father, wasn't she? Maybe it comes from her," Madle said. She had a clear memory of

Johannes' mother, a stern-faced woman of whom she'd been a little afraid. "How tall was her father?"

But Johannes had never known that grandfather.

They fell silent, each looking backward. Madle's mother had died young also. Madle kept of her only an impression of sweet softness. As so many times in the past she wondered, *What did she really look like? Was she also small? Father, I know, was small for a man. Barbara is slim and slight. I've always thought she must be most like Mother. . . . Oh Babeli, wherever you are. . . . Dear God, let me see her again!* Madle turned from Johannes to hide her pain. But he was thinking of the grandfather he did remember.

Of all his children, he thought, Georgi had most the look of old Johannes Lienhardt. Old Hans had been square, short, strong, and usually cheerful. Yes, Georgi had that sturdy Lienhardt look. As had Heiri. But Hans and Andreas were more like Madle's people. . . . Easier to break? *But Heiri was shaped like me and it didn't help him.* Grief and fear plunged down on Johannes. *Oh God, bring an end to this war!*

He decided he'd go to the Rieders' tomorrow afternoon to see what he could learn.

On August 22, Greene broke camp on the High Hills of Santee. A letter from General Washington had informed him of highly secret and critical plans to march into Virginia against Lord Cornwallis, who was presently encamped on the coast at Yorktown. Washington had decided to advance toward the Virginia coast because of the projected autumn movements of the French fleet.

On receiving Washington's letter, Greene immediately determined to take the offensive against Stewart, who was camped across the Santee. Greene hoped to bar any assistance from the British in South Carolina to those in Virginia. Accordingly he sent orders to all militia and State troops to gather at Friday's Ferry on the Congaree, where he and the Continentals would meet them.

When Stewart learned of Greene's orders, he moved farther down the Santee about forty miles below the forks of the Wateree and Congaree to a place called Eutaw Springs.

Joggi and Nissi sat close together in an empty room of the big house by the Road. They were there for privacy. Joggi had already stopped by Savana Hunt and he had only the hour left.

Nissi saw change in him. He was still gaunt, but his frame seemed more substantial. He would be twenty-three years old in December.

He spoke with certainty of what was to come. "You look back over the last year, Nissi, and you'll see. We're driving 'em out. We're driving 'em down to the water."

"Then pray God you do it soon."

"It may take more time than we'd like, but we'll do it."

They sat on an empty chest in the big ell room by the side porch. This room had been familiar to Joggi since childhood, though mostly as a place to escape from because of his elders sitting or working there.

"You be ready," he said.

She nodded, murmured against his shoulder, "I will." She looked at him and thought, *How can I ever be any more ready than I am now?*

She was as drably and poorly clothed as usual, but since she could do nothing about it, she had stopped thinking of it. She would always let his voice and his look and the closeness and feel of his body clothe her with their own beauty as they were doing now. She did not know how the reflection of it all intensified as it passed between them.

"Where's Herr Pastor these days?" he asked. "Do you know?"

"I believe he's still up at Herr Adam Summers'."

"Then we'll go to him."

"Joggi—" She took a deep breath. "It will be a big battle?"

"If we fight it, it will be."

"And could it be the last?"

He shook his head. "I can't say that."

She bent her head to hide a rush of emotion, and he felt her body shake. "Come back," she whispered, gasped, "make sure you come back!"

His hold tightened. Once he would have said strongly, "I will." The one thing he had known how to do was to elude his enemies. Now he found himself no longer in or even near the hiding place above the scuppernong arbor, for that place was gone or if it was still there, he was too heavy for it. Now he was on the ground with everyone else.

"I'll try to, Nissi. God willing, I'll come back."

They were only vaguely aware of where they were. This empty room—smoked, scoured, scarred by some thirty years' use—seemed not just vacated but forsaken.

"What I've been thinking of—we talked about it once, you remember? Land to the west? You still want to go there?"

"Oh yes. Wherever you want to go, Joggi."

"Your Papa, I don't know what he'll say."

"It won't matter what he says. I'll go. But I don't think he'll object."

"Why do you think that?"

"I just do." She did not really know why. She did not understand her father that well. She knew only that he and Herr Lienhardt were friends. As for her mother's sure objection, she would not think of that.

Joggi said, "You know I have nothing. But myself."

"And you think that's not enough for me, Joggi Lienhardt? Oh dear Lord!" She pushed him away momentarily, her eyes flashing, and he glimpsed her fire.

He laughed low, caught and pulled her back. "You know what you're getting?"

She gazed at him under half-closed lids, through long and silky lashes.

He knew now why ballad-makers sang of love's arrows and of captivity—except that it was more like a charger bearing down on you. Or a rifleman who'd got you in his sights and demanded surrender. And you wanted to surrender! Strangest of all, he was glad to! . . . Were the eyes that were trying to probe through the leaves of the arbor only the eyes of love? "Nissi, God help me, I *will* be back," he whispered.

They had not much more time. Loud steps sounded on the porch outside, a perfunctory knock, and in came Hans Jacob.

Joggi and Nissi drew apart.

Hans Jacob paused, surveying them. Joggi rose and stepped forward just as Hans Jacob did. Joggi bowed. "Herr Rieder."

Hans Jacob stretched out his hand to grasp Joggi's. "I'm glad to see you, my boy, glad to see you!"

Joggi bowed again slightly. "Sir."

"Well, no need to ask why you're here." Hans Jacob's voice was loud and hearty. "My eyes tell me that. If I didn't know already." He talked loudly because he was not sure what to say. "And so do others. Your grandmother, Nissi, she's been dinning a sermon in my ears this last quarter hour, not to mention your mother about other matters, but soon as I could get out, I did, and I said, 'I'll just step over here and speak to Joggi while I can.' Joggi, they tell me you don't have long to stay."

"No, Herr Rieder." Joggi turned to Nissi and met her look. He said, "I wish to marry your daughter when I return. With your permission."

Hans Jacob's eyes brightened. His face broke up in smiles. "Well, Joggi! Well, my boy! I can't think of a better—I don't know what could please me more! I'll be happy to have you; yes, my boy, I will. Happy to have you!" He moved to draw Joggi and Nissi, who had risen also, into a loose double embrace.

He released them and stepped back. "Yes, my boy, she's—" his voice broke, "she's—" he tried a third time, "she's a good child. God knows she never deserved—but I'll give her to you with joy for I know—your father and mother, salt of the earth, well, and you're the one I know she wants, and I couldn't have chosen a better for her, these times and things as they are—well, I wish you joy." He was finished to his and their relief.

Suddenly Nissi moved forward and kissed her father. It was the first time she'd ever kissed him of her own will that she could remember.

"Yes, yes, my good little daughter, I can't let her go so easy as you might think, Joggi. There are other matters we'll need to discuss, but they can wait, for I know you have little time now." He rubbed his hands together, looked from one to the other. "Now I know you'd rather, since there's so little time—but sometimes private afairs must give way to public ones, and that's partly why I broke in on you, though now I'm glad I did, but, Joggi, you must tell me now. Who's in camp up there, who's coming, and what are the plans?"

Joggi controlled his expression, did not even glance at Nissi. "I'll tell you what I can, Herr Rieder, though it's no more than everyone else knows."

Joggi said the ones gathering at Granby were Pickens' Brigade and what was left of Sumter's. Sumter himself was in North Carolina procuring supplies. Already here, of course, were the newly raised State troops under Colonel William Henderson. Some North Carolina militia under Colonel Francis Malmedy were coming, but Marion's Brigade would join them farther down the country. Greene's Continentals were expected to cross the Congaree tomorrow or the next day, and almost the entire Patriot force in South Carolina would be gathered at Granby. After that, everyone presumed they would be moving down the west bank of the Congaree and on down the Santee.

"Can you tell me anything else about Willi? His mother said you thought he was still with Thomas."

"Yes, sir."

"Think there's a chance we'll see him?"

"It may be. It depends on their orders and how soon they get here. He may not have a chance to stop. It wasn't easy for me to—"

Hans Jacob interrupted, "But he'll come this way? They'll all come by here?"

"Oh yes, we'll all come down the Road, there's not much other way—unless something changes we don't know about."

"Then we'll see him. I'll go to Granby myself and if I learn nothing there, I'll stand by the Road. I'll see him one way or another."

Joggi said, "He'll want to see you I know, but with so many people and so much movement—"

"Oh, I'll find him. I'll go to Granby today. I'll see Hampton, and if I can't find him, I'll find out about him."

Hans Jacob stood a few minutes longer until finally he embraced his daughter, then Joggi again. He said God's blessing on him, then hurried out. The two listened to his receding steps, heard him shout from the yard to someone distant.

Their own parting was quieter and somehow simpler even if it took longer, though in the end it was swift. Nissi did not cry. To Joggi she looked tall standing on the porch, where twice before she'd watched him go. He thought it was this last sight of her that would bring him back.

50

Late that same evening Jem Boyd came to Savana Hunt as he'd promised. He spent the night, and early the next morning Hans left with him. Though Jem had a musket for Hans, he did not bring him a horse. Johannes was on the verge of giving Hans Roker but something held him back.

Jem said he understood. "It was wonderful how it all come about, you getting him back here again. And him being Heiri's and all. I can see how you'd rather not send him off again."

That was not the reason for Johannes' reluctance, but he did not say so. However, in order not to overburden or delay Jem, Johannes did allow Hans to ride Roker to Granby, where Hans hoped to join a company of foot soldiers, and Johannes would follow and bring back the horse.

Even so, for Johannes there was something almost unbearable about watching his third son ride off on that horse. As for Madle, she could barely see her child in this dry-eyed boy, thin as ever, though no longer weak and pale. She let him go as she had let Joggi go. And Heiri. She had learned the outer if not the inner art of saying goodbye.

Cathri's mouth trembled until she finally broke down and hid her face in her apron. Jem Boyd looked at her pityingly, but Hans, trying to be angry, did not look at her at all. He did not dare to look. Nor did he look at the fields where he'd thought he slaved or at the familiar woods, nor did he look back at his parents.

Johannes followed Jem and Hans on foot as soon as he could get away, but he returned much later than he'd promised. It was mid-afternoon, and as soon as Madle saw him, she knew.

She spared him the ordeal of telling her. "I know." Her mouth and chin were firm. "I know," she repeated in a clear, remote voice.

They stood at the side gate, the one he'd gone in and out some fifty thousand times for toil and homecoming, for grief and joy. They did not face each other. They could not have stood it. Johannes looked across the broken field that sloped to the creek, toward the fields on the other side of the creek, toward the stock he could not see in the woods. Madle saw only the cruel pines on the far horizon, the flat, bright August sky.

He said, "I go as a volunteer. It's not a long-term enlistment. I go under the same colonel as Hans so you can be comforted I'll be near him."

"I'm glad of that."

"I go to do what I can, Madle. Maybe not much. But I owe it."

"You'll not go on foot, will you?"

"No, I'll ride Roker." He did not need to tell her that at forty-seven he was not as sure of his ability to endure long marches as he had been at twenty-seven.

She waited for him to tell her when.

"Soon as I get a bite to eat I'll leave."

She made him a packet of most of the bread left from the week's baking although he did not want to take it. "Madle, they'll give me rations. Keep it for yourself and the children."

"With the two of you gone we won't need as much."

"I'd feel better not to." His eyes were drenched in misery, his mouth a gulley of pain.

She turned away. "Do as I say," she said faintly but in such a tone that he had to obey. This bread my hands have made, this one thing from me, she wanted to say, take at least this one thing from me.

The four children stood with her outside the front paling. Once there'd been ten of them here. Now there were only five.

Like Hans, Johannes did not look back. His body trembled as wave after wave of fear and grief coursed through him, weakening him so that he could hardly sit upright. The horse plodded heavily through the sand. Without even knowing when he did it, Johannes turned left onto the Road.

But Madle could not stand looking long. Even before he disappeared, she had Anneli to enfold. "Hush, darling, hush," she crooned. "Papa'll come back soon. He'll be back."

She straightened up and took the little girl's hand. "Come now, we'll go and hunt guinea eggs." She reached toward Georgi. "Georgi, you come too. Cathri, Andreas, you go and see about the cows. Go ahead and drive them back toward the milking rail."

They usually went later for the cows, but the other chores would take longer this evening, and besides it was a way of turning their minds.

As Madle walked with the two young ones around the barn, the garden, and the orchard, she saw him go before her up the road. Stooped as he often was by work, he always tried to sit up straight in his saddle. She had seen that back ride off a thousand times. Ever again, oh God?

All things end. All things have their ending.

She tried to push off the thought of the empty room tonight and the empty bed. She thought, *I'll let Anneli sleep with me.*

It was almost sundown. Andreas and Cathri were still at the milking. Madle had thought of going to help though she did not often milk, but Andreas had been learning and did a good job, Cathri said. His hands were already larger and stronger than his mother's. Madle sent Georgi to help with the calves. She was thankful the two cows now gave plentifully. Only Anneli was with her at the house. Often now they were the only two there, but this evening their aloneness had a different feel to it.

Anneli hoped the others would soon come back. She thought about tonight at the table. Would anyone sit in Papa's place? She always stood at Papa's right hand to ask the blessing because she was the youngest and that was the custom. Where would she stand tonight?

Everything was *so* still. If only they had another dog. Or even a cat or a kitten or anything. A long time ago they'd had cats, but things kept happening to them. Something got the last batch of kittens and then the mother cat just disappeared. You had to feed cats and dogs to keep them tame, Papa said, and they didn't have enough extra to feed them. There weren't even any little biddies or goslings or anything, just the few old hens and the mean geese. And the guineas that were almost wild. The calves were kept so far away she never even saw or heard them. It was all *so* still. She kept listening for sounds, but she heard only the chirps and cheeps of a few wild birds.

Then she caught another sound. It was like a far off—clinking? She listened. "Mama, what's that?" It was like—creaking and wheels in the sand and like. . . . "Mama, listen!" Anneli touched her mother's arm. Madle stopped still.

Excitement tinged the little girl's cheeks as the two of them hurried around the house, though fear paled Madle's.

In the long shadows of the oak they stood at the front gate, where they'd stood three hours ago, and watched an unusual vehicle roll slowly, heavily toward them—a closed carriage drawn by two old horses. A carriage? The last carriage they'd seen was over a year ago in the churchyard. Who could it be? And why were they coming here? *Oh God*, Madle implored, *let it be nothing worse than somebody lost.*

An elderly black driver pulled on the reins shouting, "Whoa! Whoa!" and a slim white hand from inside the coach was opening the door.

A lightning thought struck Madle. With trembling fingers she unfastened the gate and at the same moment a figure slipped down, almost tumbled from the side of the carriage. Both figures rushed together.

"Barbara, Barbara!" Over and over, "Oh my child, my Babeli!"

"Mama, Mama. It's been so *long*. So *long*."

Both were crying. "Oh, I thought you'd never—" "I've waited so long—" "Oh, let me look at you."

The old man on the high box seat drew a tired sigh. The horses stood still and slowly swished their tails. Mother and daughter kept murmuring, crying, and embracing until suddenly from inside the carriage came the unmistakable sounds of someone small waking up. Both women moved simultaneously, and Barbara opened the door and lifted out a little girl.

"Ohhh!" Madle held out her arms.

"It's my little Vroniggi, Mama. Her name's Veronica, but we call her Vroniggi. My baby, it's your own grandmama!"

Oh, the feel of her! And again to hold such a small sweet body!

The baby had dark silken hair, and although the light was going, Madle could see she had brilliant blue eyes. "She looks like you," Madle whispered, "just like you at this age."

"Like you, Mama, I thought."

"And you named her 'Veronica,'" said Madle softly as she kissed the baby's cheeks and temples, "after your own grandmother." Veronica had been Madle's mother, whom she thought Barbara must look like. "Veronica?" Madle whispered. The baby gazed back, stiffened a little and said, "Down."

"Oh yes, she can walk," Barbara said proudly.

"And talk too?"

"Some words she knows. Set her down, Mama. She's independent."

The child was a small and dainty one-year-old. Standing alone, she saw Anneli and headed straight toward her.

They'd forgotten Anneli, but it didn't keep Anneli from holding out her arms to the baby. Barbara greeted and hugged Anneli too although it meant hugging both children, for Anneli would not let the baby go.

Barbara rose and turned toward the carriage where its driver sat stoic and still.

"Matthew—" she began, then asked, "Mama, where can he take the horses? Also I've brought—I didn't know how it would be—we brought what food we could, though it's not as much as I wanted. I didn't know what you'd have or how it would be."

"Oh yes, surely, surely—everything's empty in the barn and stables so there's plenty of shelter. Though as to grain for the horses—we'll see when the children come in, they're at the milking now. Tell him to drive around—"

"Where's Papa?"

"He left this afternoon. To go with the army. Hans went too."

"Oh Mama!" Some of the light left Barbara's face. Madle saw it was thinner now with marks of strain. "Oh, I'd so looked forward—"

"Yes, but it can't be helped." Madle's voice was firm and controlled. "Let's just be glad you're here safe." Madle bent to Anneli, who knelt in bliss by the child. "Come now, let's go inside. We've much to tell but it can wait." She made her tone light, loving. "And I must see more of this baby. No, Anneli, you'd better not try to pick her up." She hesitated. "Let me."

But the child would be carried only by Barbara, who after giving the old man directions came into the yard with Anneli on one side and her mother on the other and Vroniggi on high, prattling her repertory of words.

Why, I've never seen such a smart child, marvelled Madle. . . . *Except Joggi.*

Anneli's face was as pink as a rose.

They had been coming all day, Barbara said. They had come up the Road from below Sandy Run, having crossed the river at Howell's Ferry.

"No, we met few people. Several riders passed us both ways but they seemed in a hurry. I have a letter for safe passage, but no one stopped us. In fact, it seemed strange to meet so few people."

"That may be because they're all now gathered at the Congarees. But they'll be going soon down the Road. Oh, how glad—oh my child, you cannot know, that you should come today of all days!"

Barbara said she had been living at a plantation near Raiford's Creek since March. Conrad was no longer satisfied for his family to stay alone.

"Your father went in June to see you," said Madle, "but no one was there and he could not find anyone to give him direction."

"No. Most of those—loyal to the King were gone by then. And they're moving again. That's why I came here."

"Where is Frau Meyer?"

"She died, Mama, three weeks ago."

The shadow froze on Madle's face. Frau Meyer was only a few years older than she was. Madle thought that though Anna Meyer had not been a happy woman, she had seemed to be a vigorous one. "How—how did she die?"

"It was a wasting sickness. It began in winter, then she got better, but it seized her again in late spring. When she went—I could not sorry, Mama. At the end she suffered so much."

"I'm sorry, Barbara. I'm sorry for Conrad's loss. And yours. . . . And where now is Conrad?"

Barbara said he was still in the South Carolina Regiment of Loyalists but not at present with those under Colonel Stewart. His company was farther down the country below Charlestown.

"We talked about where I'd go if things got worse, and he agreed at last for me to come here. I've thought since then—perhaps I should try to go on to Charlestown, but Conrad says people like us are camped in huts and conditions are not good. And to take our baby there, well, he knew how I longed—and with Frau Meyer gone, I decided to try to come back here." Barbara spoke more haltingly. "I hope—I was thinking as I came—I hope it won't bring trouble?"

"No, no, no, child! You don't know how I've prayed, your father and I, how hard we've prayed and longed—and now your coming today, this very day of all days, of your Papa's leaving—and Hans too and the sorrow—oh, I thank my God, it's like a miracle! You could not have come at a better time for us!"

"If I could just have seen Papa. Why, why didn't I try to come yesterday?"

"Barbara, it might not have been safe then. I'm sure more people were on the Road yesterday, and some of them, all kinds of people, you never know. . . . No, I know today was better."

Madle thought of the stir last night with Jem's coming and Hans getting ready to leave. Then she wondered if Johannes would have gone if

Barbara had been here. If only he could have seen her and his grandchild. Oh, pray God he'd have yet that joy. . . . But she must fix her mind on the ones who were here. Her face softened as she gazed at Anneli and the little one with their arms around each other, looking at each other teasingly. She thought of the pleasure awaiting Cathri, wondered how the boys would feel.

"It was the good God brought you to us, Barbara, when we need you most."

As they went up the front steps, Barbara glanced about. She saw the same little benches on the porch against the wall, but something was missing, she could not think what. Later she would realize it was a dog. The house looked unexpectedly small and homely, for she'd been used to bigger houses lately, but its logs were as strong and square as she remembered, just as her father had cut them years before she was born. Home. Nothing else on earth was like it.

Inside, though the doors and windows were open, it took a few moments for her eyes to adjust to the twilight gloom, and as they did, she was unprepared for the contrast between what she remembered and what she saw. She swallowed hard.

"Yes," Madle sighed, "much has happened. But we're still here—Cathri, Georgi, Andreas, and Anneli. I thank God we're still here. Though—" Madle broke off to keep her control.

"It's how it is everywhere," Barbara said low. "I'd no reason to expect—but as you say, we're here. Oh Mama," she said in a rush, "we've so much to tell and talk about. Tell me now—" She hesitated. "Tell me about Joggi and Heiri. When have you last seen them? What have you heard?" She paused again. "I knew of Heiri's going last summer, but I've heard nothing of Joggi. When have you last seen him?"

Madle had turned away. "We'll talk after supper, Barbara. We'll wait till the others come in so we won't have to tell things twice." But she could not hide the change in her voice.

There was another silence. Many a time Barbara had prepared herself for hard news from her family, especially about Joggi. She prepared again. But Anneli's soft clear laughter and the baby's chatter broke into her fear. How those two had taken to each other. Barbara put her dread away and asked no more questions for the time being.

Madle was not alone in her room that night. She had the distraction and joy of her lost daughter and her own grandchild beside her.

Barbara would have stayed awake longer, thinking of Heiri, but she was suddenly too exhausted, even for grief, from the long tense day that had begun before sunup.

Madle saw now how her oldest daughter had lost her girlish roundness. Though only nineteen, she'd already had too many of a woman's cares.

"And Joggi," Barbara asked again tiredly, "you say you saw him only yesterday?"

"For a few minutes. He was on his way to—"

But Barbara could not take in what her mother was saying, something about the Rieders. Barbara's eyelids drooped as she looked down at the baby asleep beside her. She felt a moment of thanksgiving, closed her eyes to rest them, and then she too was asleep.

It had been hard for Cathri and Anneli to go up to bed, and, once there, they could not go to sleep for quite a while. It had never crossed Cathri's mind that of all the expected events in the world there could be such delight in being an *aunt*! Who would have thought it?

As for Anneli, Vroniggi was the best, best thing that had ever happened in her whole, whole life! She could hardly wait till morning.

Andreas and Georgi too were somewhat bemused at the presence of a baby in the house, but they gave no thought to being uncles. They were glad for the excitement of their sister's coming and they liked the feel of two more people at home. But Hans' bed was empty again. And the whole house felt twice as empty, no matter how many were in it, without Papa.

The driver, Matthew, was given the straw tick off Hans' bed to take to the barn. It was a warm night. No cover was needed though he had a blanket of his own he'd brought along. He didn't know what to think of this place. It looked poor to him, and he wondered how they'd fare. But he'd worry about that tomorrow. He was just glad tonight he had a place by himself for his poor old bones. He was worn out.

The old carriage was large and, when unpacked, it was found to have brought a trunk of clothing and a good-sized chest of small household goods such as candles, thread, linen, and tableware, which to the

Lienhardts were now luxuries. But more important were two large kegs—one of rice and one of flour—and the hampers of potatoes, dried fruits, and beans. No wonder the horses were so tired and the wheels had made such deep ruts.

In the bedroom that night Barbara had shown her mother the dozen gold sovereigns hidden in her trunk.

Madle was stricken. "You must hide them again. Don't let anyone else see this, Barbara, and don't speak a word of it to anyone!"

Tomorrow they would remove everything from the house that Barbara had brought, and they must think of somewhere else to hide the gold pieces.

51

People stood along the High Road to watch them pass. Cathri and Andreas went running when Georgi yelled from beyond the woods where he'd gone to watch and listen, and they ran up just in time to see the light-clothed, plumed cavalry sweep by and then the approach of flags and drums. Breathless they stood there watching rank after rank of infantry march by, the first time during the whole war they'd been allowed to watch such a sight. So many men! There must be a thousand of them! "And look at those big guns on carriages!" said Andreas. "Four of them, just like Joggi said!"

Most of the soldiers wore light-colored breeches. It did not seem strange that some of the men marched barefoot or that some of their shirts were sleeveless, but the children were surprised, even troubled, to see some go by without shirts and with only rags wadded under the straps of their bullet pouches and packs. Why did they go half-naked? Didn't they have shirts? Or was it the heat? Their faces were already glistening from the morning sun. Some looked pale as if they'd had the fever.

Here and there rode uniformed figures with swords and blue coats and gold fringes on their shoulders. They'd be the officers, Andreas said. And, oh, that drumbeat! It made you want to march right alongside them. Georgi kept hopping from one foot to the other.

The last of the infantry passed and now came a train of wagons, and their creaking wheels drowned out the drums ahead. They moved at a good pace and were followed by more cavalry, but after them the road was empty.

Was that all? Where were Papa and Hans? Had they missed them? "Oh, look! Here come more!" cried Cathri.

The approaching troops on horseback were of different ages, some shaven, some bearded, and they wore only everyday clothes. Yet most of their faces were set and stern and their horses were good.

Georgi was beginning to exclaim when Andreas cried, "Look! It's Roker and Papa!"

Jumping and craning this way and that, the three caught glimpses of their father on the other side of the road. "Papa!" they cried, but he seemed not to hear, for he kept his look straight ahead. They wanted to call louder, but the sight of the other grim-faced men silenced them. They looked after him as long as they could. So intent were they that Cathri did not see Anneli until she felt her pull at her arm.

"Do you see Papa?" cried Anneli. "Where is he? Where's Papa? I don't see him!"

Cathri stooped and pointed. "There, Anneli. See? Way down there on the other side."

"Oh, I can't see him!" Anneli cried in distress. "Mama, hurry, hurry!"

All the children looked back to see their breathless mother hurrying up.

"Mama, you just missed him!"

"Who?" she panted. "Joggi?"

"No, Papa! He's already gone! See? Way down there? Crossing the creek."

Madle stood on tiptoe searching among the drab shoulders and dark hats, but she could not make out her husband's back. He was merged into the mass.

"And, Mama, guess what?" said Georgi. "I saw Herr Rieder!"

"Who? Herr Rieder? You mean Hans Jacob Rieder?"

"Yes, and he was on Diamond, that's how I knew him! He was a little ahead of Papa."

"Hans? Have you seen Hans?"

"No, not yet."

A troop of infantry passed at a quicker pace. It was not yet nine o'clock but their faces shone with sweat.

"Oh, look, Mama, look!" Cathri grabbed Madle's arm. "There he is! There's Hans! See, there's Hans!"

Almost hidden by the men around him, the boy marched straight as a wooden rule, his face set in one expression. He gave his family a quick glance when they called, but his expression did not change. Scared, proud, thought Cathri. For a few moments they saw his head and shoulders, his head not reaching the height of those around him. Then he too vanished.

Oh, why, cried Madle in agony, *why would they take one so young?* Such children, she mourned. She saw two others who looked no older than Hans.

These infantry were fewer than the Continentals. More wagons came grinding and creaking. The Lienhardts were startled to see women in some of the wagons and even walking alongside.

The next body of horsemen, in spite of their nondescript clothes, looked more soldierly and yet more relaxed. They seemed to have more of a common likeness among them. Bronzed and strong, they rode easily, and their faces were not so stern.

"Oh Joggi! Joggi! Joggi!" yelled Georgi.

Joggi's face brightened and he raised his hand and smiled his curving smile.

The children surged close to the road and would have reached out to touch him if they had dared. Eyes brimming—they did not know why—they smiled proudly. Madle drank in his look and gazed after him all the way to the creek till he too merged into the mass.

"There's Willi!"

"Willi! Willi Rieder!"

"Hi, hi! Willi Rieder!"

Willi's somber glance flicked over the little family. That girl there, Heiri's sister. For a moment he saw Heiri. For a moment he was pierced by pain and joy together. He smiled at Cathri, a crooked, hurting smile.

Because they were looking at Willi, they missed seeing Jem Boyd, but he saw them. He too saw Heiri among them.

After the horsemen came another long gap, then a marching troop and more horsemen following at a walk.

Madle stood unseeing. Her husband and sons gone on down the Road, gone to some place of fear and dread she could not follow, back down the way they'd come up. She herself had come up that way. Long ago.

She did not see a burly rider draw rein and move out of his troop until he dropped beside her. "Madle," said a deep voice.

She looked up startled. "Rudi! Oh, dear Rudi!"

"I don't see Johannes with you. Where's he?"

"He's gone on ahead. He goes with those ahead."

"What? Johannes? He's with us?"

"Yes. And Hans. And Joggi. Oh Rudi," her words tumbled out, "I thank God for this sight of you!" Her voice broke as it had not broken once these last few days. She put her hands on his shoulders, then her arms around him, leaning against him hard. "Oh, you give me strength when I need it most," she whispered. "Come back safe, Rudi. I'll pray for you as for them. Oh, come back safe."

As she withdrew her arms, he caught her hands in his. "I've thought of you often, Madle, grieved for you. For Heiri." They looked into each other's eyes and exchanged pain.

"And your dear wife," she asked rapidly, "and your children?"

"They were well, when I left them. Pray for them too."

She sensed a shadow in his voice, but it took on strength as, turning to gather his reins, he said, "And Madle, I have now a new son!"

"Oh, have you? Yes, and I a grandchild! Oh, Rudi, please tell Johannes if you see him that his little granddaughter is here and Barbara too! Tell him Barbara's come back to us! Tell him, Rudi, if you see him!"

"I will." Rudi mounted lightly for one so heavy as he. "You do me good, Madle! Always! More than I can tell you!" He spurred his horse, cried back, "I'm glad you're my kin!"

"And I you! God go with you, Rudi!"

He's himself, thought Madle, *always himself. Oh, thank God for Rudi Näffels, my blessed kin. Oh thank You, God, for letting me see him again.*

A few more wagons rattled by, then a last troop of mounted men, and after that the earth was bare—trampled, rutted, spotted here and there with horse droppings. Dust coated the weeds and grass at the edge of the road, the speckled willow leaves down by the creek.

Each of the Lienhardts stood emptied. Anneli was the first to turn away. None of them spoke, not even Anneli, as they started back to the house. Madle was last to leave, Cathri walking slowly beside her.

Pickens' command veered off to Orangeburg, sent by Greene to see what the British and Tories were doing there, but the rest of the army marched on down the Road to what had been Fort Motte, then slowly toward Eutaw Springs, where Stewart and his men were camped. On September 5 at Halfway Swamp, Pickens' veteran militiamen rejoined Greene with little to report from Orangeburg. On September 7 Francis Marion's brigade of scouts and swamp fighters also merged with the main army at Henry Laurens' plantation, some seventeen miles above Eutaw Springs. Greene's army now numbered more than twenty-three hundred men, less the two hundred camp guards left up the Road. It included over thirteen hundred Continentals and over eight hundred militia, State troops, and volunteers.

The baggage and convalescents had been left at Motte's, also some newly joined privates to strengthen the guards. Among them to their mingled relief and dismay were Johannes Lienhardt and Hans Jacob Rieder.

"Might have known I'd be good for nothing but to dawdle around wagons and cattle," growled Johannes.

"Hell, I could have stayed home and done this," said Hans Jacob in a hard, angry-sounding voice.

The thought of their sons gone on made them feel old and powerless.

Oh Hans, Johannes mourned, *if I could just have stayed near you, kept an eye on you. Though what good would that do? The time's past for my doing good to Hans. And to Joggi. Whatever good I could do to either was done long ago. Or not done.* Johannes yearned over his sons, surrendered them again and again.

The able-bodied men left as guards were a motley sort, some of them recent volunteers, many of them older men like Johannes. Most were inclined to grumble. They're hiding their mixed-up feelings, Johannes thought, like me. Some were downright surly—till a one-eyed sergeant took them in charge.

"Now you slack-jawed, sourfaced lunkheads, you listen to me!" the sergeant shouted when he'd lined them up. "Somebody's got to be here, and if it wasn't you, it'd be somebody else that's gone on down the road and somebody can move a bit faster'n you or me either one! You think you can shoot better or move quicker'n the fellows gone on down? I sure as hell can't. Might could have four years ago but not today. And where they're headed every last man of 'em's going to be needed and the best they got! But you're needed here!" He paused. His voice dropped to a gently reasoning tone. "Make no mistake. Don't you know it was never an army yet didn't need its camp gear guarded?" Again he paused, then resumed at a full roar. "Hear what I say! You think you're here to decide what you do or where you do it? Then why didn't you stay home! Nobody roped you up and drug you here! Nobody blindfolded you and marched you here with a gun to your back! You 'listed to *serve* and not to decide how! Hear me! Why, you grizzle-pate, lardheaded, drag-footed stragglers! you pie-faced, thick-shanked laggards, you slugs! you sheepheads!" He paused a full ten seconds, during which his one fulminating eye bored into each one straight to his backbone. He snapped, "Now you step quick and every man look to his duty or I'll know the reason why."

Their eyes widened. A few suppressed grins. It was true. Somebody *did* have to stay; it was essential. And they *were* here of their own choice. And it *was* their place to obey. Everybody knew that.

Be glad you can do this much, Johannes told himself. *You knew how it might be before you came. What more can you do than you've always done?* he asked himself again. *Serve where you can. That's what you came out for, wasn't it?*

Still he yearned after his sons.

Hans was back where he'd been seven weeks ago, lying on black earth under dark trees in air so heavy with heat and damp you could almost cut it. It was not the shrilling and booming of night creatures that kept him awake tonight but thoughts of tomorrow. Tomorrow he knew he'd not be left behind for camp duty.

He lay near the two big fellows he always marched between. "Stay by us, Sparrow. You look out for us and we'll look out for you," they'd told him.

George Granger and Jess Jervey. For some reason they seemed to like him. Oh, they joshed him a good bit—about his speech, of course; about his skinny arms and legs; and—they said—his ferocious look. But he knew how to take it now. They called him "Sparrow Hawk," sometimes "Sparrow," sometimes "Hawk." He tried not to grin when they called him "Hawk."

He was surprised they liked him. He didn't know why they did. Maybe it was where he'd been, especially that place he'd learned now the name of, Quinby Bridge. "I heard it was a right smart of ourn got killed down there," George said.

Perhaps it was a new humility in Hans or perhaps only the Lienhardt coming out, but he did not try to hide the fact that he'd been only a horseboy before.

"Well, you come back, that's the main thing. You're more'n a horseboy now."

"How old are you anyhow, Sparrow Hawk? You must be all of thirteen."

But he would not tell them his age.

He wondered if Jem had mentioned him to them, but, no, they didn't know any Jem Boyd. Or Joggi. Or Willi either. Hans did not ask about Heiri.

George and Jess were from above Camden near Granny's Quarter Creek. They'd fought off and on with first one bunch, then another. "We was at Hanging Rock with Sumter. Almost got captured one time. After that we lay out nigh on six months in Wateree Swamp."

Gradually Hans realized that their families, or what was left of them, were very poor. George and Jess were even more dumbstruck than he was by the wealth they glimpsed in this low country—the great houses, the pleasure gardens, the vast fields worked in normal times by slaves.

"If an this thing's ever over, if I live, I aim to get me some *good* land. They tell me it's good land over to Georgy. If an we can ever get rid of the damn' redskins, I aim to go there. Get me something I can work and make something on."

"Aye, something better'n that sand and blackjacks where I come from."

But to Hans land was only a taskmaster. Unless you had slaves. And with Papa the way he was. . . . Well, he wasn't sure he'd ever go against Papa now.

I want to go some place I can learn more, he thought. *Learn even more than Joggi, be somebody different. A city? Why, I've never even seen a city. Or the ocean. Papa has, and Mama too. Why can't I? They say at the North it's cities all up and down the land. Oh, I want to see more, do more, be more! Somebody better than I am now.*

Maybe it would start tomorrow. If only he could do something brave, something outstanding. He might be younger than Heiri and Joggi but he knew he was as smart as they were—or had been, thinking of Heiri. He knew he had a good head on his shoulders. Once Herr Pastor had told him so. If only he could be brave.

He tried to say the prayers he'd been taught, but the ones he could think of seemed to have nothing to do with now. "Our Father" was only words. Finally all that would come was just, "God, help me! Help me to make up for running away! Oh God, help me to do something brave!" Over and over, gritting his teeth, he prayed this prayer till unaccountably he fell asleep.

Joggi thought how different it was from a year and a half ago, even a year ago. In April of '80 he'd been with those caught like rats in that church at Moncks Corner, which was only some thirty miles down the

Road from here. Those who'd escaped had spent the rest of April and early May skulking and running in these very swamps. And on May 12, sixteen months ago, an American army of six thousand, six hundred men had surrendered to a British armada and an army of twelve thousand men at Charlestown.

In May 1780, from the British point of view and almost everyone else's, South Carolina was recovered for the Crown. All the British and the Loyalists had to do was to fan out over the Province, station themselves at strategic places, and wait for everyone to come in and swear loyalty to the King.

And they did come, most people, Whig and Tory alike. They thought the war was over in South Carolina. Thousands came in to surrender—or proudly affirm their allegiance—and to take protection.

Even I took parole, thought Joggi, *that time at Ninety Six. Though I knew I'd break it. But it was do that or stay there and rot.*

He remembered the months afterward: the hard riding, the semi-starvation, the skirmishes, flights, pursuits of late last summer; sometimes a dozen of them lurking to spring from the bushes, sometimes fifty, occasionally a hundred or more. *At Musgrove's Mill we were two hundred, he remembered, and at Kings Mountain we were nine hundred. But even after those victories we melted away.* He remembered the dark fierceness of such victories. Blackstock's. Then the Cowpens.

There were a thousand of us at Cowpens counting the Continentals. We fought alongside Continentals for the first time since Charlestown. Yes, it was the greatest victory of all because there we beat Regulars. . . . But no victory for me.

Well, he'd just about gotten over it now, though in some ways he knew he'd never be the same again, and maybe that was good. He'd learned that much about himself when he fought at Augusta in May. He'd started yearning for the war to end. He'd begun to see as never before that it was no way to live.

Oh yes, he'd wanted to rejoin. "The spring of the year when men go forth to war." Last spring had brought its series of little victories with the taking of small posts. . . . *But we sure failed at Ninety Six though we outnumbered 'em three to one. God knows, some of 'em can fight. And we've lost bigger ones than that: Camden a year ago was the worst of all. And Guilford Courthouse in North Carolina, where they say we fought hard but couldn't beat 'em. Hobkirk Hill in April—Continentals outnumbered 'em there too, but they outfought us. So how is it if we lost so many big ones or at least we didn't win—how is it we're here and they're there?*

For now the British and their Loyalist troops—and you had to admit the Loyalists were a sizeable force—were pulling back into an ever-shrinking ring around Charlestown. The back country and the middle country were just about clean of 'em, at least of troops, though God knew there were bound to be plenty of Tories still up there.

How did we do it? General Greene? We never won any of the big ones except maybe at the Cowpens. And Greene wasn't even at the Cowpens. Yet here we are. Still. Even if we lose tomorrow we'll be here still.

It was strange . . . even mysterious, some might say.

Joggi remembered his words to his father after the surrender of Charlestown. "It's not over! It's just started!" How had he known that?

He remembered the feeling he'd had the night before he left home out there in the dark by himself, that mysterious feeling he'd never forgotten. It came from—and yet it didn't—from the ground and from the stars, and he'd exclaimed with power, "Mine!" Yet not his power. He remembered. Not his power.

And he wasn't the only one who felt it. For he knew that he had to say "ours," not "mine."

It had been given to him and to Heiri and to others like them to make it so. And Papa? And poor little Hans? Oh God, why hadn't they stayed home?

Well, why shouldn't Papa be in it? He's been part of this country longer than I have. And that poor little rail of a brother—why begrudge it to him? But does he know what it may cost him?

It does cost. Joggi felt a shiver of unaccustomed fear.

He knew now he didn't want to pay that much. Oh, he'd always been one to try and save his own hide more or less though sometimes he'd wondered why it mattered, but most of the time he hadn't even thought about it. But now. . . . *Oh God, I want to see the last of these fever-swamps and take Nissi with me to new country and live by running water and see high places. I want to live, God! To see Papa and Mama and my brothers and sisters again. . . . Savana Hunt.*

It was strange that he should care so much when now he fought on the ground like everyone else, where there was no evasion from those who came looking for him. He was on the ground with friend and enemy alike. Tonight he was one of an army of twenty-one hundred men. A year and a half ago it had been only a handful. Was that what made the difference, that now he was with so many? Was that what made him see it as so much bigger than he was?

Heiri had said, "I thought men fought together. And helped one another out."

And he'd told Heiri, "It's what you are in yourself that matters."

He still believed that. It *was* what he was in himself that would make a difference for him tomorrow. And yet—everything was bigger than he was. He knew that too.

Maybe we were both right. Helping each other out. Heiri did it. He did it to the end.

And if Heiri hadn't done it. . . . *Oh God, I thank you for my brother! Help me—help me to be more like him.*

Strange. . . .

52

At four o'clock in the morning, the great moss-draped oaks and cypresses hung black and still. The early hours had brought a touch of cool but with the rising sun yesterday's heat would return.

Willi had dreamed last night of his grandmother. She'd come chasing after him with a switch while his father walked away. Willi couldn't dodge or get away from her, but when she cornered him, she held him firmly between her knees, forcing him to face her, her strong old hands on his shoulders. She mumbled, "First time I ever saw you—" then changed it to "last time." Her drone dragged on, "I said, 'No, Willi Rieder, you'll never be the man your grandfather was, never hold a candle to Hermann Rieder,' and so I told your father, aye-God, many and many a time, 'never be the man. . . .'" Her face came fearsomely close. "But he's now gone and you're now gone and never again will I see you." She drew back, her dark face lightened, and she looked just as she used to. "But hear me, you Willi! Listen to me! You *are* now a man! You hear me? You *are* now a man! May a good God forgive me." Her grip failed. Still she held him with her look.

It stayed with him in the night and the sense of her strong old hands on his shoulders. Then toward dawn it loosened, merged into the gnarled cypresses above him.

As they formed for the march in the half-dark, he glimpsed Joggi Lienhardt. Joggi moved quickly, competently, self-absorbed as always.

They set out along the Charlestown road and it came to Willi: here they were at last, he and Joggi both, where he'd so feared to be a year and a half ago. But neither Joggi's urging nor Joggi's example had anything to do with where he was now. It came to Willi like the growing light. He was where he was because of choices he himself had made. From the day he'd left home with Heiri Lienhardt, he'd kept coming on, stumbling maybe, but of his own will.

He began to feel a powerful sense of release. The grip on him was gone. Not his grandmother's grip. Not his father's lack of grip. He knew today that his father had his own kind of courage just as he, Willi, had his. She had told him so.

Red streaked the sky. Light grew. He marched with a strong and swinging step. Where Joggi Lienhardt was, where Eph Giles was, had nothing to do with where he'd go or what he'd do this day.

The men marched in four columns. Lee's Legion and William Henderson's State Troops went ahead, followed by the four artillery pieces. Next marched the entire body of militia: South Carolinians under Francis Marion and Andrew Pickens; North Carolinians under Francis Malmedy, a French colonel whom his troops did not know very well. After the militia, came the largest part of the army, the Continentals: Marylanders under Otho Williams with John Eager Howard next in command, North Carolinians under Jethro Sumner, and Virginians under Richard Campbell. The rearguard column consisted of Robert Kirkwood's small company of Delaware infantry and William Washington's Virginia cavalry.

Except for the North Carolina militiamen and a few new South Carolina enlistees, the men were veteran fighters. They went to challenge the British and Loyalists at Eutaw Springs, most of whom were also veterans. They had some seven miles to go.

Oddly Stewart did not know they were coming. Even when two American deserters appeared in his camp about seven o'clock, Stewart refused to believe the story and had them arrested. However, he did order a cavalry troop to ride up the road. Earlier that morning he had sent out several hundred unarmed men, protected by a small escort, to dig sweet potatoes along the very road by which the Americans were advancing. But when his cavalry and the potato diggers not killed or captured dashed back into camp, Stewart believed them. He prepared for battle.

Stewart had about twenty-three hundred men, slightly outnumbering his enemy. They included the Third Regiment of Guards—the Buffs—some of whom as new recruits had arrived from Ireland in late spring. One of its flank companies, along with those of the Nineteenth and Thirtieth Regiments, had lost fifty men in one day to heat stroke on the march from Ninety Six, but now those three flank companies, commanded by a Major John Marjoribanks, were better used to the climate. So, of course, was the well-seasoned Sixty-Third, which had chased after some of these same militiamen last fall from Fishdam Ford to Blackstocks and had also beaten these same Continentals at Hobkirk Hill in April. In fact, the Sixty-Third had been in South Carolina since the siege of Charlestown, as had the Sixty-Fourth, which had tangled with Marion's men numerous times. For that matter, so had the Third. Most of these British knew the country and knew their enemy.

But about half of Stewart's army were Loyalist Americans, as battle-hardened as any British regular or American Continental. Battalions from the New Jersey Volunteers and the New York Volunteers and a cavalry troop from the South Carolina Regiment had been fighting since Savannah, the northern Loyalists longer than that. John Harris Cruger still commanded a battalion of DeLanccy's New York Brigade as he had at Ninety Six. The American Loyalists were impassioned fighters. They too fought for their country.

The land near Eutaw Springs was pleasantly wooded with little underbrush. Stewart had called it a "salubrious" situation. His army was encamped on the other side of the road from a large, strong brick house with twelve cleared acres around it and a large palisaded garden behind it. The garden backed up to Eutaw Creek, which flowed from the springs. The steep-banked creek was bordered by a thicket of blackjack oak.

Speedily Stewart deployed his men in one line under the tall trees in front of his camp. He placed his New Jersey Loyalists across the road in the center, flanked by cannon, with the British regiments on each side. The South Carolina Loyalists he held as a reserve in the woods on their left, but on their right to the front of the line and in the thick woods along the creek bordering the battlefield, he sent the three British flanking companies under Marjoribanks.

Greene's orders were for the Carolina militia to lead the attack as at the Cowpens—but this time they would fire many more than three rounds before falling back. Lee's Legion would advance on the militia's right, and the State Troops, cavalry and infantry, would attack the enemy on the left along the creek. Behind the militia the Continentals bided their time. Washington's cavalry and Kirkwood's infantry waited in the rear as a small reserve.

Skirmishers from both sides advanced and fell back; the artillery boomed. Officers barked commands, drums rolled, and the militia advanced, shouting, into a heavy fire of musket balls and grapeshot, giving what they got, some falling but the rest going on. As steady as Prussians, Greene wrote later. Both the Continentals and the British were amazed.

Rudi Näffels dodged among splintered and broken trees and used what cover he could to fire. Thank God the British mostly shot high, at least at first, though the damned Tories didn't. As good as we are, Rudi acknowledged grimly. The yelling and the roar of cannon were so deafening he heard hardly anything else. The heat, the smoke, the din and crash smothered his senses. He strained for targets. He did not shoot as quick as some men, not always even on command, but most of his shots counted. As with deer he aimed to kill, not wound. The way he'd want it for himself. Or so he'd always thought.

They kept moving up as they had been for the last—half hour, two hours? who could tell? Except for when they'd had to fall back after the North Carolina militia broke in the center, poor devils. They'd never known anything like this. Well, he hadn't either since Guilford Courthouse. And they didn't have anybody like old Longnose looming up everywhere in front of 'em, old Wizard Owl. Or that little knock-kneed, iron-jawed Swamp Fox over yonder either. Why the hell would anybody put a foreigner over new men? Thank God for the North Carolina Continentals sent in to stiffen 'em.

The partisans were still moving up through torn ground, but some were having to retire with empty ammunition pouches. Rudi had a few more rounds though somehow in the confusion of having to give way, he'd gotten separated from his company and had drifted more to the right. He tried to avoid the bodies in his way, a clawing hand, a mouth stretched wide in screams inaudible because of the roar. Dimly, occasionally he noted gory well-clad forms alongside ragged ones.

Their own little three-pounders were already out of commission, but the six-pounders weren't. Thank God at least one of the enemy's was silenced. Once, through the haze and broken trees, Rudi's keen eyes spied a cleared space far ahead. Light. Tents. The British camp! Great God Almighty, they surely were beating 'em back!

But even as he squinted and aimed, a bullet crashed into his right shoulder. He fired, knew he'd missed his mark, then glanced down and saw blood spreading on his shirt. He dropped the gun, grabbed his shoulder, saw blood pouring between his fingers. Stooping, still clutching his shoulder, he managed to pick up his gun with his right hand and turn to stumble toward the rear, knowing he had to stay up to keep from being trampled by the onrush of Continentals. He gritted his teeth so as not to yell against the swelling pain. The gun dropped from his hand; he stumbled and fell. In the tumult and roar his scream came out as soundless as everyone else's.

Hans felt a little lightheaded but he felt good. He knew it was partly the spirits they'd had earlier that morning. Just before forming their lines the General had ordered the rum casks emptied. It wasn't very much for most of the men, but for Hans, who could count on one hand the drinks he'd had in his whole life, it was enough. So far he'd felt not a twinge of fear, even with all the booming and crackling around him; in fact, he felt joyous at being where he was, moving up with the best of 'em. He'd show 'em! He might not be big and he couldn't yell like they could but, *Herr Gott*, he could shoot! He knew he was good at it. He'd show 'em, he *was* showing 'em, now!

Enveloped in the din and roar, he moved and fired on command, amazed at how easy he could do it. All that drill had helped, what he'd needed all the time, he thought, for now he paid little attention to what was around him, what came at him, just concentrated on loading and firing. *I always knew I could!* he exulted.

He'd never been in anything like his. All before was just skirmishing, but this was *so* big! He was exhilarated by the greatness, the importance of it, being with all these Continentals that had seen so much, got ready just as cool— Once Jess reached out to yank him down. He felt like laughing as shot whistled over his head.

They were on the left of General Pickens' men. He'd not laid eyes on Joggi or Willi this morning, but he was sure to see them sometimes.

But, oh God, it was hot! If only sweat wouldn't keep getting in his eyes. He couldn't half see. His eyes burned from smoke and from dirty sweat, and he shook his head, rolled his eyes to clear them.

He didn't see Jess. Where was Jess? Were they spreading out? But there was George; who could miss him? In the haze men were darting shadows. He kept his gaze fixed level ahead, tried to be careful of his aim. Trouble was you couldn't see! Those woods were so thick you couldn't *see* anybody! Oh, they'd have to go in those woods. He was ready, he'd go!

A trumpet blared and for a moment Hans was confused. For us? For them? Or for somebody else? Was it advance or fall back? He couldn't think. Where was everybody? He saw none of his company! He had a moment of panic. Had they moved up and left him? But he'd kept up, he knew he'd kept up! He rubbed his wrist across his eyes to try to see better, and then with a wave of relief recognized a man to his right, two men, and they were motioning back. Glancing behind him, he saw George, who also motioned at him. Fall back. But where were all the rest?

He stumbled over something and had to glance down, had to look where he went. Had to do more than glance. He saw the twisted shapes, men crawling, clutching at themselves, blood-soaked. Oh God, that's where they were; that's why he couldn't see them. A six-foot body, head thrown back—the staring eyes.

Emotion burst inside him, knifed his belly and breast. His pain turned red and black. Earlier reasons for being here—pride, grief, anger— left him. This present pain was all.

He could not cry for Jess. His own face was too hard; his eyes were too small and hard; every angle in his body felt sharp and hard.

. . . They said Colonel Henderson was wounded, could no longer sit a horse, and now Colonel Wade Hampton commanded.

Where was Captain Goodwin? Another captain was joining two companies together. Didn't matter to him, whoever it was.

Horses wheeled and plunged. A horse galloped back riderless and he wanted to seize and mount it, but without a sword or pistol. . . . Horses screamed, some were down kicking, men kept tumbling off.

Hans stood trembling, his blood draining from around his heart, flooding back, and he thought his head would burst. He did not understand what was happening, but when at last the order to move came, he flew forward with such a spring of release that his feet did not even feel the ground.

At last Greene loosed his fierce Marylanders and Virginians, and in the center of the battle the lines were locked, man against man, bayonet against bayonet. Pairs died in lethal embrace. Finally, with the Legion at their right flank, the Continentals forced the Loyalist center, then the British regulars on their right to give way. With their backs to the camp the British had to give ground.

The Americans pressed forward. They were beating 'em. They knew it. Slowly the British retired, abandoned their camp, moved back toward the brick house.

The Americans surged into the camp, full of victory. With red-rimmed eyes they stared about them. Clothes! salt beef! spirits! Suddenly they began to dart here and there. Half-naked, half-starved, parched, who could resist it? They'd won the battle, hadn't they? Rum! Hands began to grab and mouths to guzzle and gorge. It happened instantaneously.

The officers ahead looked behind them and shouted in dismay, then turned to rush back among the joyous ones, to curse, to threaten and plead—but even Continentals had only so much discipline. Meanwhile, the British were barricading themselves in the two-and-a-half-story house and taking positions in the palisaded garden against the few who pursued them. Later when shots cracked from the attic windows of the house, the revelers in the camp were too drunk to care. Besides, the tents protected them.

Nor did they know how little headway their comrades had made on their left. Those British in the scrub oak thicket by the creek could not be so easily dislodged.

Jem Boyd had done all he could. He willed to go on but he was out of powder. Back in the woods with the other survivors of Pickens' Brigade, he knew no ease. Too much hung in the balance for the price they'd paid. The sun beat down murderously through the smoke.

This was as bad as anything he'd ever seen. Worse.

If they could just get around that thicket with fifty good riflemen. . . . That calvary charge had been fatal. They should have known it would be. Washington himself was down and captured. Many another was not lucky enough merely to be captured. But militiamen like him who could only watch, maybe they saw what higher-ups couldn't see. He hoped to God that Kirkwood's infantry could drive out those flankers.

My God, how many were on the ground!

And there was Hampton rallying the State Troops again. Poor little Hans Lienhardt. Jem found himself hoping the boy had been shot in the arm or wounded in some lesser way to get him out of it if he was still up. Jem couldn't help feeling responsible. If it hadn't been for him, the boy might be safe at home. Or might not be, Jem sighed. He'd been so determined.

No! Somebody said Pickens was killed! He wouldn't believe that, no!

The battle was moving away from the woods. Thank God, than, God, the British flankers had been driven back along the creek, but they were still in the thickets. And probably behind those damned palisades with the cracks between them, just right for a gun barrel.

Now the fight was out in the big field. It looked as if the line, what you could see of it, was skewed aslant of where it had been; the left was still close but the right was farther away.

The big brick mansion loomed in the background. Such houses down here had many windows, high windows, too many of 'em and too damned many Tory marksmen behind 'em. Occasionally you could see in the smoky glare the work of muskets thrust between those high palisades. Thank God, the big guns were silenced.

Now the British were attacking again! Where were all the Continentals? Why were the British able to keep coming back?

Stewart's men were resolute inside and in front of their fortress, where Stewart was rallying them personally. Those inside the house kept up a steady fire from the windows. Those in the garden shot from between the pickets. American artilleryman, who'd dragged their guns and the captured British guns too close to the house, were almost all killed by upper-story marksmen, and the captured artillery was retaken by the British. Now Marjoribanks led out sortie after sortie from behind the house and garden against the Americans.

The Americans still fought hard, but the British kept counterattacking, and at last they drove the Continentals out of the camp even as Hampton led a bold but costly drive to protect their withdrawal.

Then, as so many times in the past, Greene made a wise but disappointing decision. He must pull his army back while he still had it. Almost a third of them were killed or disabled.

The British were glad to see them go. They had a strong fortress and had retaken their own camp, but they too had lost about a third of their own, not so many killed as the Americans, but more wounded or captured. They had not the strength to do more. They had fought for four hours.

Greene's army gathered up as many of their wounded as they could, those not close to the house or in the British camp. Greene would make arrangements with Stewart later for the burial of the dead.

The Virginians mourned the death of Richard Campbell. Campbell was the colonel who had led the costly assault on Ninety Six. William Washington was wounded and captured; John Eager Howard was wounded; so was Henderson. Though picked up for dead, Pickens was saved by the sword buckle which a musket ball had driven into his breast bone.

Never, it was later said, never had this army fought better, fought harder. If only some of them hadn't. . . And the Carolinians had fought so bravely.

In the afternoon as they dragged themselves back up the hot road, they came to a little pond that cavalry had splashed through that morning. Now as many men as could jumped in to drink, and those who couldn't crowd in threw themselves over the shoulders of the ones in front to get to the muddy water.

The men lay down that night on the same black earth they had lain on the night before.

Usually, even in the thick of a fight, Joggi had felt somehow shielded by his own skill or his burning will. Today, just as at Savannah, as at King's Mountain, men fell all around him, but this time he was conscious of something he'd never felt before—the dread and horror of darkness. He knew himself for a fighter. And so was a catamount—with a bullet between its eyes. But he was no longer a catamount. He knew himself a man with a man's yearnings.

So when it was over, he dropped down, spent like everyone else, and, also like some others, he thanked God to be alive. How hell could be any worse he did not know. Except they said hell never ended. And this *was* over. For the time being. But he had no joy in it. And it wasn't because they hadn't really won the ground. In some ways he thought maybe they had. But they'd left too many lying on it.

Willi was dead. Died at the edge of the clearing, skewered by a bayonet. Through the breast. It looked like a clean death. His face didn't even show pain. Just calm and even—noble. Joggi would never have thought of using that word for Willi Rieder before, but now it came to him. *Like one of those old Roman heroes Herr Pastor told us about*, he thought. He remembered Willi at Charlestown. Willi after the Cowpens. It came to Joggi suddenly that Willi was very brave. Kept on going. No matter how he felt. Not like me.

Joggi gazed at the thin and darkened face—quiet and dead—and thought, *Willi Rieder was braver than I ever was.*

A big fellow came to tell him where Hans had fallen. "I made sure you'd want to know. So you could tell your Daddy and all."

It was threatening rain next morning. Joggi asked for duty with the burial party, and the big fellow led him to the place where Hans was, not too far from Willi. He said the boy had been killed that last hour.

"Don't look like he's no more than a—reed of cane." George dashed his hand across his eyes. "I lost my best friend back yonder a ways, but seems like this'n—"

Joggi turned Hans' body over. The face was smashed. He glanced at George questioningly, allowed himself a moment of hope.

"Oh, it's him all right. I knew him by that tear in his jacket he mended that funny way hisself."

Yes, the rest of him showed who it was. Joggi was thankful his mother and father would never see it.

At least he went quick. Joggi thought, *This was a smart boy. But I never tried . . . though he was my brother . . . he never told me anything, anything he thought or felt. Oh, how I wish. . . .*

"—we called him Sparrow Hawk. I think it tickled him. We tried to look out for him."

"Thank you," said Joggi. "*Danke.*" He did not know why he must say it in German. "I'll tell my father."

Tell his father. How could he do that again?

It was beginning to rain. When he and George lifted the body to take it to the mass grave at the edge of the clearing, it seemed no heavier than a toppled cornstalk.

The battle of Eutaw Springs was not a victory for either side although both sides claimed victory, but afterwards the British moved farther down the road toward Charlestown. Their army never again came up the country.

Greene moved back to the High Hills with his ragged, hungry men, taking the wounded with him. They would stay there till mid-November, for during October over half of them were down with fever.

Toward the end of October came news of Cornwallis' surrender at Yorktown on October 19. But the war was by no means over in South Carolina.

53

Grief after grief. And joy. How could you bear it all? Such a mixed cup. Harder perhaps than grief alone . . . and even the joy was mixed with fear.

Johannes came home and found Barbara and the child there. Joggi had been home a few days before that. Nissi received his coming as a gift, received also the news of her brother's death. Elsbeth did not receive any of it. She had died on the ninth of September.

She had waked in the sleeping house early that morning and gone outside, gone out in her night clothes for a breath of air, gotten up without anyone hearing her and managed to push through the tangle of mosquito netting and feel her way through the stuffy room to the low porch. She stood a moment to face the gray east, thought longingly of cool sunlight and a crisp breeze. Home. Her own high room. She was going home.

Sand stuck to her feet, for she'd forgotten to put on her shoes. Well, she'd find a pair at home. Not like some poor souls, thank God, she had more than one pair of shoes.

But she did not have her stick. As she tottered near the young oak in the yard, she groped for its trunk to steady herself, thought for a moment of lowering herself to the ground. No, if she was to get home before sunup, she'd have to go on. . . . Where was Primus? Never where you needed him! Oh, she'd give him a fine raking when she saw him! . . . No, Primus was. . . . She could not think where Primus was, gave up the thought of him and knew she'd have to go on by herself.

She got out into the field road, lurching, swaying, was moving on in the growing light till a sudden dizziness overcame her, a giving way of every limb. She reeled and fell. Her last conscious thought was of Hermann as they'd found him that morning lying in the leaves.

Maria and Nissi sent out word as best they could. The burial was in St. John's churchyard the next morning. Only a scattering of people were there, few of the young and few men. Hans Jacob was still with the army, of course. At the Congarees nothing was known yet of the battle, not even that it had been fought.

By a special dispensation of grace, Pastor Christian Theus was in the neighborhood staying with the Fridays and visiting members of his former congregation, whom he did not consider "former," although with their meetinghouse destroyed they had not met together in over a year. Frail and thin were the singing voices and responses in the churchyard, but Pastor Theus' voice was not frail. He had gained in authority these last years. He held his worn little book open, but he did not need it. He had performed many such an office lately.

Madle attended. She was thankful for Barbara's carriage and the old horses, also for Matthew to drive them. She had nothing to ride and doubted she could have walked the four miles there and back. Cathri and the boys went with her, but Anneli stayed home with Barbara. Barbara was reluctant to go about in the neighborhood.

Madle herself had not been so far in over a year. She had not seen the desolation of the Theus place, or the weed-grown sand between the brick pillars where the church had stood. Parts of the churchyard were overgrown with seedlings and vines. She thought, *Have I been so long in this land that what I've known here has fallen already into ruin?* After the burial she was distressed to see the weeds on her little children's graves. She looked for Matthys' fieldstone marker but could not find it. She thought, *We must come back here soon, some of us, and clear away—I'll tell Cathri.*

The funeral feast was scant. Maria and Nissi were half-embarrassed and Elsbeth would have been indignant, but no guest wondered at it. What more could anyone provide? Apple cider, peach brandy—who could expect more? The big house was opened and chairs brought up from the other house and the scarred mahogany table dusted.

Madle felt like a ghost herself as she stepped inside Elsbeth's open room off the hall. She stood a moment remembering where everything had been, remembered Elsbeth's English teaware and wondered what ever happened to it. Broken, stolen, or hidden?

Vigor and will. Broken, stolen? Or kept somewhere?

Madle heard a step behind her and Nissi stood in the doorway. Her face was settled in somber lines, her mouth drooped, yet in the eyes—could it be a fleck of relief?

All at once Madle felt a surge of angry pain. *And what do you know of how it was?* She remembered Elsbeth's own words, "—how we laughed, how we sang, how we danced—" *And what do you know of the great sea and the awe and the coming; the terror and the grief? And slow-won peace and later that gush of joy. You'll never know. Nor memory of peaks and valleys either and bells and snow-hung eaves. . . .*

Nissi said, "Frau Lienhardt—"

Madle waited. The girl was silent. Then a wave of love and pity swept into Madle. She moved to take the girl, taller than she was, into her arms. "My dear, my dear, we have her goodness still."

Nissi did not answer.

"Oh yes, there was goodness. For her and in her. It was maybe hard to see because of the words, but she had goodness in her life. And great understanding."

Nissi gasped and bowed her head on Madle's shoulder.

"Remember the good in her, Nissi, always. Remember it." Madle stroked the girl's hair and thought how silken it was.

Nissi sighed and drew back, wiped her face and eyes. Each gave the other a grief-hung smile. Madle thought, *I'm glad he'll have her. I pray God he'll have her. Oh God, bring him back!*

Nissi thought, *I see now why they love her so much. God help me to love her too and not be jealous.*

After her father came home, Barbara grew more and more anxious about many things.

Her father's homecoming was profoundly moving for both of them. No weariness or grief could destroy his gladness in embracing her and in taking up his little grandchild in his arms. Moreover, everyone felt great relief to have him home again and safe. He came with the yellowing of the tulip poplar leaves, the return of cool nights. His service had been only six weeks.

But the news of Hans' death had preceded him, for Joggi had brought it, and Barbara was unprepared for the intensity of her family's mourning, especially Cathri's and the children's. For a while the younger children wailed uncontrollably, and not for many days did their wan looks disappear. Up until then, Barbara and Cathri had been enjoying a new companionship. Now Cathri turned silent, her face haggard.

But it was her mother's condition that worried Barbara most. In late August Madle had seemed much the same as always, although of course older and more worn, a little gentler perhaps with not so much energy as formerly. But soon Barbara began to miss her mother's crisp edge. Madle did only handwork that she could do sitting. Her steps were never quick. Outwardly she was calm. She suffered Hans' death without great display of emotion but exerted herself to give what comfort she could to her children.

When Johannes returned, it was the only time Barbara saw her mother's face wet. It had not been so even when Joggi came, only full of light.

Barbara hoped, oh how she hoped, that with the changing of the season and the return of the blessed cool, the outward events that promised more peace, at least up here—oh, how she hoped her mother's health would return. Her mother must have sensed her anxiety, for she kept saying, "What a blessing you are, my child. What would we ever have done without you?"

Perhaps she kept saying it because Barbara had other anxiety. She'd had no word from Conrad. They were fairly sure he had not been at Eutaw Springs. Joggi said only a troop of cavalry from Conrad's regiment was engaged there. The main part of that regiment was supposed to be somewhere along the coast, so he'd heard. Her father, of course, knew no more than Joggi did.

He looked at her with sad and loving eyes. "My daughter, you're welcome to stay with us always. You know that."

She answered his look with a difficult smile. How could she ever live anywhere else than with Conrad—if he still lived? But where? She tried to hold fast to every remembrance of him—his tenderness, his deference to her, and his gentle courtesy, that others seemed not to appreciate. Oh where? The dark pines brushed the sky with remote indifference.

October's air brought cool light and warm noons, crisping leaves, darker greenery, and crimson, yellow, and purple.

One evening the whole sky flamed with sunset. Later the sky and the sand were old, old.

Madle remembered the daintiness of lace-edged garments, tiny limbs and the warmth of tiny bodies against her breast and on her knees;

small curved lips, small perfect hands. The warmth of fires. She remembered winter fires. . . . Hot fires, towering, smoking, dreadful, dread of fire and blade—

She remembered the free unburdened movement of walking swiftly across a field, acres and acres of fields; rich, ripe, green, or gold for harvest. . . . The monotony and the flatness of it all.

Then she'd remember height and depth and rock, mighty almost as God, where you could climb up and up. She thought, *If only I could climb again to breathe that air, deep long breaths of that cold air, I'd be renewed maybe, remade.*

But nowhere here to climb. Even if she could. A riverbank once a long time ago. She remembered the scrabbling of her sweaty arms and legs, her growing triumph through thick heat and clouds of insects, and at last below her, small yellow butterflies sipping from river-washed sand. *But I climbed, oh, I climbed*—here.

Here.

She could feel the smooth-planed wood beneath her feet. Wood he planed. *He smoothed it for me. He made it mine. Here.*

And she knew the covering of his deep wide body sheltering her and enriching her beyond any expectancies. . . . She knew its absence, her terror, her unreasoning fear.

Setting out on that road alone.

And now again she thought, *How can I? I'm not ready yet, God! My Andreas, my Georgi, my darling Anneli—so long I've sat with one or the other tucked up under my arm, close against my side!*

Old hen. You know what must come. . . . She thought of Heiri. Hans. *And, oh, my dear little Verena we laid that day in the rain-soaked earth. . . .* Her own mother, her father, all those she'd never known, generations and generations ago.

How did you come here, Madle? Remember?
I came alone.

Jem Boyd stopped by again. This time he brought the Lienhardts dressed venison and another small bag of salt. He said he was on his way back down to Dorchester, where Pickens had returned from his sickbed to join Marion. The militia who were able to travel had been furloughed in September, but some, like Joggi, had rejoined their old companies. Joggi

was at Dorchester. Shortly before Eutaw, Joggi had been promoted to sergeant for the second time, and after the battle he was commissioned lieutenant. Johannes was proud of him, thought that one day, if he was spared,
Joggi might be a great man in the country.

Johannes thanked Jem for his gifts and asked him to spend the
night if he would, and Jem accepted. It was late afternoon in mid-November. The air was soft and mild again after the first frosts. The two men
stood talking by the fence of the empty barn lot. Johannes asked about the
army in the High Hills.

"Some of 'em's still down with the fever," Jem said, "but I look to
see 'em move out in a week or so."

Johannes had already heard the news from Yorktown, Virginia.

Jem said, "No, I don't see anything for it now but for the country
to be free."

"But when?" asked Johannes. "You tell me King's men are on the
coast still. What will make them leave?"

Jem shook his head. "They're still in other parts, I hear. I fear it's
like to take a deal of words and jangling before such bigwigs agree."

"Yes," Johannes sighed, remembering how long it had taken the
bigwigs in Charlestown and London to agree on courts for the middle and
the up-country. And most of those courthouses were now destroyed. "How
is it up the country?"

Jem hesitated. Afternoon sunlight slanted against the fence rails,
against the weathered side of the house, silvering it around the ragged
shadows of the oak tree. Jem knew there was need in that house. And
sorrow. Yet here, of all the places he knew, he felt an essential peace. Until
he looked at the face of the man beside him.

"Sir—" he never knew quite how to address Johannes, "—I heard
tales I mislike to tell you—but then—have you e'er heard of any
Cunninghams?"

Johannes shook his head.

"Well, one of 'em—mind you, they were men of good name once,
for all they've stuck to Britain, but one of 'em, he's took up terrible ways."

"What? Plundering, burning? Murder?"

Jem nodded. His face was as grim as Johannes'. "He's a man, if
'man' you can call him, as has no mercy. Well, he's got a great pack of
Tories together—"

"Where?" Johannes interrupted.

"They started back up beyond Ninety Six, but now, well, he moves so fast you can't tell where he'll be next. He's caught people unawares, men just come home, caught 'em in their beds and killed some as they lay, dragged out others and hanged or shot 'em. He burns houses, and they say he's vowed to kill every Whig American he can lay his hands on ere he's done."

Johannes stared beyond Jem with unseeing eyes. Never an end. What was it about this country?

"'Bloody Bill.' 'Bloody Bill' Cunningham they call him, and he's well named. And the trouble is there's too many others like him. And another thing—" Jem stopped himself. No use to repeat that tale. The Cherokee nation was a long way from here.

"What more?" Johannes asked.

Jem sighed and shook his head. "You just keep you a sharp lookout. Though it's not like, I judge, they'll come down here, but then again— Oh, we'll take care of 'em, never doubt that! It's just that they've caught us with so many of us down the country and those not—well, who would ha' thought once we'd drove the British almost to the Neck of Charlestown, there'd be those to fight again up here?"

"It wasn't just British you fought down there," said Johannes.

"No, I know that."

Both men fell silent. They thought of the brokenness of old neighborhoods. A number of men were now returned to the Congarees, but Johannes had seen few of them.

"Anyway, we got us a governor taking charge," said Jem. "Rutledge, John Rutledge. At least, he's one of us."

Johannes wondered. *Big Charlestown lawyer, according to Hans Jacob. How much will he understand about us up here?*

"They say he's ordered all the Tory families to leave, to move on down to Charlestown," Jem said, but the moment he spoke he wished he hadn't. He remembered the Lienhardt daughter with the Tory husband.

Johannes' face was grayer than the fence rails.

Jem said quickly, "But I don't see how they can force anybody to leave, say in a case like yours. That would go against anybody's conscience."

"Conscience? And when has that—" Johannes broke off. "One thing I tell you, Jem. My daughter will have the shelter of my rooftree long as I do, long as she wants it. Let no one think to drive her out. Or her child."

"Now, sir, I tell you," Jem answered warmly, "it's men like you will make a difference in this country one day. When we settle down to our natural lives again."

Johannes looked away, not even asking this time, When will that be? The silence lay heavy between them. Finally Jem asked, "How—how is Mistress Lienhardt?"

Johannes merely shook his head.

"I—we buried our daddy three weeks ago."

As Johannes turned to look at Jem, the lines of his face softened. He touched the young man's shoulder. "I'm sorry, my boy."

The change in the older man's voice took Jem by surprise so that he had to swallow hard to clear away his own sudden emotion. "It was that old hurt he got at Blackstock's never would heal right," he said huskily. "Just drained away his strength."

"Some hurts—don't heal." Johannes looked off. The fields around them that day lay derelict and brown. Would they ever be plowed and green again—by his hand?

"How's old Roker?" Jem ventured at last. "Stout as ever?"

"I hope so. My youngest has now most of the tending of him."

"Got back from his service all right then?"

"Oh yes. *He* got back," said Johannes. And how many times he had agonized, *If only I'd given that horse to Hans.* But then he had to ask, Would Hans have fared any better if he'd ridden to war? Roker was no charger and could never have carried Hans into battle even if Hans could have served as a trooper, which Johannes knew the boy could not have because of his size. Besides, look how many of *those* were killed. . . . Still, if he'd gone with mounted infantry. . . . And then it might have been some comfort to have his father's horse, Heiri's horse. . . .

Johannes bowed his head over his forearms on the fence rail.

Doves called cool and minor in the oak. The air was so still that far sounds were near. Johannes caught the faint sound of lowing. He lifted his head. Sometimes the sounds would carry, he thought, no matter how hard they tried to keep the cattle at a distance. Cathri and Andreas ought to be going for the milking. Surely they'd know to go ahead by themselves since there was company.

Yes, there they came down the back steps now, Cathri with her pail and Andreas behind her with his. And Georgi going to help manage the yearlings. Johannes' face cleared a little. They were good children, he thought.

The procession veered off to the side of the barn lot as they approached. Georgi grinned, flipped up his hand, and Andreas smiled shyly. Cathri did not exactly smile but there was a kind of bright curiosity in her look. A question?

Jem's heart moved as it always did when he saw her. What moved him most was not beauty, although he admired her young shapeliness, but it was something about the curve of her mouth, her cheek, which was so like Heiri's, yet hers alone. So generous, he thought, with a promise of— No, she was not too young! His eyes deepened, darkened with his smile.

Quickly she looked away and hurried on. Suddenly, she wanted to run, whirl, dance down the field! Suddenly, she could fly almost in this living air!

As Johannes looked after her, for the first time ever she reminded him of her mother, a girl running up an alpine meadow.

54

Madle went up in late November just before daybreak. Whether anyone was near to say "Come" her family did not know. They were too enclosed in their own numb selves for such discernment. There was not overmuch crying. Her husband and children had few tears left, or else the tears were too deep. Once Andreas thought she looked as if she were about to wake up.

Washing and preparing their mother's body in the winding sheet was the hardest thing her daughters ever had to do in their lives. No one was there to help. No help had been sought. Later in the morning Johannes asked old Matthew to take the news to Rieders with a request that word be sent to Herr Pastor if possible. He would bury her, he said, at St. John's.

Early that afternoon Johannes went with his shovel, hoe, and rake to the churchyard. He thought bleakly that unless the meetinghouse was rebuilt, and it looked unlikely, few more graves would be added there. Most people now buried on their own land. He took the boys with him, not for their help but in pity for their forlornness, but as they neared the old churchyard, he realized he should never have brought them. He just wasn't thinking right. Perhaps he could set them to work weeding in another part of the churchyard. When he arrived, however, he was surprised to find a number of men waiting for him.

They greeted Johannes and spoke condolences, though with few words. Several were men Johannes had not clasped hands with in almost two years. He saw they'd brought tools. He scanned the seamed, unemotional faces with wonder. "I thank you. I thank all of you."

"Rieder said to tell you he'd see to the box. He said to tell you he's already sent word to Matthias' old Quince. They'll bring it in the morning."

"Please thank Hans Jacob for me." Johannes' voice broke. He had brought two of Barbara's sovereigns with one of which he'd hoped to hire a joiner if he could find one.

"And Herr Pastor, he'll be here tomorrow."

"I thank God for all your kindness," Johannes said huskily.

He found the fieldstone marker near the edge of the cemetery not far from the small Lienhardt graves. "Here," he told them. He called Andreas. "Here, and here will be my place by hers on the other side. Remember now. And tell Joggi. Georgi, you remember too. Tell the girls. Mine will be here." He added, seeing Georgi's face, "Someday."

If the men thought it strange that her grave should be there, no one said so, though probably few if any remembered whose the old marker was.

"Matthys Tschudi. He was our friend," said Johannes. "We three were children together in the Toggenburg. He and I came together."

The men took up their tools. "No use you to stay, Johannes, now we know the place; we'll see to it. Unless you want to."

No, he'd be glad to take the boys away. Still he hesitated. Perhaps he should give Barbara's money to Theiler or Buser to give to Hans Jacob and ask him to procure food and drink for tomorrow. Until now he had not even thought of anyone coming to the house. Perhaps—yes, perhaps he should. But it might be better to send Matthew this afternoon. Old Matthew was becoming a godsend.

As he left, the men were already clearing the area with rakes and grubbing hoes.

Later in the afternoon other neighbors did come to the Lienhardt house. The surprise of their coming was a distraction to the children and to Johannes too. Again they were men and women Johannes had not seen for many months. Of course, he and Madle used to go also to a mourning house, he remembered, but it all seemed so long ago.

In the evening the Rieders arrived with provisions for tomorrow. Food and drink, though still dear, were easier to obtain now than they had been three months ago. Even so, Hans Jacob returned a sovereign in spite of Johannes' protests. "No, one was a gracious plenty."

Hans Jacob's condolences were brief. "I know it goes hard, old friend." He stayed in the yard talking with Busers, Köhlers, Stegs, and Theilers, most of them men his own age, but Maria and Nissi went into the house.

"We've come to sit up with you," Maria said to Barbara. Maria's hair was gray all over. The lines about her mouth were deep.

That night five men sat with Johannes in the shadowy room where the fire burned brightly, glowed and crumbled, flared again. Maria, Nissi, and three other women sat with Barbara and Cathri in the adjoining room. Tears kept clouding Nissi's eyes, and once she went outside for a long time. But Madle's daughters were tearless. The still form on the cold, smooth bed already seemed remote. Yet sometimes it seemed the only presence in the room.

What little speech there was was low. Someone asked, "What do you hear from Joggi?"

"We've heard nothing for almost a month," Barbara answered.

One woman was about to speak of a fearful thing that had happened last week but caught herself in time.

The men in the outer room were less reticent. They too spoke low but not too low for Johannes to hear although he did not join the conversation.

"Aye-God, it was a hard thing. They got back the cattle but what a price they paid next day."

They spoke of the massacre of Captain Sterling Turner and twenty-three men some forty miles from here. Pickens had sent them against Cunningham, and they'd surprised a band of Tories at Tarrar's Spring eleven miles west of Granby. They'd driven off the Tories and recaptured horses and cattle but foolishly let themselves get caught on Cloud's Creek next day, where they had to surrender, then were cut to pieces by Bloody Bill and his men. Only two escaped.

"And you heard what happened above the Fork? Between Bush River and Saluda?"

Two of them hadn't.

"Place called Hayes Station. House set afire and all forced out to surrender. Then all either hanged or cut to pieces."

"*Herr Gott, Herr Gott!*"

"And just when it's started to look like peace."

Johannes half-rose to get another log, but someone touched his shoulder, "I'll get it," and Johannes sank onto the bench again. A log crashed, sparks flew up, and he thought dully of how many times her small strong arms had fed this fire.

And how many times, he thought, he'd tried to stand between her and just such tales as were entering the house tonight. But time and again they had come in. And each time taken their toll.

Oh, she'd seldom shown her fear. Oh yes, she'd fought it with all her strength, over twenty years she'd fought it. Till at last her body gave way. But not her spirit. The lines of his face deepened, his mouth drew back in a deep grimace, and he wanted to go outside, go up the creek and yell into the woods as he had a few nights ago.

At length someone's movement caused him to raise his head, look dimly about him. Conversation had ceased. One or two men were gazing into the fire but the others were looking at him.

Vaguely at first, Johannes recognized what he saw. These men were concerned about him. They were friends. Neighbors. It was a long time since he'd had neighbors.

They talked of their fields. Most of them, like Johannes, had been clearing newground away from the road.

"It bears rich in there next to the branch."

"If it didn't next to mine, I don't know what we'd do this winter."

Talking sporadically, they sat and watched until daybreak. Only the children slept.

In the morning the number of people who came continued to astonish Johannes. What did it mean? Madle would have been amazed. There were more people here than ever at any one time before, he realized—at least peacefully—more than at Barbara's wedding. Or at Rudi Näffels'. Remembering that old, ill-fated marriage, Rudi's first, Johannes felt a thrust of unease, wondered where Rudi was, and if he'd yet gotten able to travel. Of all who were not here today, Johannes thought suddenly, Rudi should be most missed, her only kin from the old country. . . . And Joggi. But before new grief could take him, other people claimed his attention. He welcomed each one, received their words of sorrow, and in a strange unexpected way they bore him up.

Barbara and Cathri too were astonished, especially at the food that appeared. Where had it all come from? Older women took charge of arrangements for receiving and later serving it. Cathri was distressed at first because of the fewness of their own serving vessels until she realized that women were bringing their own, mostly wooden, though a few were crockery.

It was a cool November day. The light frost melted early. All the doors and windows were open.

Cathri went up to the loft-room, where Anneli was keeping Vronnigi, into a separate world where she longed to stay with the children prattling and dressing and undressing a little wooden doll Johannes had made for his granddaughter. Cathri stepped into the boys' room. Andreas lay face down on his bed. No, he didn't know where Georgi was, he mumbled. Cathri hurried down the steps, hurried outside, finally found

Georgi doing something, she didn't know what, but his legs and hands were dirty, and he ran when he saw her. She caught him by the old empty pigsty, gave him one look and dragged him down to the spring. There she scrubbed him mercilessly again with a rag kept there for that purpose.

"Stay clean, Georgi!" She was half crying. "I told you you must stay clean!"

Georgi would not look at her, kept tugging at her hand, and she thought his eyes were wild. She would not let him go, but dragged him to the front porch, where her father stood talking to people. "Papa, please keep Georgi with you," she pleaded in a low voice.

Johannes caught Georgi's hot hand in his own and sat Georgi on the bench behind him. From time to time he put his own hand on the boy's shoulder, and finally Georgi quieted in the shadow of his father.

The morning passed in a dream, slowly, endlessly, and then swiftly into a long procession up the road.

Gathered in St. John's churchyard, people looked about them and at one another. Here they all were. Oh, there were faces missing. Members of the Gallman family. Young men like Willi Rieder they'd never see again. But here were more of them gathered than there'd been in many a long day. For the first time in many a day they were gathered as a people, a community. Was that why so many had felt impelled to go down to Johannes Lienhardt's yesterday and today? Sorrowful as the occasion was, they felt that something was being restored.

Johannes looked at the coffin, saw it clearly for the first time in the open air. It was good workmanship, the kind he'd have wanted to make himself if he could have. The wood was planed smooth and evenly beveled. She had always appreciated smooth polished wood. He was satisfied to have it for her. Or for her body. She was not in it. He'd affirmed that knowledge again to his children this morning. He thought that he could not have borne it if he had believed otherwise.

He and the five of them stood for the final rites and they knew they were being moved into a different life from any they had ever known.

Christian Theus had difficulty with the service. Rarely did he let memory intrude as it insisted on doing today. He kept seeing her as the young woman he'd met on the road that day, setting out from the stockade fort at Gallman's. Going home for an hour of privacy, she'd said, with her husband, who was working there. A very private woman. Yet a sweetness and an elegance rarely to be met here. It refreshed him every time he saw her. . . . He knew he had no gift for poetry, yet every time she brought one of her babies for christening her eyes made him think of alpine gentians, the blue *HerrGottsblumen*. . . . On the road that day they'd talked of home, the home they'd left that was no longer home. She'd come here a year or so after Johannes. After Johannes and his poor friend Matthys Tschudi. Came alone on the ship. . . .

Today he kept thinking of a ship. . . . A small ship with unfurled sails.

55

As soon as Rudi slipped off his horse, Johannes saw the man's pain and exhaustion. It was a God's mercy Rudi still had his own black gelding, Johannes thought, and was able to mount, but it was evident that even riding was almost too much for him. Johannes suspected that was one of the reasons Rudi was willing to stop and spend the night.

He said his shoulder was healing. The bullet had chipped off a piece of bone, and movement still pained him, but he was glad for no worse. He'd had a long spell of fever and one time thought he was done for. He'd still been down in mid-November when the army broke camp in the High Hills, but the people roundabout took over the care of those who couldn't leave, and finally he'd started to get better.

"You can believe as soon as I could get in the saddle I left."

But he still ought not be traveling, Johannes thought, *at least not alone. I've never seen him look this bad. But, here it's the middle of December, and he's been gone—how long? Since August? It's a wonder he's waited this long. No, I'd do the same.*

Johannes asked, "You've heard nothing from—that place you left your Margreth?"

Rudi shook his head, lips compressed. "No, and I tried to send her word but. . . ." He shook his head again.

Johannes looked away, afraid Rudi might read his face. He wondered if Rudi had heard the tales he'd been hearing from up the country. Well, no use to alarm him further, maybe unnecessarily.

But if Johannes was troubled for Rudi, Rudi was pierced with grief when he learned about Madle. His first thought was he'd go on and try to bed down somewhere else, but, looking at Johannes, he knew he couldn't.

It was hard for Rudi even to enter that house, much less be in it, when his every memory of it included her. He'd helped Johannes build the house. He remembered that August afternoon twenty-three years ago, when she'd stood looking up through its rafters at the blue sky. It was the same day he'd met her, and he remembered yet the wonder of her clean young arms embracing his filthy self, her open delight in having an "own cousin" in this alien country. That was also the first time his far away people and native land became real to him. . . . He'd lived here until after Joggi was born.

Too many memories. . . . And she never even knew Margaret, he thought sadly. Or Margaret her. And it was too late now. . . . She'd said once, "I'm so glad for you, Rudi, that you have a dear wife." Thank God he'd stopped when he saw her that last time on the Road.

He sat with Johannes by the fire that night, sat a long time without talking, neither trying to divert the other's thoughts. Rudi saw how hump-shouldered and beak-faced Johannes was now. *He's beginning to look like an old man*, thought Rudi. *Soon we'll both be old men. . . . I ought to lie down.* But somehow he felt he shouldn't, not yet.

Finally he asked, "When did you first know, Johannes?" and Johannes told him of all that had happened since Eutaw: the outward signs and the course of her illness; their efforts, her responses. The end.

Rudi asked only an occasional question or drew a sigh.

And then Johannes found himself telling Rudi other things, things he'd never told anyone else, unburdening himself of memories of grief and regret. He told of his earliest love for Madle, the pain and the joy of it. He spoke of his boyhood when she was a thin, eager-faced little girl, who'd once climbed almost up to the summer pastures, where no little female was supposed to go. "She loved Matthys Tschudi even then." And told how Matthys was the reason she'd come here—Rudi shook his head, "I never knew that"—and told how she'd married him, Johannes, because Matthys was dead when she got here and she had nowhere else to turn. "But she turned to me, to me she turned. To me she always turned."

"Oh yes, I saw that. I saw always how she turned to you, Johannes." As Rudi gazed at Johannes under drooped eyelids, he was unconscious now of any pain of his own, only of Johannes.

"But I never thought to have her. When I was a young man. . . ."

They sat up late, far too late for Rudi, Johannes realized suddenly with compunction. "Rudi, I don't know what's got into me!" He clapped his hands on his knees. "Here I've kept you up and you already tired! It's just—I've got so used to sitting up. I never used to do that." He stood up.

❦

"No, I know you never used to." Rudi swayed slightly as he rose.

Johannes wanted to reach out and take his arm. He said abruptly, "Now look here, you'll have to stay tomorrow. Get yourself a good rest-up. Take another day with us, Rudi."

"No, I've got to go on, Johannes. You understand how it is."

Johannes was silent, then sighed, "Yes. . . . But I wish you could stay. I'm so sorry I—"

Rudi interrupted gruffly, "You needn't be. You gave me part of her. Gave me part of both of you. Something I didn't have before." He turned as he made his way around the end of the bench, smiled one-sidedly. "I loved Madle too, you know. She made me feel I—belonged to people. At a time when I belonged to no one. You—both of you. Don't think I ever forget it." He looked into the darkness of wall and ceiling. "But I always saw you as one. Like this house."

Johannes stood silent a moment. "Yes, but—never quite, Rudi."

"Well—no." Again Rudi half-smiled, thinking of Margaret. "A man never is—quite."

For the first time in weeks Johannes went easily to sleep in the loft-room, where he usually lay awake until almost daybreak, trying not to turn and creak the ropes and wake Andreas, a light sleeper. Tonight the whole family slept upstairs, Barbara and the baby too, so Rudi would not have to climb the steep steps. Johannes was a little surprised that Rudi accepted his place downstairs without protest. That just showed how worn out he was.

To Rudi, being in Johannes' and Madle's bed was only more of the terrible sadness of this house. But he was too tired to be aware of it very long.

When Rudi awoke next morning, Johannes had been up over an hour. The girls, busy at the hearth, greeted Rudi shyly. Outside, Rudi's breath was frosty in the gray air. He met Johannes coming with a pail of milk.

"Ready for breakfast?" Johannes spoke with at least a semblance of his old heartiness.

As they sat around the table, Rudi felt surprise at the traces of pleasant familiarity still here. Again he was touched as he'd been last night when the little girl stood by her father and asked the blessing. He'd forgotten that old custom. Yes, it had been a long time since he'd sat here. And there was something else unchanged. Something to do with that toddling little prattler.

He liked the boys, who were both like and unlike their older brothers. Georgi was Jemmy's age. *I wish my boy could know these two,* he thought; *they'd be good for him.* Rudi hardly thought of Hans for he'd never really known him. He remembered the older girls only as children. The dark-haired one had the look of her mother but was more constrained in her manner. *Poor girl, she had something to make her that way*, he thought. As for Cathri, it was easy to see she was a Lienhardt.

Last night Anneli had been very shy, but this morning when Rudi said, "I have a little girl almost as almost as old as you," she flushed and wanted to know how old.

"She's five years old."

"I'm six going on seven. And this is my niece, she's already one year old." Anneli drew close to Barbara, who had the baby on her lap. "Vroneggi, my sister's girl. What's your girl's name?"

"She's Katy. She's your cousin."

"Oh, I didn't know! Cathri! I have a cousin!"

"And you have two more," Rudi said smiling. "One is just six months old—and named Johannes, same as your Papa."

"Oh, is he named for Papa?"

"Well, it was my Papa's name, but I don't remember him much—so in my mind he's named for your Papa." Rudi did not look at Johannes.

"Oh Papa! Oh, I wish I could see him! Cathri, I just wish we could see our baby cousin! Oh, I wish, I wish!"

Even Georgi smiled, but no one said anything.

"Who is our other cousin?" asked Anneli.

"He's Jemmy," Rudi nodded toward the Lienhardt boys. "He's nine years old. His leg got hurt last summer. But I'm hoping it's better now."

Their food was simple if not abundant. Rudi found himself enjoying the milk and butter and raised bread and just sitting down with a family in a warm room. He said so.

"Yes, we're better provided than I thought we'd be four months ago," Johannes answered. "If the locusts will leave us alone." With neighbors mingling more freely they could help one another more, he explained. The Lienhardts had swapped a calf for a half dozen more hens; a sack of sweet potatoes for some dried apples and peaches. Not all orchards had been stripped.

But Johannes did not say that two more of Barbara's sovereigns had helped to increase their provisions, also bought them cloth and shoes. He had been reluctant to use her money and very secretive about getting it exchanged, trusting only Hans Jacob.

Hans Jacob had also helped to provide for Matthew. When the weather turned cold, Johannes wanted the old man to sleep in the house, but Matthew was strangely reluctant. He said he couldn't climb those steep steps and he didn't want to sleep in the big room either. Johannes was perplexed. The old man had to have a warmer place than the barn. Then he thought of the empty cabins at Rieders. After some negotiation with Hans Jacob, Matthew agreed to go there for the cold weather if he could have a place to himself. Hans Jacob would provide food, shelter, and fuel in exchange for Matthew's help with the stock. "Now I'm still a Meyers," the old man told Johannes sternly. He wanted everyone, Barbara included, to understand that if she went away, he would go too. Johannes promised.

Later he admitted to himself he was relieved to have the old man gone. His presence never seemed quite right there. There were times Johannes had been glad for his help, but yet. . . . Now if he'd been a free man. . . . There seemed no way out of the tangle.

But Rudi knew nothing of such dilemmas. He asked, "What's the last you've heard from Joggi?"

"Not much," said Johannes, his face suddenly shadowed. "He's been here only once since his mother left us."

"Is he still with Pickens? Or is he gone with Sumter again?" A force under Sumter was trying to get the Tories at Orangeburg under control.

"Pickens, I believe." Johannes did not want to say more, yet felt compelled to add, "I hear there's still trouble beyond Ninety Six."

Rudi felt a sudden urgency to be gone. "Yes, and I must be on my way." Half-rising, he bowed to Barbara, then to Cathri. "I thank you for the best food I've had in many a day. You'll forgive me if I hurry away."

Johannes nodded to the children, who began sliding down the bench after their elders. Barbara and Cathri were already busying themselves near the hearth as Johannes touched Rudi's elbow. "Come this way." He steered Rudi toward the front door. "Something I want to tell you."

Rudi felt a lurch of fear, but once they were out in the light and he saw Johannes' expression, his fear became annoyance.

Johannes shut the door behind him. "Rudi, I've made up my mind. I'm going with you. At least across Saluda."

"What? Why, Johannes, there's no need—"

"Maybe not, but you'll have to bear with me. I'm going."

Rudi stared, first in amazement, then in exasperation. "But, Johannes—"

"No, now listen to me. I know how you are. I know how independent-minded you are and all that, but the country's too unsettled for you to be going alone and you not many days out of your sickbed either."

"I made it here all right." But Rudi knew that was not strictly true. He'd almost despaired of getting across Wateree. He'd had a time just finding the ferryman and if he hadn't found him—

"Rudi, I don't say you might not make it to where you're going. God knows you've gone through things I never have. Still—and I know I'm not the woodsman you are either, but at least I can get up firewood and rig up shelter if we need it. And, no, I don't doubt you'd be able to do it better than I can, but, Rudi, you never know—what you might run into, and it's just good sense to have somebody else along."

Normally Rudi would have disputed him, might even have said, "Johannes, you'll slow me down." But he knew that today he couldn't cut across ridges through rough ways. Mounting and dismounting took too much out of him. He looked at Johannes' earnest face, not knowing whether to laugh or frown.

"Besides," Johannes said low, "she'd want me to. I'm doing it for her too, Rudi." He looked away but not before Rudi saw his eyes cloud up. "And another thing," Johannes said more abruptly, "what's a family for? You think because she's gone, you're not now our family? And you never helped me? You never did anything for me? That's your trouble, Rudi Näffels, and I can hear her say it too—it's all right for you to work and hunt for us, help my boys, help me a hundred ways, you think I forget? but for me to help you one time, oh no—"

"Johannes, hush!" Rudi was grinning. "Go catch that wonderful horse and hurry up. Let's go."

"He's already caught. I sent the boys out first thing this morning. I've talked with Barbara and Cathri. They're both good sensible girls and they're not afraid, though I do want to stop by Rieders for a minute. I know—" as Rudi made an impatient gesture, "but I must leave word. And, Rudi—another thing—" Johannes voice sank, "I—" He took a deep breath. "I want to go away for a while. For myself. You understand?"

Rudi did not speak but their eyes met. *Maybe I do*, Rudi thought.

They left the children standing on the front porch. Anneli called, "Cousin Rudi, please bring our little cousins to see us!"

Johannes looked back one last time, then spurred Roker.

The morning was gray, but once they emerged from the screening woods and turned up the road, Johannes was conscious of a slight easing of his heaviness. He was glad to be done with talk.

Later that morning when they left Granby and the road turned west, he found himself looking around him with interest. He had not gone this way in years.

They crossed the Saluda at Kennerly's Ferry, where Heiri and Willi had once feared to cross. No King's troops or Tories guarded it now. Nevertheless the ferryman seemed wary.

Rudi paid him with salt from his discharge pay, although Johannes protested, wanting to pay his own fare. But at least he could unsaddle and manage the horses that swam alongside. As they climbed the north bank, the sun came out and its promise of warmth cheered them somewhat. Neither said anything about Johannes turning back.

They followed the road winding west above the river, then after an hour branched off to the right, but still going west away from the river.

Many trees were already leafless. Some sweetgum still flamed red, but whiteoak leaves hung ragged and brown. The large hardwoods were interspersed with pines and quite a few cedars. The few fields they saw were wasteland. More than once Johannes saw houseless chimneys in the distance, though sometimes in the farther distance he glimpsed wisps of smoke.

Late in the afternoon a steep-sided hill reared itself up on the right. Johannes had heard of it but never seen it; the "little mountain," they called it. It amused him that anyone would call it a mountain.

Soon afterward they stopped for the night. It was still light enough for Johannes to gather wood and make a big fire, but he observed that although Rudi didn't say anything, he looked uneasy, so Johannes stopped feeding the fire. They were in a fairly sheltered place about a quarter of a mile off the road up a branch of Camping Creek. Johannes tended the horses, but there was not much forage, so he gave them a measure of corn. He was glad for the bread and meat he'd brought and saw that Rudi was too. They spoke little. Johannes remembered that Rudi had once settled on

Camping Creek. It was during his first marriage, but with its dissolution Rudi had let his claim lapse. That was when he'd lost just about everything he had and later almost his life.

Yes, Rudi had known hard times. But always a man to go his own way. Until he met Margaret. Johannes wondered about her as he and Madle had wondered so many times before. *Named a son Johannes*, he thought. *I'd like to meet her at last.*

He slept very little that night. It was not the cold or even sleeping on the ground, for he now had a blanket as did Rudi, and he'd heaped up beds of dry leaves for both of them and kept the fire burning low all night. But even though his body relaxed, his mind would not grow still. He kept seeing the road, the interlaced trees and the dead leaves and wondered where it would take him. How far should I go? He heard Rudi groan several times. He was glad for the paling of the sky.

In the flaring firelight both men looked haggard, but Johannes feigned cheerfulness as he mixed water and meal and made four corncakes—two for now and two for later, he said—and fried two sausages. As they finished eating, Johannes said, "Something I didn't take time for yesterday morning was see to my gun. If you don't mind, I'll take this chance to do it."

Rudi nodded, "You'd better," and reached for his.

The best reward for his six weeks' service, Johannes thought, was this musket. Many volunteers had brought their own, but some, like Johannes, had none to bring. After Eutaw, at least some of the officers agreed it would be unconscionable to let a man go home unarmed, and Johannes was very glad to keep the gun he'd been issued.

By the time their gear and provisions were packed, the sun edged the horizon. Johannes observed Rudi's slowness, the obvious effort with which he heaved himself into the saddle.

Out from under the trees, frost roughened the ground, but the sun shone red between the branches and it looked to be a fair day. Johannes was glad for his coat and the thick stockings his daughters had knitted. Four months ago they'd not known where winter clothing would come from. She'd worried so. . . . He wrenched his thoughts away. ... Dear little Babeli. But he feared she'd be leaving them soon. She'd gotten a letter at last from Conrad. Her husband wrote of their taking up residence elsewhere. But how? Where? Somewhere I'll never see her again.

The road rose northeast and ran along the side of a ridge, dry stony ground, and now it was more like a path than a road. The two rode single file. Still they saw signs of travel.

Yesterday they had met few riders although there were numerous tracks and even signs of wagons. Once they'd seen a man on foot disappear into the woods ahead of them. Johannes had felt uneasy as they passed the place. Today, only the scuttling of a squirrel among the branches, the distant hammering of a woodpecker, or the whirr of some startled groundbird broke the stillness.

It was about mid-morning when Rudi halted in front of him. Johannes drew rein. Rudi sat motionless. Then Johannes too caught sounds ahead. Rudi began edging his horse among the trees on the right, motioning Johannes toward the opposite side of the path.

Again they sat still, listening. Whoever it was must have stopped too. It had sounded like more than a couple of riders. Johannes stared up the path. Then he was aware that Rudi had slipped from his horse and now stood facing the path with his gun leveled.

Johannes dismounted and pulled Roker back, tethered him to a low branch, and moved nearer the path, though not without noise, for there was more brush and understory on his side than on Rudi's. However, because the trail wound slightly toward the right, he had a better view of it than Rudi had, and about this time he saw three men on foot slipping along the edge of the woods on the other side. As he signaled to Rudi their number and whereabouts, the men faded among the trees. Slowly Rudi turned to face into the woods. Again they waited.

Suddenly, Rudi felt the silence deaden. He whipped around and saw a man about sixty yards away stealing down the ridge through the trees. Rudi had a clear view of the man's head and shoulders, and as he recognized the face, a huge triumph surged through him. The man drew nearer. Rudi felt his body swell with the rush and darkness of blood. He shouted, "Micajah Fonder! It's me, Rudi Näffels!"

The man looked startled, and before he could raise his gun, Rudi yelled, "Lame my son, will you?" and shot.

And missed. A split second before he'd fired, a spasm in his shoulder ran down his arm.

A moment later Fonder's bullet whizzed by Rudi's ear. Panting, Rudi moved behind a large oak and furiously began trying to reload, trying to will strength into his trembling arm as the man came toward him with the butt of his rifle raised like a club, roaring, "Hear that, boys? Come on in! We got him!"

"Wait, Mike!" a voice yelled. "You don't know how many—"

"Well, I got this'n!" The man came bounding on, a big, broken-nosed fellow, and Rudi felt rage and despair engulf him. He dropped his musket, drew his knife and crouched.

Just then a shot exploded from close behind him. The man pitched forward, arms flailing, and his rifle slid away.

Someone kept calling, "Rudi! Rudi Näffels!"

Rudi glanced up the ridge. Johannes was reloading his musket.

"It's me, Rudi! It's Bill Lee!"

Rudi kept trying to work with his gun. The man called again. Rudi muttered, "Bill Lee." Suddenly he yelled, "Fonder's got his! You want yours!"

"Not from your piece I don't. Rudi, I got no quarrel with you!"

"Then why you ride with this vermin?"

"A man can't always choose his lice. You ought to know that!"

The man moved into view about eighty yards off. After a short silence Rudi cried, "But you burn my house!"

"No, I didn't! You know I wouldn't burn Margaret Allen's house!"

"You burnt the one she stayed in!"

"We burnt Aleck Fraser's house. Fraser killed my brother. I had nothing to do with burning your house. Or hurting your boy."

Margaret's words: "It was Bill Lee pulled him off."

Rudi called, "Then why you come at me now?"

"Man, I'm not coming at you, I'm trying to tell you! I—we didn't know who it was! You ought to know it's too many on the roads now it's worth your life to meet up with." He paused. "It was sure worth Fonder's."

Rudi's gray face was expressionless.

Lee called, "You let us by, Rudi, we'll let you by."

"Go back then," Rudi said finally, tiredly. "We'll stand here till you pass. . . . But wait, how do I know you won't turn around and follow us?"

Lee began cursing but finally broke off to yell, "You watch us pass and then I'll tell you a thing so you'll know why I won't come back!"

Johannes, who still stood behind Rudi, caught a clear view of the man. He was heavyset and red-faced, but he did not have the ruffian look of the other one. Johannes lowered his musket.

He and Rudi stood where they were a few more minutes. Then Johannes crossed the path and took cover on the other side again. It seemed a long wait before a single file of horsemen came trotting down the path with a riderless horse behind them. The five men were well-armed with good horses. Except for Lee, who rode last, their black hats were pulled low over their faces. Johannes was glad for the brush in front of him and wished Rudi had more cover.

The men came on so fast that it looked for a moment as if they would not stop, until suddenly Lee drew rein and wheeled his horse with a scattering of pebbles. The others did the same. Lee peered into the woods.

"All right, Rudi, I'll tell you a thing you'll maybe not want to hear, and if it's how I think it is, you'll see why I got no wish to hinder you today."

Johannes did not perfectly understand the words but something in their tone disquieted him.

No answer came from the woods.

"Rudi?"

"I hear you."

"You going to Gilchrist's?"

After a moment Rudi answered, "I am."

"It's no use to go there. Or maybe you heard?" Lee waited. When no answer came, he said, "Fort was burnt a week ago by the Cherokee. Them they didn't scalp they carried off."

The woods were silent.

"You see now why I won't waste a bullet on you, Rudi. Even if I was your worst enemy. Which I'm not."

Rudi's voice sounded thin and high-pitched. "Who got carried off? You know?"

"No, I don't know. I heard it was a few women. Maybe some children. You know how they do."

"Who did it?"

"As to names I can't tell you. I heard it was a party from the Overhills. You'll have to find out names for yourself. But one thing—if you should find her. Tell her Bill Lee would never ha' let such a thing happen. If he could ha' helped it."

Lee gathered his reins to turn his horse. "Oh, one more thing. I heard the Laird boys are back on Indian Creek. I heard their mammy was supposed to be at Gilchrist's too. You can make sure they'll know the straight of it."

Lee clapped his heels to the sides of his horse. The others let him edge by them to the head of their column; then all rode off down the path, their faces still half-hidden.

56

There was no question now of Johannes leaving Rudi even though the man did seem newly supplied with strength. They galloped much of the time, especially after the ground became smoother and the path widened although it was still rolling country. They forded a number of small creeks, barely pausing. They passed more fenced farmland but saw only two houses standing. They came to various forks but Rudi did not hesitate. They rode due north.

Finally, seeing a large creek ahead, Johannes called, "Rudi!"

Rudi slowed and looked back.

"Rudi, we need to stop awhile! Old Roker's a steady goer, but I'll be damned if I want to kill him. Unless I have to."

Rudi drew rein, looked as if he would say something unpleasant, but when he glanced at the foam-streaked neck of his own horse, felt the heaving of the dark sides, he dismounted.

Johannes was already leading Roker to the creek. He said, "My throat's parched too."

Neither spoke as they watered the horses and drank for themselves. Johannes opened a saddlebag and got out the corncakes he'd made that morning and handed one to Rudi. Rudi stood eating with the reins still clutched in his other fist, until he noticed Roker snatching at some cane; then he loosed his own horse.

Johannes said, "I couldn't understand all that man said. Tell me, did he say—Margaret could be alive?"

Rudi's jaws champed the bread as the horses champed the brown-edged cane. "It's a chance. Depends on who was in the war party."

Indians. That's what I thought. Johannes' face was seamed like the boles of the great hickories. Finally he asked, "Where you going?"

"Find somebody. To tell me something. Old Mistress Laird, she was there. You can depend on it, the Lairds will know. Who it was. Where they went. Not that they'll find *her* again."

Johannes did not need to ask why. Old people, the weak and infirm, they had no chance. But sometimes women and healthy children were spared and taken away. Maybe the oldest child and the little girl—but wait, what had Rudi shouted about his son being lame? Oh, God have mercy.

"You know where they are—the people of that older woman?"

"I know where they might be. If I can't find them, I'll find somebody. Oh, I'll find out. What's to be found." Rudi spoke in jerked, rasping phrases.

Johannes thought, *What good am I to him now? . . . But I can't leave him.* He stared past the trunks rising above the tangled creek bank. "Rudi, God knows what you got ahead of you. But I'm keeping with you. You hold up now. Hold on." But his words sounded weak and foolish.

Then Rudi looked at him and Johannes saw his eyes and could hardly bear what he saw. Rudi began to turn his head from side to side, moaning high, whimpering. "And she wanted to leave there. Oh God, she saw it. And I—" His voice cracked, loudened. "Goddamned fool—I told her, No!" Rudi yelled. His shoulders shook and he made sounds almost like laughing.

Johannes was still. Suddenly he said, "But, Rudi, maybe she did leave. Maybe she wasn't there."

"If I thought that— But I put my foot down. See, I never did that before. I thought it was just some—contrary notion. I thought—" Again Rudi twisted his head from side to side as if to break free of an impaling rod or spike.

"Rudi." Johannes' voice came strong. "Maybe she didn't obey you. If she did foresee—and thought first of her children, then maybe she felt she *must* leave."

Rudi looked up. "If I thought that—God! I'd go down on my knees every day I live! and thank Him for every contrary word she ever said to me. God! if only—"

"Now, Rudi, maybe she did." Johannes tried to speak matter-of-factly. "I don't know your Margaret but—where would she go?" He moved toward the horses.

"Oh, she'd go with Martha Laird. They'd go together. To Martha's house. If it was still there. She said that's where they'd go. But Lee said—"

"Did he know for certain?" Rudi didn't speak. "Now, Rudi, maybe—"

Rudi interrupted, groaning, "Johannes—the woods alive with painted devils and white scum—you've never—you don't know—"

"But it's a chance! If they left soon enough. And I do know some things, Rudi. You forget?"

Yes, Rudi thought wearily, *Johannes did know. Some things. But the raids twenty-three years ago down where Johannes lived were nothing like the raids up here. . . . Yes, Johannes had gone on that march into Cherokee settlements. And lasted out better than I did*, Rudi remembered. He looked at the worn face of the older man. He thought of that man's losses. Thought of what he'd already done this morning. Rudi made a half gesture toward Johannes, almost stretched out his hand. *Maybe some day I can thank him.*

It was late afternoon when they turned up the trail by Indian Creek. They had met only two pairs of travelers since they'd stopped. Rudi had drawn up and hailed the first, but they'd hurried by, shaking their heads and barely touching their hats. However, the next two men knew Rudi and stopped.

Their looks were gloomy. Yes, they'd heard what happened at Gilchrist's, heard it five days ago, but they knew little more than Rudi did. They'd heard it was six women, three young boys, and two girls carried off. They'd thought it was—but, no, they didn't know who they were and, no, so far as they knew, nobody'd gone after 'em yet, but did Rudi know, they asked hurriedly, that Pickens had ordered Colonel Sam Hammond to take command up here and that Joe Towles was raising a new company? "But who we need is Pickens himself. Though I don't doubt he'll come when he can get loose from down there."

No, they hadn't heard anything about the Laird boys, but you could make sure if their mammy'd been tomahawked, they'd not be slow to go after the ones that did it, whether with Towles or alone. But what about Bloody Bill, had Rudi heard anything of him?

Rudi shook his head.

"We heard he's been run clear down to Charlestown, but somebody else said, 'No, he's gone to the Cherokees.' You've not heard anything?"

"Very few people we've seen since yesterday morning."

"Where'd you come from, Rudi?"

"From the Congarees. Before that—it's too long to tell. Down near Santee. This is my kin, Johannes Lienhardt, from the Congarees."

"How'd you find out about Gilchrist's?"

"We met six men this morning. Near the head of Cannon Creek. One of 'em told me."

"Who was it?"

"Bill Lee told me."

"Bill Lee! Then I'm surprised to see you."

"He let us by."

The men glanced at each other. Rudi understood their looks. As long as he'd lived among them, he'd never quite become one of them.

"I got no quarrel with Lee," he told them wearily. "I thought once he burnt my house. He said he didn't. I took his word. But the man rode with him that lamed my boy, Micajah Fonder. Fonder got killed this morning." Rudi nodded toward Johannes. "He killed him when I couldn't. Johannes Lienhardt. He killed him for me."

"To save our lives," said Johannes. "That was why I shot."

"After that, Lee told me—what happened at Gilchrist's stockade fort. And let us pass."

The men were silent. They shook their heads, looked as if they wanted to say something more, shook their heads again and compressed their lips.

"Well, we got to get on, Rudi, day's so short. It won't do to get caught out late if you can help it. I hope you find out something."

They sat there awkwardly a moment longer until one raised his hat to Johannes and smiled fiercely. "It was good work you did to kill that Fonder. Many a one'll thank you for it." They picked up their reins and the other cried as they passed. "And Lee, he'll get his too, one day!"

Johannes nodded but had no answering smile. He thought of the sprawled body in the leaves, wondered if anyone would come back to bury it. No. They wouldn't. But he had no regret for what he'd done, only heaviness that he'd had to do it.

Long shadows streaked the path. Sometimes Johannes glimpsed the steep-banked creek below it. Again they passed derelict fields and chimneys. He saw that fields were smaller up here and he wondered if, like him, the people had hidden fields. Clearing land would be harder work up here.

They passed a bare hilltop with two charred trees. Johannes asked about it and Rudi said it was where the meetinghouse had stood.

At a fork they took the trail to the right. Rudi might have said, "That other way goes to our place." He'd been there only once since June, had thought then, We'll come back. Now his mind barely touched the thought. He bent it only on the hope he might find in that low-lying house ahead. If it still stood.

They climbed and descended an endlessly winding trail. The tired horses could not be spurred to more than a walk.

The December sun was sinking as they turned into what had been a wider lane but was now overgrown at the edges with blackberry briars. Rudi caught a whiff of smoke.

He felt a leap of hope but curbed it, remembering. But surely there'd be something to catch onto—if the boys were there.

Johannes smelled it too. "Somebody must be home!" he called.

The horses plodded down the eroded path. The trees thinned. Now the men could see the clearing and see the dark of a house. The air lightened beneath the yellowing sky, and flame of sunset was already spreading upward from the horizon.

They saw no lights in the house but made out a wisp of chimney smoke. And saw and heard other signs of occupancy. A cow lowing. A horse up the slope beyond the house. Somebody— And inside the dooryard paling—

Rudi was off his horse, began to run, great leaping strides that Johannes marveled at.

Johannes heard him shout a loud incoherent cry, saw the child in the dooryard turn, the woman— And come running toward him.

Johannes stopped where he was, got off his horse. He leaned his head against Roker's dusty neck, his face streaming. *"Danke, danke! O, Du mein Gott, herrliebster Gott, ich danke!"*

It was a long time before Rudi or Margaret could speak coherently or the children could speak at all. Katy kept winding her arms around her father and Jemmy pressed close to his side.

Martha was the one who said finally, "We'd about give you out."

"You didn't hear—" His voice was still thick. "I sent word by. . . " Now he couldn't even call the man's name.

"No, for we ha' been here nigh on six weeks. When we left Gilchrist's, it was thought best not to give out our direction."

"Here? Six weeks?" He turned to Margaret again, lost himself in the living feel of her, drew back to look at her and then at Katy and at

Jemmy. Six weeks! Their faces were beautiful in the afterglow, transfigured, yet so thin. The baby. "My little—my little—" He couldn't finish, afraid to ask.

"Hannis!" Margaret exclaimed.

"I'll get him," said Martha. "I'll bring him out." She had seen the other man at the gate with the horses.

Rudi turned. "Johannes! Come in!" he shouted. He swung his free arm in a wide, welcoming arc, not even feeling the pain. "Come in!"

Johannes looked at the little family—Rudi and his wife still in half-embrace, the dark-haired child in front looking up at her father, and the slim boy under his father's other arm.

"It's Johannes!" said Rudi loudly. "You'll never know, Margaret—all—he's done for me!" And to Johannes those halting but clear words were a medal of honor.

He looped the reins on the two gateposts and came inside. *Oh God, Your mercy endures forever!*

Rudi said all their names and Johannes bowed to each. He asked, "And your little one?" He spoke English in courtesy to Margaret.

"He's right here." Martha had returned with a well-wrapped bundle in her arms. She gave it to Rudi. "Here's your Hannis. Stout as can be. Said it was about time his Daddy got here."

Rudi took the little fellow, and clumsily letting some of the wrappings fall, he raised the baby's cheek to his and cried some more. Then Hannis joined him.

Gideon and David were away hunting, Martha said, but hoped to be back sometime tomorrow. Their families were still in Virginia and would stay there till it was safe to come home. "Though the Lord knows it's little for 'em to come back to." She said Gideon's house was lately burned. David's still stood, though stripped bare with broken shutters and doors.

"I told both they're welcome to stay here, all of 'em, long as they will. But whether Becky will, I do not know. It's between her and Gideon, but you can make sure they'll go *her* way." David's Susan was more biddable, however, and would no doubt be glad enough of this roof till her own was fit to live under.

Rudi asked how many children each had now. Martha said Becky had eight and Susan five. The last she'd heard. "One or both the boys intend to go up there soon. They hope to bring some or all of 'em back by spring."

Johannes shook his head slightly. *I wouldn't bring mine here*, he thought.

"They want me to go up to Sarah's on Fairforest while they're gone, but I said, 'No, long as Margaret's with me, I'll stay here.' And now with Rudi come—"

Martha kept the talk going, for Margaret said very little. Though it was not her nature to be at all demonstrative in company, tonight more than once she let her hand rest on Rudi's good shoulder or touch his head or cheek as she and Martha moved between the hearth and table. Many and many a time their looks locked and held. Rudi cradled Hannis till he went to sleep, then drew Katy onto his lap. Jemmy, like Margaret, kept looking at his father, and Rudi, glancing at his son from time to time, saw that his eyes were clear and smiling.

But, oh, they were all so thin—except Hannis.

They had rabbit stew thickened with corn meal for supper. Her boys had brought her two bushels of grain, Martha said, back in November. And though the cow was about to dry up, she still gave a little milk for the children.

"And I'll tell you one thing, Rudi. Your Jemmy's a wonder when it comes to snaring small game."

"Wonder where he learned that?" asked Margaret softly.

Rudi's chuckle was deep and rich. It was a long time since anyone had heard that chuckle. He and Jemmy elbowed each other.

"And Margaret, I'll have to say a word for her too. She's turned out to be a right good fisherman."

"And, Daddy, I helped Mammy, too." Katy was suddenly wide awake, twisting in Rudi's lap to look up at him. "We catched a *big* fish!"

"'Caught,'" murmured Margaret.

Their sleeping arrangements that night were simple, being mostly on the floor. Only one of the bedsteads had been re-roped, and tonight Martha shared it with Katy, for Rudi and Margaret would not hear of displacing her. The house had three rooms: two big rooms and an ell.

Johannes was glad to lie down near the hearth on a pallet with Jemmy. Tonight he slept soundly, did not awake even when Jemmy backed up close to him for warmth. His ponderings of the various ways and means he'd been thinking about all evening did not keep him awake more than three minutes.

The two Lairds came home the next day, and within a few hours it was decided that David and another man would ride with Johannes as far as the Saluda River. It was soon apparent that Johannes and the Laird boys were hitting it off rather well. Unlike most of his Swiss or German neighbors, Johannes had always been able to warm up to the "Irish," as they were called. Once he'd had a very good friend named Jesse McGowan. He'd often wondered whatever happened to Jesse. In these times, God only knew.

Before Johannes left, he and Rudi had a long talk in which Johannes used argument after argument to persuade Rudi to his will. Again he had the feeling, This is what *she'd* say.

"There's room! As much or more than I see here. It was built for more than us five. Oh yes, it'll soon be just the five of us. I doubt Joggi ever lives there again.

"Oh yes, Barbara, she'll go. I see it in her face. You know, Rudi, the Meyers, they have means we don't have, and Conrad Meyer, he'll find a way to get her to him or somewhere near him. I know that. Conrad's a good boy or I wouldn't have given her to him. He's faithful. 'Loyal,' that's the word for him, all right." Johannes sighed. "But loyal to her too and I thank God for it. I thank God also none of us ever faced him on the other side. That I know of. But he said in his letter he'll send for her soon. And I can't wish her not to go. . . . Oh, I may *wish* her not to, but I know what's right.

". . . And another thing, Rudi, that house needs another boy." Johannes was silent a moment. "It needs another little child. . . . Why, your little Hannis and your little Katy, they'll be the best thing in the world for us. My Anneli will be so lonely when Barbara and the baby leave. I—I don't like to think of it. . . . And then, Rudi, there's Cathri, and she'll need. . . ." His voice trailed off. "Rudi, you know we'll never get over missing. . . ." Johannes could not speak for a moment or so. "But think about the comfort you'll be to us, you and Margaret together." He spoke low. "Now talk to Margaret. I know you can't leave Frau Martha alone, but if her sons' wives return and all their children—I wish you could come before hard cold sets in. But if not then, come anytime. Come in the spring."

Rudi did not answer for a long while. He could imagine what living in the house with Martha would be like, and if Gideon and David were out much of the time, he thought he could bear it, at least until he got his strength back. But what then? And what if that other crowd moved in—though it might be a while yet. . . . And another thing, with him and Margaret here, how would the boys feel about bringing their own families home? No, it wouldn't be right for his family to displace theirs. . . . But say they all came anyhow, and all or even some of 'em tried to crowd under this one roof. Now he didn't have to ask Margaret how she'd feel about that. . . . But what about her and the Lienhardts? How would she like them?

All at once he thought of Margaret's little Granny. Now what would Granny advise?

A safer place. Maybe. Yes, unless something unexpected happened, it will be a safer place, he thought. Then came an even more compelling truth: *It's a gentler place. Meg needs that now. Granny would say so. There'll be more of the gentleness of her Granny there.*

From the moment he'd first seen little Granny bending over him, tending him, she had brought back that almost forgotten brightness from his own childhood, far away and almost lost.

He remembered the little girl Anneli's parting words.

Well, why shouldn't we? Why shouldn't I take my children to see their kin? We won't have to stay forever. Once I get my strength back. . . . But even then he knew he'd have a hard time managing everything alone. It all came down to whose help he'd rather take. *Why is it so much easier to give help than to take it?* he asked himself.

He glanced at Johannes. *Johannes is the same way. Trouble is, we're alike. Is that good or bad?*

Rudi said, "Well, Johannes, it may be you'll come to regret what you've started. You know me, but you don't know the rest of us." He meant Margaret. "But I'll talk to her. And if she's agreeable—soon as I'm fit to go and the weather's good enough, we'll come. For a while."

Johannes' only answer was a smile that lighted his whole face. *Loving, that's what it is*, Rudi recognized. Then he realized that losing love was not the end of love. *Would it have been so with me?* He wondered.

Later Rudi knew he wronged Margaret in being so apprehensive about her, especially as he observed her quiet courtesy toward Johannes and heard her expressions of gratitude. After all, she'd had Granny to teach her, hadn't she? He remembered she'd seemed to like Heiri and even Joggi. And that little Cathri and Anneli, who could help liking them? But as for the boys—and none of them except their father speaking any English as far as he knew . . . and then his talkers. . . . Well, it would be interesting.

The next morning Rudi, Margaret, Jemmy, and Katy stood shivering in the gray dawn to watch the men leave. Rudi thought, *There goes the best friend I'll ever have in this life, barring Jamie Fraser. But Jamie's too high and he's gone away from us now. And this man's my very own blood, I don't care if he's not blood kin.*

That night Margaret said, "Well, I'll say this, Rudi. Now that I ha' learned to live with one Dutchman—and from what I ha' seen of others so far—it's fair like I can live well enough with the rest of you."

"You'll like them better, Margaret," Rudi said warmly. "They're different from me."

"I hope not too different. And I doubt I'll like 'em better."

Her voice was as soft and bright as the sheen of Hannis' fuzzy hair in the firelight, he thought. But he would not say it now. He'd save it till later—if it seemed appropriate.

EPILOGUE

The year 1782 brought little peace to the back country. True, Bill Cunningham had rejoined the British at Charlestown, although rumors persisted that he had gone to aid and abet the Cherokees. The British confined their activities to the coastal region, but Patriots and Tories still fought near the Congarees and in the Edisto swamps. In the upcountry, Indian attacks continued.

Early in the year Andrew Pickens and Elijah Clark led an expedition into the mountains of north Georgia, but because of heavy snow and lack of food—the Cherokees had fled with their corn and stock—the South Carolinians and Georgians withdrew. They burned thirteen towns, killed forty Cherokees, and finally found forty bushels of corn. Nevertheless, the expedition was considered a failure.

Emboldened, the Cherokees, Creeks, and Tories were soon planning an attack that would sweep the country all the way to the city of Savannah.

To forestall them, three hundred South Carolinians and a hundred Georgians under Pickens and Clark met on April 1 northwest of Augusta on the Oconee River. This time they were more successful in breaking up and scattering their enemies, and for the time being Tory and Indian forays ceased.

But summer would bring no quiet. Bands of "outliers," some of them Whigs with families safe in Virginia and North Carolina, kept coming out of the mountains to plunder, burn, and murder indiscriminately in the upcountry. They no longer used revenge as a pretext. The outliers had turned outlaw.

When would it end?

Not until late summer, when Captain William Butler under orders from General Pickens organized a company to destroy and banish the outlaws. Not fully until mid-October, when Pickens led a last expedition into the north Georgia mountains. On October 17, temporary peace terms were signed by the Cherokee headmen and General Pickens. The terms involved renewed trade between whites and Indians and a new cession to the whites of Cherokee lands in north Georgia. At last the militia could come home—to a desolate countryside. But to fourteen hundred widows and orphans in the Ninety Six district no one came home.

On an April day in 1784, Johannes Lienhardt sat in the Sabbath sunshine behind his old barn. The remains of last year's harvest, his part of it, were stored inside. Joggi's share was gone as was Rudi's, on the way to parts unknown, unknown at least to Johannes, somewhere over the mountains on the Cumberland River. Johannes could only guess where they'd be by now. He'd never been so far north or west, nor had Joggi, though Rudi had been partway to their destination, and three of their party had gone all the way. *But from what I've heard*, Johannes mused, *that country's as rugged as any I saw in '61*. Remembering the steep rough ways, he prayed they'd get through. He kept thinking of the little children.

Johannes stirred restlessly. His hands felt empty, for he'd gotten accustomed to using his rest time for whittling little wooden toys. He rose and looked vaguely about him, thought of walking down the field to get his mind on something else.

No use to wonder and worry. All he could do was pray for them. He'd never see them again; the way was too long. He'd never see again that little black-haired, blue-eyed boy, the very image of his father at that age, mischief and all. Johannes never said to Hans Jacob that the child was Joggi all over again, it was so obvious. Still Hans Jacob *would* claim its bright, adventurous ways came straight from old Hermann Rieder, the onetime Indian trader. "And now you're going up there where your old great-grandpapa Hermann used to go." Hans Jacob would poke the little fellow's stomach and make him laugh.

Johannes never commented. The child's Lienhardt grandparents hadn't been exactly stay-at-homes, he wanted to say. And, Hans Jacob, you never saw a mountain in your life.

Hans Jacob had not opposed their going although Maria had. In fact, Hans Jacob had given them a great deal of help—Nissi's dower, he said.

Johannes gazed across his smooth green wheatfield. It had taken years to get all the stumps and roots out. But with oxen it ought to be easier to clear and break new land. *I must admit*, Johannes mused, *Hans Jacob was generous at last in spite of himself*.

What Hans Jacob had opposed was the two years Joggi spent farming and raising stock on Savana Hunt instead of on the Rieder place. What made it worse was that, at the time, the young couple were living in the same low-roofed house the Rieders had recently occupied, and also Joggi's parents for a short unhappy time many years ago. Joggi's stay there had not been very happy either. Eventually a coolness had grown up between the Lienhardts and the Rieders.

But it was over now. "Let 'em go," Hans Jacob said to Johannes. "No use to oppose it. They'll never be satisfied here." Both men knew Hans Jacob meant "he," not "they."

No, Johannes told himself as he had a dozen times, *it's in him to go, and always has been. Who am I to oppose it? Danger? Well, what account did I take of the dangers of the way? . . . But I came alone; I did not expose a family. . . . Oh, didn't you, later? Well, not intentionally. But there were dangers even here.*

Aye-God, it's how we're made.

Johannes walked out the back gate of the barnyard but stopped again to lean against the rails of the new fence Rudi had helped him put up when they'd had to enlarge the lot.

Yes, Rudi too had settled down well enough here for a while, clearing, claiming, and improving land, but he'd said at last, "I guess I'm too much an upcountry man, Johannes, to stay here. I've lived in red clay too long."

But Johannes knew it wasn't red clay or the land itself. It was something inside him just as it was in Joggi. Well, his wife was a good match for him. She'd know how to manage everything and keep him straight.

Johannes wished they'd been willing to wait for this year's wheat harvest. Yet he understood their anxiety to get through the high places as soon as the snow melted in hopes of reaching the Cumberland by early summer. They knew the work waiting for them.

Again Johannes gazed across his wheatfield, deep and green before him with never a stump, and edged by tawny broomsedge up the rise. This year even with Jem's help he might have to hire another reaper and binder. Andreas and Georgi were good binders for a fourteen- and a twelve-year-old, but that would make only four of them. Anneli must not do such work; her mother would never have approved it. And even though Cathri was more than willing, she must not help either, not this year. Thank God, he himself could still do a longer day's work than any of them.

Yet his body did welcome the Sabbath rest. Slowly Johannes came back inside the lot and sank down on the bench under the eaves of the barn. Absentmindedly he felt about him for the little chunk of applewood he'd pushed up under the bench one day to dry.

Long ago he'd stopped feeling guilty about not attending divine worship. There was yet no meetinghouse and it looked as if there'd never be one again, at least not on the old site. He didn't know why. Pastor Theus still performed marriages, baptisms, and funerals up and down the Congaree and sometimes held divine service in someone's house. Herr Pastor was stretched too thin, Johannes thought. With his home destroyed as well as his church, maybe he felt too old to rebuild. He must be in his late sixties. God knows I'd give my labor if somebody else would take the lead. Trouble is, we're all too wrapped up in building up our own again.

Johannes was fifty years old, strong as ever, he believed, though troubled sometimes with pains in his joints, which he ignored. He thought more often these days about his own father and his grandfather. *To think I'm now older than Father when he died and almost as old as Grandfather. And I'm now a grandfather. But the three I have*—he shook his head—*one I'll never know in this life and the other two won't remember me. But at least I knew them. And God willing, they won't be the only ones, will they? Please God?*

Johannes drew out his knife and turned the wood in his hands. A horse? Or a rabbit? A boy or a girl would like a rabbit. Vroniggi loved hers.

The letter from Barbara had arrived in September, written just before they left Charlestown, sailing north to far away Nova Scotia, she wrote, to a port called Halifax. It would be very cold in winter, but in summer green and beautiful, it was said, good rich land. Conrad hoped to do well on his grant. Johannes hoped and prayed they were on it now. If they'd had to build, he wondered what help they'd been given. . . . Vroniggi was almost four and the baby he'd never seen, another Georgi, would be a year old. If they'd made the journey safely. All through the autumn with every threat of storm, Johannes had thought of the little ones on that long voyage, and for some reason of old Matthew. If they'd taken him; she hadn't said. In the winter on every frozen morning he'd prayed they'd all be under warm shelter.

Johannes wondered: *Is this how they felt in the old country, the ones we left behind?*

It was not only the wondering and the half-grieving, but it was missing them because of the place they'd had in his own life so richly only for a short time. And it wasn't just Joggi and Barbara and their children he missed. It was Rudi and Margaret and theirs. He loved those children of Rudi's. That Katy now, she was a little trick. She'd twined herself about him as tightly as one of his own. He'd never known a child quite like her. Johannes smiled and shook his head. "Uncle Hans, tell me about my daddy in the olden days."

And Jemmy, how his own boys missed him. He wished Jemmy could have stayed. Johannes thought he almost would have if—but, no, it wouldn't have been right.

Well, thank God for the time you had with them, he told himself. *How else could you have borne the hard seasons?*

It was hard still. You could reach out in thought and prayer to those still in the world, but for the others, Heiri and Hans. . . . Oh Madle! . . . Barbara, Cathri, then Margaret and all the little ones might fill up the house-space, but no one, *no one* could ever fill her place. He'd never bring another woman here, he thought fiercely, no matter how much advice or how many hints and suggestions.

He still saw and heard her. Oh, not in the house, too many other voices and echoes of voices there; in the house she was only an absence. But when he crossed the creek sometimes to hoe or plow, there in the sweetness of bay bloom and the freshness of fern and moss and the rush of water he could see and hear her. She'd ever loved the beauty of wild and growing things. Even as a child. . . .

His lined face softened. He laid the wood on the bench and leaned his head against the old log barn and closed his eyes. Wrens were building in the eaves above him. He heard their light arrivals and busyness. A partridge called at the far edge of the woods. The scent of young leaves drifted on the warm wind, and the smell of new-turned earth.

"Papa, Cathri says dinner's ready. You can come on."

As Johannes opened his eyes, a wet tongue swiped his hand; a long tail wagged the end of a slick black and tan body. Carlo, brother to Charco, both named by Katy for a boy called Charles from up the country. The girls had wanted the puppies named alike. It didn't matter that their names sounded alike, said Katy, since Charco was going to Tennessee.

As Johannes absently rubbed the dog's head, then pushed it back, he looked at the sweet, serious face of his little girl. Soon they'd have to drop the "-li" for "little." Fraulein Anna. Miss Anna. Too serious, too quiet. Too much taken from her in too short a time. . . . Yet much given.

But the more given, the more to be taken. She was learning early. . . . Yet maybe the more taken, the more to be given again. Did it work that way too?

Johannes rose stiffly. "Wait for me, Anneli." She'd turned to go and Johannes reached out suddenly to hold her back, to draw her close, trying to feel still a child's body, but it was already angular and somewhat resistant. *My last chick gone.*

Then he thought of October. He caught his breath in sudden joy, only faintly tinged with fear. A new grandchild, God willing, in Wine-month! Cathri not really leaving him. And Jem as fine a boy as you'd see anywhere, even if he was Irish, almost like a new son. And Georgi and Andreas. *Lord, Lord, You're good to me!*

He breathed deeply. And the new-plowed fields, the ones yet to plow, and the wheat growing. The things he would make for Cathri and Jem.

He was not forsaken; he knew that. As it said in the Bible: "Seedtime and harvest; cold and winter. . . ."

Anneli, now walking beside him, took his hand, hers slim and soft in his. Surprised, he glanced at her, gazed at her neatly braided hair. It was the color of Heiri's. Anneli was slender like her mother and Barbara, though she was not like them in her countenance. She favored . . . who? They'd never quite decided. . . . Why, Brother Heinrich in Wildhaus! For the first time he saw it! She had the same long, thoughtful cast to her face. Heinrich had been two years older than Johannes, mild and generous as a young man, easy to get along with. Johannes had not heard from him in many years.

How many sons and daughters, my brother, and how many left you? Johannes' heart yearned backward across the years.

The dog, running ahead, yipped, turned and raced toward them again, one ear flung inside out, and Anneli gave a little tug to her father's hand.

And your sons and daughters, my Anneli, if God spares you and gives them to you, who will they be? Will I see them? Will one of them maybe look like your mother? Or your brother Heiri?

From the small window near the fireplace Cathri saw Anneli and her father coming, and she called Jem from the porch along with the boys.

The dark waters flowed strong around the ice-rimmed rocks. The breaths of the travelers whitened the air. An unbidden picture came to Joggi: purling riffles, sunlit shallows, the overhang of sweetbay and titi and the tangle of greenbrier up the bank. Willows and alders would be leafing out and crayfish turrets bubbling up in the mud. In the woods above the creekside, white dogwood would be floating, fraying, and beneath the scattered long-leaf pines, little brown catkins would litter the sand. He let himself see and feel it for a moment.

Here in the rhododendron thickets, leaves hung vertical in the cold, tubular in the sunless draws where old snow still lay deep, though a little way up the slope the dark leaves were beginning to lift and spread in the pale sunlight. Thank God it looked to be a fair day. Surely this spell of cold would be the last. But Easter was late this year.

They were threading their way through the New River country, whether in North Carolina or Virginia, no one could say with certainty. They were headed for the Holston Valley and the road that would lead them through the mountains to the land on the other side. The Wilderness Road, some called it. Others called it Boone's Trace. Whatever its name, many had traveled it these last ten years. But their own party, once they got through the Gap, would take a southerly road from Boone's, for their goal was the French Lick on the Cumberland River, where there was already a settlement called Nashborough. It was fine, rich country, full of game, and good for stock and farming; a country of gentle hills and well-watered valleys. A Promised Land.

The hardest part of their journey was still ahead. And the most dangerous. She knew it as well as he did. He glanced at Nissi. She could have been riding more warmly behind him in the wagon, but every morning she took her place on the seat beside him. Once when he'd remonstrated with her, she said, "I want to see what's ahead the same as you do, Joggi. And," glancing at the child in her arms, "he does too."

Her hood was pushed back from her forehead. She no longer wore those deep bonnets that hid her face. Her hazel eyes sought each new turn and unfolding of rock, stream, and peak just as her husband's did. But the baby was so swaddled in wool and fleece that Joggi could not see his face.

"He asleep?"

"No, and he's not thinking about going to sleep." Nissi tightened her hold against the sudden squirm and pull of the child's body. "But you'd better be still, young sir," she admonished, "or I'll have to put you in your basket."

Young Andrew Pickens Lienhardt quieted at the word "basket," and gazed up through the bare-limbed oaks, hickories, and chestnuts. His eyes were a deeper blue than the sky. "Like yours, Joggi," Nissi said. "Like his grandmother's," Grandfather Johannes had said.

Eighteen men, twelve women, and seventeen children, some half-grown, their party was large enough that they felt fairly confident in risking the Warrior's Path, which turned southwest on the other side of the Gap. As always the greatest danger would be when they were strung out in narrow places or in the early morning before they broke camp. But it was hard to keep danger in mind when they came out onto a high rock ledge and saw the misted blue folds before them. Such a mighty land! they marveled. Surely it's meant for more than death and danger. A few men among them noted signs of past events: a heap of stones, a scarring of a rock or a tree. But for most of them the grim old places were far behind them—their ruined or forsaken houses; rainwashed battlefields with broken trees already hidden by bushes and vines.

The road was deepened and rutted by much traffic. Because of the thawing and freezing again it was hard to get the wagons through some places. Sometimes the women and children had to walk or else ride horseback, with the smallest children in split-oak baskets suspended on the sides of the horses. People had told them they'd never get the ox-drawn wagons through the Gap. Maybe they wouldn't, but if they could get the oxen and gear across, they could build new wagons.

Deeper they wound into the mountains; higher they climbed.

At night for Joggi and Nissi it was the same—deeper, higher

If they talked before sleep—not long because they were too tired—it was of the next day or of time to come, of what they would do on the Cumberland.

"We must open up the seed tomorrow, Joggi, and examine it. We must take no chance with the seed. . . . And, Joggi, I've decided. We ought to keep sheep. I must learn to weave and to spin better too."

"Do you know anything about sheep? I don't." Joggi was half-amused, half-dismayed. Nissi was becoming an unexpectedly practical woman.

"No, but we can learn. Margaret will teach me to weave."

"Where'll you get your loom?"

"You can build me one."

He laughed as he drew her close. "Let's just hope I can build you a house." But he wondered if he might not one day find hims trying to build a loom. Nissi was not Frau Elsbeth's granddaughter for nothing.

"Joggi, we'll need warmer clothes where we're going with the winters colder and longer."

"Maybe Simmi'll know about sheep," Joggi answered drowsily. "He knows so much about other things. Knows more about horses and stock than anybody I know."

"He may," she murmured but said no more.

Nissi never spoke directly of her half-brother. Joggi often wondered what her feelings about him might be, but he never probed.

Simmi Rieder went with them as a free man. In the spring of '83 he'd returned to the Congarees, apparently of his own will. His mother, Calli, did not return. They never knew what happened to her. Elsbeth's prediction that she'd find her way home did not come true.

Once Joggi ventured to Nissi, "If it hadn't been for Simmi's mother, I wonder if we'd be here now together."

Nissi shook her head and did not answer. He thought he saw pain in her face.

When Hans Jacob had broached the subject of Simmi's going with them, Joggi interrupted tersely, "We'll be glad to have him with us, Herr Rieder, but only as a free man. Nissi and I, we'll take no slaves."

Hans Jacob flushed, opened his mouth, shut it. He was silent a full minute.

"I'll draw up his papers. He'll go free. But I'll give him a woman. He can take Marti, I'll deed her to him." He looked defiantly at Joggi. "Unless you want to tell Simmi she can't go?"

Joggi stared back at his father-in-law. At last he said, "If Simmi wants to go, I've nothing to say about who or what you give him."

"You didn't let me finish awhile ago, Joggi. I intended to free him. Simmi wants now to leave. And I want him to go. And provide for him too."

Hans Jacob walked off and Joggi felt a little ashamed, though at the same time nettled. *How can he expect me to understand such a tangle?* Suddenly, Joggi remembered a scene from a long time ago—Herr Rieder holding the little boy Simmi in front of him on his horse as he rode off somewhere. Joggi never remembered seeing him with Willi in front of him like that. And Willi dead. The oldest son, George, was still more or less estranged from his father as he had been for years. But there was still other son, Uli, much younger. *Maybe they'll learn. . . . Oh, who am I to judge the man when I don't even understand him? Who knows, if I could understand him, I might even start liking him.*

But free or slave, Simmi Rieder was a valuable member of their party. He was a bigger and stronger man than Willi, although a more silent one. How much of his silence was because of his own dark difference, Joggi wondered, and how much because of his nature? It was no Rieder trait, to be sure. Yet one Rieder trait Simmi did have, and that was a dogged determination to hold on to things, and not only to his own goods but to Joggi's and Nissi's for them. So far they'd lost nothing to spills or runaway animals or other mishaps, though some in their party had. Once Joggi asked Simmi about his freedom paper. Simmi said he had it safe but didn't say where. Yes, strange as it seemed, he was Elsbeth's grandson too, Joggi thought.

Brother even to me. But never a whole brother. And not just because of the half-blood, but because of how we both came here, how we came into the world. Joggi could not understand such things. No use to try. How life was ordered. But it was ordered. There were patterns. There were ordinations.

"He telleth the number of stars. He calleth them all by their names."

Who knew how many like him and Nissi and their little Andrew were moving across this darkened earth? Ordained. And Simmi and Marti. And Rudi and young Jemmy. And that little rascal Hannis.

In the daytime the creak and clank and scuffle of wheels, chains, and feet were sharp in the bright cold air, yet small in the silent reaches of mountainside. The dogs ran ahead, nosing scents and occasionally giving tongue until called in. They found signs of travelers gone before them—a rag, a broken packsaddle. Their own train would leave signs too, Joggi thought. How different this going from the way he'd used to envision it—just him and Nissi seeing it together in wonder for the first time. A child's dream.

How did I ever imagine we could go alone? We're on our way to make something bigger than we are. We can't go alone. We have to help one another out.

Who first said that? Heiri that night on the bridge. "Well, I thought men fought together and helped one another out."

Then came another echo, older than that one. "Well, Joggi, I found you."

Never. Other brothers maybe but not that one. Ever.

Or has he? Did he?

In the afternoon Cathri and Jem walked up the creek. They followed the way that Hans had led him on an August night almost three years ago. The path was wider now and Cathri and Jem walked side by side. Late yellow jessamine still softened the air. Crimson honeysuckle rambled over stumps and small shrubby trees. The great pines and most of the gums had been taken out but not the hickories and the oaks. Through the misting of new leaves, sunshine warmed the brown floor beneath.

Suddenly, Cathri gave a cry of delight. Hundreds of blue bird's-foot violets looked up from among the dead leaves. "Oh, I must pick some on our way back! Mama loved them, Jem."

They grew at the edge of a large new clearing that stretched up a gentle slope. Cathri had not been to the clearing for several weeks. Jem was working hard here with her father helping as he could, and planting had already begun among the stumps. For the hundredth time Cathri marveled at how things happened.

To think he'd wanted to stay here.

When he'd first kept coming by, she'd thought it might be because he'd known Heiri and Hans. Later she'd wondered if it was because of Joggi being here or maybe even Rudi, for they'd all been soldiers together.

She'd listened to their talk of moving west, what she could understand, and was terribly afraid he might go too. But was there a chance he might ask her to go? Sometimes she thought so. If he did, she knew she'd have to even though she dreaded to think of what it would mean to leave Papa and Anneli and the boys—and here. But maybe she wouldn't ever have to. Maybe he wouldn't ask her.

He didn't. He asked Papa. He asked Papa about settling on Savana Hunt.

"Somehow I can't find it in me to want to live up home anymore. There's still too much of—hate-spirit. Maybe it's because we lost so many. But down here—I don't know how it is, but here it feels—well, peaceful. So if you think I could get hold of a good tract on up the creek, I'd like to come here and build. If Cathri would be agreeable."

This statement of intention was long, long overdue, everyone else thought, considering how much he came and went. But they couldn't understand how hard it was, thought Cathri, with her speaking so little English and him no German.

It was before he'd talked to Papa that she'd asked Margaret to help her learn better the English. Margaret understood and tried to encourage and advise her.

"You're learning fine. But I tell you, child, the time's come, you'd best give him a sign. If you mean to have him. Do you?"

Cathri turned quickly, her bright face asking what her tongue could not.

"Well, do you?" repeated Margaret.

"But, Margaret—he says nothing."

"Child, child, don't his looks say enough?"

"Oh Margaret, you think so, you think so?"

"Pshaw, if you'd look him straight in the face a time or two, you'd see."

"But I did! One time I did."

"Well, a word or two might help."

"Oh Margaret, you're so good, you tell me!"

But when he'd finally spoken to her father last spring, it was not looks or words that precipitated it but what had happened up the country. He'd felt obliged, he said, to make some provision for his mother and his younger brothers and sisters, but he hadn't been able to settle in his mind how to do it. Now he didn't have to. His mother had remarried. "A good enough man and one well-fixed for these times, but I think it better not to try to live amongst 'em. To speak the truth, I don't want to. I want to live here."

From that time on, their looks and words were merely a froth upon their joy.

They had married in August. Anneli and Katy moved downstairs to sleep on the trundle bed in the big room with Rudi and Margaret, and the girls' room became Jem's and Cathri's. And now even the big room was theirs. Yet Cathri never felt right about it. She'd tried to get Papa to move back into his and Mama's room, but he wouldn't. Not yet. *But when we go to our own house. . . .*

At home she tried to put away thoughts of leaving, but now as she and Jem moved farther and farther from her father's house, her thoughts rushed forward.

They spoke little as they trudged up the edge of the newground. From time to time Jem took Cathri's arm to steady her in rough places, and at last they walked hand in hand. Then they saw it.

It stood in its own clearing on a slight knoll. It was about the size of the Lienhardt house, constructed on much the same plan. The floor sills rested on great blocks of heart pine, which were set on rock foundations. The corner posts, roof beams, and ridgepole were already weathered

were the lower tiers of great squared logs on the outer wall, which was
already seven feet high. The upper tiers and rafters gleamed new in the
sunshine.

"Ohh," Cathri breathed. "So much since last time! You didn't tell
me!"

"Well, it couldn't ha' been done without your Papa to help me."

"Oh Jem!"

Cathri's lifted face was pink-radiant. "So high!"

"See, this side's the front. This is our front door."

The ground was rough in front of the house, the sand soft and
uneven from much trampling.

"We'll have two wide porches, front and back. See, over here's
where I'd thought to build the chimney. What do you think?"

The door sill was three feet off the ground, too high for Cathri to
climb over, at least now. She looked up. "Oh, I want to go in!"

"That's easy enough." Jem lifted her over the doorsill, lifted her
high and kissed her rosy again before putting her down. "You've got to be
a right good armful."

He said the floor would not be laid until after the roof was shingled
although the joists were already in place. "No, you'll not have to contend
with a dirt floor. I said from the start I'd have you a smooth floor to walk
on like the one you been used to."

The pine logs were at the sawmill waiting to be planed into boards
as he was able to pay with labor or money. There'd be inside paneling too,
he said, just as in her father's house. "And maybe one day I'll be able to
clapboard it like some of them at Granby."

They moved about, Jem helping Cathri over the joists. She reached
out to flatten her hand against the wall.

"Now for our windows," Jem said, "I want more than one or two.
Where do you think we'll want our windows?"

They talked of the stairway and doors and windows.

"One day I aim to glaze your windows for you."

Cathri could hardly speak. The wonder of it. And for her to choose
and to make decisions.

"Your Papa said he'd help with the shelves and such. And when
our crops come in and we can start to accumulate. . . ."

She saw herself sitting in the doorway to the porch, churning fine
yellow butter, bringing to perfection all she'd been taught about washing
and shaping butter. She saw shelves and cupboards with bowls and plat-

ters, not much to begin with, of course, but, oh, her own! And a kettle and pots and skillets . . . and her very own hearth!

Another thought struck her. "Jem, you think—" She broke off. "No, it won't be ready by then, will it? Not soon as that."

He shook his head with his slow smile. "No. But if I can just get the shingles on this fall and the walls finished and the chimney built before next spring, then maybe—maybe by the next fall. But I'll not move you in till it's floored and ceiled the way I want it." He put his arms around her to draw her close. "No, it'll have to get borned the same place you did."

"But he'll learn to walk here."

"Or *she* will," said Jem.

"Oh Jem, you don't care?"

"Nah. Just so it looks more like its mammy than me."

Cathri leaned against him, faint with love. Then suddenly in an upsurge of strength, she broke away and whirled in the sand, flung up her arms and cried, looking up through the new yellow rafters at the bright sky, "Oh Jem, I could sing! I could shout!"

Already the oak trees heard her song and her cry.

AFTERWORD

In 1986, a year or so after I began searching out historical materials for this novel, I realized that I could read for years and still not amass all that was available. Yet even as I read, a number of facts eluded me. The years of 1780-1781 in South Carolina was a fluid and complex time. And so as the story progressed, as in other works of fiction, I had to rely on imagination. Many people referred to in the novel, and most places and events are real. However, the reader will surely recognize that Heiri's conversation with General Sumter, for example, is a work of the imagination.

To the best of my ability, I tried for historical accuracy, although I cannot have done justice to the many aspects and events of the time. I am especially indebted to Terry W. Libscomb of the Caroliniana Library of the University of South Carolina for reading portions of the novel and finding a number of questionable details and errors. One possible inaccuracy Mr. Lipscomb called to my attention, but that I retained, was the time of Nissi's small pox. He pointed out that the smallpox epidemic followed rather than preceded the route of the war as it spread up the country after the fall of Charleston. Another seeming inaccuracy: the Tory I named Bill Lee in Chapter 55 is not nearly as bad as the notorious Bill Lee of history.

Many people do not know of the important role South Carolina played in the American Revolution. Somehow we have let the events of 1860-1865 overshadow it. Nor do many appreciate the role of our upstate partisans in that war. These partisan bands included Georgians and North Carolinians as well. Therefore, I am most grateful to Dr. Hans Kuhn, former honorary Swiss consul at Spartanburg, South Carolina, for enlisting the support of other longtime Swiss residents of the Piedmont in the Carolinas, who generously helped underwrite the publication of this novel.

Also, I am immensely indebted to the Swiss-American Historical Society for its role in sponsoring *By Wonders and By War*, and to Leo Schelbert of the University of Illinois at Chicago, the Society's general editor of publications, an encourager and friend for many years.

In addition, I owe thanks to fellow members of the South Carolina Writers' Workshop, Columbia I, who suffered with me through most of the these chapters and offered valuable suggestions: "What happened to his gun?" "I don't understand that sentence." "Too many words." At last, friends, here it is, perhaps with still too many words, but I thank you.

And finally, a big thank you to my sister, Patricia Williams, who is always my first reader and critic.